EAGLE

BOOK ONE

$19.95 USA/$30.95 CAN

The Making of an Asian-American President

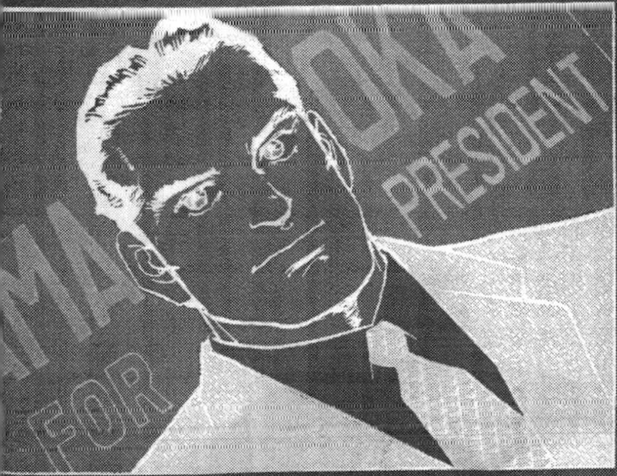

MA
OKA
PRESIDENT
FOR

enator Kenneth Yamaoka (D) New York
nnounces in Tim... esterday That
e Will S... ation to
United
2000

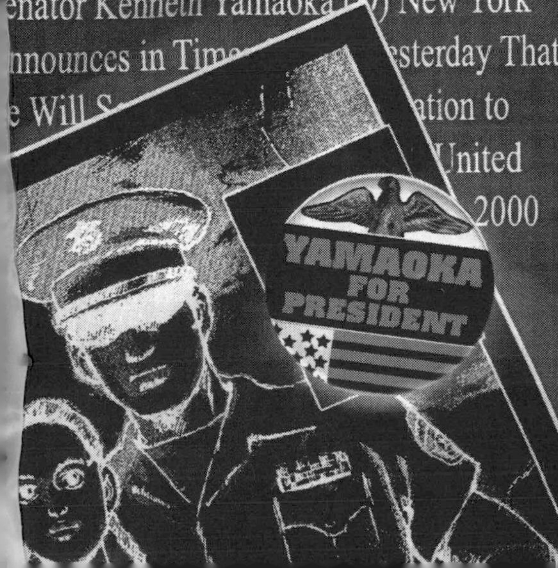

YAMAOKA
FOR
PRESIDENT

SENATOR YAMAOKA'S LAST-MINUTE CHALLENGE TO THE VICE-PRESIDENT FOR THE DEMOCRATIC NOMINATION

FIRST ASIAN-AMERICAN TO SEEK PRESIDENCY: "DON QUIXOTE?"

Who is Kenneth Yamaoka?

STORY AND ART BY
KAIJI KAWAGUCHI

"**EAGLE** GETS MY HIGHEST RECOMMENDATION... A TERRIFIC COMICS WORK THAT DESERVES YOUR ATTENTION."

—Tony Isabella
COMICS BUYER'S GUIDE

CONTENTS

STORY & ART BY KAIJI KAWAGUCHI

**ENGLISH ADAPTATION BY
CARL GUSTAV HORN**

Translation/Yuji Oniki
Touch-Up Art & Lettering/Steve Dutro
Cover Design/Izumi Evers
Editor/Carl Gustav Horn

Senior Sales Manager/Ann Ivan
Senior Marketing Manager/Dalla Middaugh
Managing Editor/Annette Roman
Editor-in-Chief/Hyoe Narita
Publisher/Seiji Horibuchi

Published by Viz Communications, Inc.
P.O. Box 77010 • San Francisco, CA 94107

10 9 8 7 6 5 4 3 2 1
First printing, August 2000

Eagle online:
www.viz.com/products/series/eagle
Vizit all our web sites at **www.viz.com**,
www.pulp-mag.com,
www.animerica-mag.com, and our Internet
magazine at
www.j-pop.com!

This volume contains the monthly issues of
EAGLE: THE MAKING OF AN ASIAN-
AMERICAN PRESIDENT Vol. 1 through
Vol. 4 in their entirety.

REPORT #1
MOTHER'S SMILE ———————3

REPORT #2
THE CANDIDATE: KENNETH YAMAOKA ——— 39

REPORT #3
THE RECEPTION———————63

REPORT #4
WHAT TO BELIEVE ———————87

REPORT #5
THE HAMPTON FAMILY ———————111

REPORT #6
GIFT OF THE FATHER ———————135

REPORT #7
SCANDAL ———————161

REPORT #8
FATHER AND SON———————187

REPORT #9
DUSTOFF ———————213

REPORT #10
VICE-PRESIDENT ALBERT NOAH ——— 237

REPORT #11
STALEMATE ———————261

REPORT #12
THE SPIN ———————287

REPORT #13
TAKING INITIATIVE ———————313

REPORT #14
BLIZZARD ———————339

REPORT #15
COUNTING THE VOTE ———————365

REPORT #16
OFFENSE/DEFENSE———————389

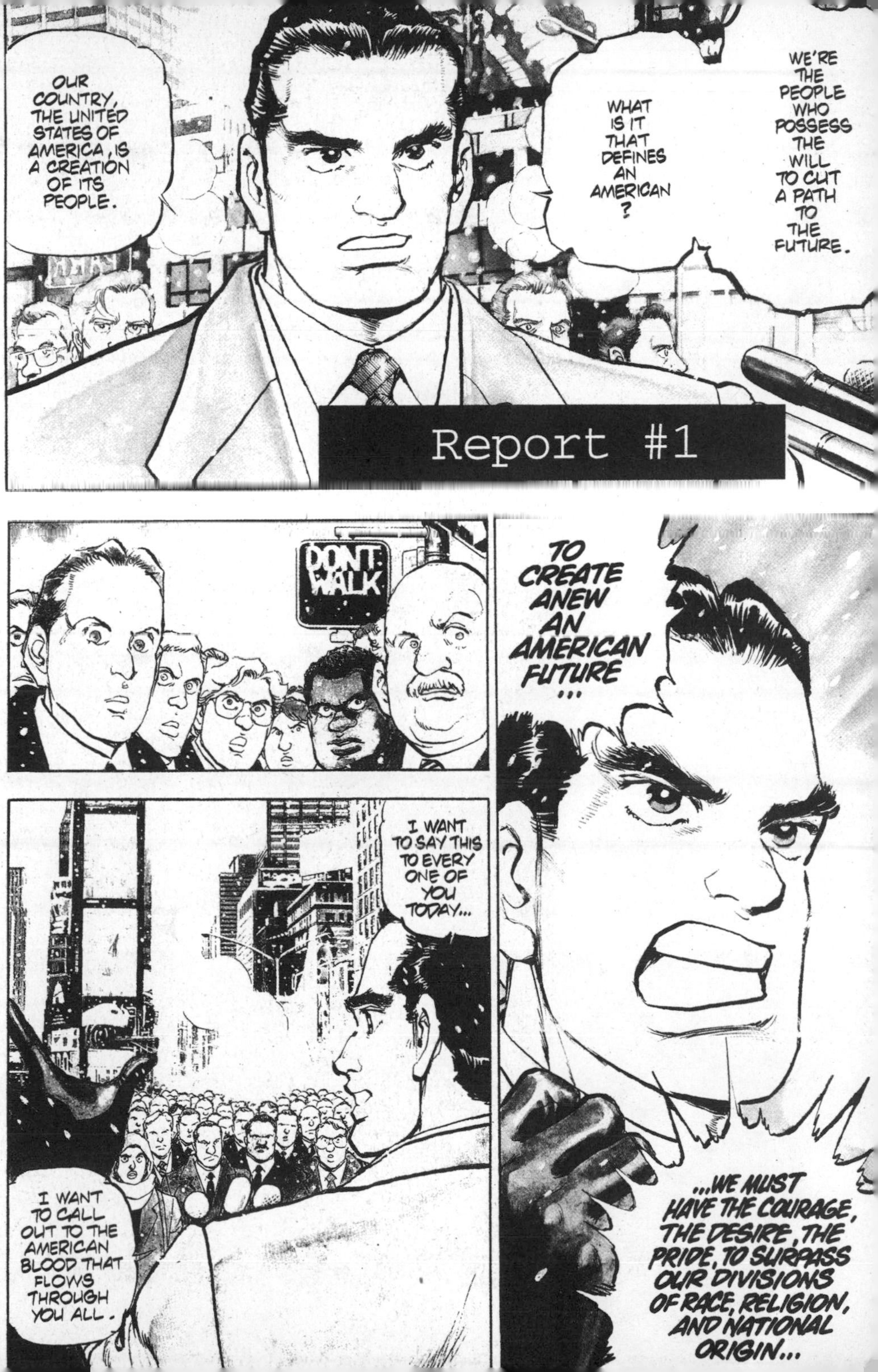

OUR COUNTRY, THE UNITED STATES OF AMERICA, IS A CREATION OF ITS PEOPLE.
WHAT IS IT THAT DEFINES AN AMERICAN?
WE'RE THE PEOPLE WHO POSSESS THE WILL TO CUT A PATH TO THE FUTURE.
Report #1
DONT WALK
I WANT TO SAY THIS TO EVERY ONE OF YOU TODAY...
I WANT TO CALL OUT TO THE AMERICAN BLOOD THAT FLOWS THROUGH YOU ALL.
TO CREATE ANEW AN AMERICAN FUTURE...
...WE MUST HAVE THE COURAGE, THE DESIRE, THE PRIDE, TO SURPASS OUR DIVISIONS OF RACE, RELIGION, AND NATIONAL ORIGIN...

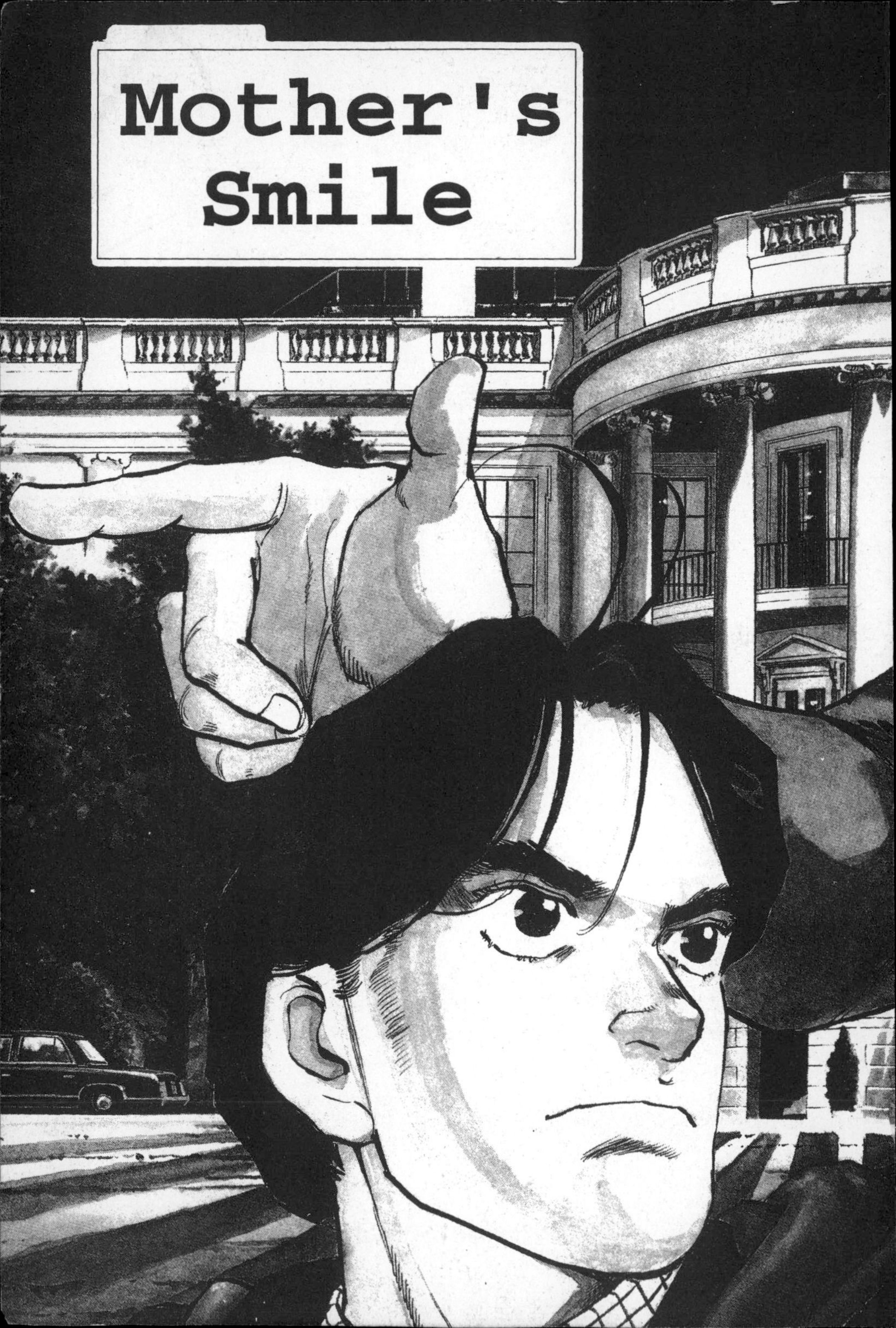
Mother's
Smile

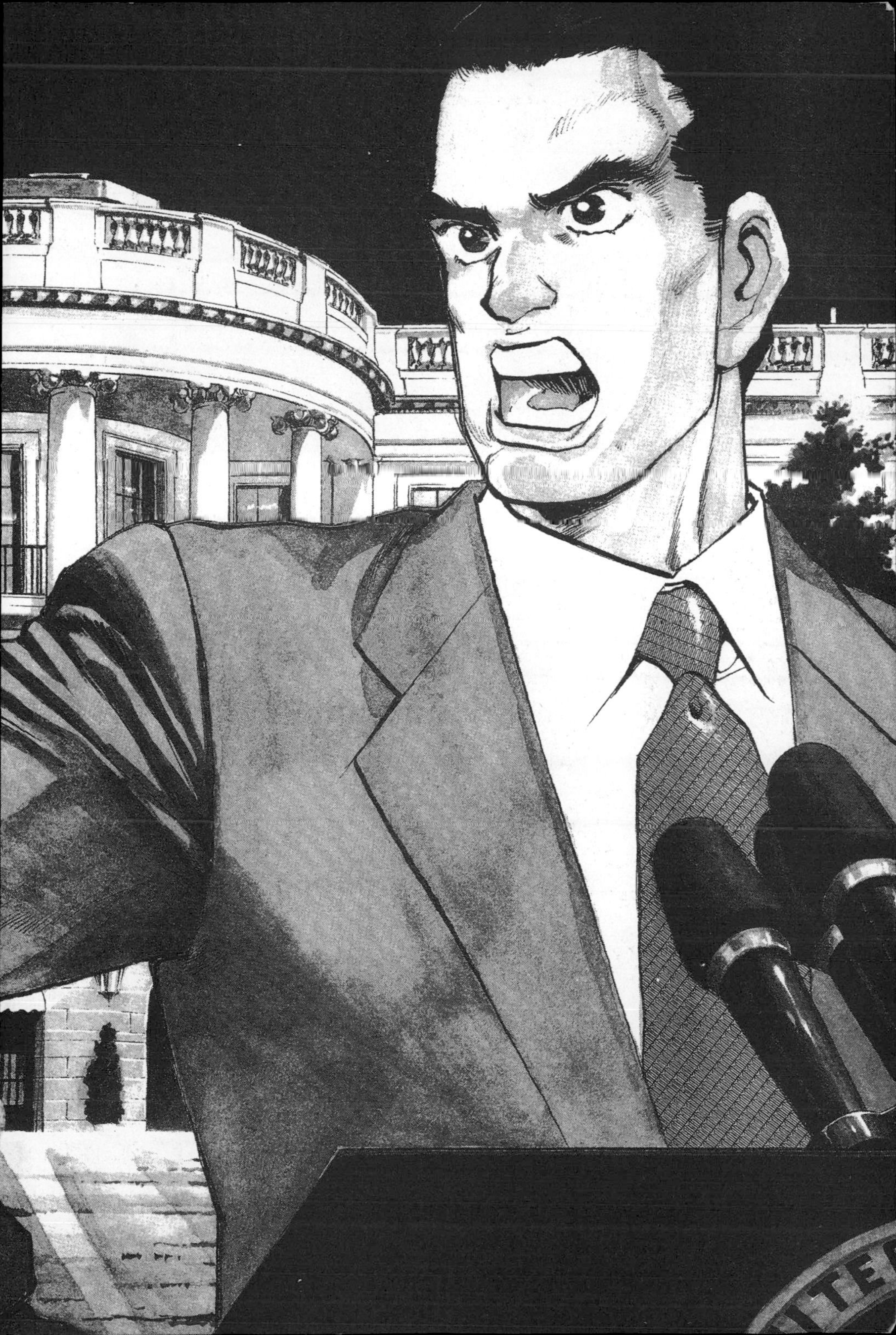

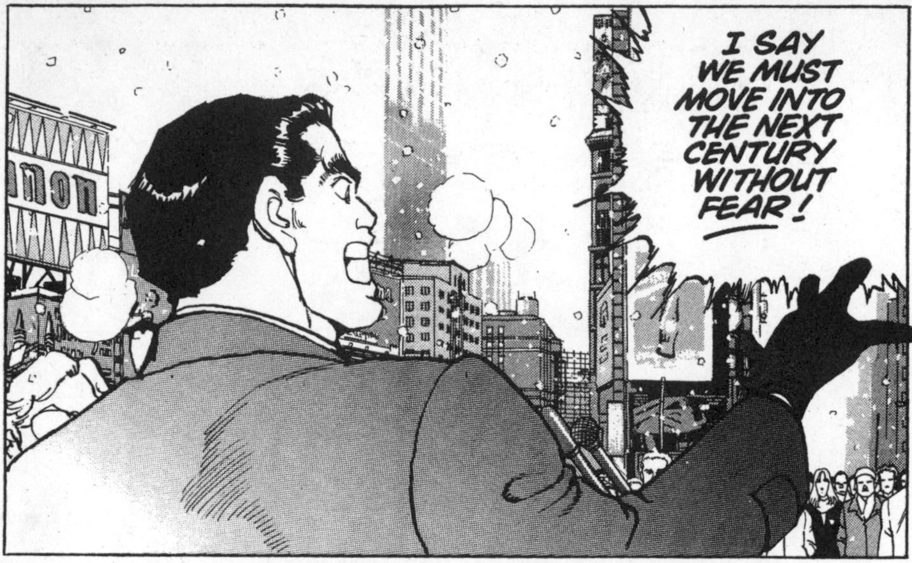
I SAY WE MUST MOVE INTO THE NEXT CENTURY WITHOUT FEAR!
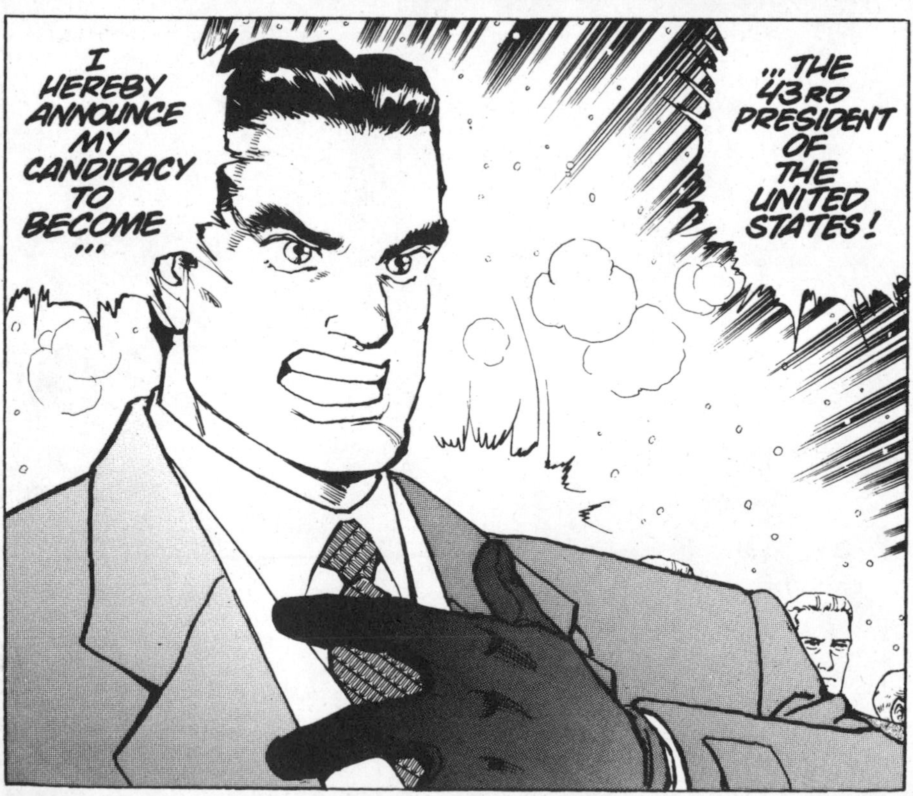
I HEREBY ANNOUNCE MY CANDIDACY TO BECOME ...
...THE 43RD PRESIDENT OF THE UNITED STATES!

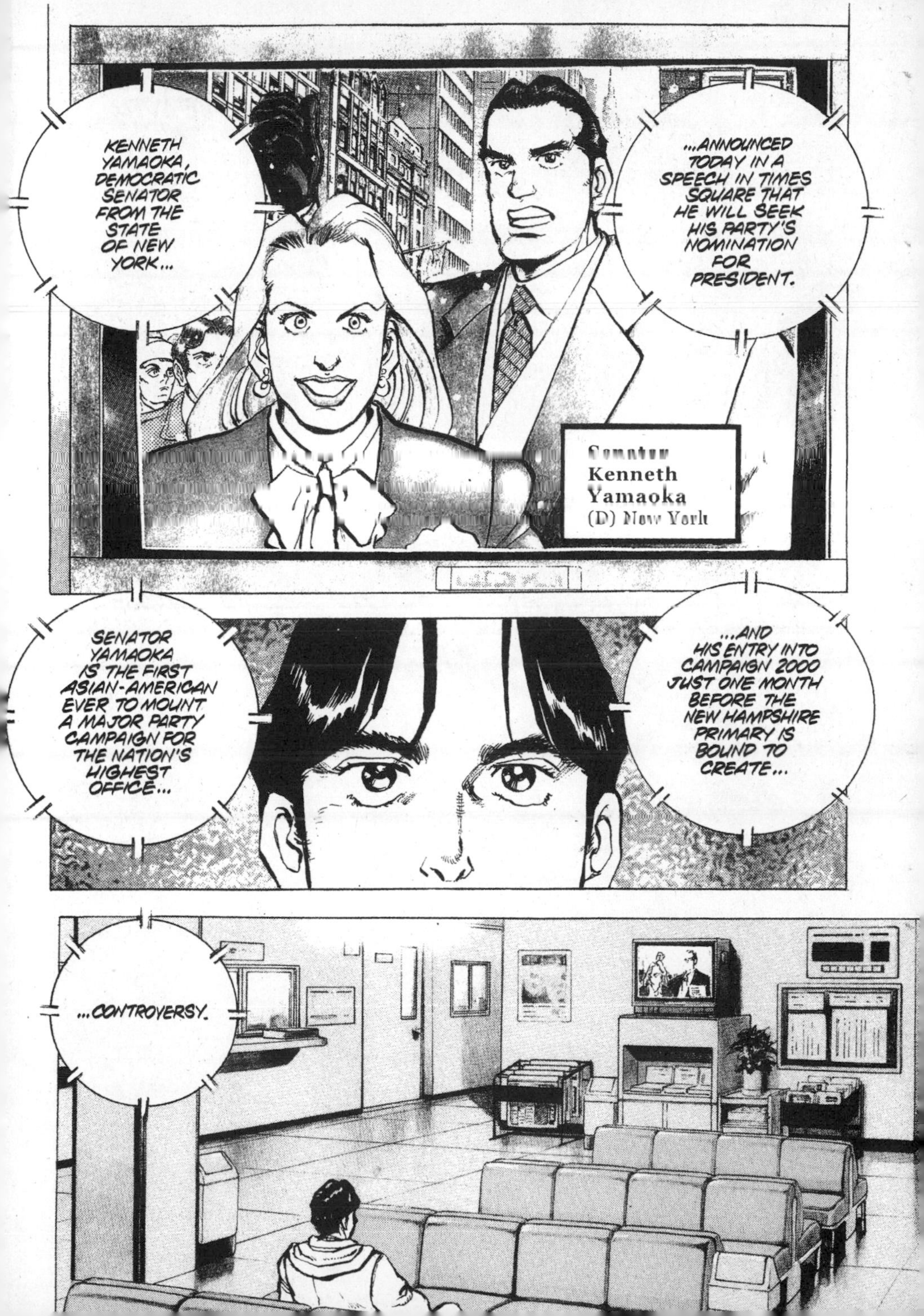
KENNETH YAMAOKA, DEMOCRATIC SENATOR FROM THE STATE OF NEW YORK...
...ANNOUNCED TODAY IN A SPEECH IN TIMES SQUARE THAT HE WILL SEEK HIS PARTY'S NOMINATION FOR PRESIDENT.
Senator Kenneth Yamaoka (D) New York
SENATOR YAMAOKA IS THE FIRST ASIAN-AMERICAN EVER TO MOUNT A MAJOR PARTY CAMPAIGN FOR THE NATION'S HIGHEST OFFICE...
...AND HIS ENTRY INTO CAMPAIGN 2000 JUST ONE MONTH BEFORE THE NEW HAMPSHIRE PRIMARY IS BOUND TO CREATE...
...CONTROVERSY.

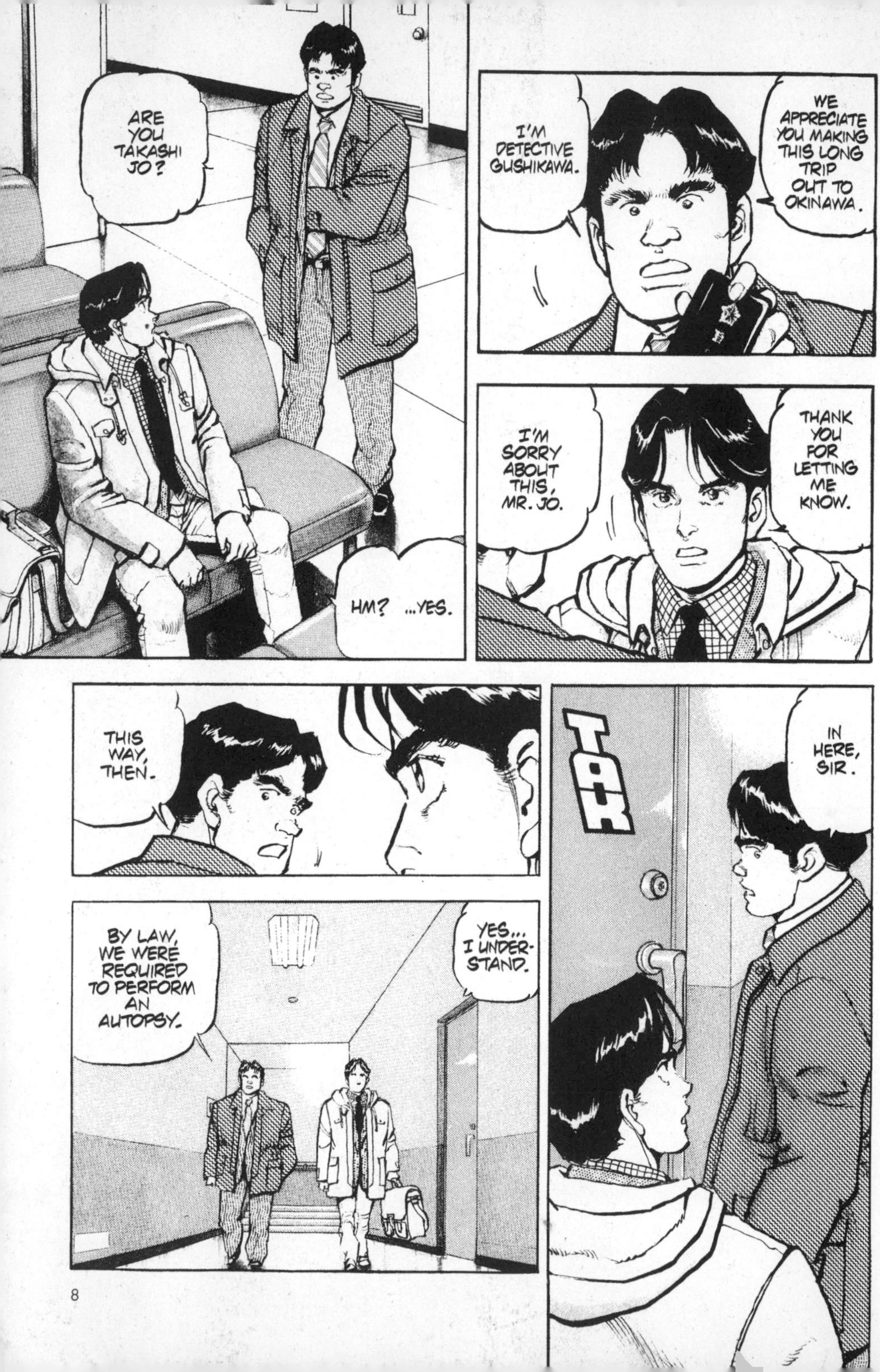
ARE YOU TAKASHI JO?
HM? ...YES.
I'M DETECTIVE GUSHIKAWA.
WE APPRECIATE YOU MAKING THIS LONG TRIP OUT TO OKINAWA.
I'M SORRY ABOUT THIS, MR. JO.
THANK YOU FOR LETTING ME KNOW.
THIS WAY, THEN.
BY LAW, WE WERE REQUIRED TO PERFORM AN AUTOPSY.
YES... I UNDER-STAND.
IN HERE, SIR.

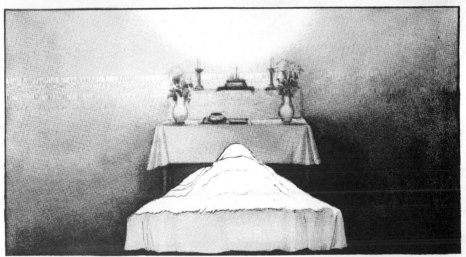

IF YOU
COULD
PLEASE
CONFIRM
HER
IDENTITY
...

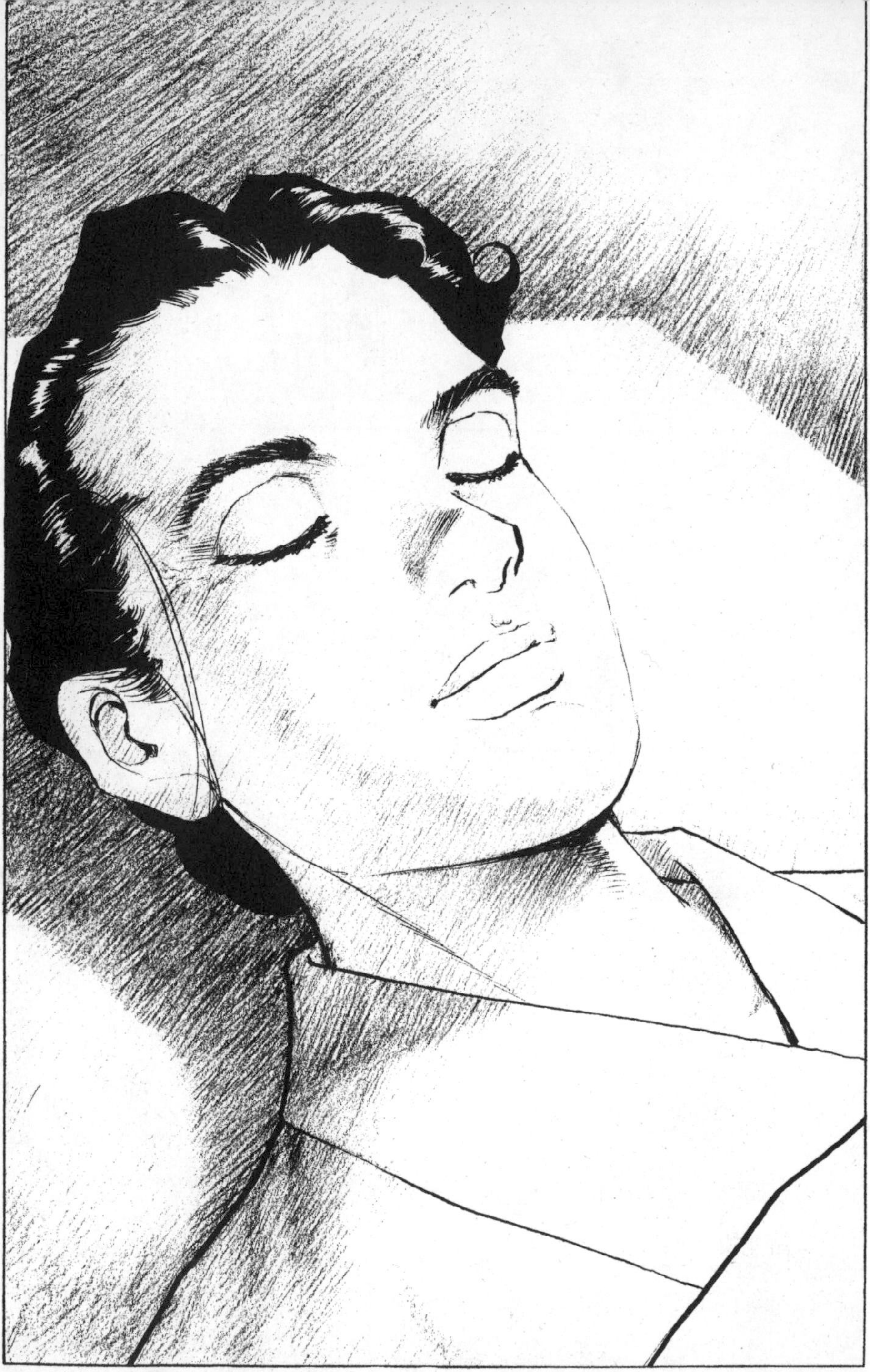

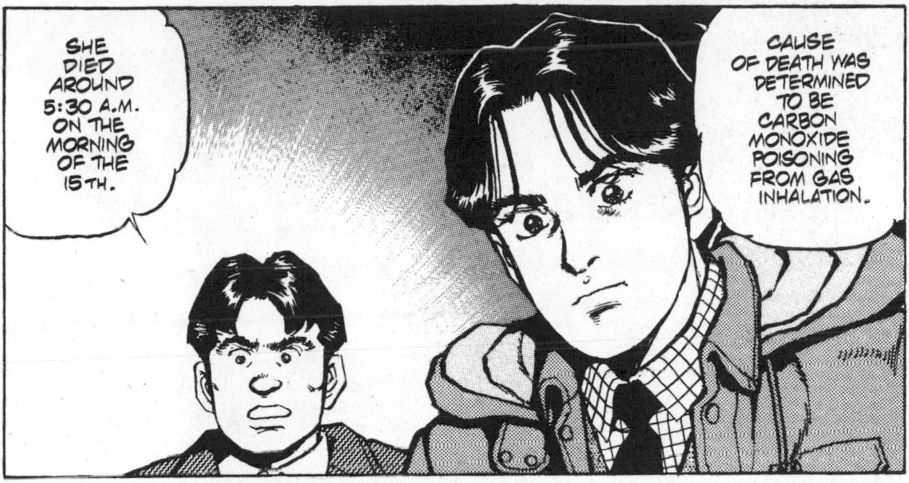
SHE DIED AROUND 5:30 A.M. ON THE MORNING OF THE 15TH.
CAUSE OF DEATH WAS DETERMINED TO BE CARBON MONOXIDE POISONING FROM GAS INHALATION.

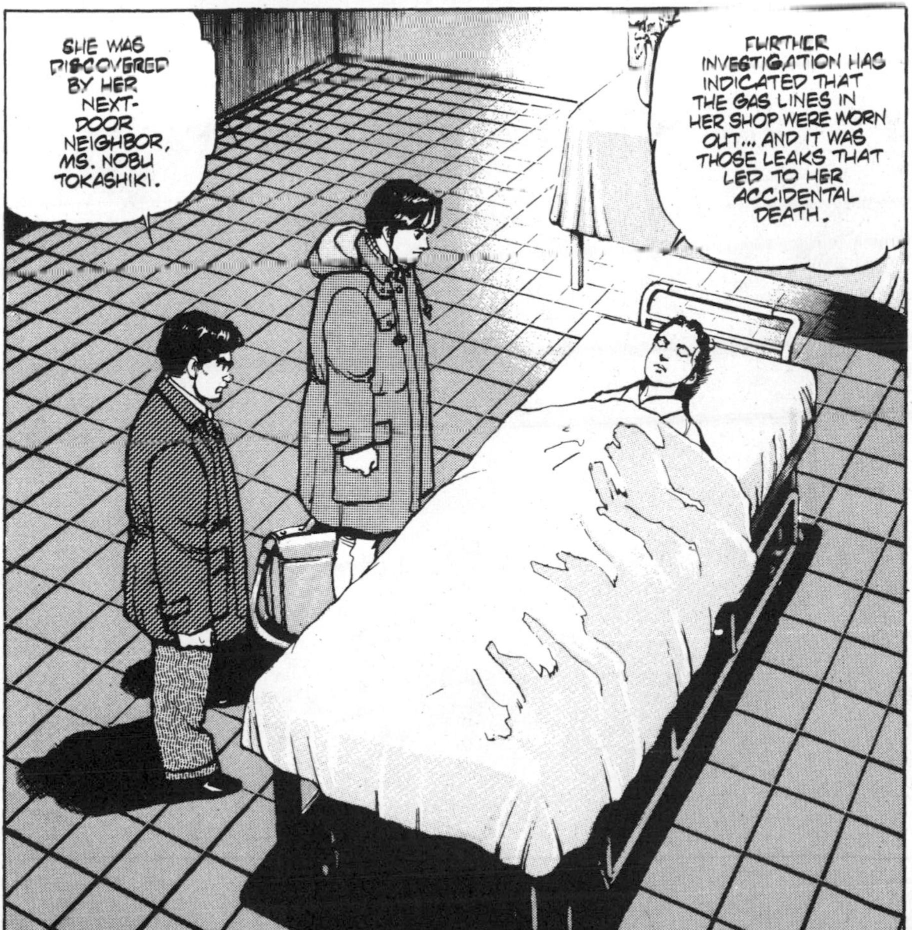
SHE WAS DISCOVERED BY HER NEXT-DOOR NEIGHBOR, MS. NOBU TOKASHIKI.
FURTHER INVESTIGATION HAS INDICATED THAT THE GAS LINES IN HER SHOP WERE WORN OUT... AND IT WAS THOSE LEAKS THAT LED TO HER ACCIDENTAL DEATH.

ARE YOU POSITIVE THIS IS THE BODY OF TOMIKO JO?

YES ...

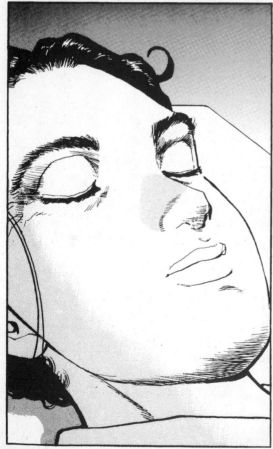

THIS IS MY MOTHER.

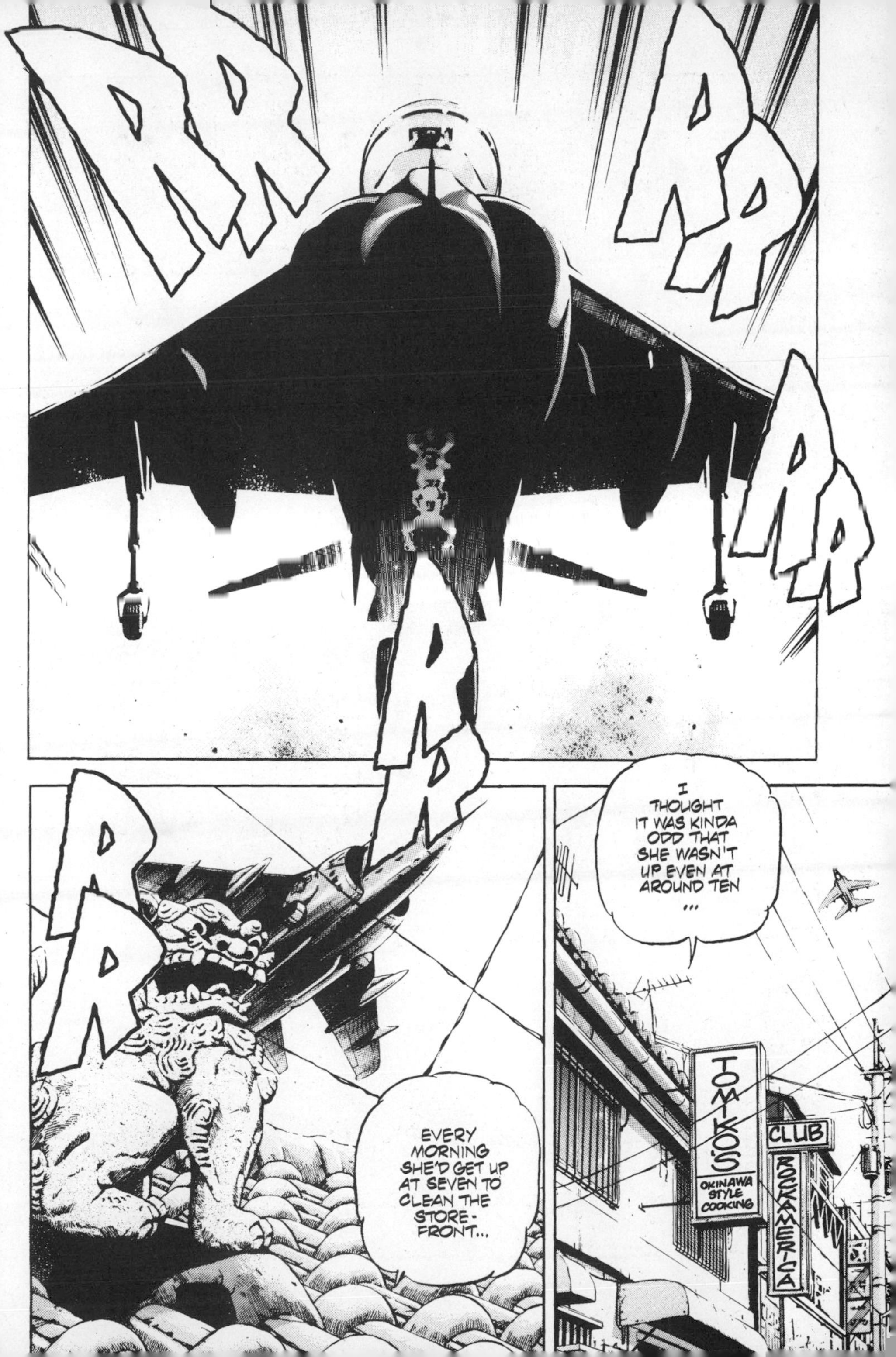
EVERY MORNING SHE'D GET UP AT SEVEN TO CLEAN THE STORE-FRONT...
I THOUGHT IT WAS KINDA ODD THAT SHE WASN'T UP EVEN AT AROUND TEN ...
TOMIKO'S
OKINAWA STYLE COOKING
CLUB
ROCKAMERICA

...BECAUSE SHE WAS ALWAYS SO HARD-WORKING.

YOU NEVER KNOW WHAT'S GONNA HAPPEN, HUH?

SHE WAS ALWAYS SO PROUD OF YOU.

SHE BOASTED HOW YOU WERE A REPORTER FOR AN IMPORTANT NEWS-PAPER. SAID THAT ALL THE YEARS OF HARD WORK TO SEND YOU TO COLLEGE FINALLY PAID OFF.

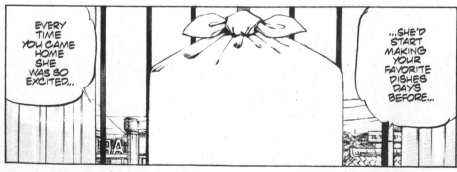

EVERY TIME YOU CAME HOME SHE WAS SO EXCITED...

...SHE'D START MAKING YOUR FAVORITE DISHES DAYS BEFORE...

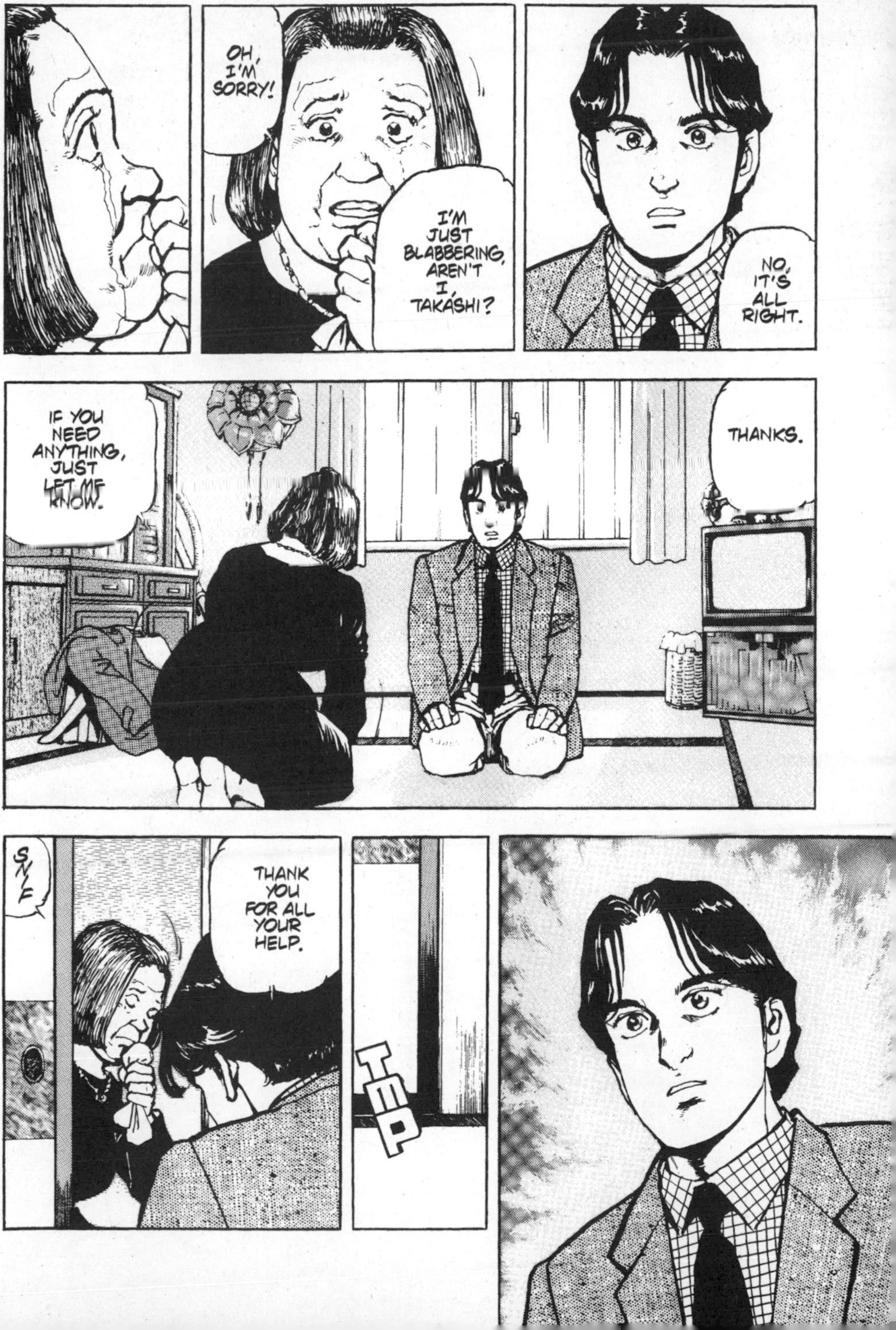
OH, I'M SORRY!
I'M JUST BLABBERING, AREN'T I, TAKASHI?
NO, IT'S ALL RIGHT.
IF YOU NEED ANYTHING, JUST LET ME KNOW.
THANKS.
SNIF
THANK YOU FOR ALL YOUR HELP.
TMP

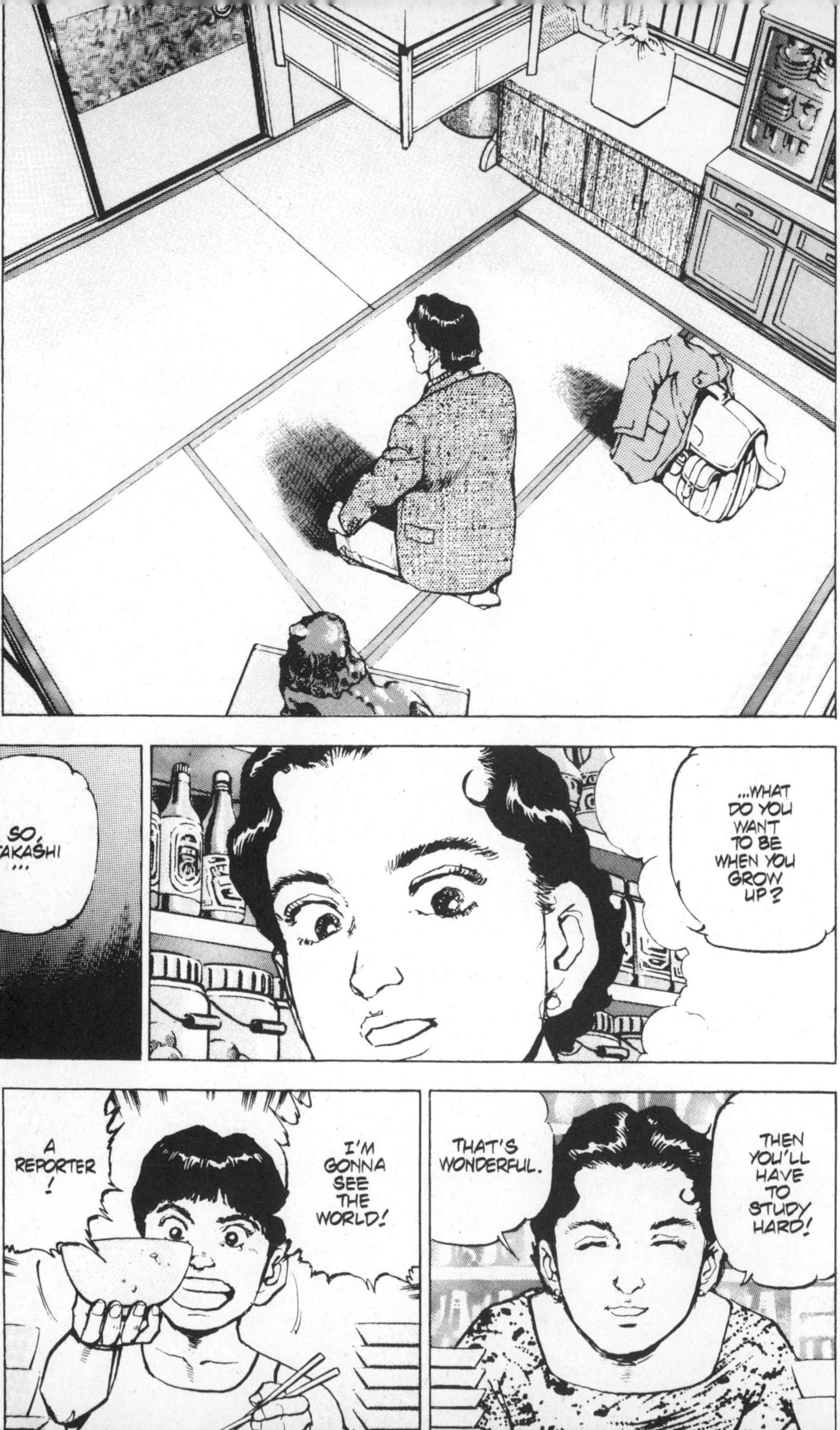
SO, TAKAŚHI ...
...WHAT DO YOU WANT TO BE WHEN YOU GROW UP?
A REPORTER!
I'M GONNA SEE THE WORLD!
THAT'S WONDERFUL.
THEN YOU'LL HAVE TO STUDY HARD!

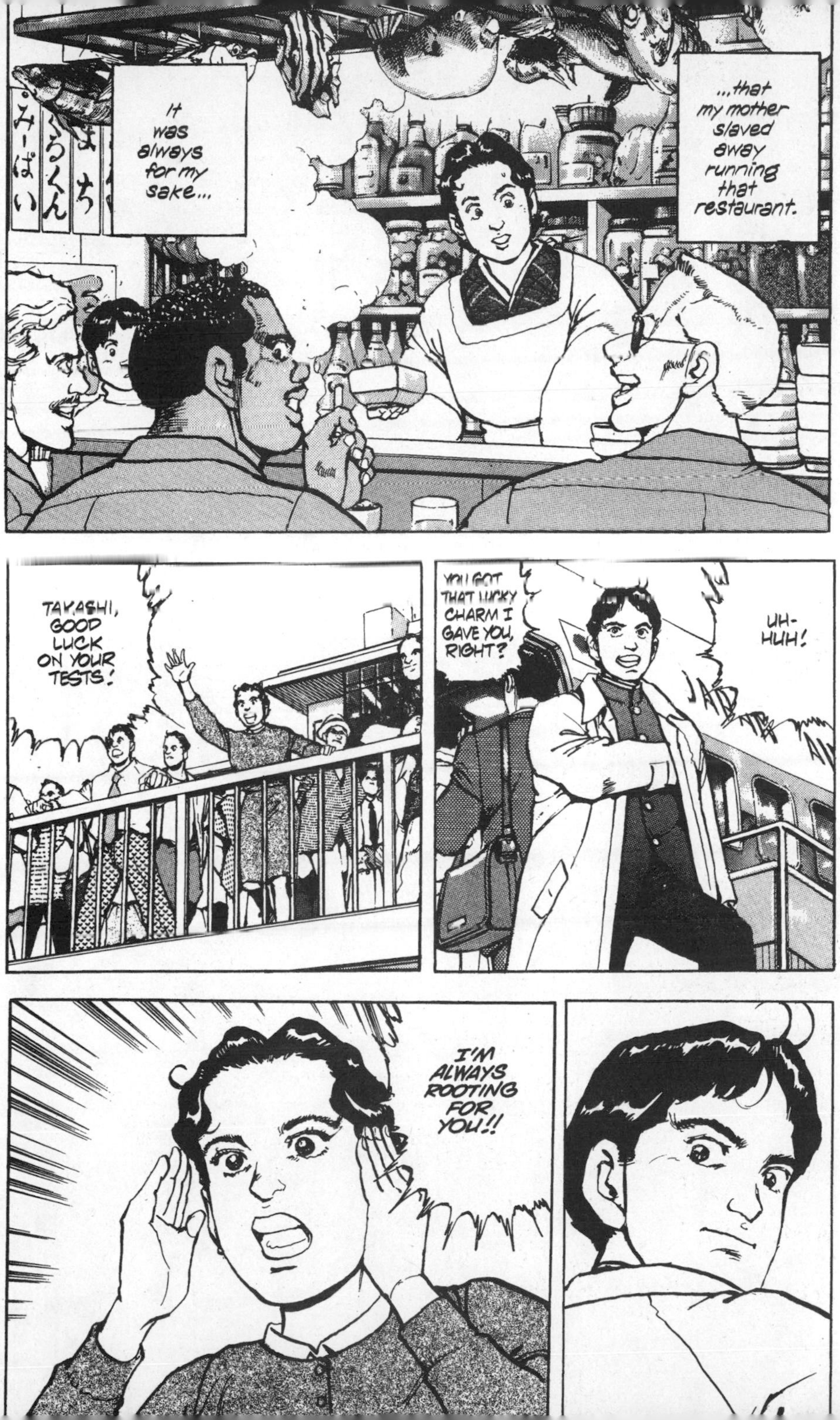

みーばい
It was always for my sake...
...that my mother slaved away running that restaurant.
TAKASHI, GOOD LUCK ON YOUR TESTS!
YOU GOT THAT LUCKY CHARM I GAVE YOU, RIGHT?
UH-HUH!
I'M ALWAYS ROOTING FOR YOU!!

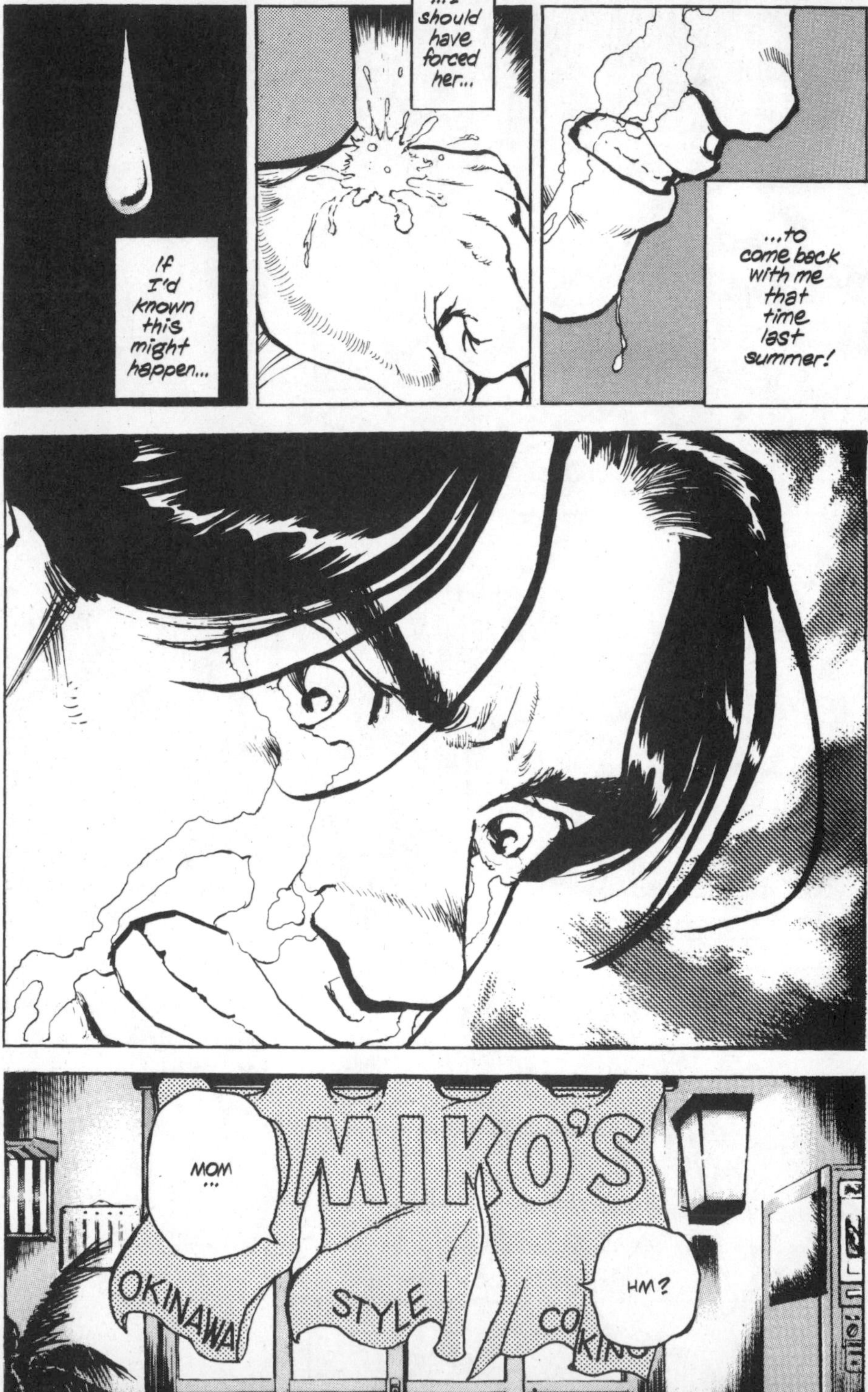
If I'd known this might happen...
...I should have forced her...
...to come back with me that time last summer!
MOM...
MIKO'S
OKINAWA STYLE CO KIN
HM?

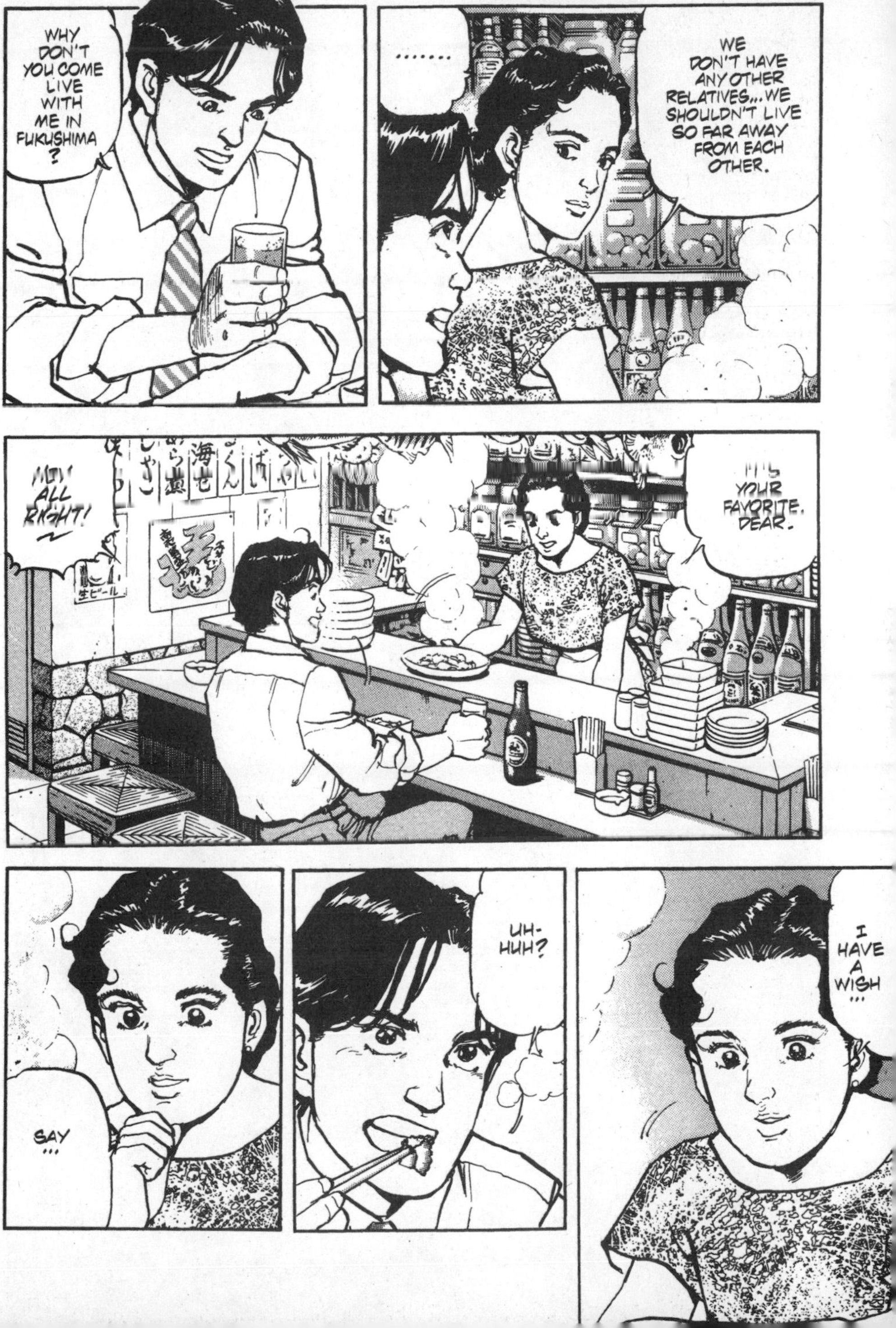
WHY DON'T YOU COME LIVE WITH ME IN FUKUSHIMA?
......
WE DON'T HAVE ANY OTHER RELATIVES... WE SHOULDN'T LIVE SO FAR AWAY FROM EACH OTHER.
ALL RIGHT!
生ビール
YOUR FAVORITE, DEAR.
!
SAY...
UH-HUH?
I HAVE A WISH...

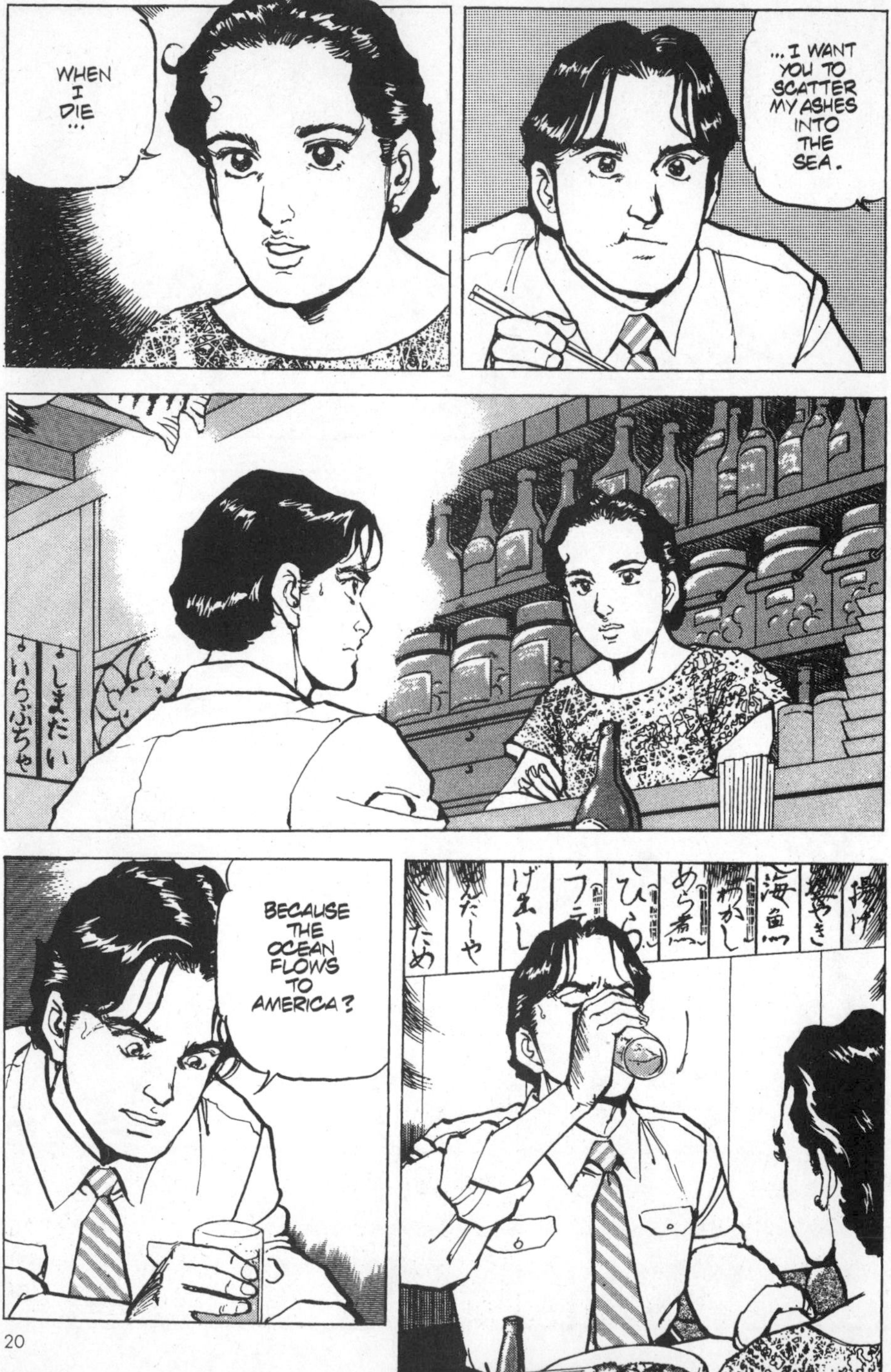
WHEN I DIE ...
... I WANT YOU TO SCATTER MY ASHES INTO THE SEA.
しまたい
いらぶちゃ
BECAUSE THE OCEAN FLOWS TO AMERICA?
あら煮

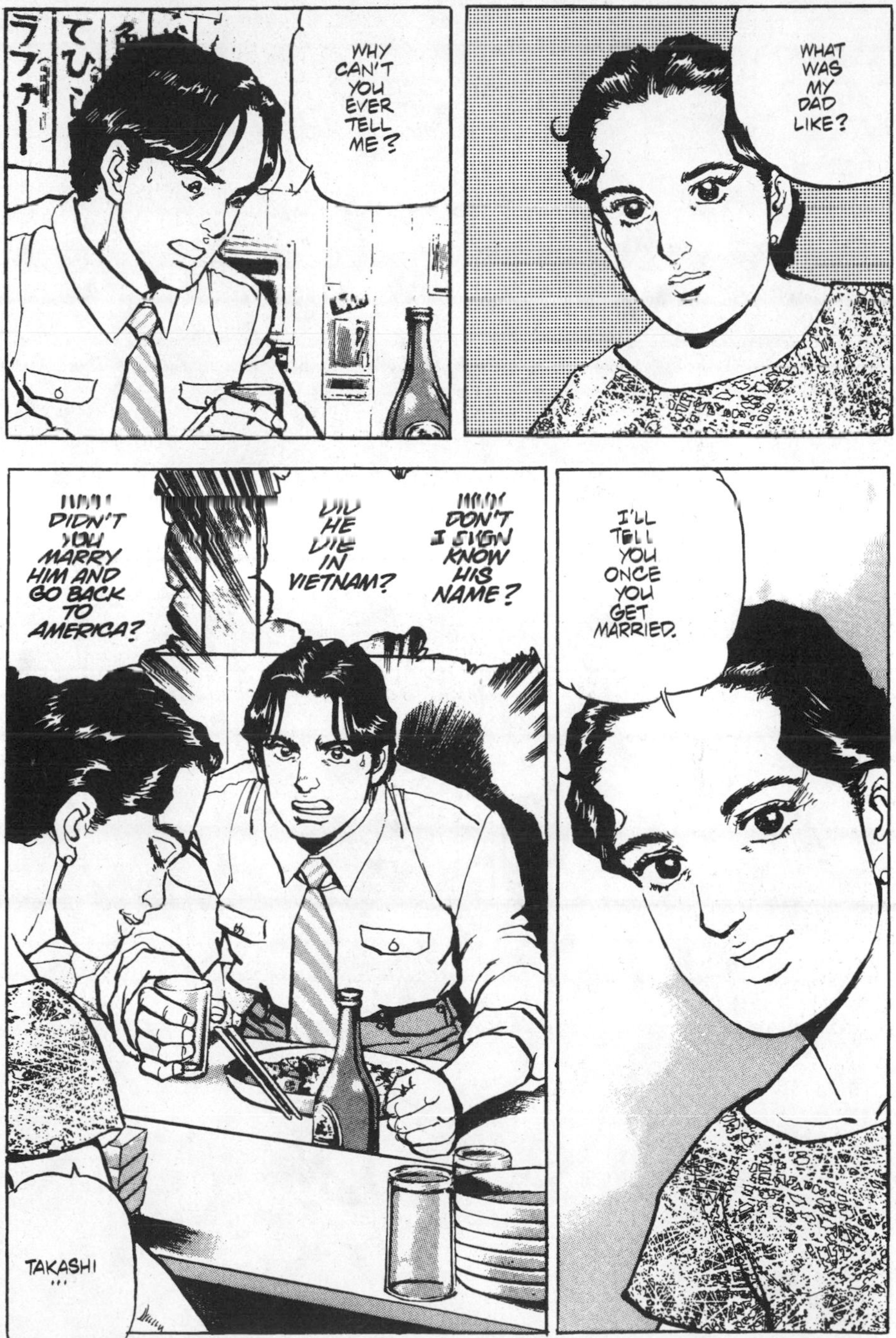
WHY CAN'T YOU EVER TELL ME?
WHAT WAS MY DAD LIKE?
DIDN'T YOU MARRY HIM AND GO BACK TO AMERICA?
HE IN VIETNAM?
DON'T I KNOW HIS NAME?
I'LL TELL YOU ONCE YOU GET MARRIED.
TAKASHI ...

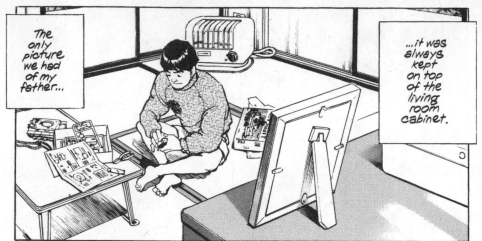

The only picture we had of my father...

...it was always kept on top of the living room cabinet.

An amateurish, out-of-focus photo in faded colors...

...a man in a U.S. Marines uniform... his features looked Japanese, too...

I grew up with that photo by my side....

...thinking, what was he like? Is he like me?

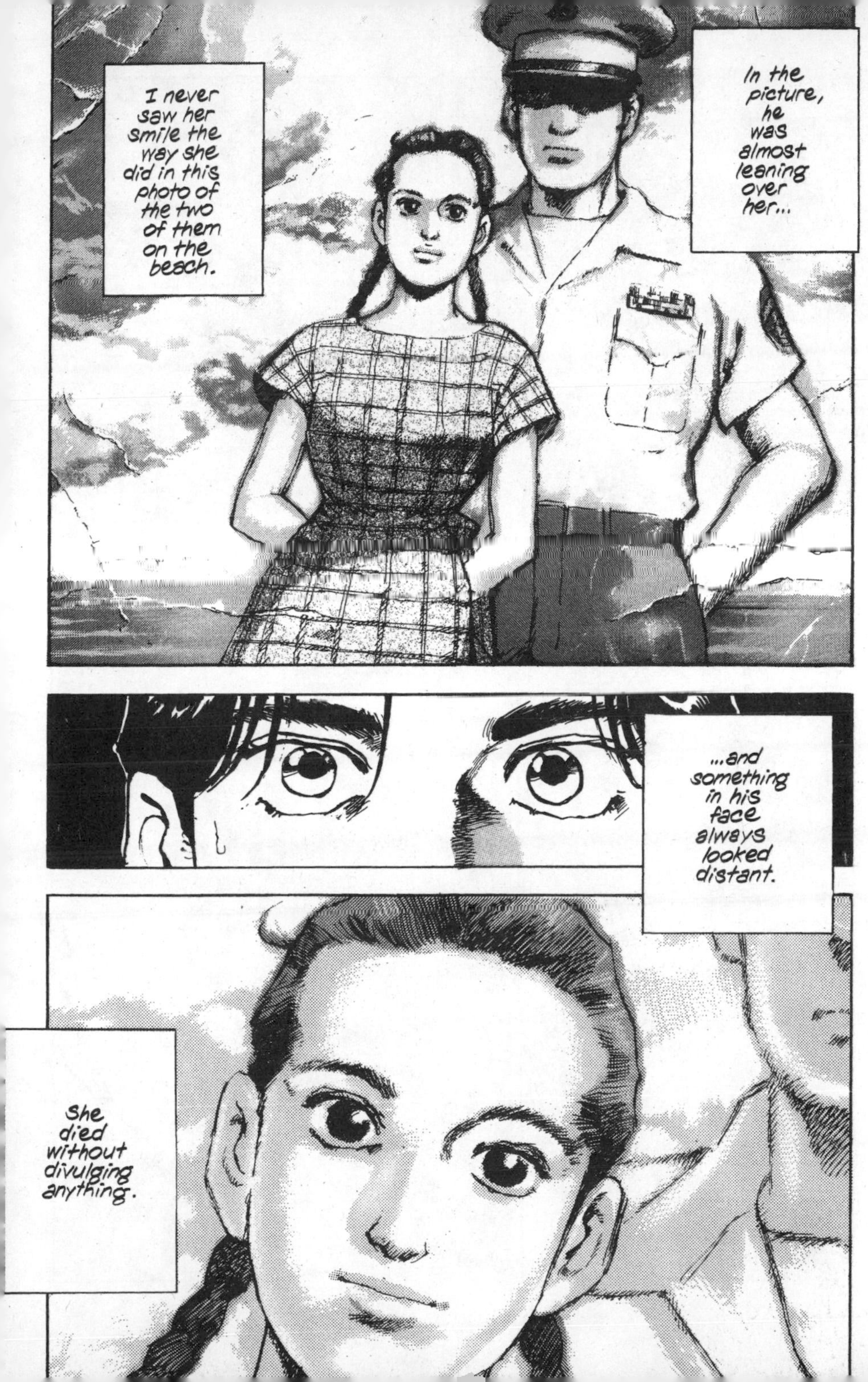
I never saw her smile the way she did in this photo of the two of them on the beach.
In the picture, he was almost leaning over her...
...and something in his face always looked distant.
She died without divulging anything.

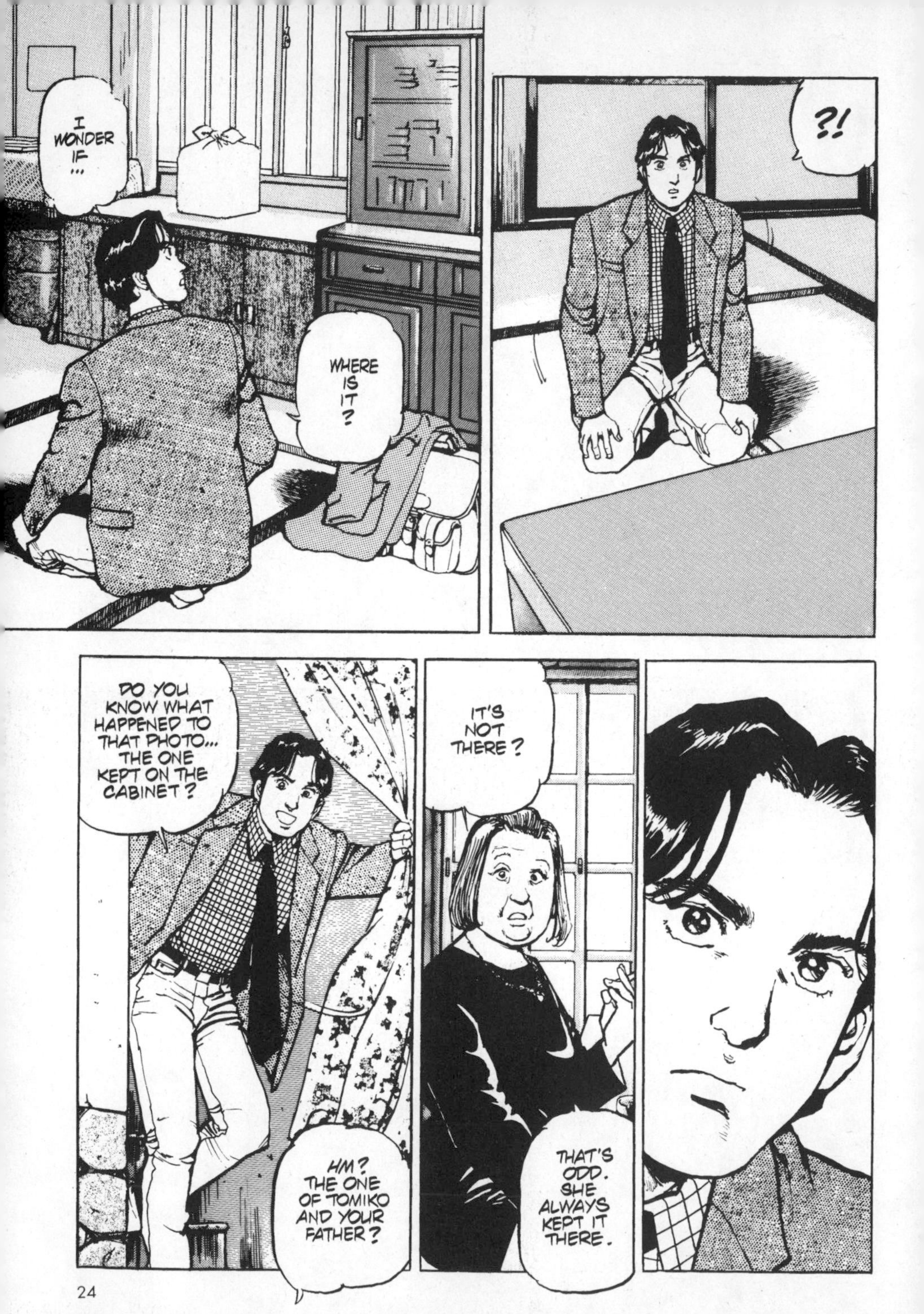
I WONDER IF ...
WHERE IS IT?
?!
DO YOU KNOW WHAT HAPPENED TO THAT PHOTO... THE ONE KEPT ON THE CABINET?
HM? THE ONE OF TOMIKO AND YOUR FATHER?
IT'S NOT THERE?
THAT'S ODD. SHE ALWAYS KEPT IT THERE.

The
police
knew
nothing
about it,
either.

SSSHHAAAA

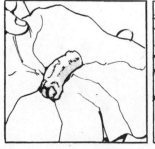

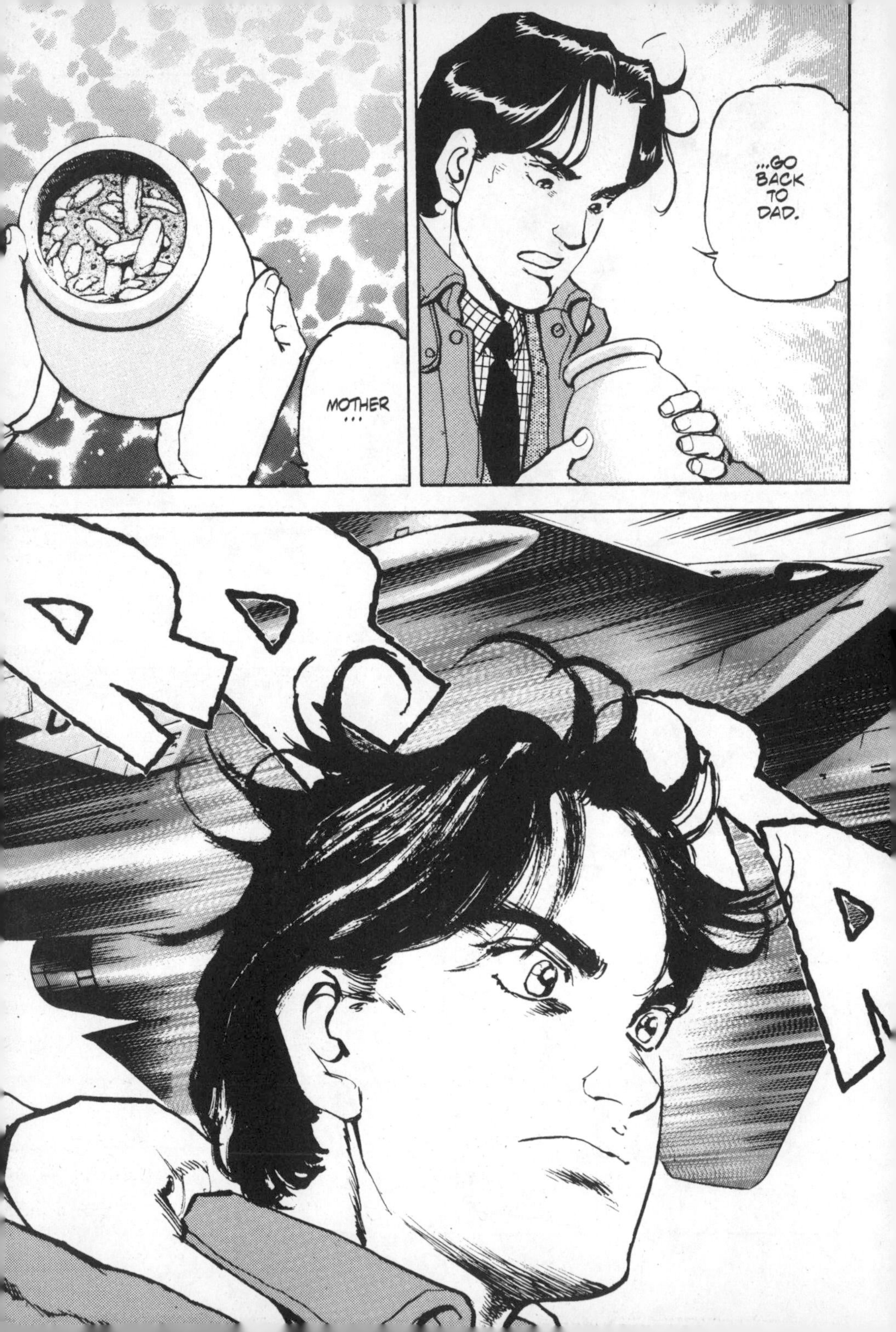
MOTHER ...
...GO BACK TO DAD.

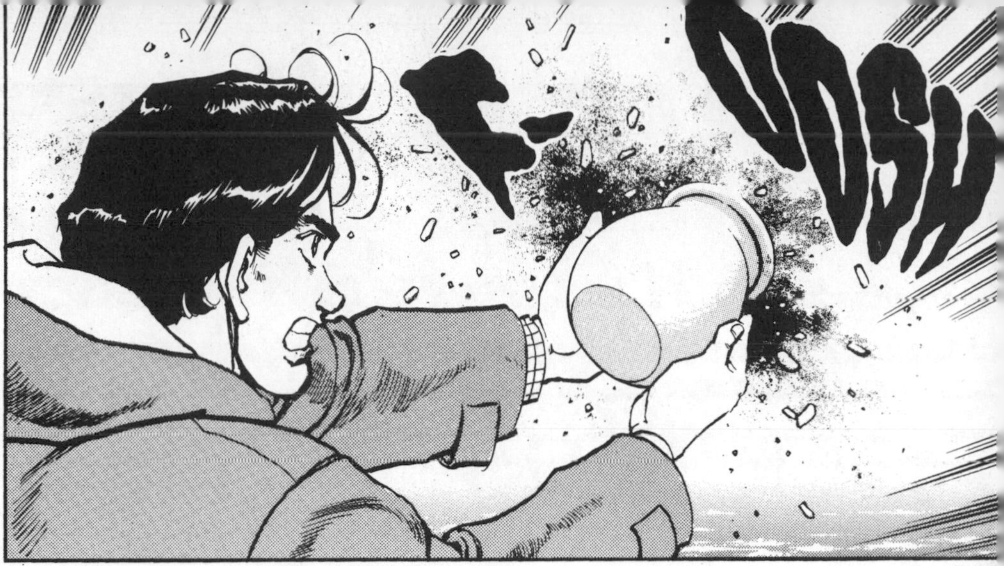
F-OOSH

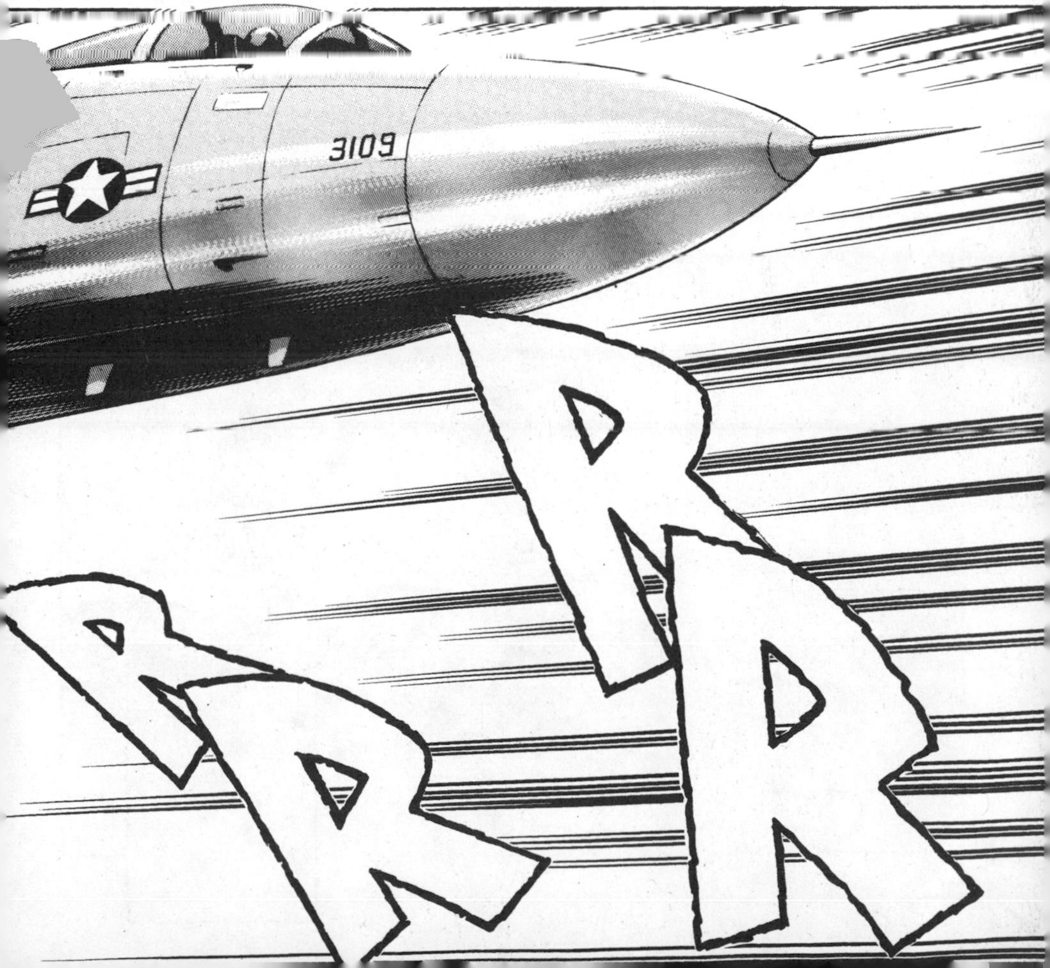
3109
RRRR

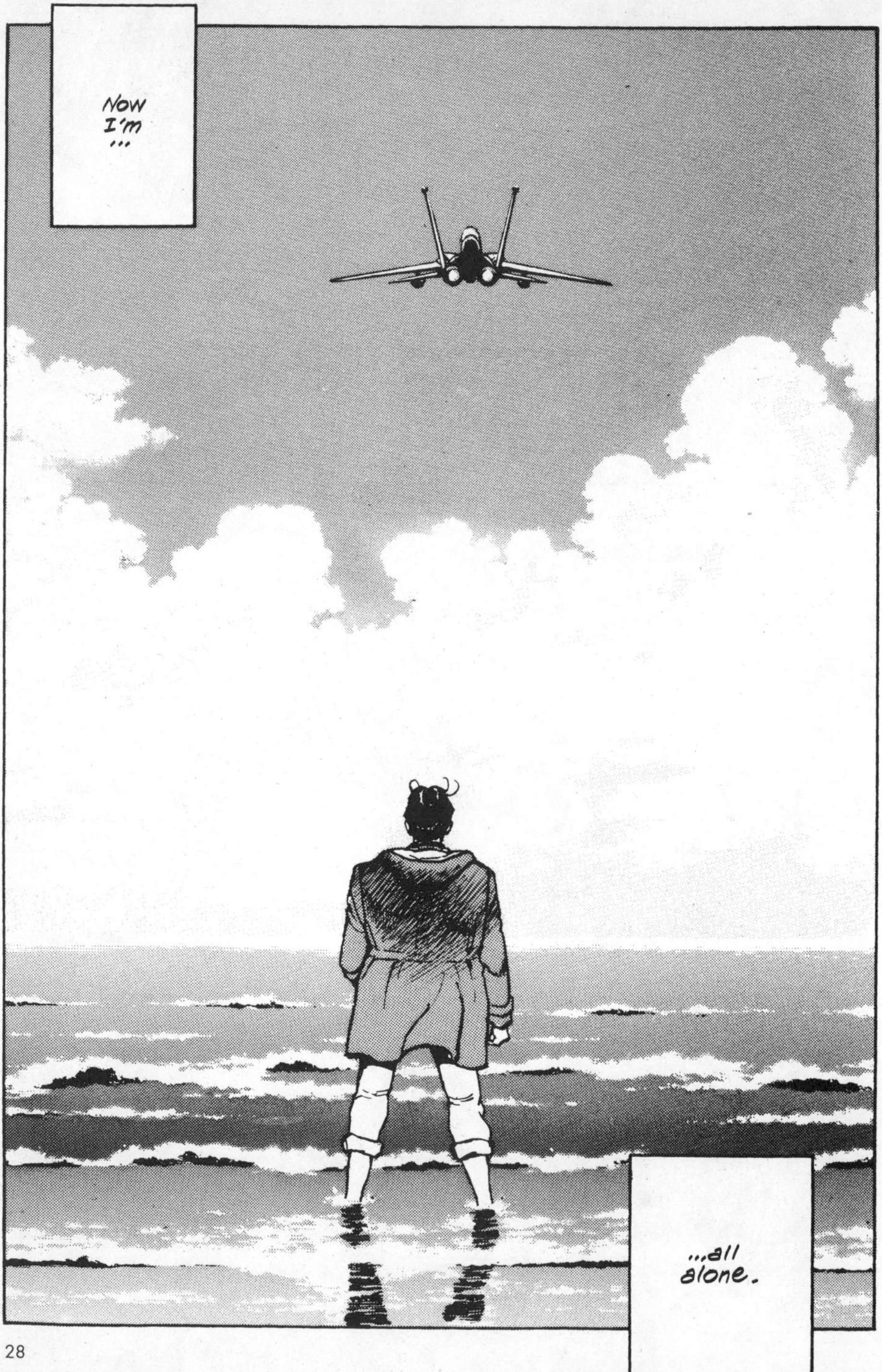
Now I'm ...
...all alone.

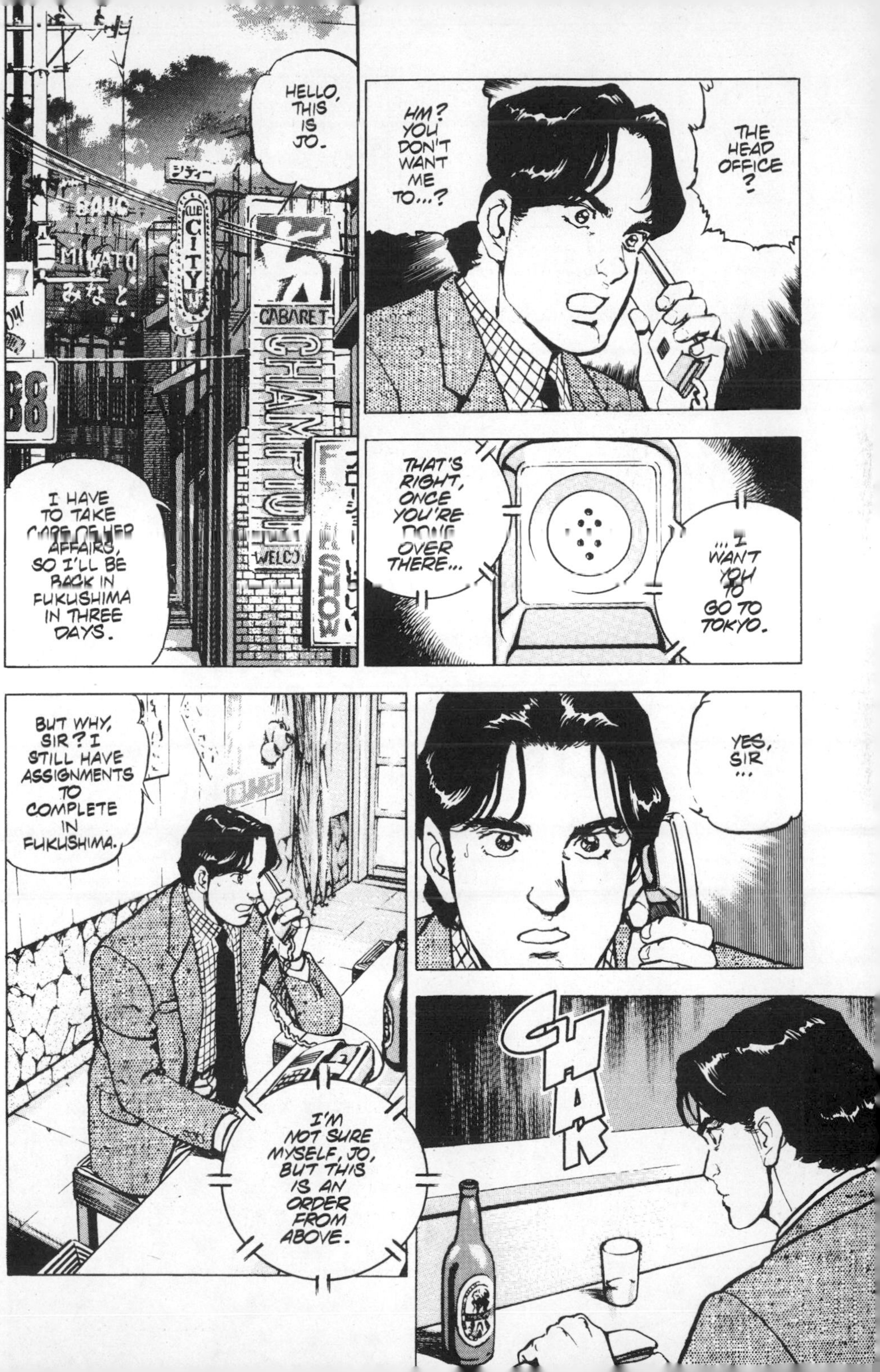
HELLO, THIS IS JO.
シティー
CITY
MINATO
みなと
CABARET
CHAMP
SHOW
I HAVE TO TAKE CARE OF HER AFFAIRS, SO I'LL BE BACK IN FUKUSHIMA IN THREE DAYS.
HM? YOU DON'T WANT ME TO...?
THE HEAD OFFICE?
THAT'S RIGHT, ONCE YOU'RE DONE OVER THERE...
...I WANT YOU TO GO TO TOKYO.
BUT WHY, SIR? I STILL HAVE ASSIGNMENTS TO COMPLETE IN FUKUSHIMA.
I'M NOT SURE MYSELF, JO, BUT THIS IS AN ORDER FROM ABOVE.
YES, SIR...
CHAK

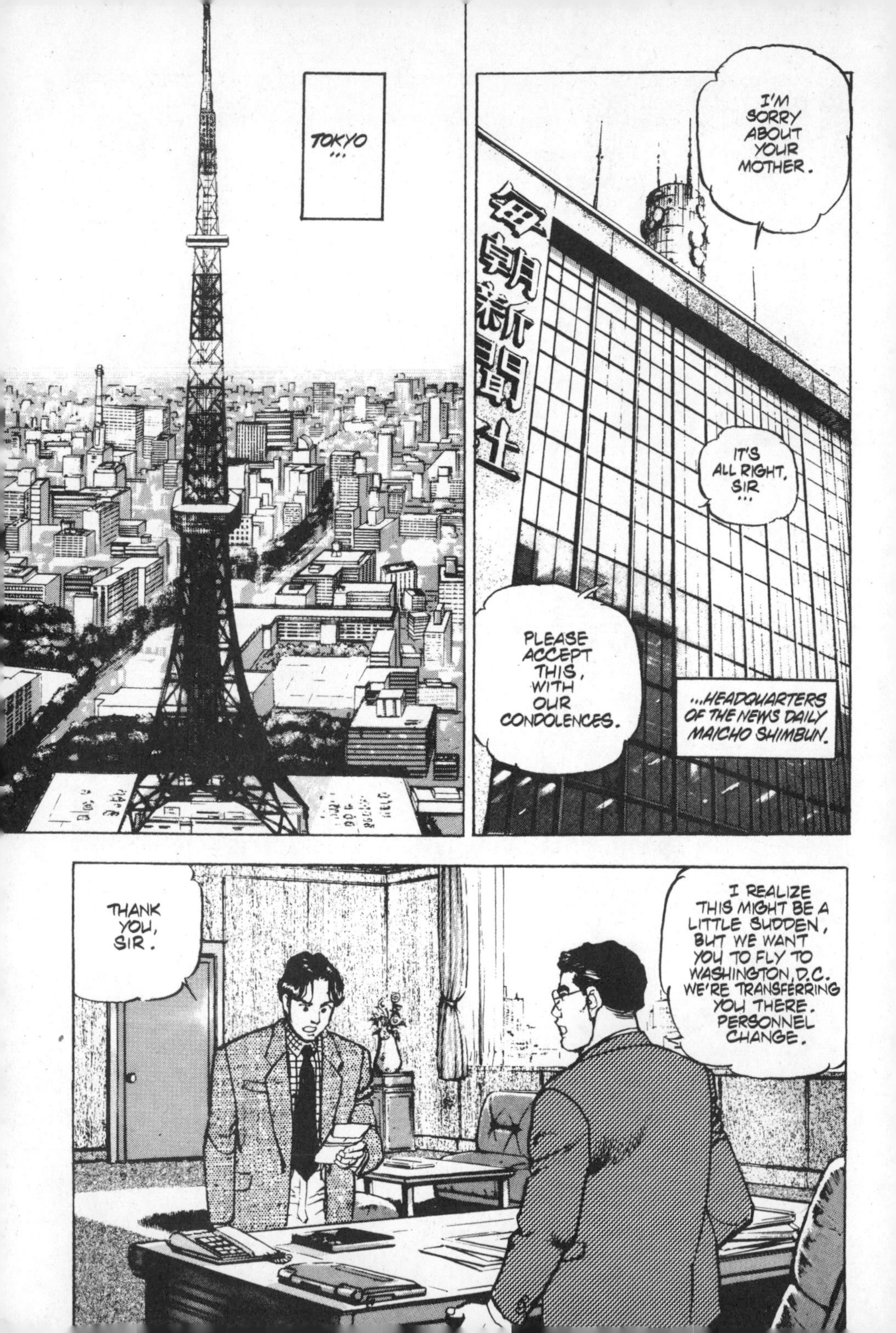
TOKYO ...
I'M SORRY ABOUT YOUR MOTHER.
毎朝新聞社
IT'S ALL RIGHT, SIR ...
PLEASE ACCEPT THIS, WITH OUR CONDOLENCES.
...HEADQUARTERS OF THE NEWS DAILY MAICHO SHIMBUN.
THANK YOU, SIR.
I REALIZE THIS MIGHT BE A LITTLE SUDDEN, BUT WE WANT YOU TO FLY TO WASHINGTON, D.C. WE'RE TRANSFERRING YOU THERE. PERSONNEL CHANGE.

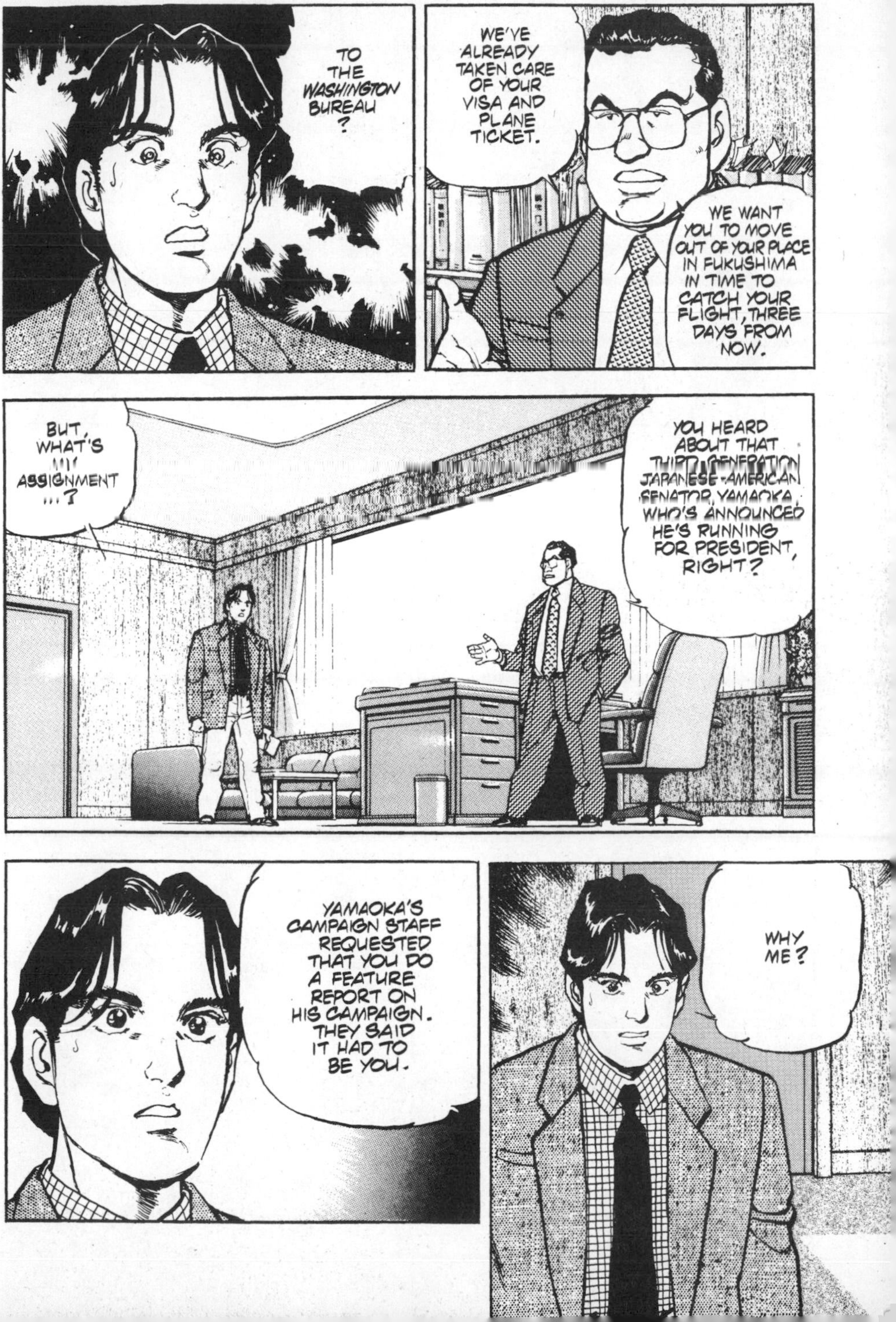
TO THE WASHINGTON BUREAU?
WE'VE ALREADY TAKEN CARE OF YOUR VISA AND PLANE TICKET.
WE WANT YOU TO MOVE OUT OF YOUR PLACE IN FUKUSHIMA IN TIME TO CATCH YOUR FLIGHT, THREE DAYS FROM NOW.
BUT, WHAT'S MY ASSIGNMENT ...?
YOU HEARD ABOUT THAT THIRD-GENERATION JAPANESE-AMERICAN SENATOR, YAMAOKA, WHO'S ANNOUNCED HE'S RUNNING FOR PRESIDENT, RIGHT?
YAMAOKA'S CAMPAIGN STAFF REQUESTED THAT YOU DO A FEATURE REPORT ON HIS CAMPAIGN. THEY SAID IT HAD TO BE YOU.
WHY ME?

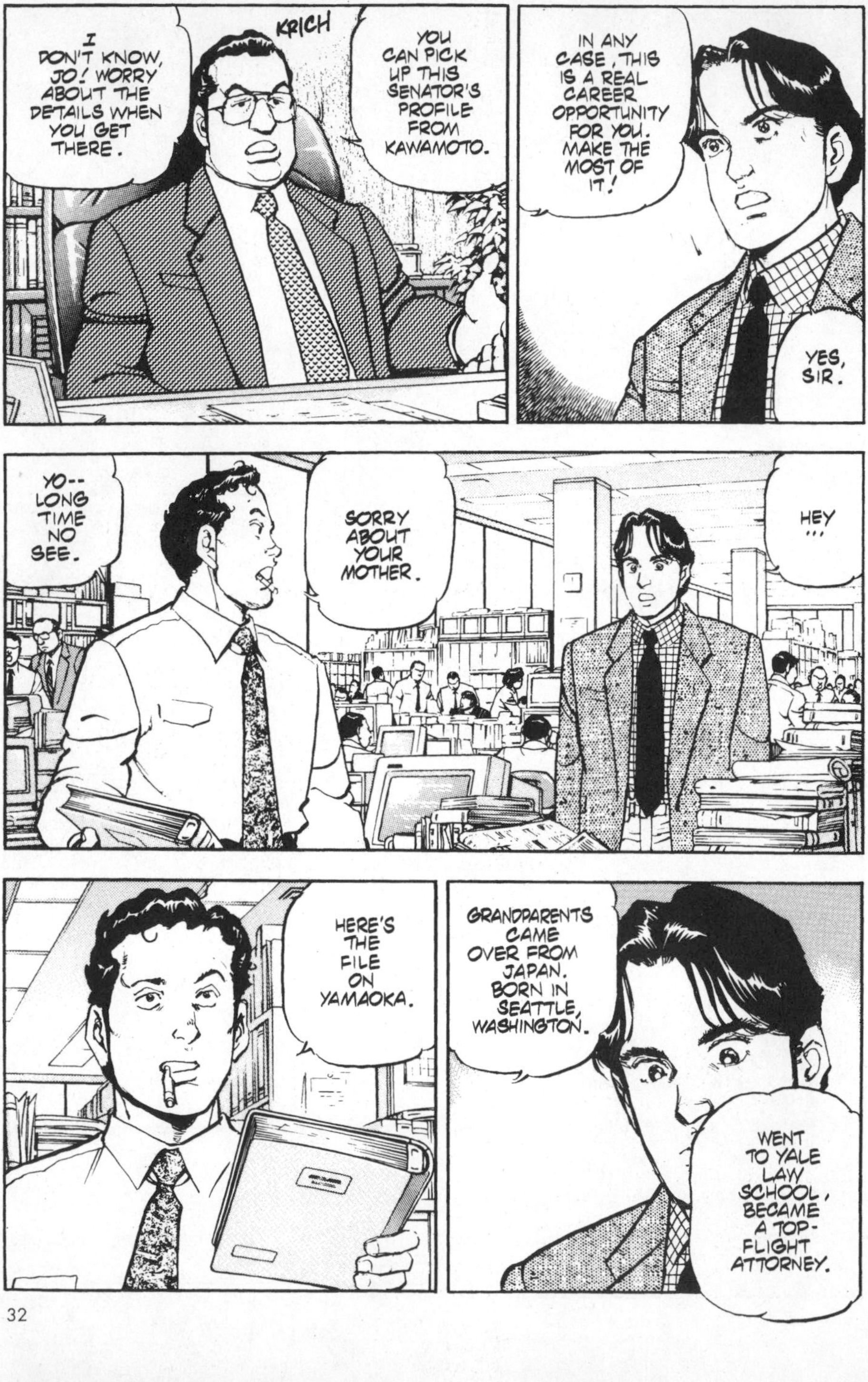
I DON'T KNOW, JO! WORRY ABOUT THE DETAILS WHEN YOU GET THERE.
KRICH
YOU CAN PICK UP THIS SENATOR'S PROFILE FROM KAWAMOTO.
IN ANY CASE, THIS IS A REAL CAREER OPPORTUNITY FOR YOU. MAKE THE MOST OF IT!
YES, SIR.
YO-- LONG TIME NO SEE.
SORRY ABOUT YOUR MOTHER.
HEY ...
HERE'S THE FILE ON YAMAOKA.
GRANDPARENTS CAME OVER FROM JAPAN. BORN IN SEATTLE, WASHINGTON.
WENT TO YALE LAW SCHOOL, BECAME A TOP-FLIGHT ATTORNEY.

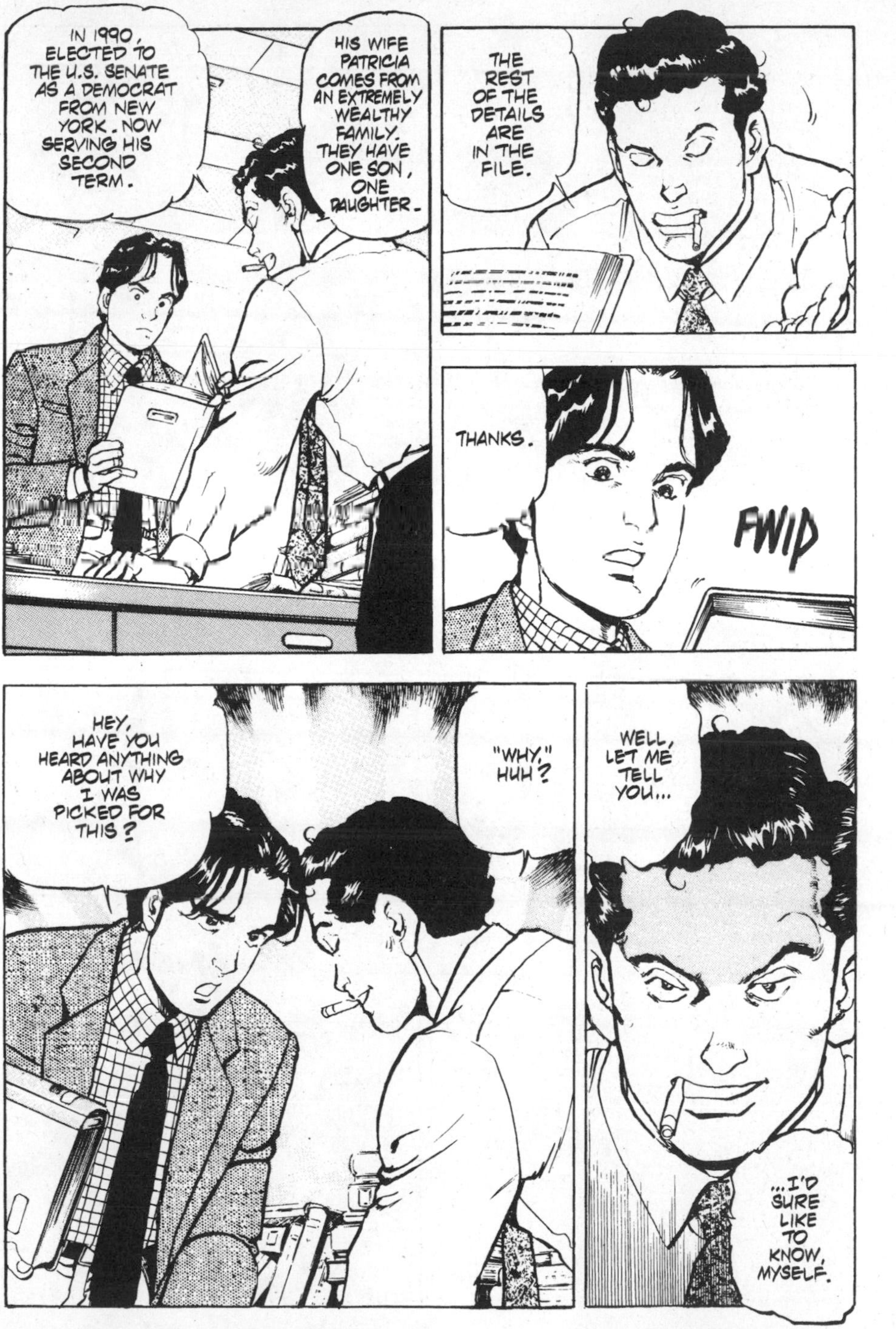
IN 1990, ELECTED TO THE U.S. SENATE AS A DEMOCRAT FROM NEW YORK. NOW SERVING HIS SECOND TERM.
HIS WIFE PATRICIA COMES FROM AN EXTREMELY WEALTHY FAMILY. THEY HAVE ONE SON, ONE DAUGHTER.
THE REST OF THE DETAILS ARE IN THE FILE.
THANKS.
FWIP
HEY, HAVE YOU HEARD ANYTHING ABOUT WHY I WAS PICKED FOR THIS?
"WHY," HUH?
WELL, LET ME TELL YOU...
...I'D SURE LIKE TO KNOW, MYSELF.

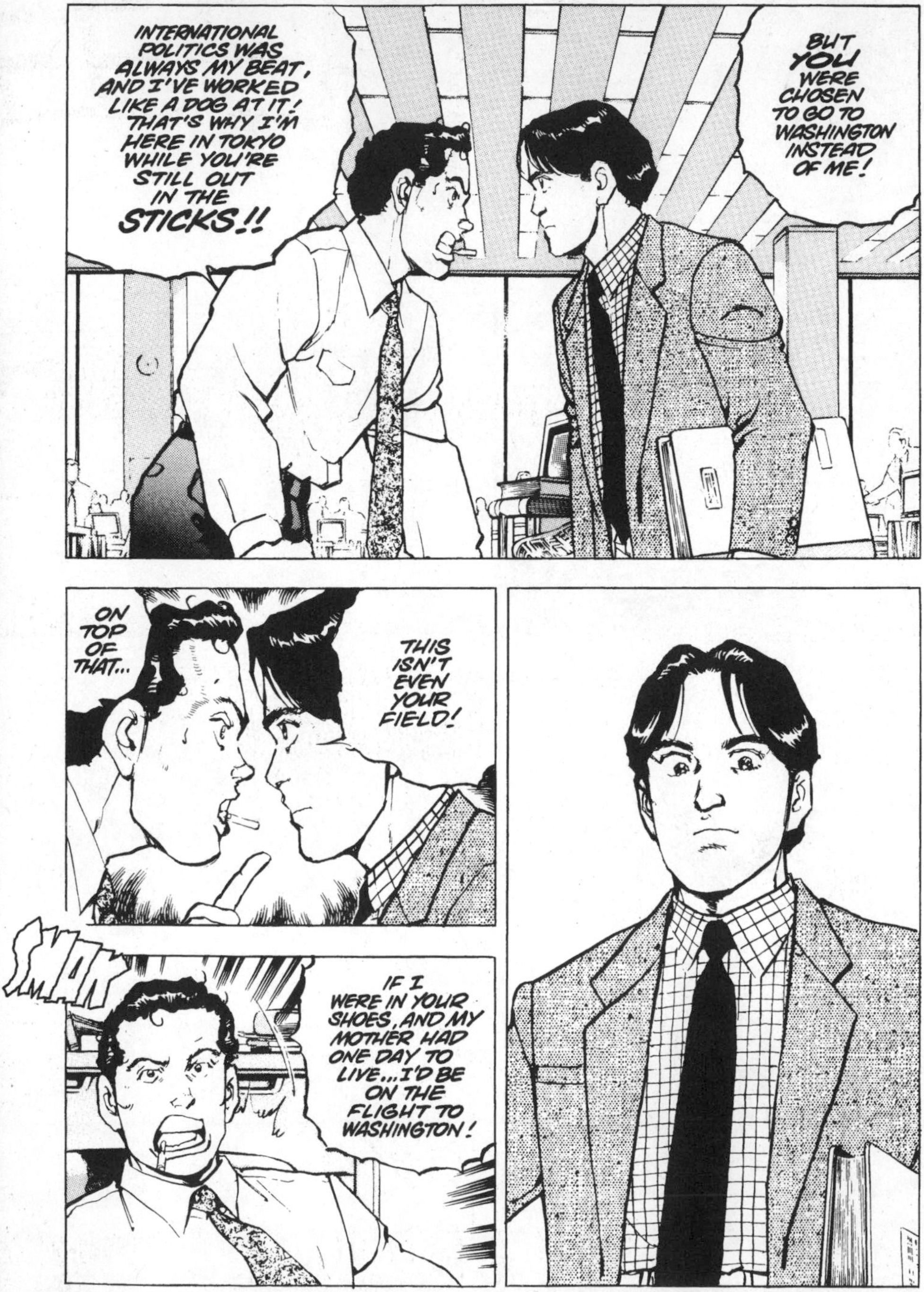
INTERNATIONAL POLITICS WAS ALWAYS MY BEAT, AND I'VE WORKED LIKE A DOG AT IT! THAT'S WHY I'M HERE IN TOKYO WHILE YOU'RE STILL OUT IN THE STICKS!!
BUT YOU WERE CHOSEN TO GO TO WASHINGTON INSTEAD OF ME!
ON TOP OF THAT...
THIS ISN'T EVEN YOUR FIELD!
SMAK
IF I WERE IN YOUR SHOES, AND MY MOTHER HAD ONE DAY TO LIVE... I'D BE ON THE FLIGHT TO WASHINGTON!

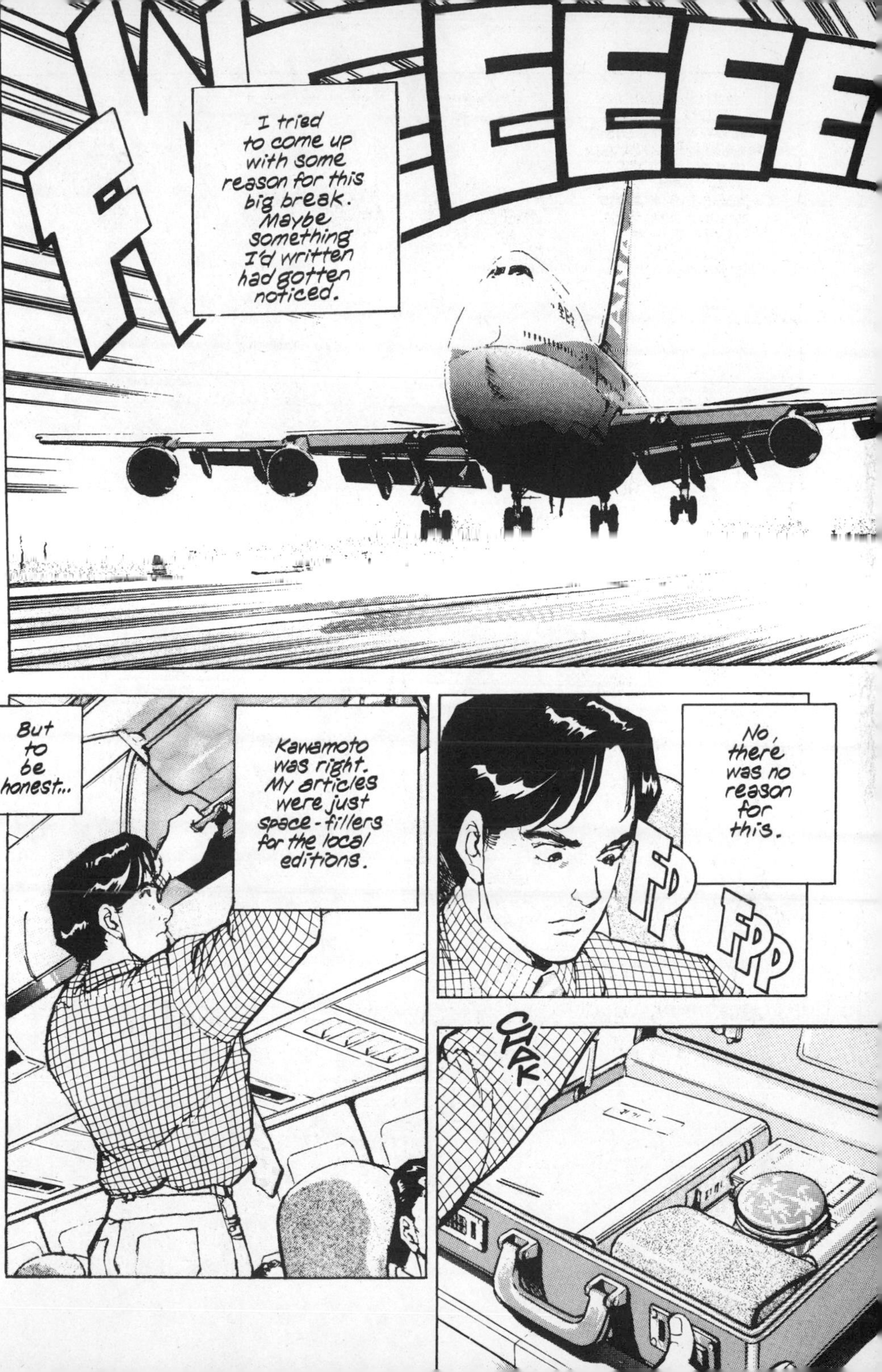
FWEEEEE
I tried to come up with some reason for this big break. Maybe something I'd written had gotten noticed.
But to be honest...
Kawamoto was right. My articles were just space-fillers for the local editions.
No, there was no reason for this.
FP
FPP
CHAK

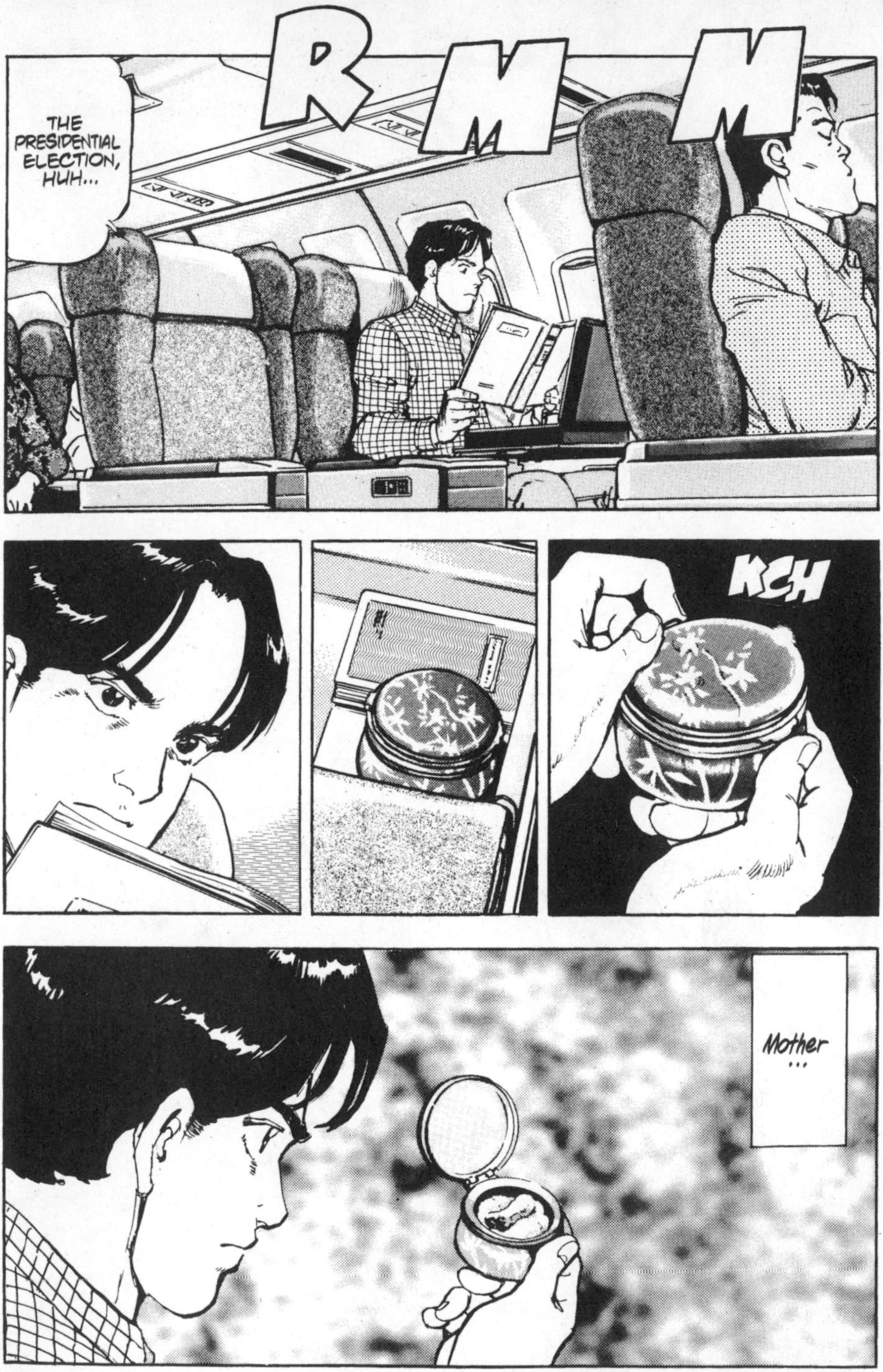
RMM
THE PRESIDENTIAL ELECTION, HUH...
KCH
Mother...

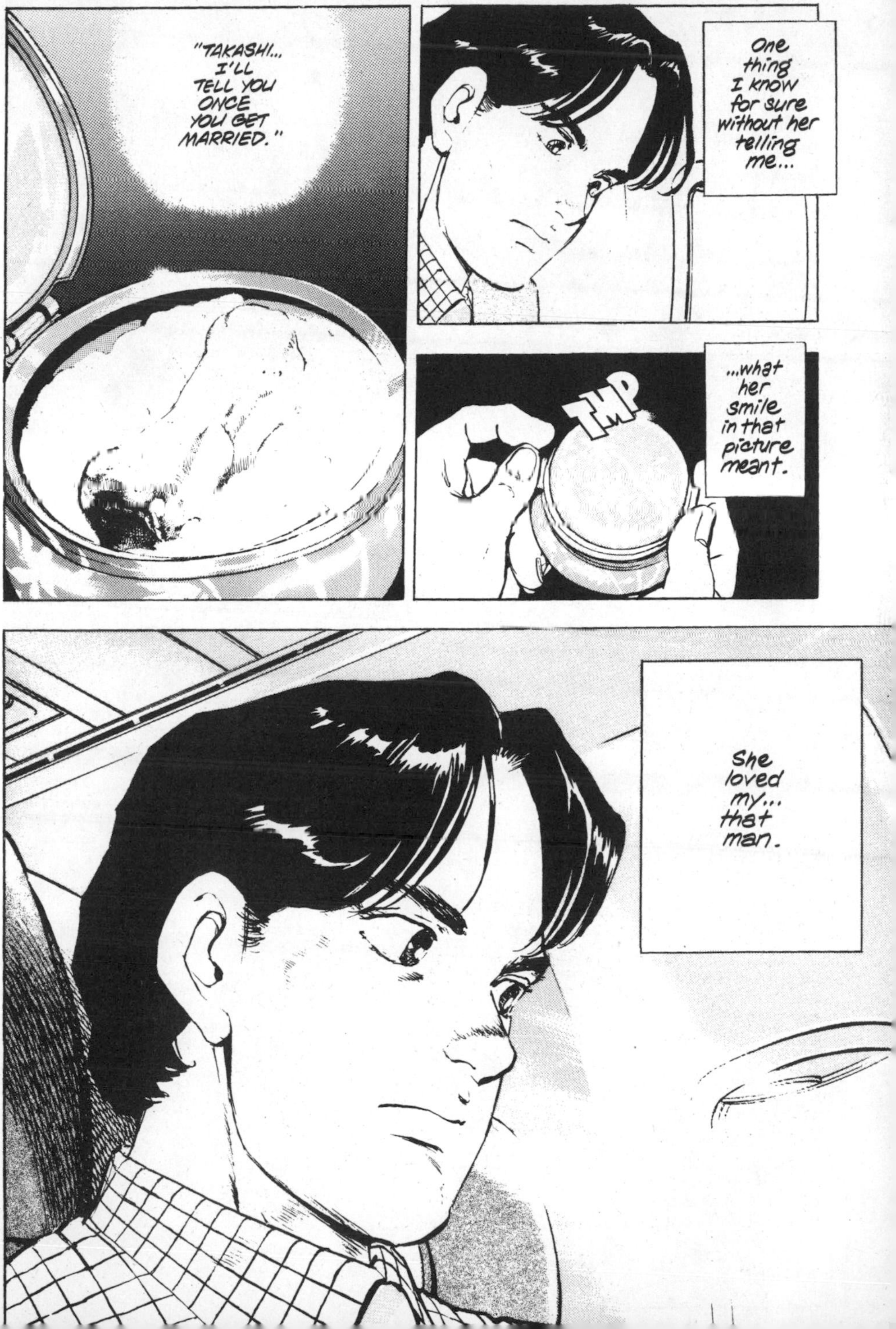
"TAKASHI... I'LL TELL YOU ONCE YOU GET MARRIED."
One thing I know for sure without her telling me...
THP
...what her smile in that picture meant.
She loved my... that man.

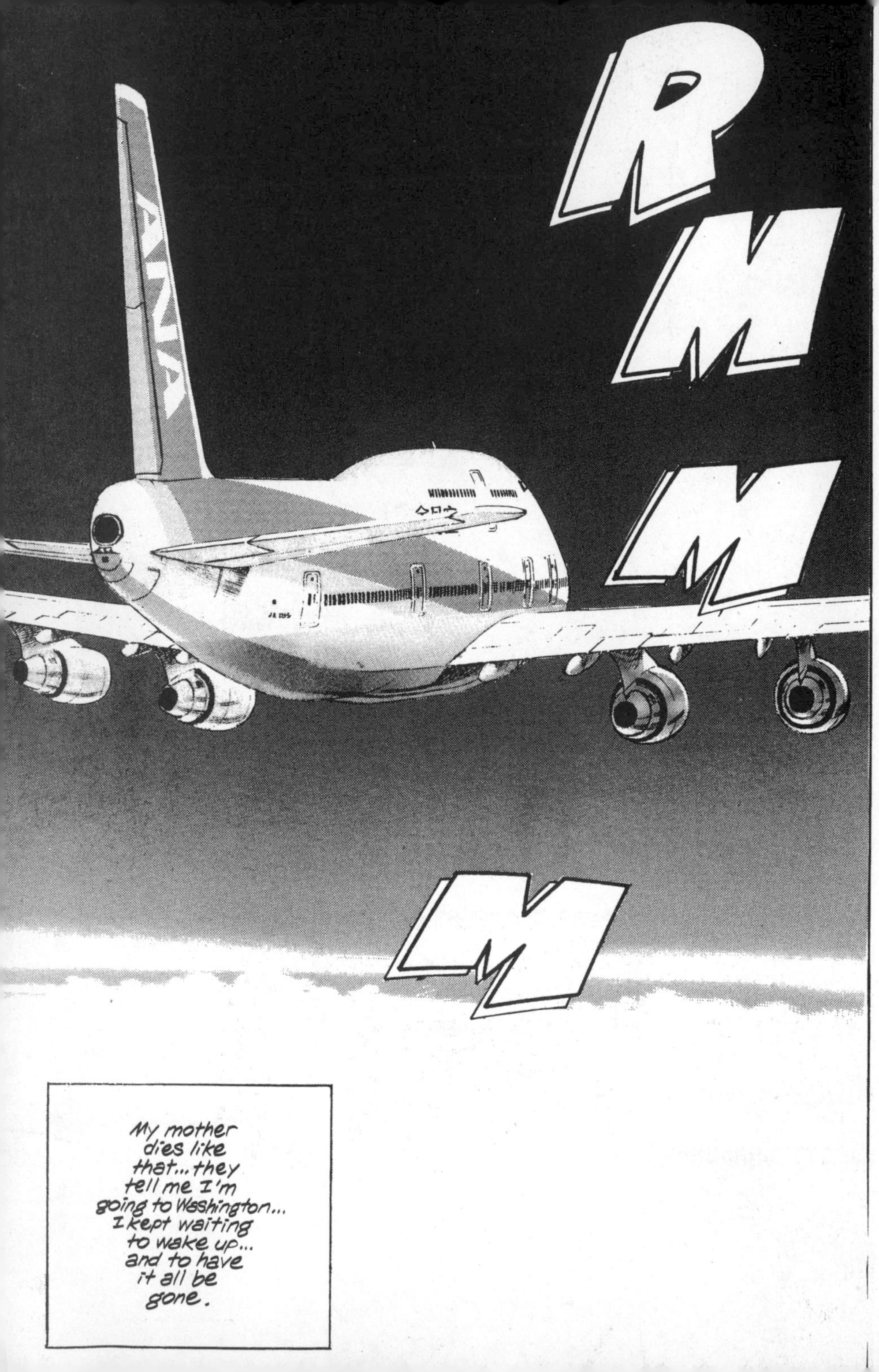
RMMM
My mother dies like that... they tell me I'm going to Washington... I kept waiting to wake up... and to have it all be gone.

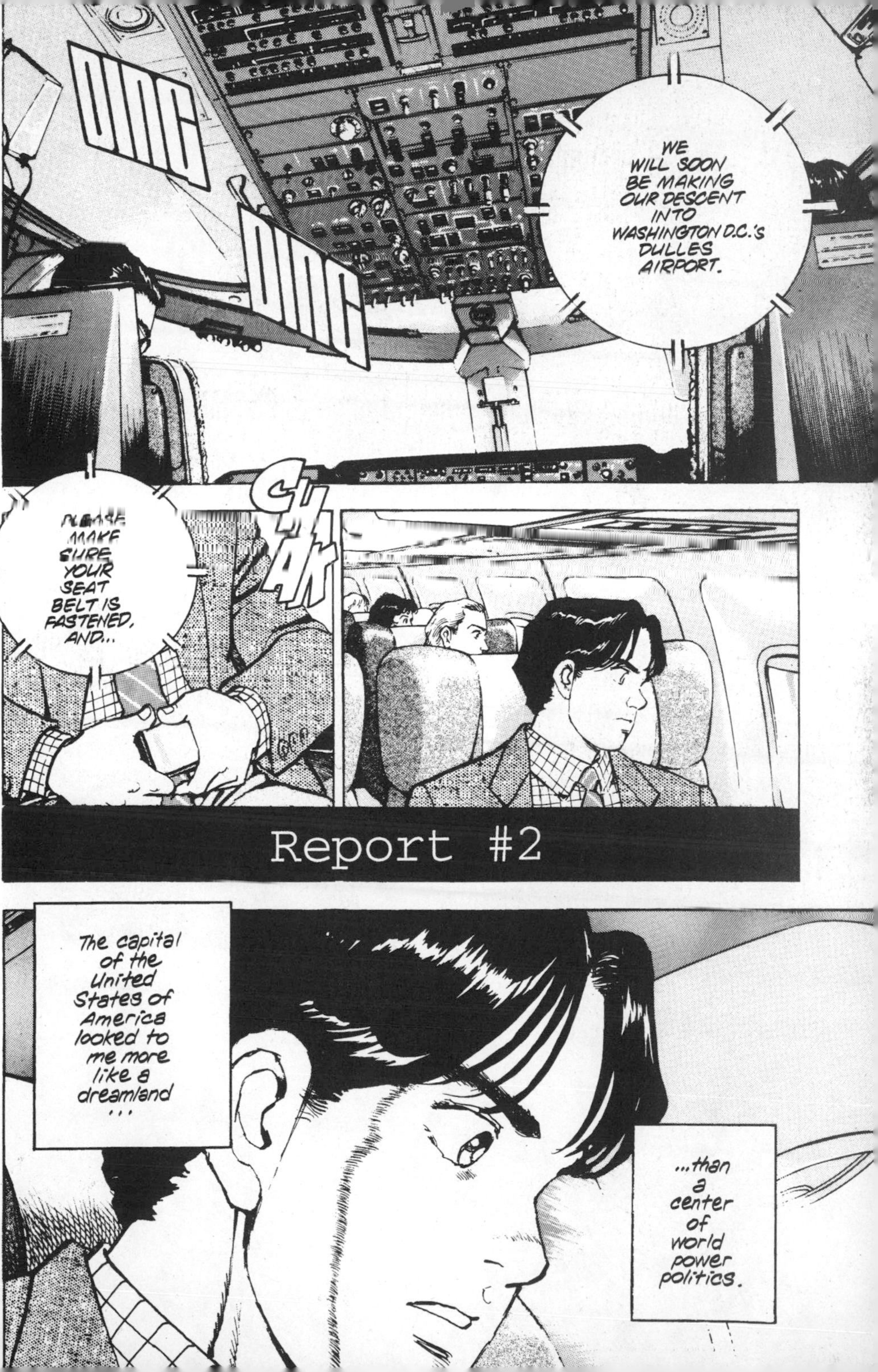
DING
DING
WE WILL SOON BE MAKING OUR DESCENT INTO WASHINGTON D.C.'s DULLES AIRPORT.
PLEASE MAKE SURE YOUR SEAT BELT IS FASTENED, AND...
CHAK
Report #2
The capital of the United States of America looked to me more like a dreamland ...
...than a center of world power politics.

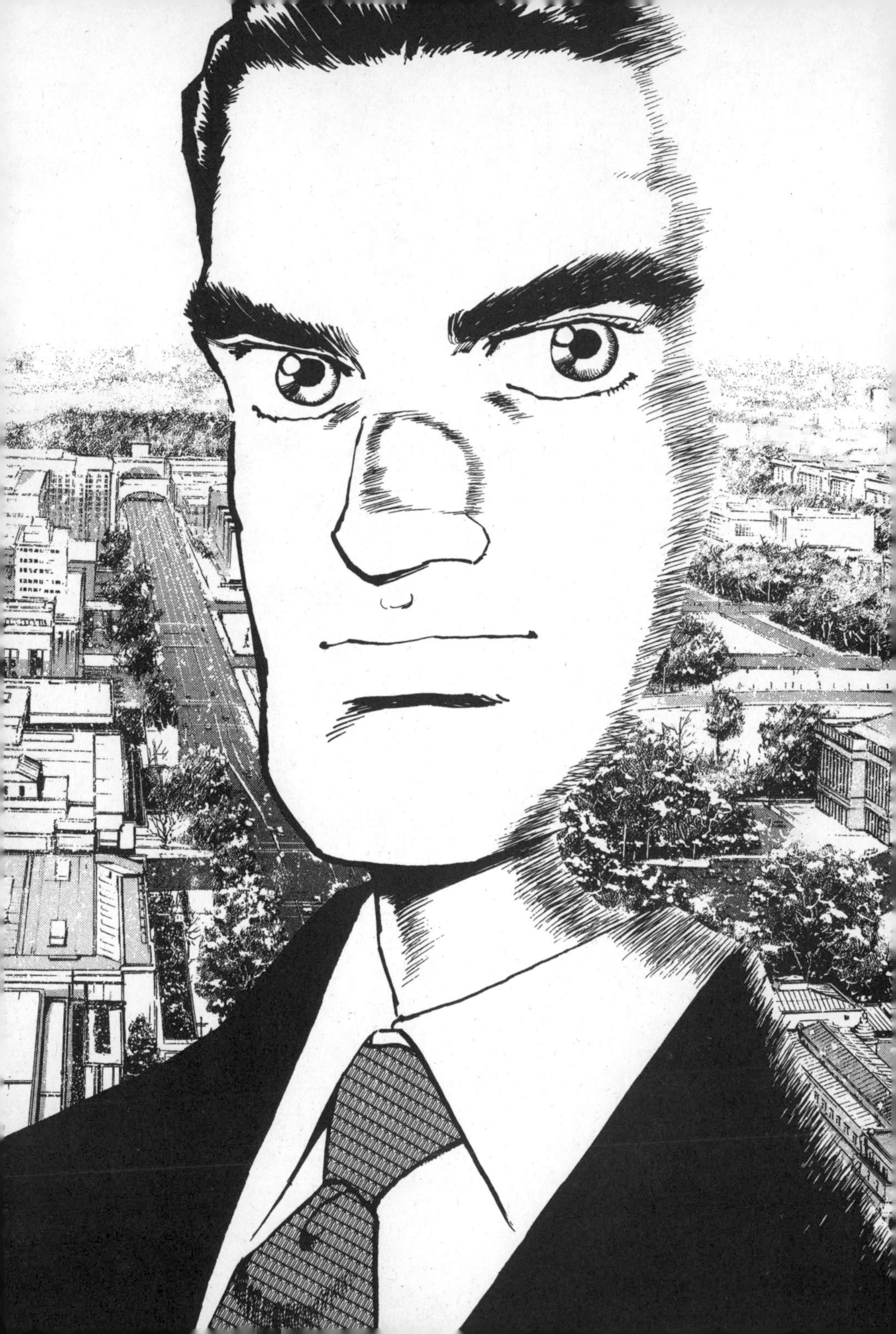

The Candidate:
Kenneth
Yamaoka

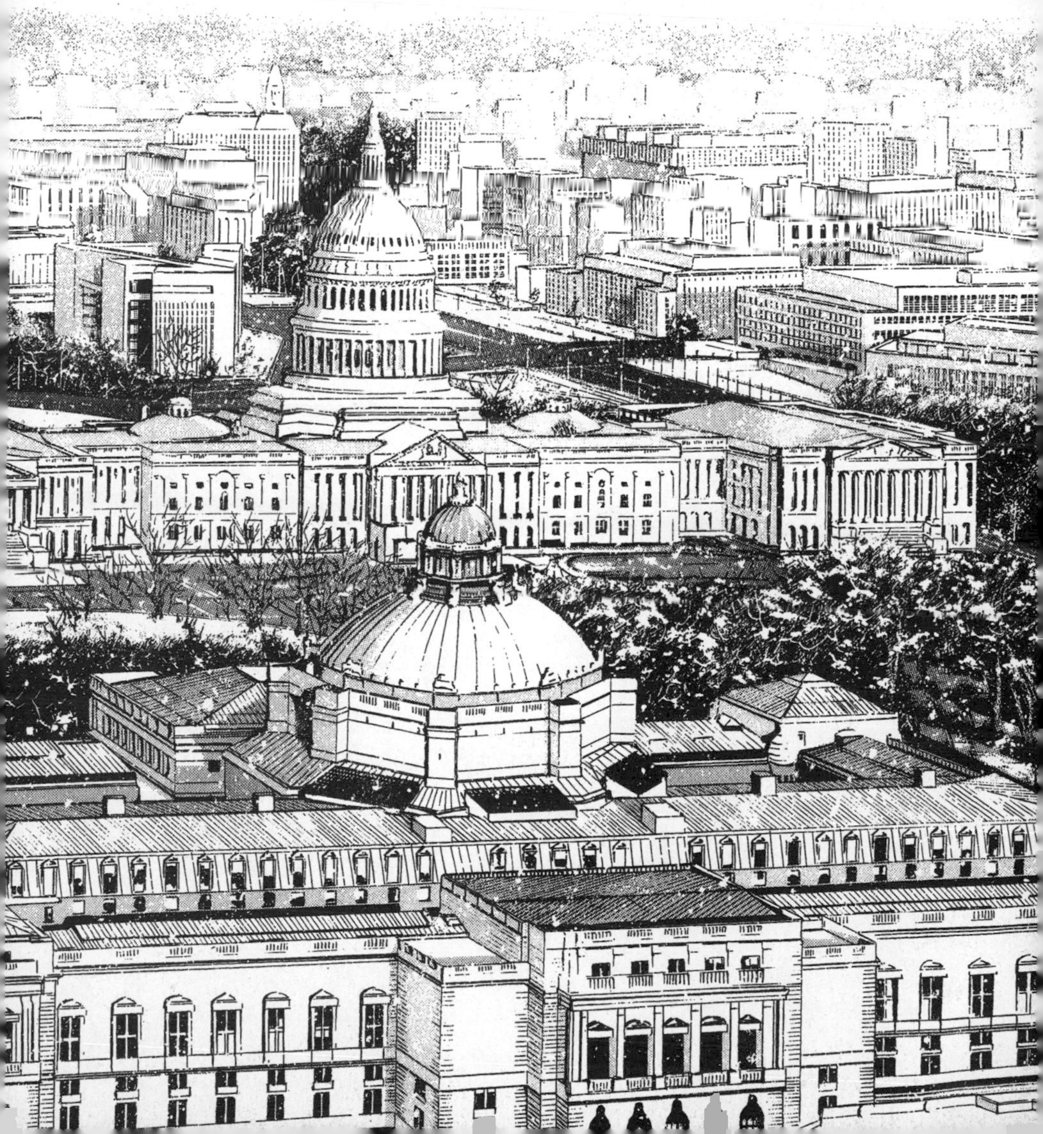

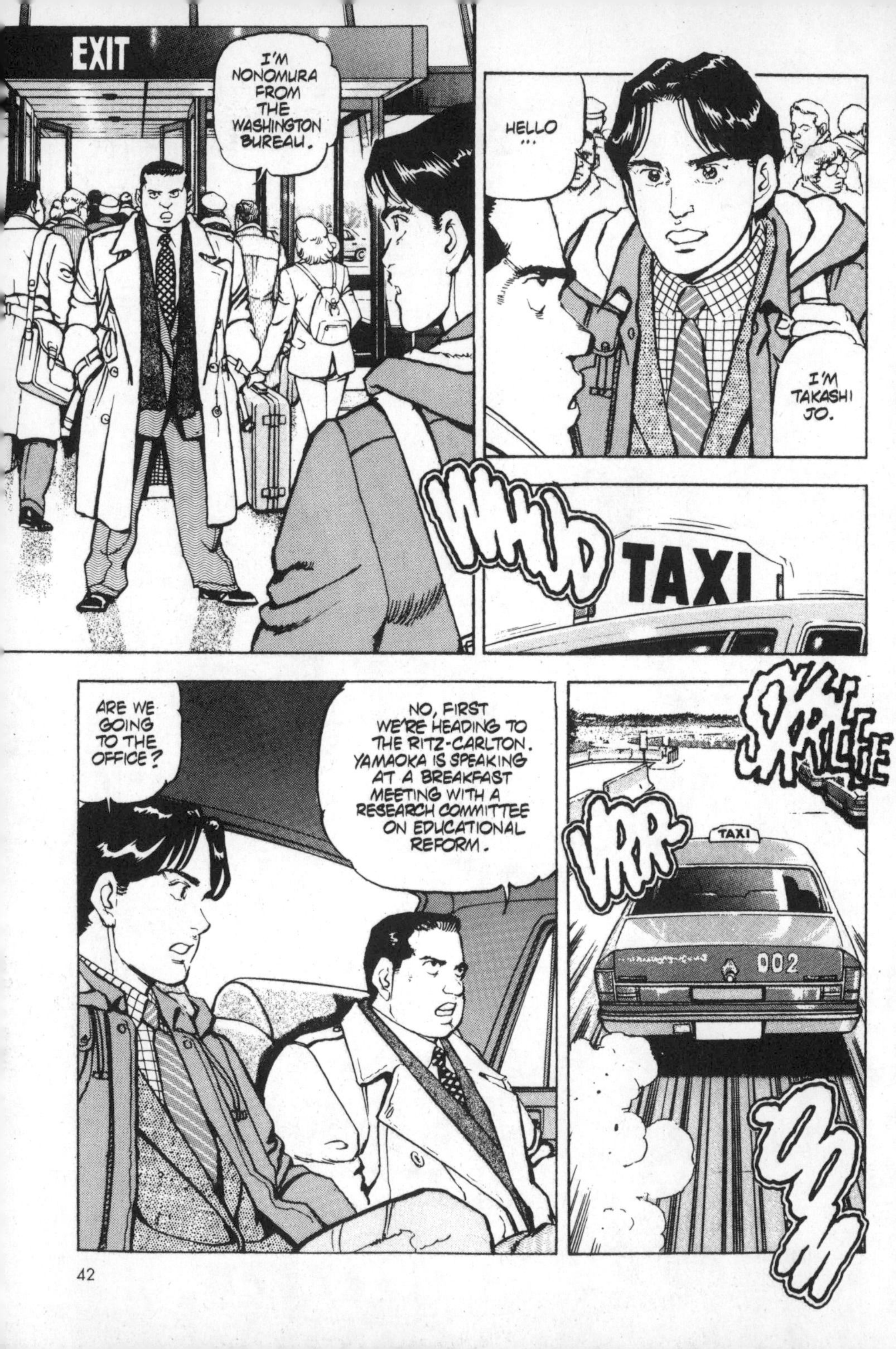
EXIT
I'M NONOMURA FROM THE WASHINGTON BUREAU.
HELLO ...
I'M TAKASHI JO.
WHUD
TAXI
ARE WE GOING TO THE OFFICE?
NO, FIRST WE'RE HEADING TO THE RITZ-CARLTON. YAMAOKA IS SPEAKING AT A BREAKFAST MEETING WITH A RESEARCH COMMITTEE ON EDUCATIONAL REFORM.
VRR
TAXI
002

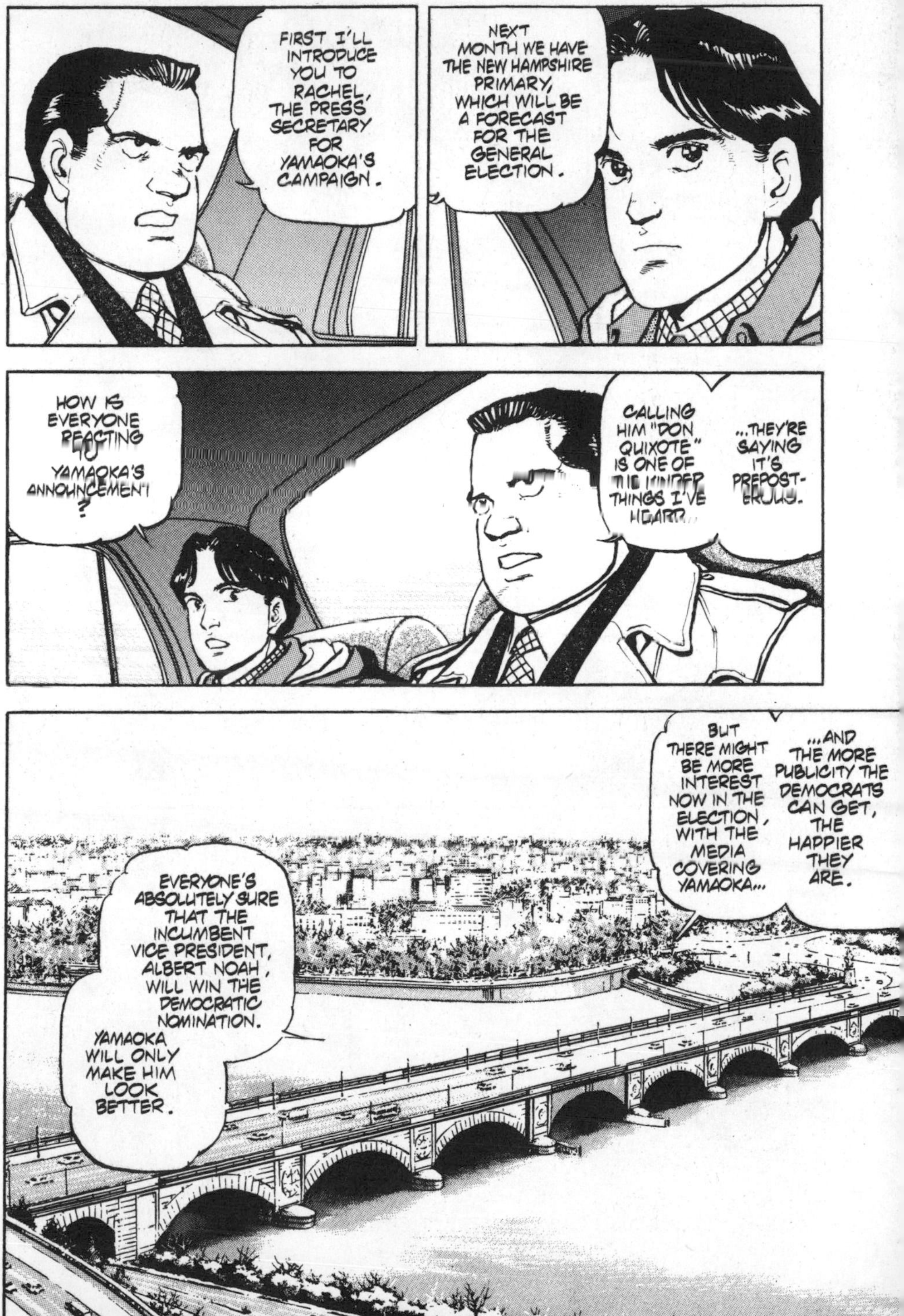
FIRST I'LL INTRODUCE YOU TO RACHEL, THE PRESS SECRETARY FOR YAMAOKA'S CAMPAIGN.
NEXT MONTH WE HAVE THE NEW HAMPSHIRE PRIMARY, WHICH WILL BE A FORECAST FOR THE GENERAL ELECTION.
HOW IS EVERYONE REACTING YAMAOKA'S ANNOUNCEMENT?
CALLING HIM "DON QUIXOTE" IS ONE OF THINGS I'VE HEARD...
...THEY'RE SAYING IT'S PREPOST-
EVERYONE'S ABSOLUTELY SURE THAT THE INCUMBENT VICE PRESIDENT, ALBERT NOAH, WILL WIN THE DEMOCRATIC NOMINATION. YAMAOKA WILL ONLY MAKE HIM LOOK BETTER.
BUT THERE MIGHT BE MORE INTEREST NOW IN THE ELECTION, WITH THE MEDIA COVERING YAMAOKA...
...AND THE MORE PUBLICITY THE DEMOCRATS CAN GET, THE HAPPIER THEY ARE.

ANY OTHER QUESTIONS?

PERHAPS YOU WOULD KNOW...

KNOW WHAT?

WHY I WAS CHOSEN TO DO THIS FEATURE REPORT ON YAMAOKA.

I DON'T KNOW THE DETAILS.

I JUST HEARD THAT HIS STAFF SELECTED YOU.

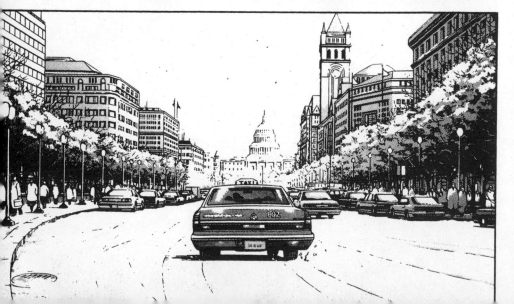

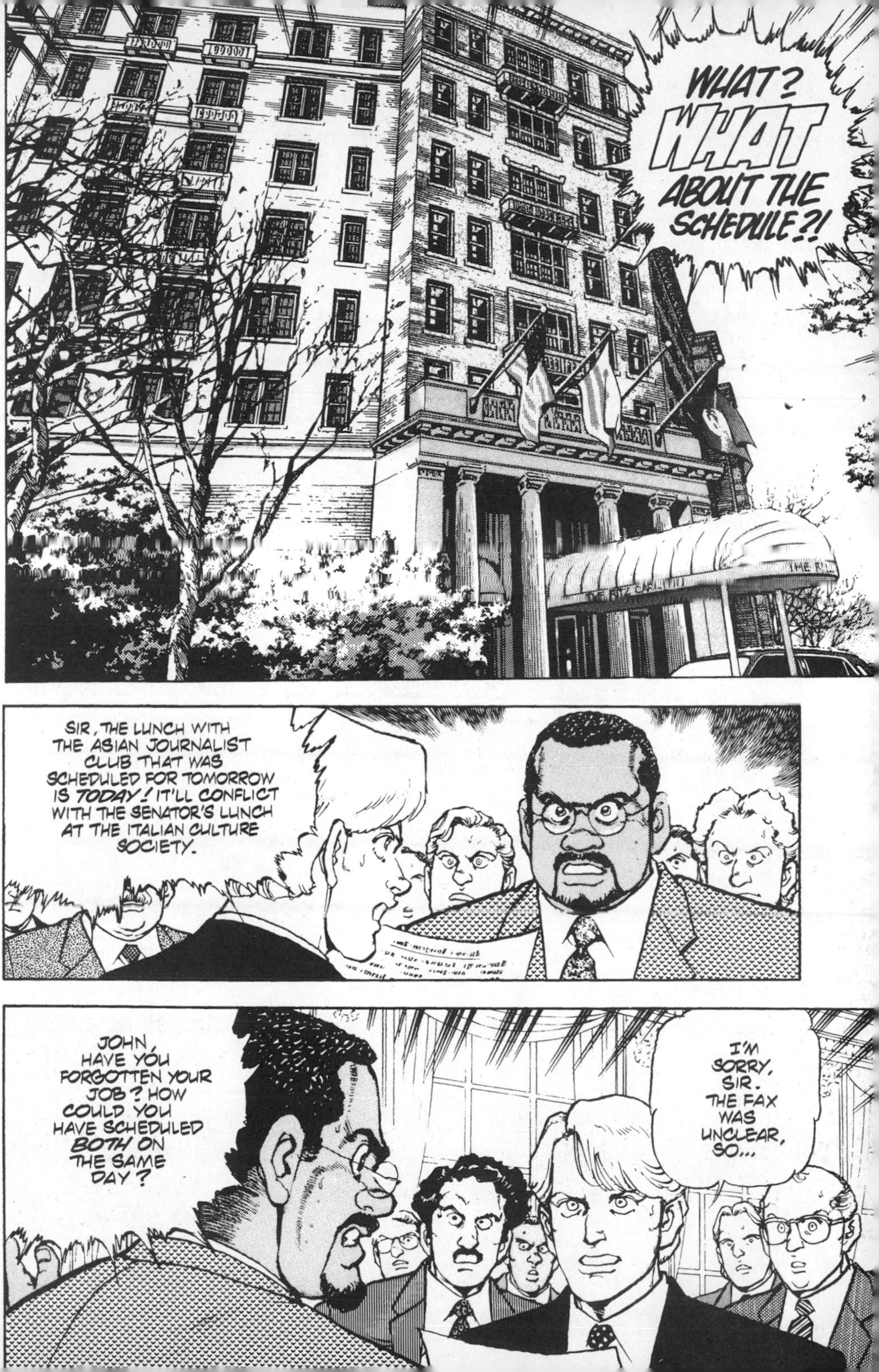
WHAT? WHAT ABOUT THE SCHEDULE?!
SIR, THE LUNCH WITH THE ASIAN JOURNALIST CLUB THAT WAS SCHEDULED FOR TOMORROW IS TODAY! IT'LL CONFLICT WITH THE SENATOR'S LUNCH AT THE ITALIAN CULTURE SOCIETY.
JOHN, HAVE YOU FORGOTTEN YOUR JOB? HOW COULD YOU HAVE SCHEDULED BOTH ON THE SAME DAY?
I'M SORRY, SIR. THE FAX WAS UNCLEAR, SO...

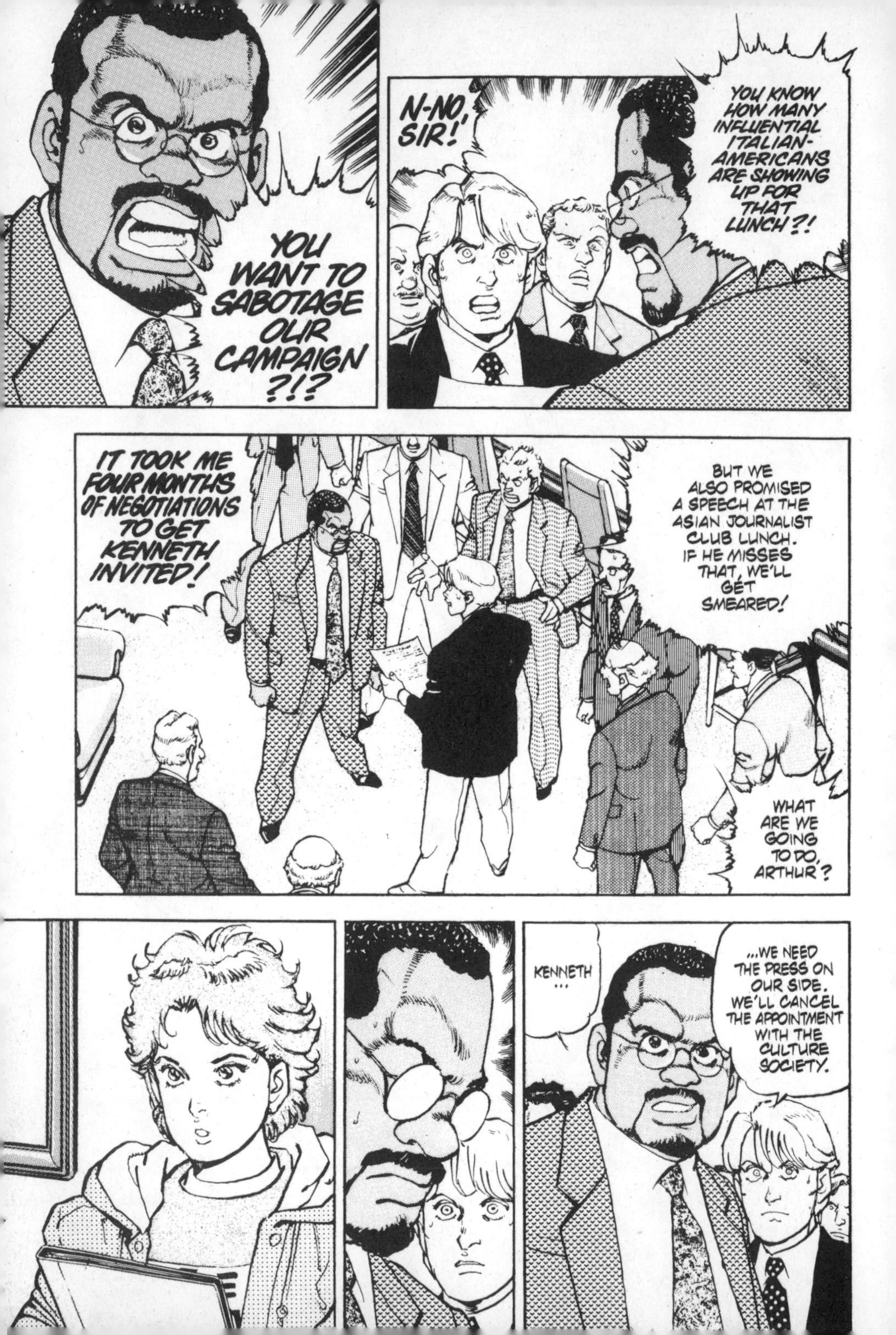
YOU WANT TO SABOTAGE OUR CAMPAIGN ?!?
N-NO, SIR!
YOU KNOW HOW MANY INFLUENTIAL ITALIAN-AMERICANS ARE SHOWING UP FOR THAT LUNCH?!
IT TOOK ME FOUR MONTHS OF NEGOTIATIONS TO GET KENNETH INVITED!
BUT WE ALSO PROMISED A SPEECH AT THE ASIAN JOURNALIST CLUB LUNCH. IF HE MISSES THAT, WE'LL GET SMEARED!
WHAT ARE WE GOING TO DO, ARTHUR?
KENNETH ...
...WE NEED THE PRESS ON OUR SIDE. WE'LL CANCEL THE APPOINTMENT WITH THE CULTURE SOCIETY.

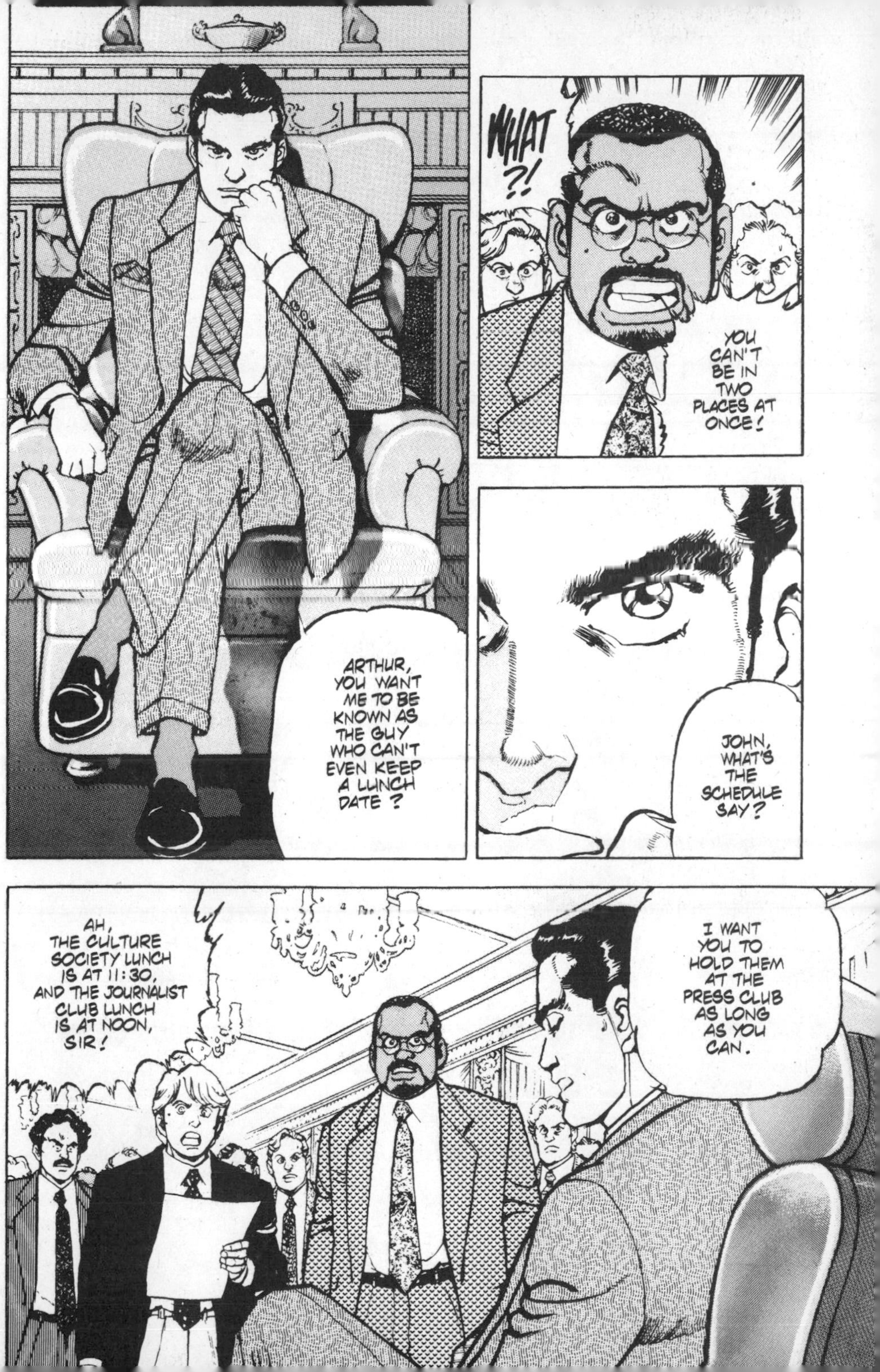
WHAT ?!
YOU CAN'T BE IN TWO PLACES AT ONCE!
ARTHUR, YOU WANT ME TO BE KNOWN AS THE GUY WHO CAN'T EVEN KEEP A LUNCH DATE ?
JOHN, WHAT'S THE SCHEDULE SAY ?
AH, THE CULTURE SOCIETY LUNCH IS AT 11:30, AND THE JOURNALIST CLUB LUNCH IS AT NOON, SIR!
I WANT YOU TO HOLD THEM AT THE PRESS CLUB AS LONG AS YOU CAN.

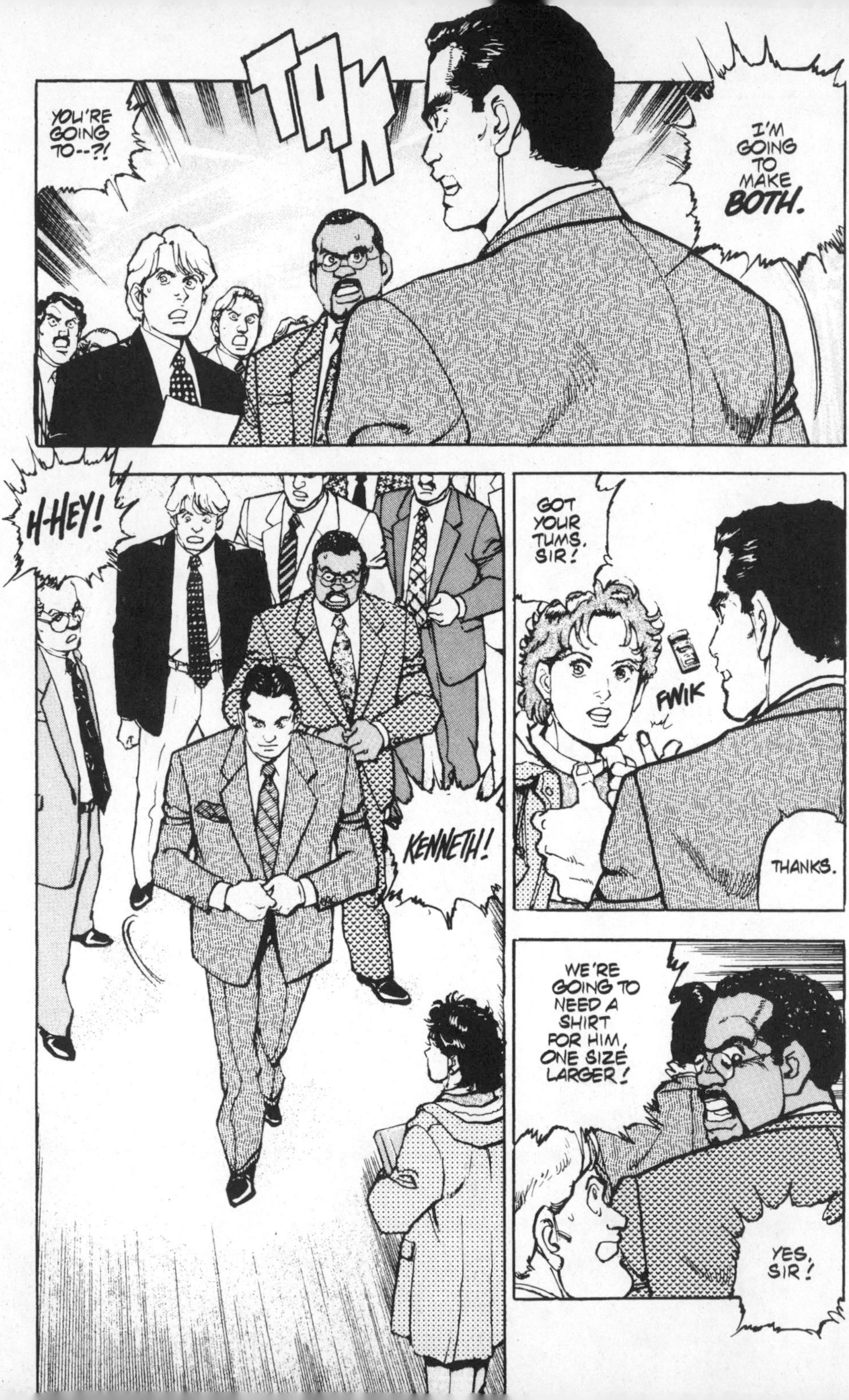
TAK
YOU'RE GOING TO--?!
I'M GOING TO MAKE BOTH.
H-HEY!
KENNETH!
GOT YOUR TUMS, SIR!
FWIK
THANKS.
WE'RE GOING TO NEED A SHIRT FOR HIM, ONE SIZE LARGER!
YES, SIR!

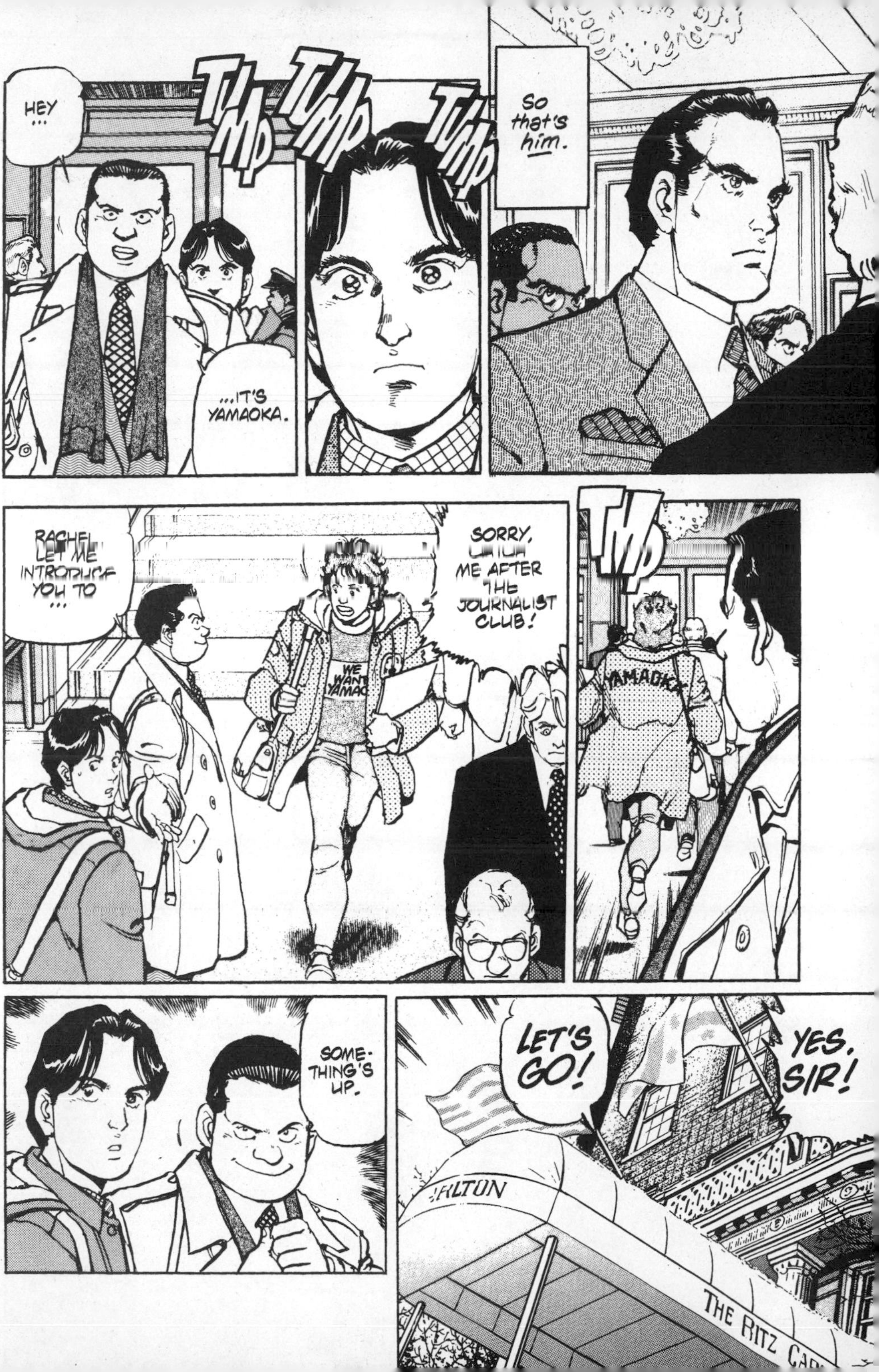
HEY ...
...IT'S YAMAOKA.
TMP
TUMP
TUMP
So that's him.
RACHEL, LET ME INTRODUCE YOU TO ...
WE WANT YAMAOKA
SORRY,
ME AFTER THE JOURNALIST CLUB!
TMP
YAMAOKA
SOME-THING'S UP.
LET'S GO!
YES, SIR!
CARLTON
THE RITZ CAR

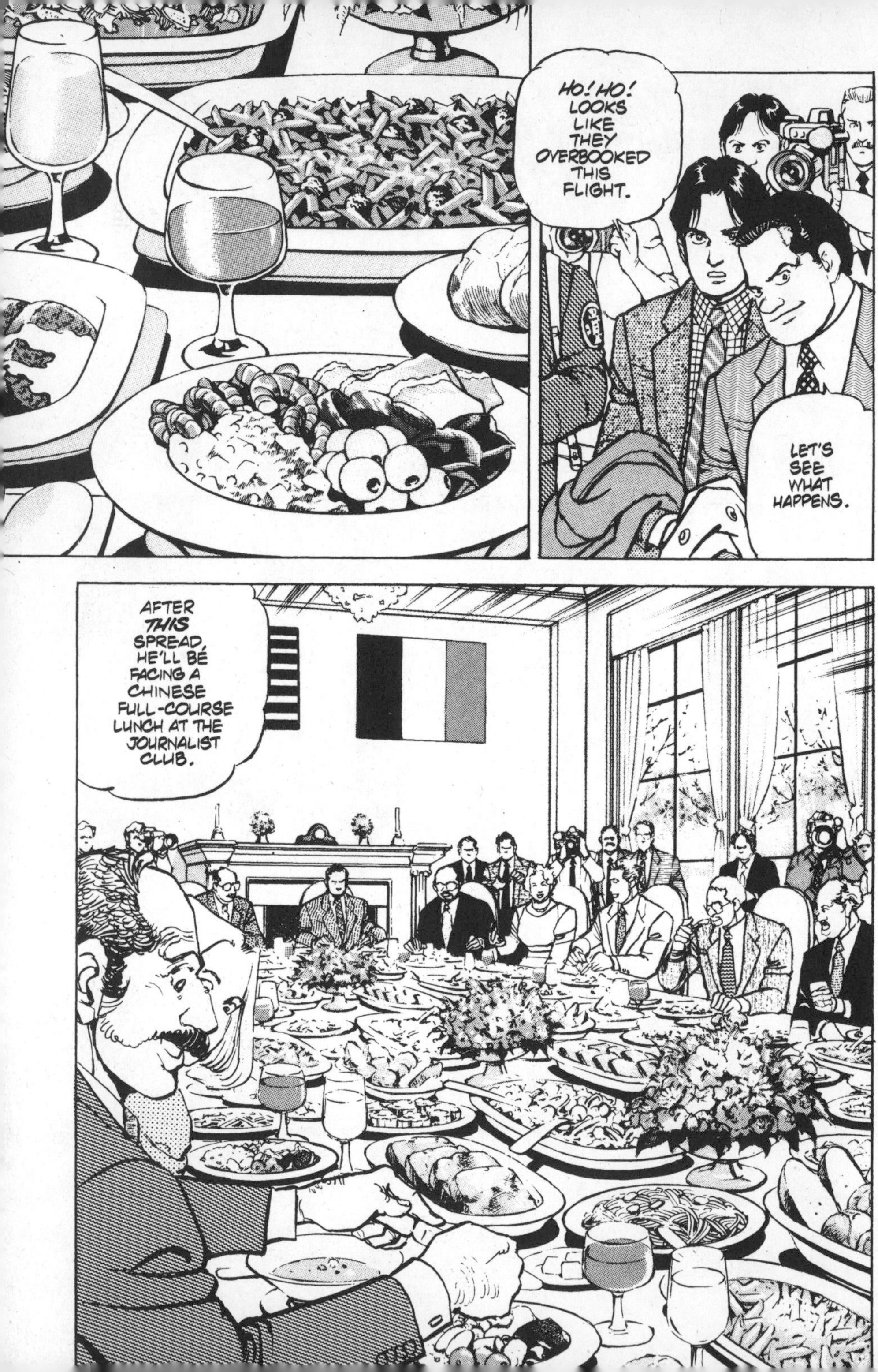
HO! HO! LOOKS LIKE THEY OVERBOOKED THIS FLIGHT.
LET'S SEE WHAT HAPPENS.
AFTER THIS SPREAD, HE'LL BÉ FACING A CHINESE FULL-COURSE LUNCH AT THE JOURNALIST CLUB.

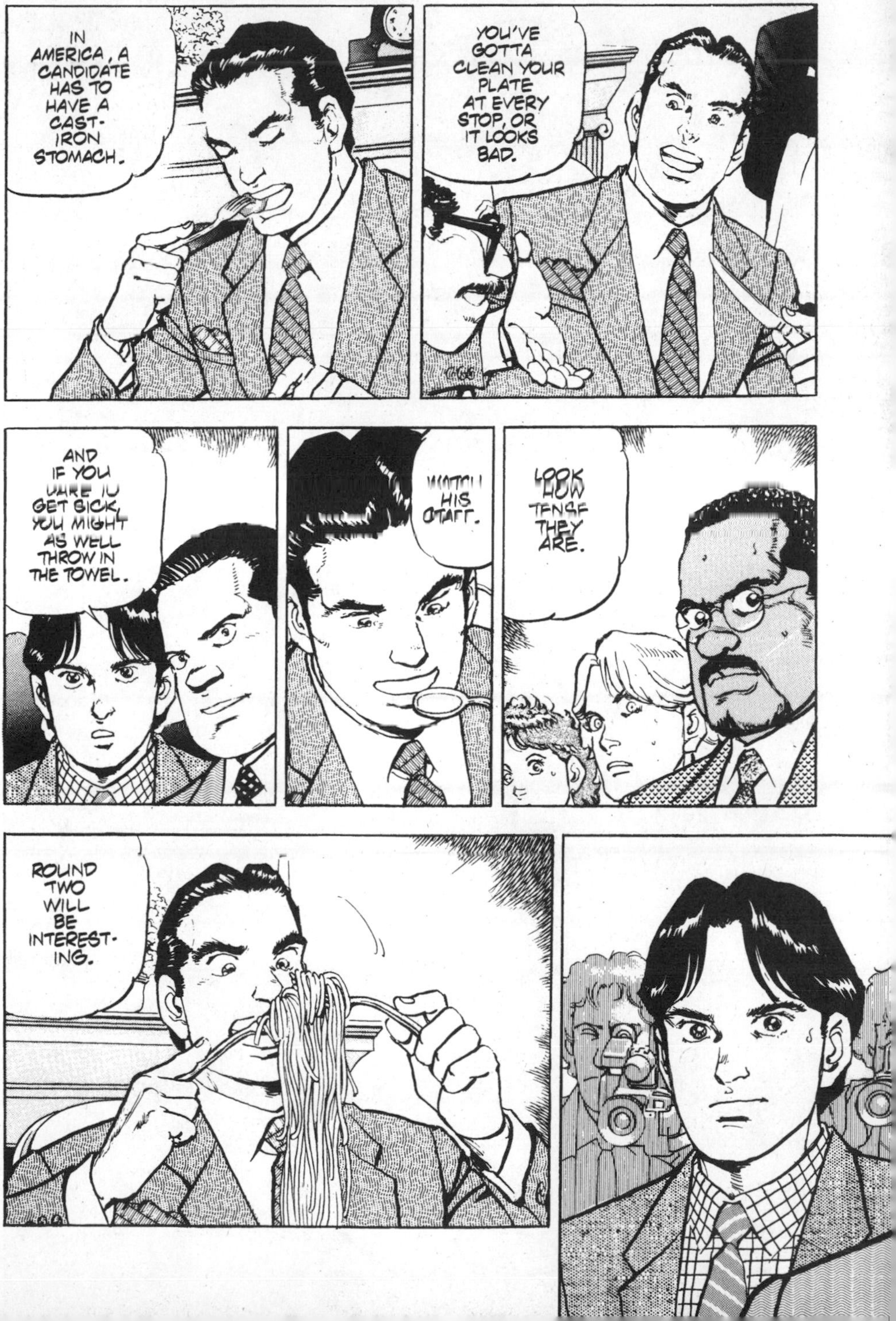
IN AMERICA, A CANDIDATE HAS TO HAVE A CAST-IRON STOMACH.
YOU'VE GOTTA CLEAN YOUR PLATE AT EVERY STOP, OR IT LOOKS BAD.
AND IF YOU DARE TO GET SICK, YOU MIGHT AS WELL THROW IN THE TOWEL.
WATCH HIS STAFF.
LOOK HOW TENSE THEY ARE.
ROUND TWO WILL BE INTEREST-ING.

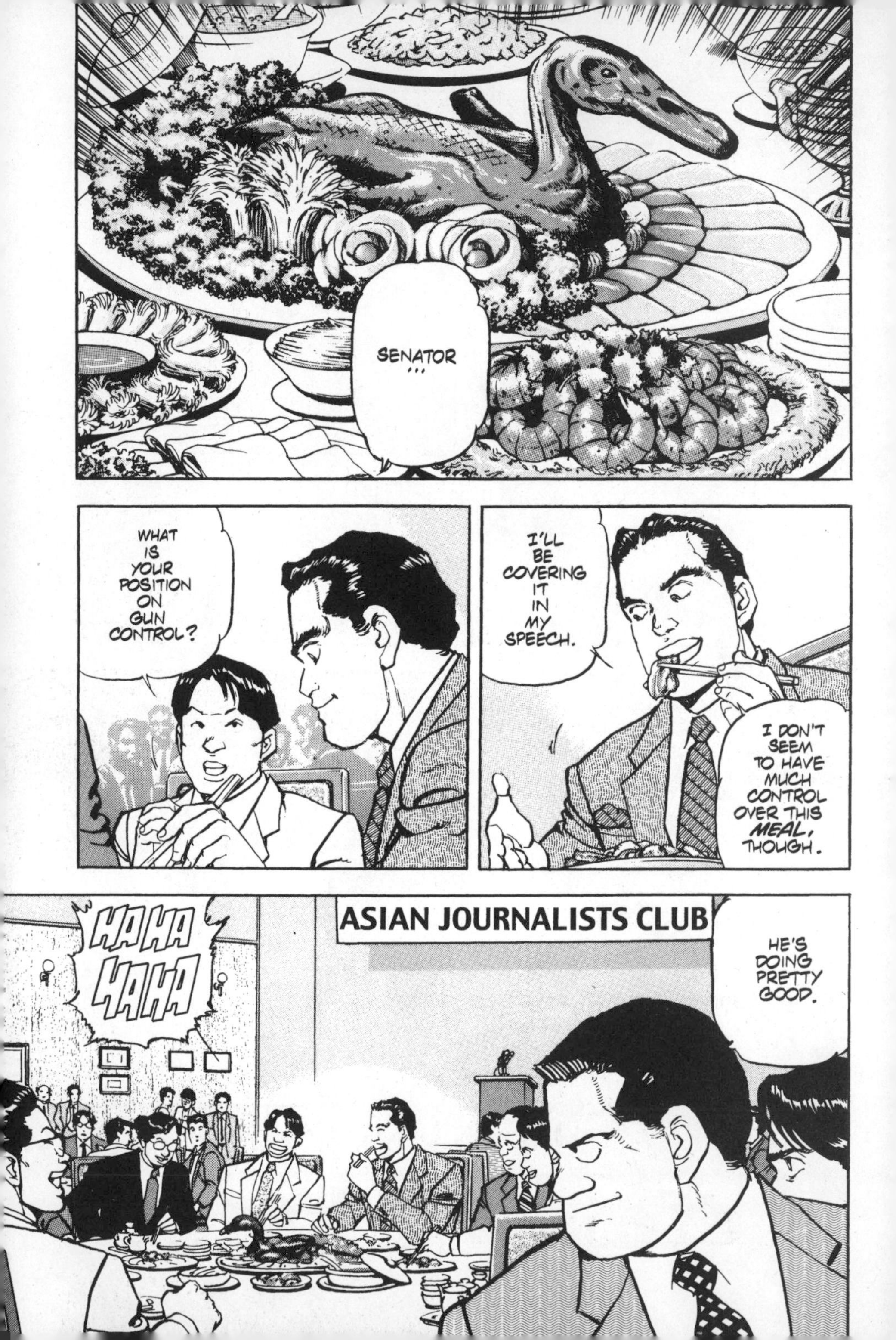
SENATOR ...
WHAT IS YOUR POSITION ON GUN CONTROL?
I'LL BE COVERING IT IN MY SPEECH.
I DON'T SEEM TO HAVE MUCH CONTROL OVER THIS *MEAL,* THOUGH.
HA HA HA HA
ASIAN JOURNALISTS CLUB
HE'S DOING PRETTY GOOD.

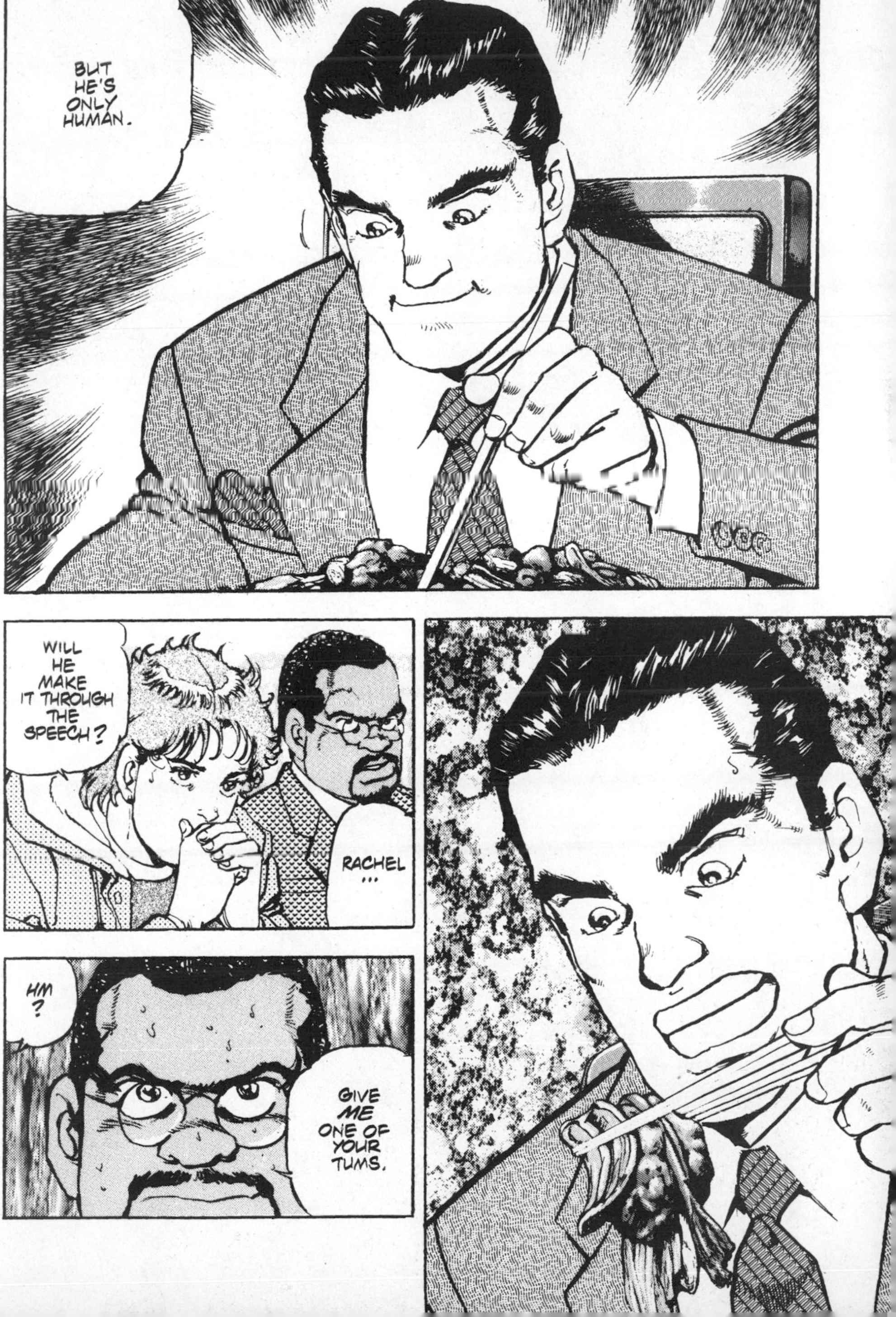
BUT HE'S ONLY HUMAN.
WILL HE MAKE IT THROUGH THE SPEECH?
RACHEL...
HM?
GIVE ME ONE OF YOUR TUMS.

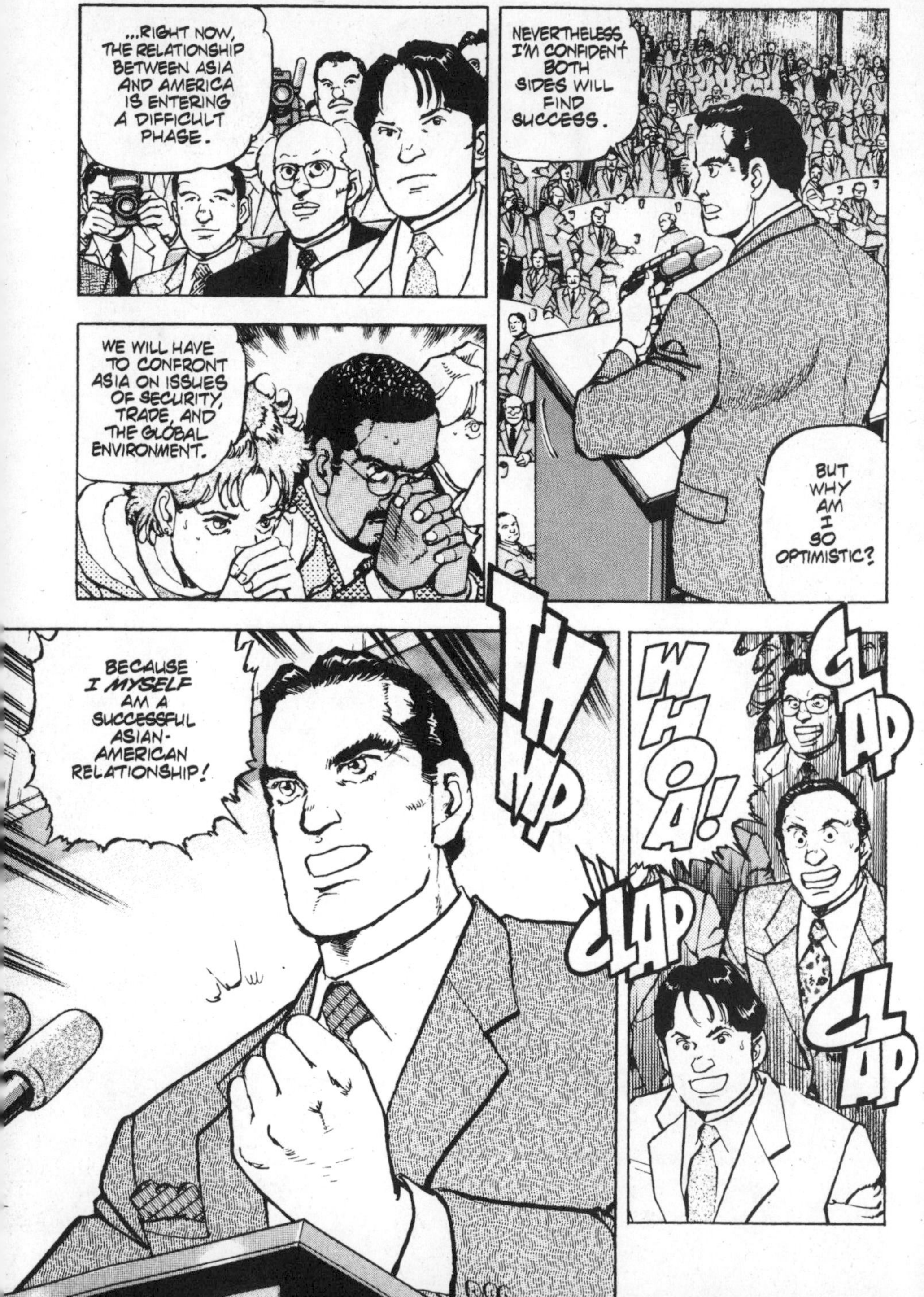
...RIGHT NOW, THE RELATIONSHIP BETWEEN ASIA AND AMERICA IS ENTERING A DIFFICULT PHASE.
WE WILL HAVE TO CONFRONT ASIA ON ISSUES OF SECURITY, TRADE, AND THE GLOBAL ENVIRONMENT.
NEVERTHELESS, I'M CONFIDENT BOTH SIDES WILL FIND SUCCESS.
BUT WHY AM I SO OPTIMISTIC?
BECAUSE I *MYSELF* AM A SUCCESSFUL ASIAN-AMERICAN RELATIONSHIP!
THUMP
WHOA!
CLAP
CLAP
CLAP

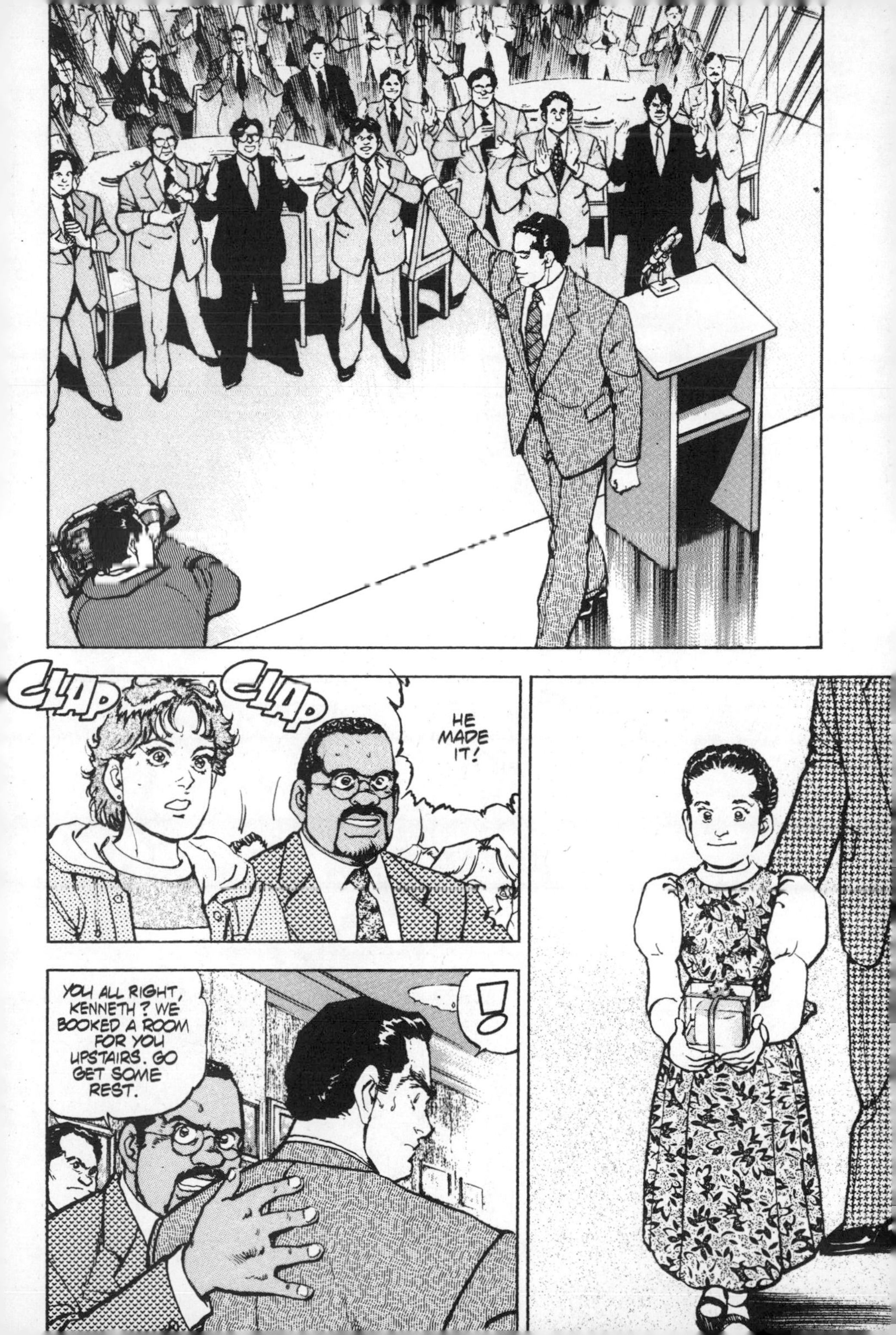
CLAP CLAP
HE MADE IT!
YOU ALL RIGHT, KENNETH? WE BOOKED A ROOM FOR YOU UPSTAIRS. GO GET SOME REST.
!

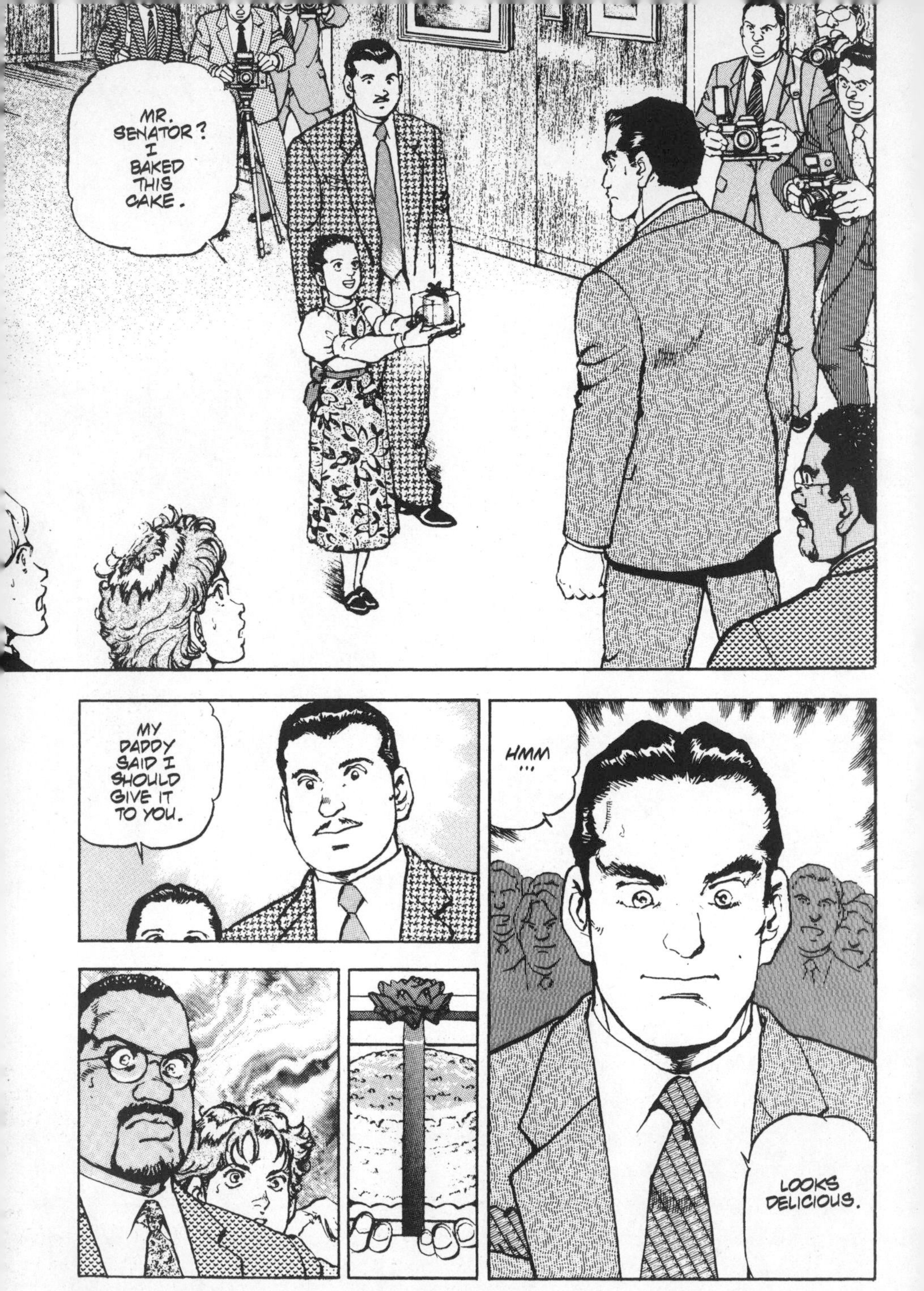
MR. SENATOR? I BAKED THIS CAKE.
MY DADDY SAID I SHOULD GIVE IT TO YOU.
HMM...
LOOKS DELICIOUS.

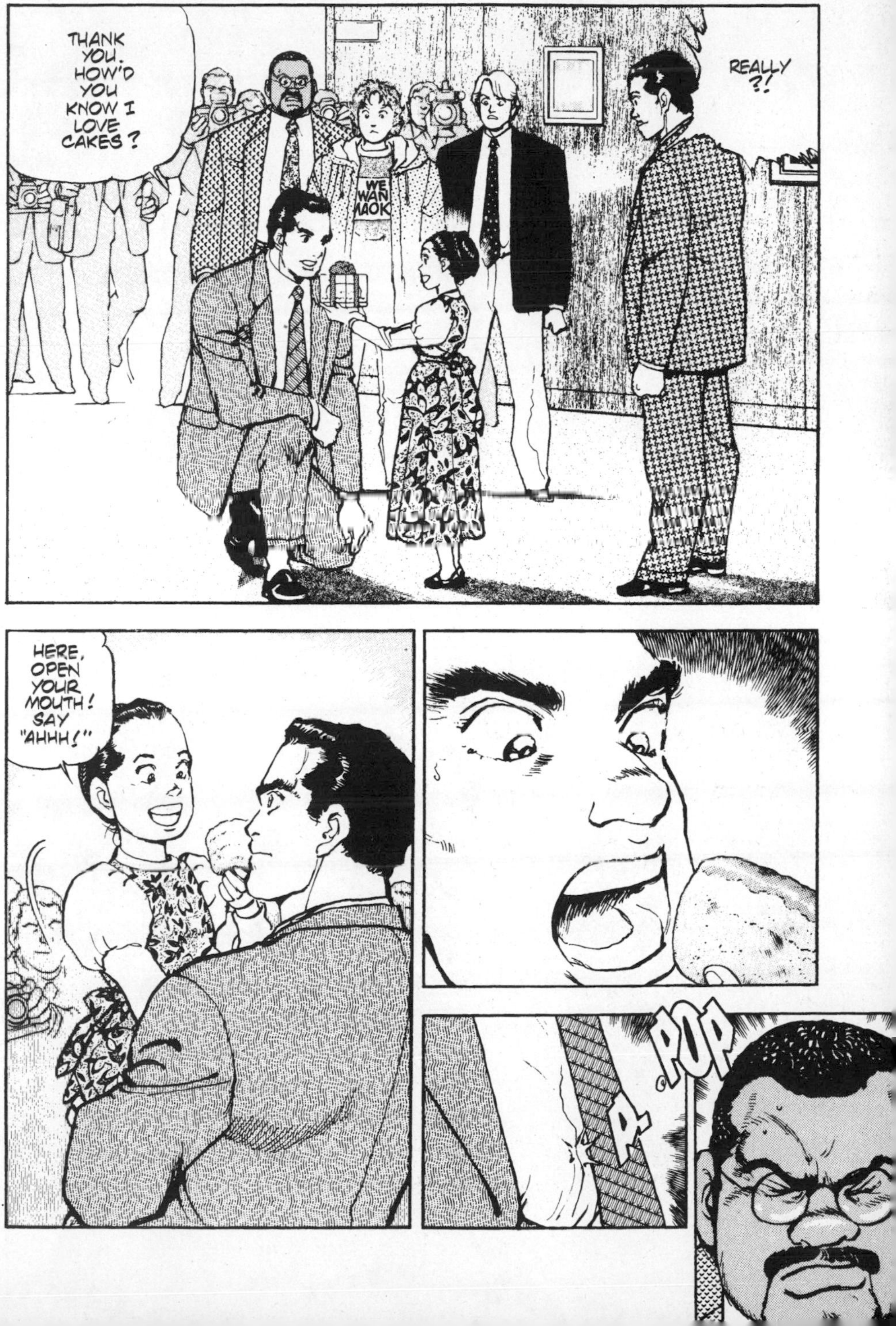
THANK YOU. HOW'D YOU KNOW I LOVE CAKES?
WE WAN NAOK
REALLY ?!
HERE, OPEN YOUR MOUTH! SAY "AHHH!"
POP

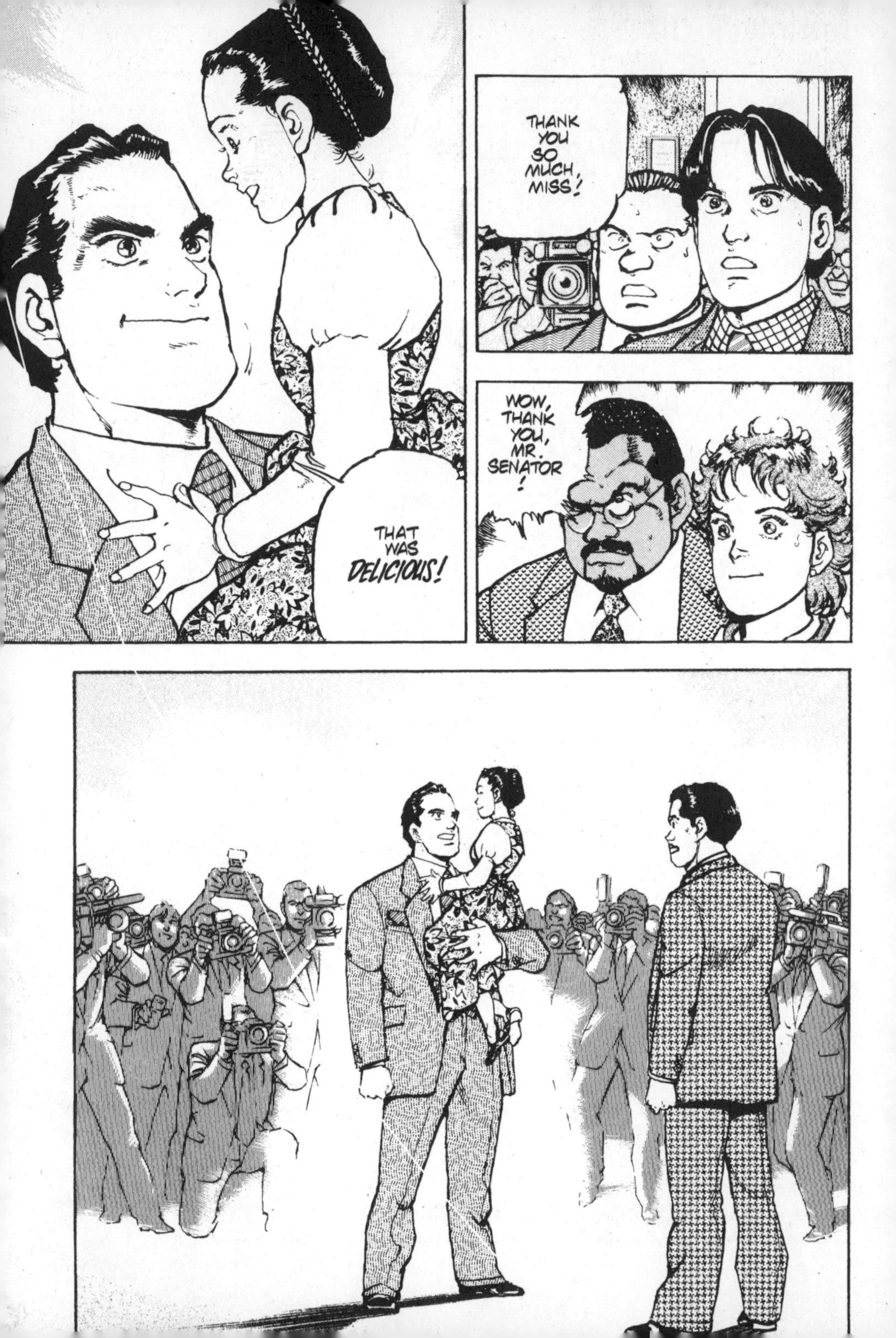
THAT WAS DELICIOUS!
THANK YOU SO MUCH, MISS!
WOW, THANK YOU, MR. SENATOR!

So this is what it takes to become president.

What stamina! Like he could swallow fifty states... two hundred seventy million people!

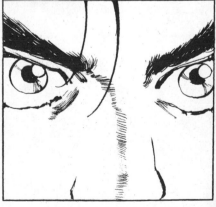

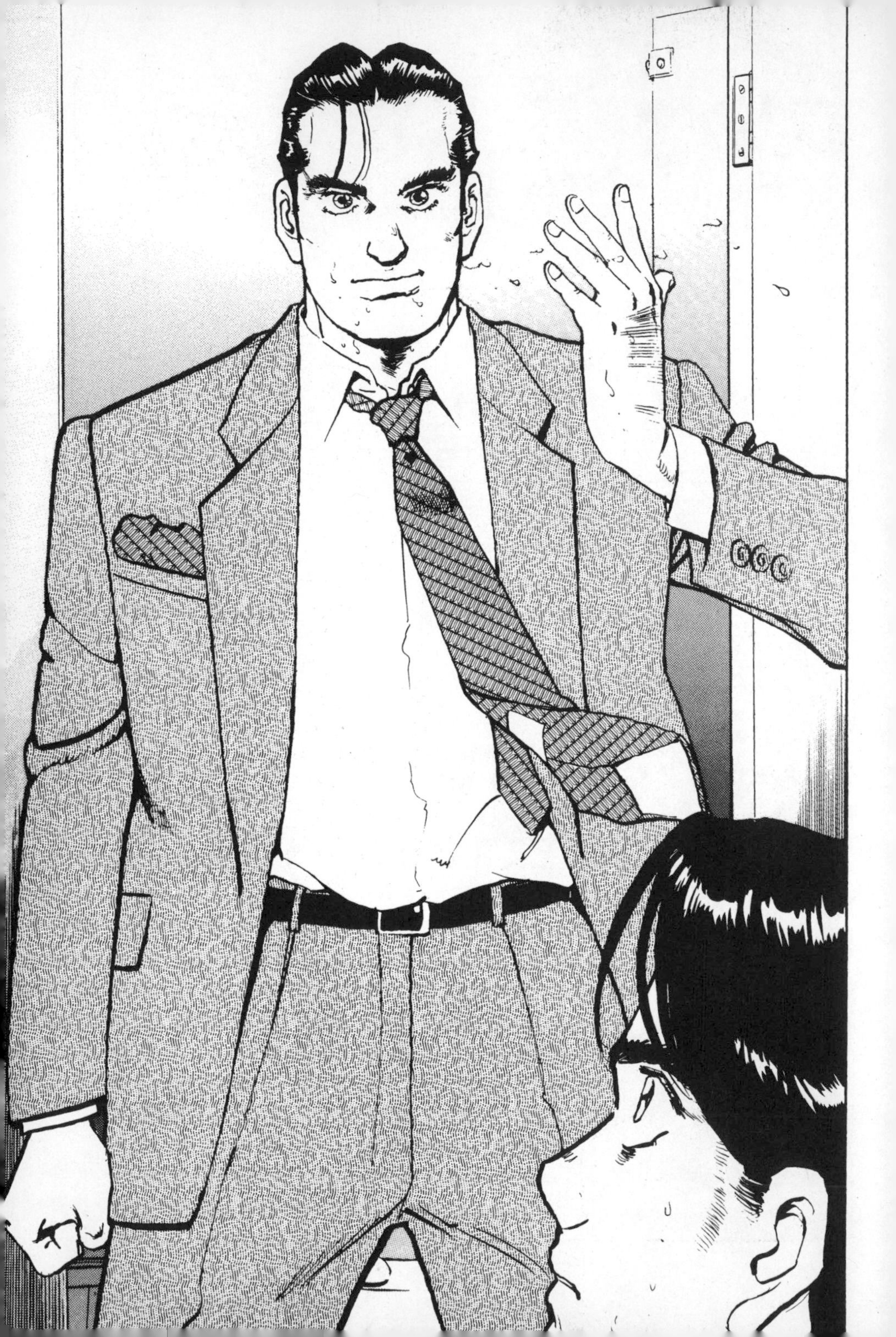

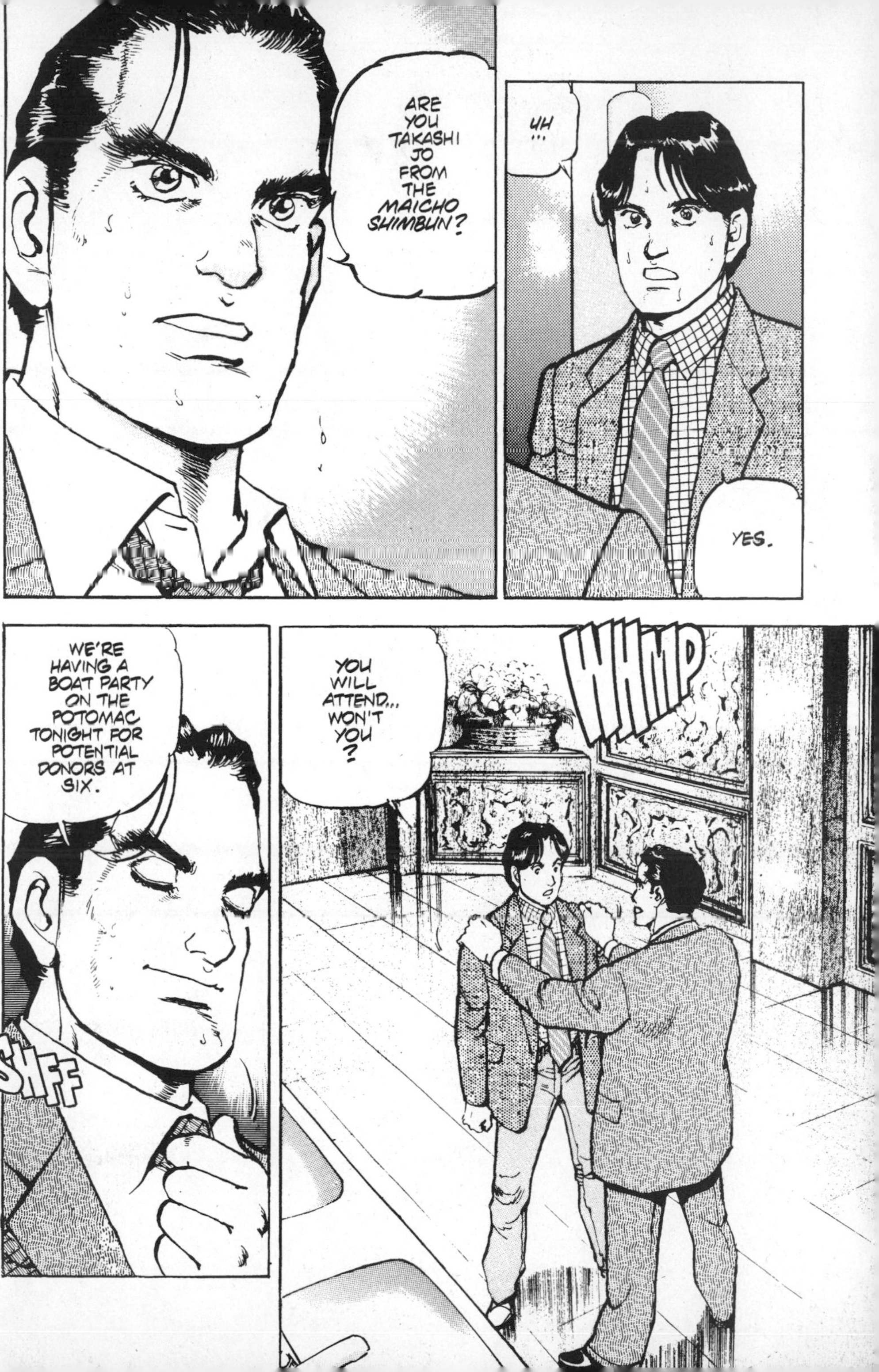
ARE YOU TAKASHI JO FROM THE MAICHO SHIMBUN?
UH ...
YES.
WE'RE HAVING A BOAT PARTY ON THE POTOMAC TONIGHT FOR POTENTIAL DONORS AT SIX.
SHFF
YOU WILL ATTEND... WON'T YOU?
WHMP

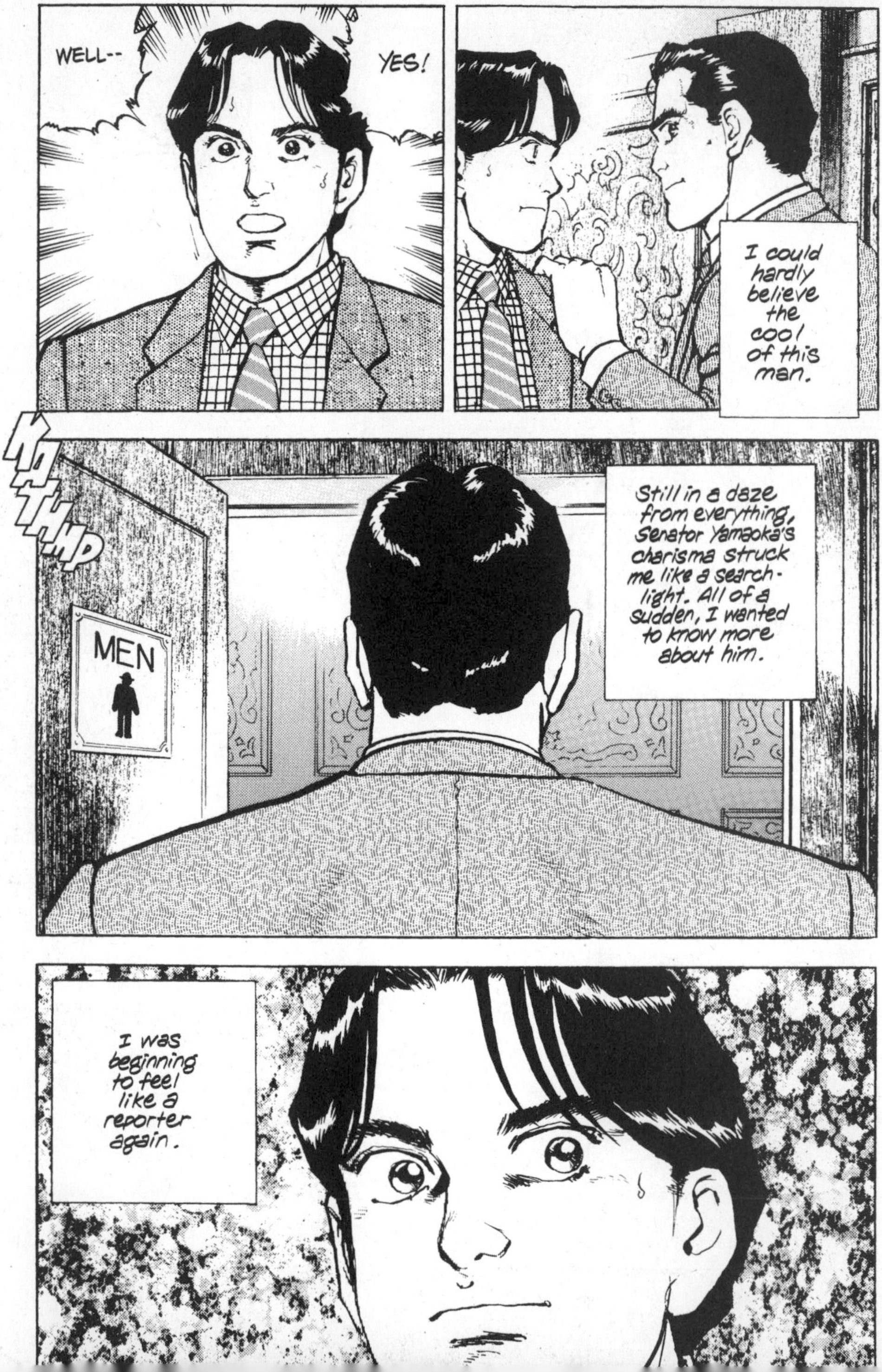
WELL--
YES!
I could hardly believe the cool of this man.
KATHUMP
MEN
Still in a daze from everything, Senator Yamaoka's charisma struck me like a search-light. All of a sudden, I wanted to know more about him.
I was beginning to feel like a reporter again.

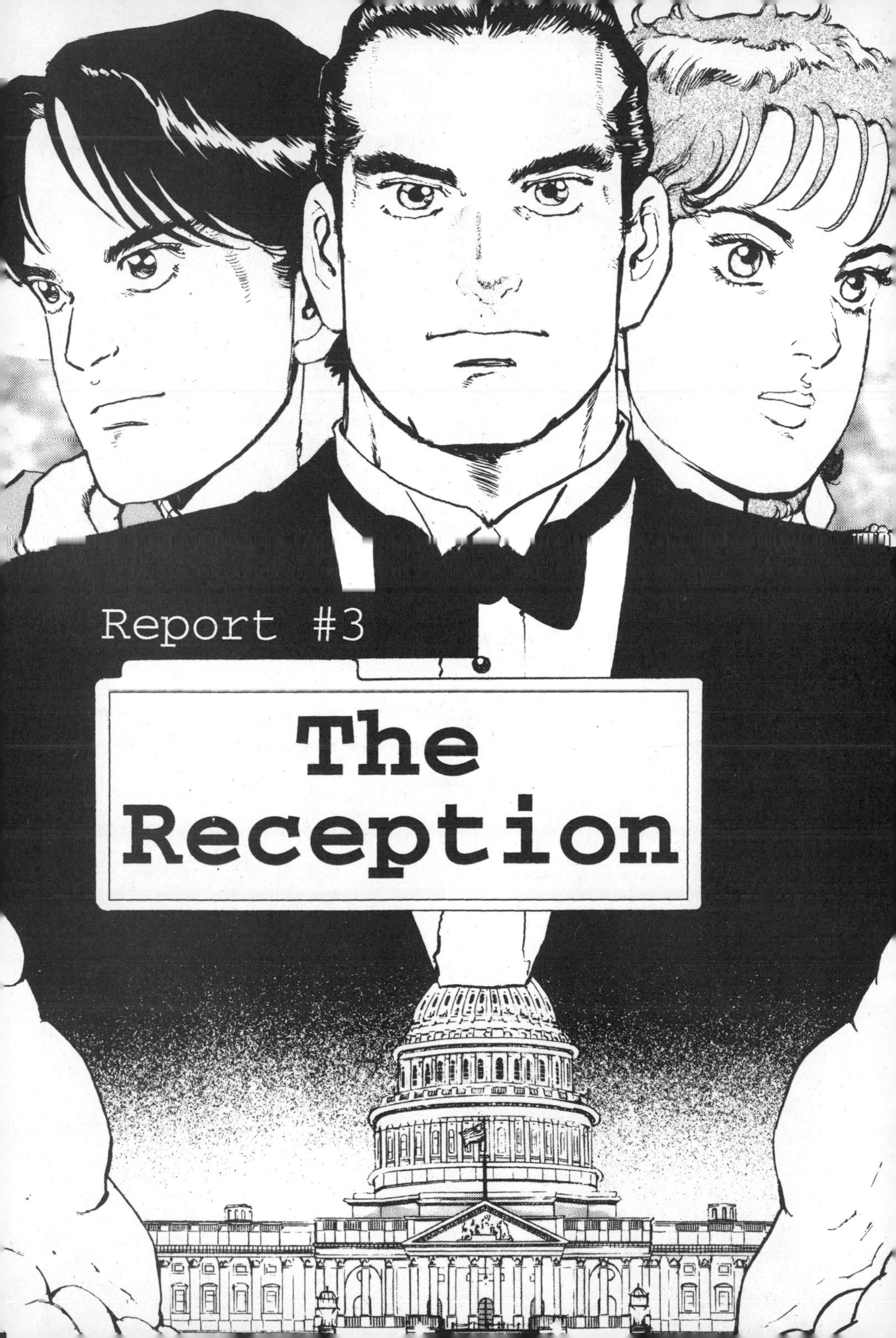
Report #3
The Reception

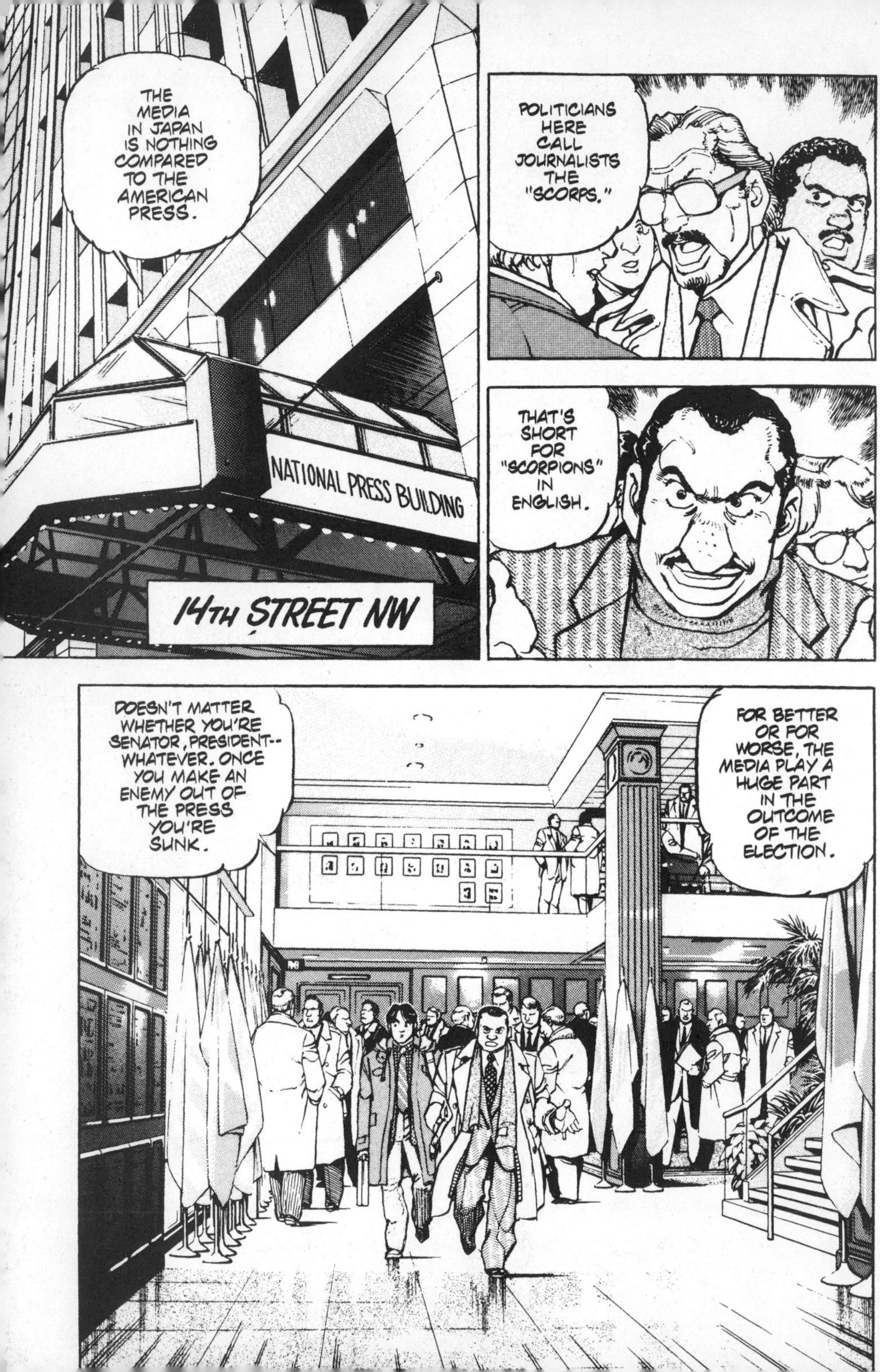
THE MEDIA IN JAPAN IS NOTHING COMPARED TO THE AMERICAN PRESS.
NATIONAL PRESS BUILDING
14TH STREET NW
POLITICIANS HERE CALL JOURNALISTS THE "SCORPS."
THAT'S SHORT FOR "SCORPIONS" IN ENGLISH.
DOESN'T MATTER WHETHER YOU'RE SENATOR, PRESIDENT-- WHATEVER. ONCE YOU MAKE AN ENEMY OUT OF THE PRESS YOU'RE SUNK.
FOR BETTER OR FOR WORSE, THE MEDIA PLAY A HUGE PART IN THE OUTCOME OF THE ELECTION.

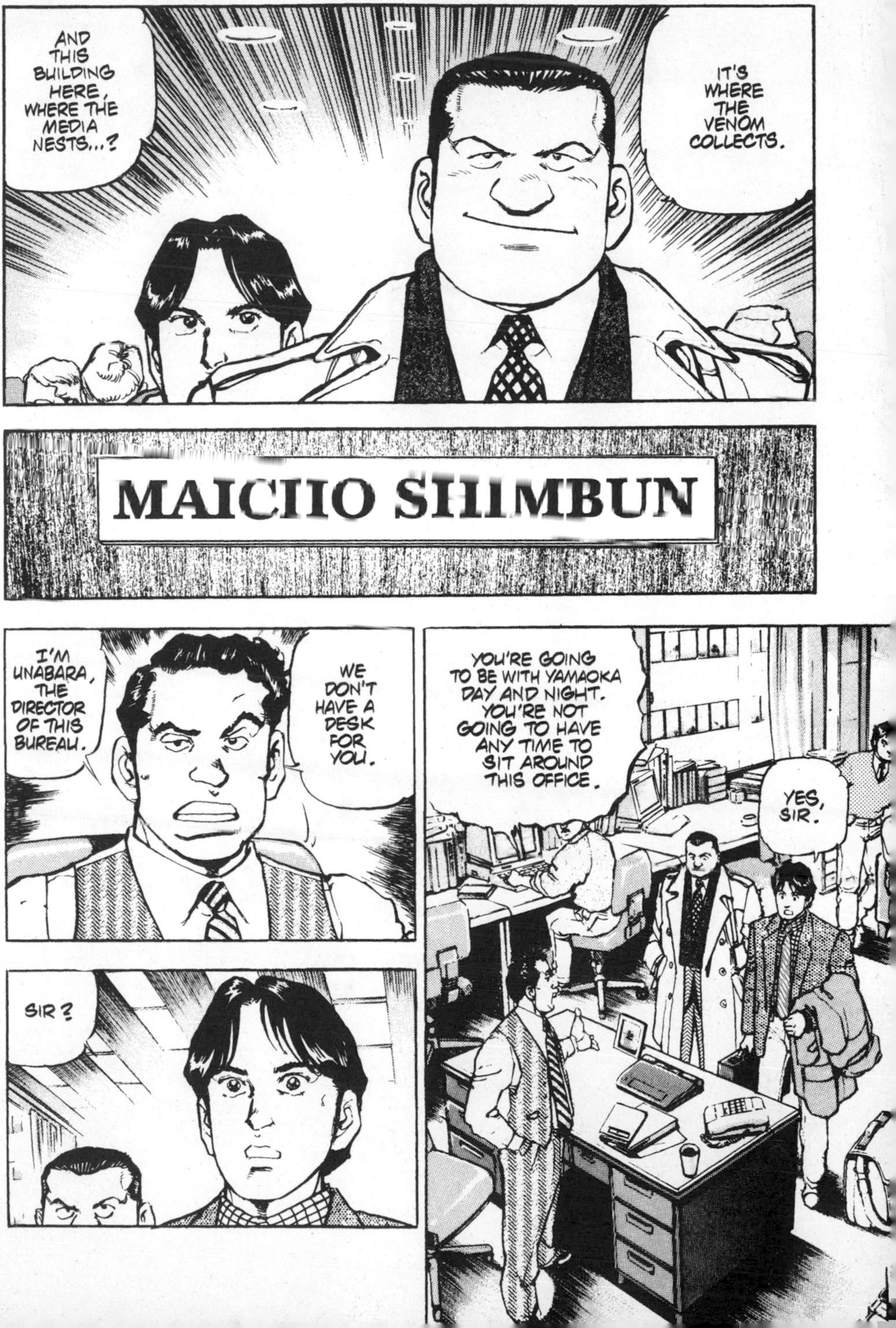
AND THIS BUILDING HERE, WHERE THE MEDIA NESTS...?
IT'S WHERE THE VENOM COLLECTS.
MAICHO SHIMBUN
I'M UNABARA, THE DIRECTOR OF THIS BUREAU.
WE DON'T HAVE A DESK FOR YOU.
YOU'RE GOING TO BE WITH YAMAOKA DAY AND NIGHT. YOU'RE NOT GOING TO HAVE ANY TIME TO SIT AROUND THIS OFFICE.
YES, SIR.
SIR?

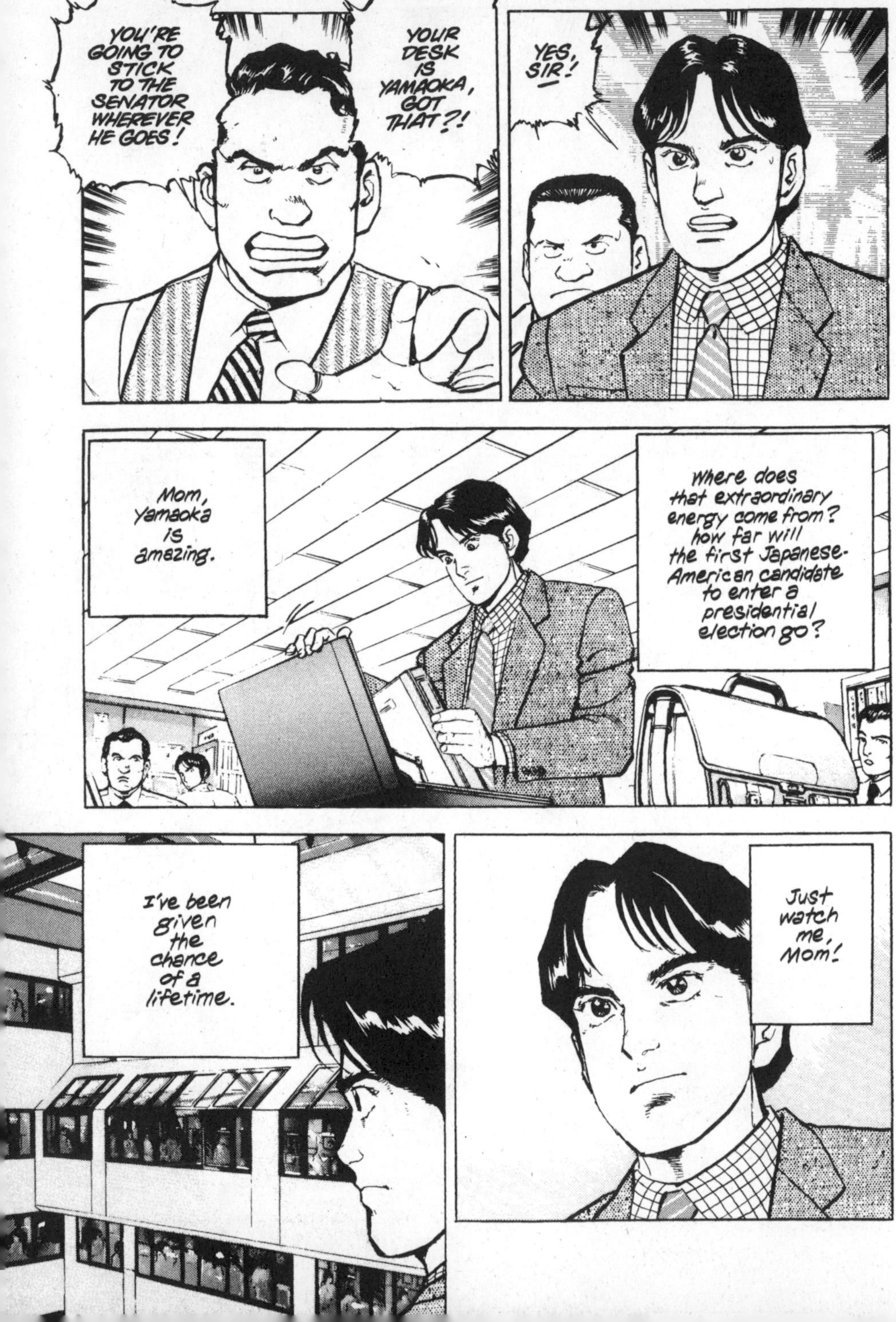
YOU'RE GOING TO STICK TO THE SENATOR WHEREVER HE GOES!
YOUR DESK IS YAMAOKA, GOT THAT?!
YES, SIR!
Mom, Yamaoka is amazing.
Where does that extraordinary energy come from? how far will the first Japanese-American candidate to enter a presidential election go?
I've been given the chance of a lifetime.
Just watch me, Mom!

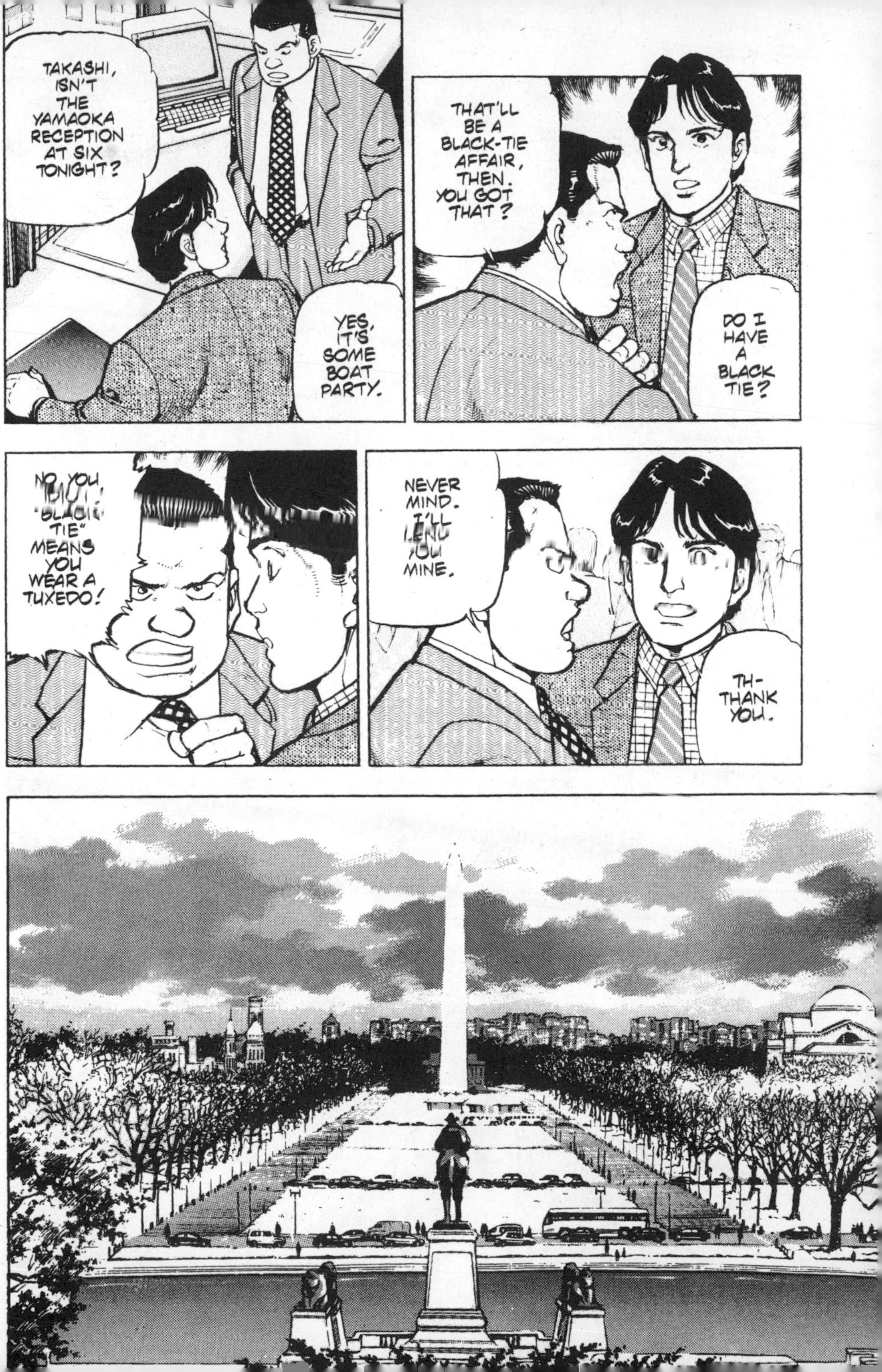
TAKASHI, ISN'T THE YAMAOKA RECEPTION AT SIX TONIGHT?
YES, IT'S SOME BOAT PARTY.
THAT'LL BE A BLACK-TIE AFFAIR, THEN. YOU GOT THAT?
DO I HAVE A BLACK TIE?
NO, YOU
TIE" MEANS YOU WEAR A TUXEDO!
NEVER MIND. I'LL
MINE.
TH-THANK YOU.

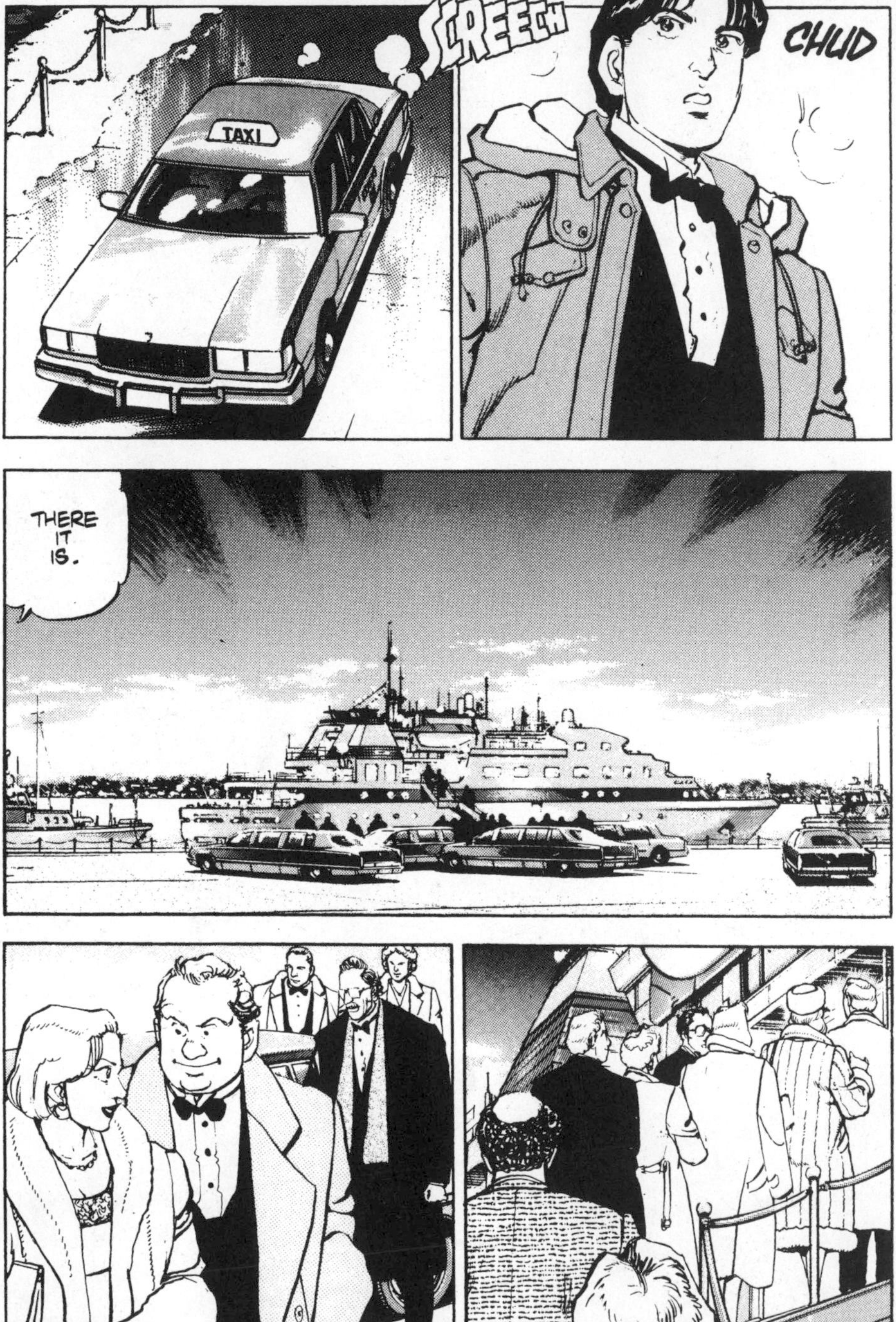
SCREECH
CHUD
THERE IT IS.

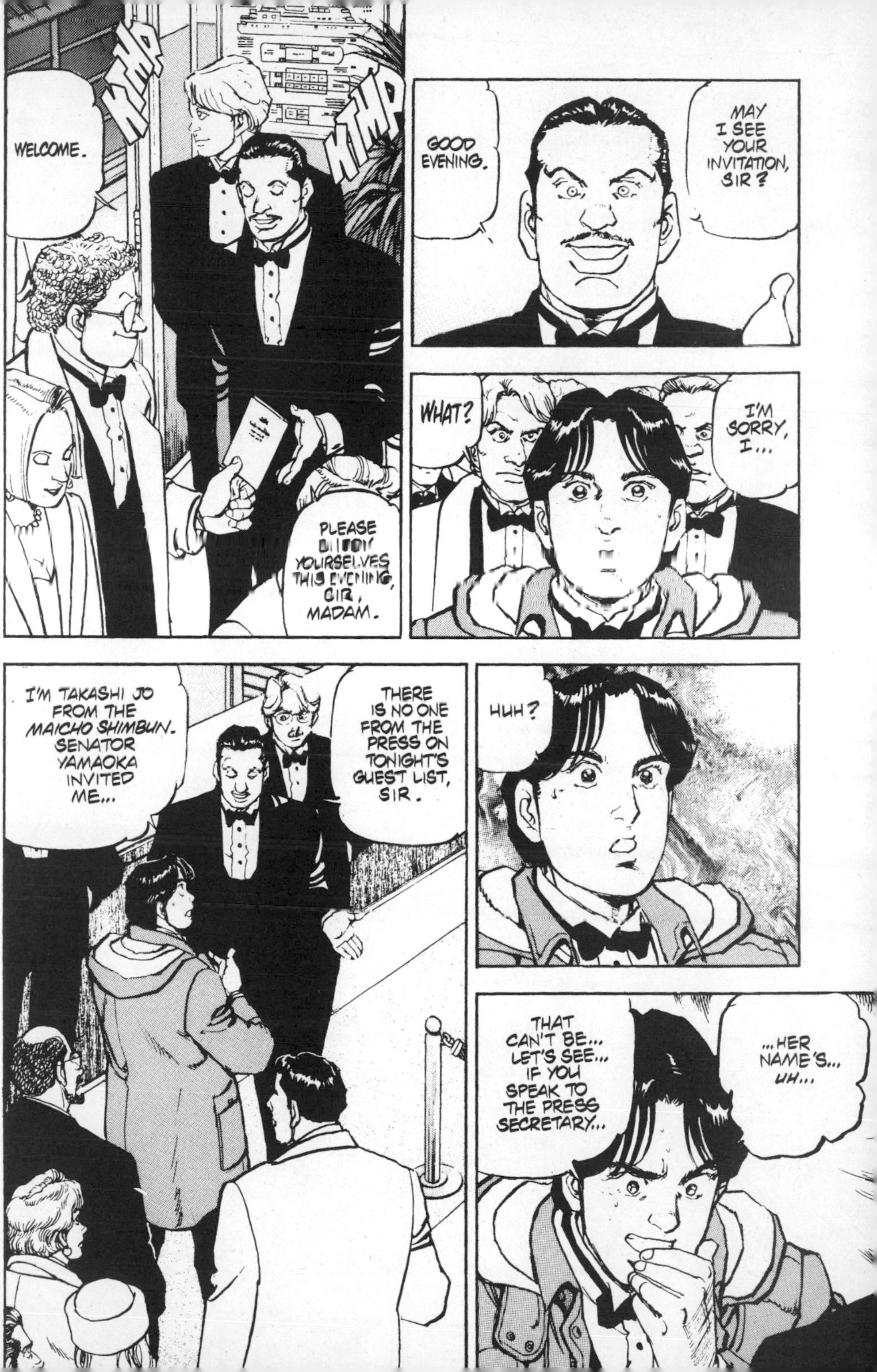
WELCOME.
KTHP
KTHP
PLEASE ENJOY YOURSELVES THIS EVENING, SIR, MADAM.
GOOD EVENING.
MAY I SEE YOUR INVITATION, SIR?
WHAT?
I'M SORRY, I...
I'M TAKASHI JO FROM THE *MAICHO SHIMBUN*. SENATOR YAMAOKA INVITED ME...
THERE IS NO ONE FROM THE PRESS ON TONIGHT'S GUEST LIST, SIR.
HUH?
THAT CAN'T BE... LET'S SEE... IF YOU SPEAK TO THE PRESS SECRETARY...
...HER NAME'S... UH...

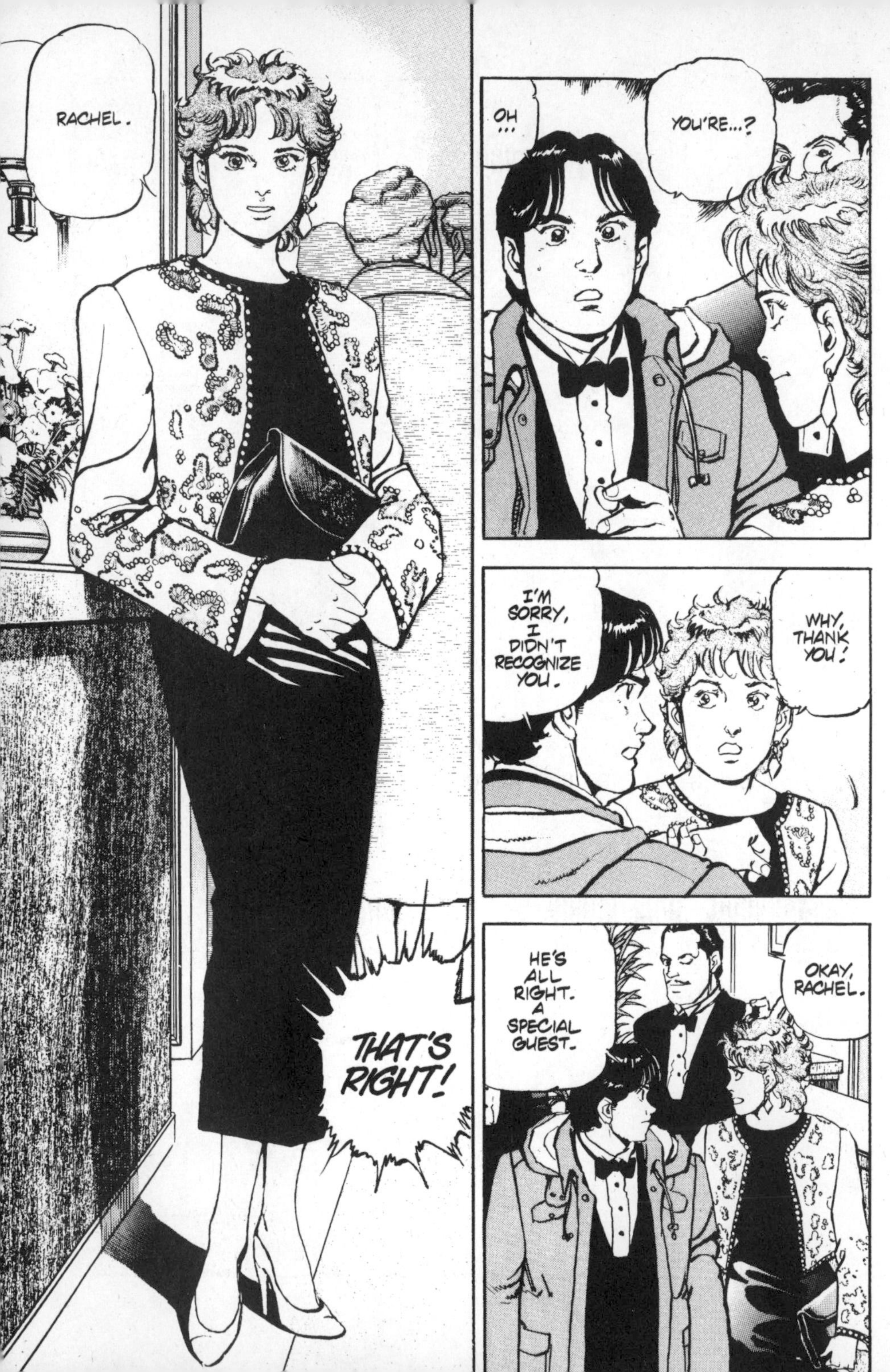
RACHEL.
THAT'S RIGHT!
OH...
YOU'RE...?
I'M SORRY, I DIDN'T RECOGNIZE YOU.
WHY, THANK YOU!
HE'S ALL RIGHT. A SPECIAL GUEST.
OKAY, RACHEL.

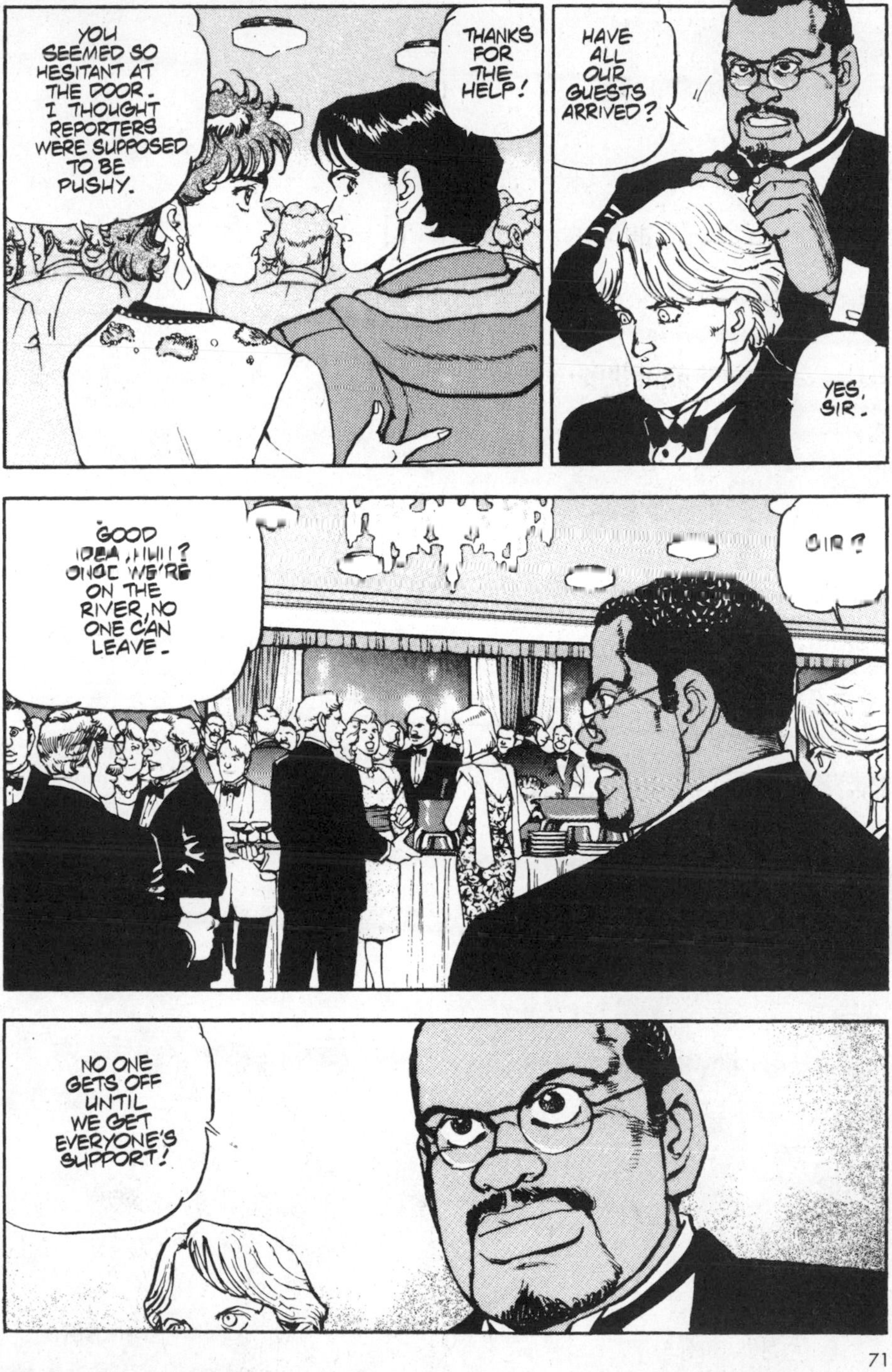
YOU SEEMED SO HESITANT AT THE DOOR. I THOUGHT REPORTERS WERE SUPPOSED TO BE PUSHY.
THANKS FOR THE HELP!
HAVE ALL OUR GUESTS ARRIVED?
YES, SIR.
GOOD IDEA, HUH? ONCE WE'RE ON THE RIVER, NO ONE CAN LEAVE.
SIR?
NO ONE GETS OFF UNTIL WE GET EVERYONE'S SUPPORT!

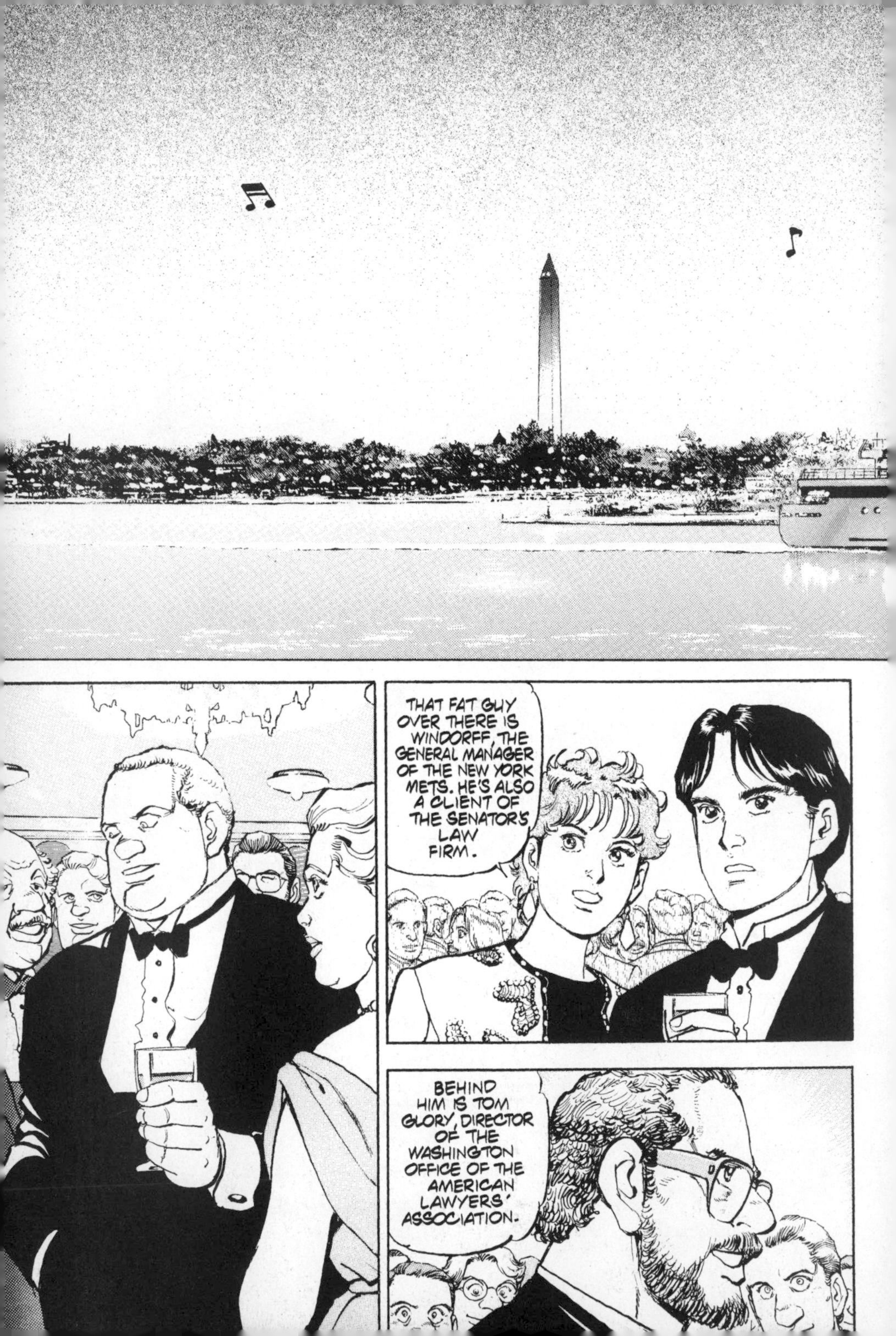
THAT FAT GUY OVER THERE IS WINDORFF, THE GENERAL MANAGER OF THE NEW YORK METS. HE'S ALSO A CLIENT OF THE SENATOR'S LAW FIRM.
BEHIND HIM IS TOM GLORY, DIRECTOR OF THE WASHINGTON OFFICE OF THE AMERICAN LAWYERS' ASSOCIATION.

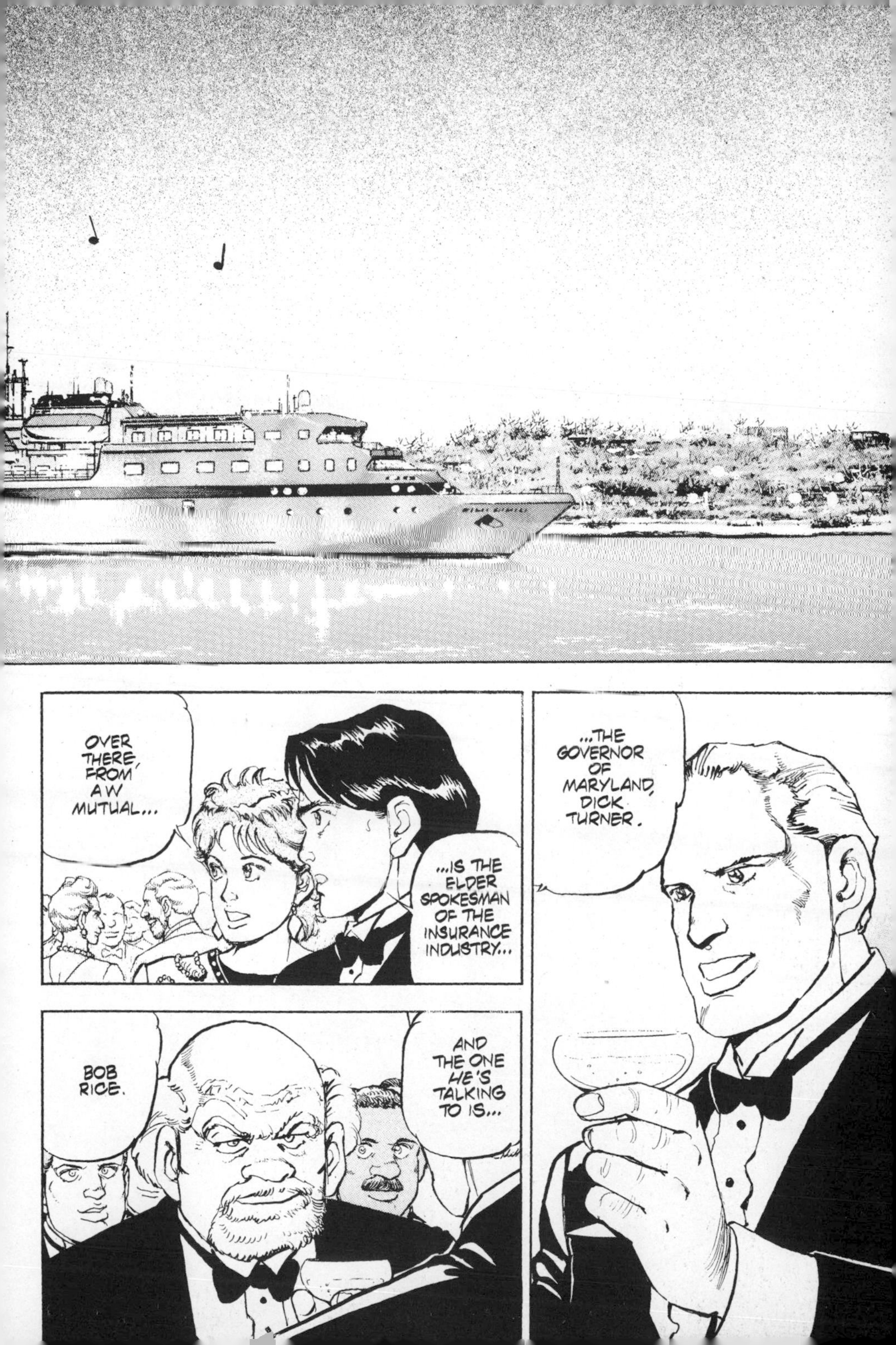
OVER THERE, FROM AW MUTUAL...
...IS THE ELDER SPOKESMAN OF THE INSURANCE INDUSTRY...
BOB RICE.
AND THE ONE HE'S TALKING TO IS...
...THE GOVERNOR OF MARYLAND, DICK TURNER.

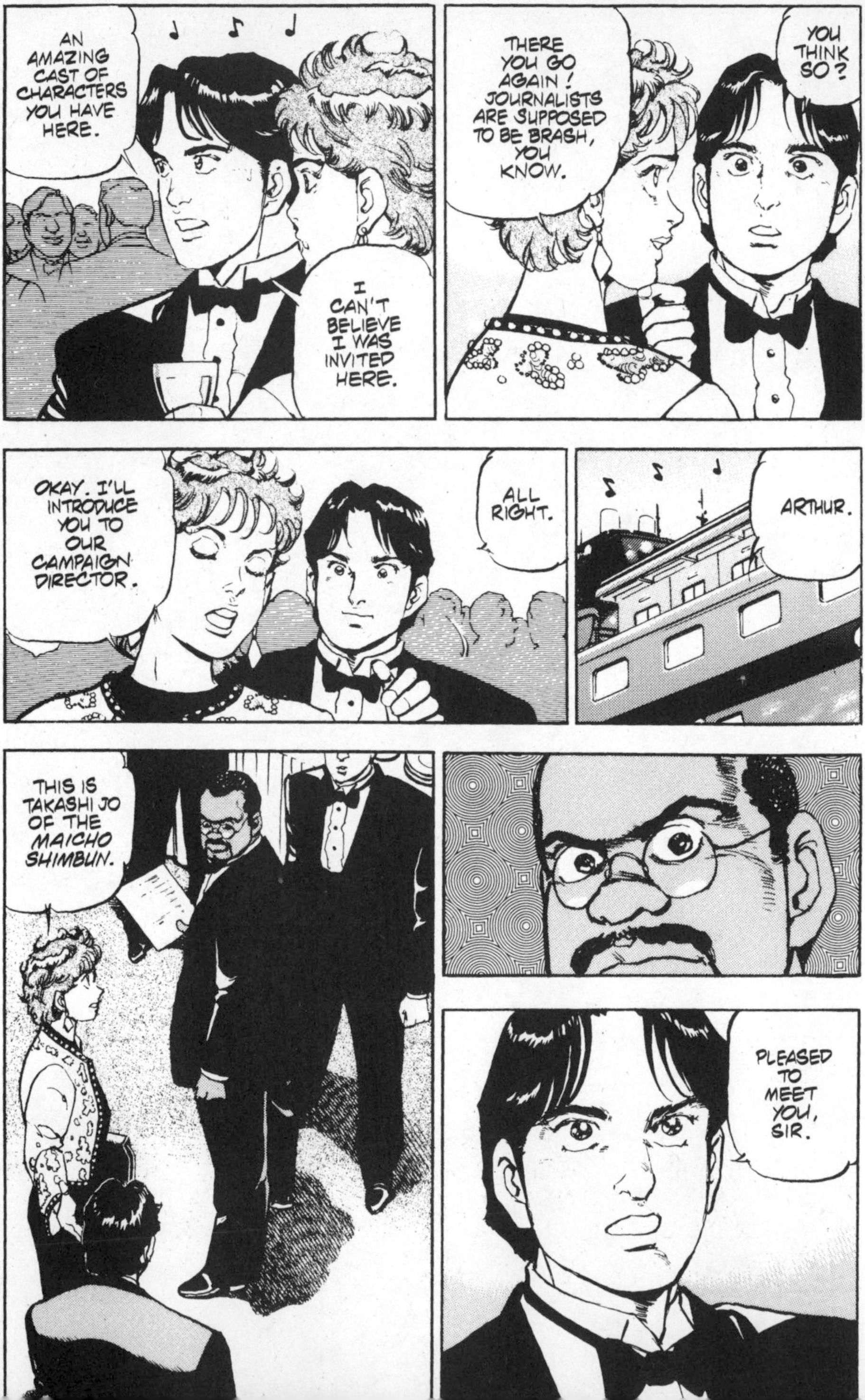
AN AMAZING CAST OF CHARACTERS YOU HAVE HERE.
I CAN'T BELIEVE I WAS INVITED HERE.
THERE YOU GO AGAIN! JOURNALISTS ARE SUPPOSED TO BE BRASH, YOU KNOW.
YOU THINK SO?
OKAY. I'LL INTRODUCE YOU TO OUR CAMPAIGN DIRECTOR.
ALL RIGHT.
ARTHUR.
THIS IS TAKASHI JO OF THE *MAICHO SHIMBUN*.
PLEASED TO MEET YOU, SIR.

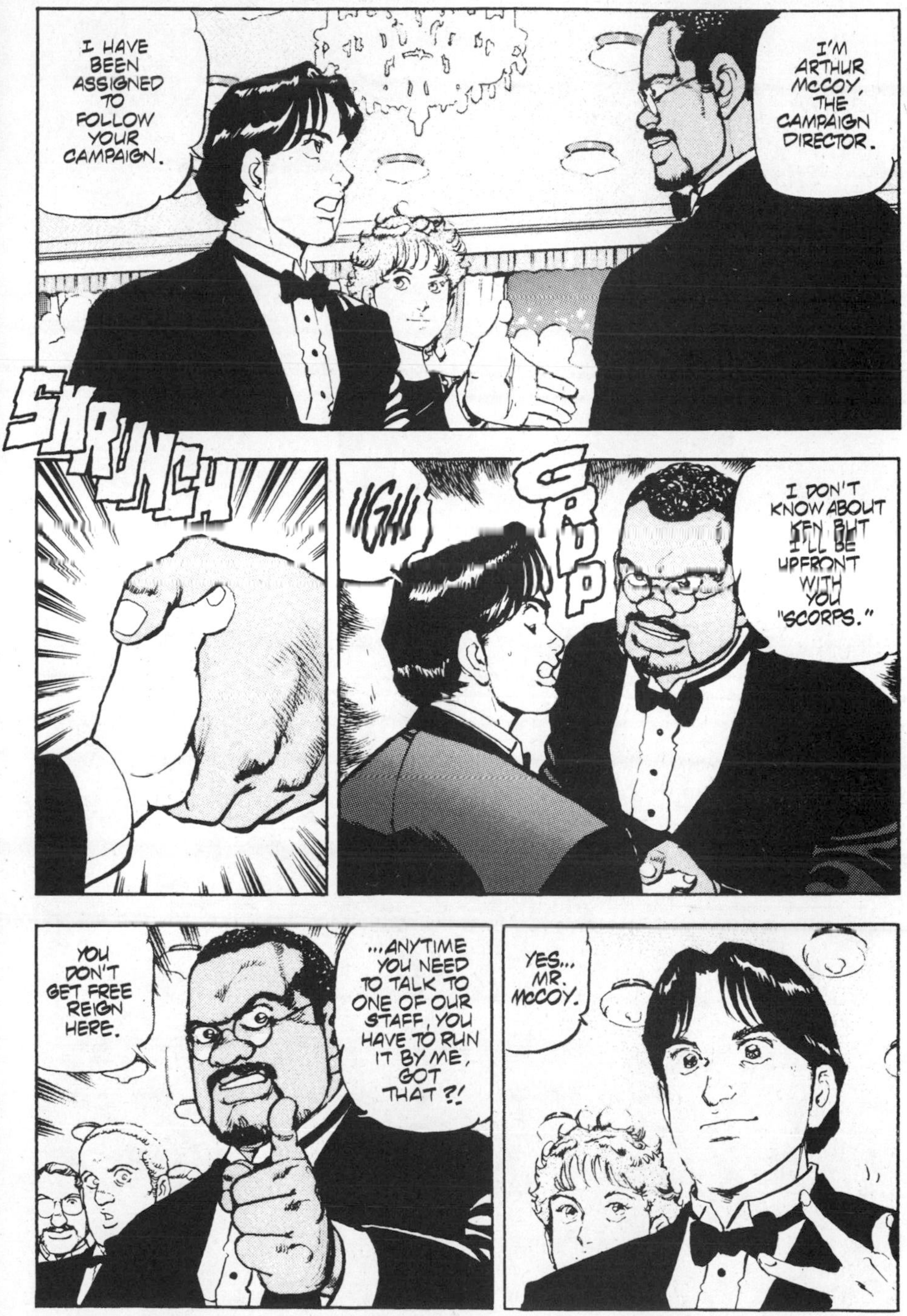
I HAVE BEEN ASSIGNED TO FOLLOW YOUR CAMPAIGN.
I'M ARTHUR McCOY, THE CAMPAIGN DIRECTOR.
SHRUNCH
UGH
GRIP
I DON'T KNOW ABOUT KEN BUT I'LL BE UPFRONT WITH YOU "SCORPS."
YOU DON'T GET FREE REIGN HERE.
...ANYTIME YOU NEED TO TALK TO ONE OF OUR STAFF, YOU HAVE TO RUN IT BY ME, GOT THAT?!
YES... MR. McCOY.

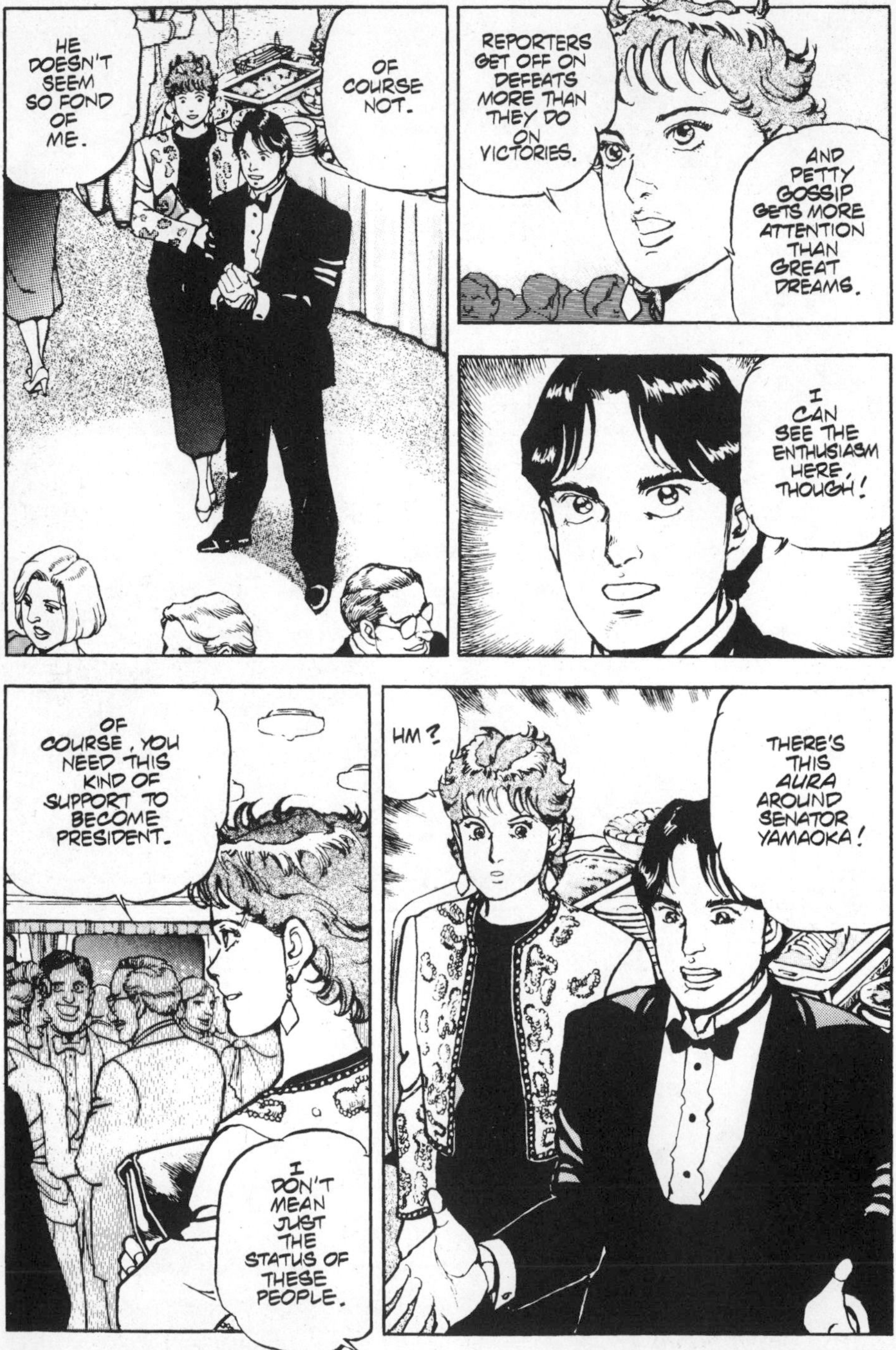
HE DOESN'T SEEM SO FOND OF ME.
OF COURSE NOT.
REPORTERS GET OFF ON DEFEATS MORE THAN THEY DO ON VICTORIES.
AND PETTY GOSSIP GETS MORE ATTENTION THAN GREAT DREAMS.
I CAN SEE THE ENTHUSIASM HERE, THOUGH!
OF COURSE, YOU NEED THIS KIND OF SUPPORT TO BECOME PRESIDENT.
I DON'T MEAN JUST THE STATUS OF THESE PEOPLE.
HM?
THERE'S THIS AURA AROUND SENATOR YAMAOKA!

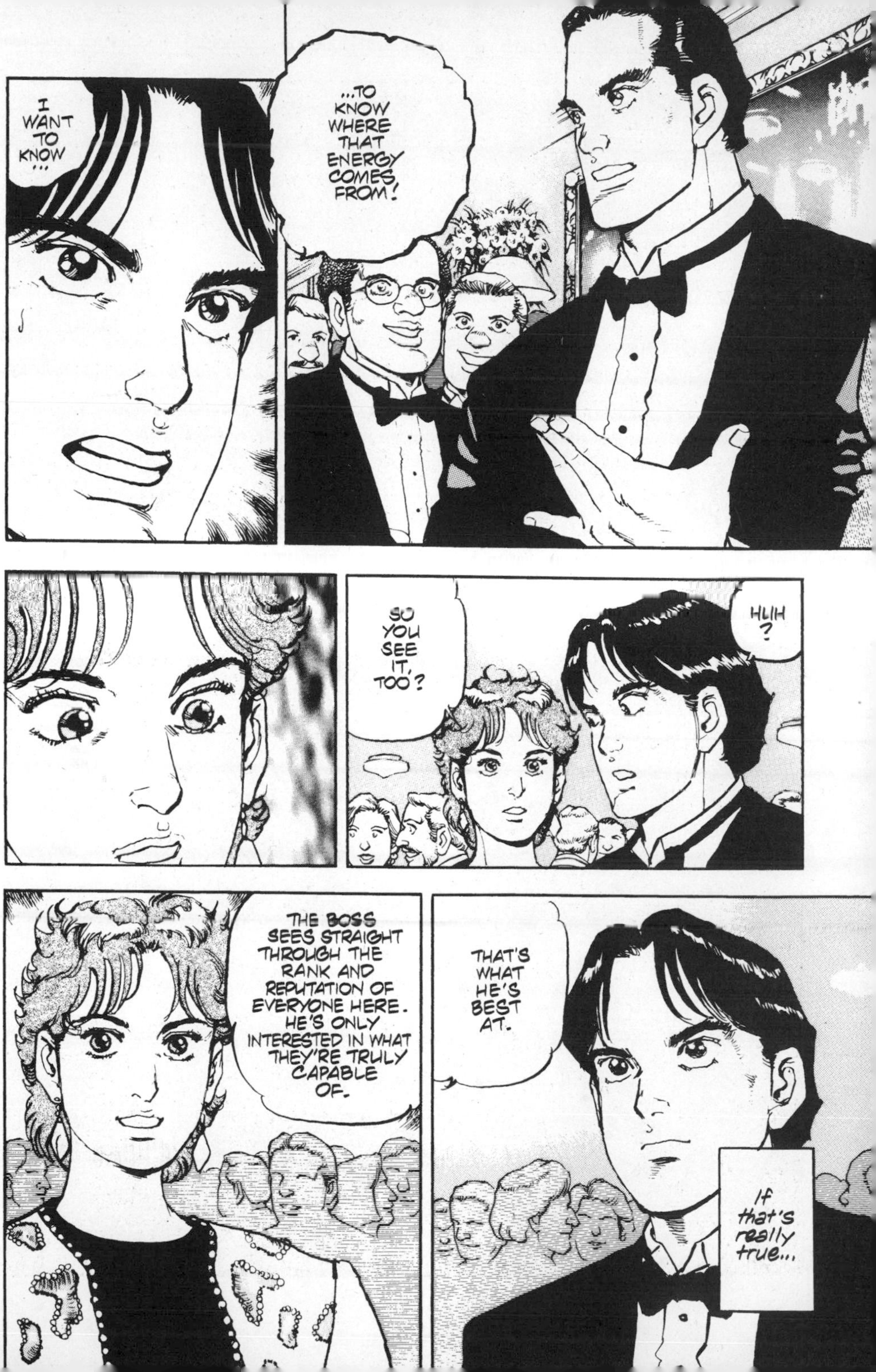
I WANT TO KNOW...
...TO KNOW WHERE THAT ENERGY COMES FROM!
SO YOU SEE IT, TOO?
HUH?
THE BOSS SEES STRAIGHT THROUGH THE RANK AND REPUTATION OF EVERYONE HERE. HE'S ONLY INTERESTED IN WHAT THEY'RE TRULY CAPABLE OF.
THAT'S WHAT HE'S BEST AT.
If that's really true...

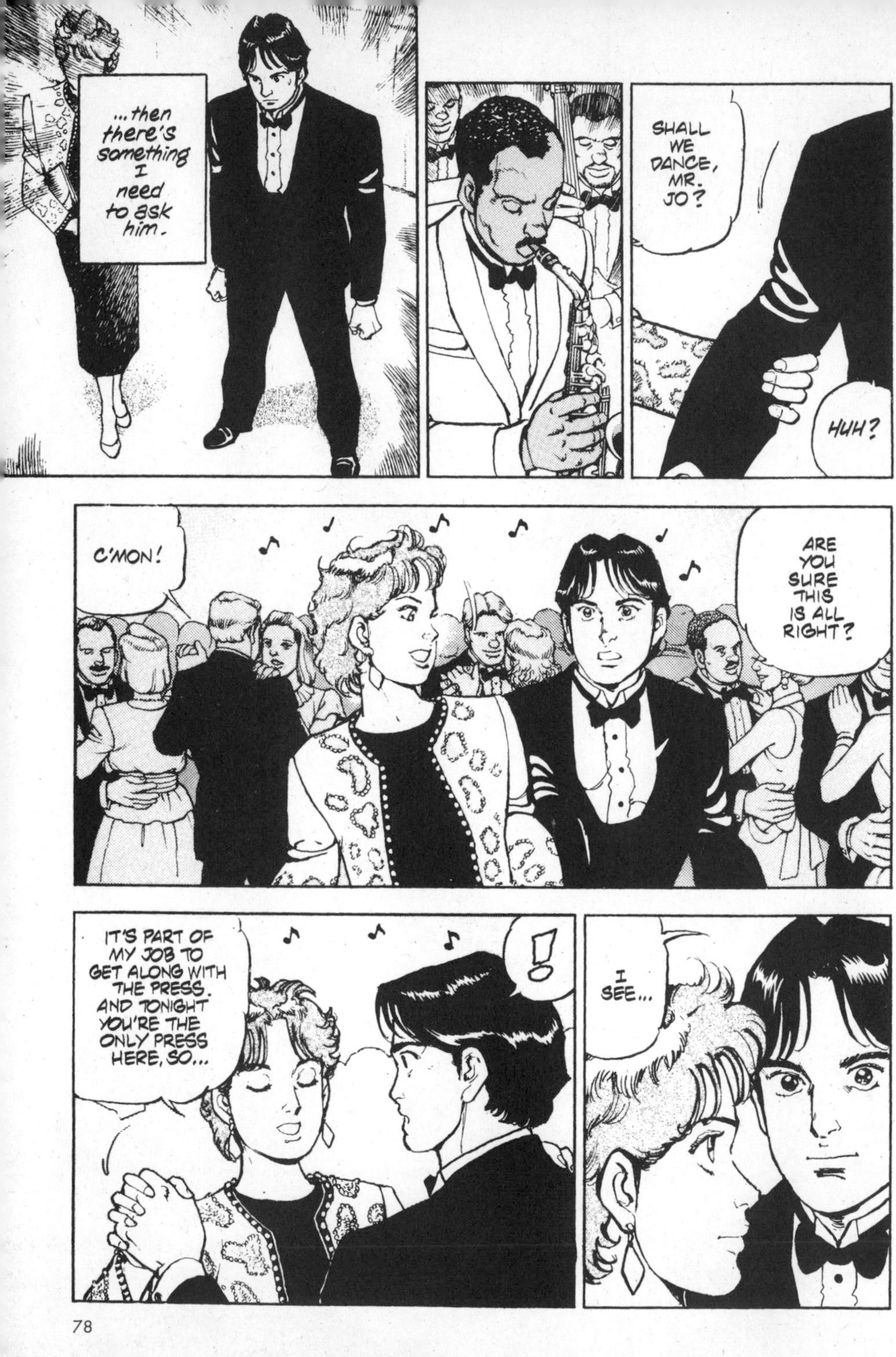

...then there's something I need to ask him.
SHALL WE DANCE, MR. JO?
HUH?
C'MON!
ARE YOU SURE THIS IS ALL RIGHT?
IT'S PART OF MY JOB TO GET ALONG WITH THE PRESS. AND TONIGHT YOU'RE THE ONLY PRESS HERE, SO...
!
I SEE...

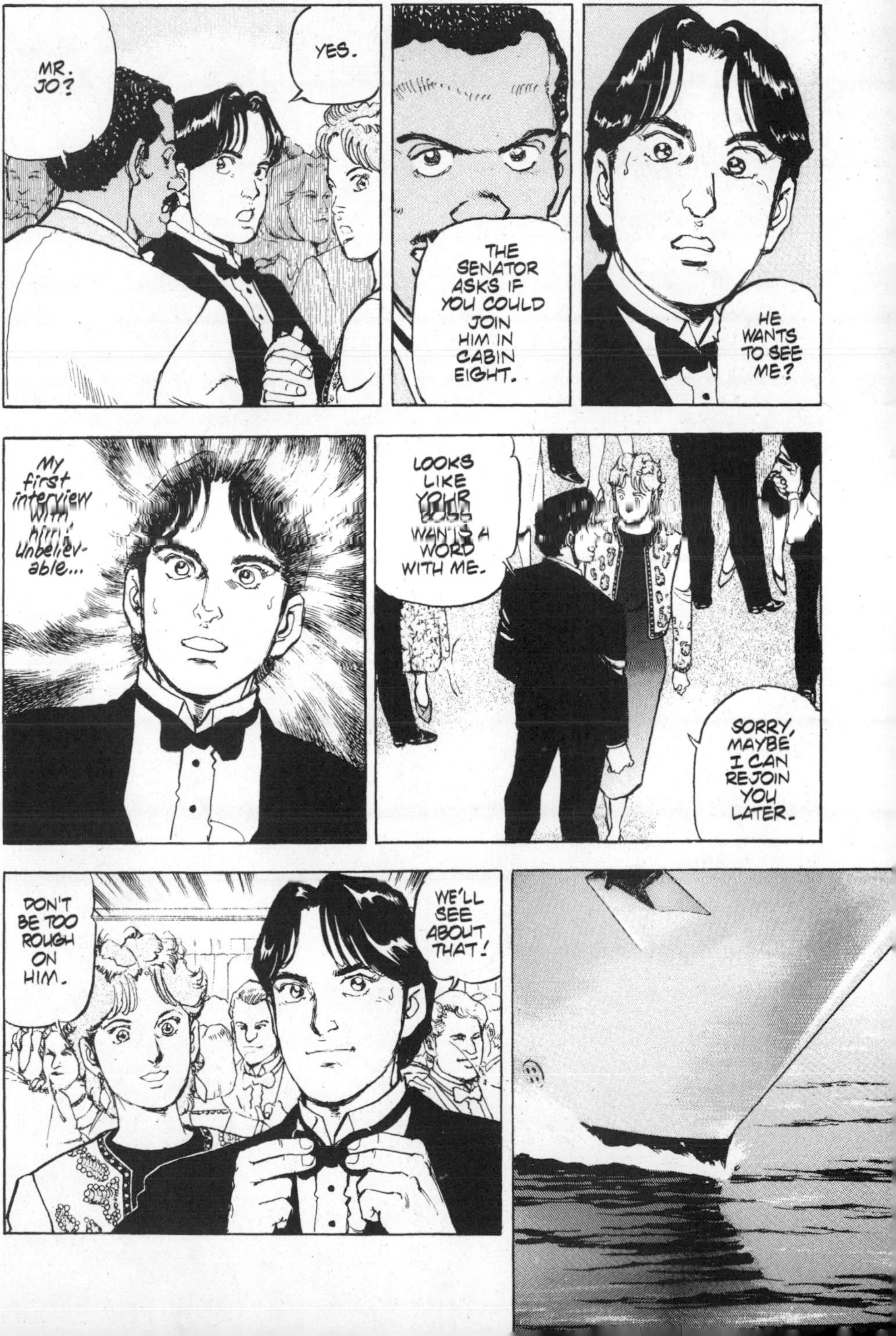
MR. JO?
YES.
THE SENATOR ASKS IF YOU COULD JOIN HIM IN CABIN EIGHT.
HE WANTS TO SEE ME?
My first interview with him! Unbeliev-able...
LOOKS LIKE YOUR BOSS WANTS A WORD WITH ME.
SORRY, MAYBE I CAN REJOIN YOU LATER.
DON'T BE TOO ROUGH ON HIM.
WE'LL SEE ABOUT THAT!

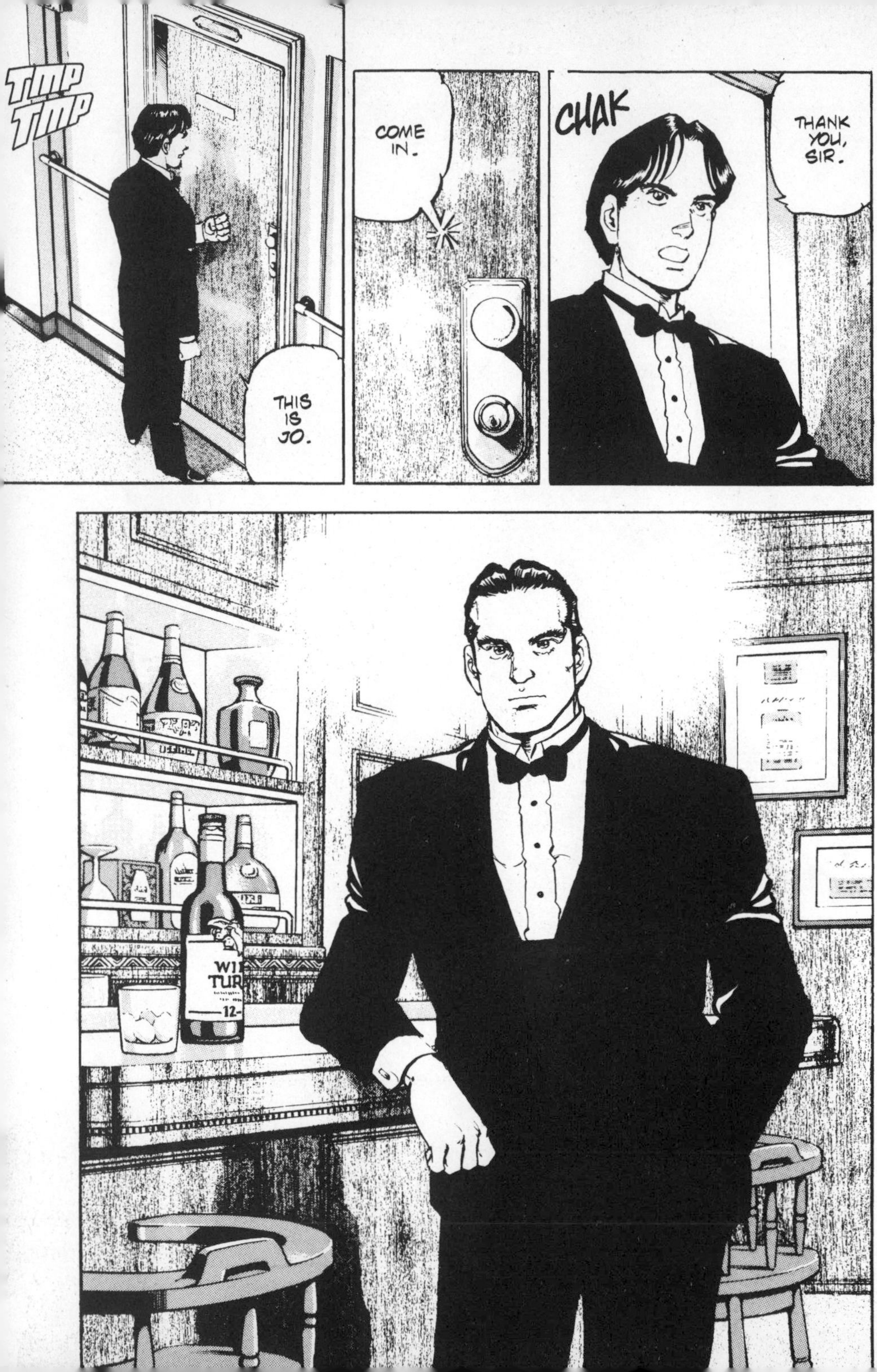
TMP TMP
THIS IS JO.
COME IN.
CHAK
THANK YOU, SIR.

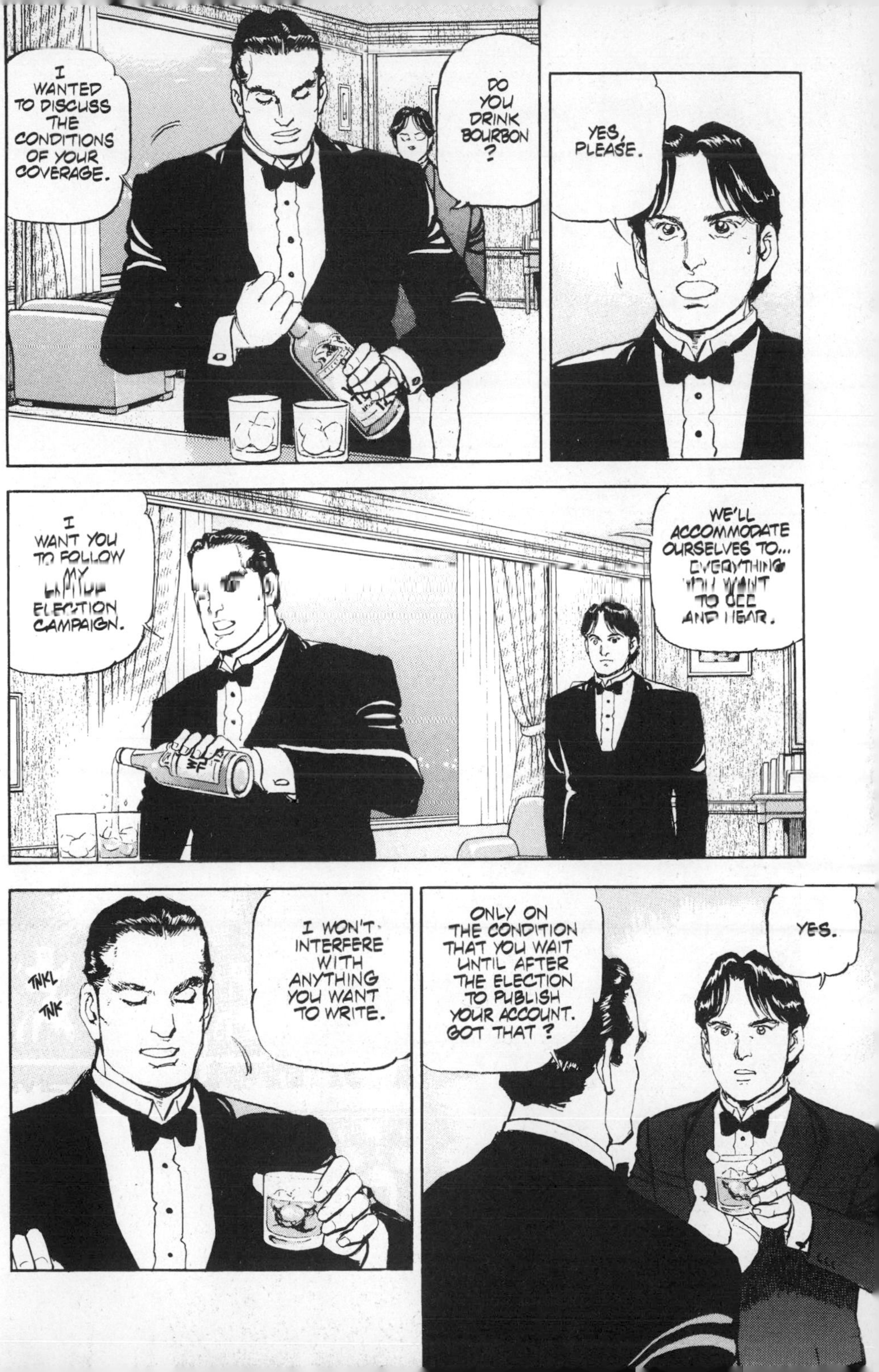
I WANTED TO DISCUSS THE CONDITIONS OF YOUR COVERAGE.
DO YOU DRINK BOURBON ?
YES, PLEASE.
I WANT YOU TO FOLLOW MY ELECTION CAMPAIGN.
WE'LL ACCOMMODATE OURSELVES TO... EVERYTHING YOU WANT TO SEE AND HEAR.
TNKL
TNK
I WON'T INTERFERE WITH ANYTHING YOU WANT TO WRITE.
ONLY ON THE CONDITION THAT YOU WAIT UNTIL AFTER THE ELECTION TO PUBLISH YOUR ACCOUNT. GOT THAT ?
YES.

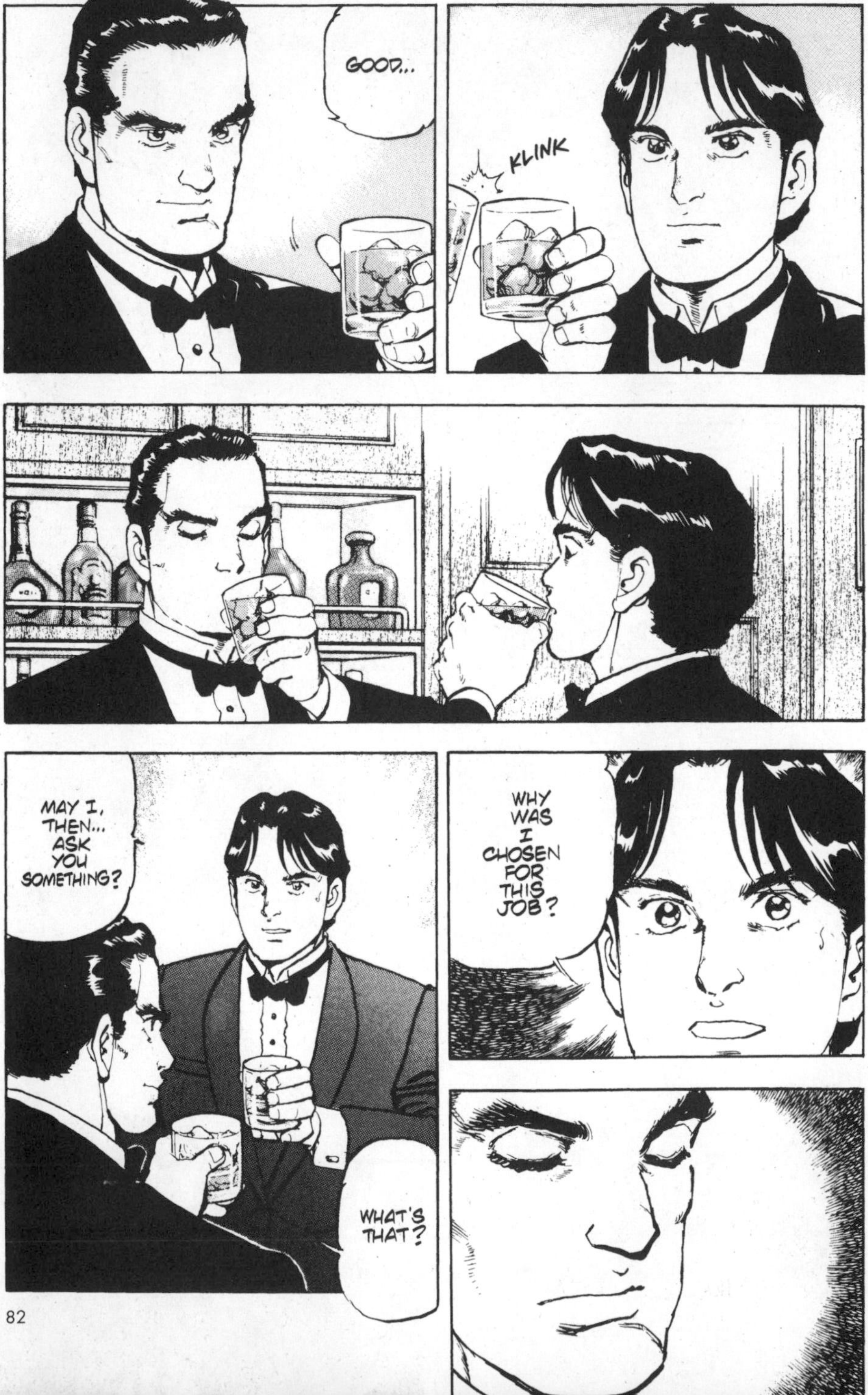
GOOD...
KLINK
MAY I, THEN... ASK YOU SOMETHING?
WHAT'S THAT?
WHY WAS I CHOSEN FOR THIS JOB?

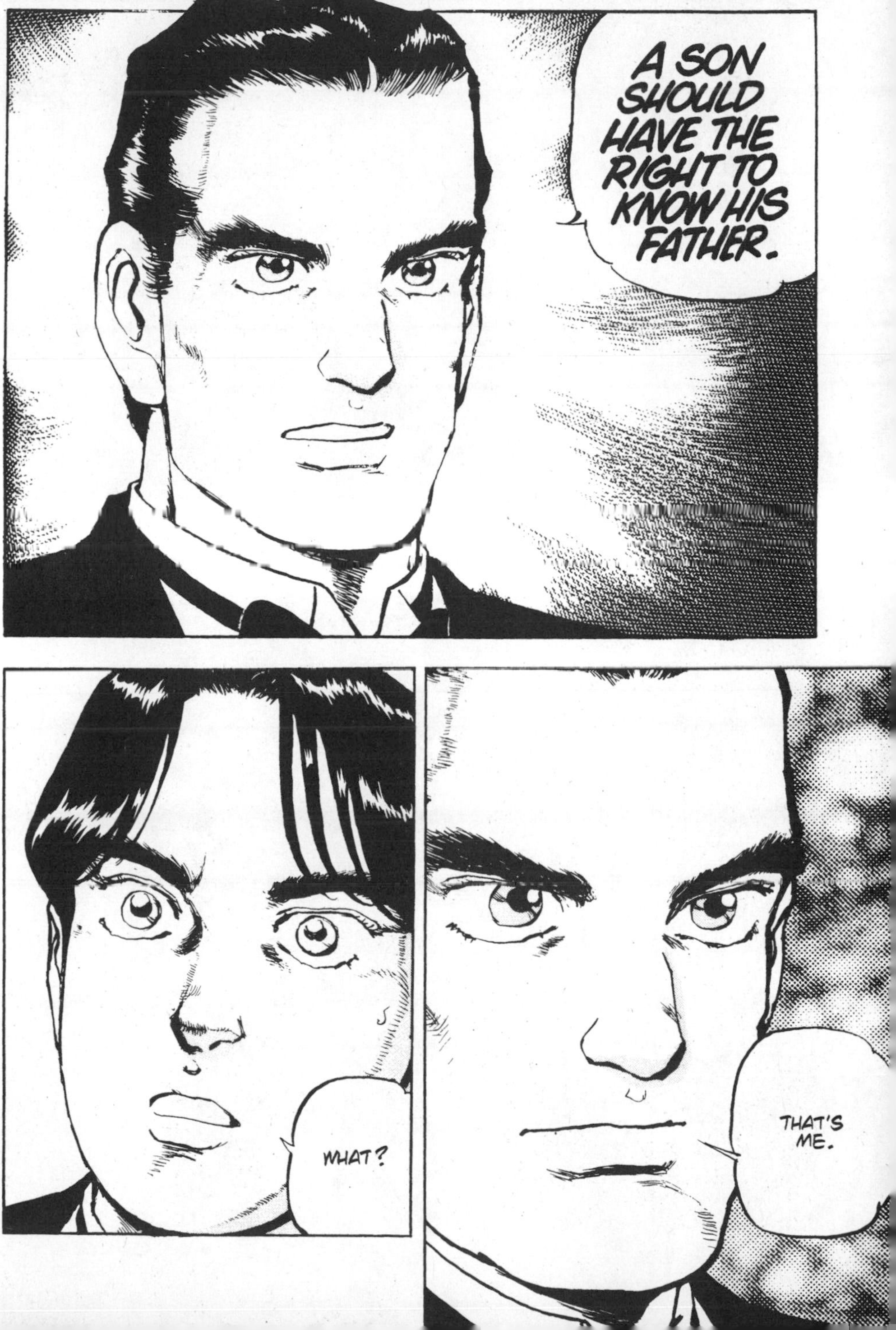
A SON SHOULD HAVE THE RIGHT TO KNOW HIS FATHER.
WHAT?
THAT'S ME.

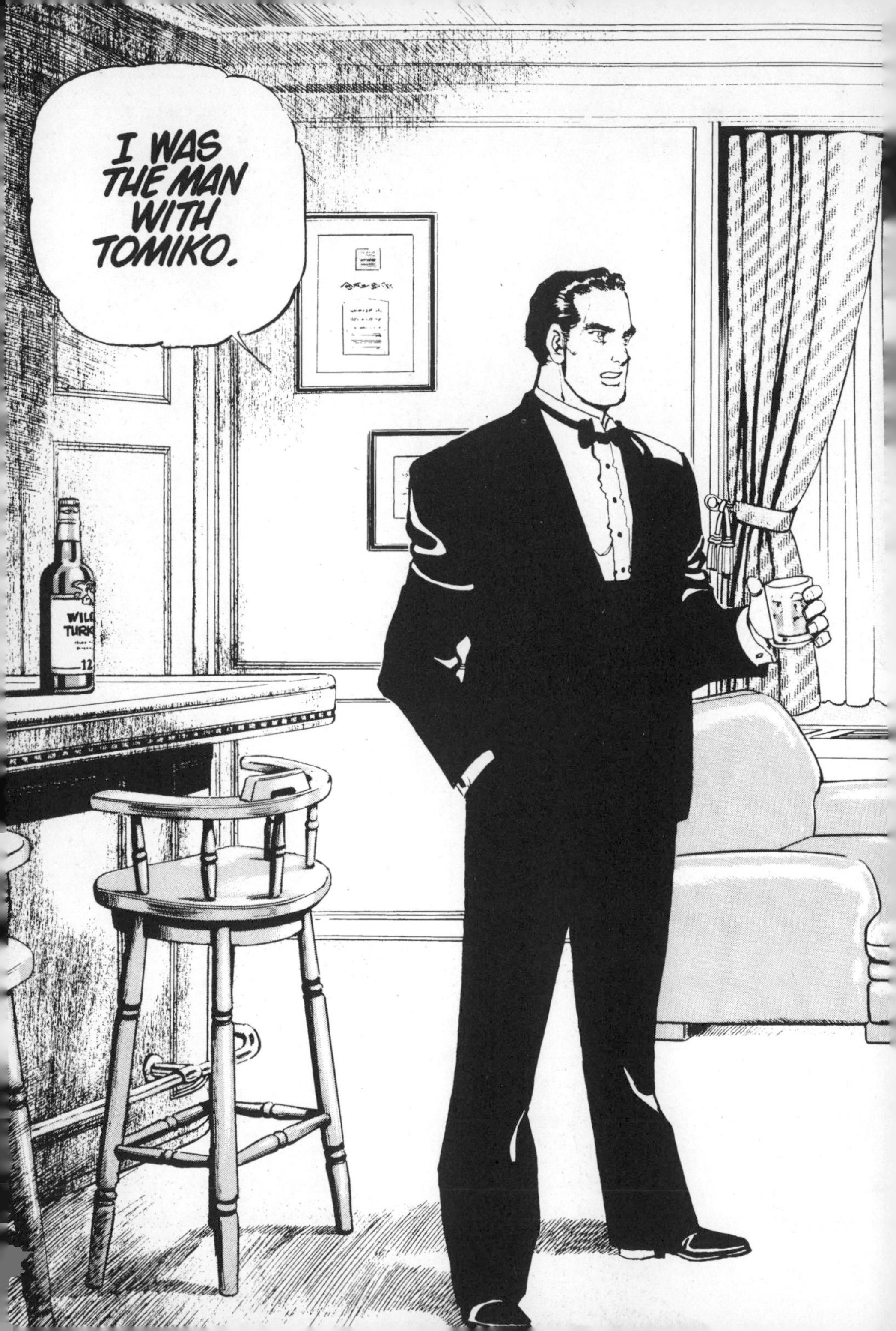
I WAS THE MAN WITH TOMIKO.
WILD TURKEY 12

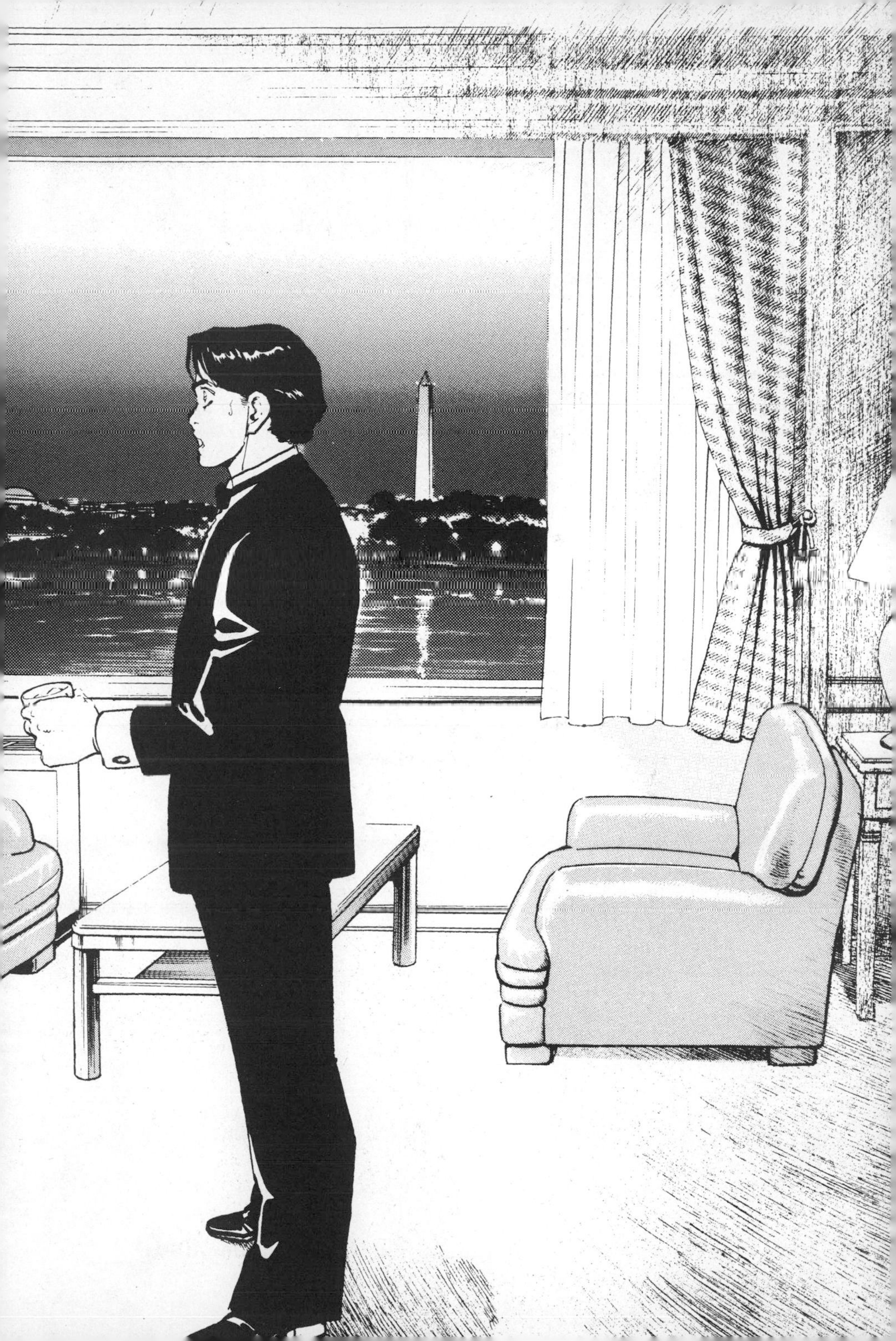

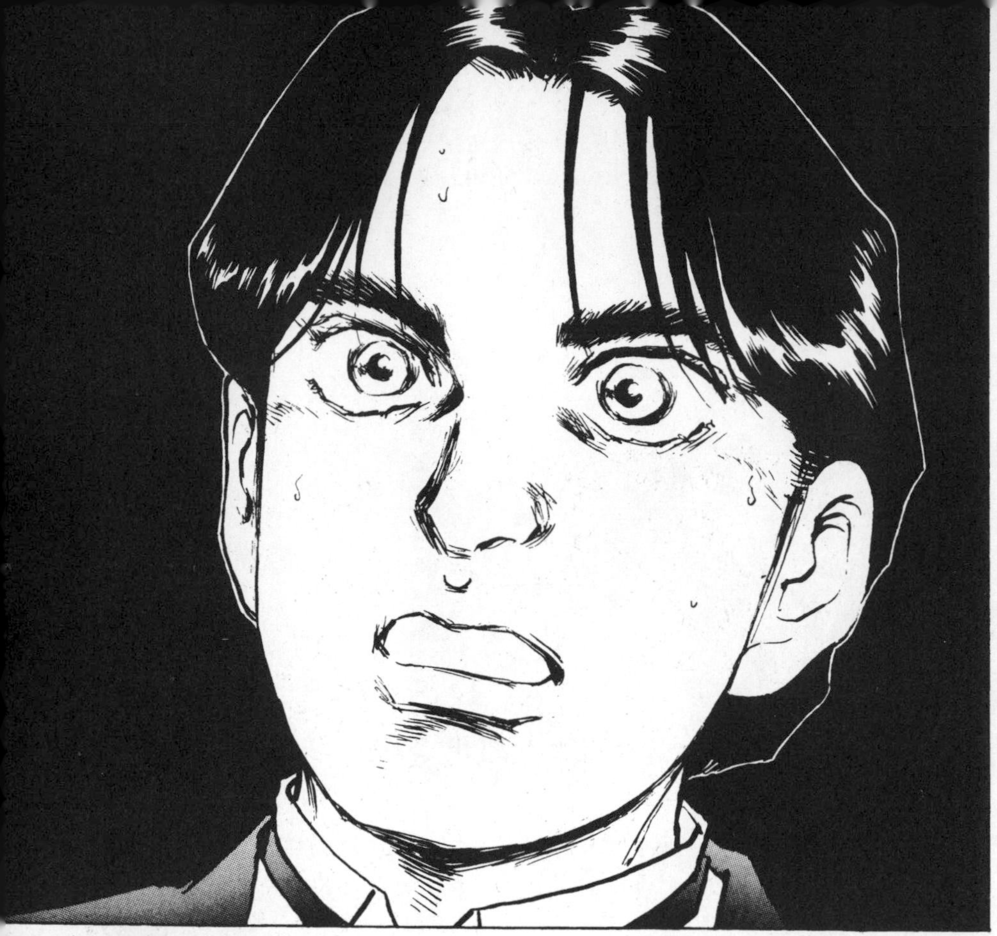
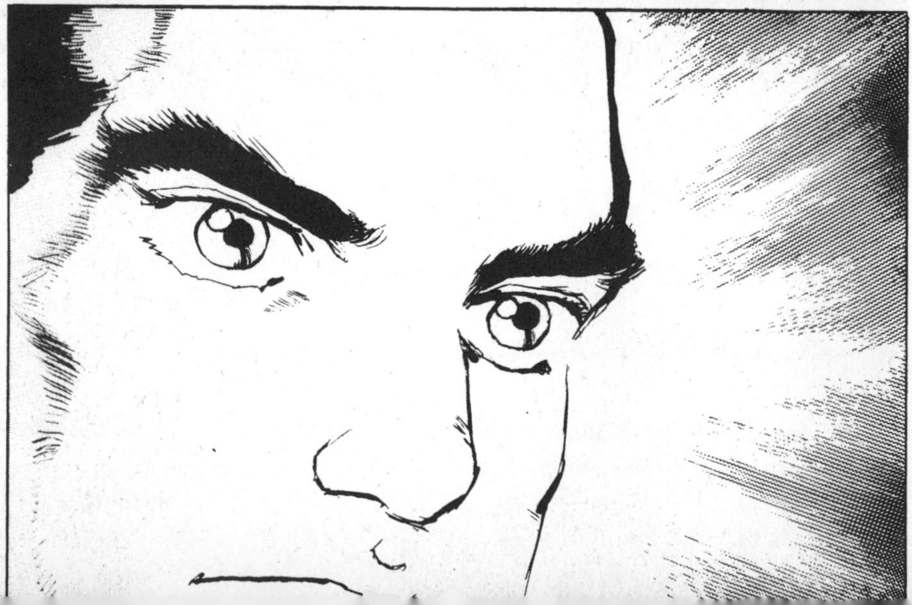

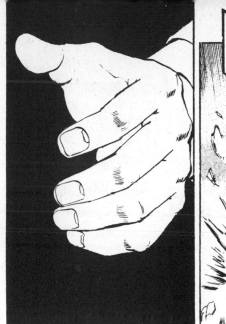

KRRSH

Report #4

W-WHAT DID YOU SAY?

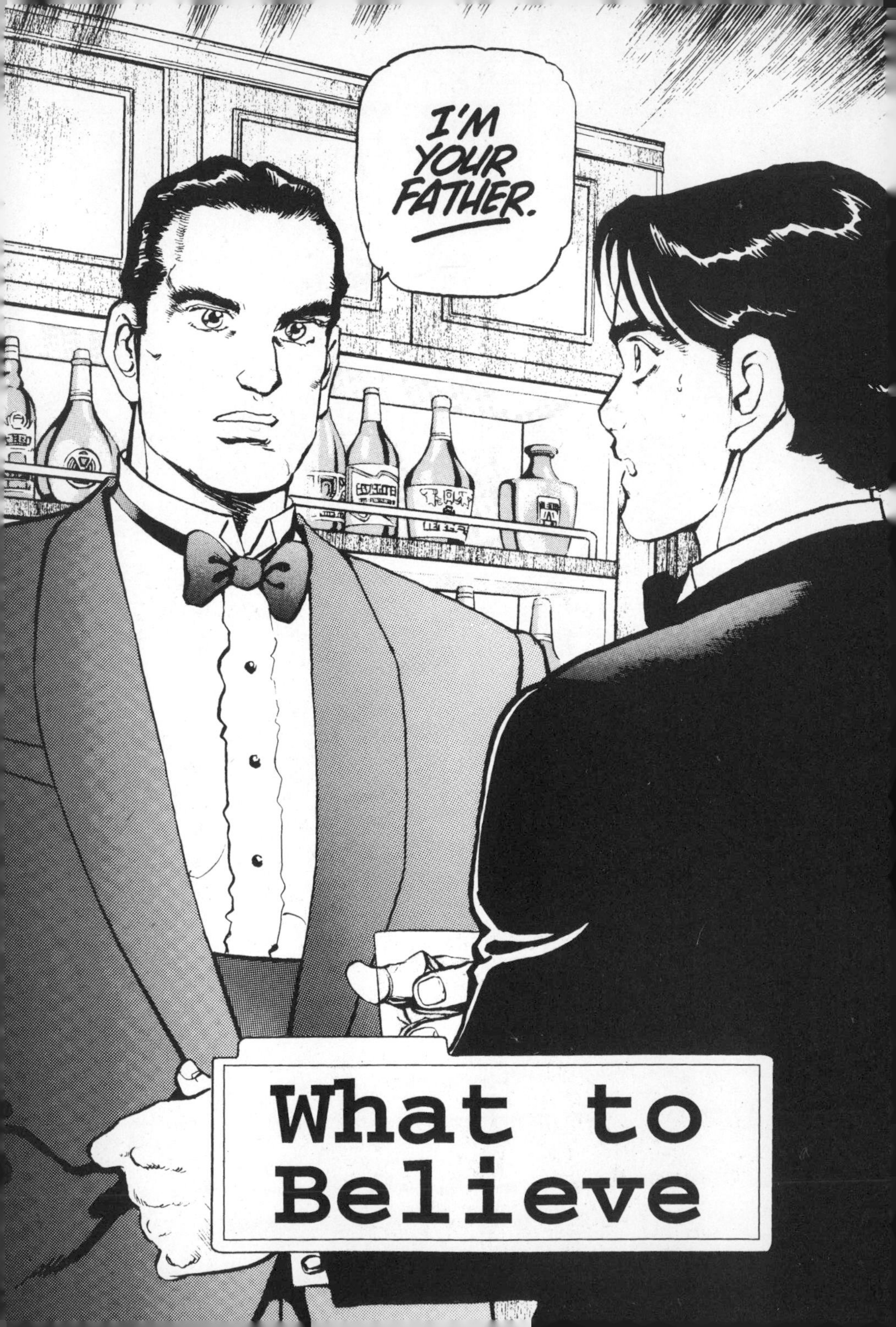
I'M YOUR FATHER.
What to Believe

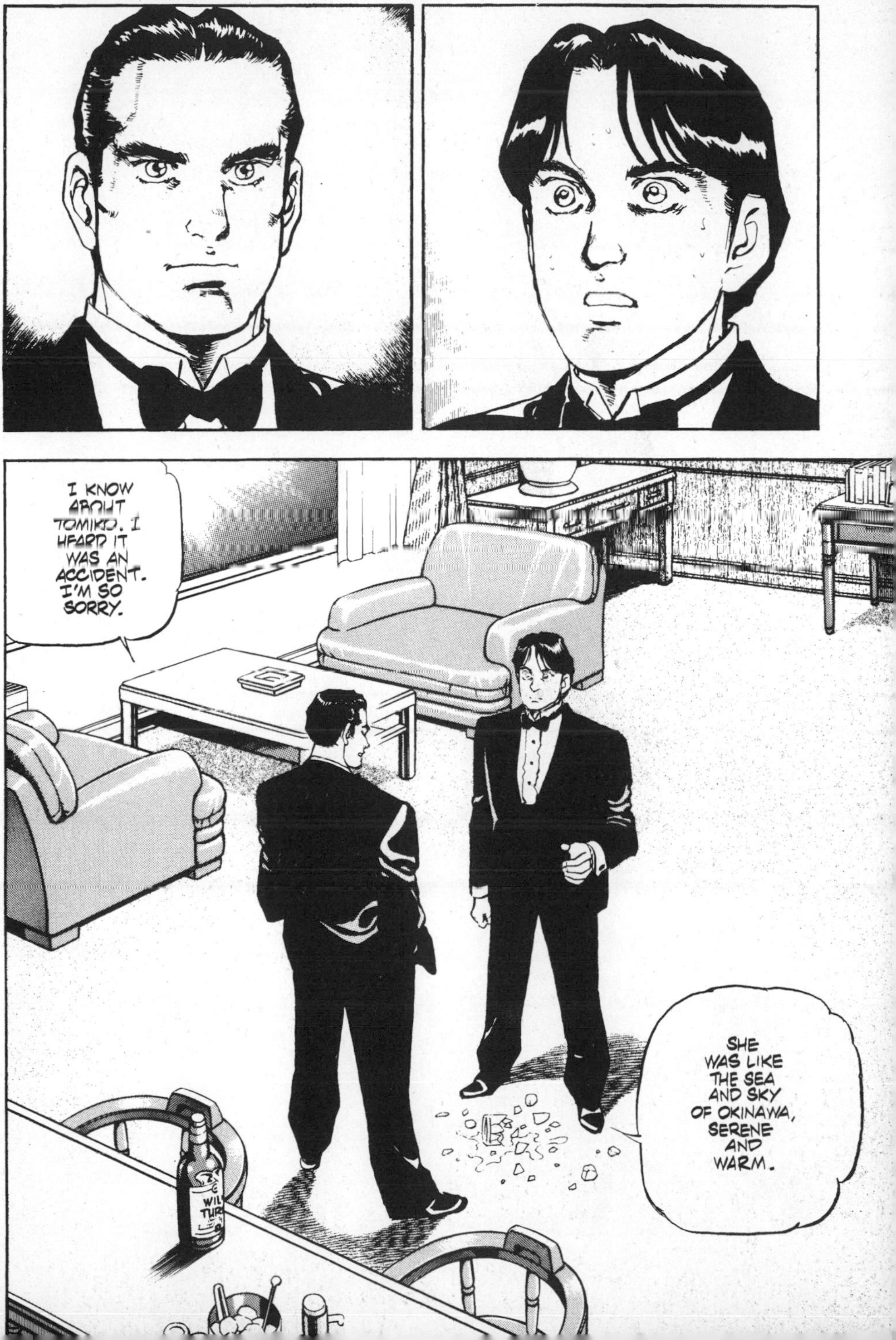
I KNOW ABOUT TOMIKO. I HEARD IT WAS AN ACCIDENT. I'M SO SORRY.
SHE WAS LIKE THE SEA AND SKY OF OKINAWA, SERENE AND WARM.

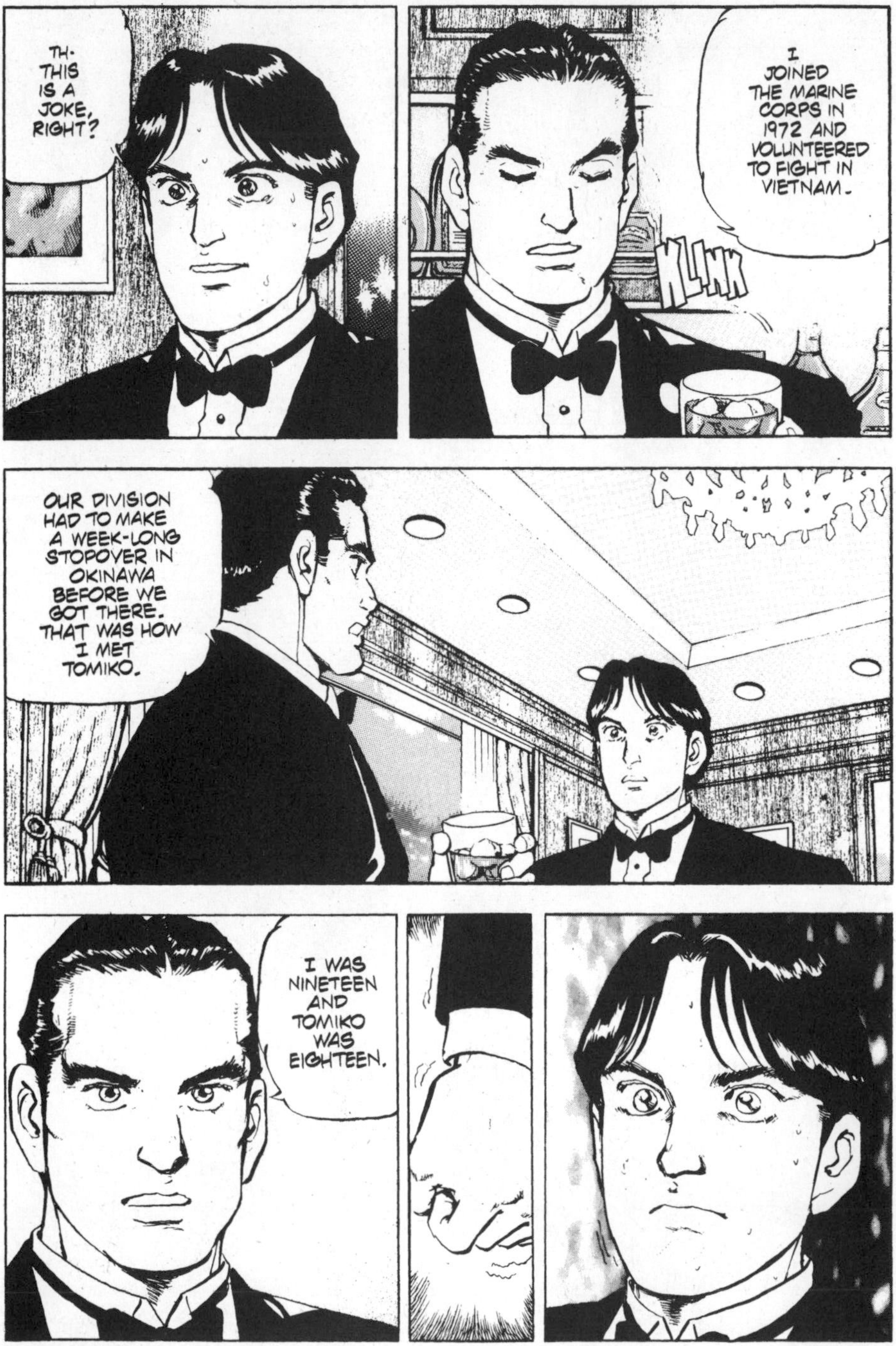
TH- THIS IS A JOKE, RIGHT?
I JOINED THE MARINE CORPS IN 1972 AND VOLUNTEERED TO FIGHT IN VIETNAM.
KLINK
OUR DIVISION HAD TO MAKE A WEEK-LONG STOPOVER IN OKINAWA BEFORE WE GOT THERE. THAT WAS HOW I MET TOMIKO.
I WAS NINETEEN AND TOMIKO WAS EIGHTEEN.

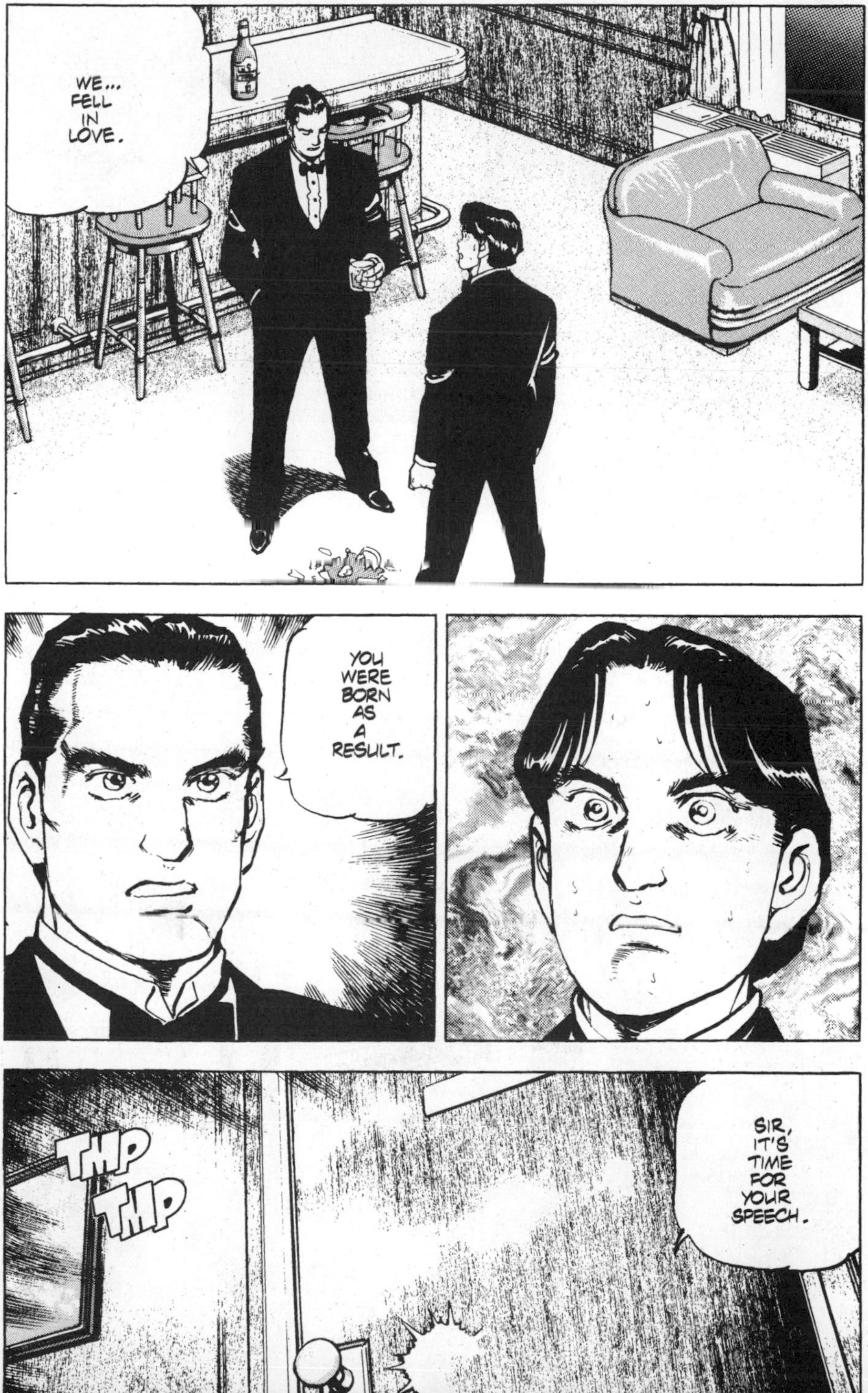
WE... FELL IN LOVE.
YOU WERE BORN AS A RESULT.
TMP TMP
SIR, IT'S TIME FOR YOUR SPEECH.

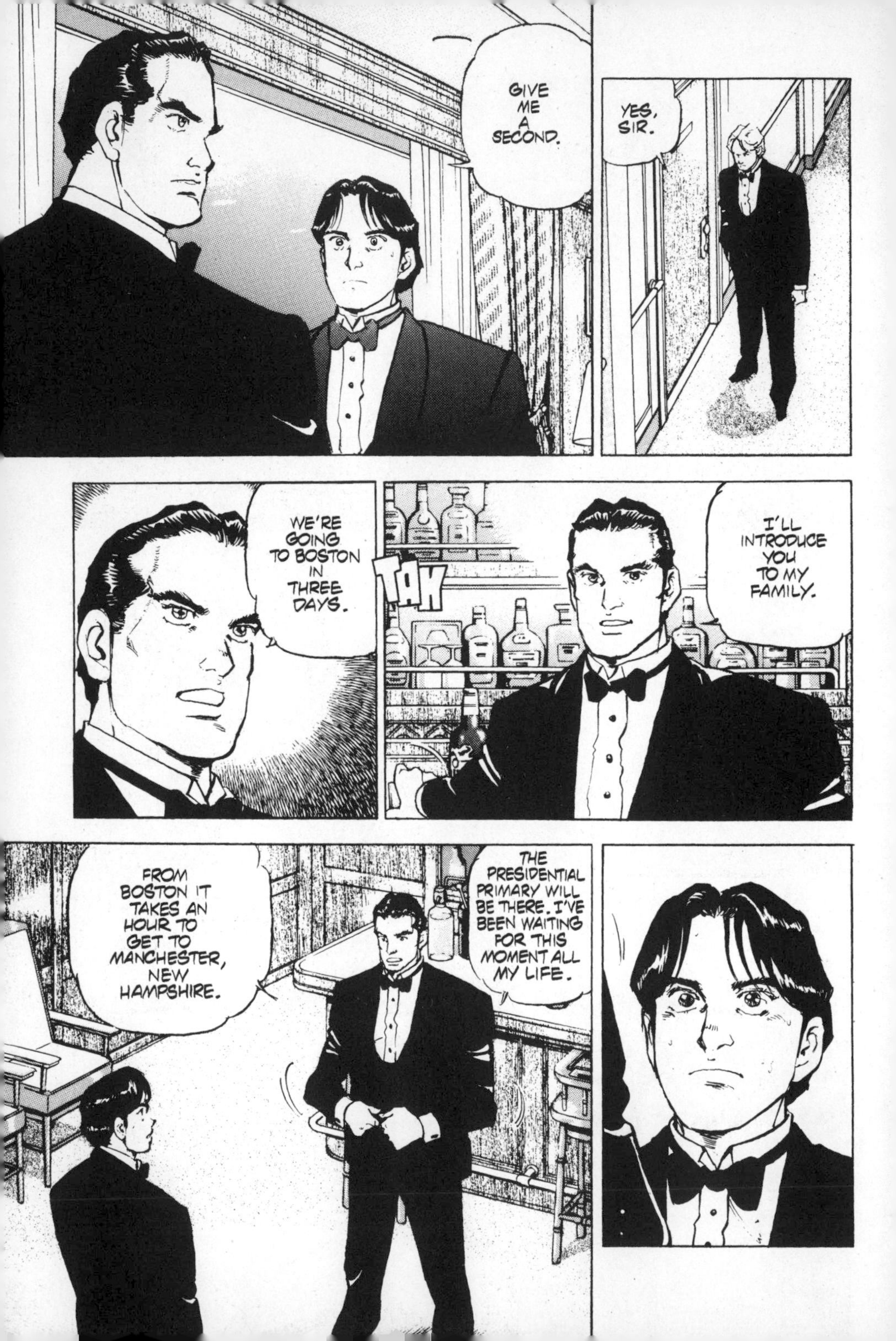
GIVE ME A SECOND.
YES, SIR.
WE'RE GOING TO BOSTON IN THREE DAYS.
TAK
I'LL INTRODUCE YOU TO MY FAMILY.
FROM BOSTON IT TAKES AN HOUR TO GET TO MANCHESTER, NEW HAMPSHIRE.
THE PRESIDENTIAL PRIMARY WILL BE THERE. I'VE BEEN WAITING FOR THIS MOMENT ALL MY LIFE.

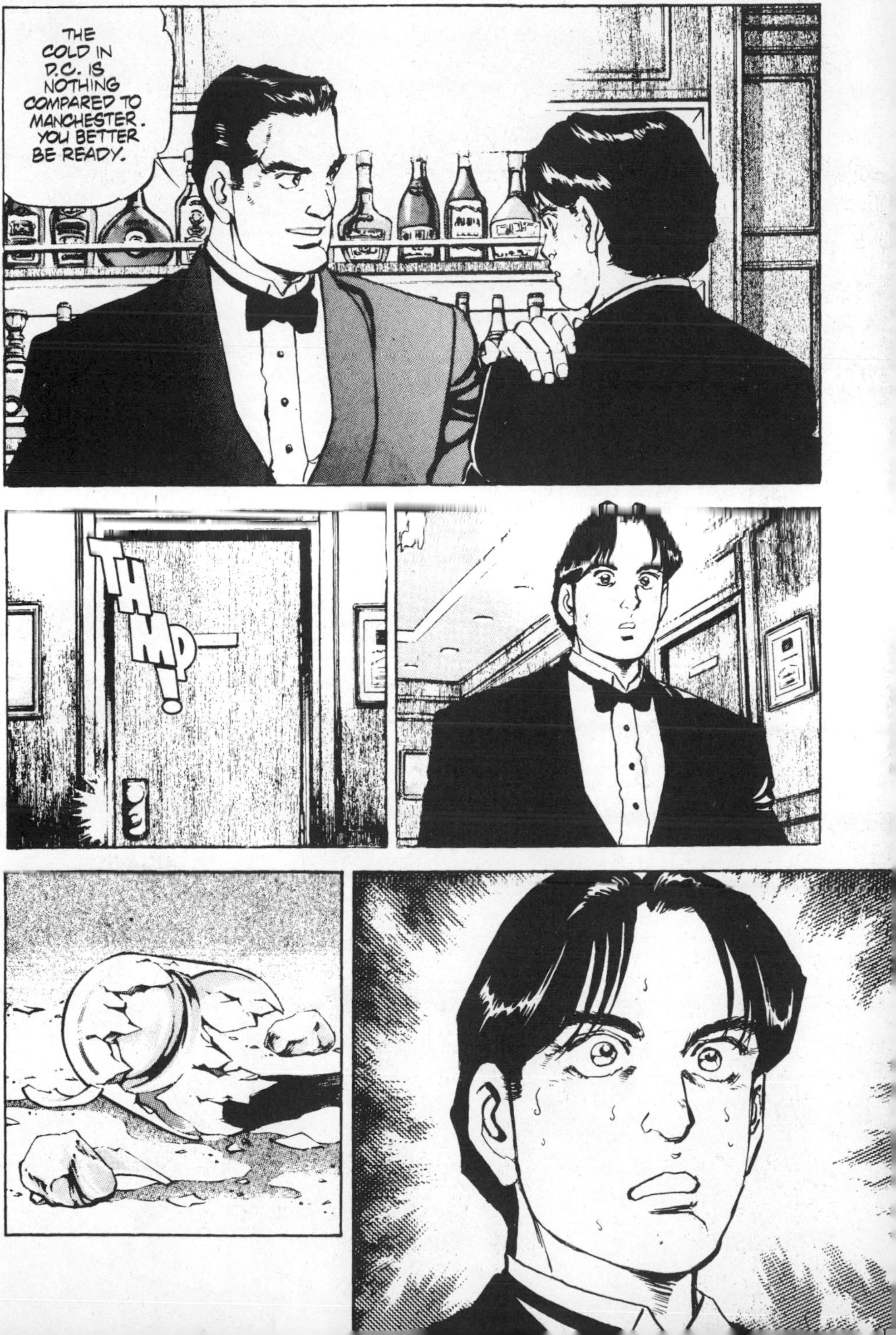
THE COLD IN D.C. IS NOTHING COMPARED TO MANCHESTER. YOU BETTER BE READY.
THMP!

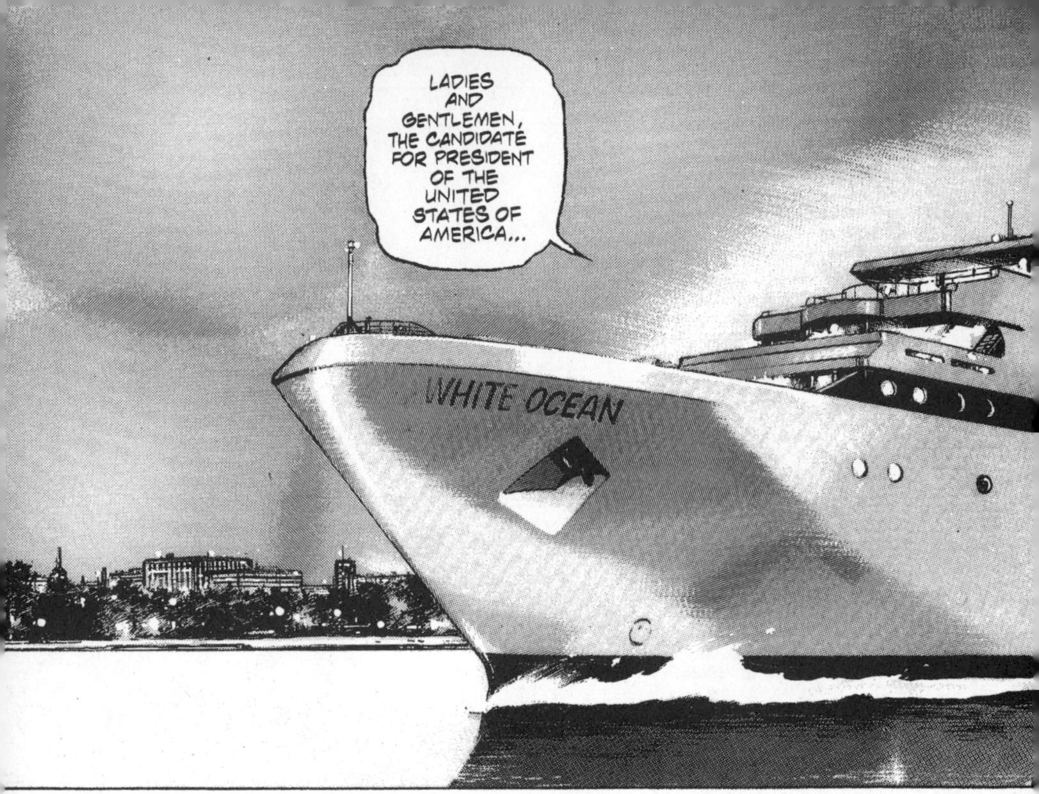
LADIES AND GENTLEMEN, THE CANDIDATE FOR PRESIDENT OF THE UNITED STATES OF AMERICA...
WHITE OCEAN
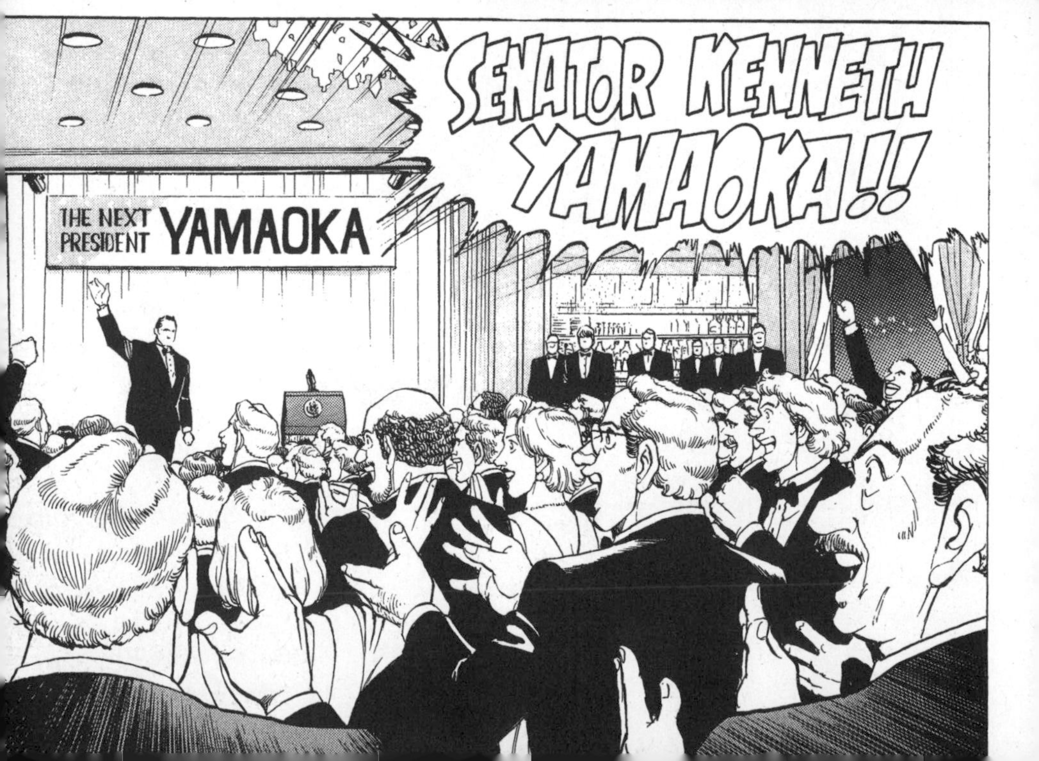
SENATOR KENNETH YAMAOKA!!
THE NEXT PRESIDENT YAMAOKA

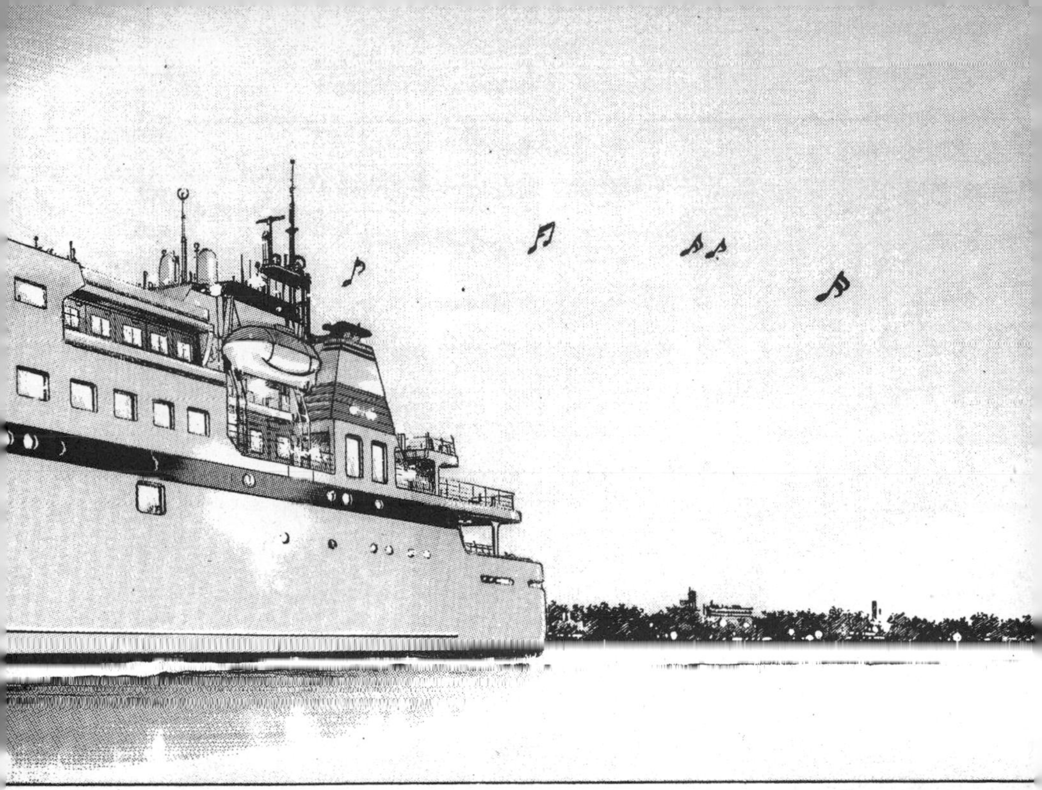

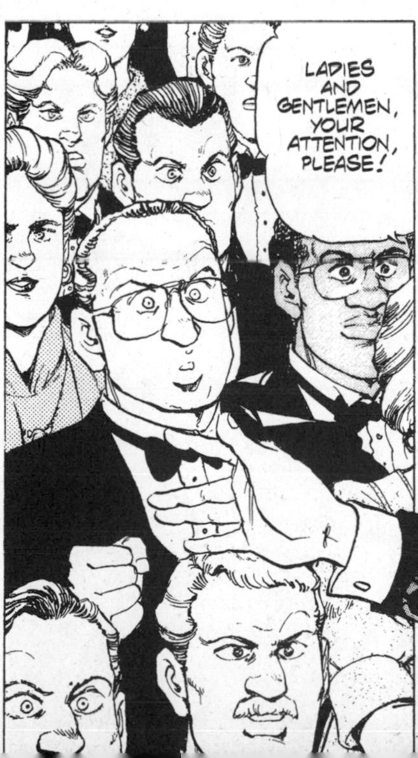
LADIES AND GENTLEMEN, YOUR ATTENTION, PLEASE!

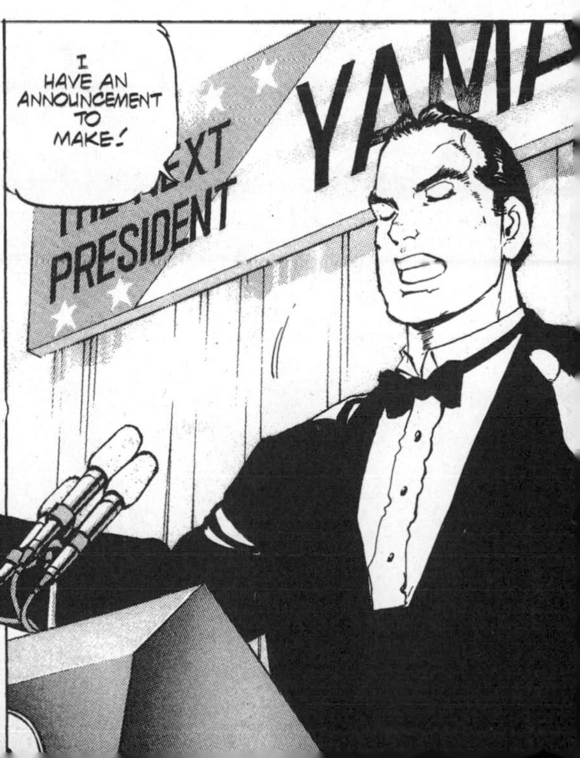
I HAVE AN ANNOUNCEMENT TO MAKE!
PRESIDENT

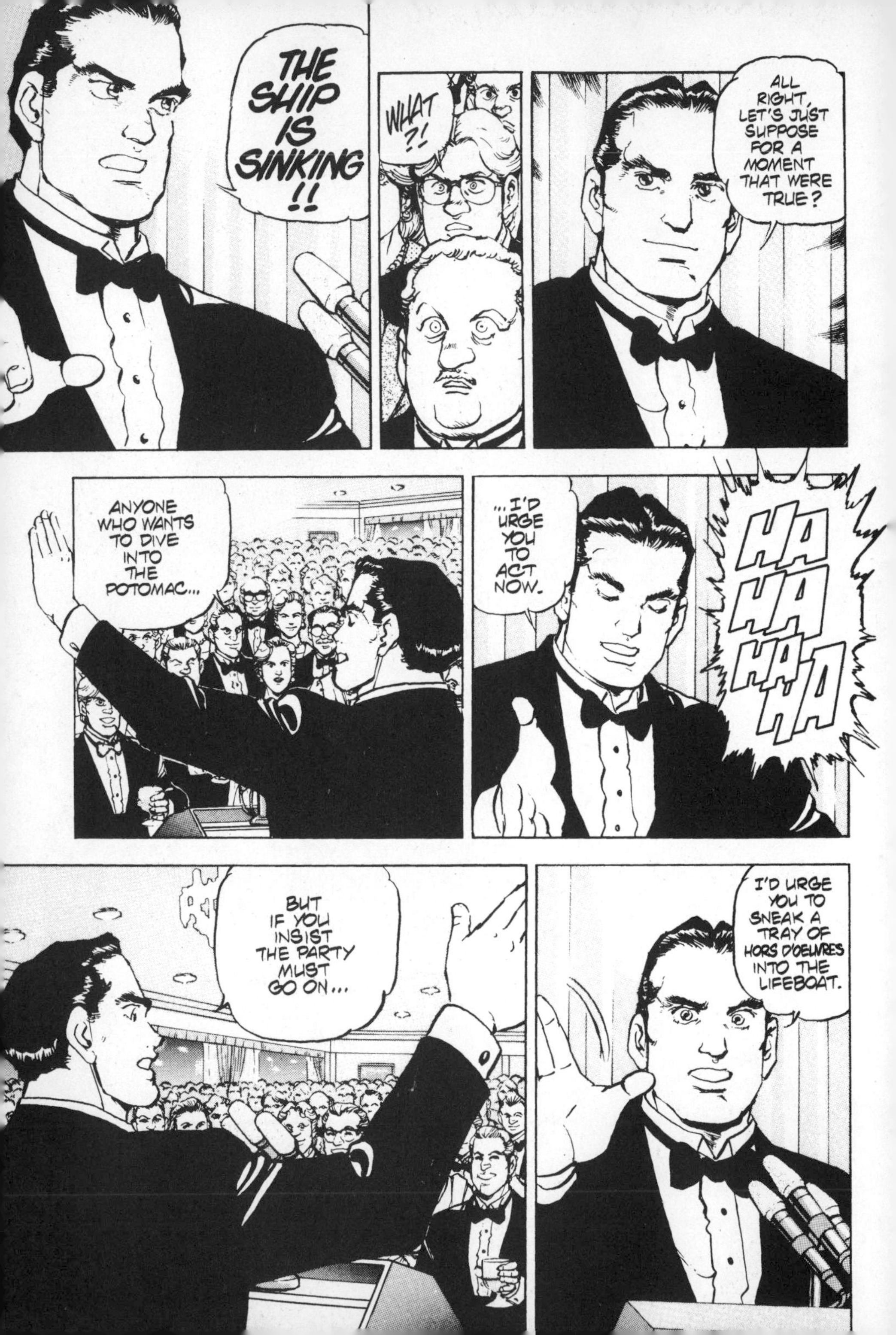
THE SHIP IS SINKING!!
WHAT?!
ALL RIGHT, LET'S JUST SUPPOSE FOR A MOMENT THAT WERE TRUE?
ANYONE WHO WANTS TO DIVE INTO THE POTOMAC...
...I'D URGE YOU TO ACT NOW.
HA HA HA HA
BUT IF YOU INSIST THE PARTY MUST GO ON...
I'D URGE YOU TO SNEAK A TRAY OF HORS D'OEUVRES INTO THE LIFEBOAT.

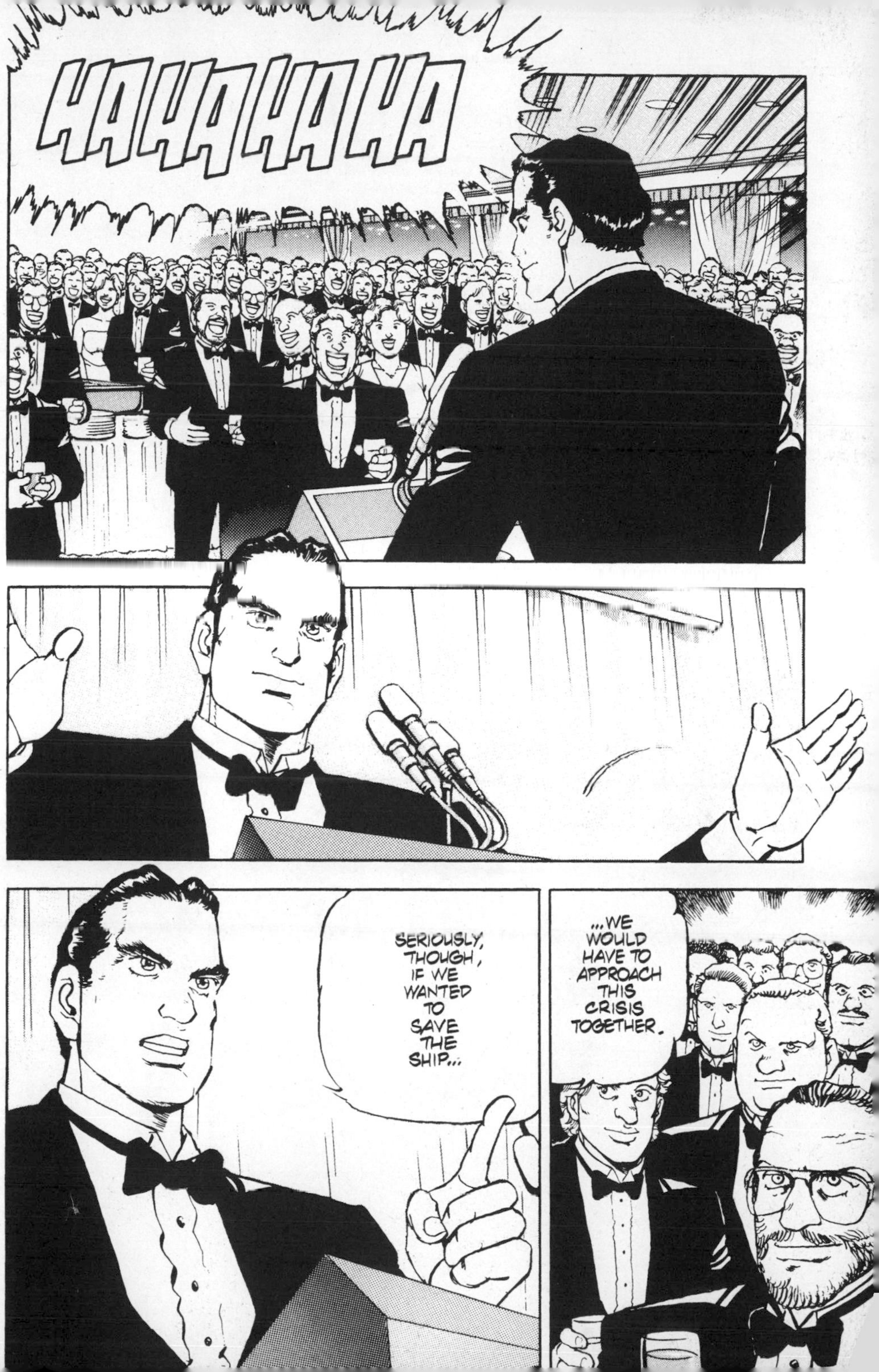
HAHAHAHAHA
SERIOUSLY, THOUGH, IF WE WANTED TO SAVE THE SHIP...
...WE WOULD HAVE TO APPROACH THIS CRISIS TOGETHER.

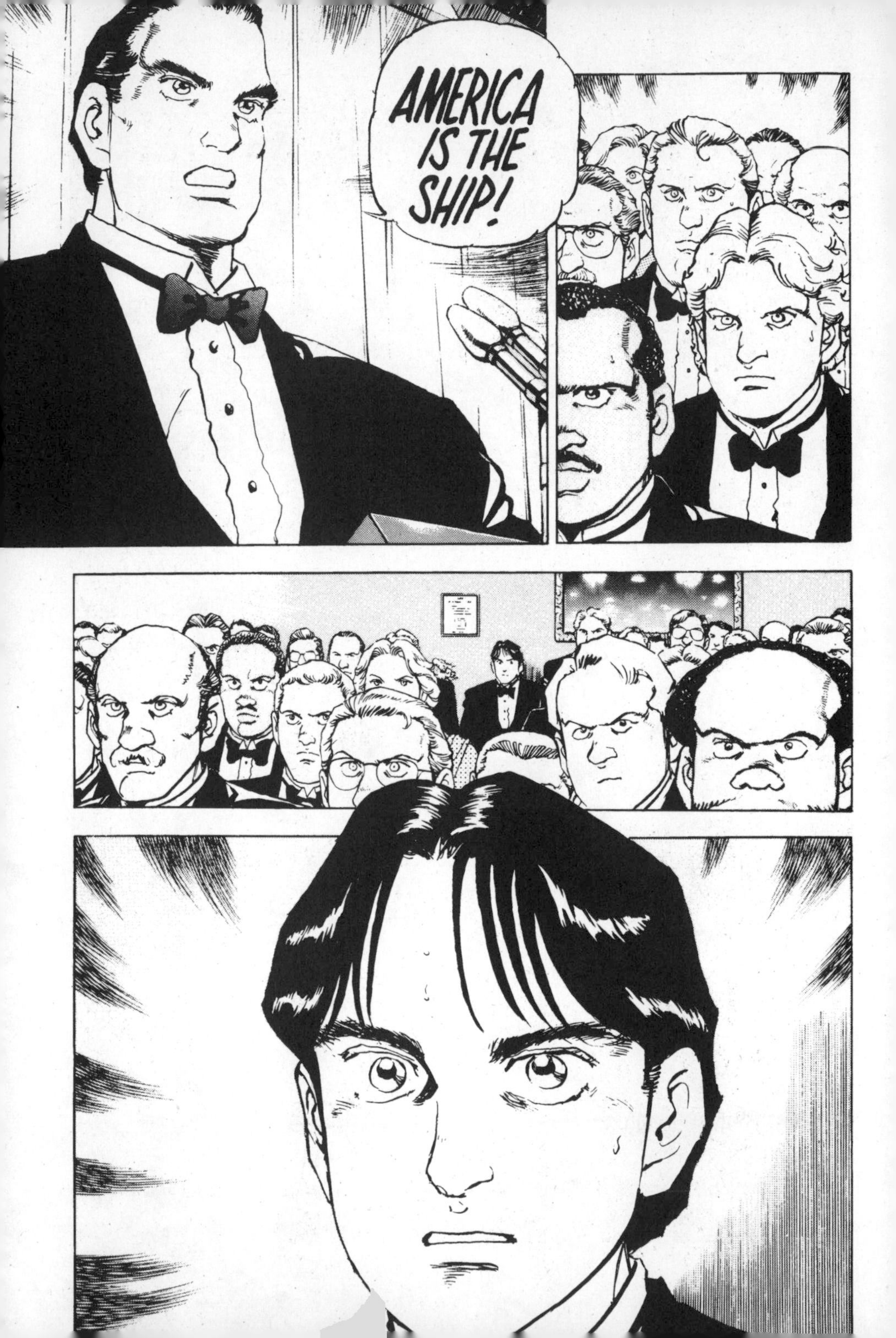
AMERICA IS THE SHIP!

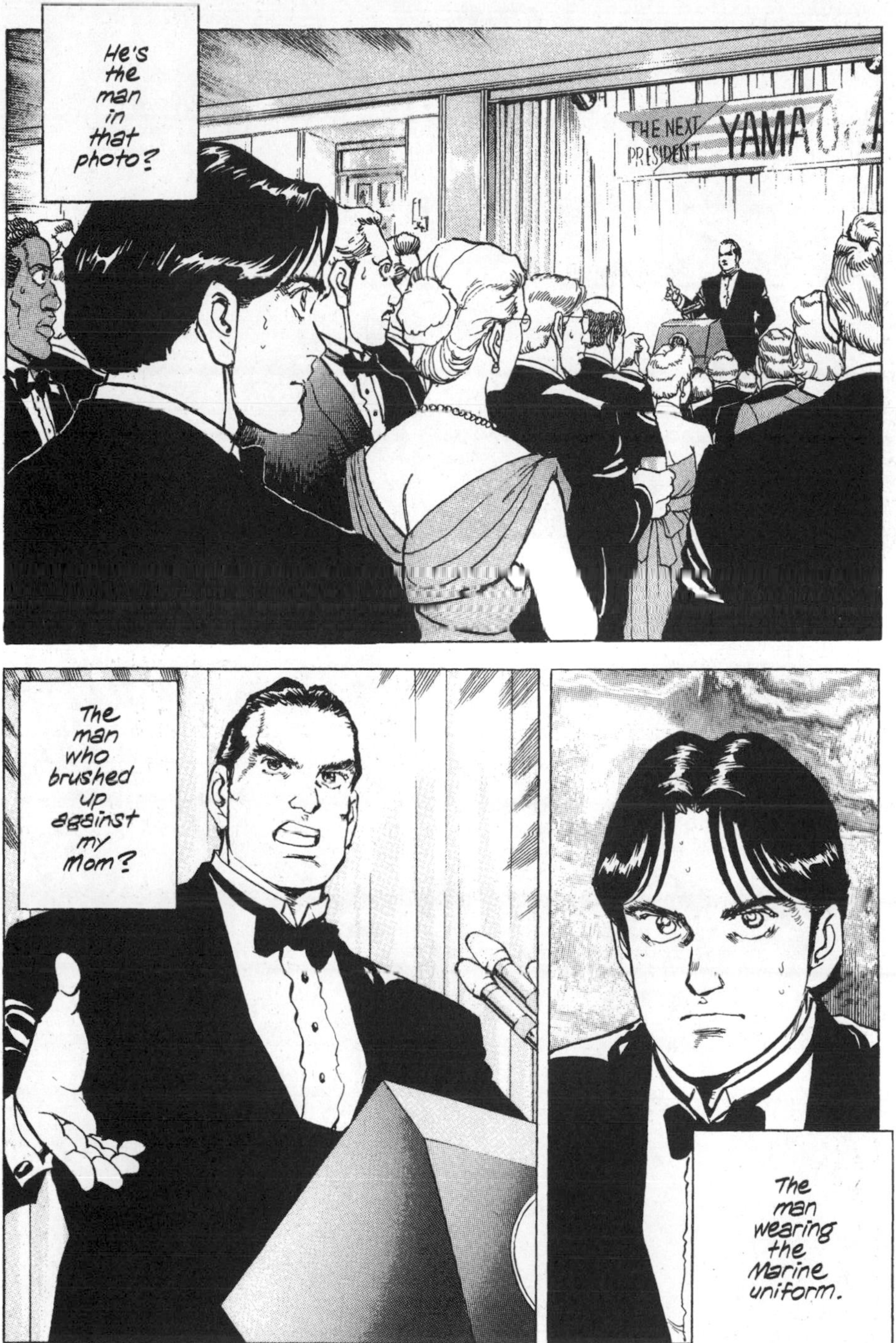
He's the man in that photo?
THE NEXT PRESIDENT
YAMA
The man who brushed up against my Mom?
The man wearing the Marine uniform.

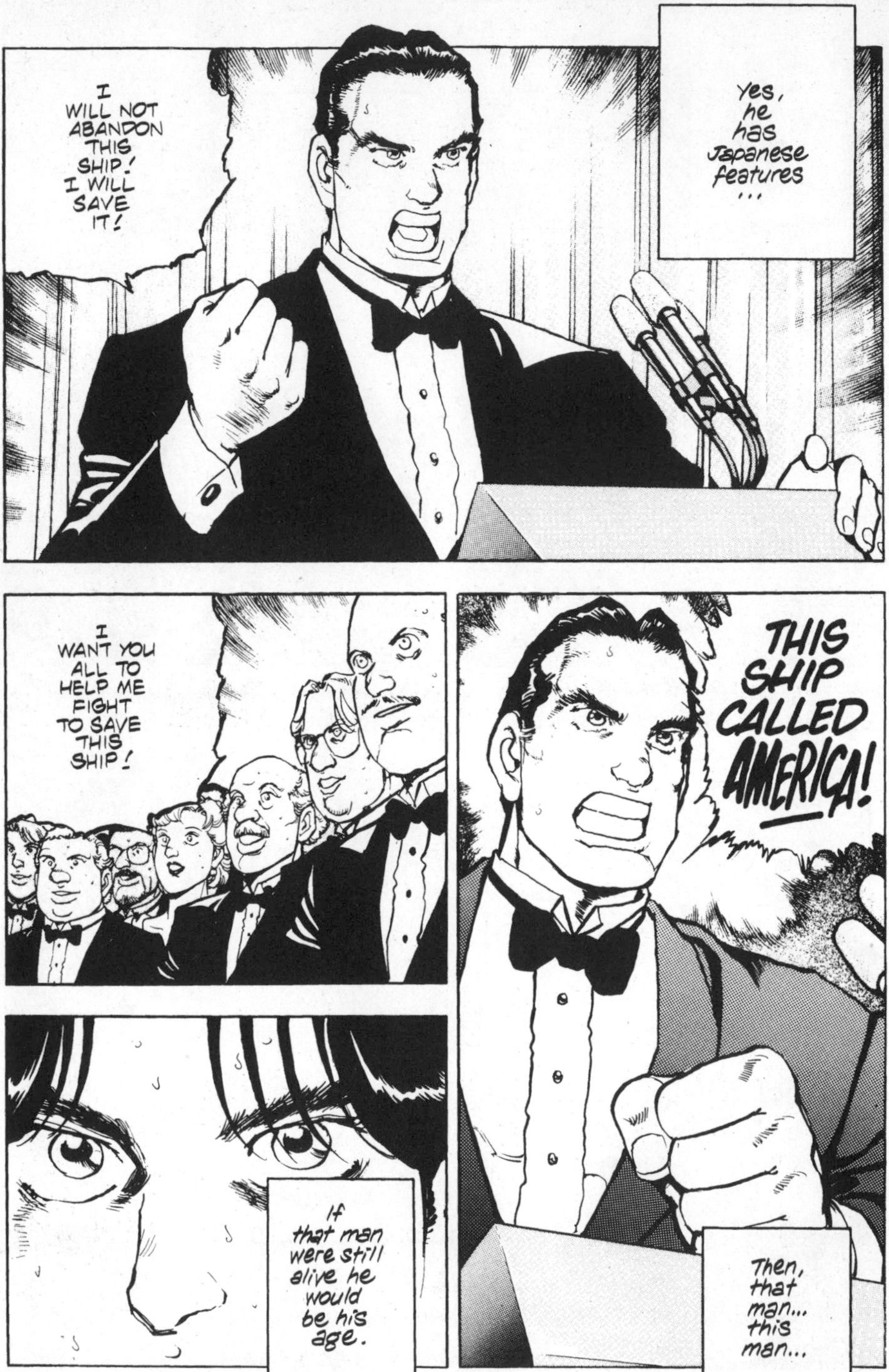
I WILL NOT ABANDON THIS SHIP! I WILL SAVE IT!
Yes, he has Japanese features...
I WANT YOU ALL TO HELP ME FIGHT TO SAVE THIS SHIP!
If that man were still alive he would be his age.
THIS SHIP CALLED AMERICA!
Then, that man... this man...

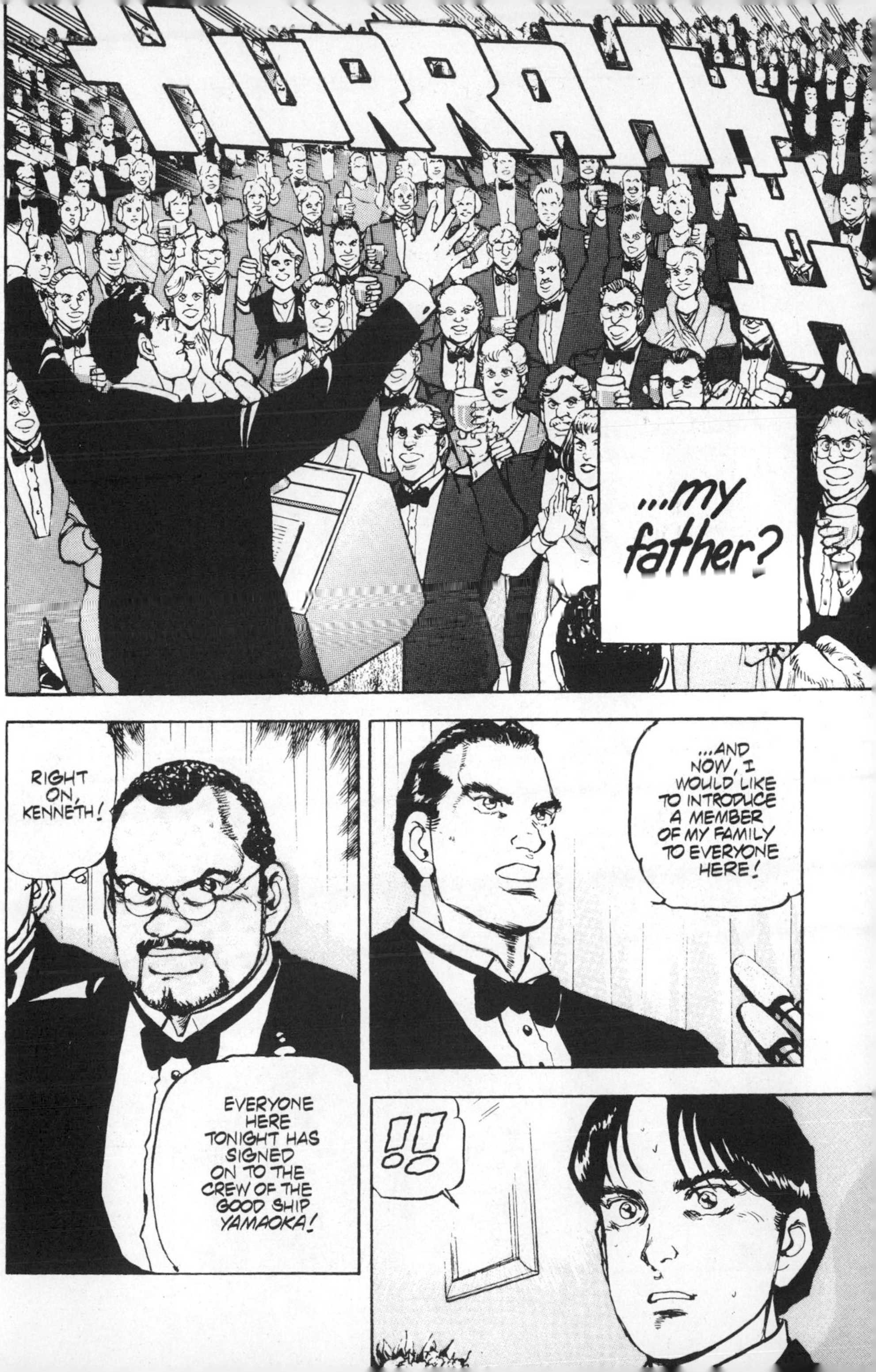
HURRAH!!
...my father?
RIGHT ON, KENNETH!
EVERYONE HERE TONIGHT HAS SIGNED ON TO THE CREW OF THE GOOD SHIP YAMAOKA!
...AND NOW, I WOULD LIKE TO INTRODUCE A MEMBER OF MY FAMILY TO EVERYONE HERE!
!!

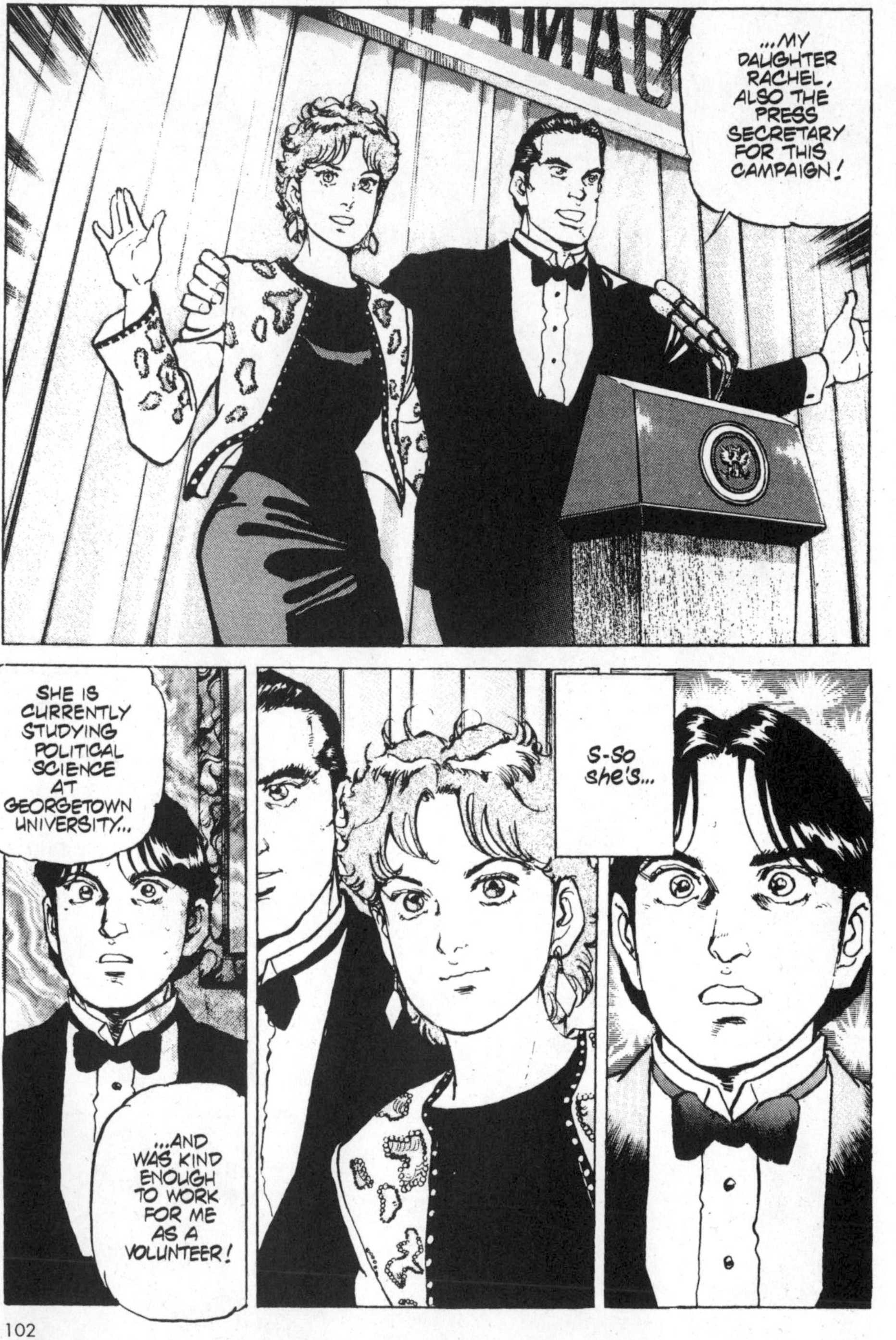
...MY DAUGHTER RACHEL, ALSO THE PRESS SECRETARY FOR THIS CAMPAIGN!
SHE IS CURRENTLY STUDYING POLITICAL SCIENCE AT GEORGETOWN UNIVERSITY...
...AND WAS KIND ENOUGH TO WORK FOR ME AS A VOLUNTEER!
S-SO she's...

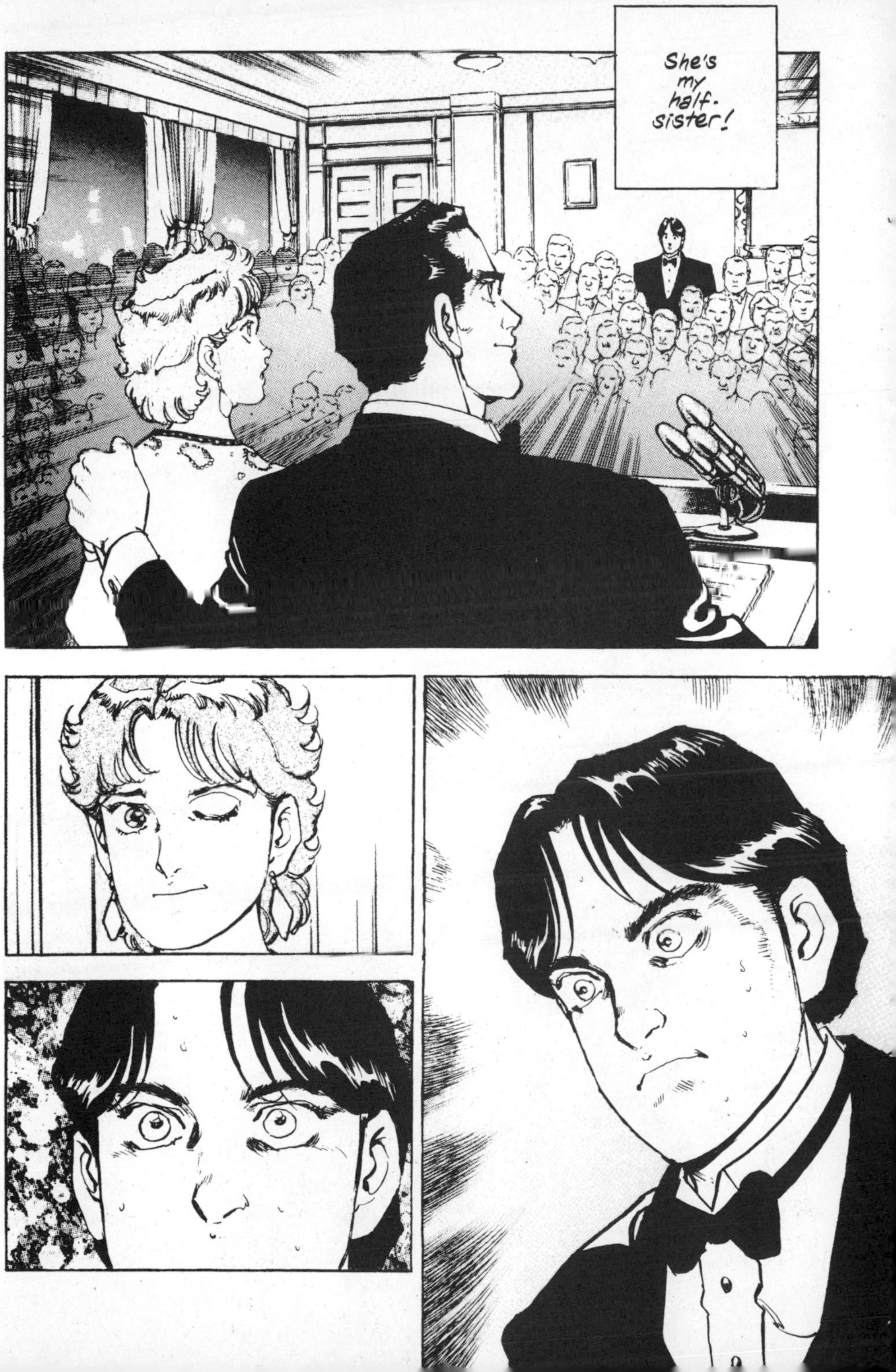
She's my half-sister!

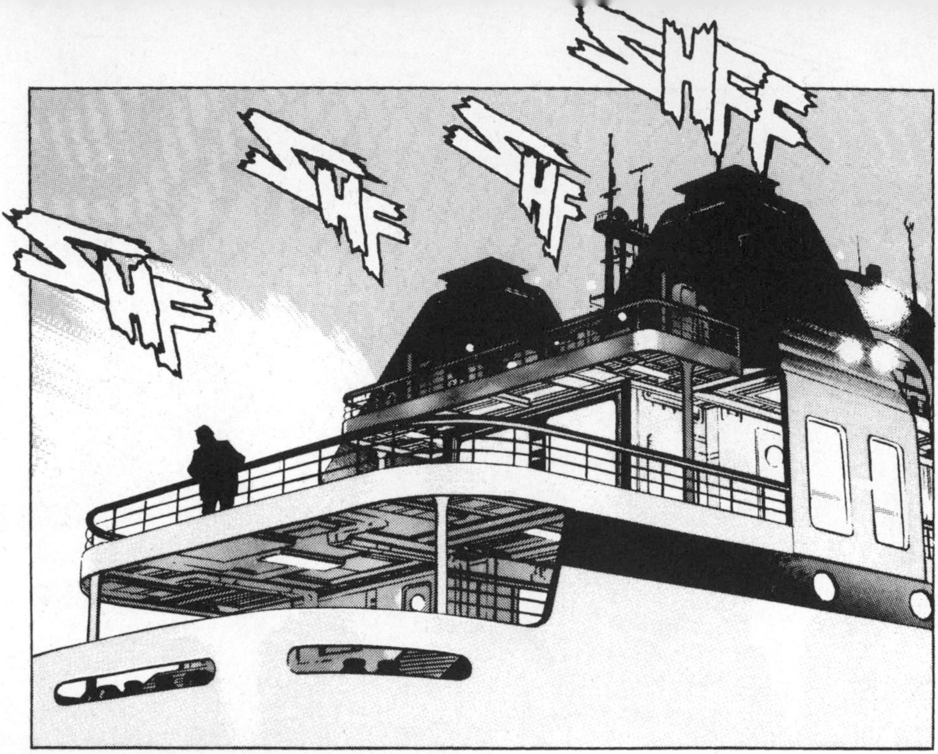
SHF
SHF
SHF
SHFF

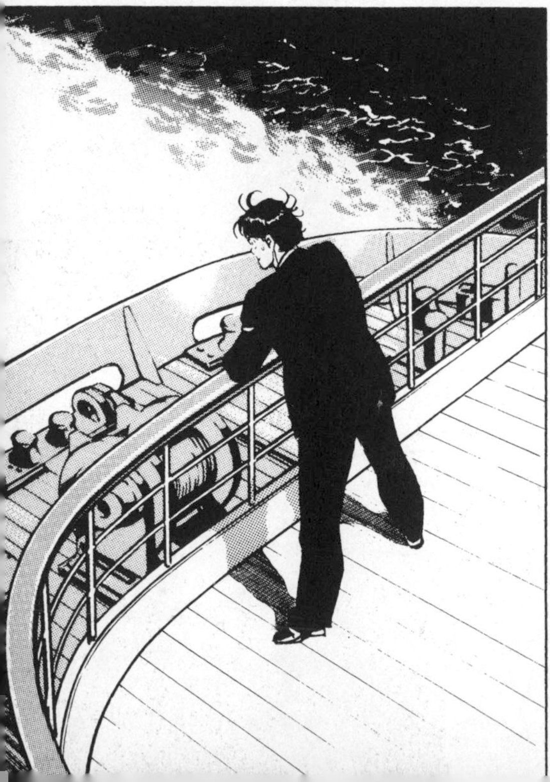

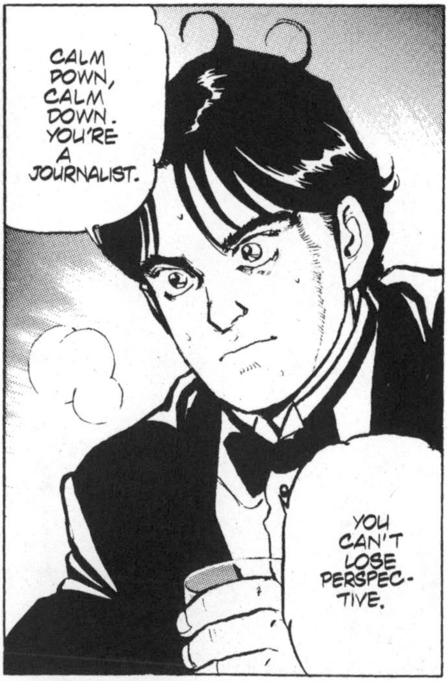
CALM DOWN, CALM DOWN. YOU'RE A JOURNALIST.
YOU CAN'T LOSE PERSPEC-TIVE.

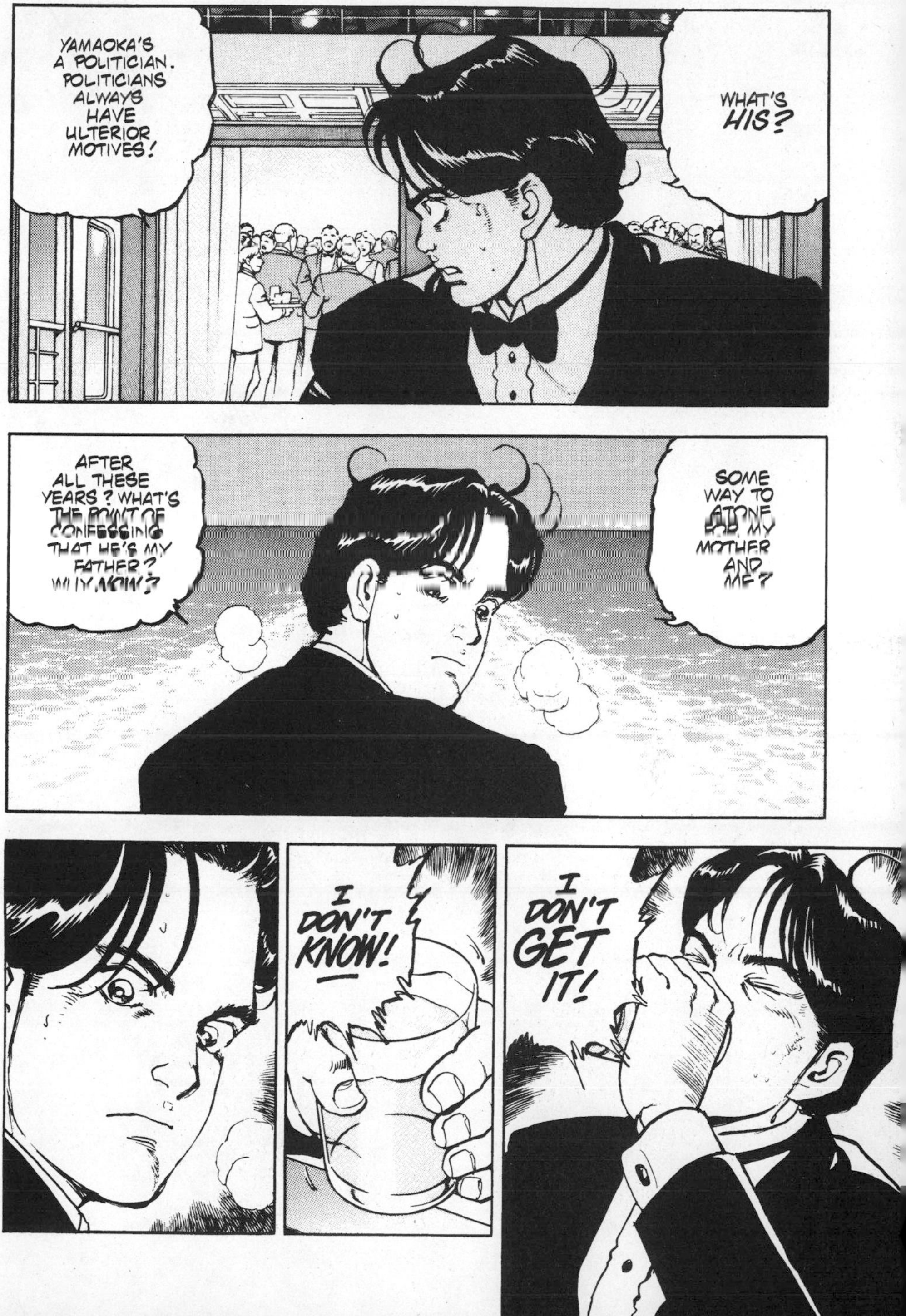
YAMAOKA'S A POLITICIAN. POLITICIANS ALWAYS HAVE ULTERIOR MOTIVES!
WHAT'S HIS?
AFTER ALL THESE YEARS? WHAT'S THE POINT OF CONFESSING THAT HE'S MY FATHER? WHY NOW?
SOME WAY TO ATONE FOR MY MOTHER AND ME?
I DON'T KNOW!
I DON'T GET IT!

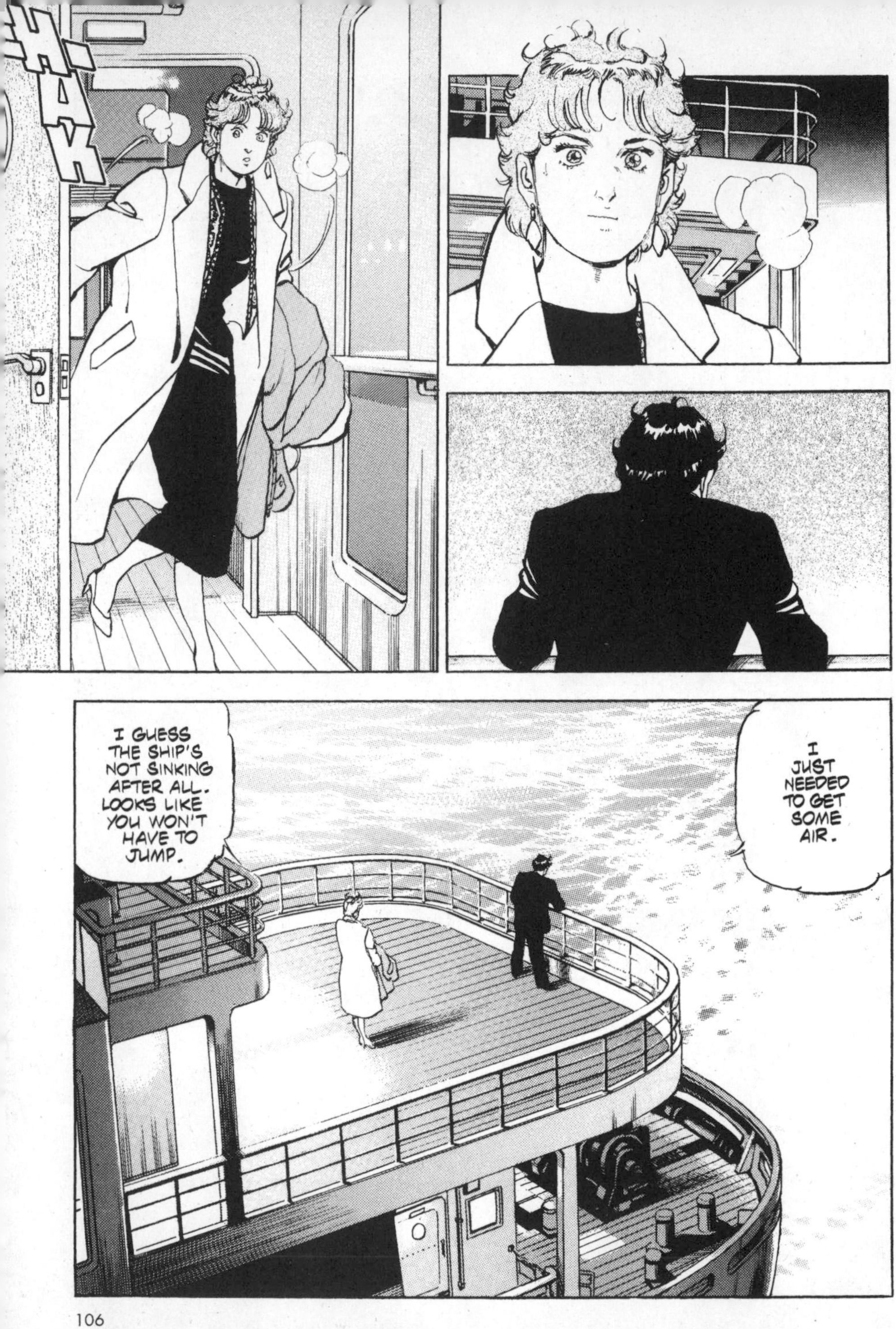
HA-AH
I GUESS THE SHIP'S NOT SINKING AFTER ALL. LOOKS LIKE YOU WON'T HAVE TO JUMP.
I JUST NEEDED TO GET SOME AIR.

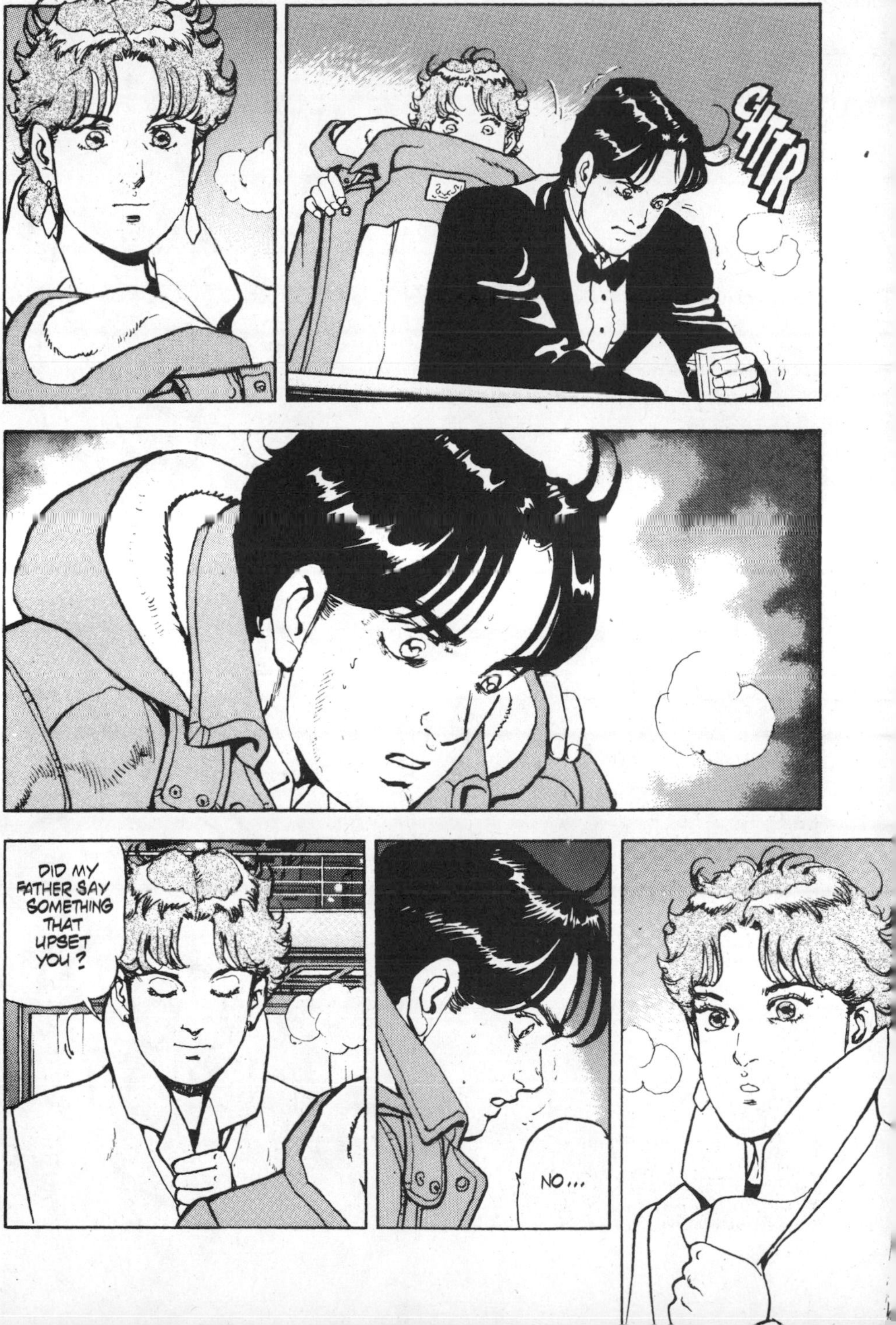
CHTR
DID MY FATHER SAY SOMETHING THAT UPSET YOU?
NO...

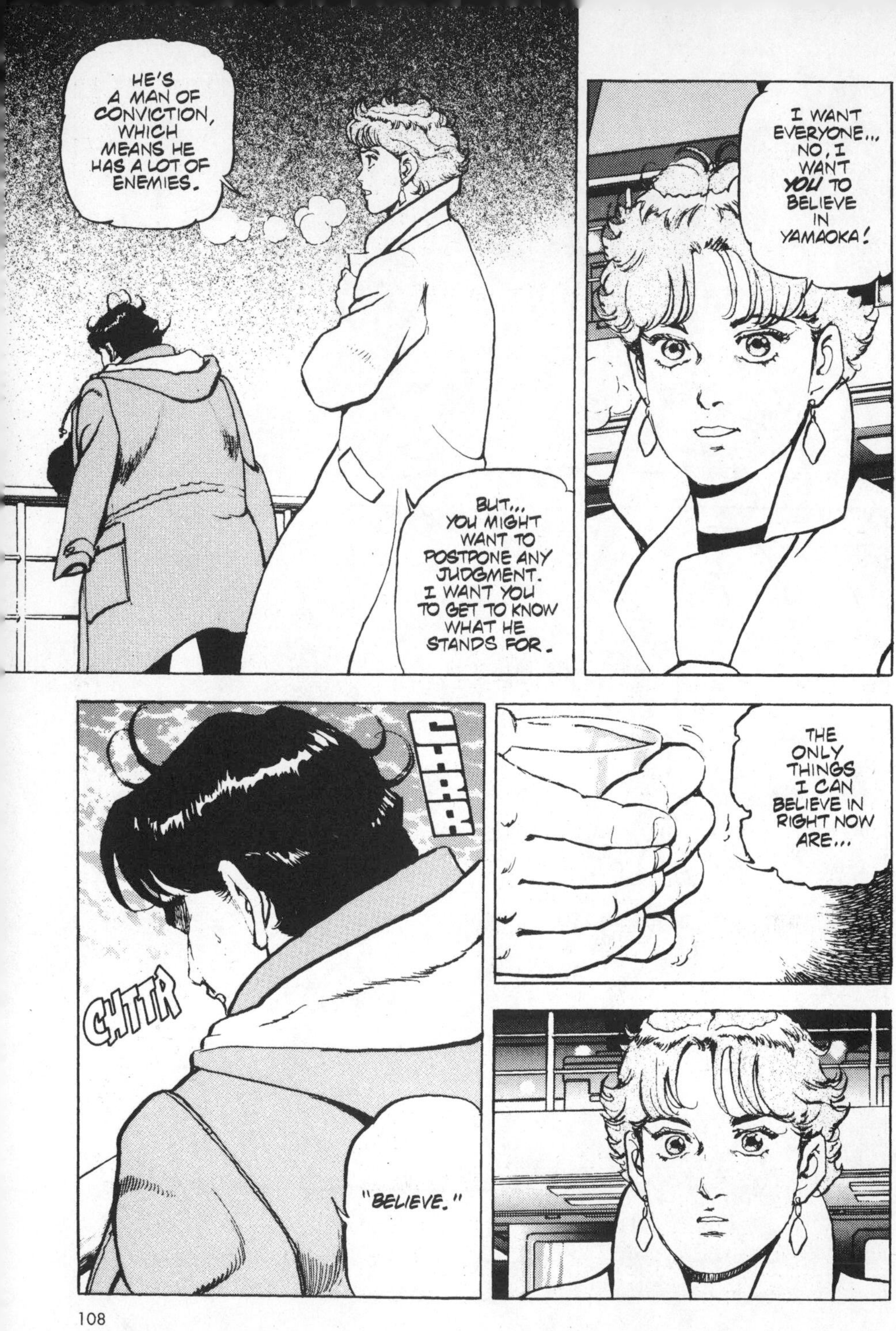
HE'S A MAN OF CONVICTION, WHICH MEANS HE HAS A LOT OF ENEMIES.
BUT... YOU MIGHT WANT TO POSTPONE ANY JUDGMENT. I WANT YOU TO GET TO KNOW WHAT HE STANDS FOR.
I WANT EVERYONE... NO, I WANT YOU TO BELIEVE IN YAMAOKA!
CHRR
CHTTR
"BELIEVE."
THE ONLY THINGS I CAN BELIEVE IN RIGHT NOW ARE...

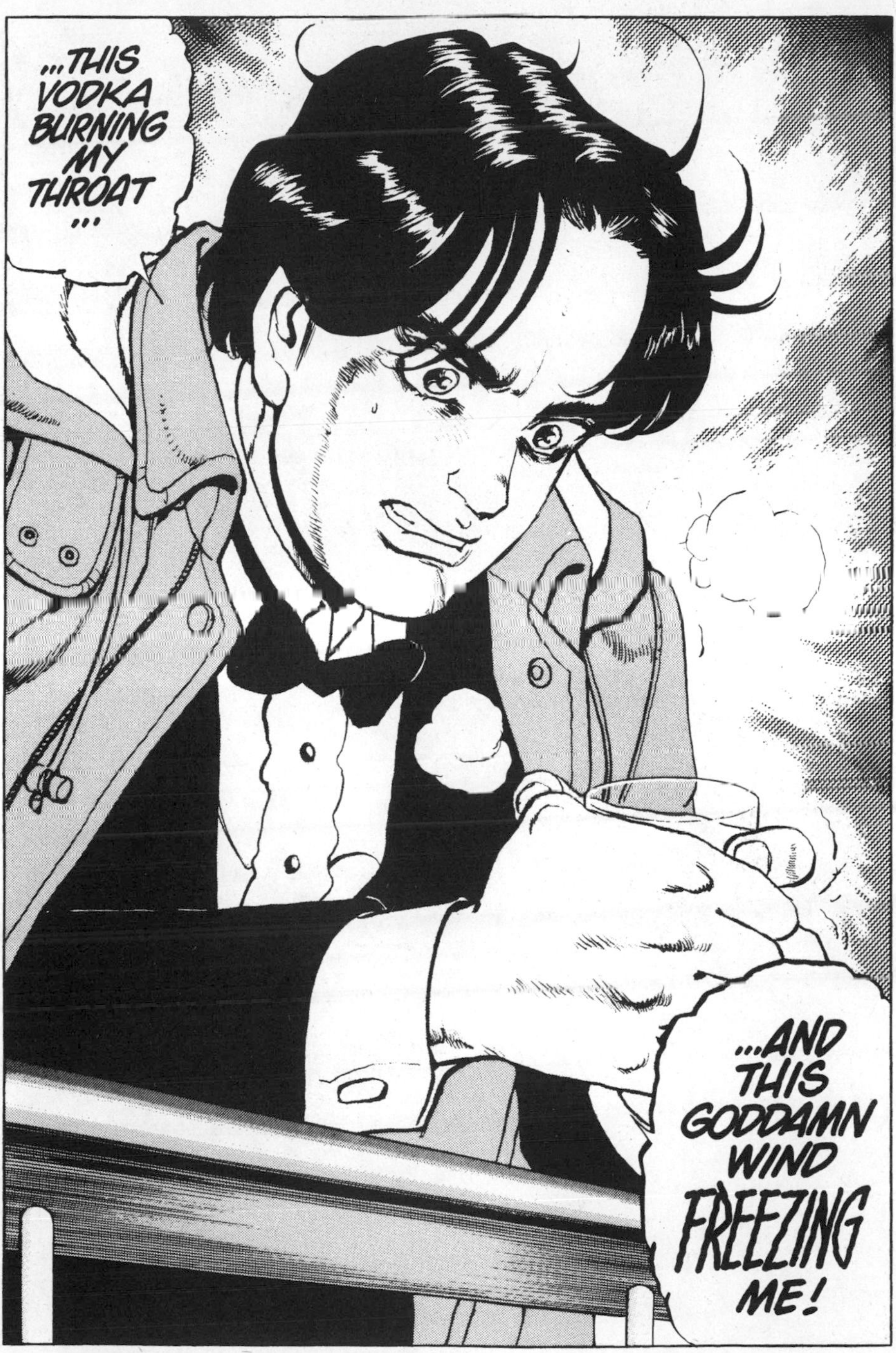
...THIS VODKA BURNING MY THROAT ...
...AND THIS GODDAMN WIND FREEZING ME!

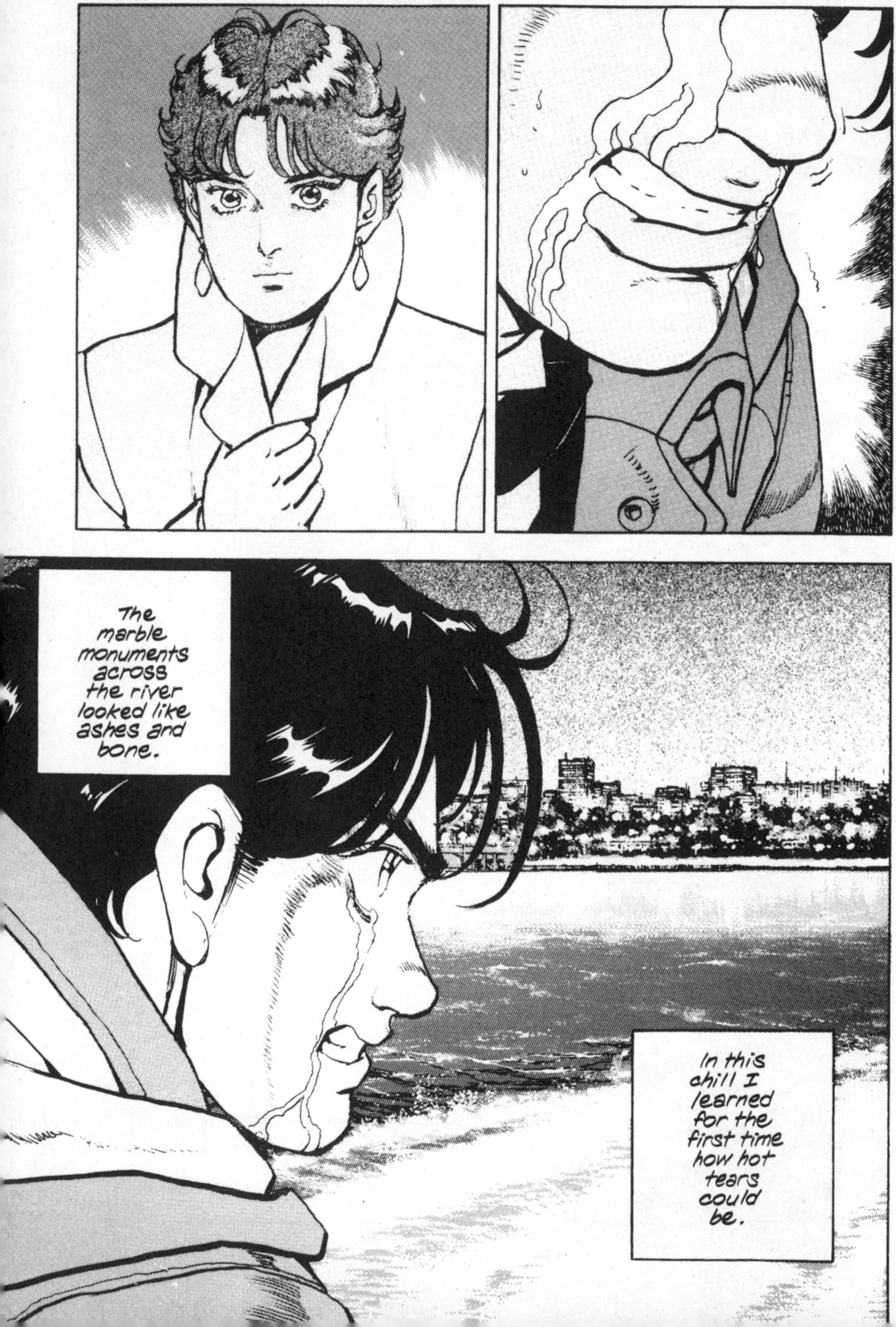
The marble monuments across the river looked like ashes and bone.
In this chill I learned for the first time how hot tears could be.

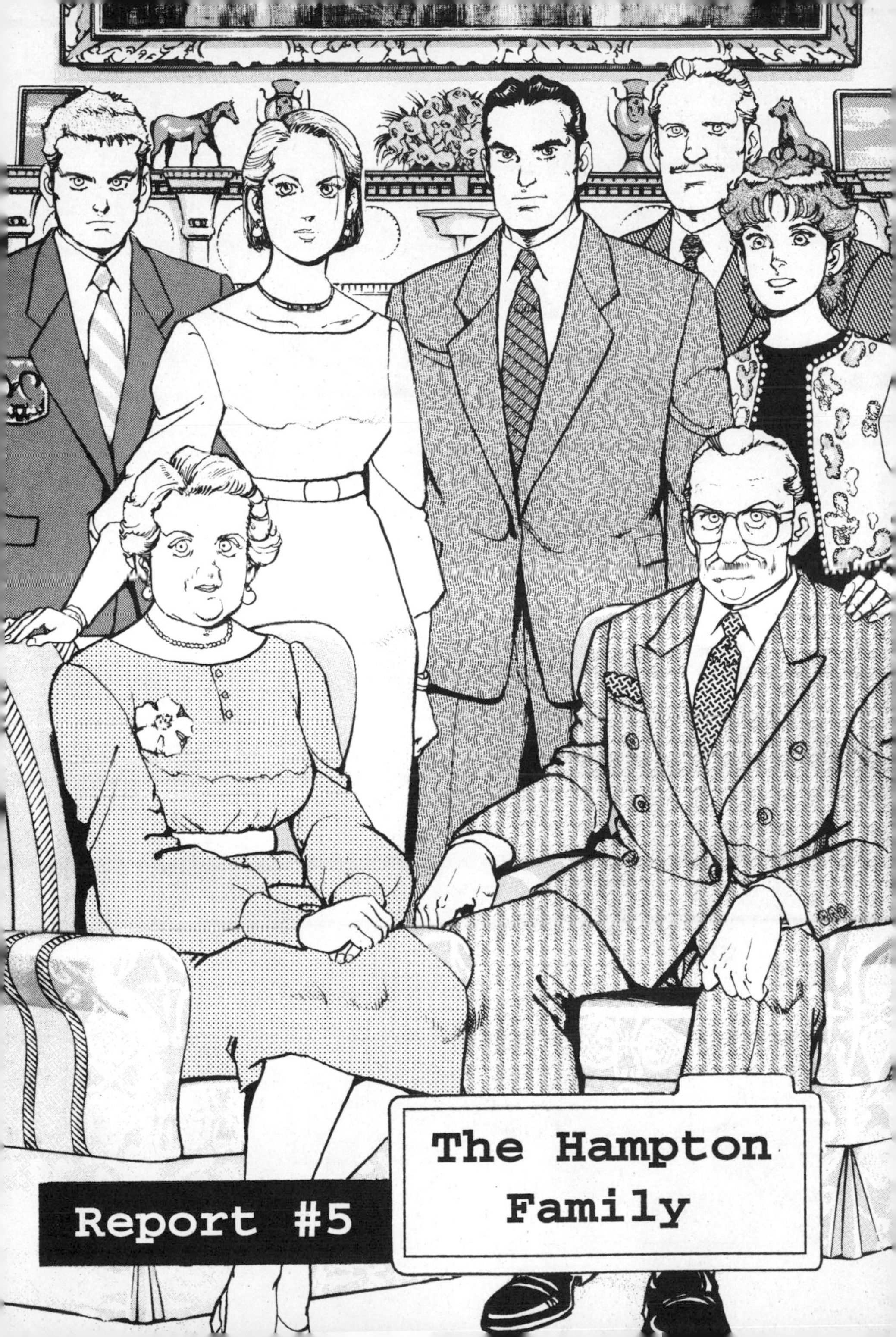

Report #5
The Hampton Family

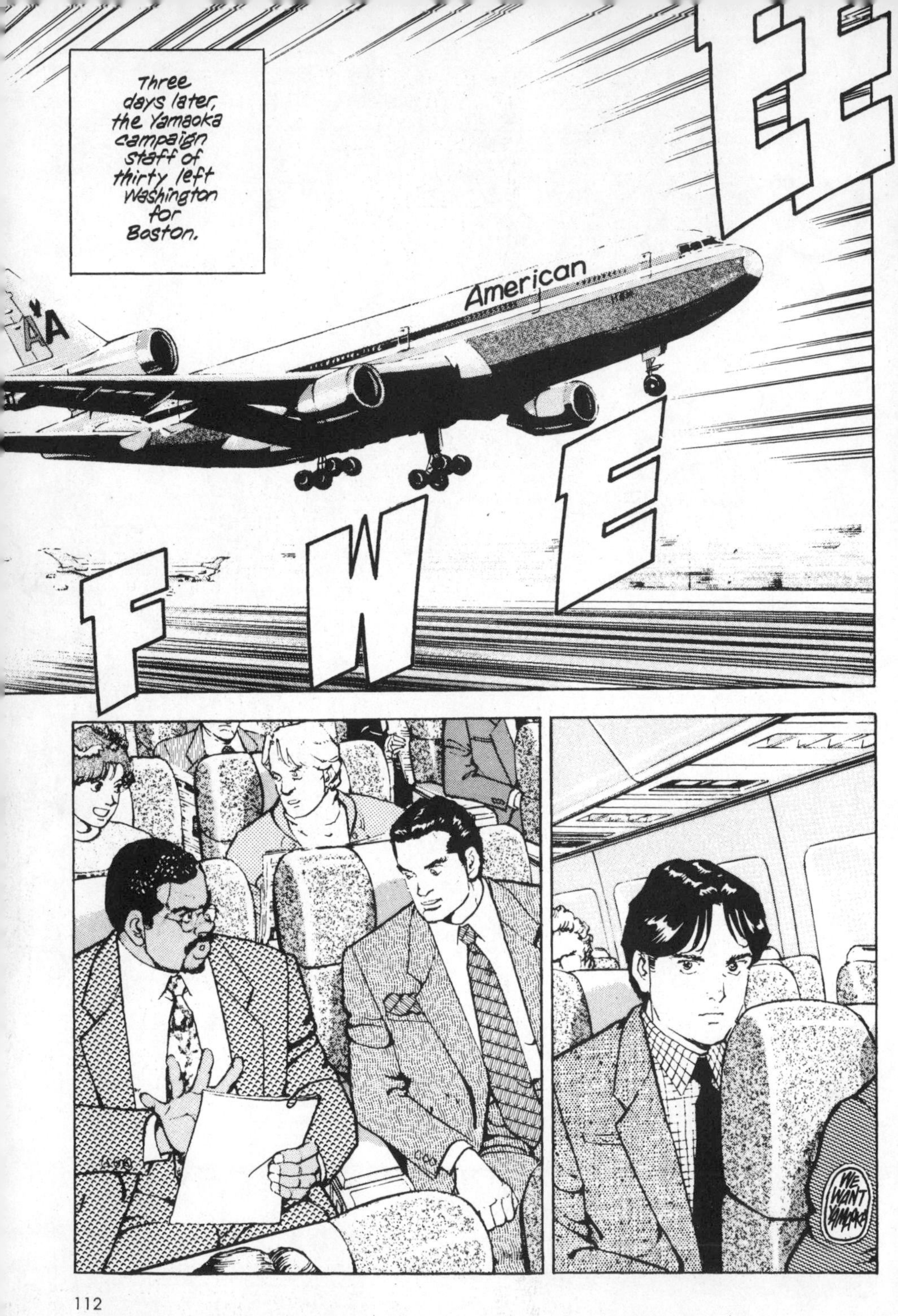
Three days later, the Yamaoka campaign staff of thirty left Washington for Boston.
American
AA
FWEEE
WE WANT YAMAOKA

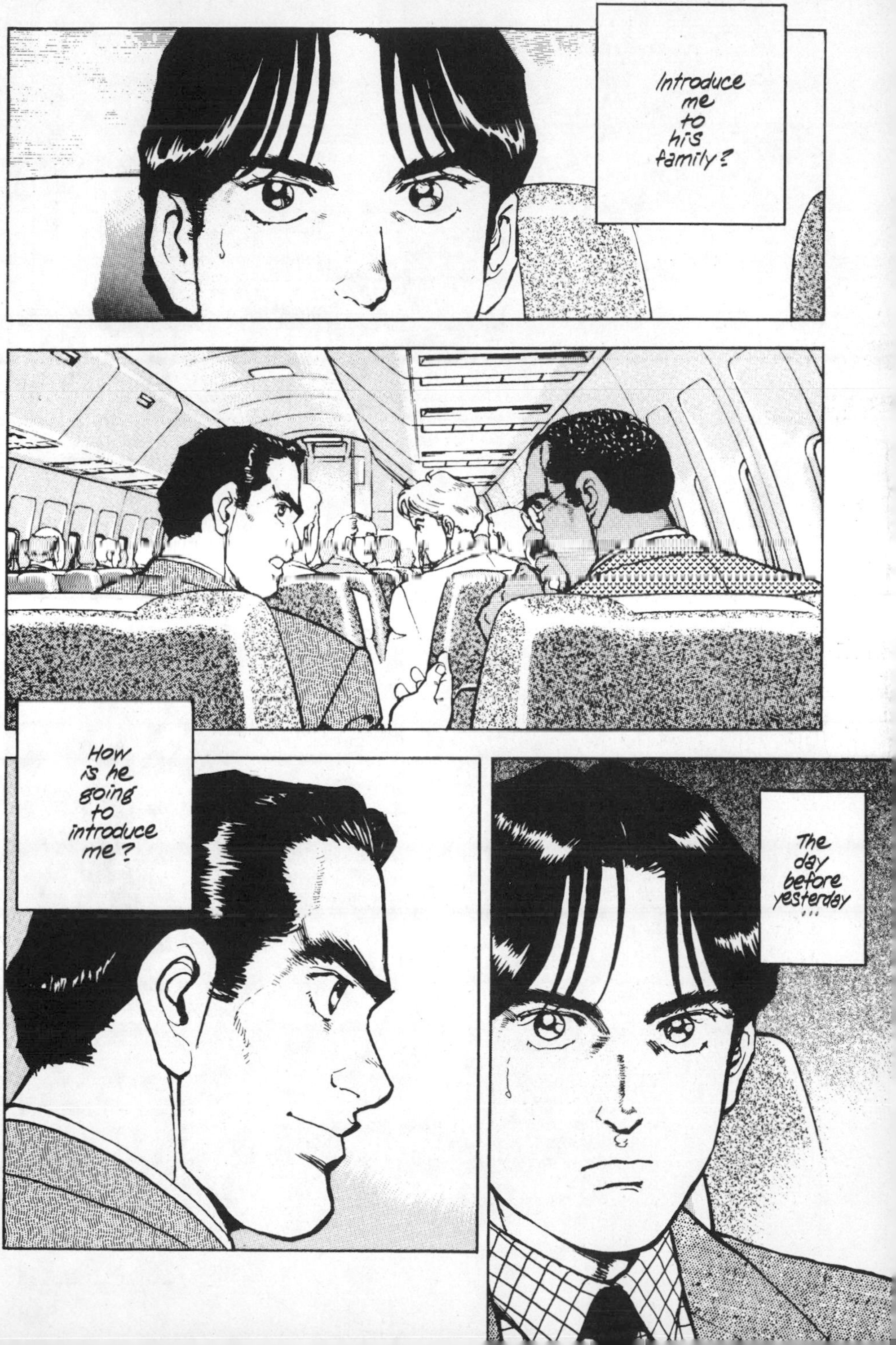
Introduce me to his family?
How is he going to introduce me?
The day before yesterday ...

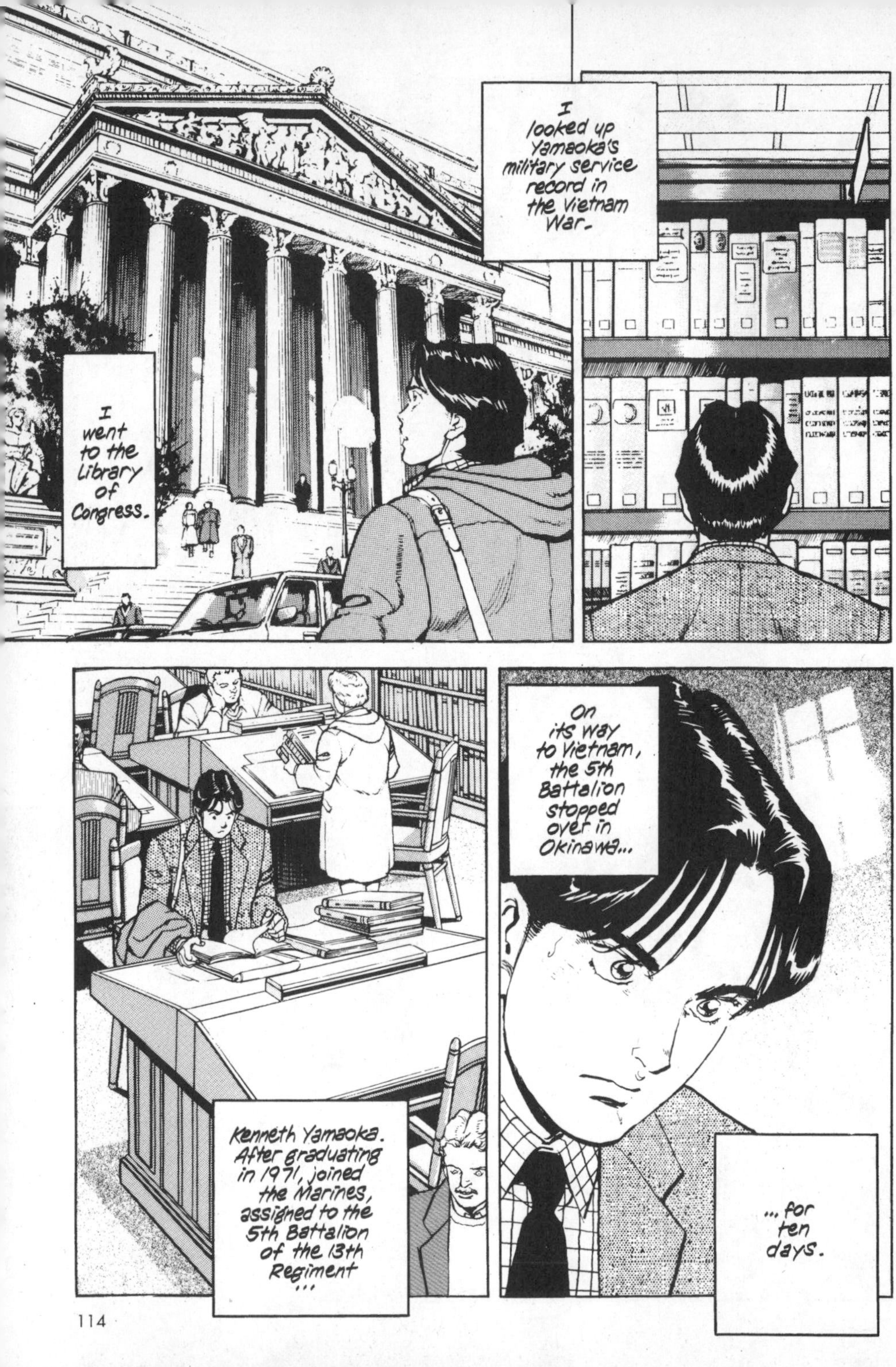
I went to the Library of Congress.
I looked up Yamaoka's military service record in the Vietnam War.
Kenneth Yamaoka. After graduating in 1971, joined the Marines, assigned to the 5th Battalion of the 13th Regiment ...
On its way to Vietnam, the 5th Battalion stopped over in Okinawa...
...for ten days.

The stopover was between March 3 and March 12, 1972.

....January 23, 1973!

My birthday is....

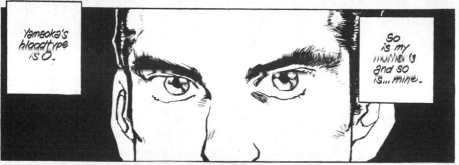

Yamaoka's bloodtype is O.

So is my mother's and so is....mine.

All the circumstantial evidence supports Yamaoka's claim that he's my father.

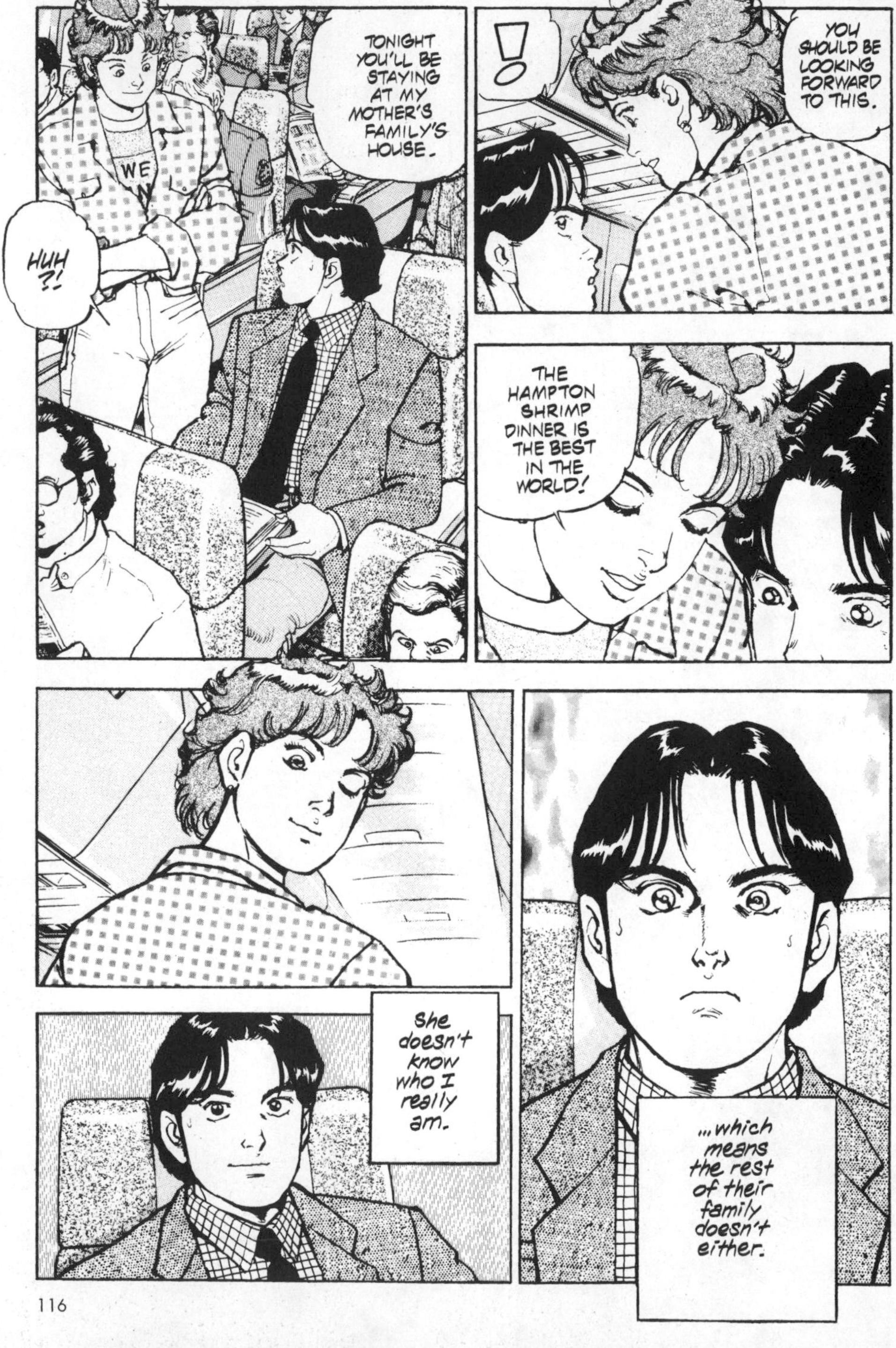
TONIGHT YOU'LL BE STAYING AT MY MOTHER'S FAMILY'S HOUSE.
HUH ?!
!
YOU SHOULD BE LOOKING FORWARD TO THIS.
THE HAMPTON SHRIMP DINNER IS THE BEST IN THE WORLD!
She doesn't know who I really am.
...which means the rest of their family doesn't either.

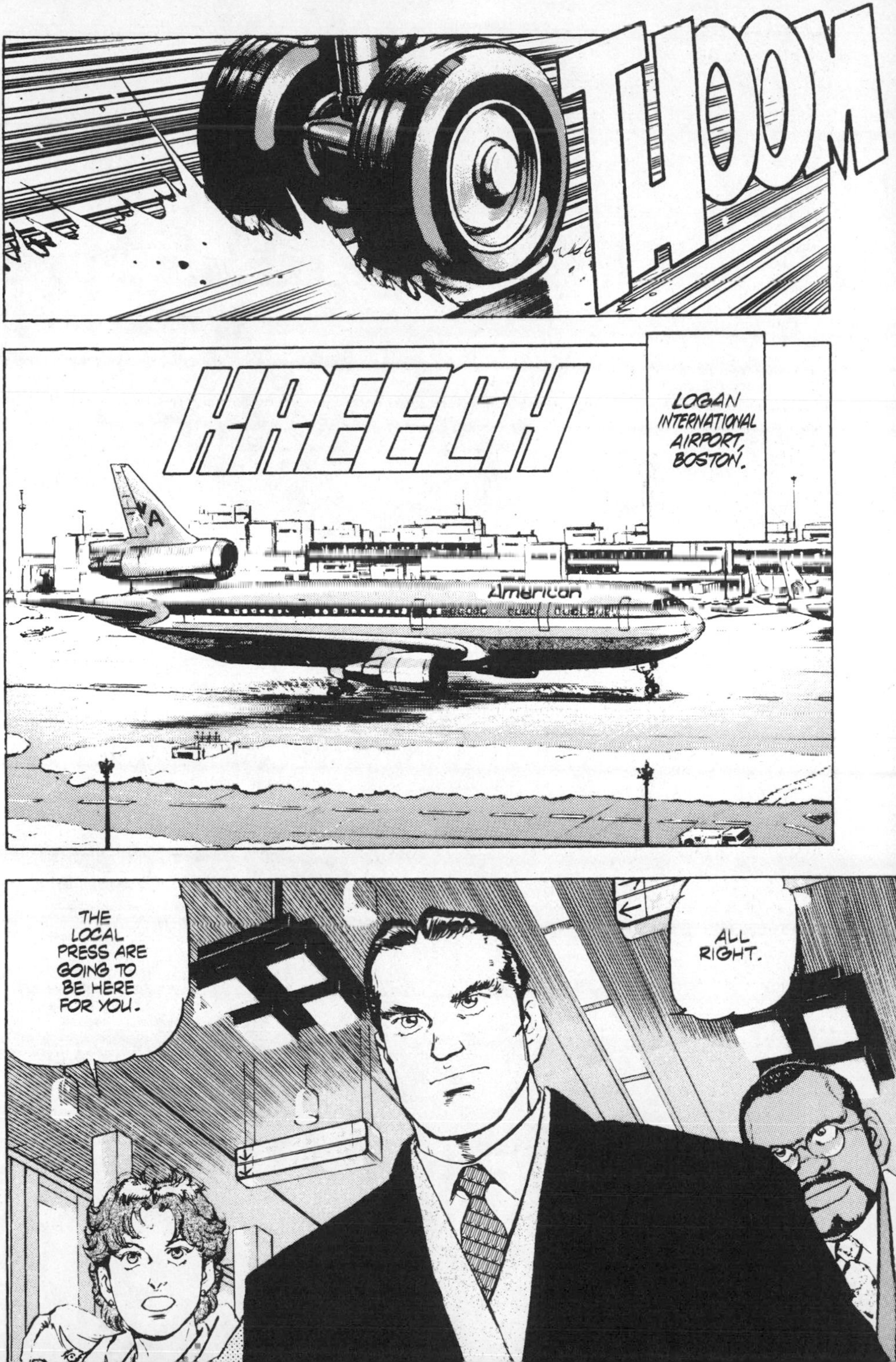
THOOM
KREECH
LOGAN INTERNATIONAL AIRPORT, BOSTON.
American
THE LOCAL PRESS ARE GOING TO BE HERE FOR YOU.
ALL RIGHT.

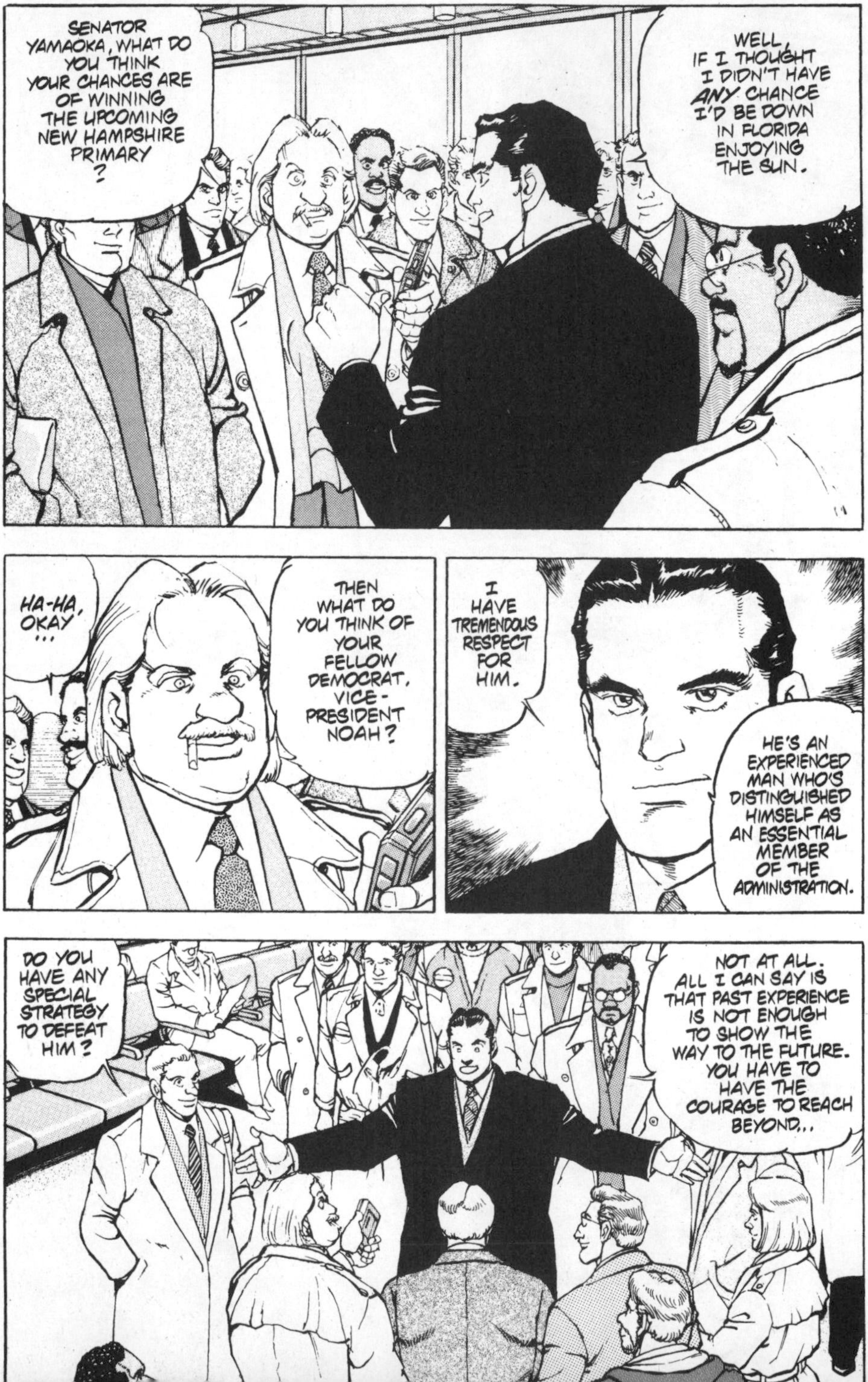
SENATOR YAMAOKA, WHAT DO YOU THINK YOUR CHANCES ARE OF WINNING THE UPCOMING NEW HAMPSHIRE PRIMARY ?
WELL, IF I THOUGHT I DIDN'T HAVE *ANY* CHANCE I'D BE DOWN IN FLORIDA ENJOYING THE SUN.
HA-HA, OKAY ...
THEN WHAT DO YOU THINK OF YOUR FELLOW DEMOCRAT, VICE-PRESIDENT NOAH ?
I HAVE TREMENDOUS RESPECT FOR HIM.
HE'S AN EXPERIENCED MAN WHO'S DISTINGUISHED HIMSELF AS AN ESSENTIAL MEMBER OF THE ADMINISTRATION.
DO YOU HAVE ANY SPECIAL STRATEGY TO DEFEAT HIM ?
NOT AT ALL. ALL I CAN SAY IS THAT PAST EXPERIENCE IS NOT ENOUGH TO SHOW THE WAY TO THE FUTURE. YOU HAVE TO HAVE THE COURAGE TO REACH BEYOND...

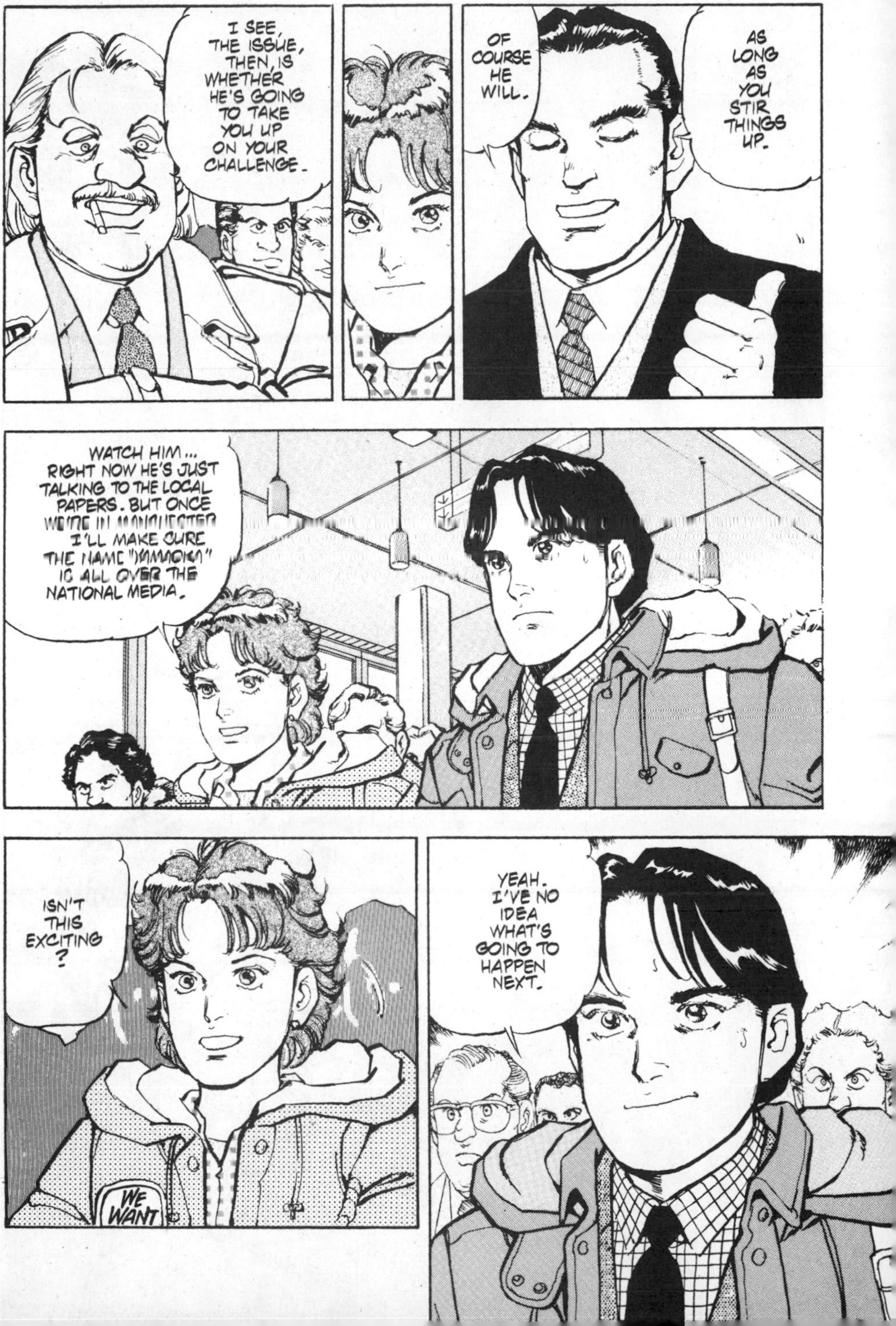

I SEE, THE ISSUE, THEN, IS WHETHER HE'S GOING TO TAKE YOU UP ON YOUR CHALLENGE.
OF COURSE HE WILL.
AS LONG AS YOU STIR THINGS UP.
WATCH HIM... RIGHT NOW HE'S JUST TALKING TO THE LOCAL PAPERS. BUT ONCE WE'RE IN MANCHESTER I'LL MAKE SURE THE NAME "YAMAOKA" IS ALL OVER THE NATIONAL MEDIA.
ISN'T THIS EXCITING?
WE WANT
YEAH. I'VE NO IDEA WHAT'S GOING TO HAPPEN NEXT.

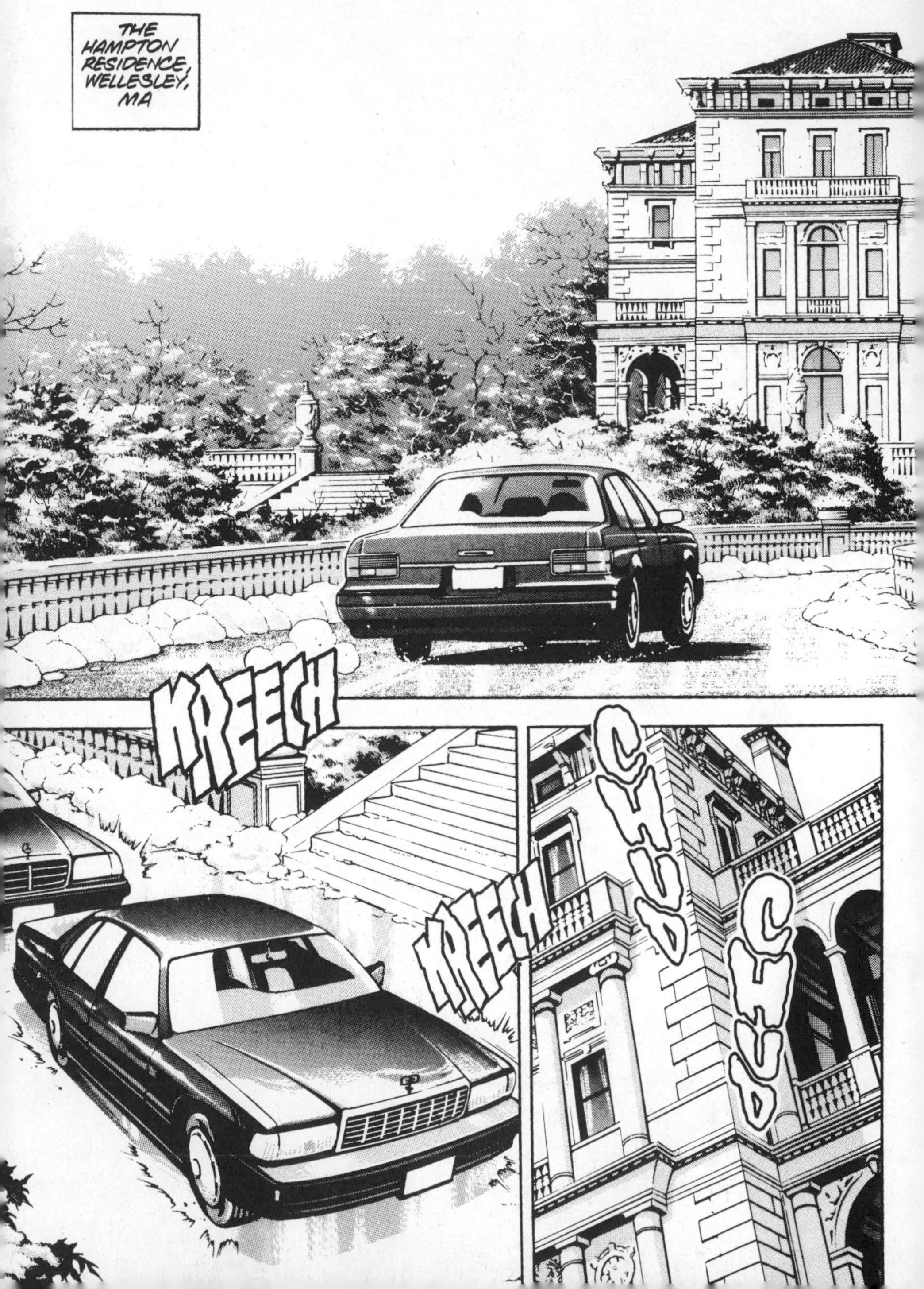
THE HAMPTON RESIDENCE, WELLESLEY, MA
KREECH
KREECH
CHUD
CHUD

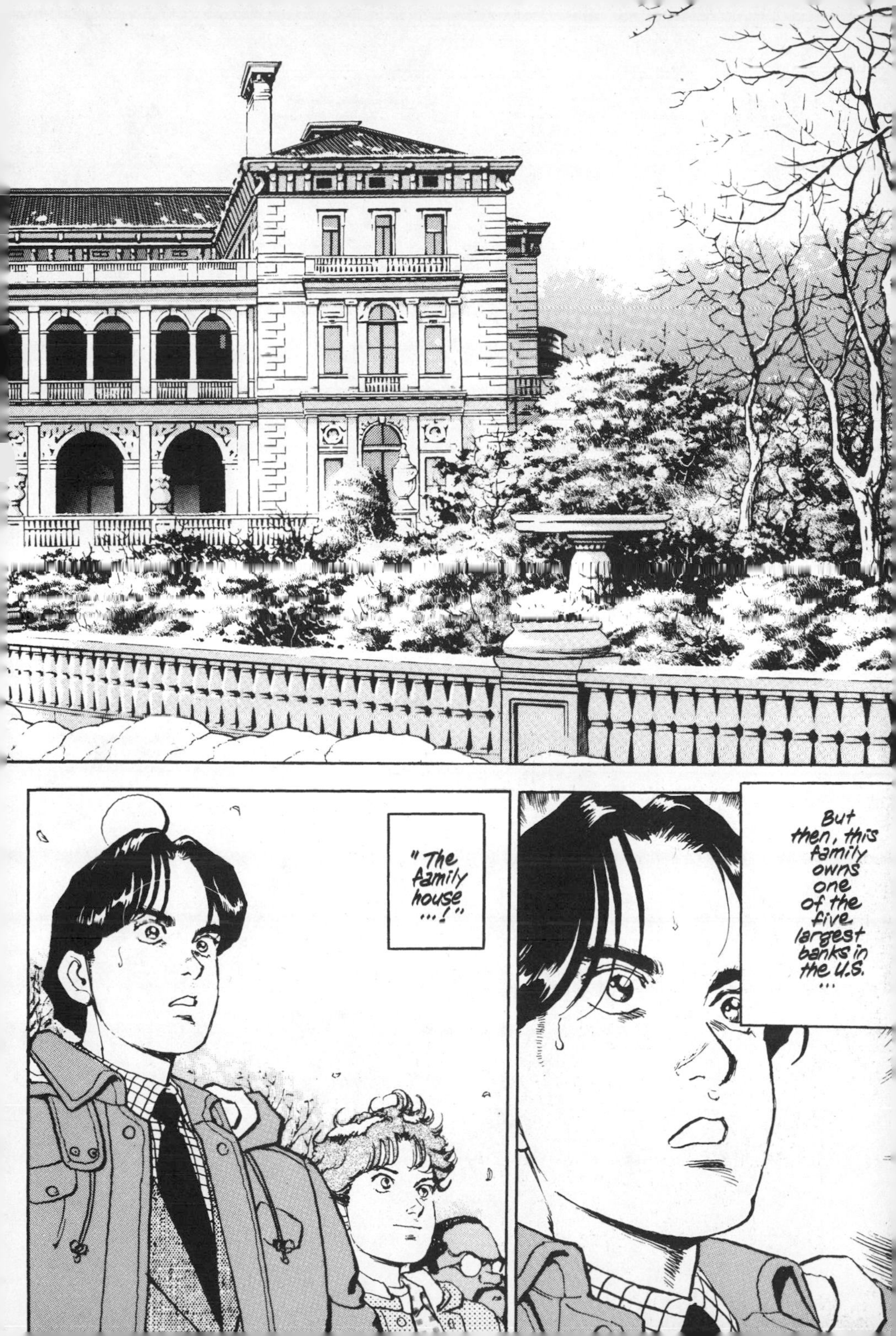
"The family house ...!"
But then, this family owns one of the five largest banks in the U.S. ...

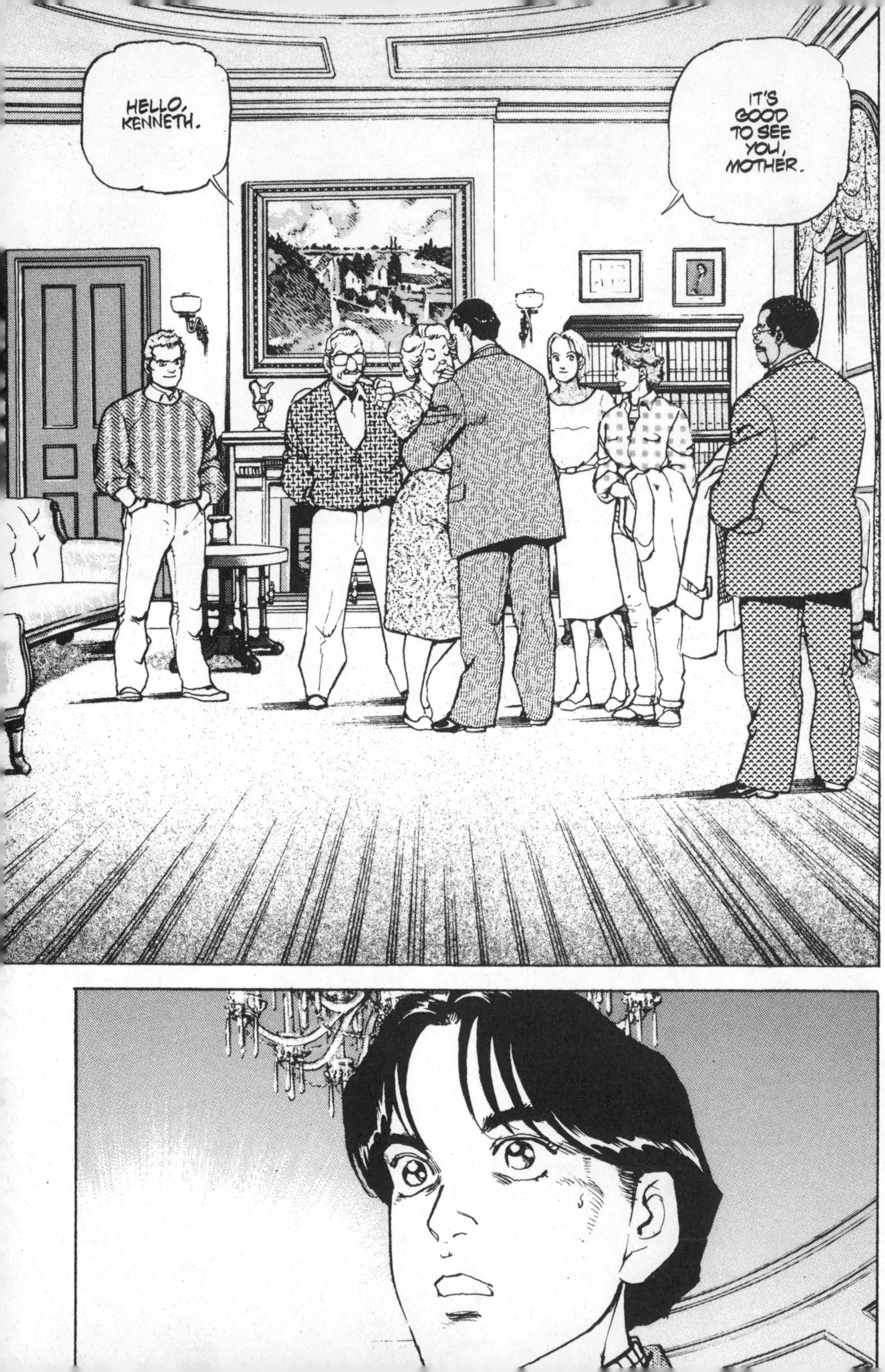
HELLO, KENNETH.
IT'S GOOD TO SEE YOU, MOTHER.

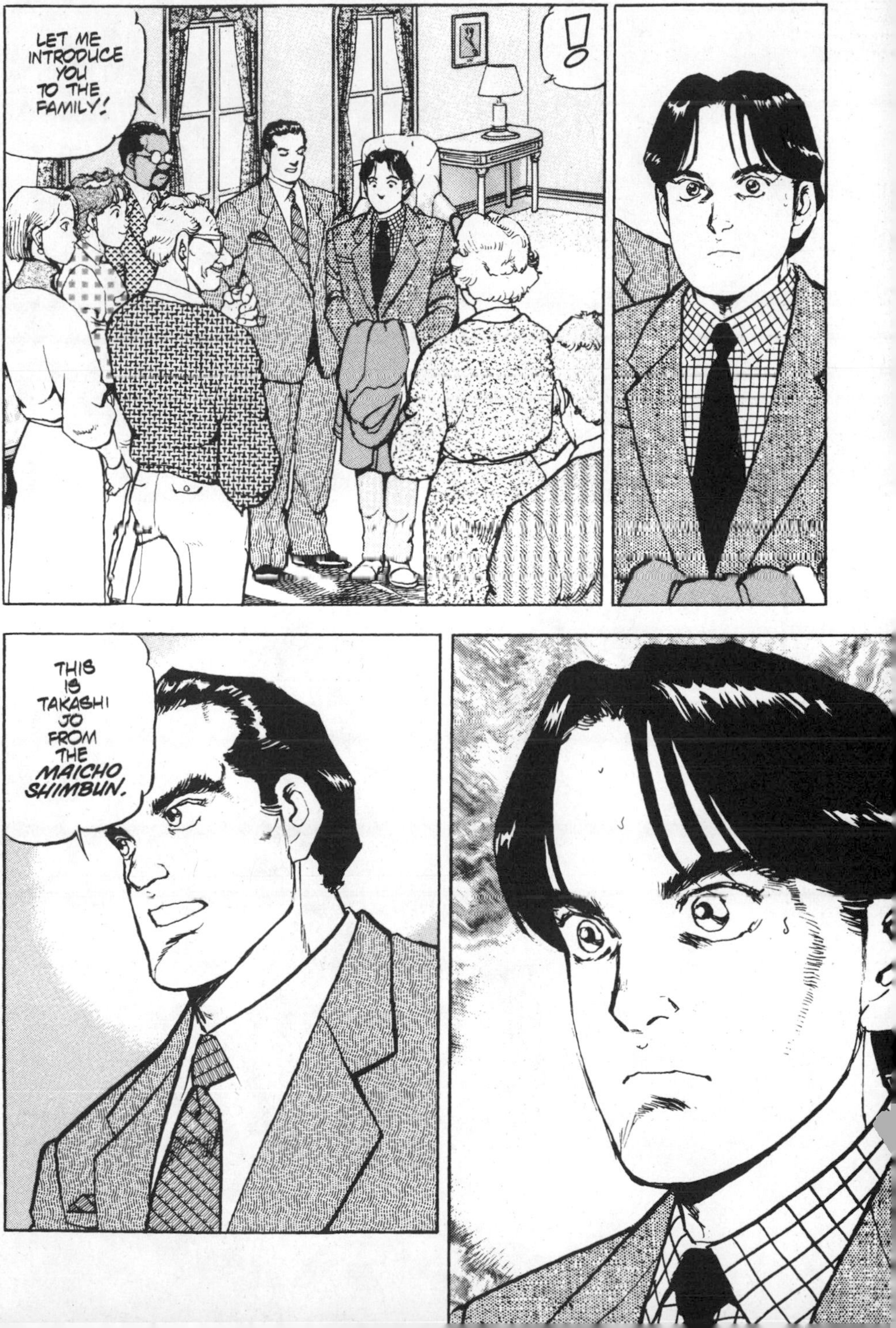
LET ME INTRODUCE YOU TO THE FAMILY!
!
THIS IS TAKASHI JO FROM THE *MAICHO SHIMBUN*.

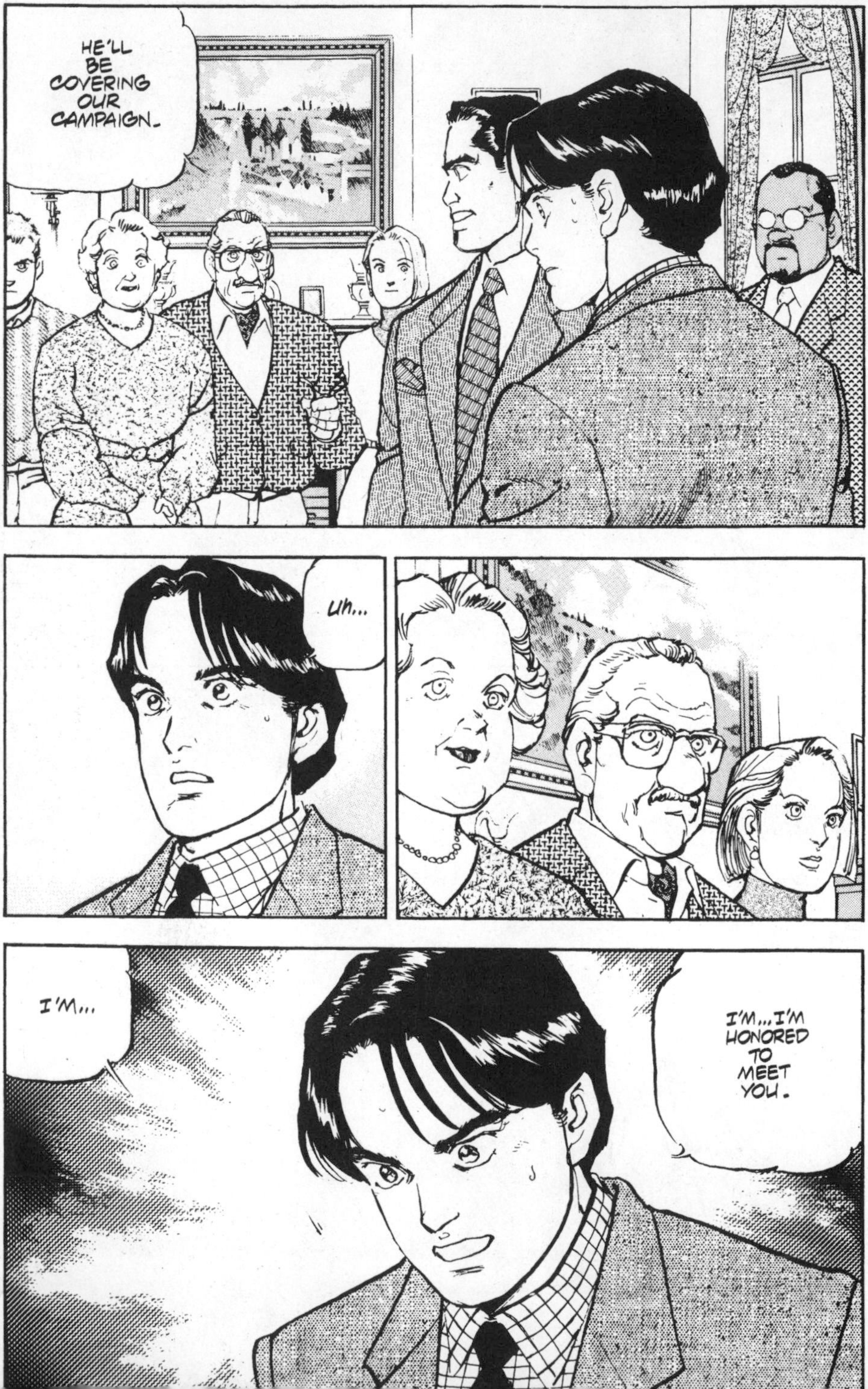
HE'LL BE COVERING OUR CAMPAIGN.
UH...
I'M...
I'M...I'M HONORED TO MEET YOU.

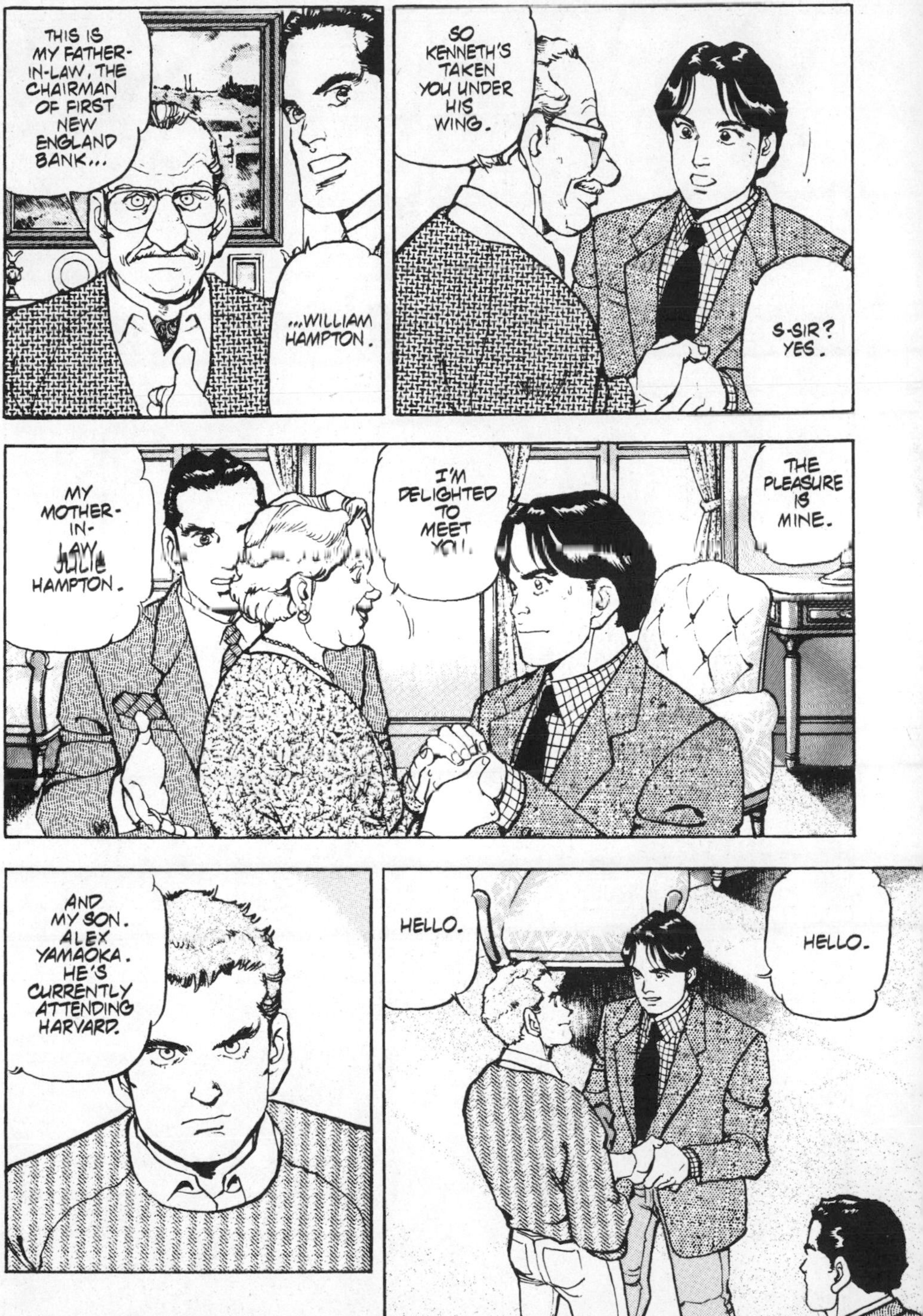
THIS IS MY FATHER-IN-LAW, THE CHAIRMAN OF FIRST NEW ENGLAND BANK...
...WILLIAM HAMPTON.
SO KENNETH'S TAKEN YOU UNDER HIS WING.
S-SIR? YES.
MY MOTHER-IN-LAW, JULIE HAMPTON.
I'M DELIGHTED TO MEET YOU.
THE PLEASURE IS MINE.
AND MY SON. ALEX YAMAOKA. HE'S CURRENTLY ATTENDING HARVARD.
HELLO.
HELLO.

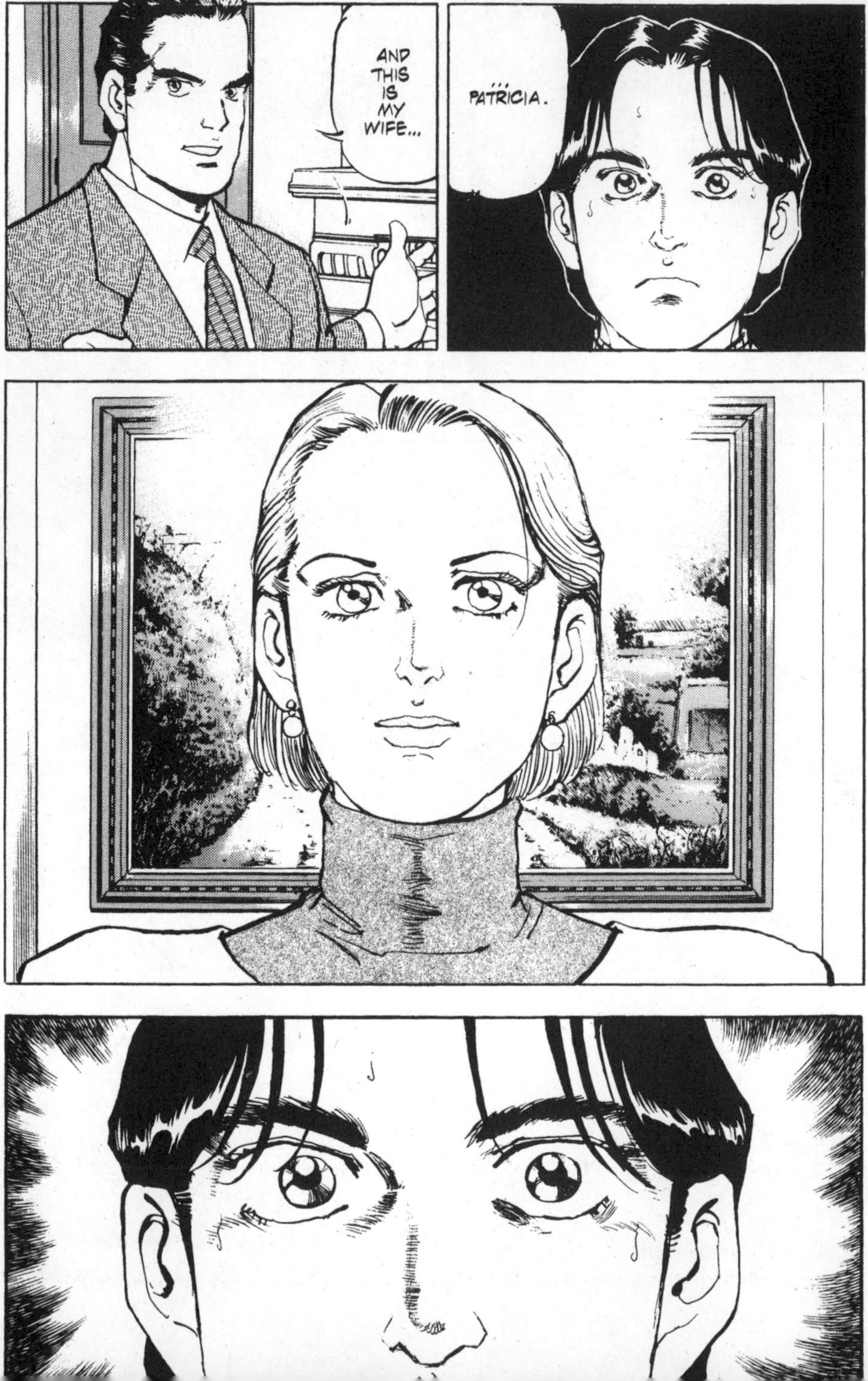
AND THIS IS MY WIFE...
...PATRICIA.

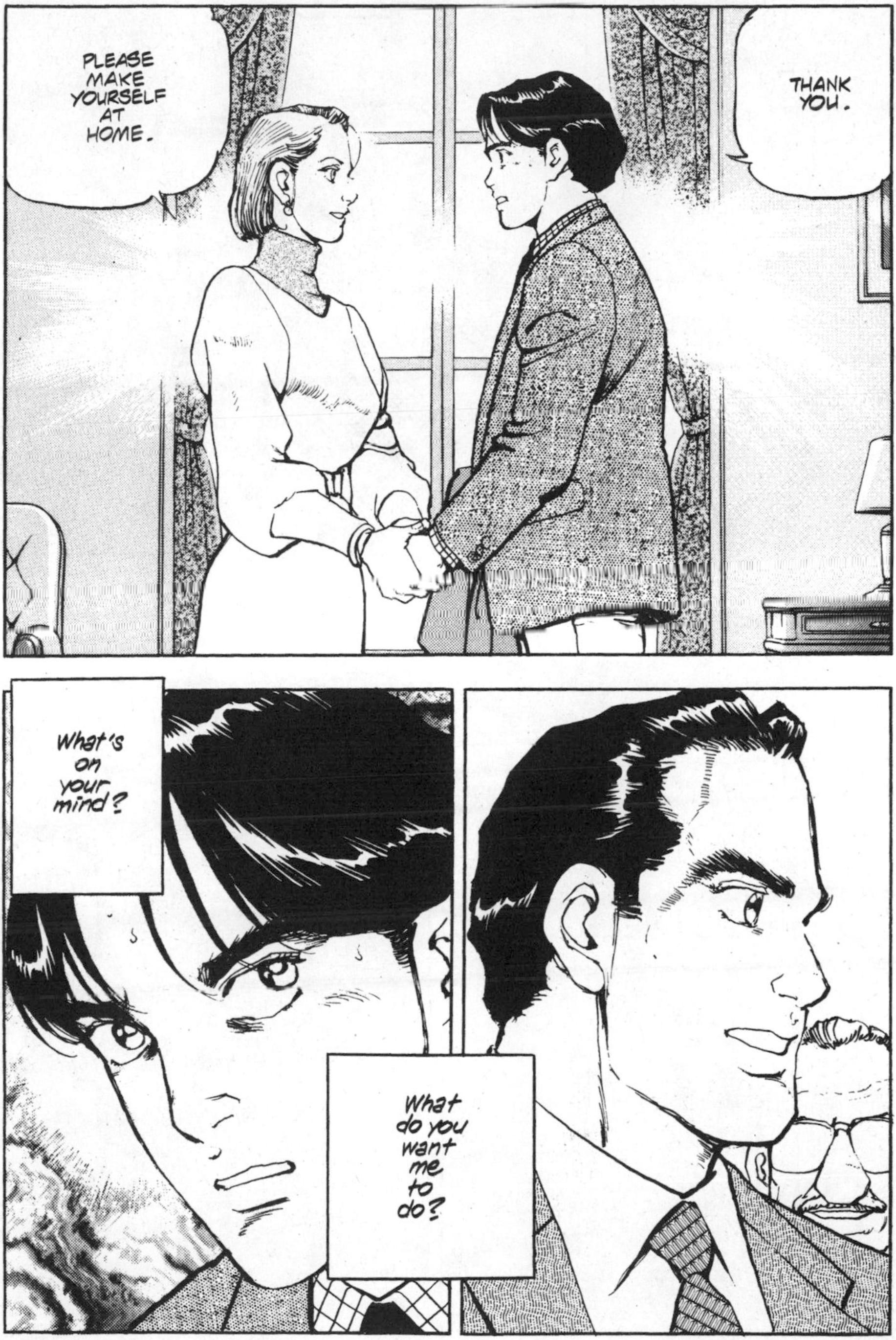
PLEASE MAKE YOURSELF AT HOME.
THANK YOU.
What's on your mind?
What do you want me to do?

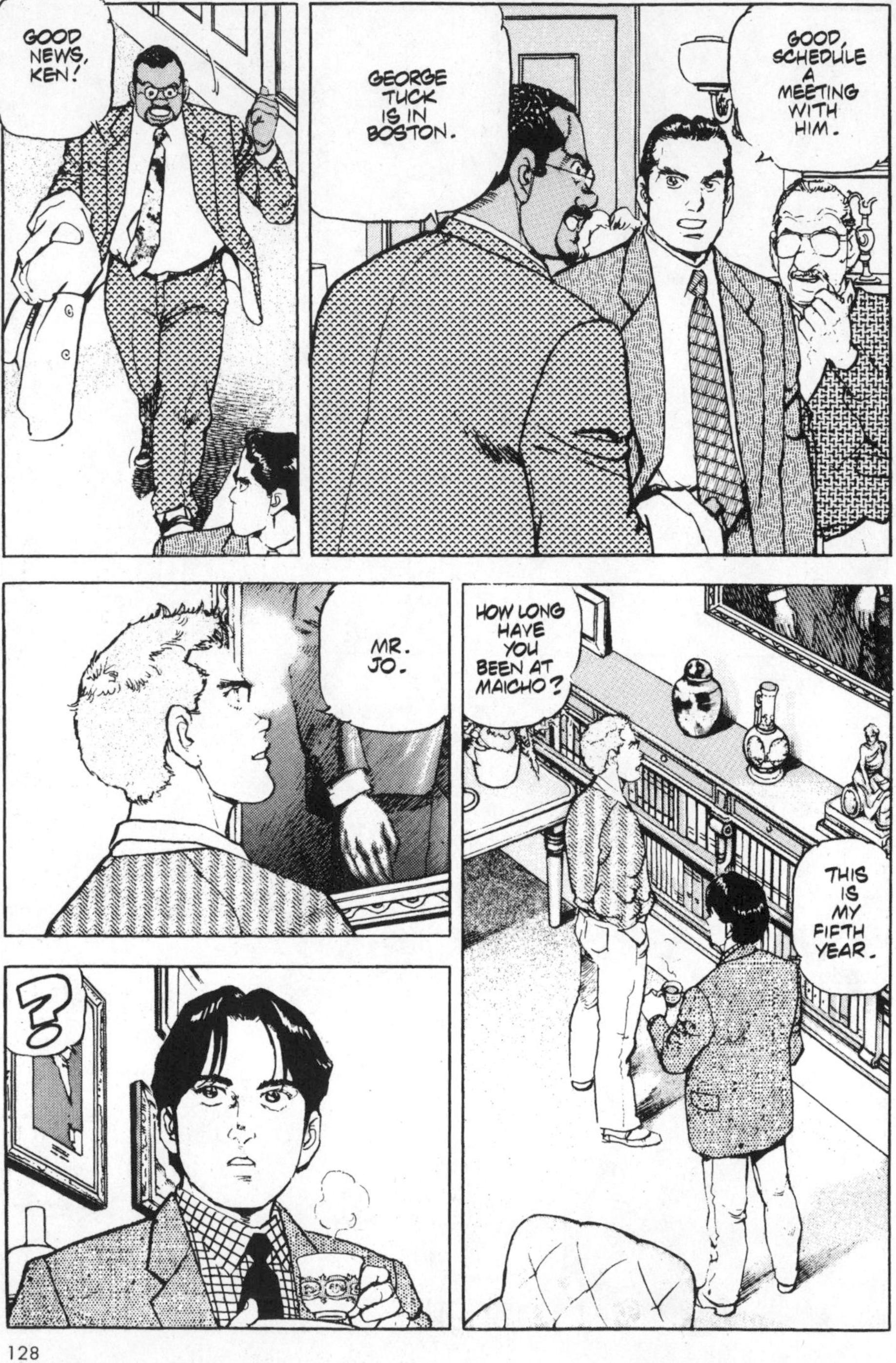
GOOD NEWS, KEN!
GEORGE TUCK IS IN BOSTON.
GOOD, SCHEDULE A MEETING WITH HIM.
MR. JO.
?
HOW LONG HAVE YOU BEEN AT MAICHO?
THIS IS MY FIFTH YEAR.

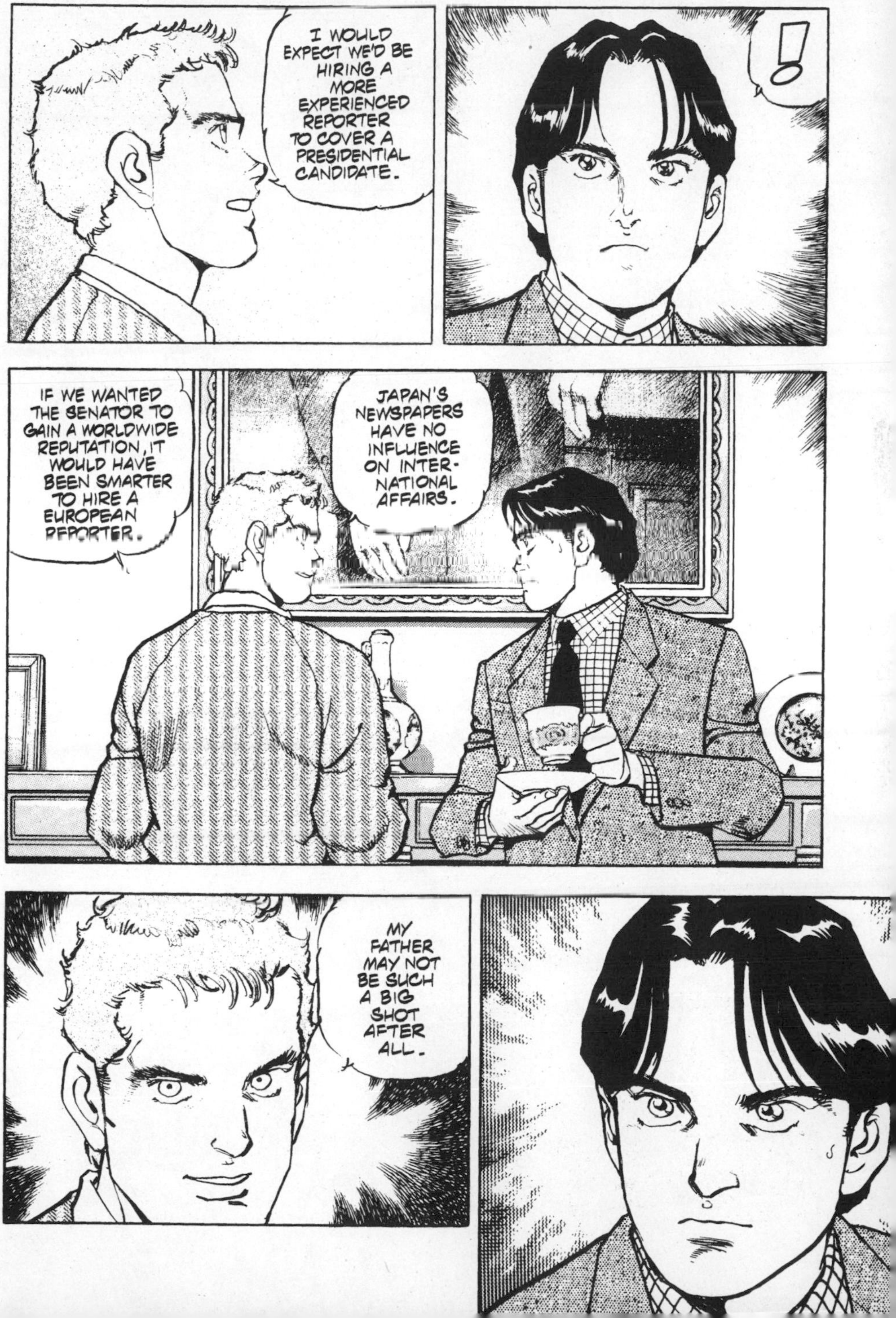
I WOULD EXPECT WE'D BE HIRING A MORE EXPERIENCED REPORTER TO COVER A PRESIDENTIAL CANDIDATE.
!
IF WE WANTED THE SENATOR TO GAIN A WORLDWIDE REPUTATION, IT WOULD HAVE BEEN SMARTER TO HIRE A EUROPEAN REPORTER.
JAPAN'S NEWSPAPERS HAVE NO INFLUENCE ON INTER-NATIONAL AFFAIRS.
MY FATHER MAY NOT BE SUCH A BIG SHOT AFTER ALL.

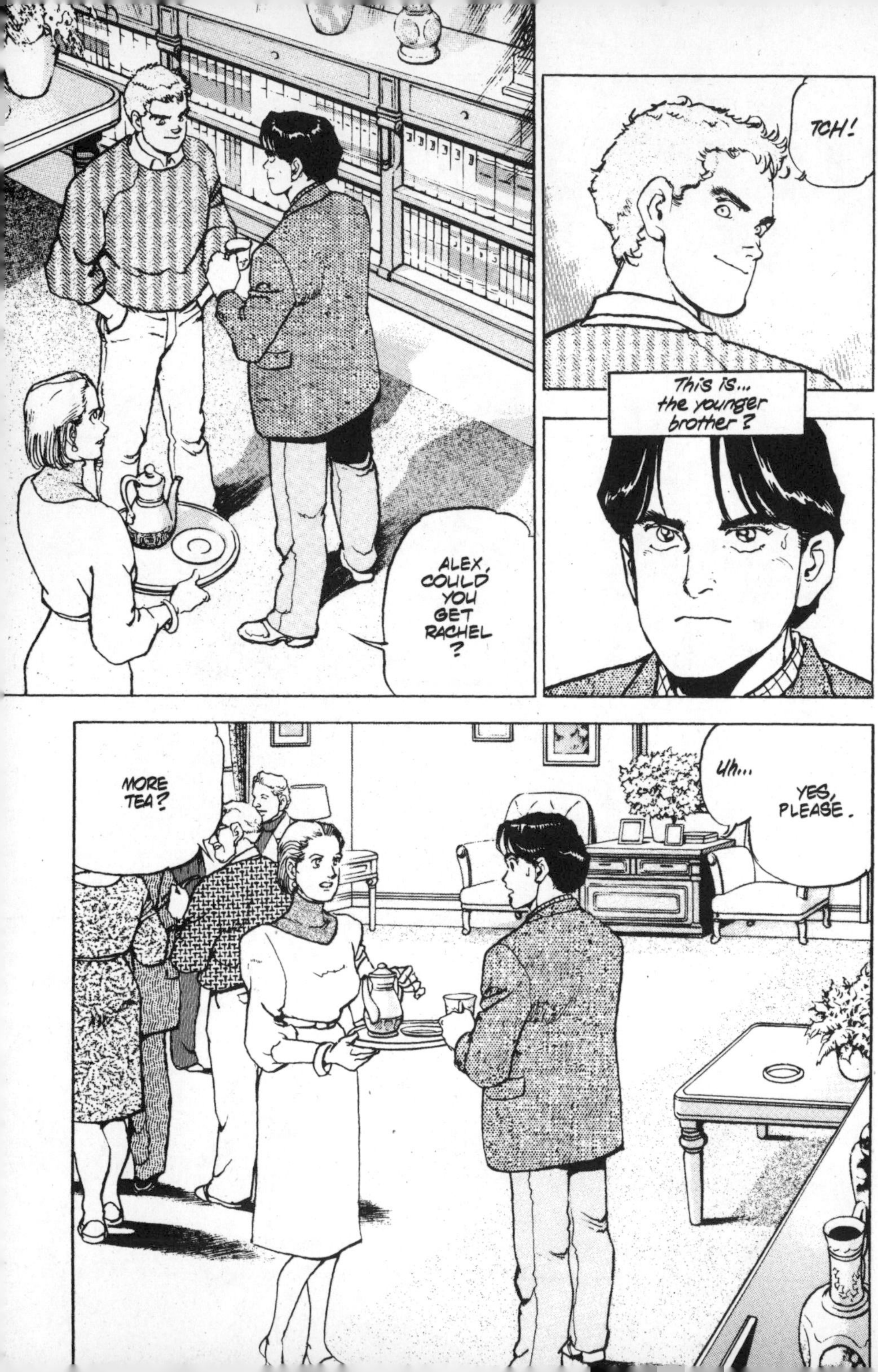
ALEX, COULD YOU GET RACHEL?
TCH!
This is... the younger brother?
MORE TEA?
Uh...
YES, PLEASE.

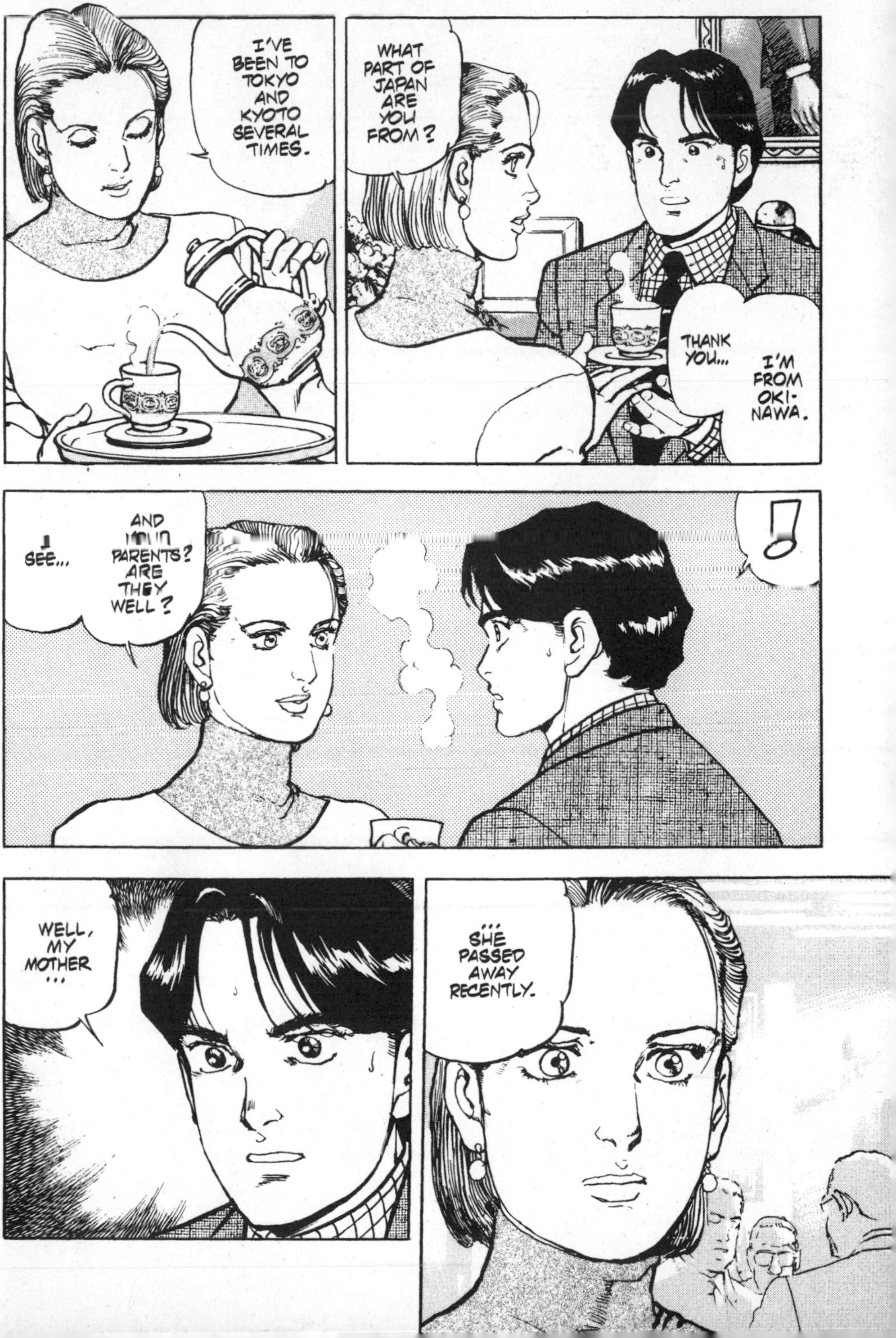
I'VE BEEN TO TOKYO AND KYOTO SEVERAL TIMES.
WHAT PART OF JAPAN ARE YOU FROM?
THANK YOU...
I'M FROM OKI-NAWA.
I SEE...
AND PARENTS? ARE THEY WELL?
!
WELL, MY MOTHER ...
... SHE PASSED AWAY RECENTLY.

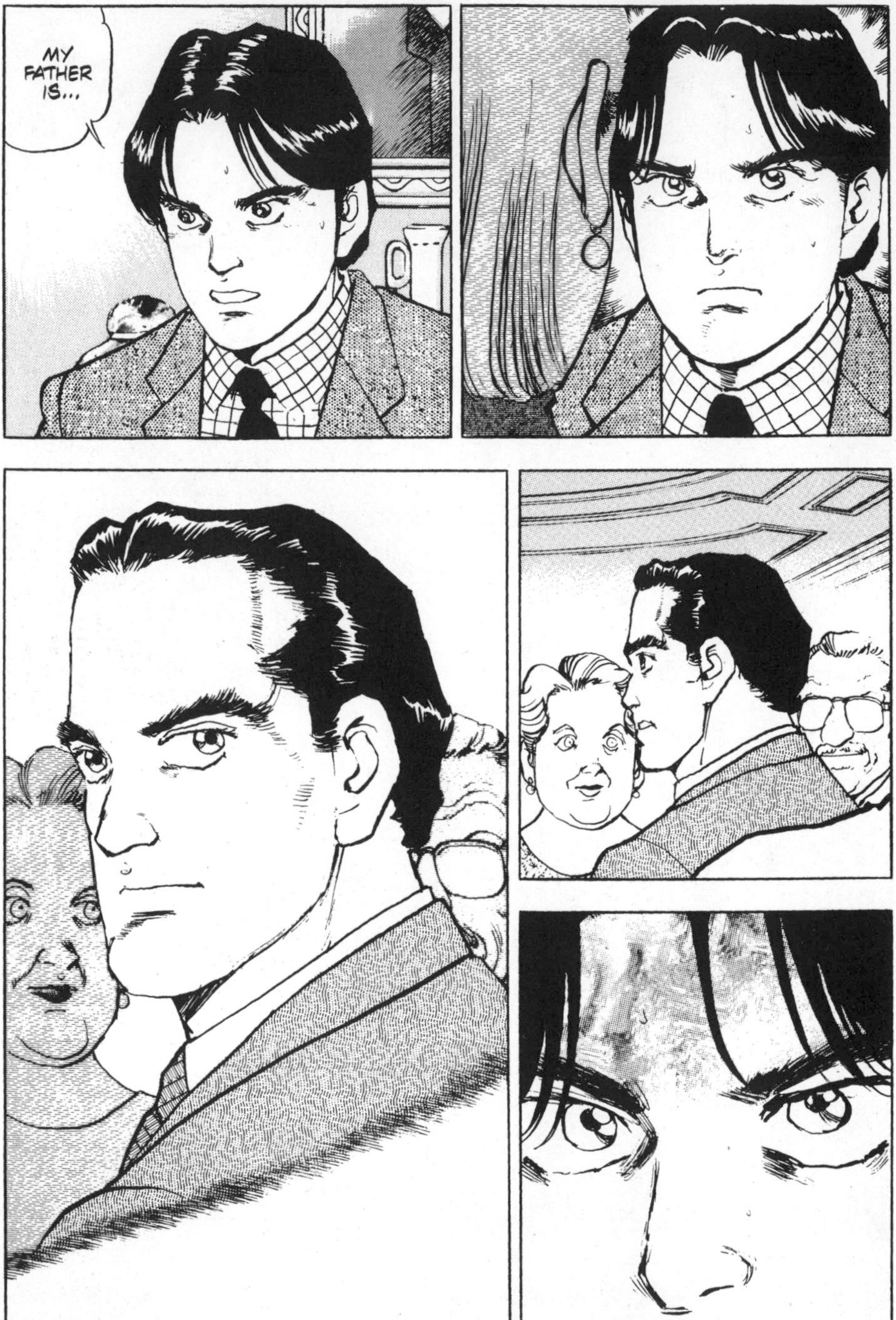
MY FATHER IS...

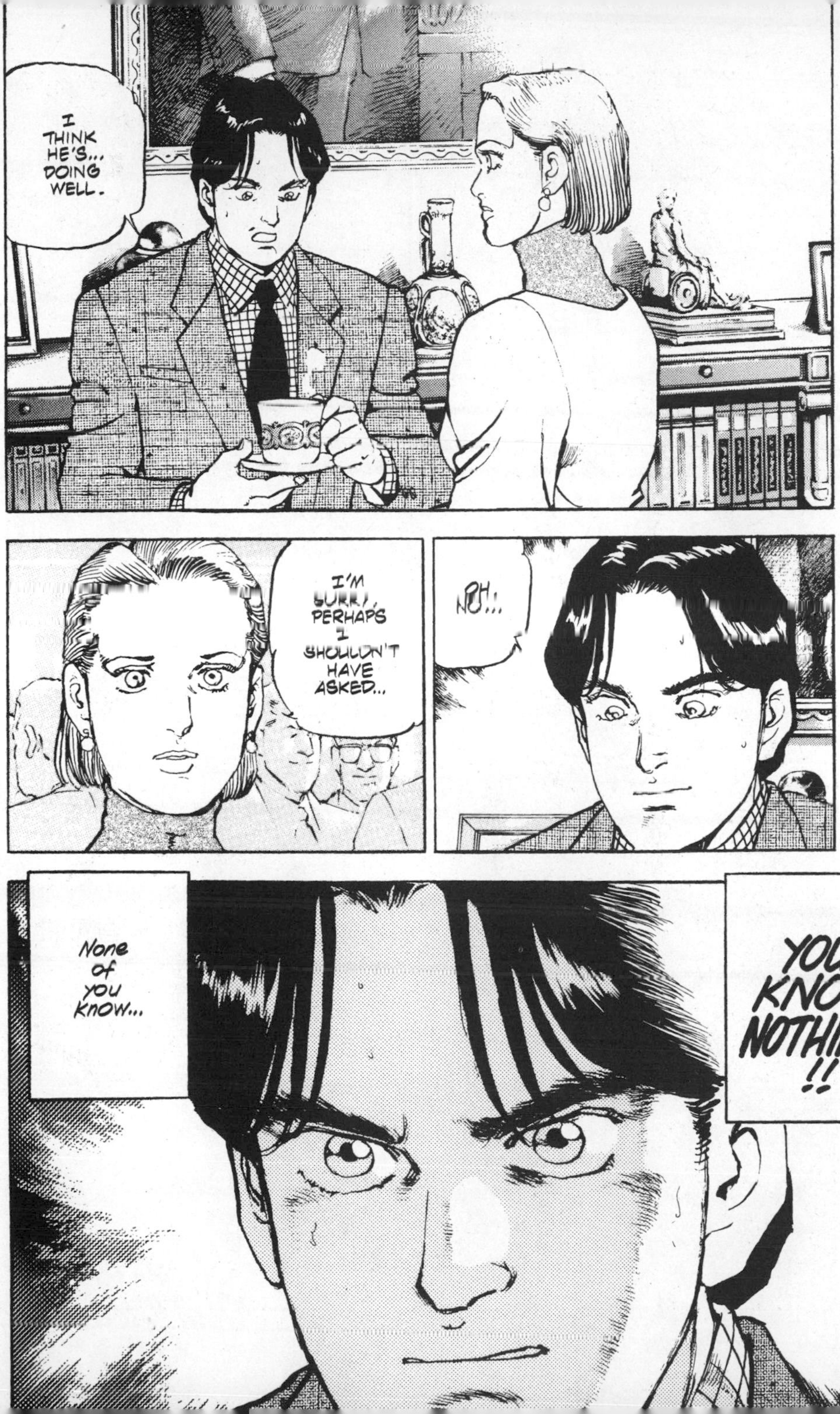
I THINK HE'S... DOING WELL.
I'M SORRY, PERHAPS I SHOULDN'T HAVE ASKED...
OH NO!...
None of you know...
YOU KNOW NOTHING !!

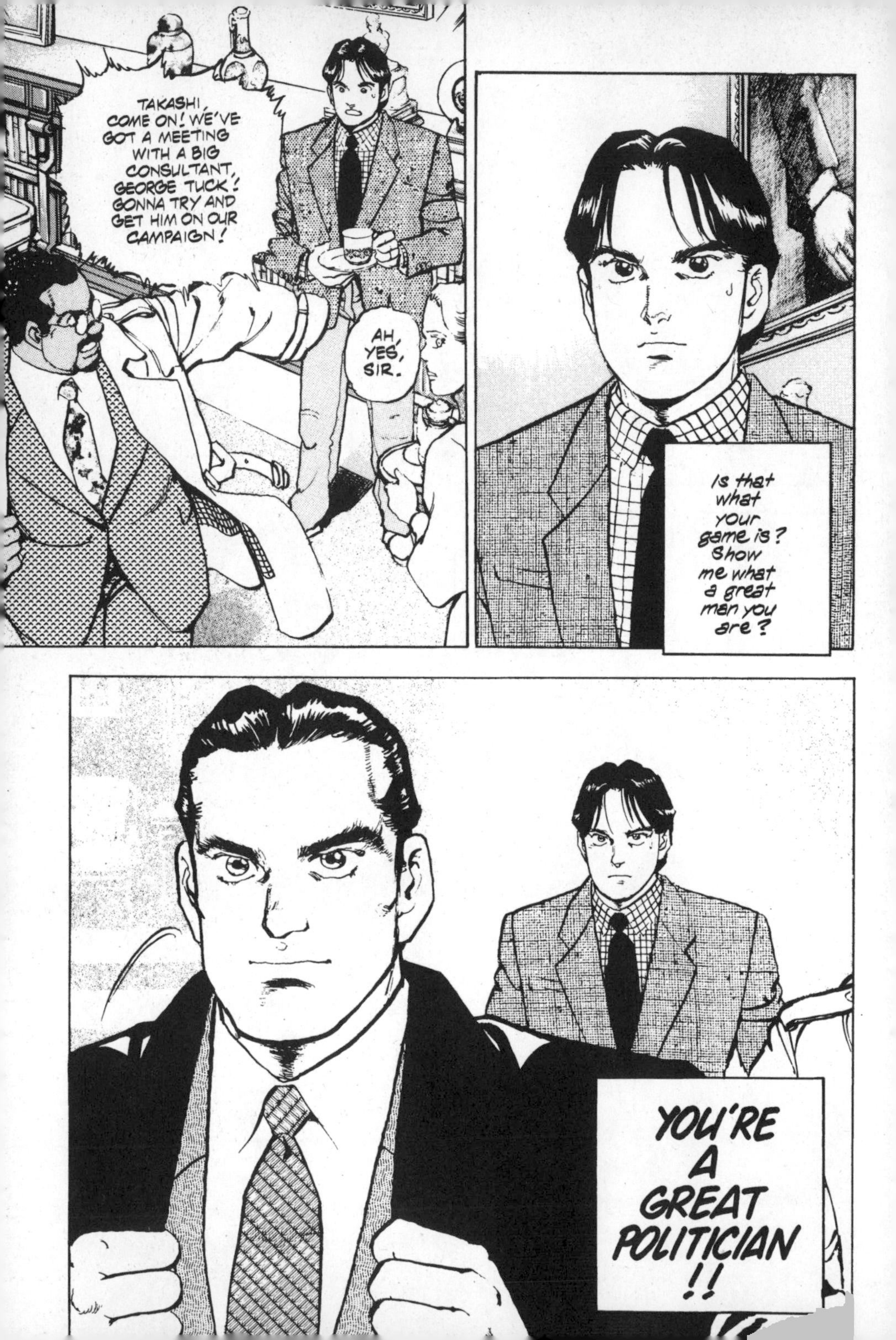
TAKASHI, COME ON! WE'VE GOT A MEETING WITH A BIG CONSULTANT, GEORGE TUCK! GONNA TRY AND GET HIM ON OUR CAMPAIGN!
AH, YES, SIR.
Is that what your game is? Show me what a great man you are?
YOU'RE A GREAT POLITICIAN!!

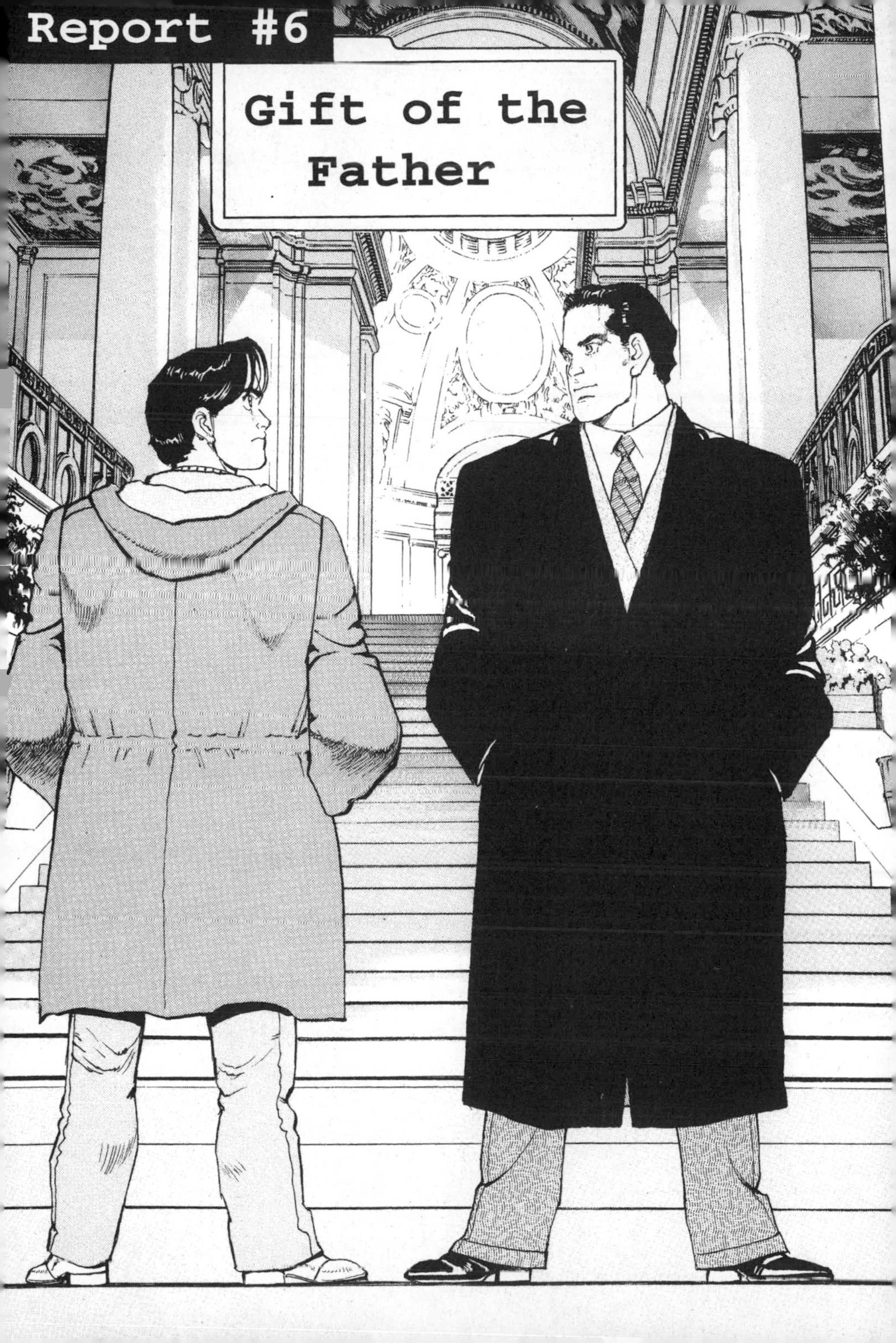
Report #6
Gift of the Father

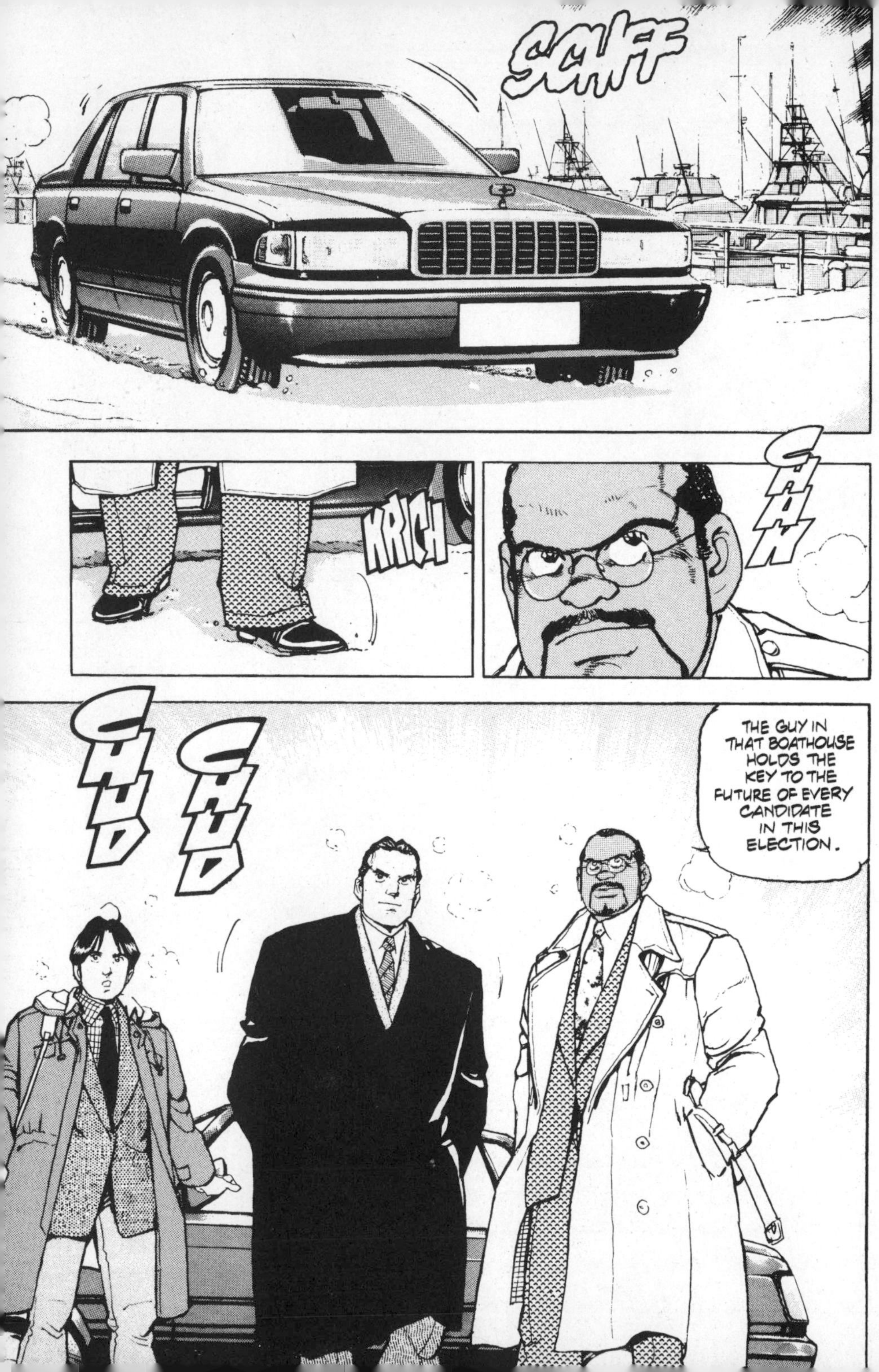
SCUFF
KRICH
CHAK
CHUD
CHUD
THE GUY IN THAT BOATHOUSE HOLDS THE KEY TO THE FUTURE OF EVERY CANDIDATE IN THIS ELECTION.

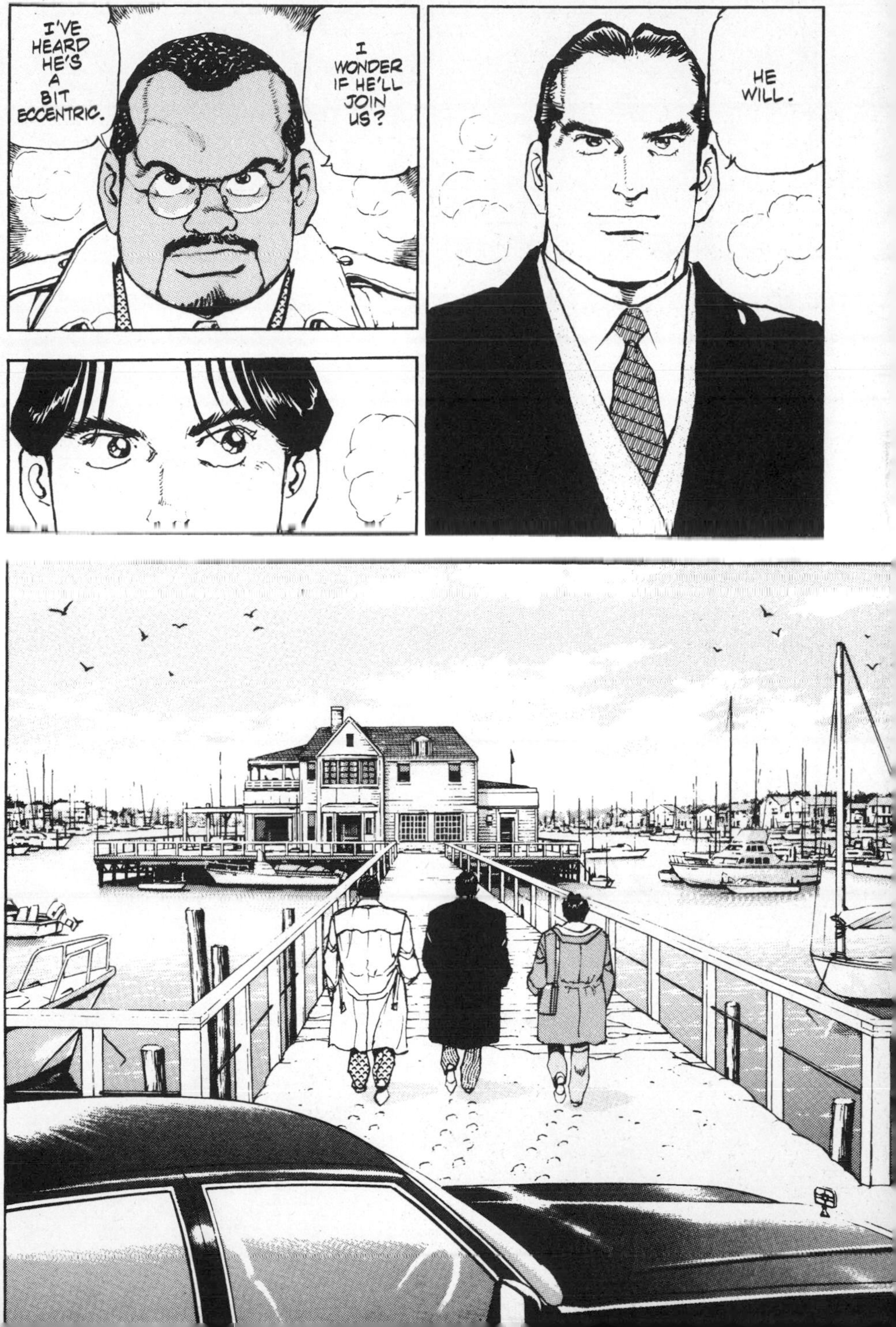
I'VE HEARD HE'S A BIT ECCENTRIC.
I WONDER IF HE'LL JOIN US?
HE WILL.

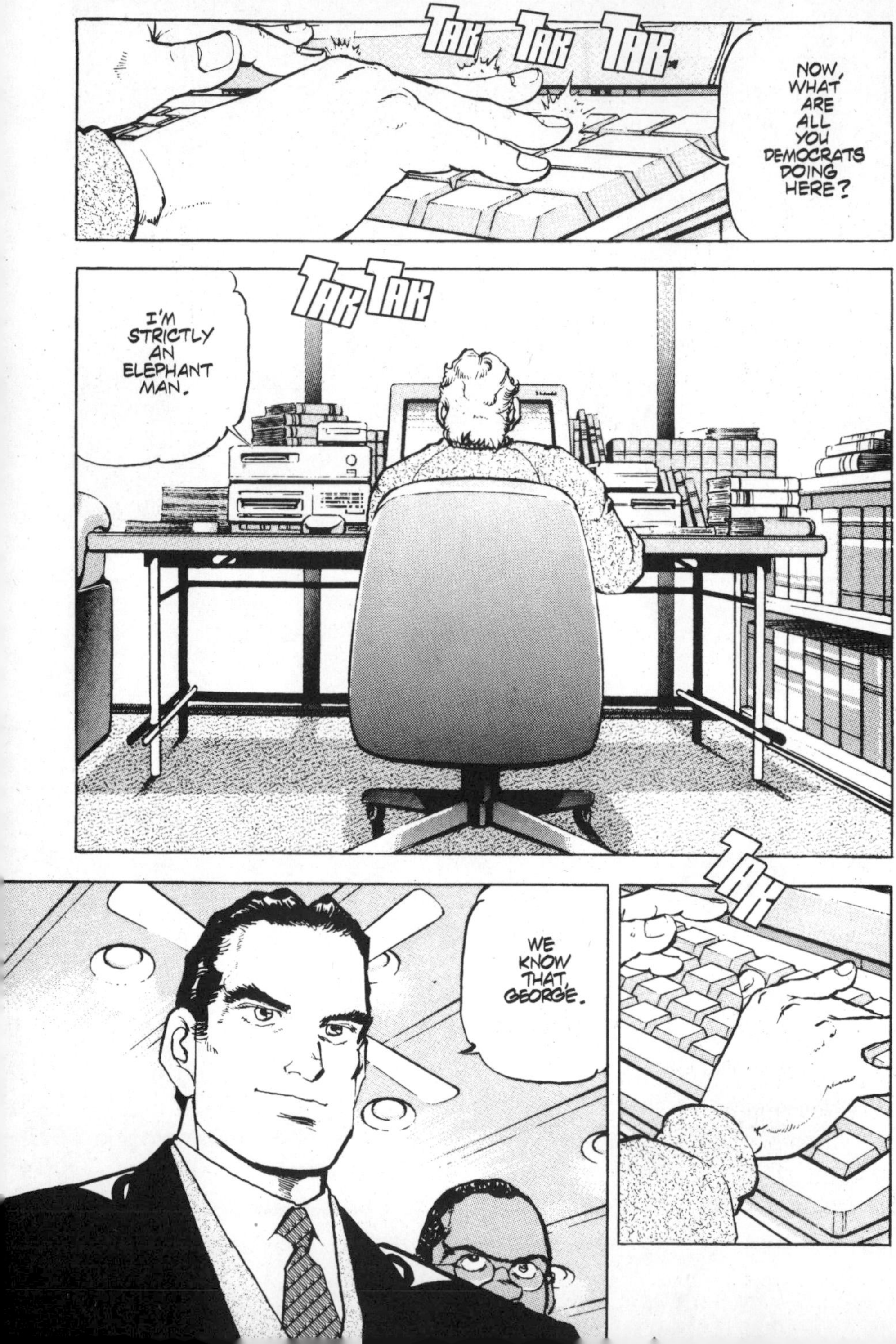
TAK TAK TAK
NOW, WHAT ARE ALL YOU DEMOCRATS DOING HERE?
TAK TAK
I'M STRICTLY AN ELEPHANT MAN.
WE KNOW THAT, GEORGE.
TAK

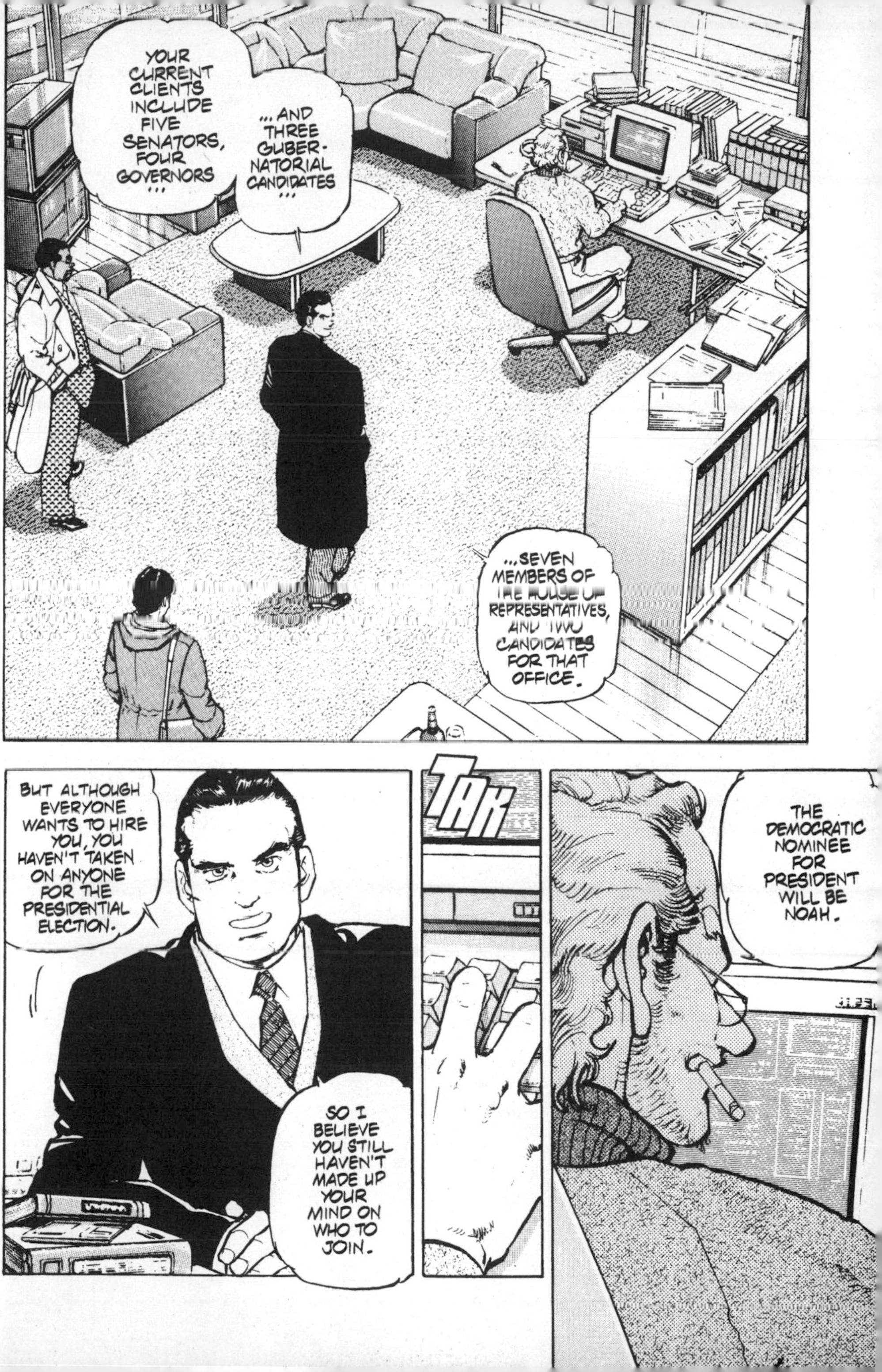
YOUR CURRENT CLIENTS INCLUDE FIVE SENATORS, FOUR GOVERNORS ...
...AND THREE GUBER-NATORIAL CANDIDATES ...
...SEVEN MEMBERS OF THE HOUSE OF REPRESENTATIVES, AND TWO CANDIDATES FOR THAT OFFICE.
BUT ALTHOUGH EVERYONE WANTS TO HIRE YOU, YOU HAVEN'T TAKEN ON ANYONE FOR THE PRESIDENTIAL ELECTION.
SO I BELIEVE YOU STILL HAVEN'T MADE UP YOUR MIND ON WHO TO JOIN.
TAK
THE DEMOCRATIC NOMINEE FOR PRESIDENT WILL BE NOAH.

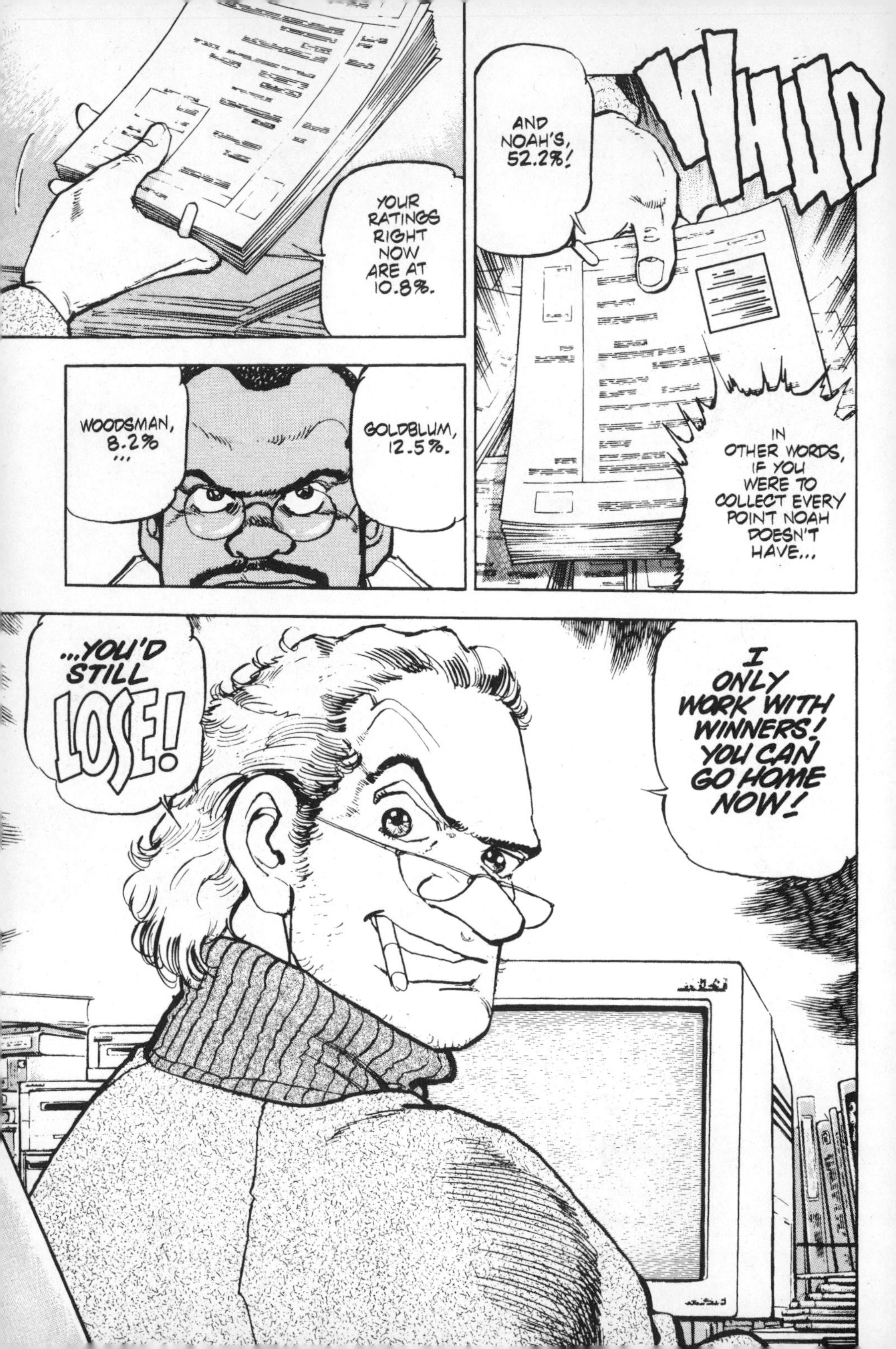
YOUR RATINGS RIGHT NOW ARE AT 10.8%.
WOODSMAN, 8.2% ...
GOLDBLUM, 12.5%.
AND NOAH'S, 52.2%!
WHUD
IN OTHER WORDS, IF YOU WERE TO COLLECT EVERY POINT NOAH DOESN'T HAVE...
...YOU'D STILL LOSE!
I ONLY WORK WITH WINNERS! YOU CAN GO HOME NOW!

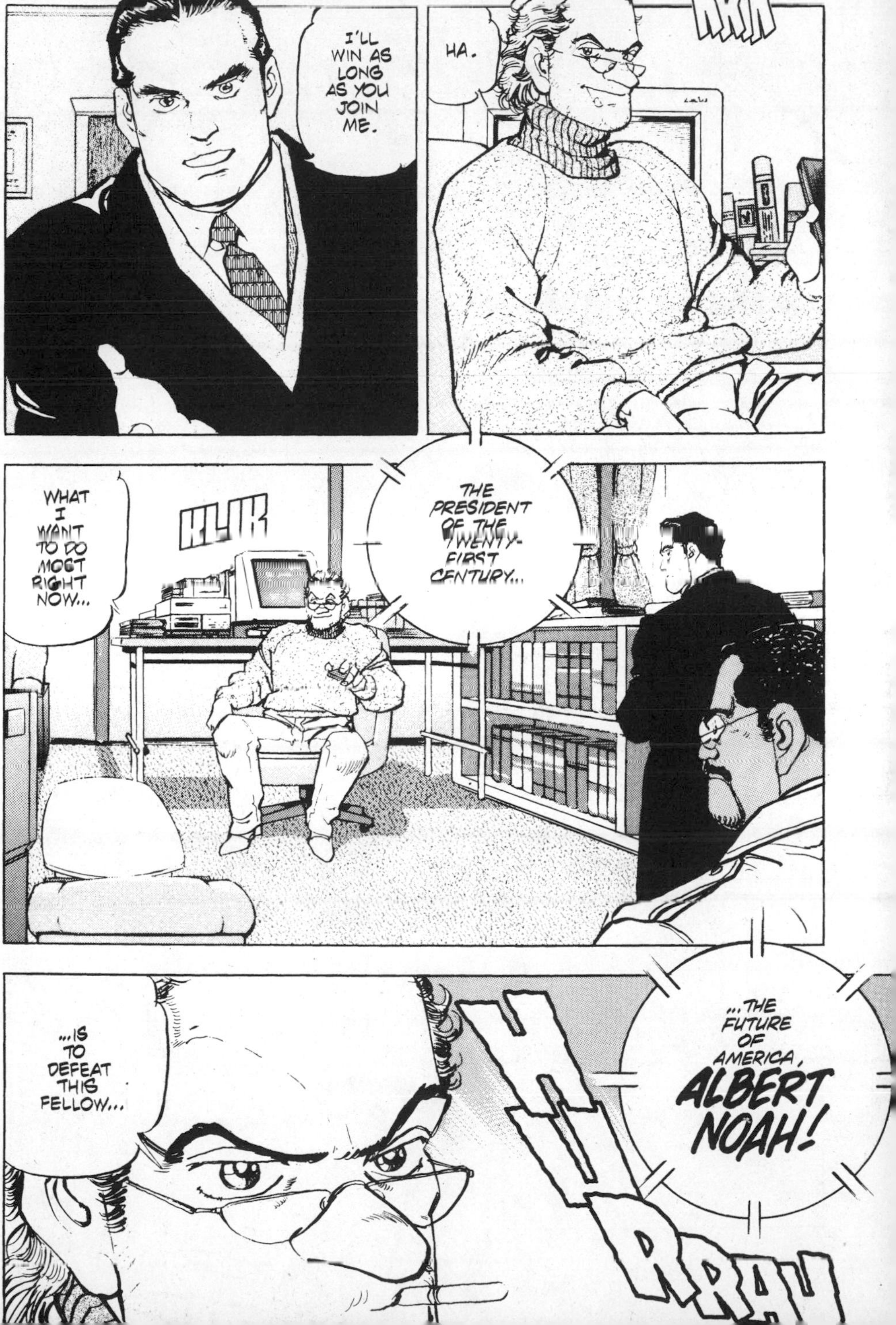
I'LL WIN AS LONG AS YOU JOIN ME.
HA.
KRIK
WHAT I WANT TO DO MOST RIGHT NOW...
KLIK
THE PRESIDENT OF THE TWENTY-FIRST CENTURY...
...IS TO DEFEAT THIS FELLOW...
...THE FUTURE OF AMERICA, ALBERT NOAH!
HURRAH

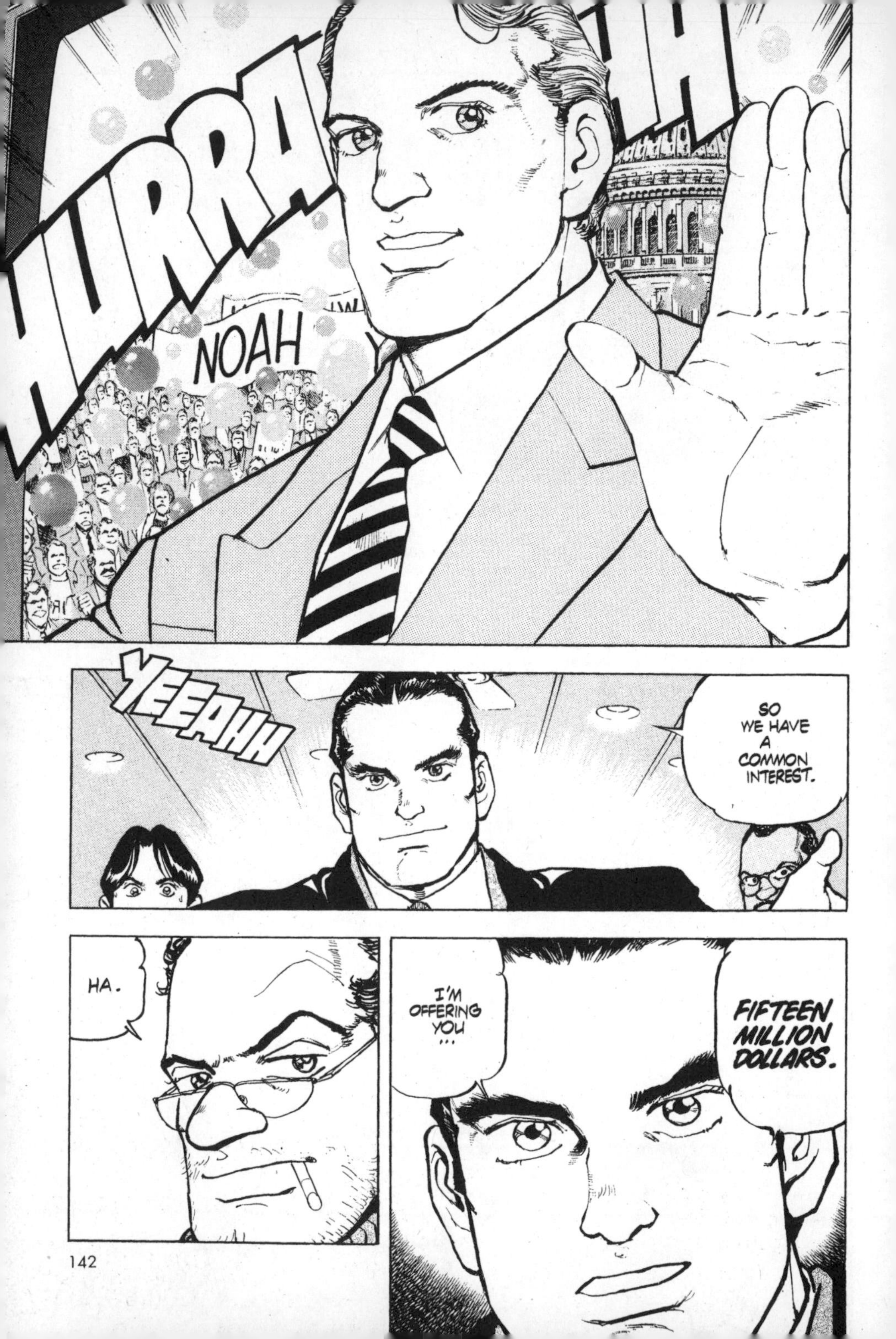
HURRA
NOAH
YEEAHH
SO WE HAVE A COMMON INTEREST.
HA.
I'M OFFERING YOU...
FIFTEEN MILLION DOLLARS.

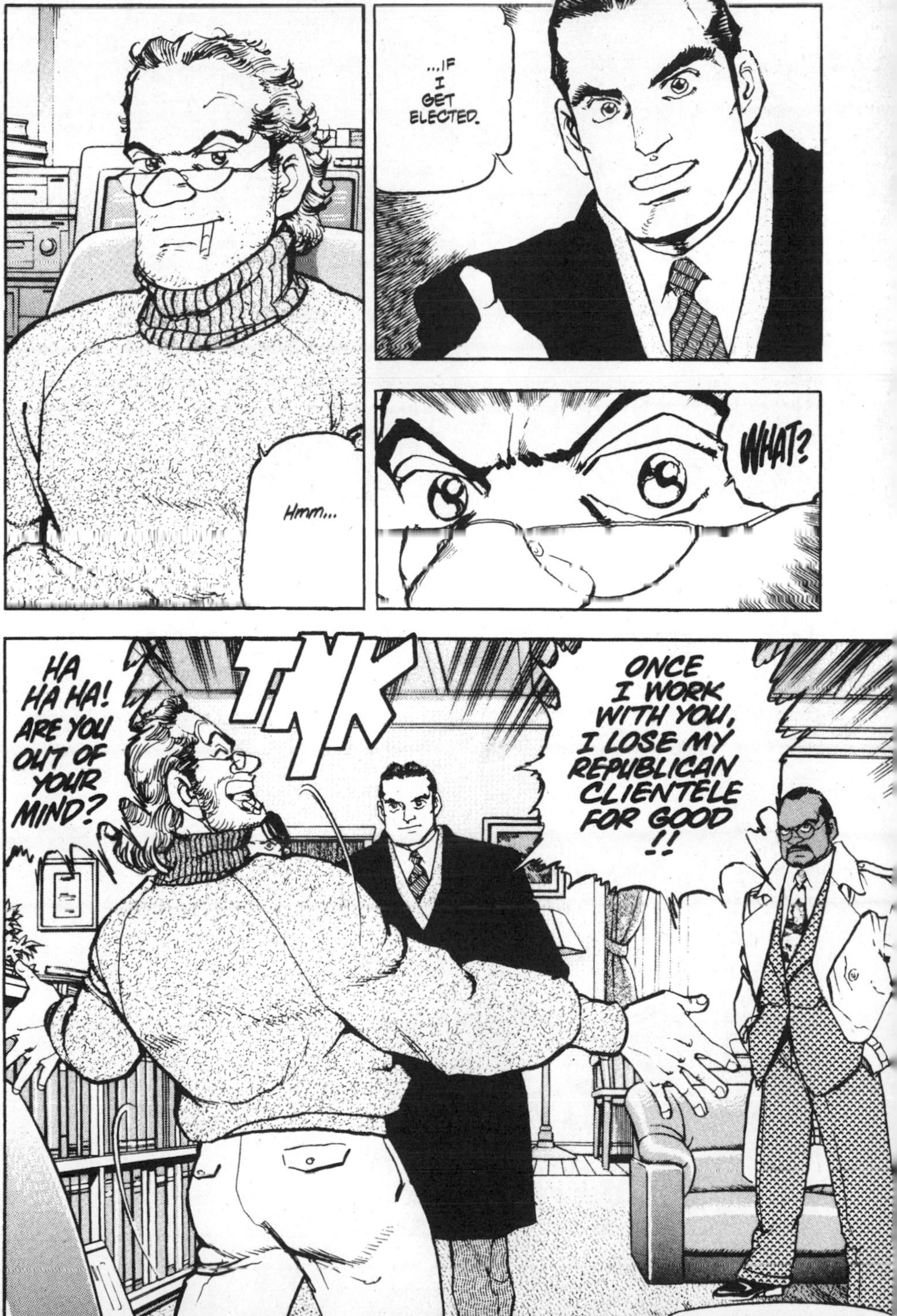
...IF I GET ELECTED.
Hmm...
WHAT?
TNK
HA HA HA! ARE YOU OUT OF YOUR MIND?
ONCE I WORK WITH YOU, I LOSE MY REPUBLICAN CLIENTELE FOR GOOD!!

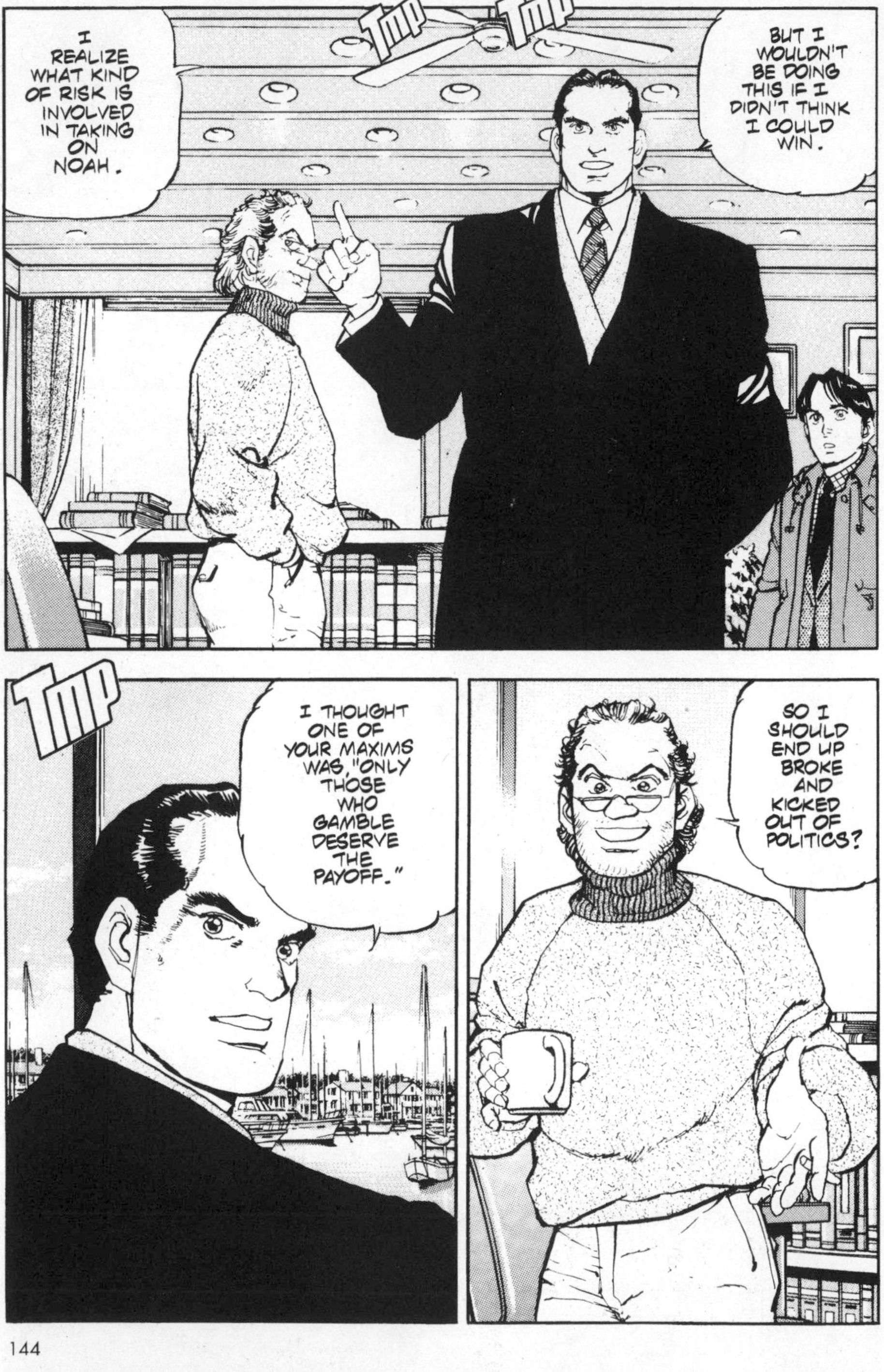
Tmp
Tmp
I REALIZE WHAT KIND OF RISK IS INVOLVED IN TAKING ON NOAH.
BUT I WOULDN'T BE DOING THIS IF I DIDN'T THINK I COULD WIN.
Tmp
I THOUGHT ONE OF YOUR MAXIMS WAS, "ONLY THOSE WHO GAMBLE DESERVE THE PAYOFF."
SO I SHOULD END UP BROKE AND KICKED OUT OF POLITICS?

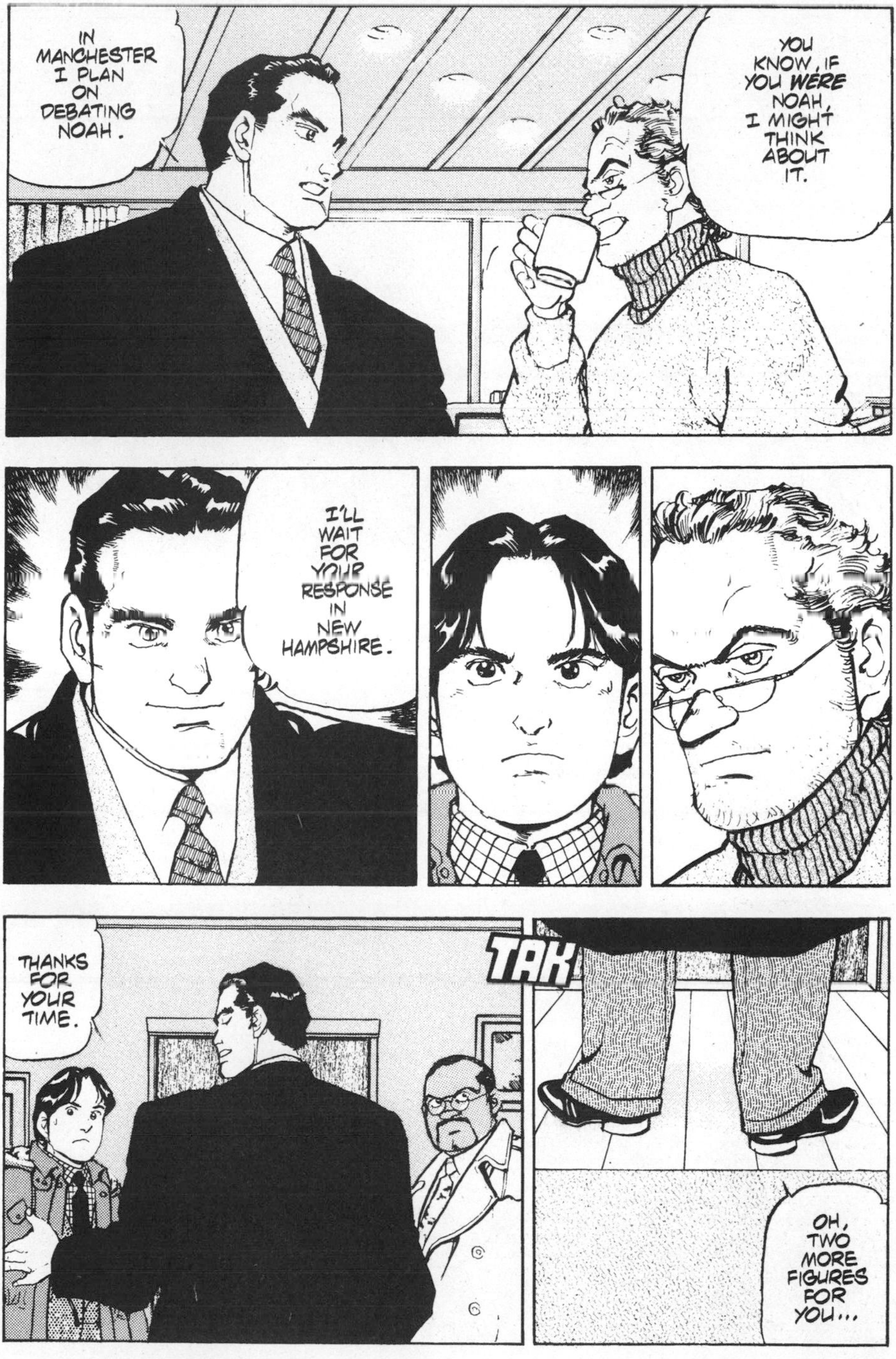
IN MANCHESTER I PLAN ON DEBATING NOAH.
YOU KNOW, IF YOU *WERE* NOAH, I MIGHT THINK ABOUT IT.
I'LL WAIT FOR YOUR RESPONSE IN NEW HAMPSHIRE.
THANKS FOR YOUR TIME.
TAK
OH, TWO MORE FIGURES FOR YOU...

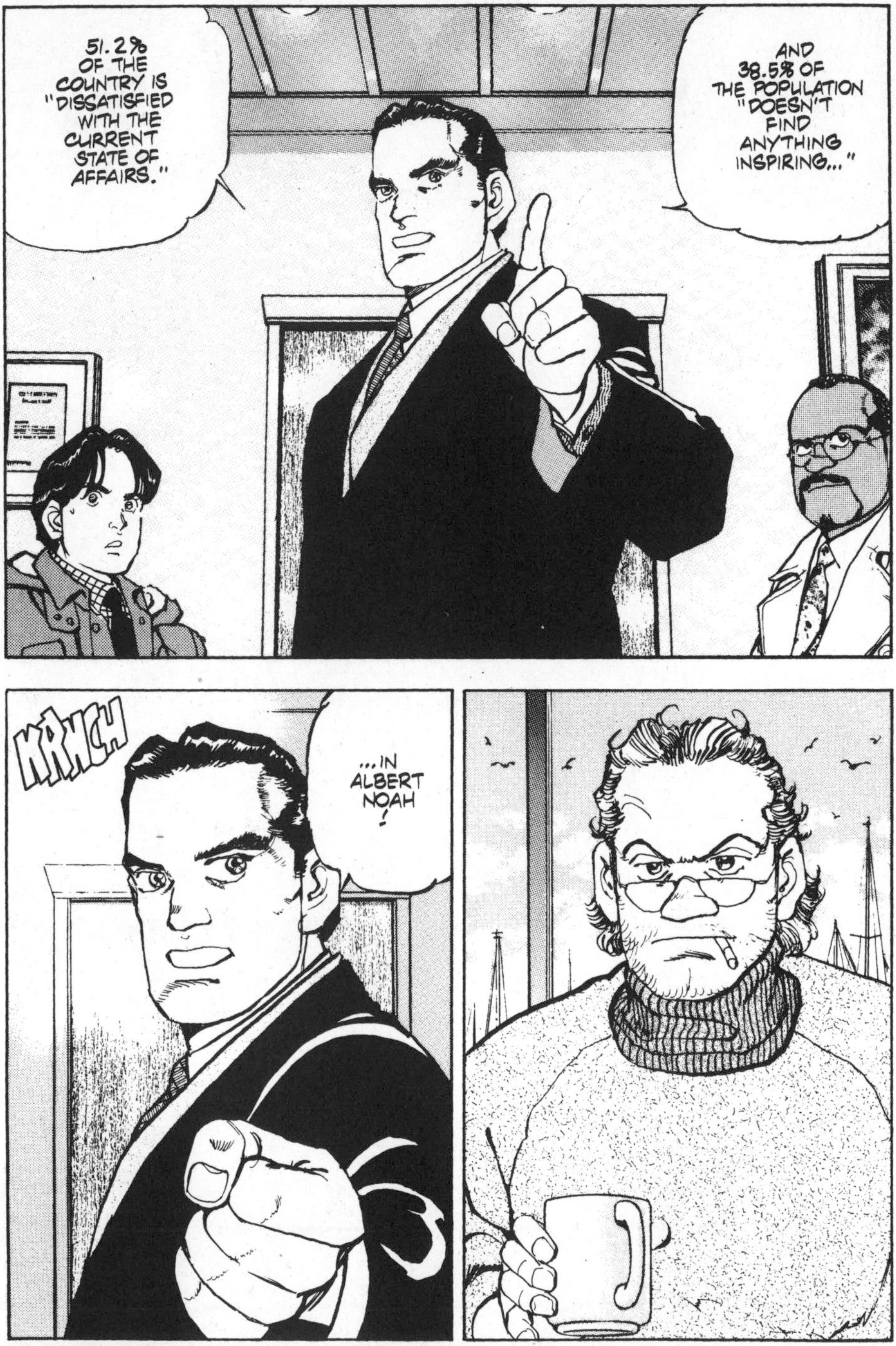
51.2% OF THE COUNTRY IS "DISSATISFIED WITH THE CURRENT STATE OF AFFAIRS."
AND 38.5% OF THE POPULATION "DOESN'T FIND ANYTHING INSPIRING..."
KRNCH
...IN ALBERT NOAH!

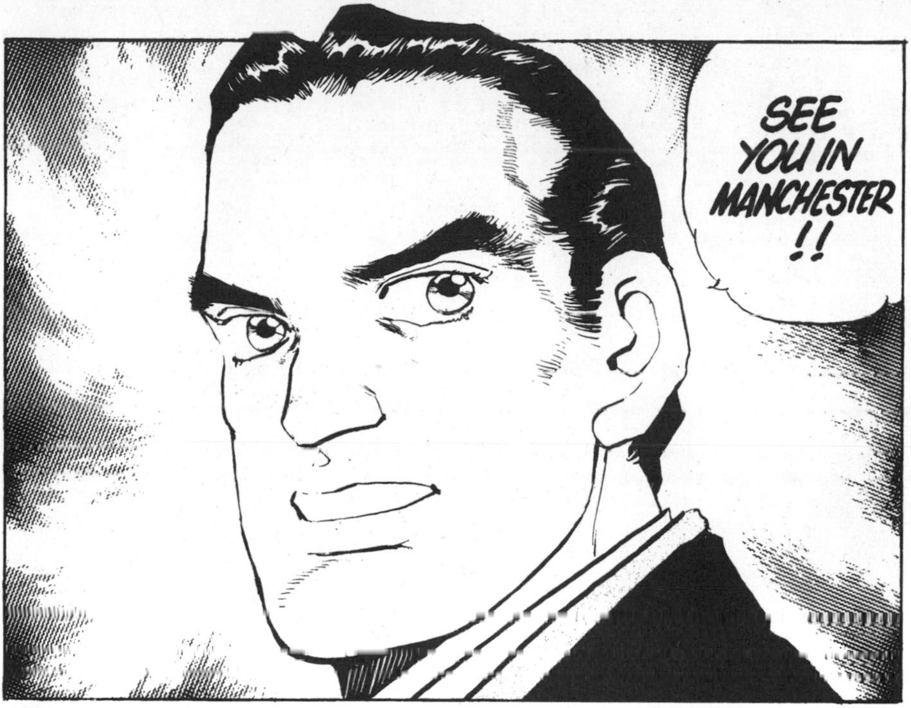
SEE YOU IN MANCHESTER !!
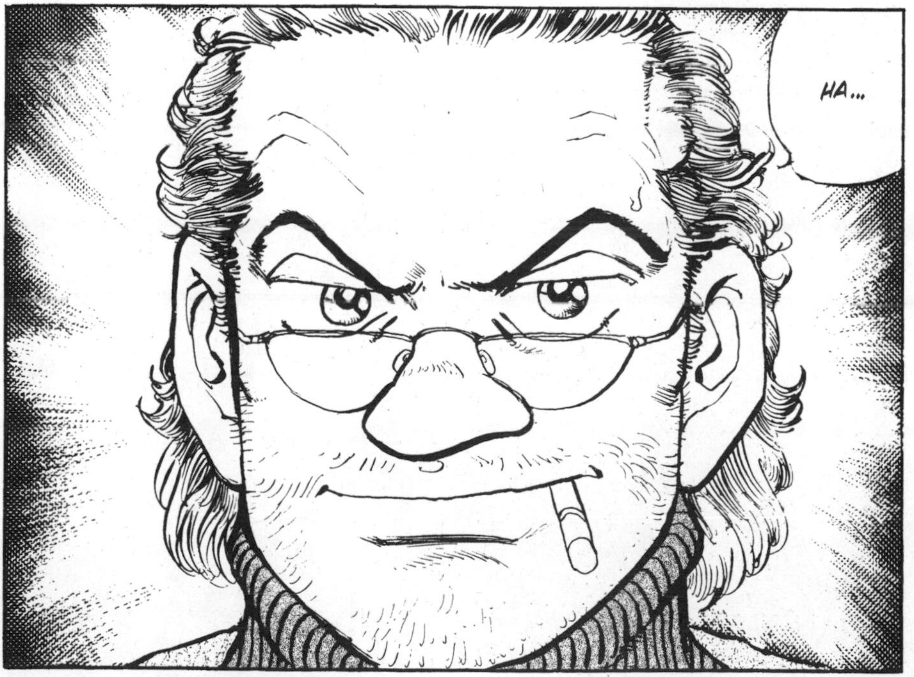
HA...

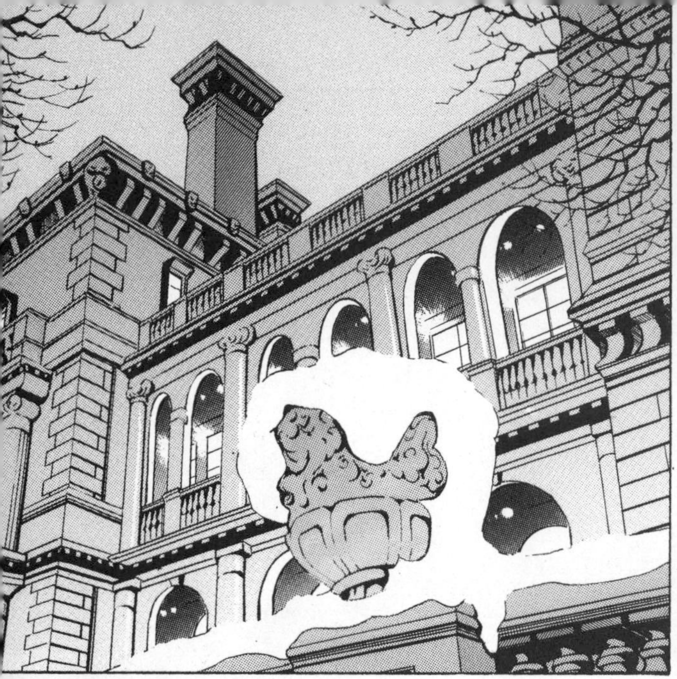

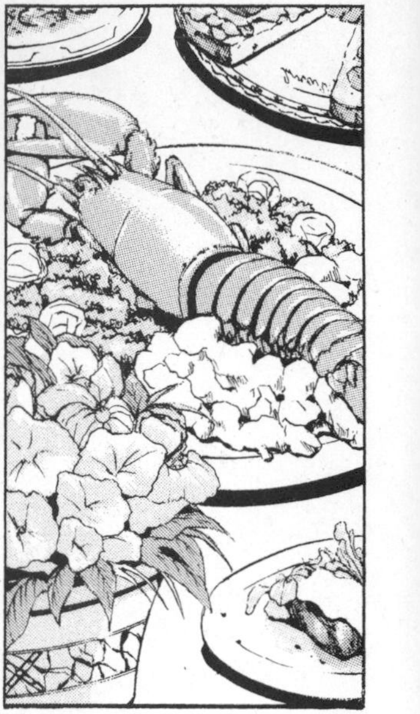

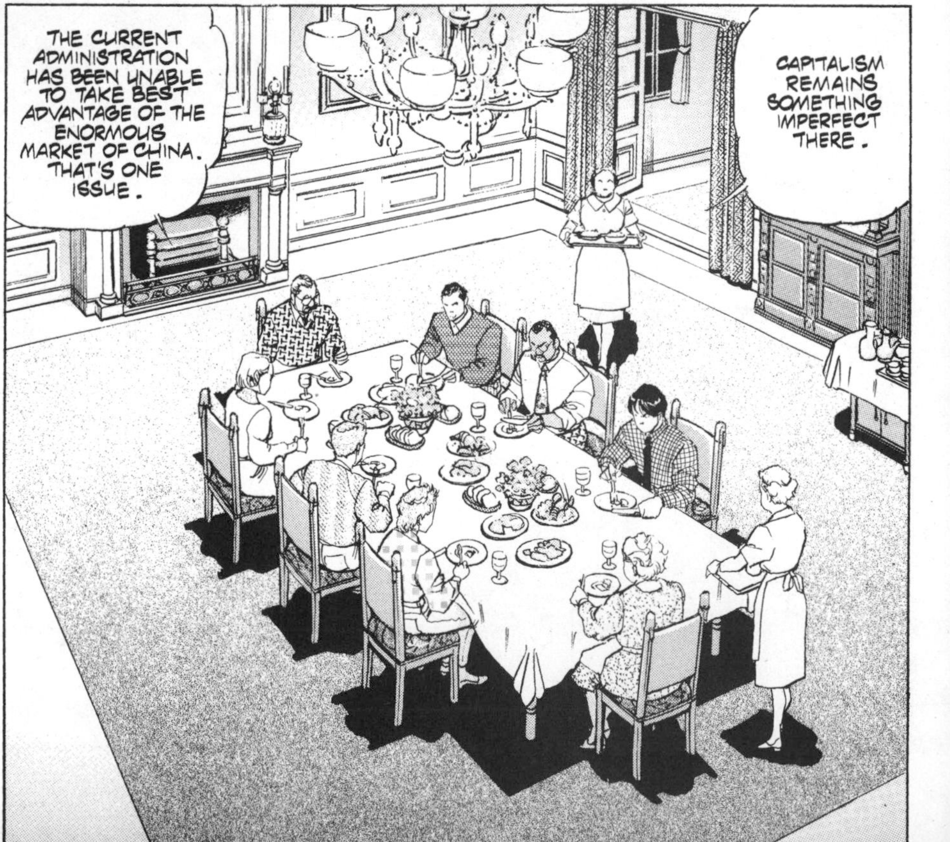
THE CURRENT ADMINISTRATION HAS BEEN UNABLE TO TAKE BEST ADVANTAGE OF THE ENORMOUS MARKET OF CHINA. THAT'S ONE ISSUE.
CAPITALISM REMAINS SOMETHING IMPERFECT THERE.

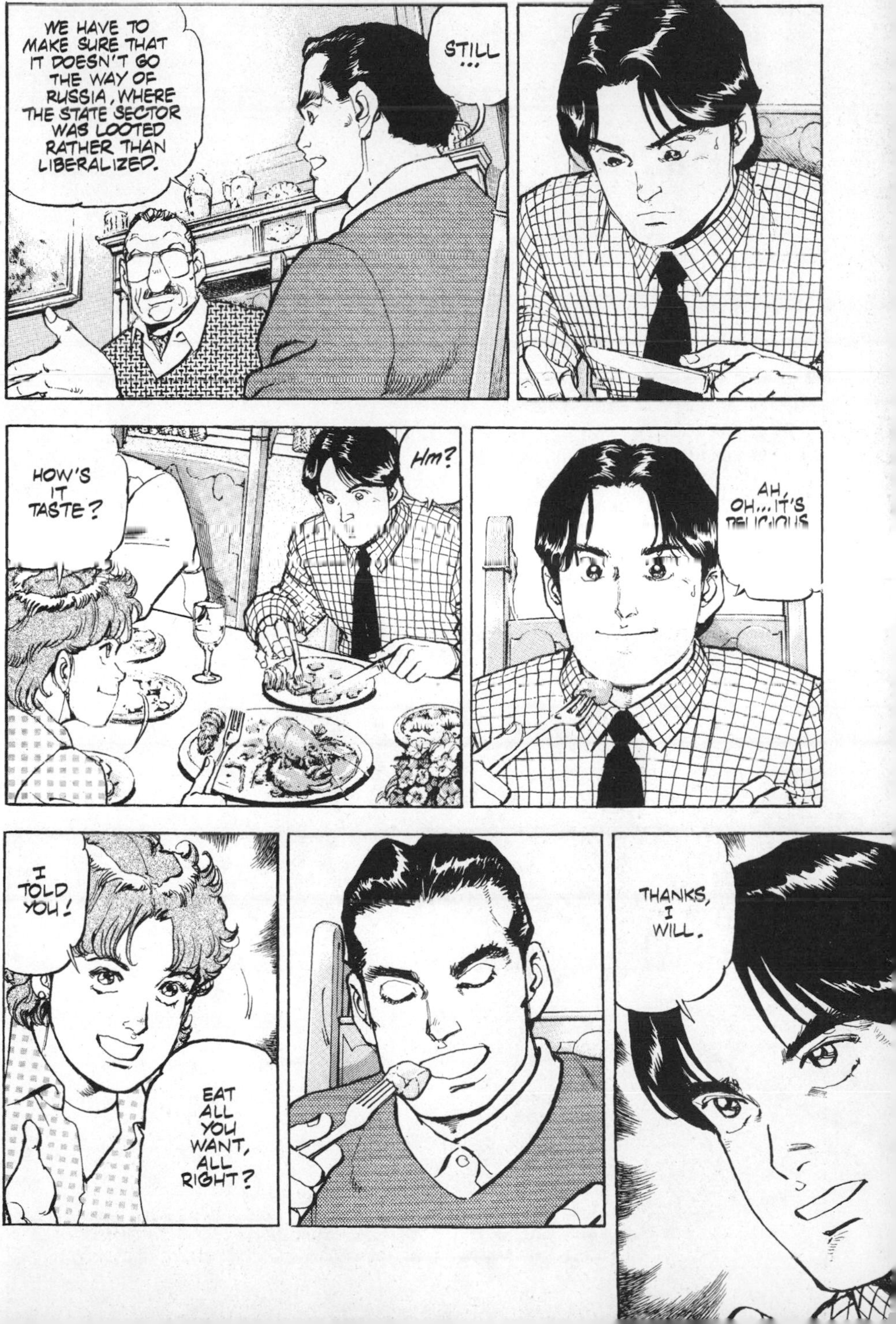
WE HAVE TO MAKE SURE THAT IT DOESN'T GO THE WAY OF RUSSIA, WHERE THE STATE SECTOR WAS LOOTED RATHER THAN LIBERALIZED.
STILL ...
HOW'S IT TASTE?
Hm?
AH, OH... IT'S DELICIOUS
I TOLD YOU!
EAT ALL YOU WANT, ALL RIGHT?
THANKS, I WILL.

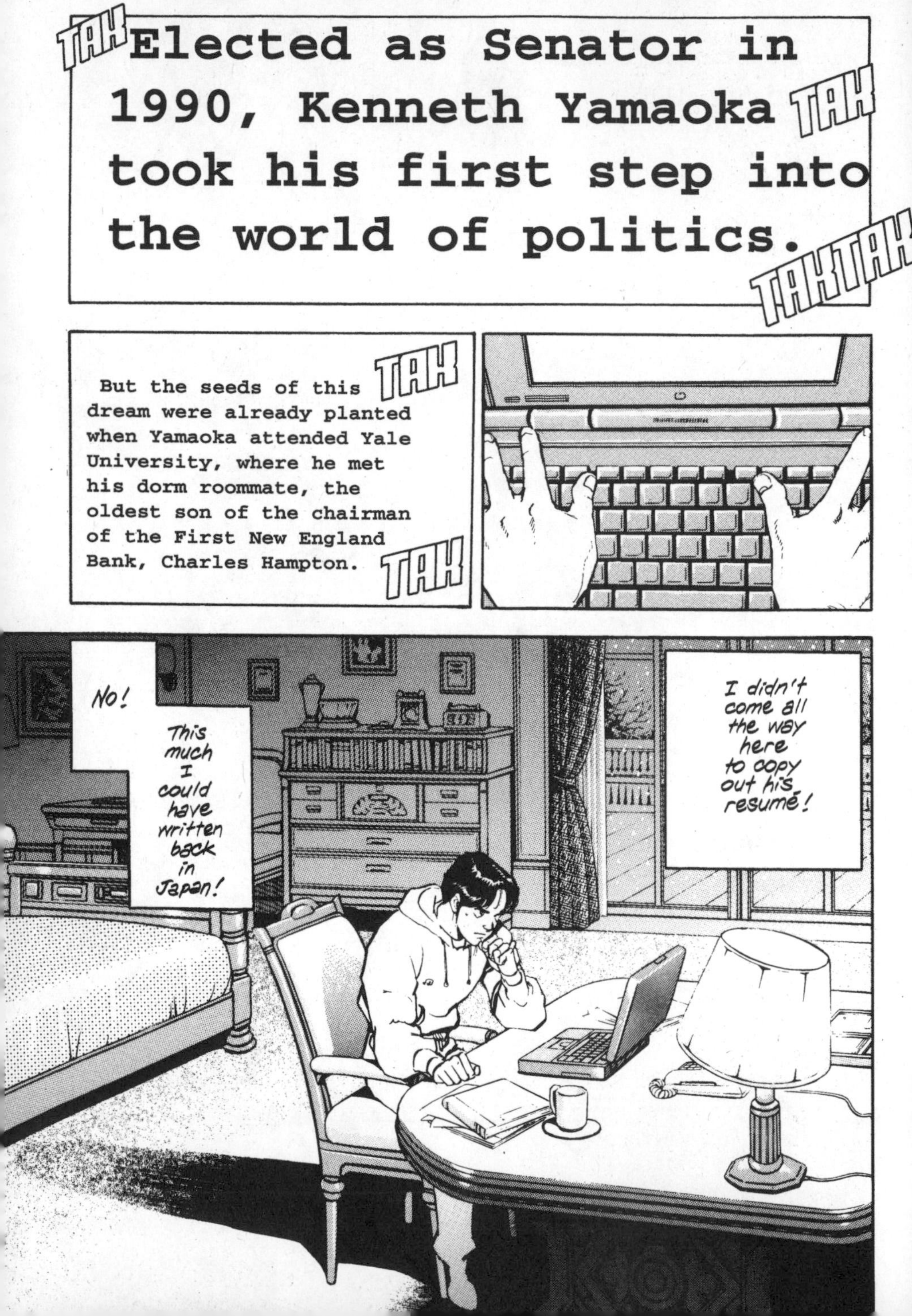
TAK
Elected as Senator in 1990, Kenneth Yamaoka took his first step into the world of politics.
TAK
TAKTAK
But the seeds of this dream were already planted when Yamaoka attended Yale University, where he met his dorm roommate, the oldest son of the chairman of the First New England Bank, Charles Hampton.
TAK
TAK
No!
This much I could have written back in Japan!
I didn't come all the way here to copy out his resumé!

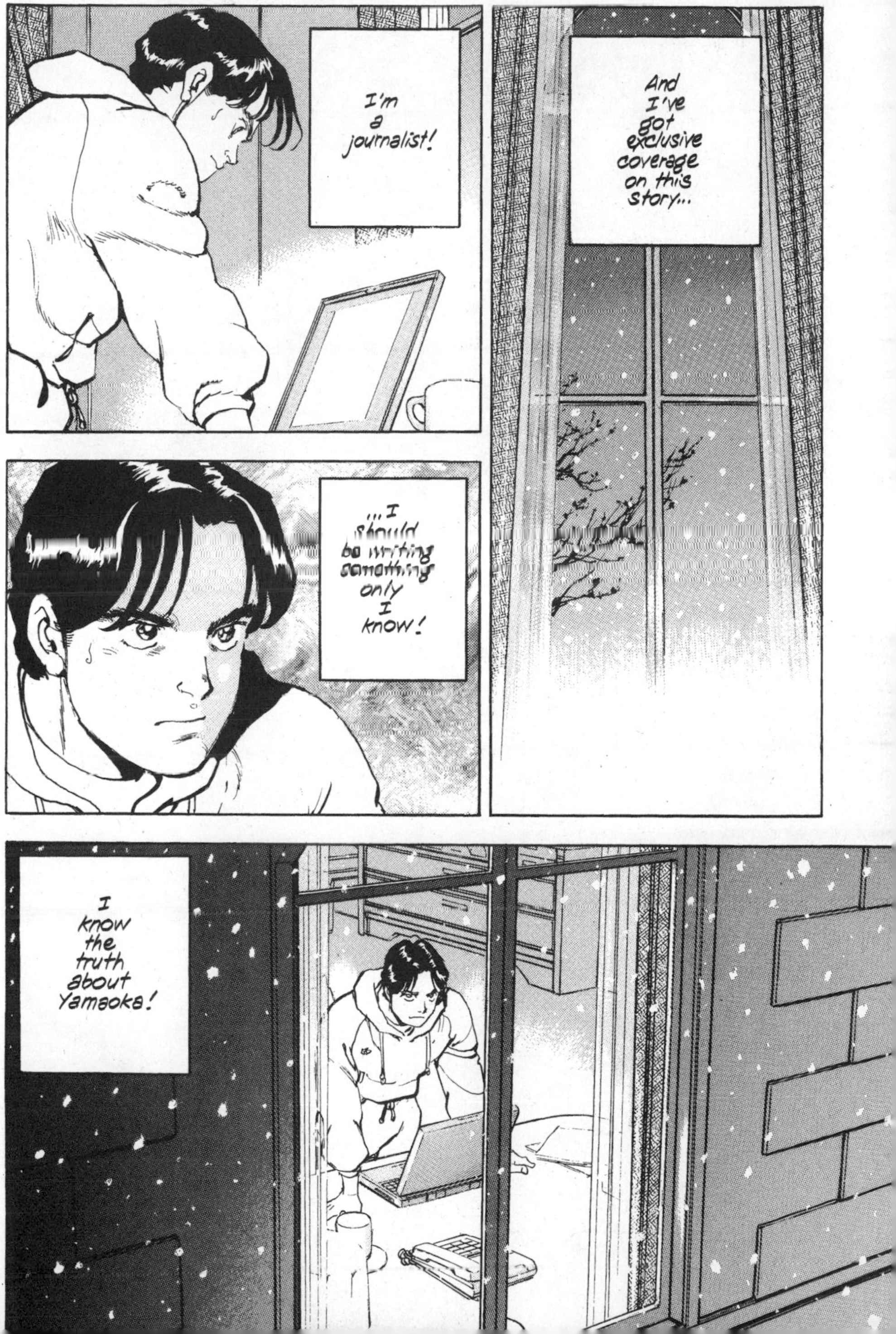
I'm a journalist!
...I should be writing something only I know!
And I've got exclusive coverage on this story...
I know the truth about Yamaoka!

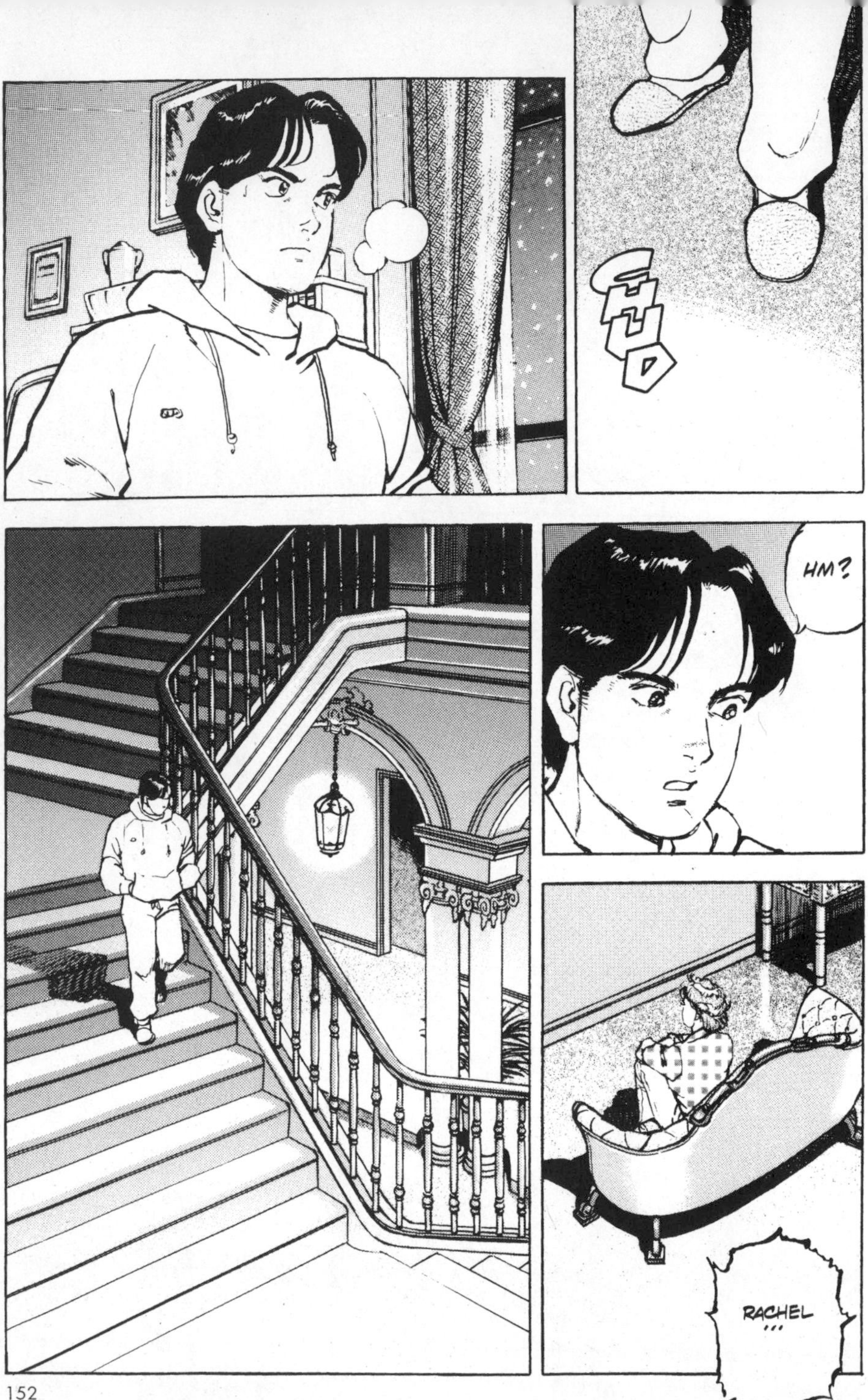
THUD
HM?
RACHEL ...

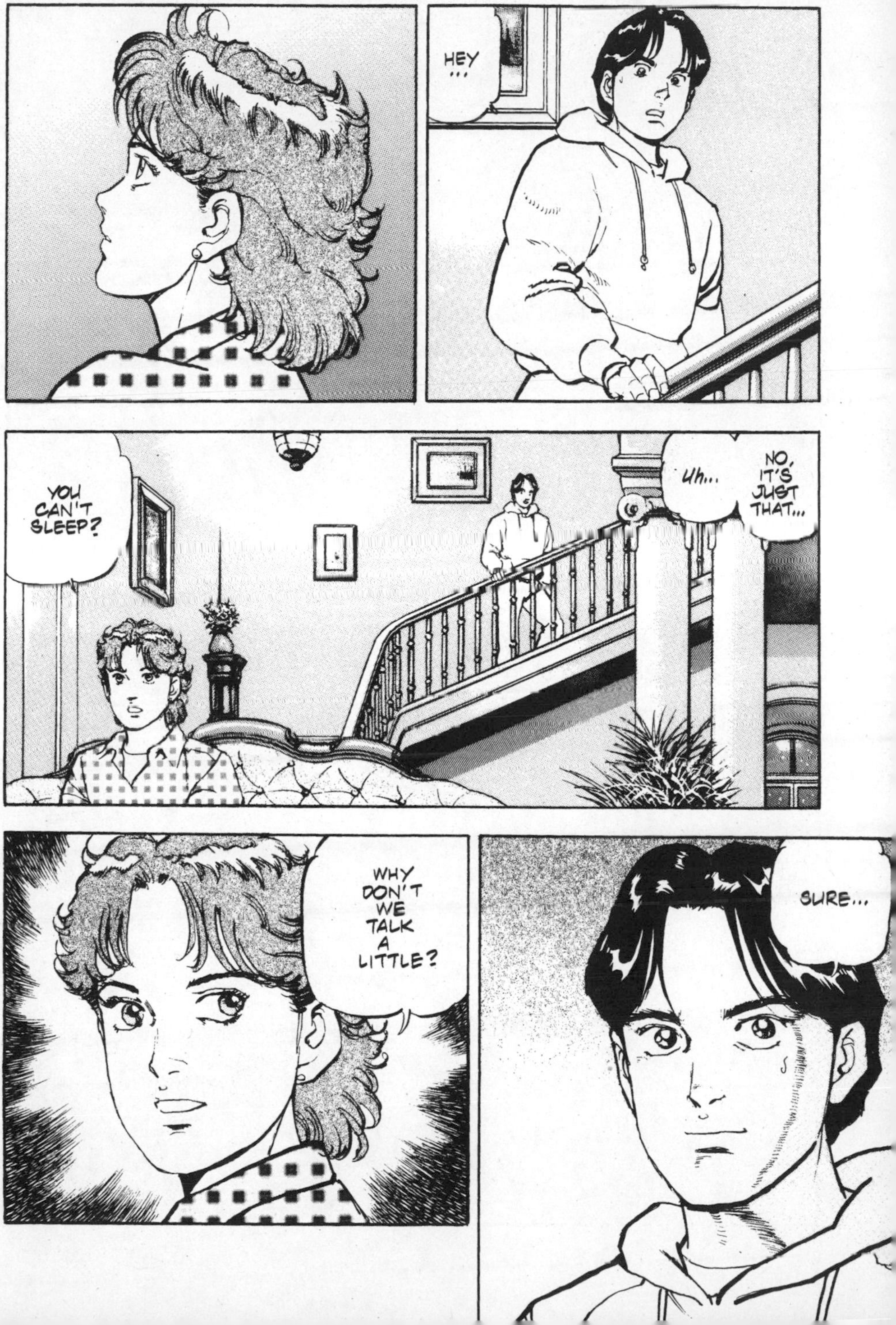
HEY ...
YOU CAN'T SLEEP?
Uh...
NO, IT'S JUST THAT...
WHY DON'T WE TALK A LITTLE?
SURE...

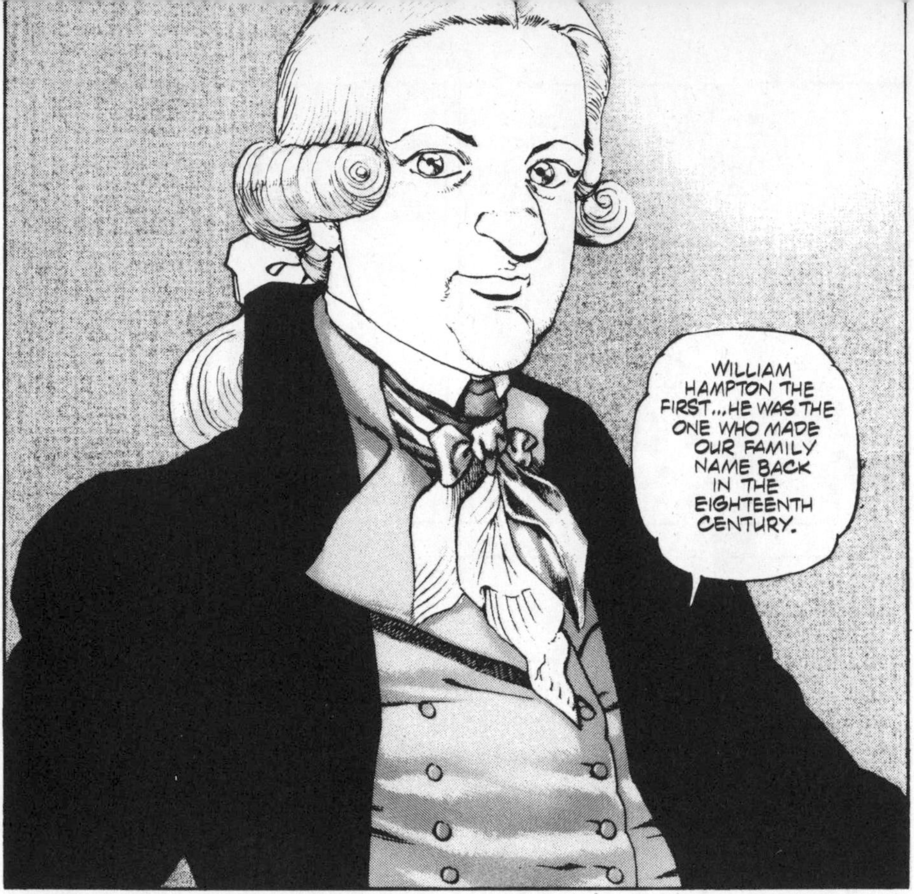
WILLIAM HAMPTON THE FIRST...HE WAS THE ONE WHO MADE OUR FAMILY NAME BACK IN THE EIGHTEENTH CENTURY.
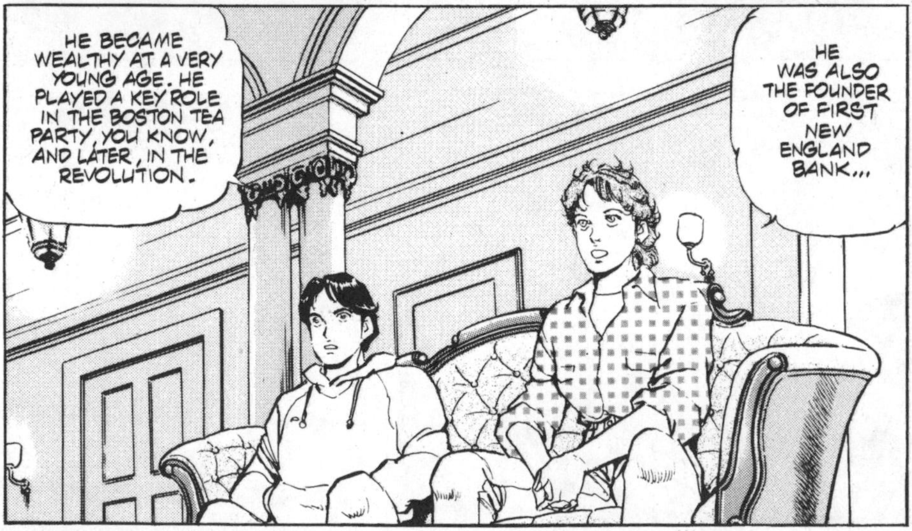
HE BECAME WEALTHY AT A VERY YOUNG AGE. HE PLAYED A KEY ROLE IN THE BOSTON TEA PARTY, YOU KNOW, AND LATER, IN THE REVOLUTION.
HE WAS ALSO THE FOUNDER OF FIRST NEW ENGLAND BANK...

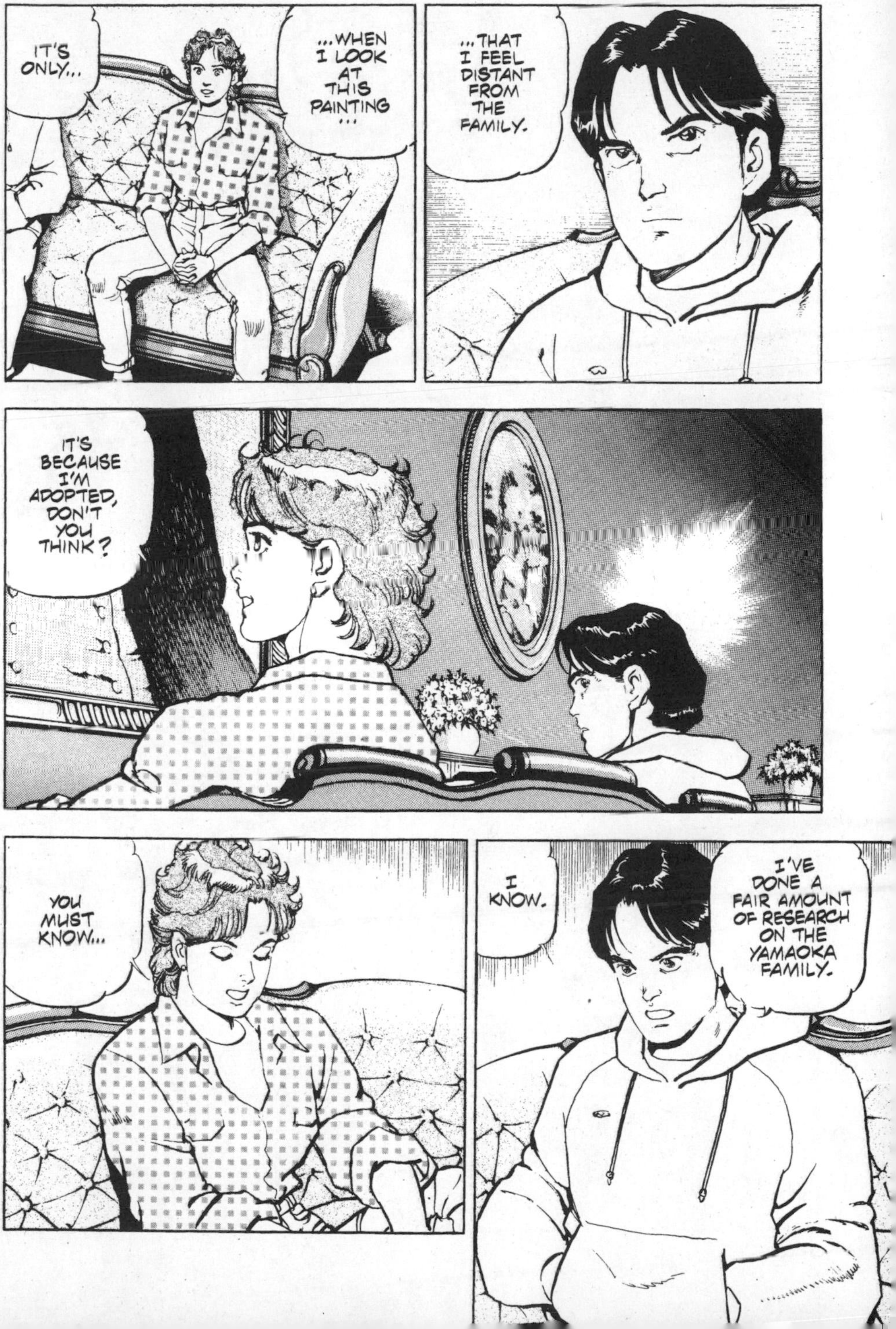
IT'S ONLY...
...WHEN I LOOK AT THIS PAINTING...
...THAT I FEEL DISTANT FROM THE FAMILY.
IT'S BECAUSE I'M ADOPTED, DON'T YOU THINK?
YOU MUST KNOW...
I KNOW.
I'VE DONE A FAIR AMOUNT OF RESEARCH ON THE YAMAOKA FAMILY.

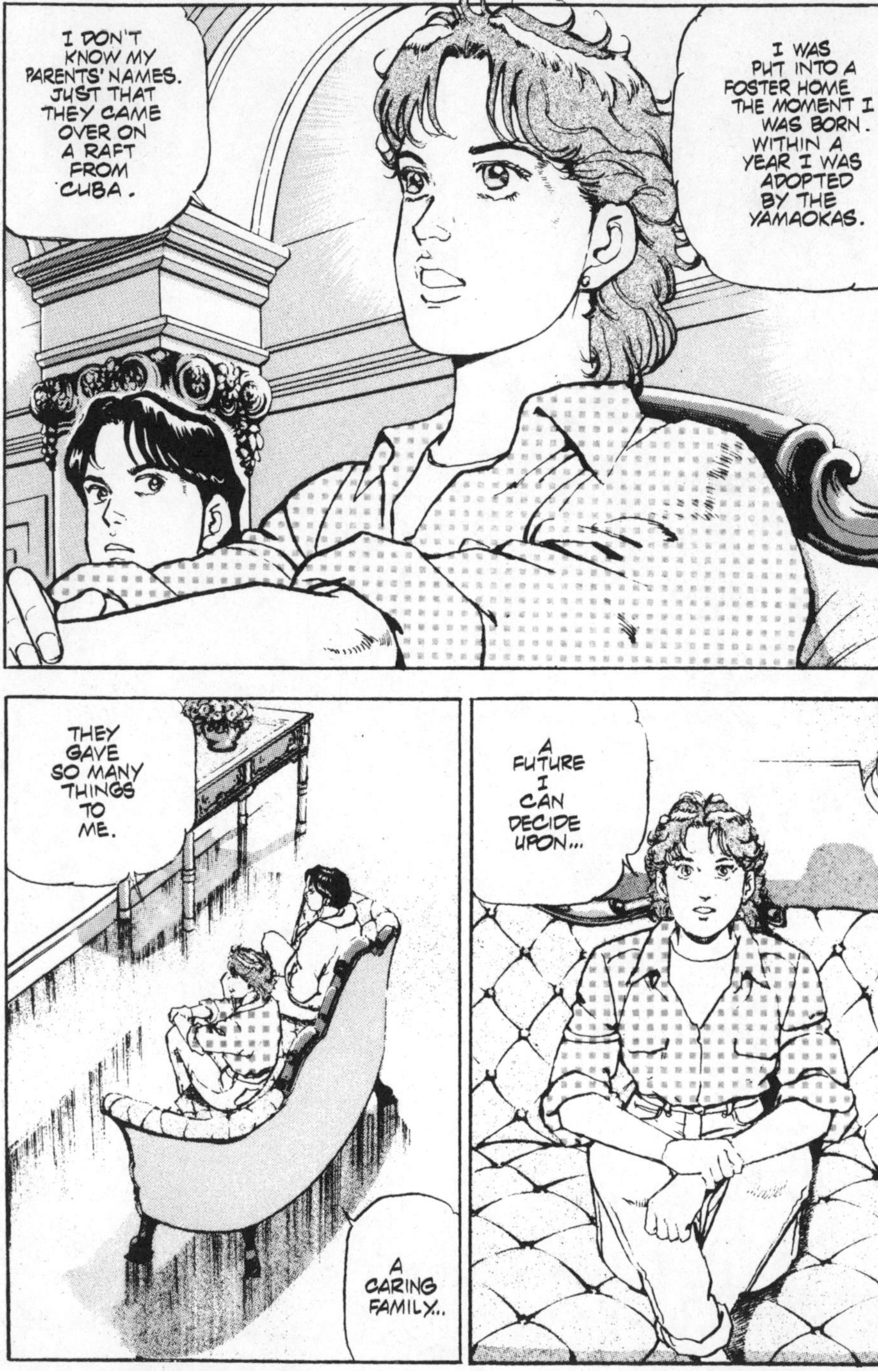
I DON'T KNOW MY PARENTS' NAMES. JUST THAT THEY CAME OVER ON A RAFT FROM CUBA.
I WAS PUT INTO A FOSTER HOME THE MOMENT I WAS BORN. WITHIN A YEAR I WAS ADOPTED BY THE YAMAOKAS.
THEY GAVE SO MANY THINGS TO ME.
A CARING FAMILY...
A FUTURE I CAN DECIDE UPON...

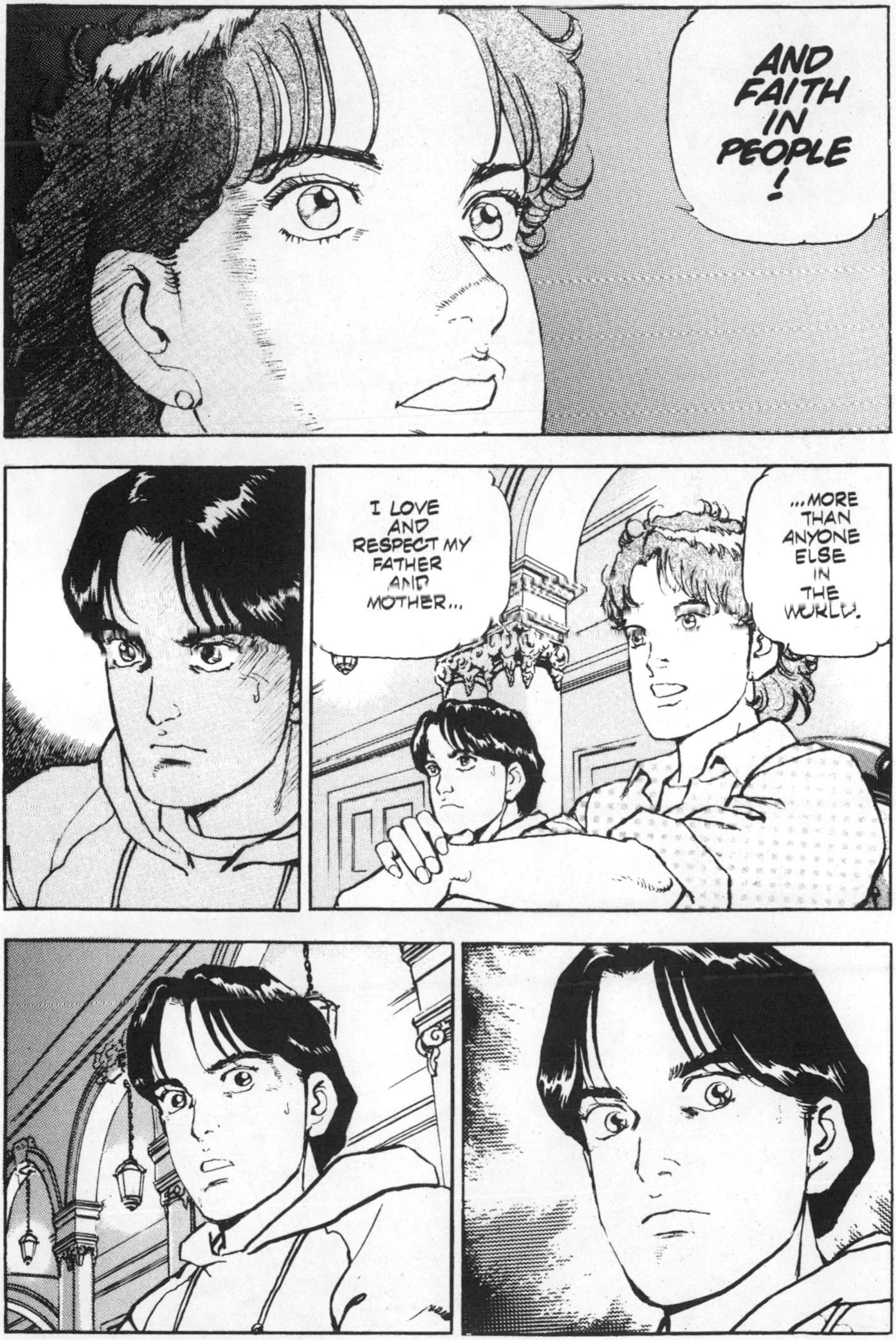
AND FAITH IN PEOPLE!
I LOVE AND RESPECT MY FATHER AND MOTHER...
...MORE THAN ANYONE ELSE IN THE WORLD.

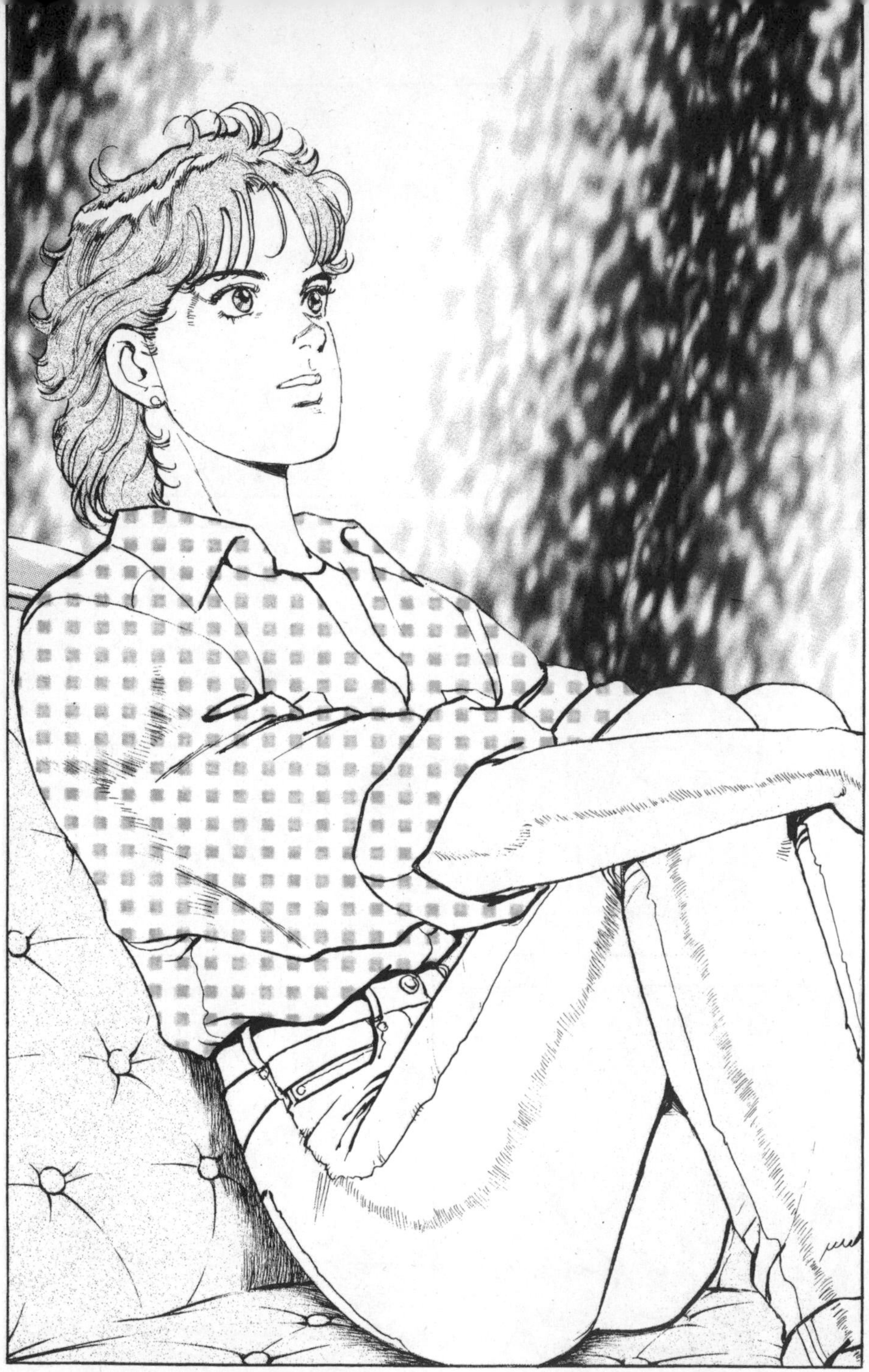

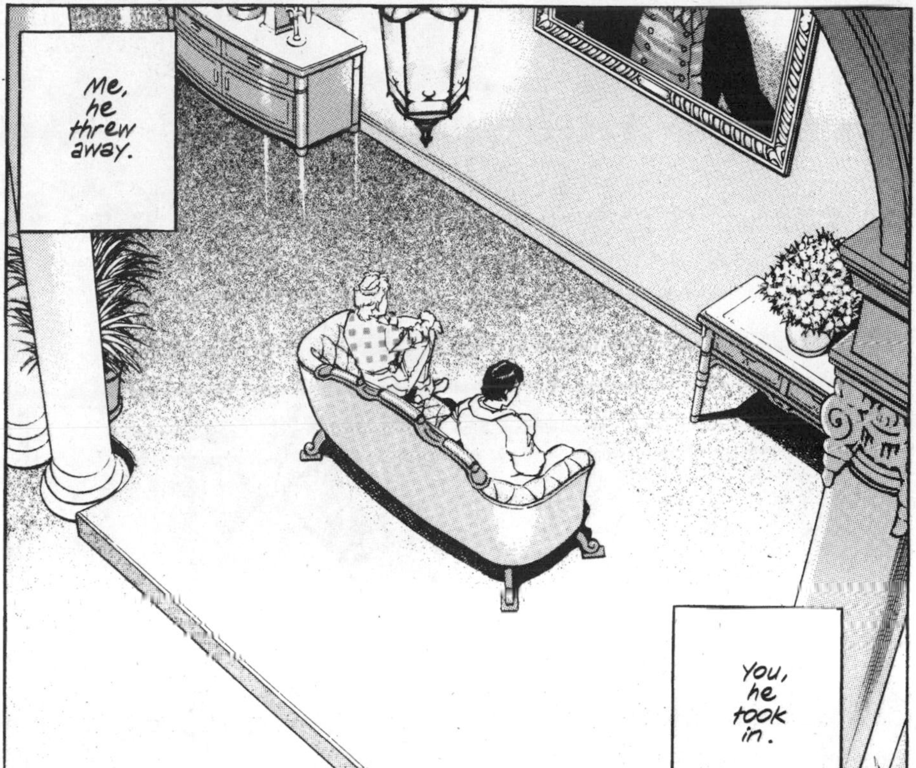
Me, he threw away.
You, he took in.

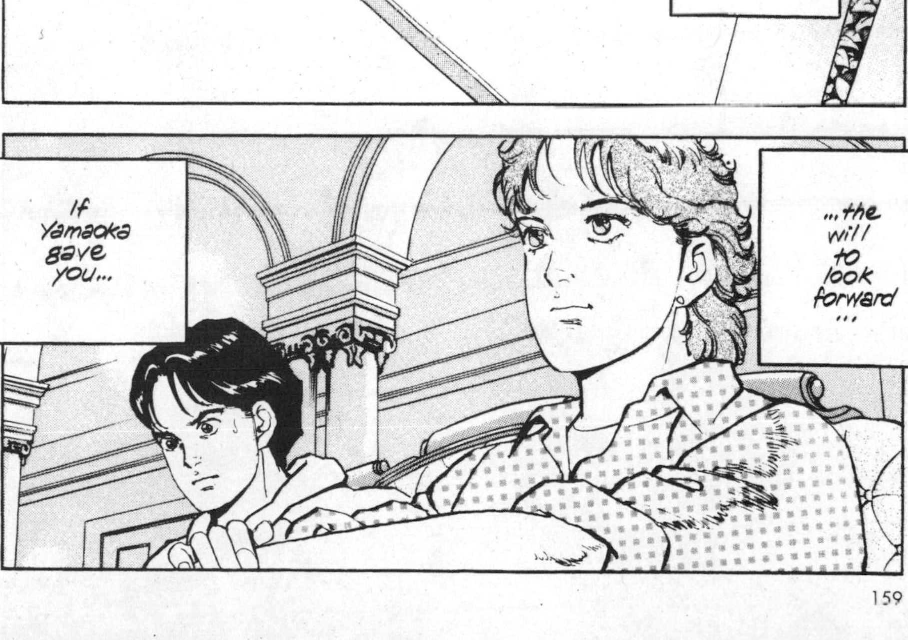
If Yamaoka gave you...
...the will to look forward ...

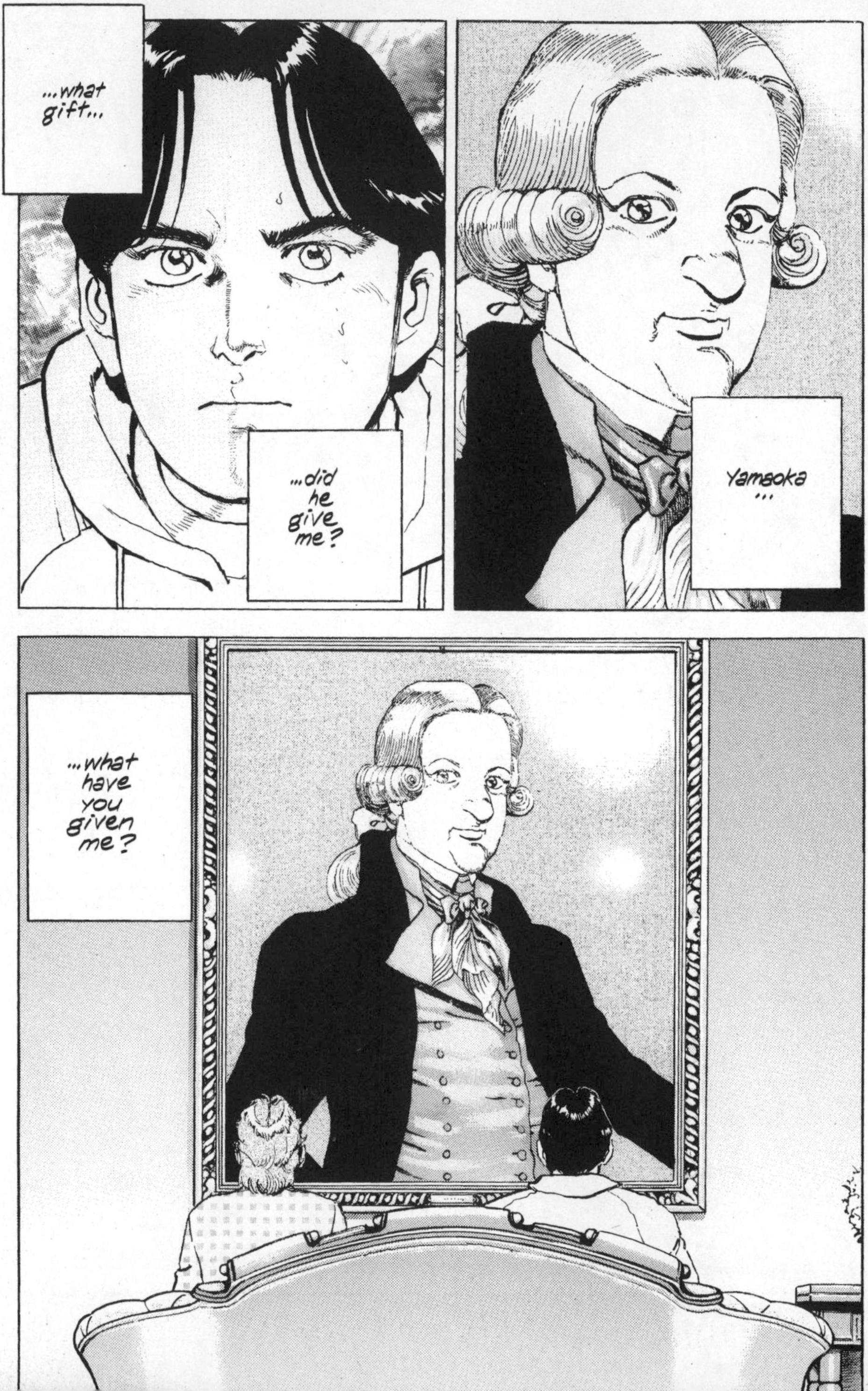
...what gift...
...did he give me?
Yamaoka ...
...what have you given me?

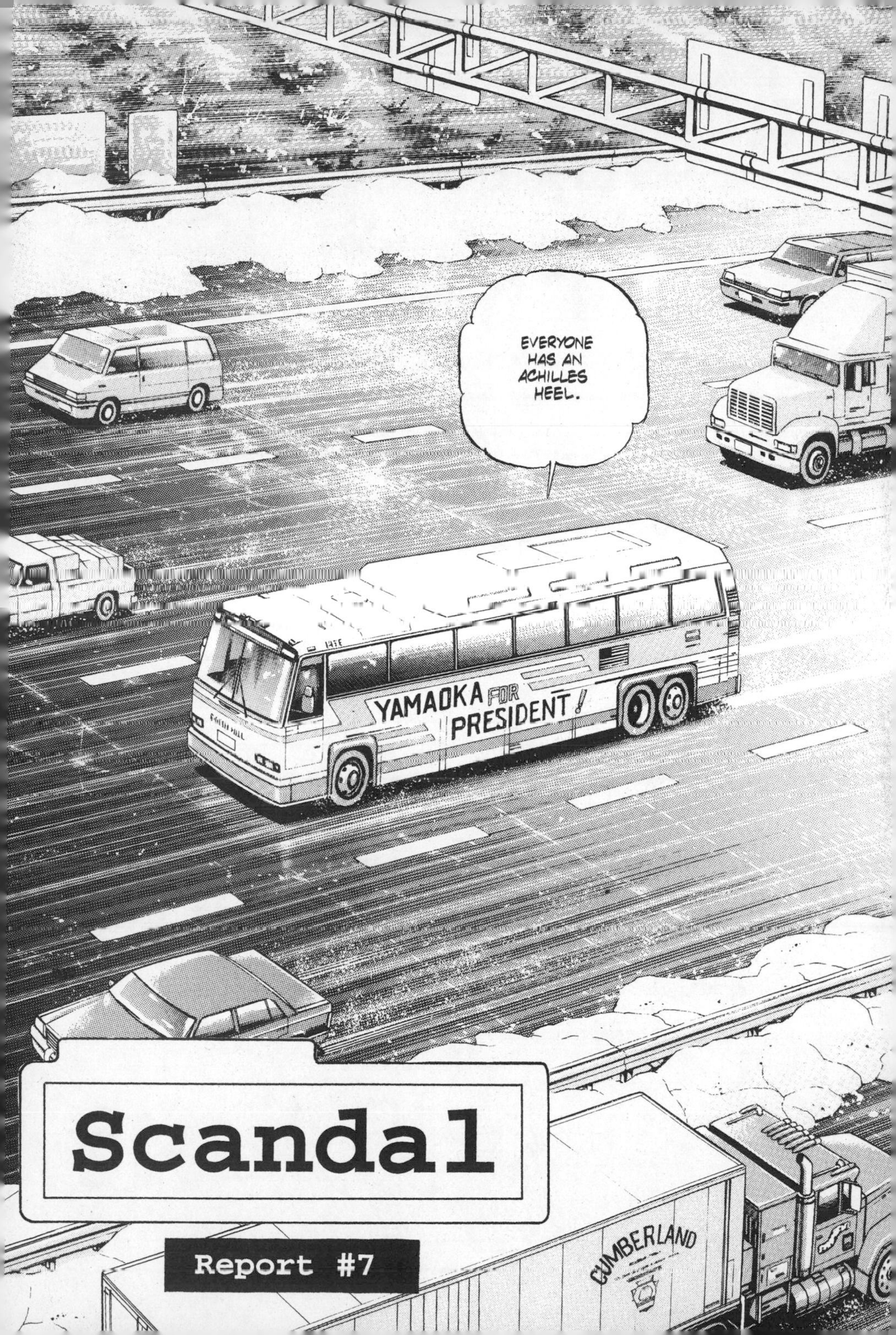
EVERYONE HAS AN ACHILLES HEEL.
YAMAOKA FOR PRESIDENT!
Scandal
Report #7
CUMBERLAND

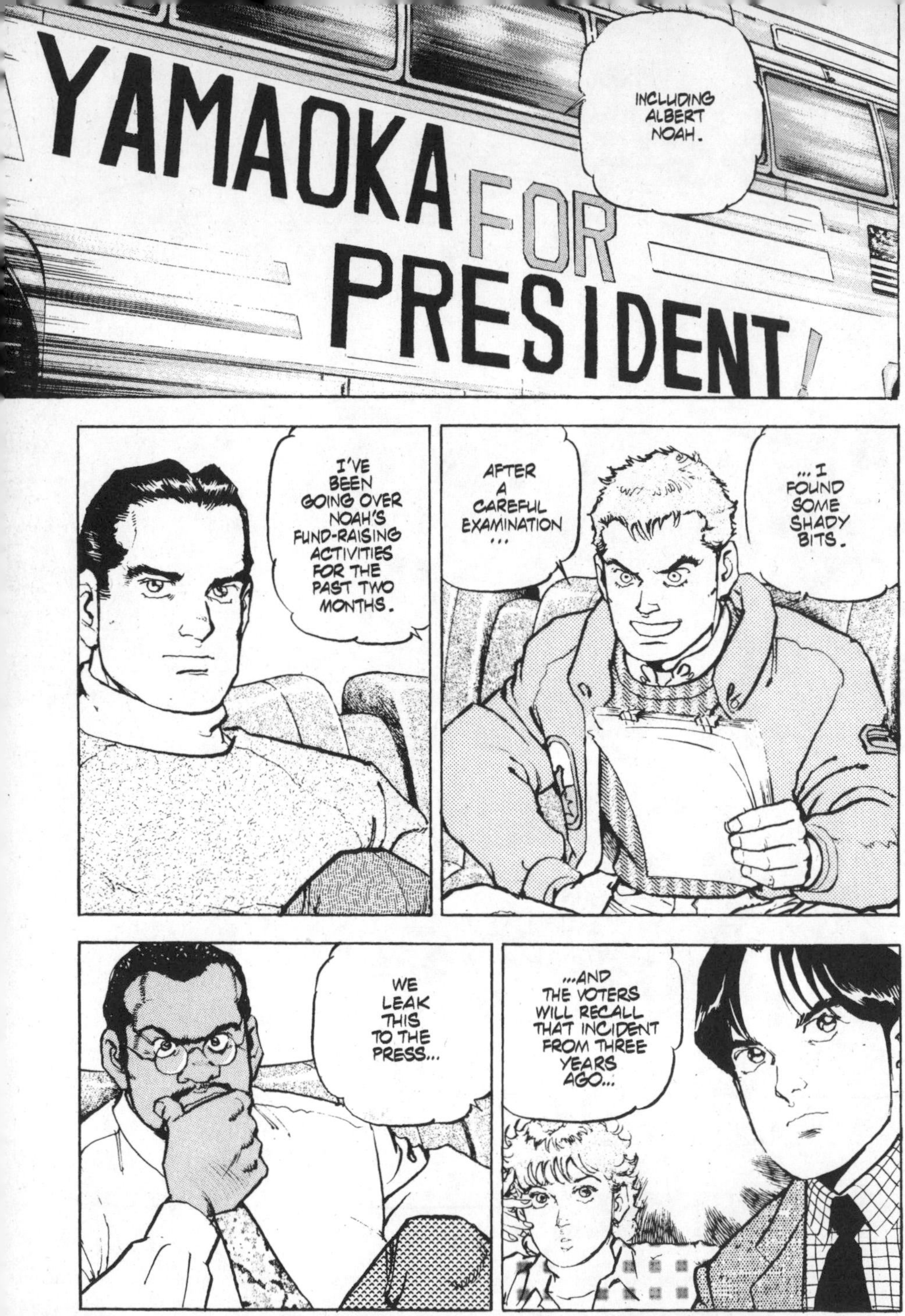
YAMAOKA FOR PRESIDENT!
INCLUDING ALBERT NOAH.
I'VE BEEN GOING OVER NOAH'S FUND-RAISING ACTIVITIES FOR THE PAST TWO MONTHS.
AFTER A CAREFUL EXAMINATION...
...I FOUND SOME SHADY BITS.
WE LEAK THIS TO THE PRESS...
...AND THE VOTERS WILL RECALL THAT INCIDENT FROM THREE YEARS AGO...

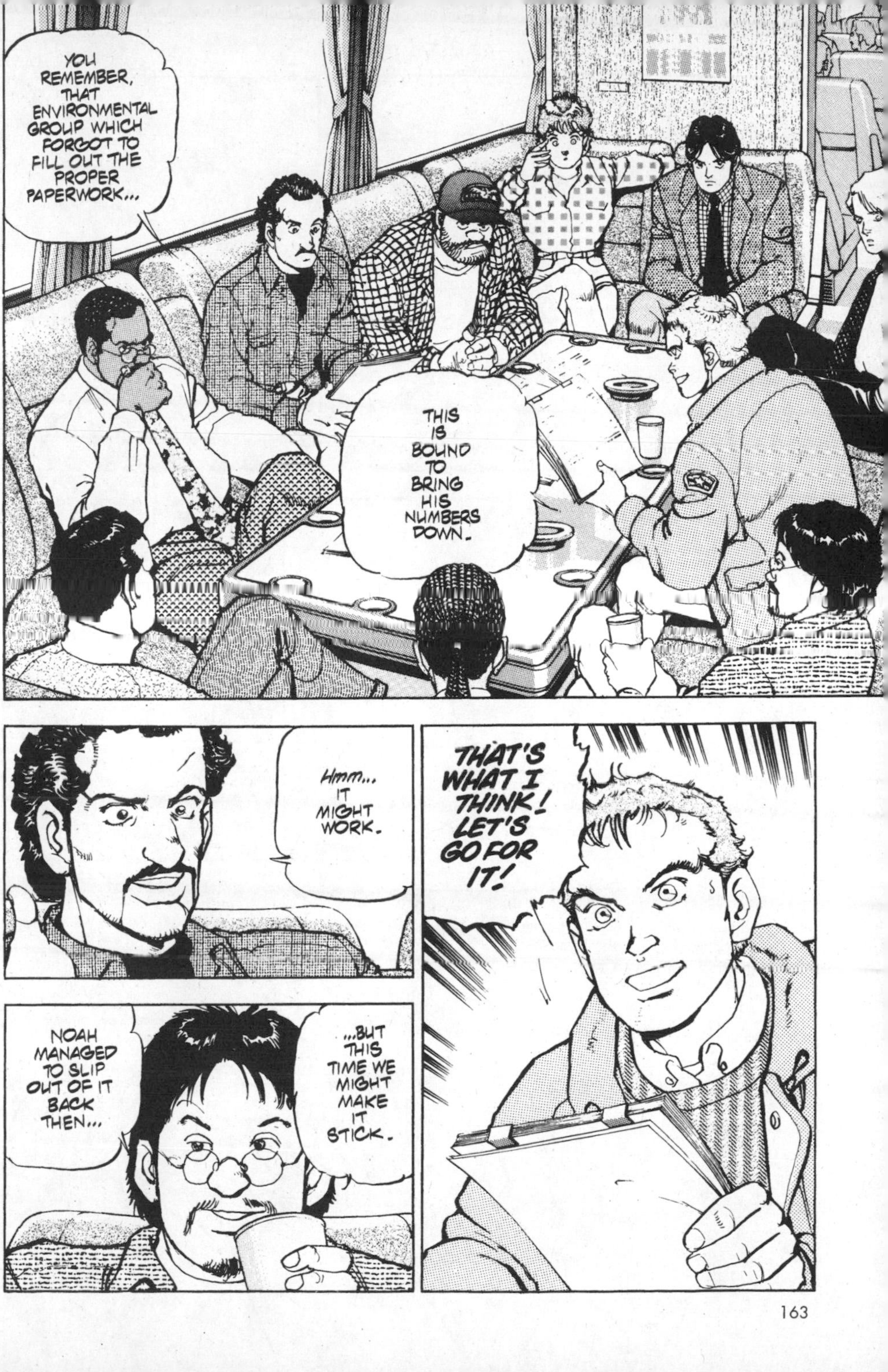
YOU REMEMBER, THAT ENVIRONMENTAL GROUP WHICH FORGOT TO FILL OUT THE PROPER PAPERWORK...
THIS IS BOUND TO BRING HIS NUMBERS DOWN.
Hmm... IT MIGHT WORK.
THAT'S WHAT I THINK! LET'S GO FOR IT!
NOAH MANAGED TO SLIP OUT OF IT BACK THEN...
...BUT THIS TIME WE MIGHT MAKE IT STICK.

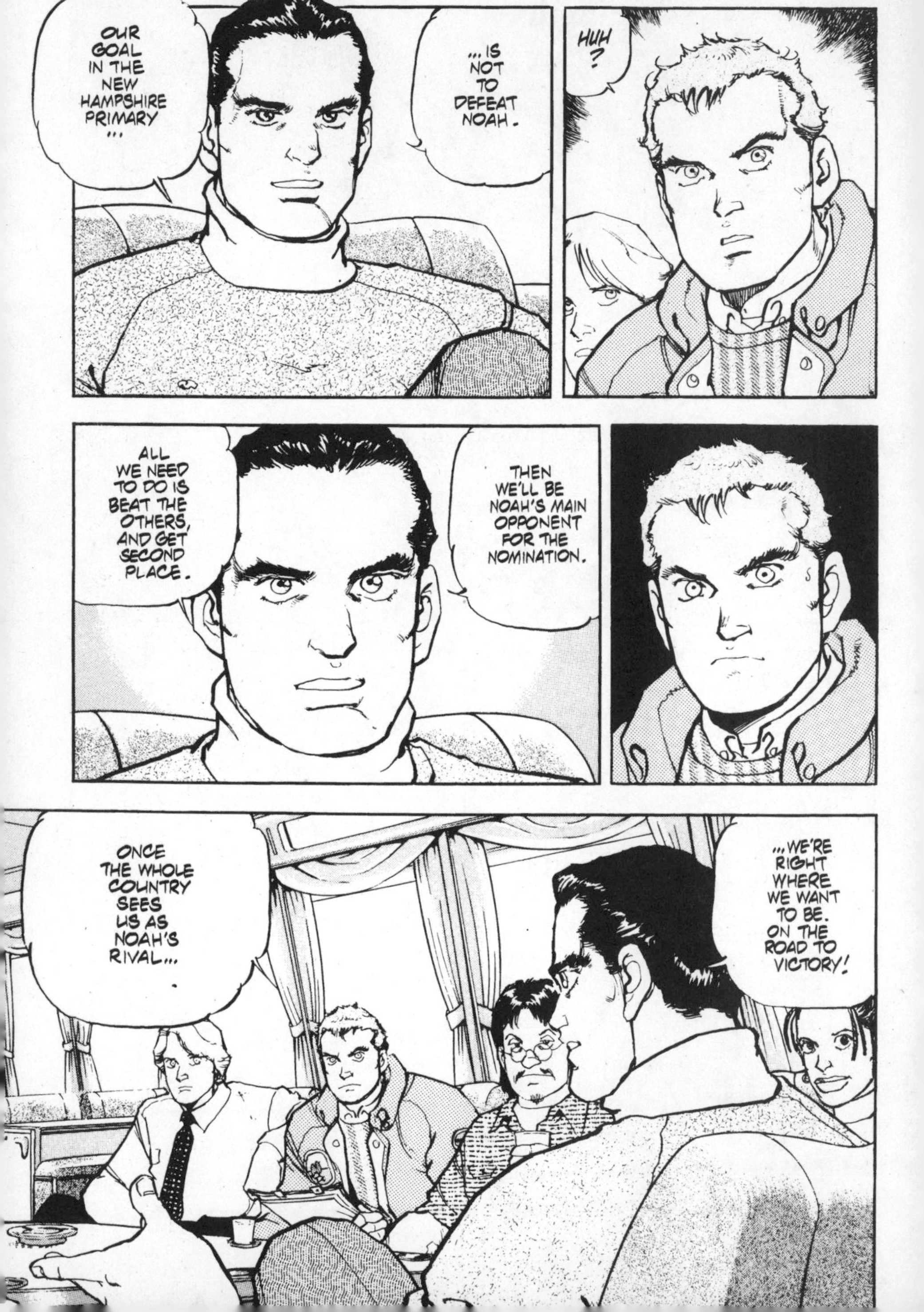
OUR GOAL IN THE NEW HAMPSHIRE PRIMARY...
...IS NOT TO DEFEAT NOAH.
HUH?
ALL WE NEED TO DO IS BEAT THE OTHERS, AND GET SECOND PLACE.
THEN WE'LL BE NOAH'S MAIN OPPONENT FOR THE NOMINATION.
ONCE THE WHOLE COUNTRY SEES US AS NOAH'S RIVAL...
...WE'RE RIGHT WHERE WE WANT TO BE. ON THE ROAD TO VICTORY!

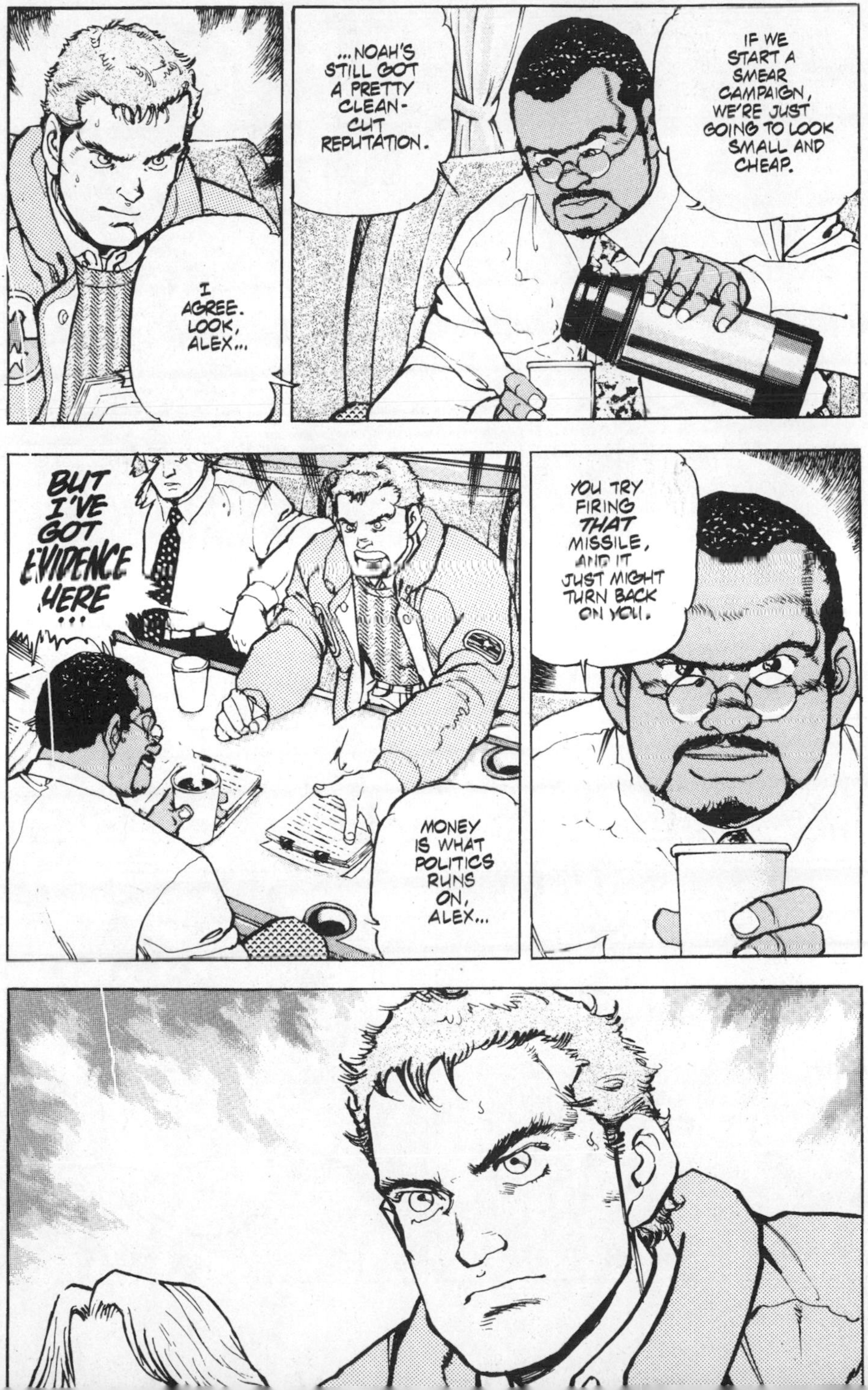
I AGREE. LOOK, ALEX...
...NOAH'S STILL GOT A PRETTY CLEAN-CUT REPUTATION.
IF WE START A SMEAR CAMPAIGN, WE'RE JUST GOING TO LOOK SMALL AND CHEAP.
BUT I'VE GOT EVIDENCE HERE...
MONEY IS WHAT POLITICS RUNS ON, ALEX...
YOU TRY FIRING *THAT* MISSILE, AND IT JUST MIGHT TURN BACK ON YOU.

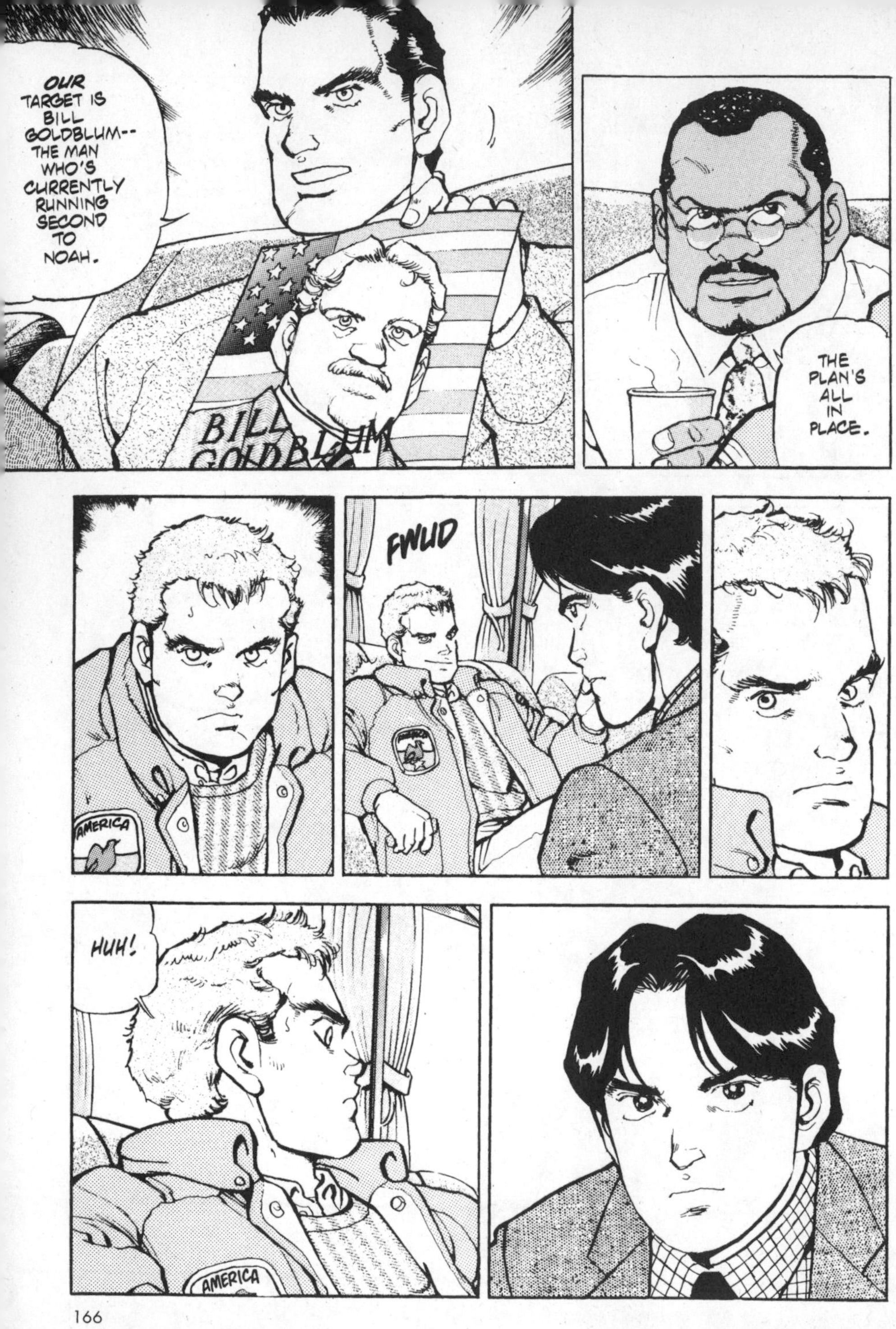
OUR TARGET IS BILL GOLDBLUM-- THE MAN WHO'S CURRENTLY RUNNING SECOND TO NOAH.
BILL GOLDBLUM
THE PLAN'S ALL IN PLACE.
FWUD
HUH!

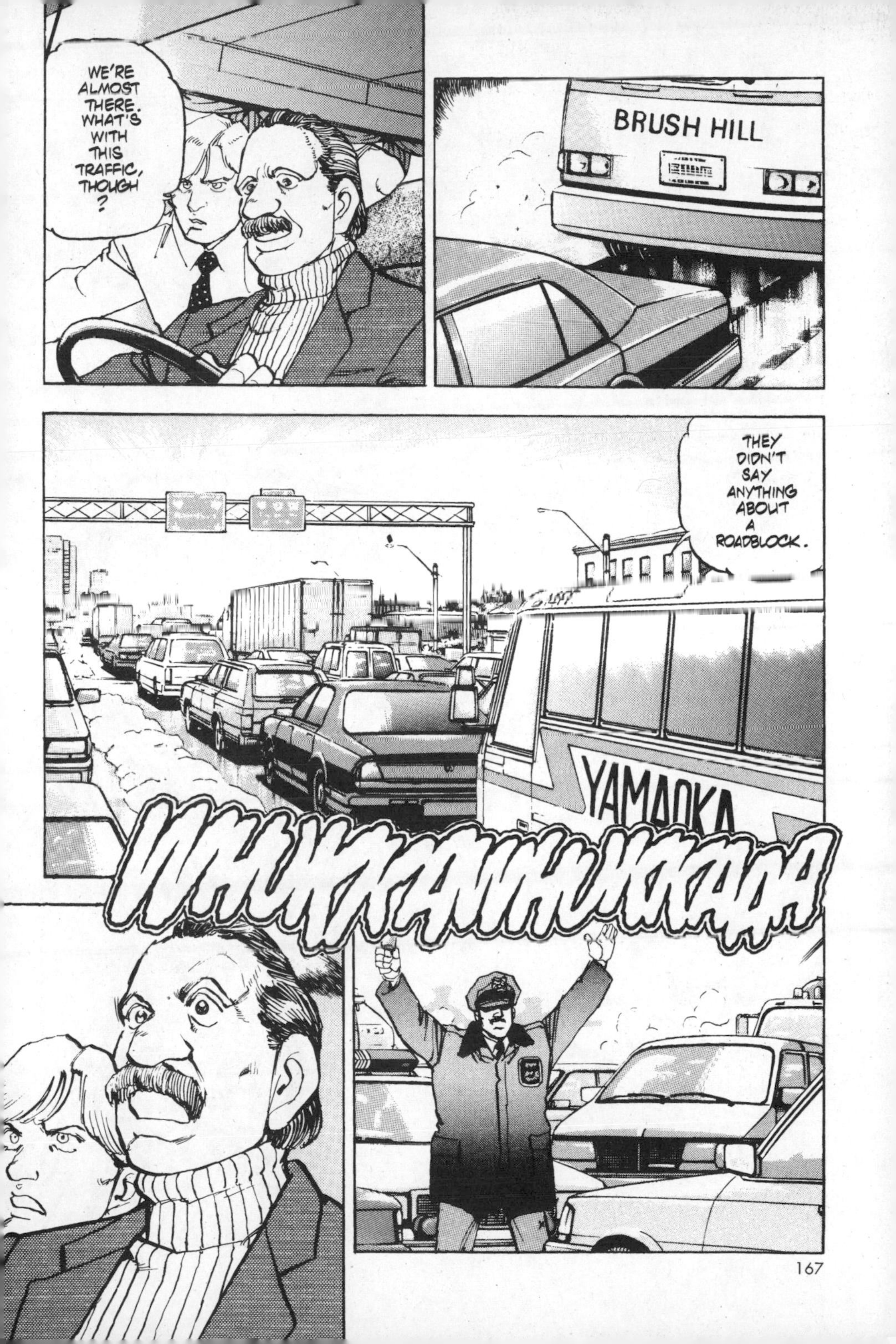
WE'RE ALMOST THERE. WHAT'S WITH THIS TRAFFIC, THOUGH?
BRUSH HILL
THEY DIDN'T SAY ANYTHING ABOUT A ROADBLOCK.
YAMAOKA

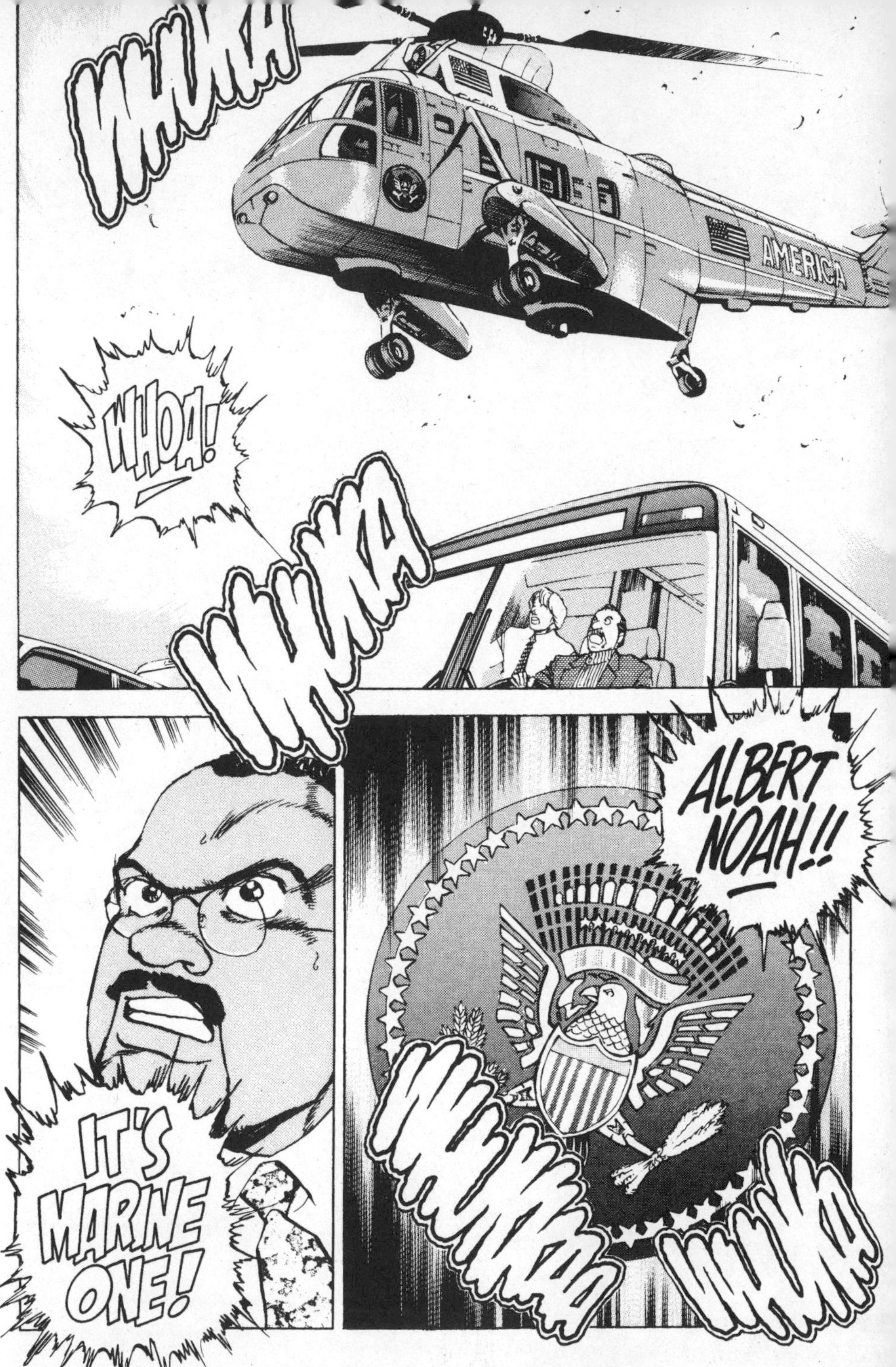
WHUKA
AMERICA
WHOA!
WHUKA
ALBERT NOAH!!
IT'S MARINE ONE!

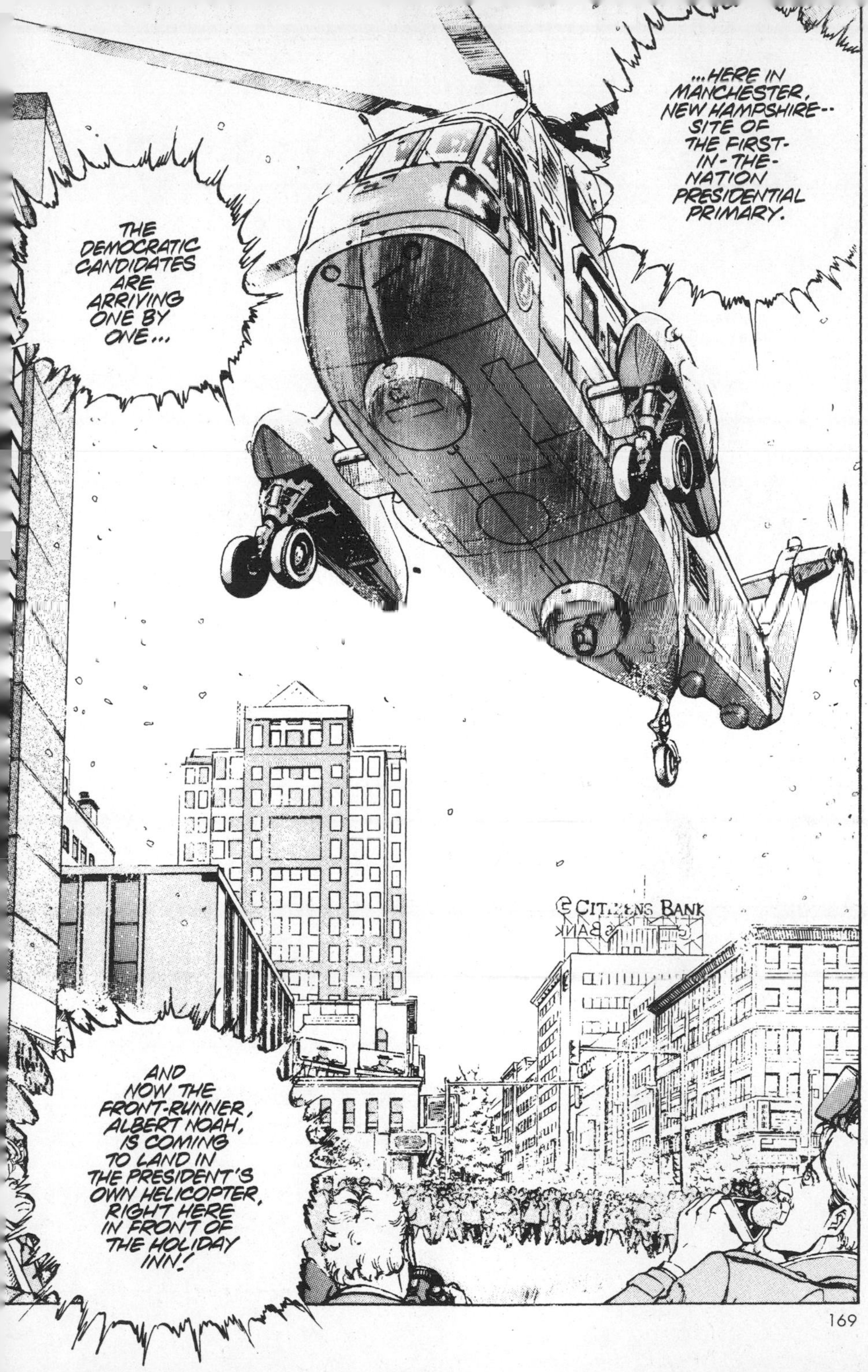
THE DEMOCRATIC CANDIDATES ARE ARRIVING ONE BY ONE...
...HERE IN MANCHESTER, NEW HAMPSHIRE-- SITE OF THE FIRST-IN-THE-NATION PRESIDENTIAL PRIMARY.
CITIZENS BANK
AND NOW THE FRONT-RUNNER, ALBERT NOAH, IS COMING TO LAND IN THE PRESIDENT'S OWN HELICOPTER, RIGHT HERE IN FRONT OF THE HOLIDAY INN!

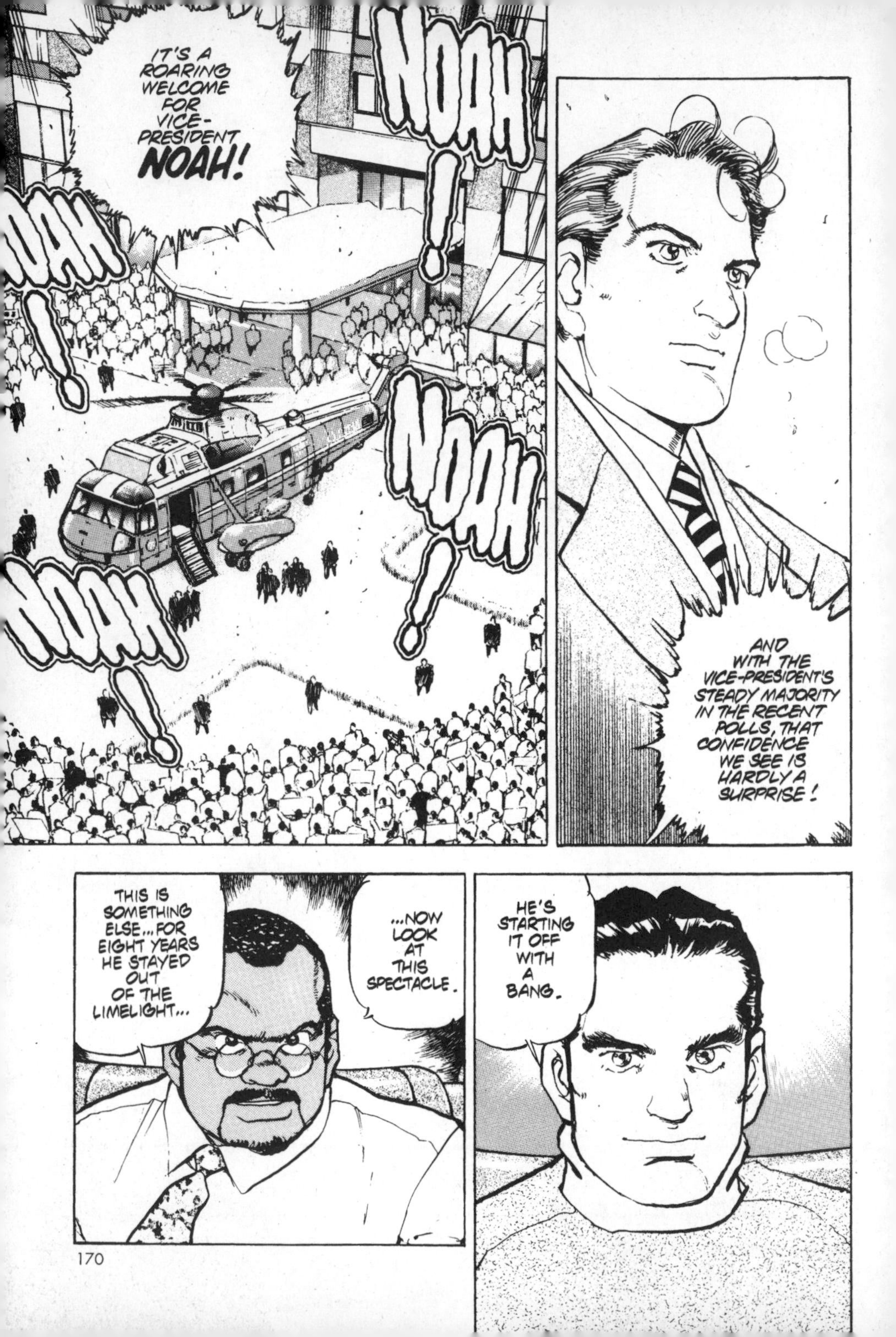
IT'S A ROARING WELCOME FOR VICE-PRESIDENT NOAH!
NOAH!
NOAH!
NOAH!
NOAH!
AND WITH THE VICE-PRESIDENT'S STEADY MAJORITY IN THE RECENT POLLS, THAT CONFIDENCE WE SEE IS HARDLY A SURPRISE!
THIS IS SOMETHING ELSE... FOR EIGHT YEARS HE STAYED OUT OF THE LIMELIGHT...
...NOW LOOK AT THIS SPECTACLE.
HE'S STARTING IT OFF WITH A BANG.

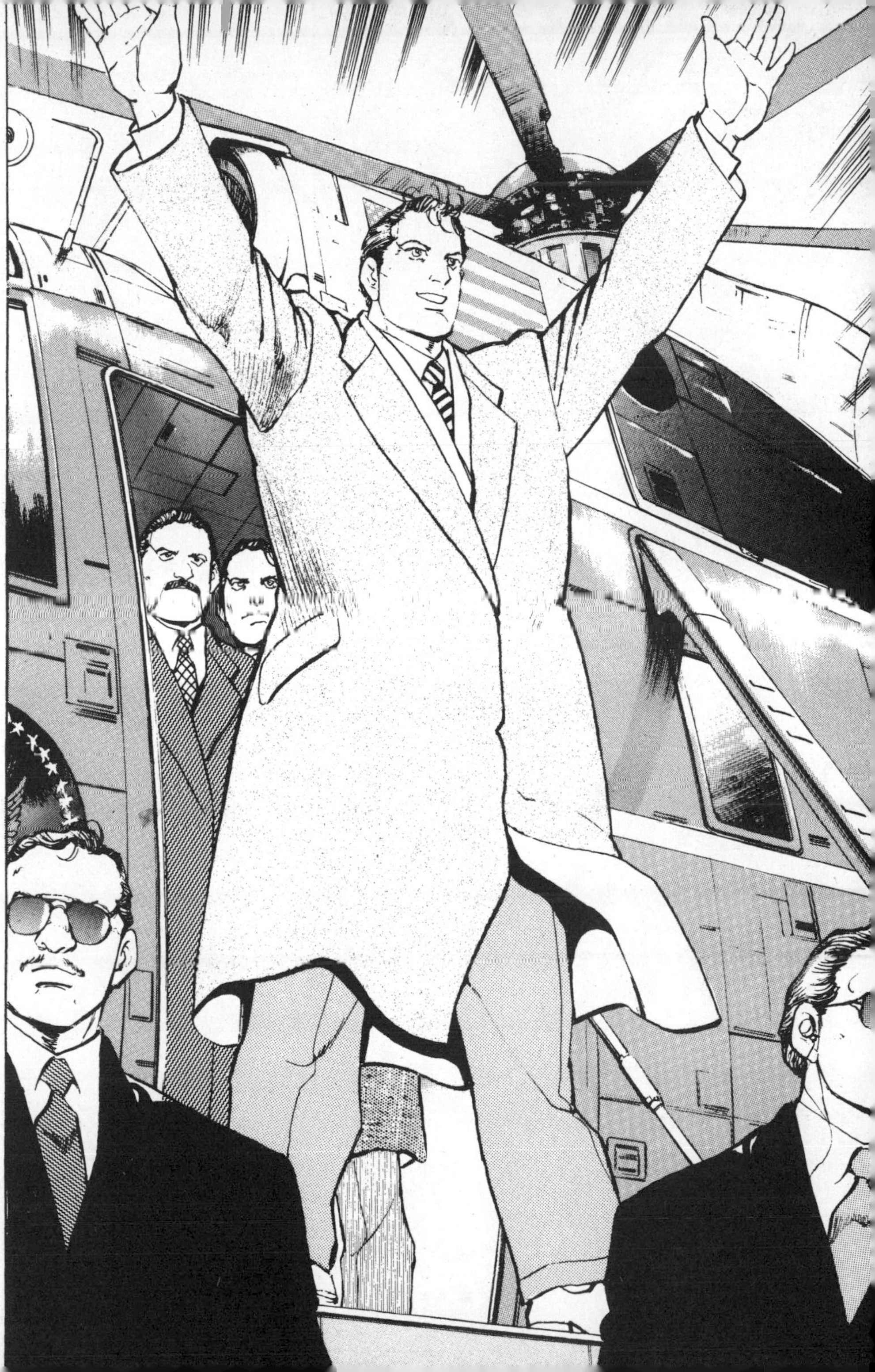

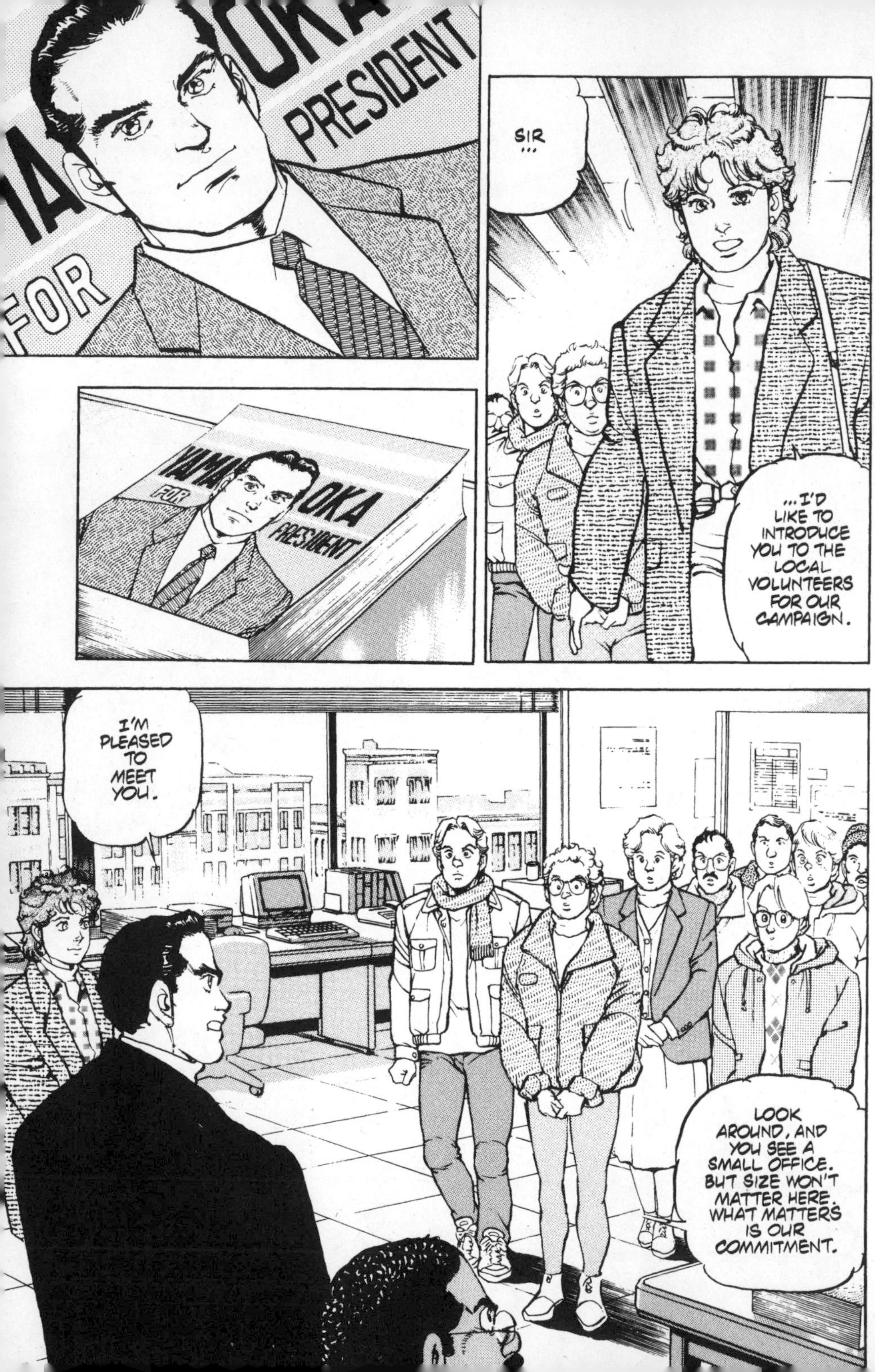
YAMAOKA FOR PRESIDENT
SIR ...
YAMAOKA FOR PRESIDENT
...I'D LIKE TO INTRODUCE YOU TO THE LOCAL VOLUNTEERS FOR OUR CAMPAIGN.
I'M PLEASED TO MEET YOU.
LOOK AROUND, AND YOU SEE A SMALL OFFICE. BUT SIZE WON'T MATTER HERE. WHAT MATTERS IS OUR COMMITMENT.

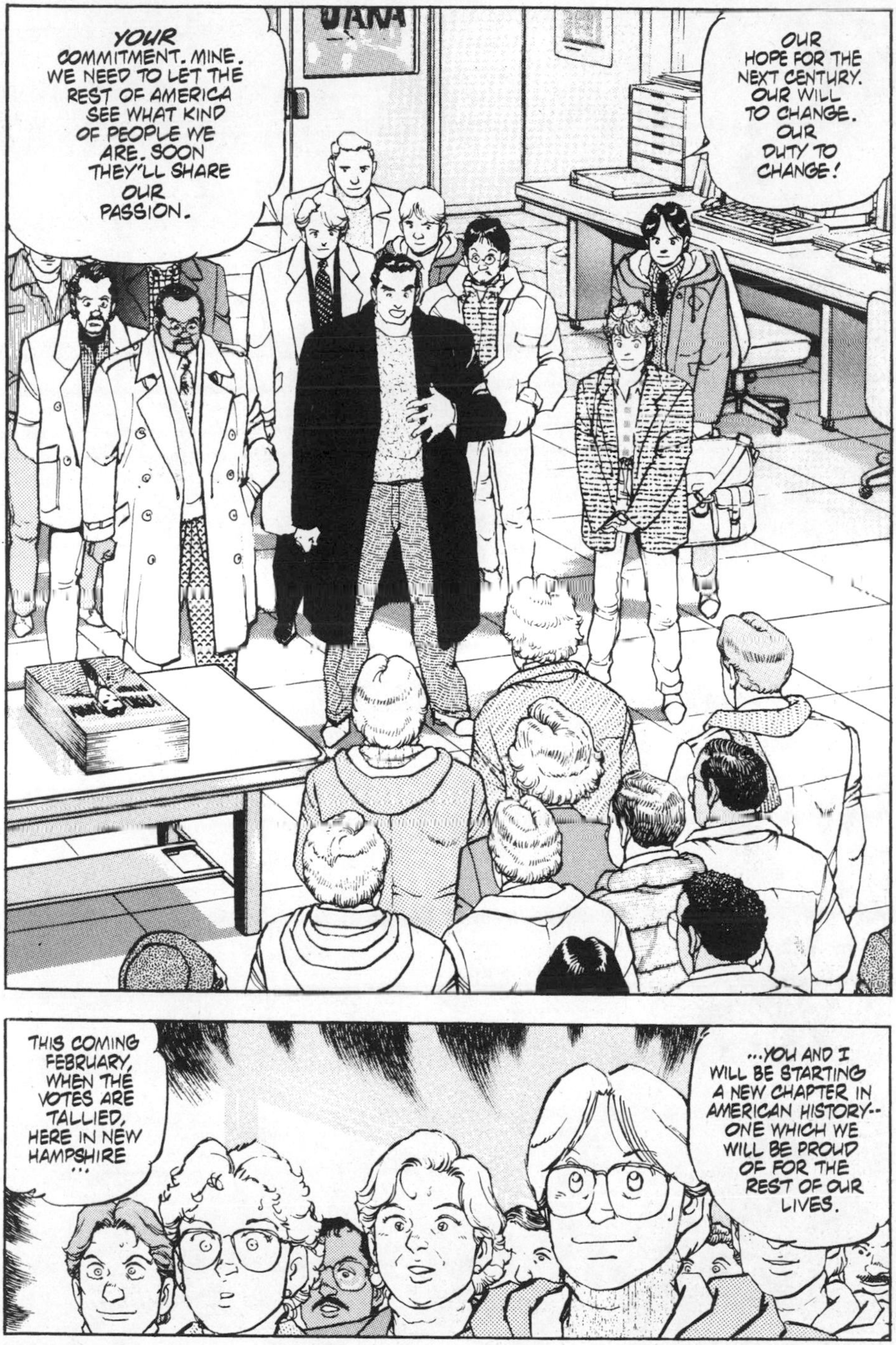
YOUR COMMITMENT. MINE. WE NEED TO LET THE REST OF AMERICA SEE WHAT KIND OF PEOPLE WE ARE. SOON THEY'LL SHARE OUR PASSION.
OUR HOPE FOR THE NEXT CENTURY. OUR WILL TO CHANGE. OUR DUTY TO CHANGE!
THIS COMING FEBRUARY, WHEN THE VOTES ARE TALLIED, HERE IN NEW HAMPSHIRE ...
...YOU AND I WILL BE STARTING A NEW CHAPTER IN AMERICAN HISTORY-- ONE WHICH WE WILL BE PROUD OF FOR THE REST OF OUR LIVES.

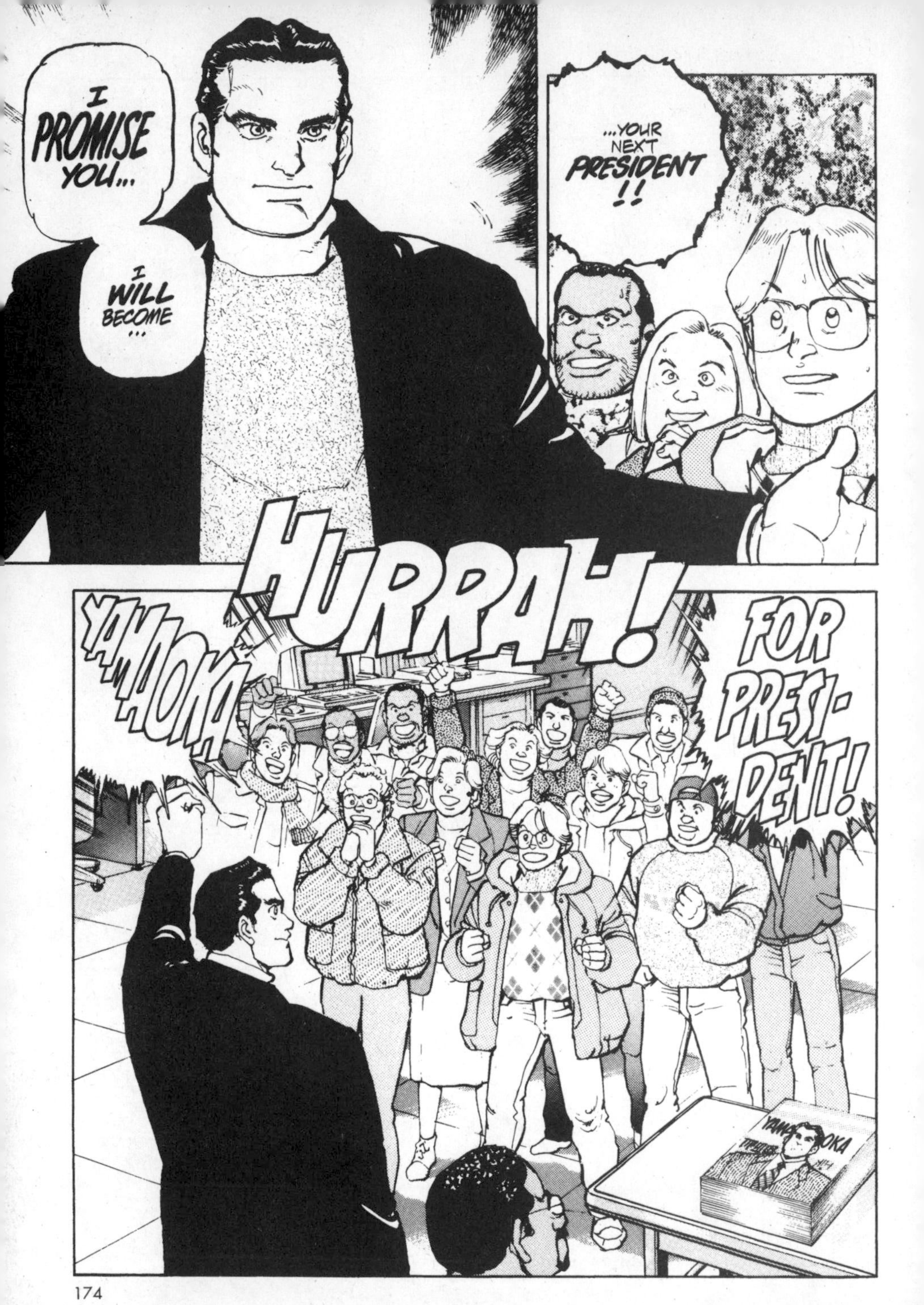
I PROMISE YOU...
I WILL BECOME ...
...YOUR NEXT PRESIDENT !!
HURRAH!
YAMAOKA
FOR PRESI-DENT!

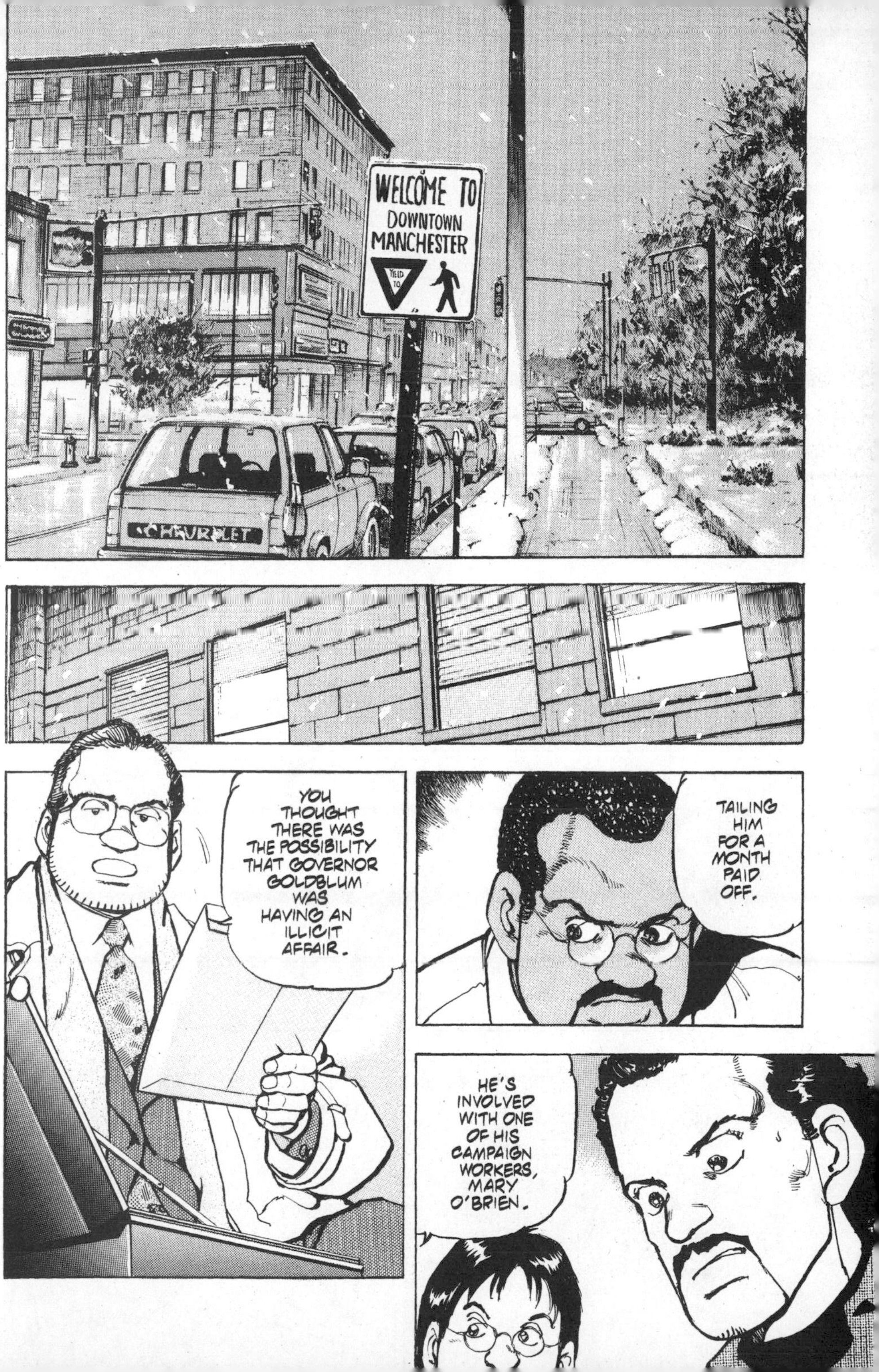
WELCOME TO
DOWNTOWN
MANCHESTER
YIELD TO
CHEVROLET
YOU THOUGHT THERE WAS THE POSSIBILITY THAT GOVERNOR GOLDBLUM WAS HAVING AN ILLICIT AFFAIR.
TAILING HIM FOR A MONTH PAID OFF.
HE'S INVOLVED WITH ONE OF HIS CAMPAIGN WORKERS, MARY O'BRIEN.

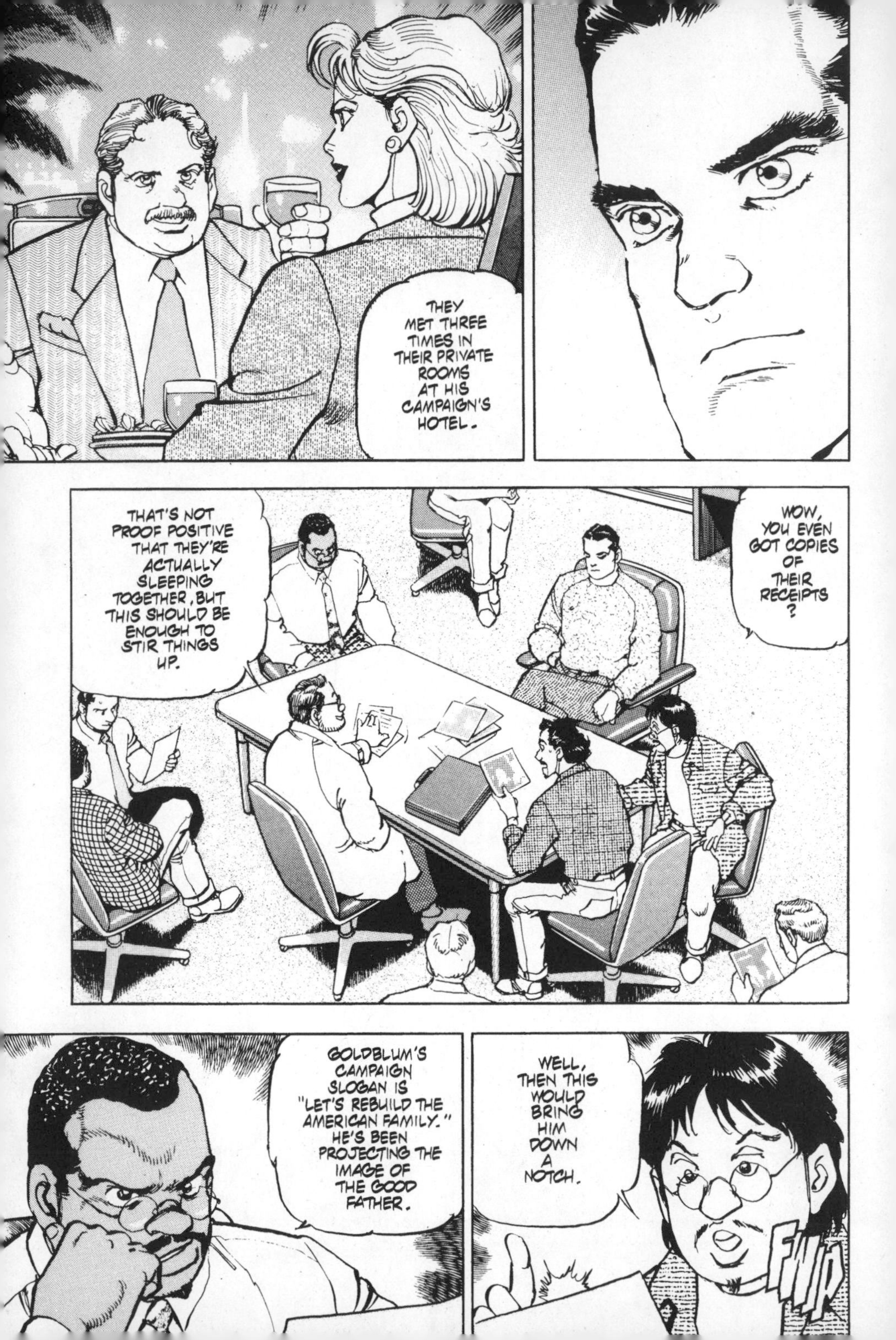
THEY MET THREE TIMES IN THEIR PRIVATE ROOMS AT HIS CAMPAIGN'S HOTEL.
THAT'S NOT PROOF POSITIVE THAT THEY'RE ACTUALLY SLEEPING TOGETHER, BUT THIS SHOULD BE ENOUGH TO STIR THINGS UP.
WOW, YOU EVEN GOT COPIES OF THEIR RECEIPTS?
GOLDBLUM'S CAMPAIGN SLOGAN IS "LET'S REBUILD THE AMERICAN FAMILY." HE'S BEEN PROJECTING THE IMAGE OF THE GOOD FATHER.
WELL, THEN THIS WOULD BRING HIM DOWN A NOTCH.
FWIP

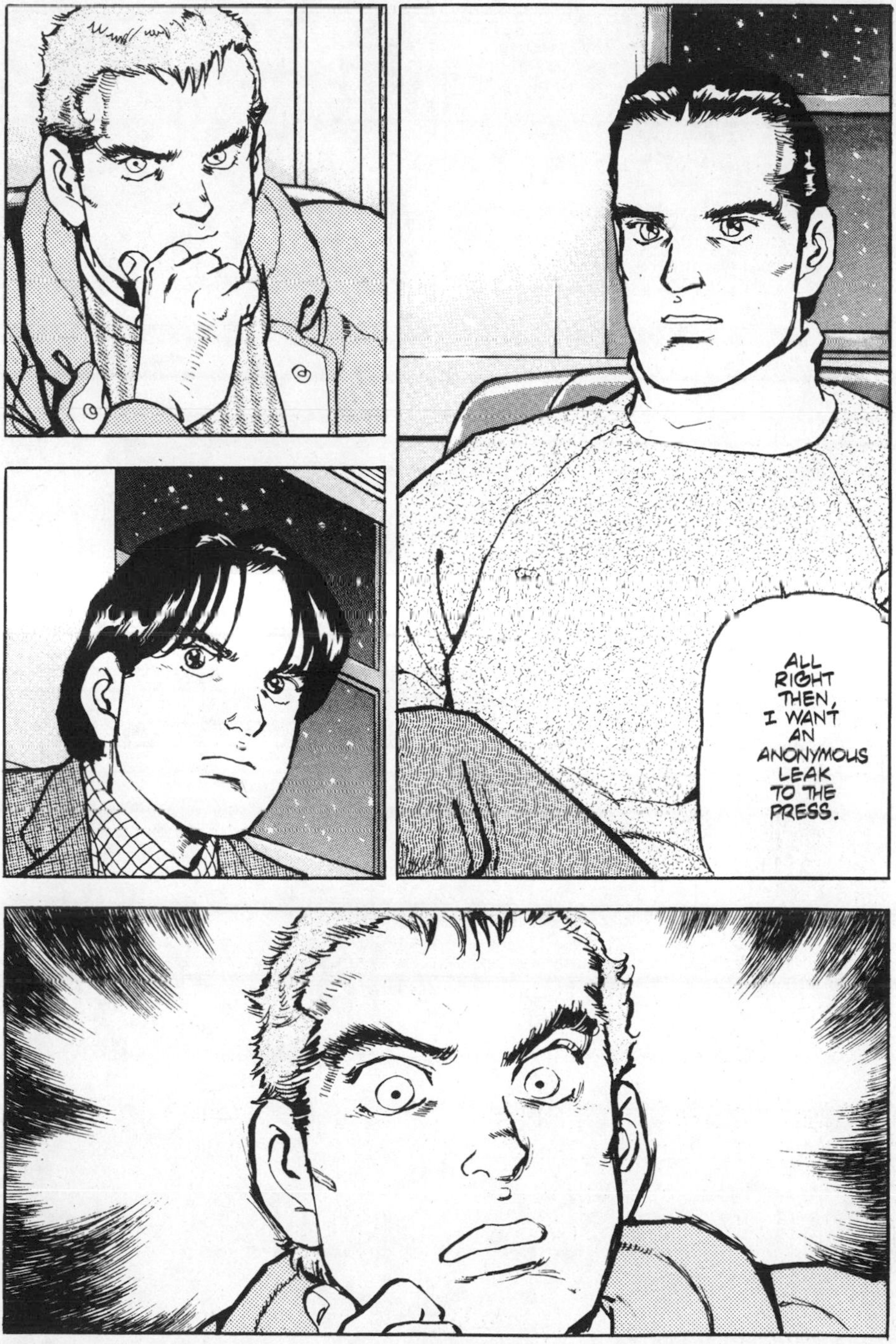
ALL RIGHT THEN, I WANT AN ANONYMOUS LEAK TO THE PRESS.

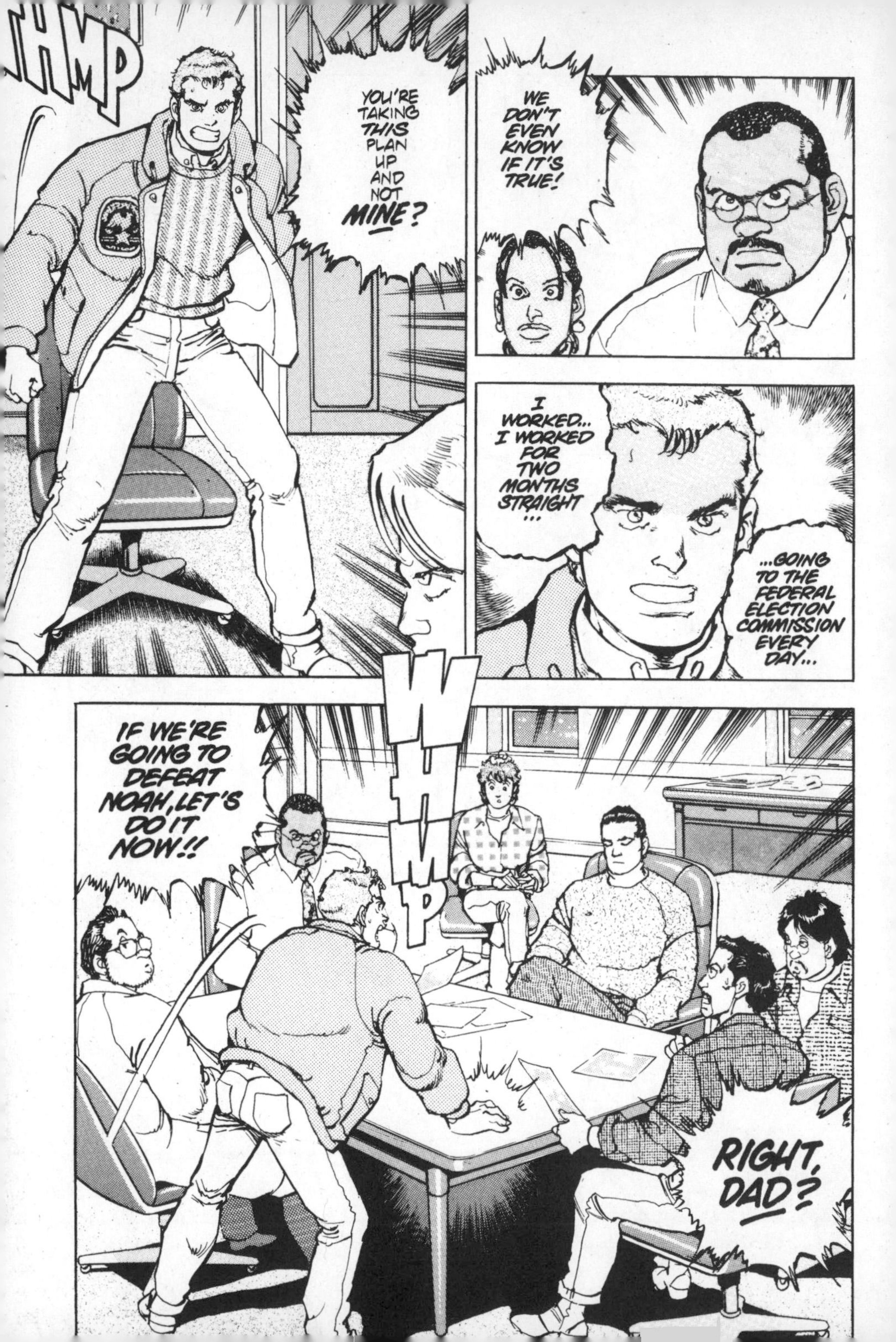
THMP
YOU'RE TAKING THIS PLAN UP AND NOT MINE?
WE DON'T EVEN KNOW IF IT'S TRUE!
I WORKED... I WORKED FOR TWO MONTHS STRAIGHT...
...GOING TO THE FEDERAL ELECTION COMMISSION EVERY DAY...
IF WE'RE GOING TO DEFEAT NOAH, LET'S DO IT NOW!!
WHUMP
RIGHT, DAD?

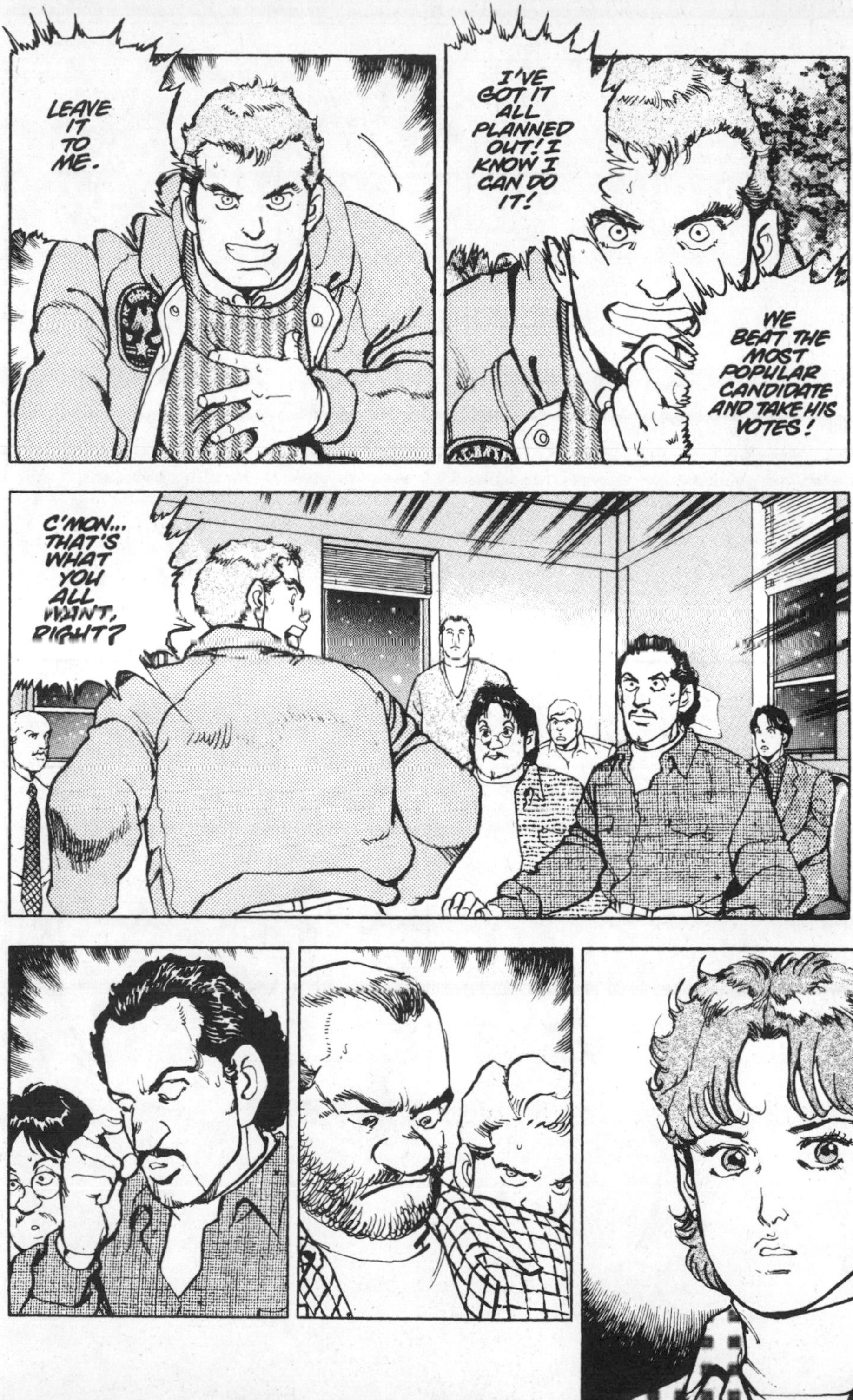
LEAVE IT TO ME.
I'VE GOT IT ALL PLANNED OUT! I KNOW I CAN DO IT!
WE BEAT THE MOST POPULAR CANDIDATE AND TAKE HIS VOTES!
C'MON... THAT'S WHAT YOU ALL WANT, RIGHT?

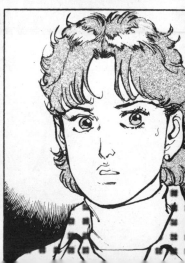

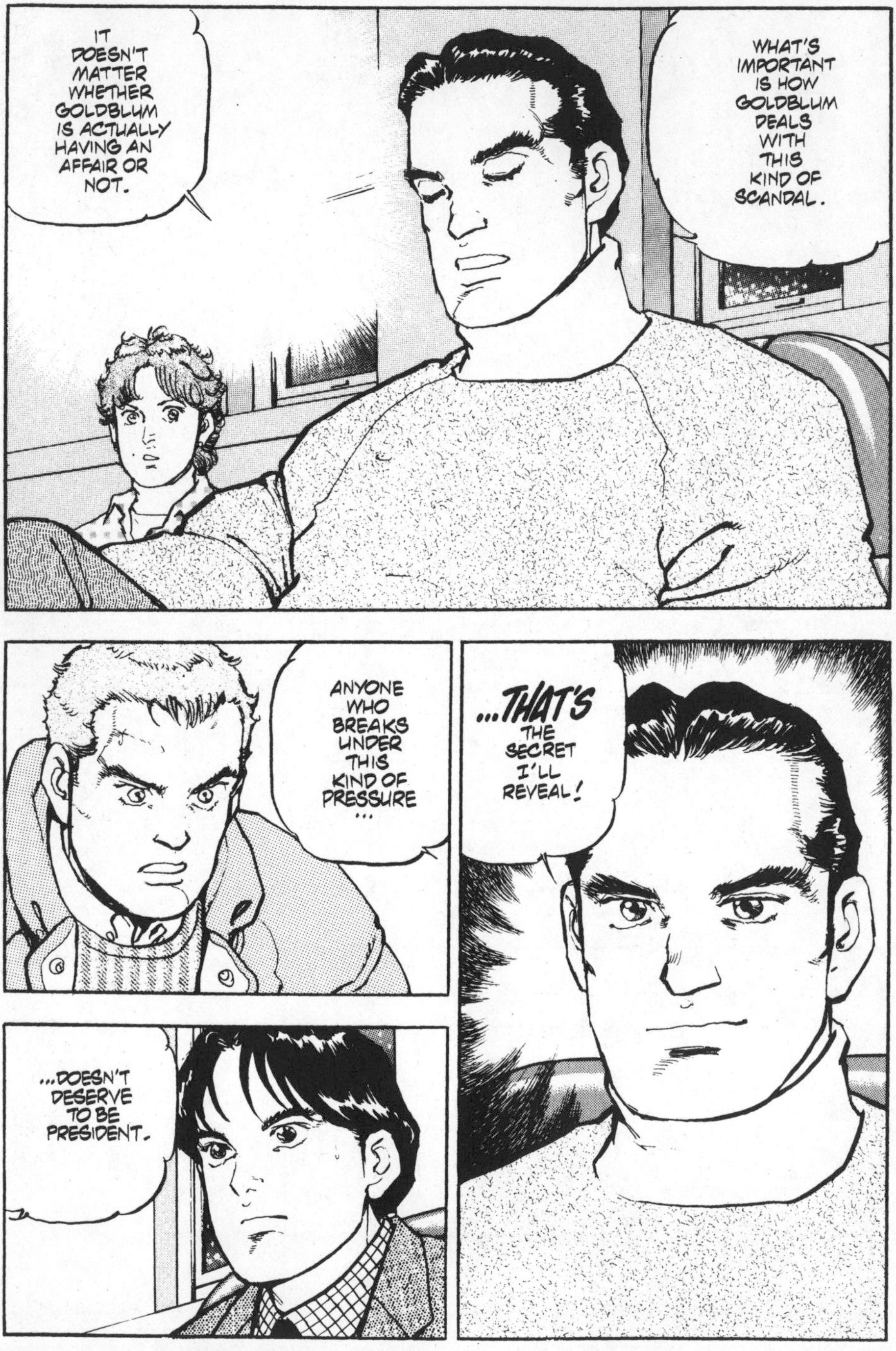
IT DOESN'T MATTER WHETHER GOLDBLUM IS ACTUALLY HAVING AN AFFAIR OR NOT.
WHAT'S IMPORTANT IS HOW GOLDBLUM DEALS WITH THIS KIND OF SCANDAL.
ANYONE WHO BREAKS UNDER THIS KIND OF PRESSURE ...
...DOESN'T DESERVE TO BE PRESIDENT.
...THAT'S THE SECRET I'LL REVEAL!

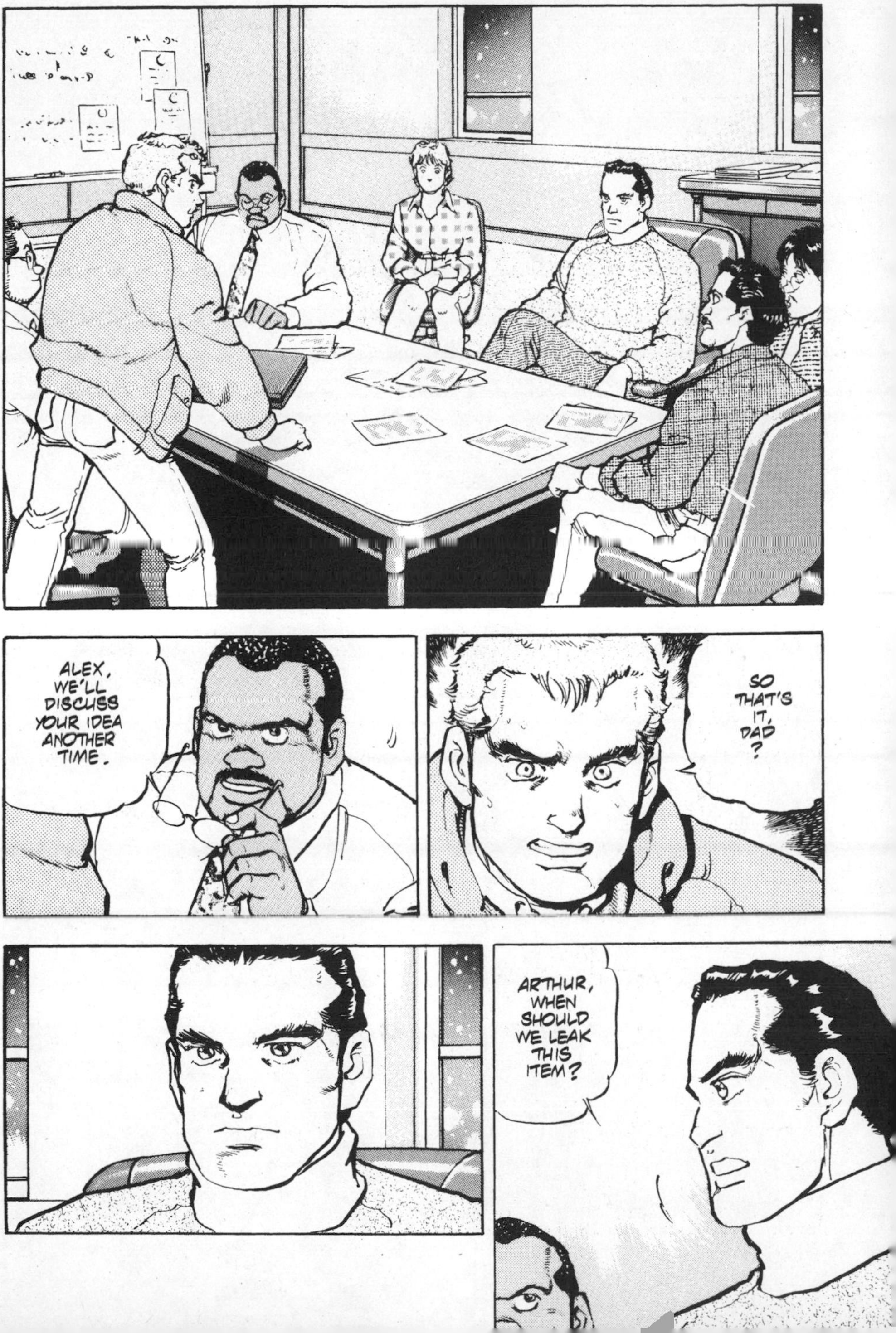
ALEX, WE'LL DISCUSS YOUR IDEA ANOTHER TIME.
SO THAT'S IT, DAD?
ARTHUR, WHEN SHOULD WE LEAK THIS ITEM?

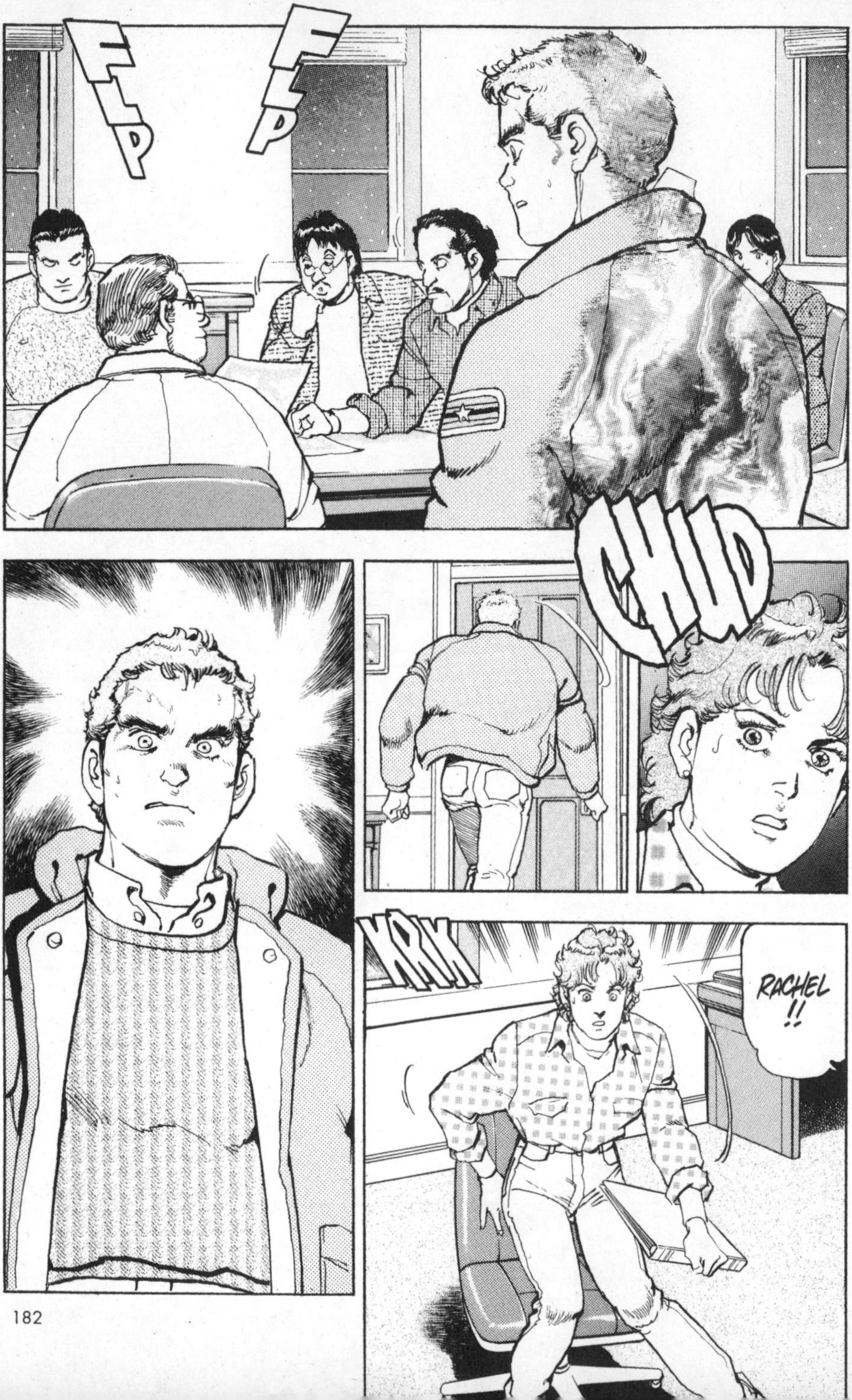
FLIP
FLIP
CHUD
KRAK
RACHEL !!

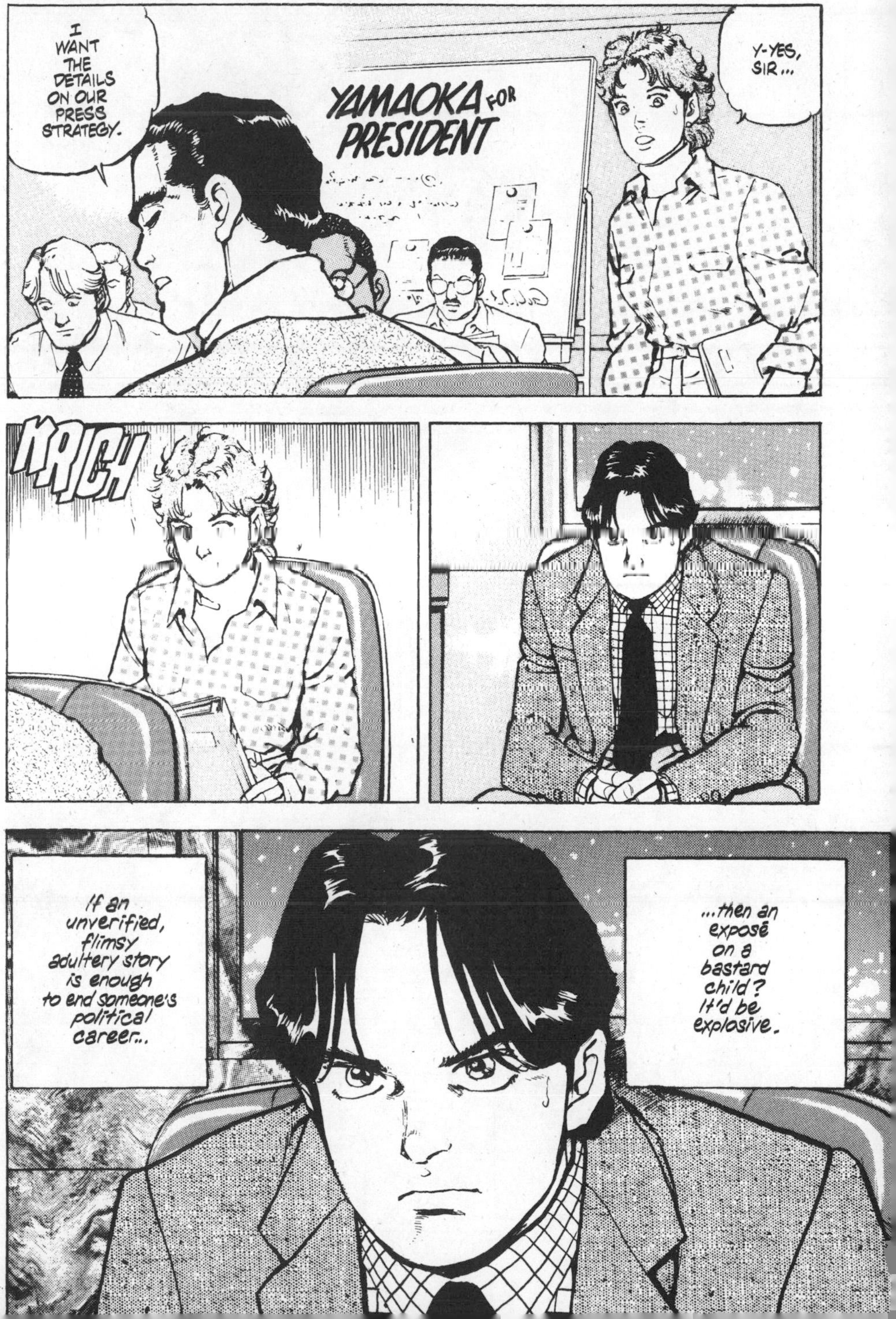
I WANT THE DETAILS ON OUR PRESS STRATEGY.
YAMAOKA FOR PRESIDENT
Y-YES, SIR...
KRICH
If an unverified, flimsy adultery story is enough to end someone's political career...
...then an exposé on a bastard child? It'd be explosive.

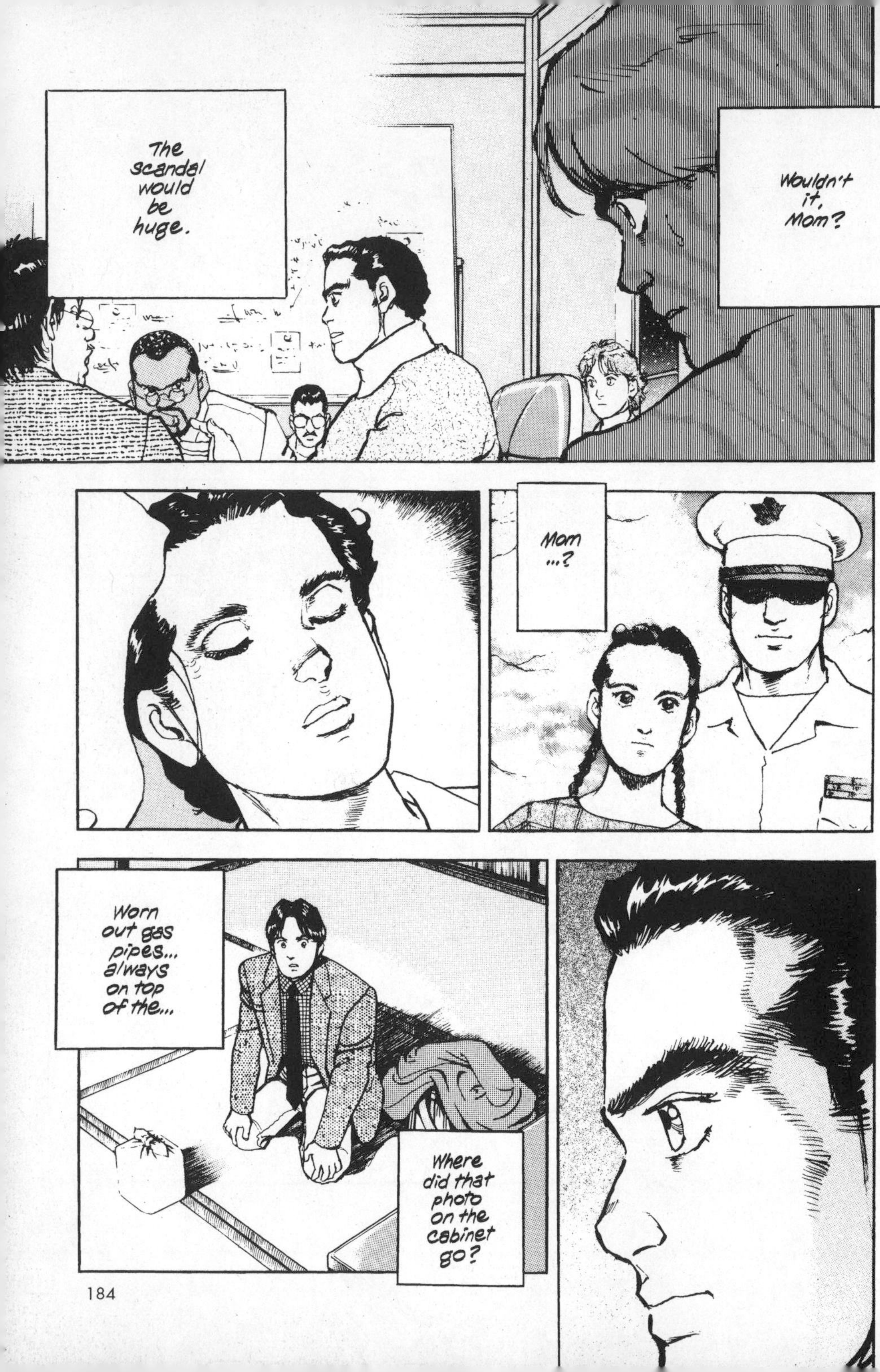
The scandal would be huge.
Wouldn't it, Mom?
Mom ...?
Worn out gas pipes... always on top of the...
Where did that photo on the cabinet go?

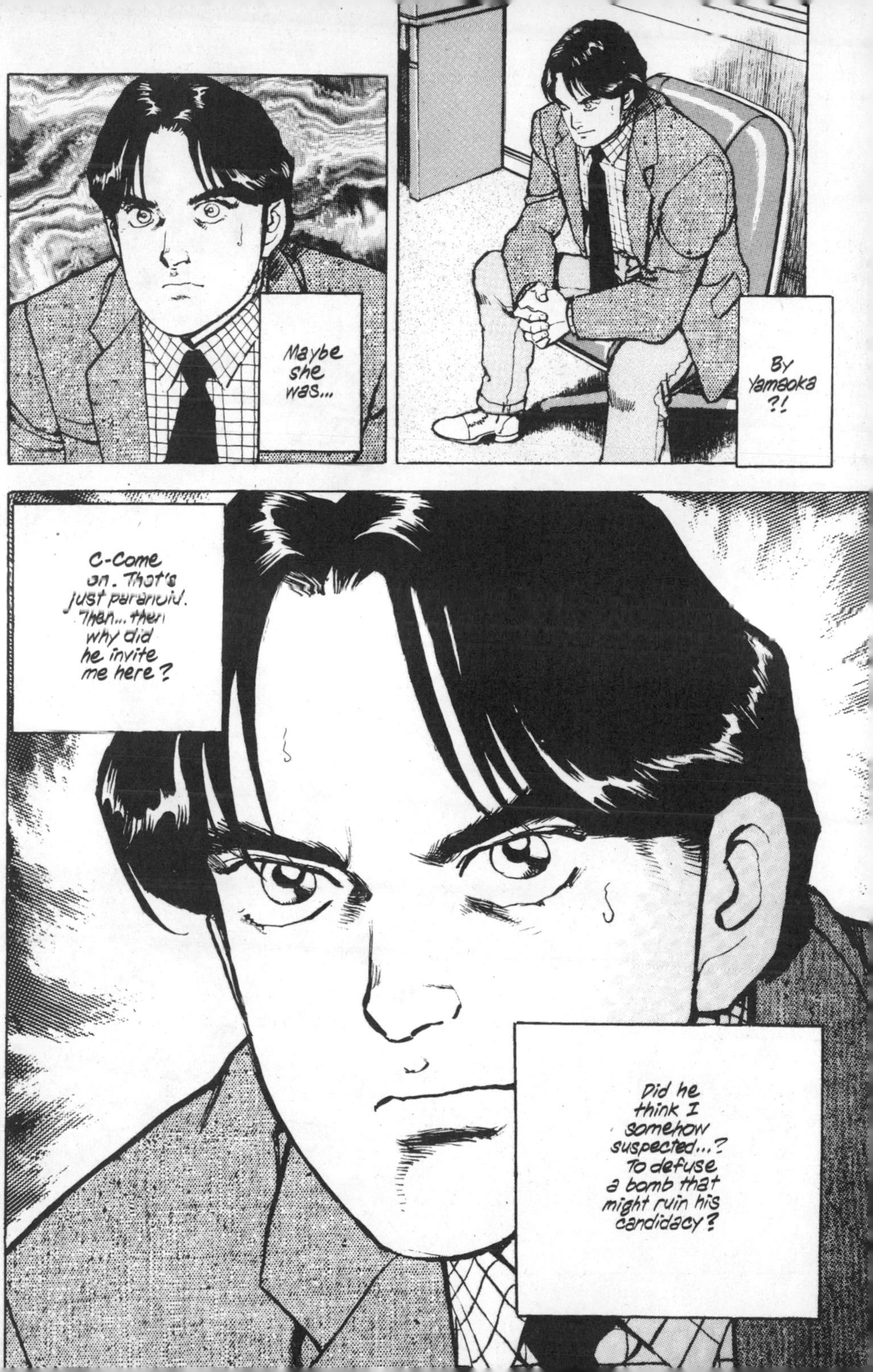
Maybe she was...
By Yamaoka?!
C-Come on. That's just paranoid. Then... then why did he invite me here?
Did he think I somehow suspected...? To defuse a bomb that might ruin his candidacy?

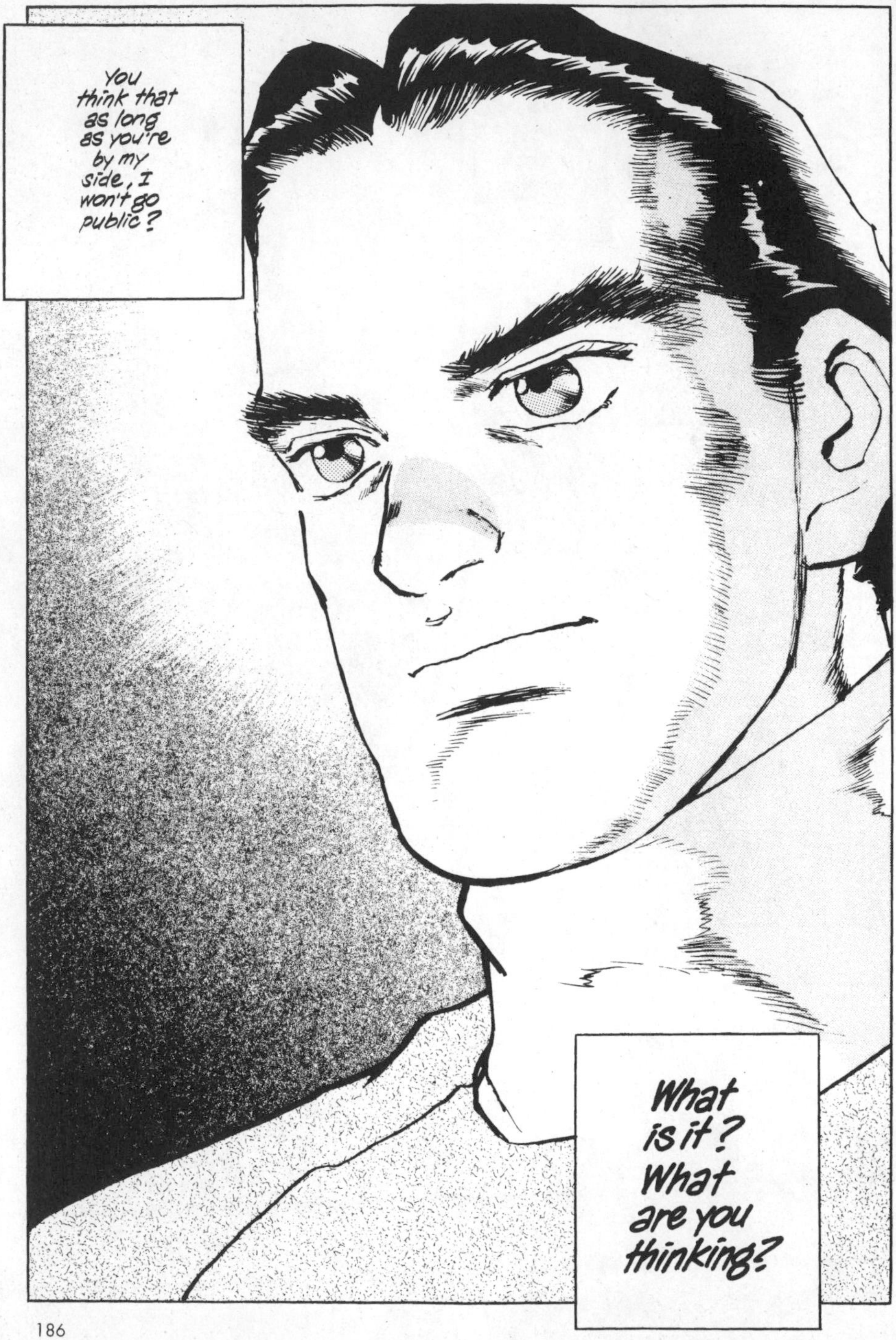
You think that as long as you're by my side, I won't go public?
What is it? What are you thinking?

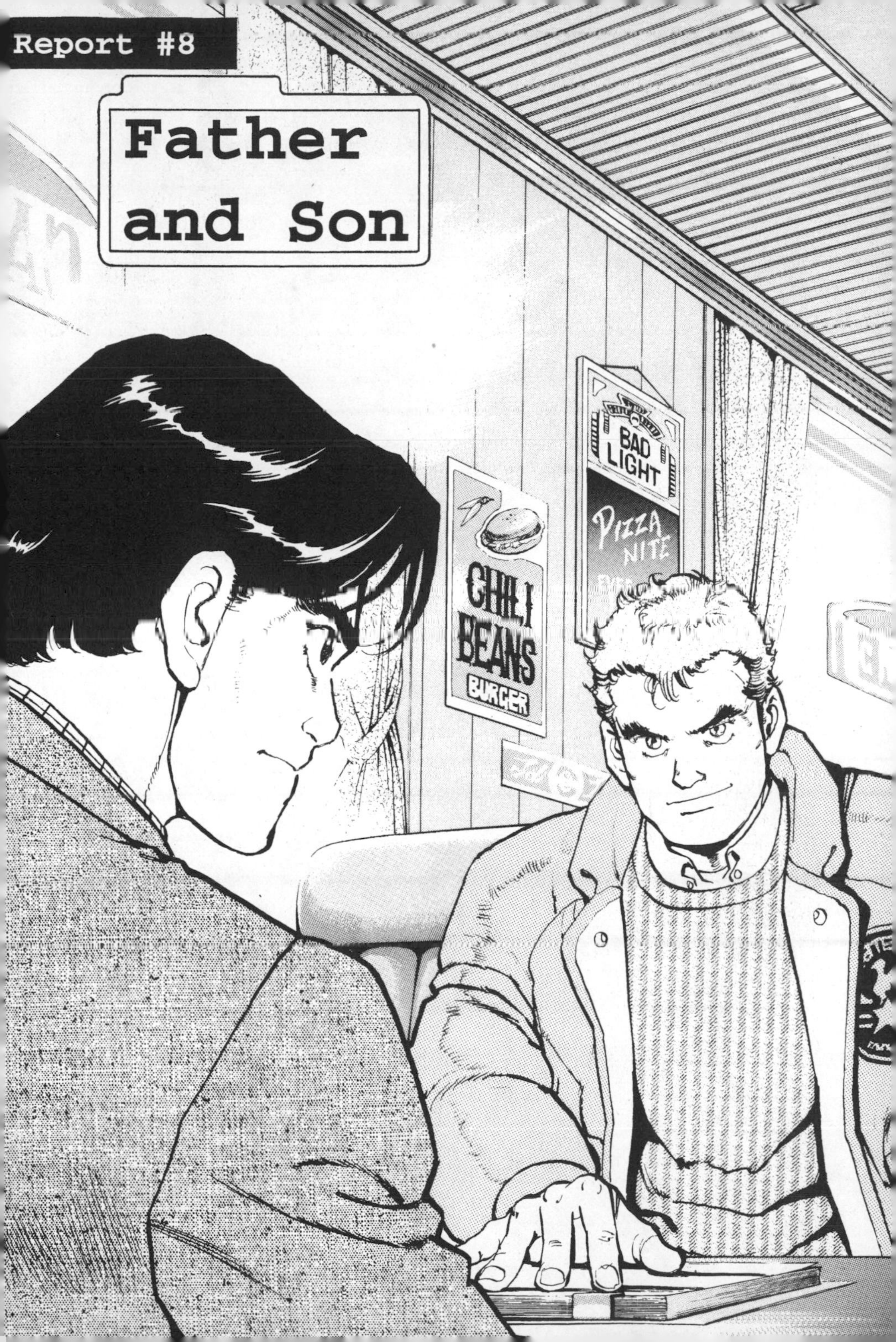
Report #8
Father and Son
CHILI BEANS BURGER
BAD LIGHT
PIZZA NITE

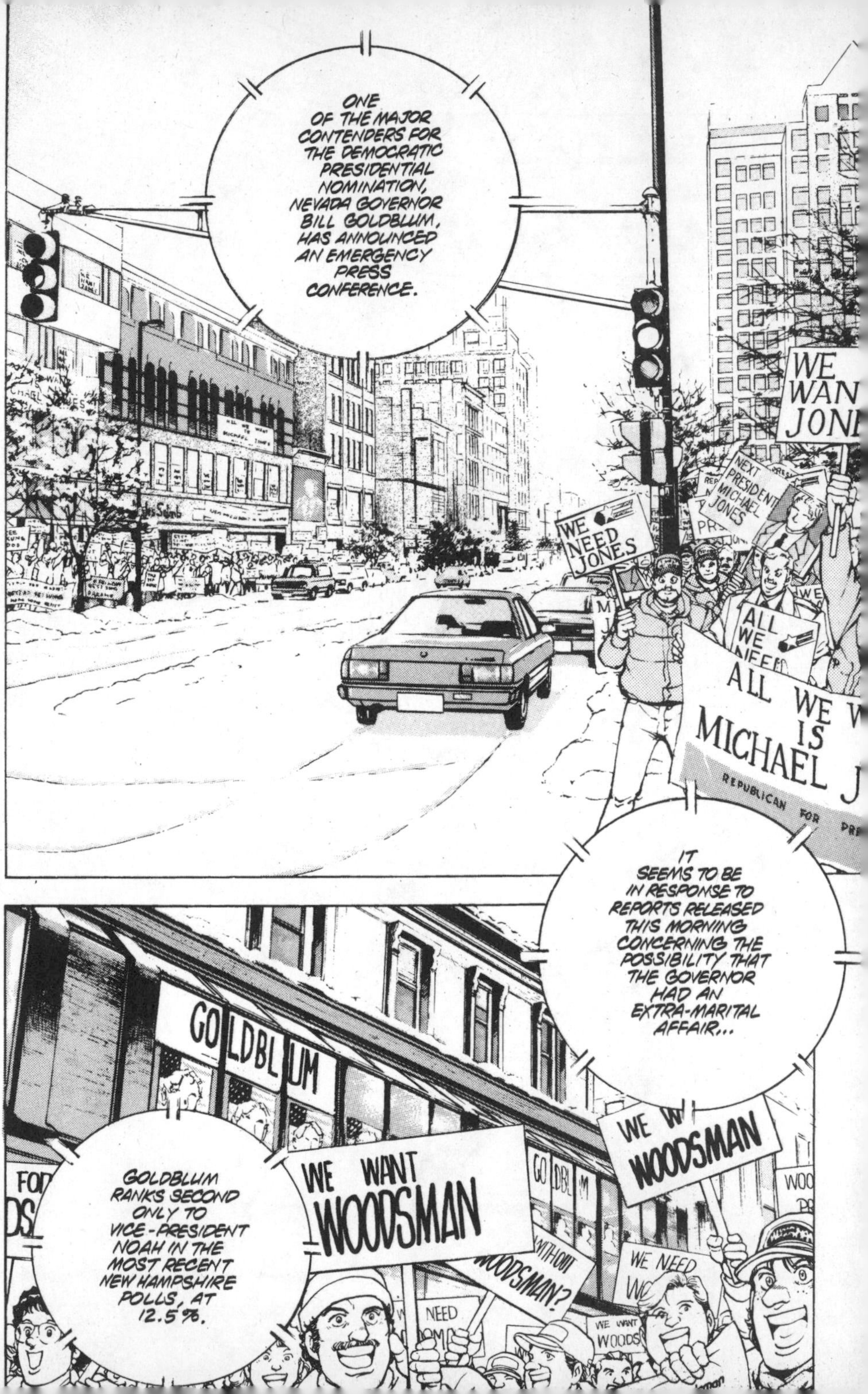
ONE OF THE MAJOR CONTENDERS FOR THE DEMOCRATIC PRESIDENTIAL NOMINATION, NEVADA GOVERNOR BILL GOLDBLUM, HAS ANNOUNCED AN EMERGENCY PRESS CONFERENCE.
WE WAN JONE
NEXT PRESIDENT MICHAEL JONES
WE NEED JONES
ALL WE NEED
ALL WE W IS MICHAEL J
REPUBLICAN FOR
IT SEEMS TO BE IN RESPONSE TO REPORTS RELEASED THIS MORNING CONCERNING THE POSSIBILITY THAT THE GOVERNOR HAD AN EXTRA-MARITAL AFFAIR...
GOLDBLUM
GOLDBLUM RANKS SECOND ONLY TO VICE-PRESIDENT NOAH IN THE MOST RECENT NEW HAMPSHIRE POLLS, AT 12.5%.
WE WANT WOODSMAN
WE W WOODSMAN
WE NEED
WE WANT WOODS
NEED

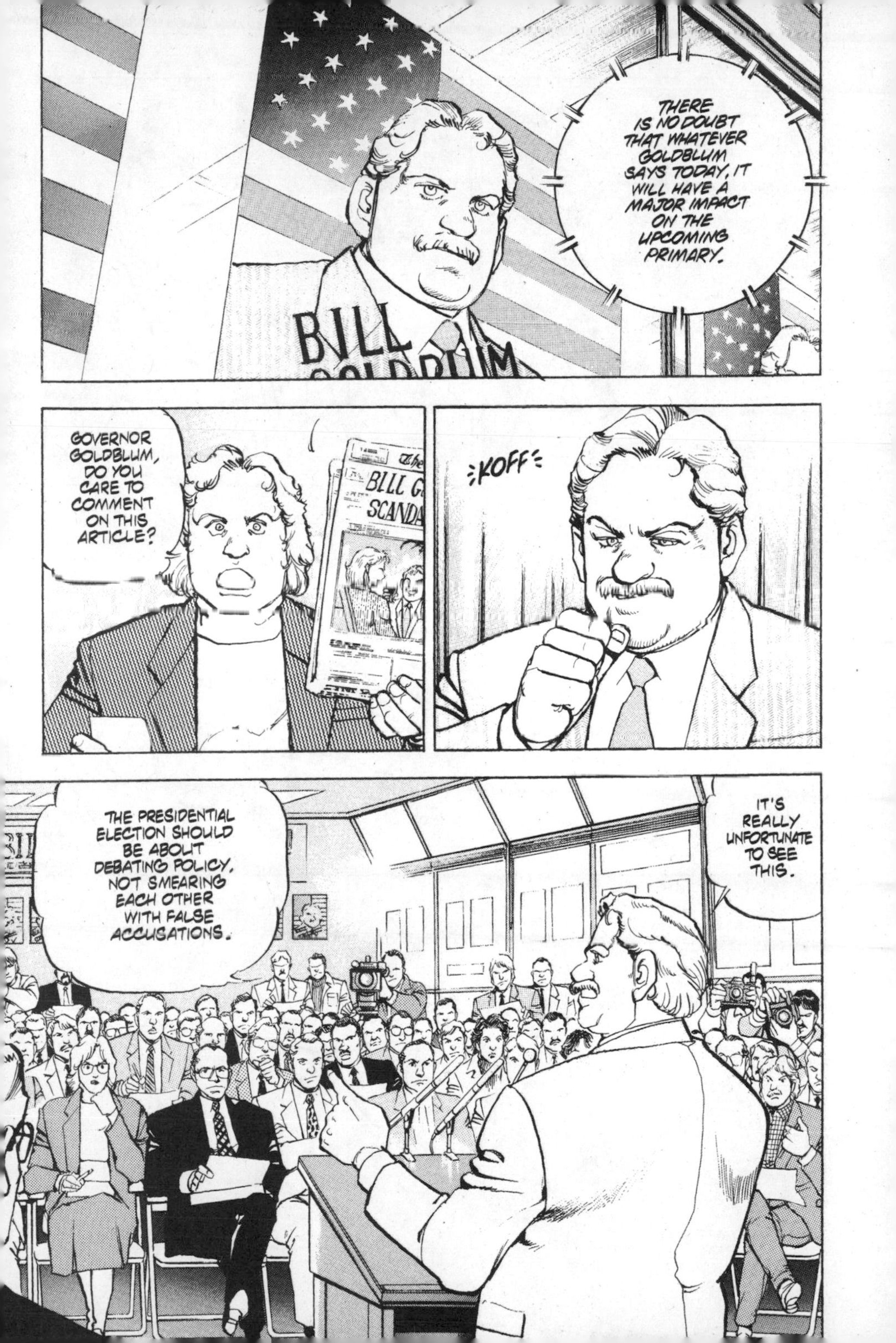

THERE IS NO DOUBT THAT WHATEVER GOLDBLUM SAYS TODAY, IT WILL HAVE A MAJOR IMPACT ON THE UPCOMING PRIMARY.
BILL GOLDBLUM
GOVERNOR GOLDBLUM, DO YOU CARE TO COMMENT ON THIS ARTICLE?
BILL G
SCANDA
KOFF
THE PRESIDENTIAL ELECTION SHOULD BE ABOUT DEBATING POLICY, NOT SMEARING EACH OTHER WITH FALSE ACCUSATIONS.
IT'S REALLY UNFORTUNATE TO SEE THIS.

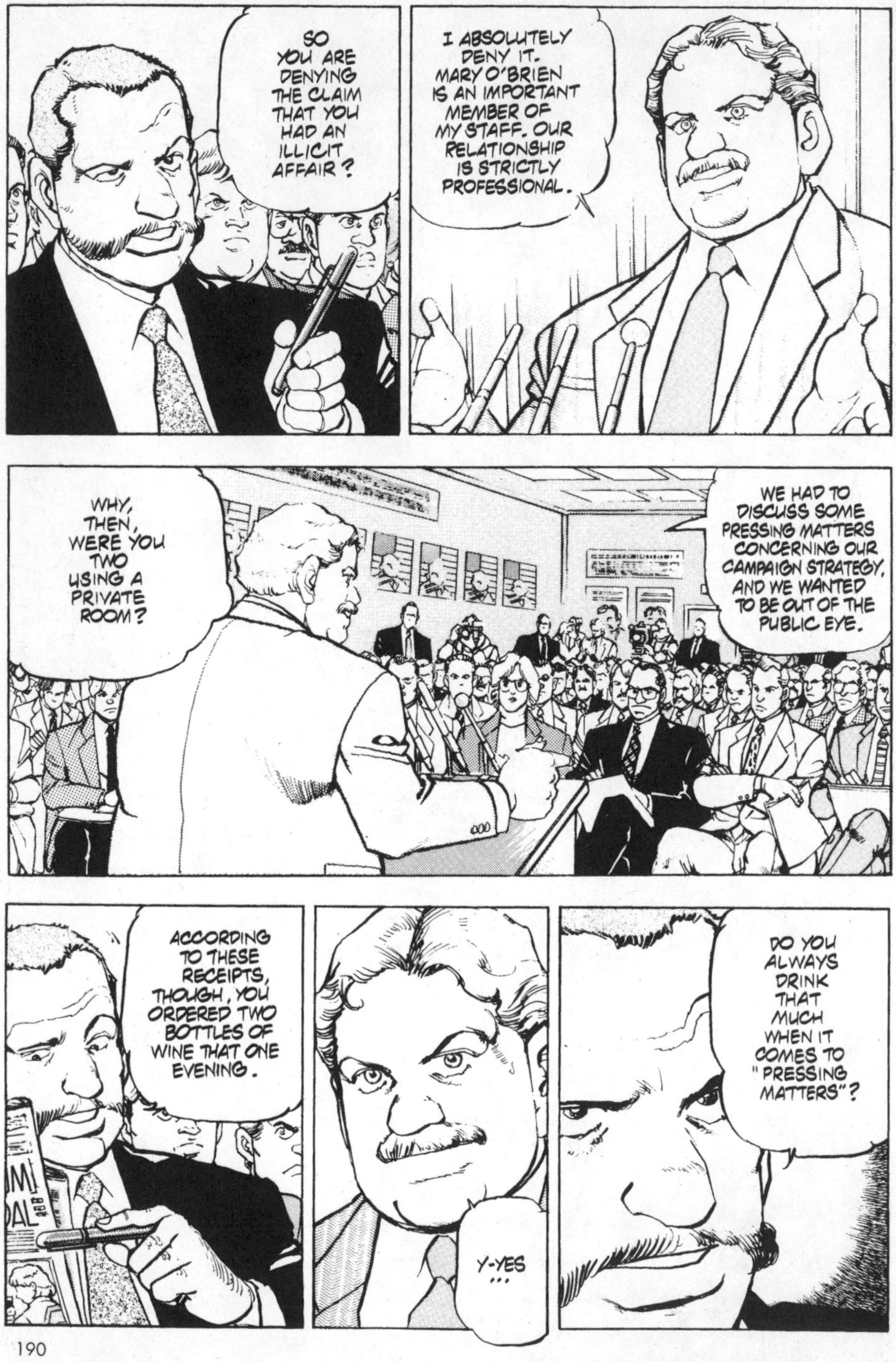
SO YOU ARE DENYING THE CLAIM THAT YOU HAD AN ILLICIT AFFAIR?
I ABSOLUTELY DENY IT. MARY O'BRIEN IS AN IMPORTANT MEMBER OF MY STAFF. OUR RELATIONSHIP IS STRICTLY PROFESSIONAL.
WHY, THEN, WERE YOU TWO USING A PRIVATE ROOM?
WE HAD TO DISCUSS SOME PRESSING MATTERS CONCERNING OUR CAMPAIGN STRATEGY, AND WE WANTED TO BE OUT OF THE PUBLIC EYE.
ACCORDING TO THESE RECEIPTS, THOUGH, YOU ORDERED TWO BOTTLES OF WINE THAT ONE EVENING.
Y-YES...
DO YOU ALWAYS DRINK THAT MUCH WHEN IT COMES TO "PRESSING MATTERS"?

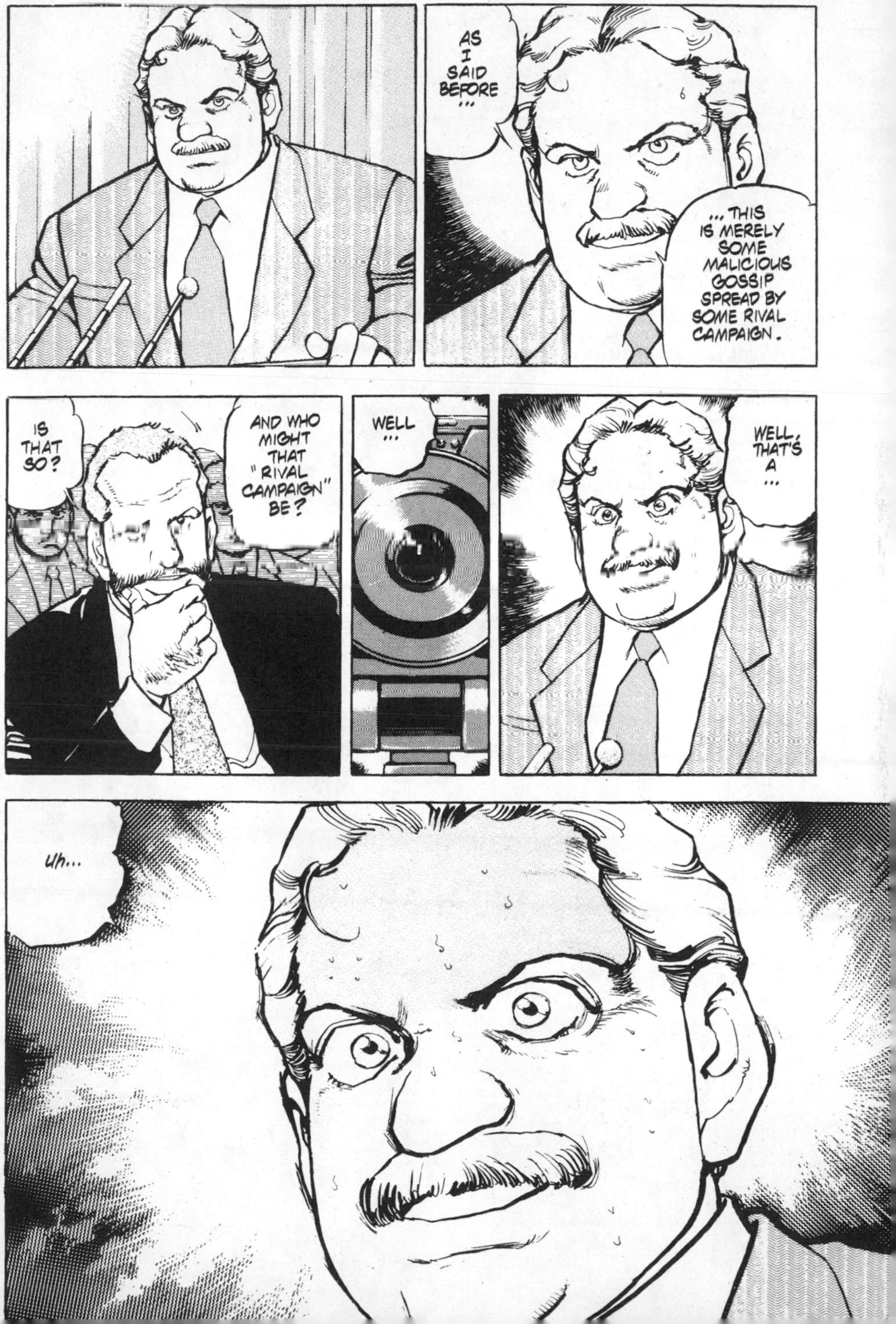
AS I SAID BEFORE ...
... THIS IS MERELY SOME MALICIOUS GOSSIP SPREAD BY SOME RIVAL CAMPAIGN.
IS THAT SO?
AND WHO MIGHT THAT "RIVAL CAMPAIGN" BE?
WELL ...
WELL, THAT'S A ...
uh...

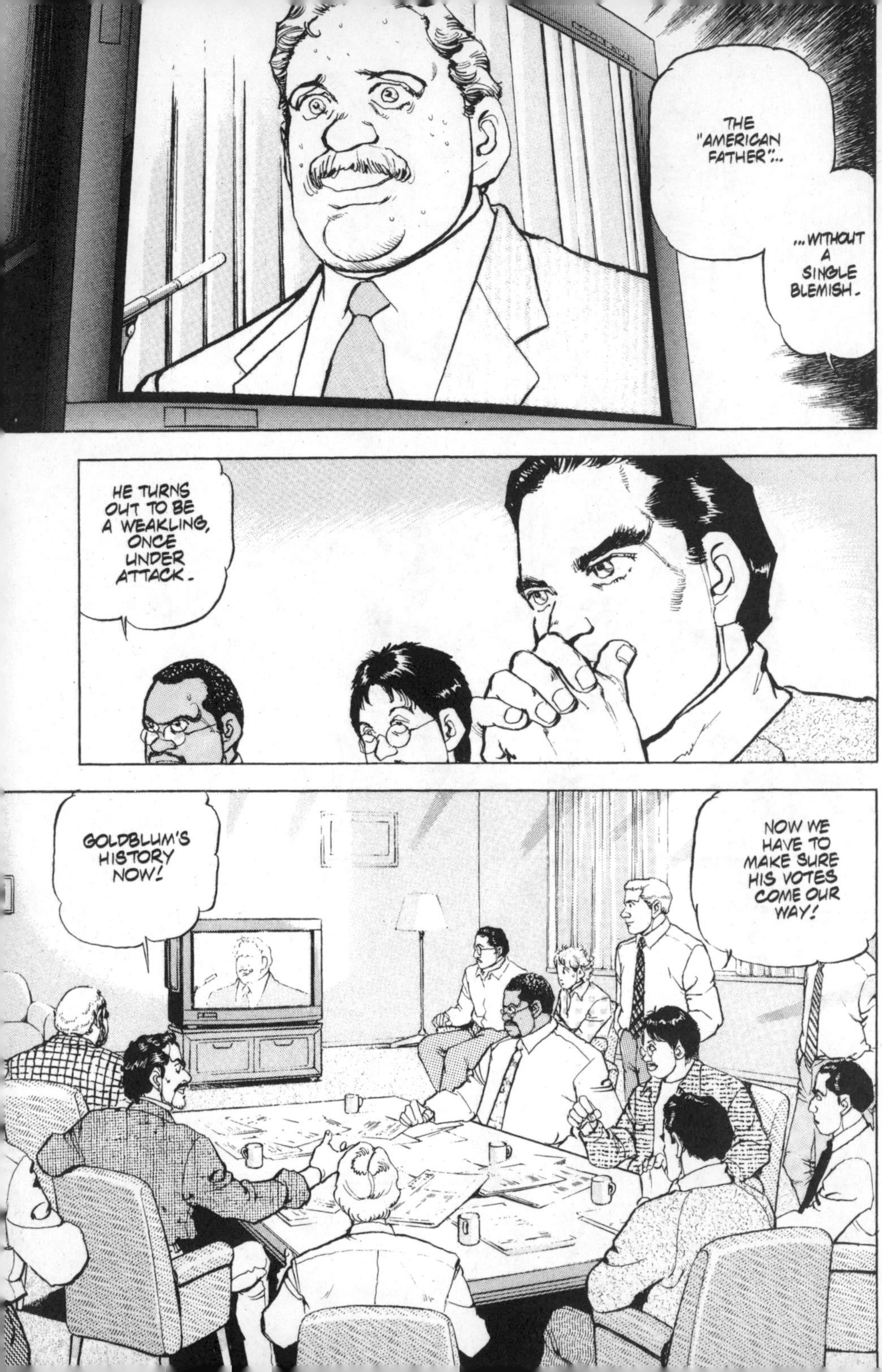
THE "AMERICAN FATHER"...
...WITHOUT A SINGLE BLEMISH.
HE TURNS OUT TO BE A WEAKLING, ONCE UNDER ATTACK.
GOLDBLUM'S HISTORY NOW!
NOW WE HAVE TO MAKE SURE HIS VOTES COME OUR WAY!

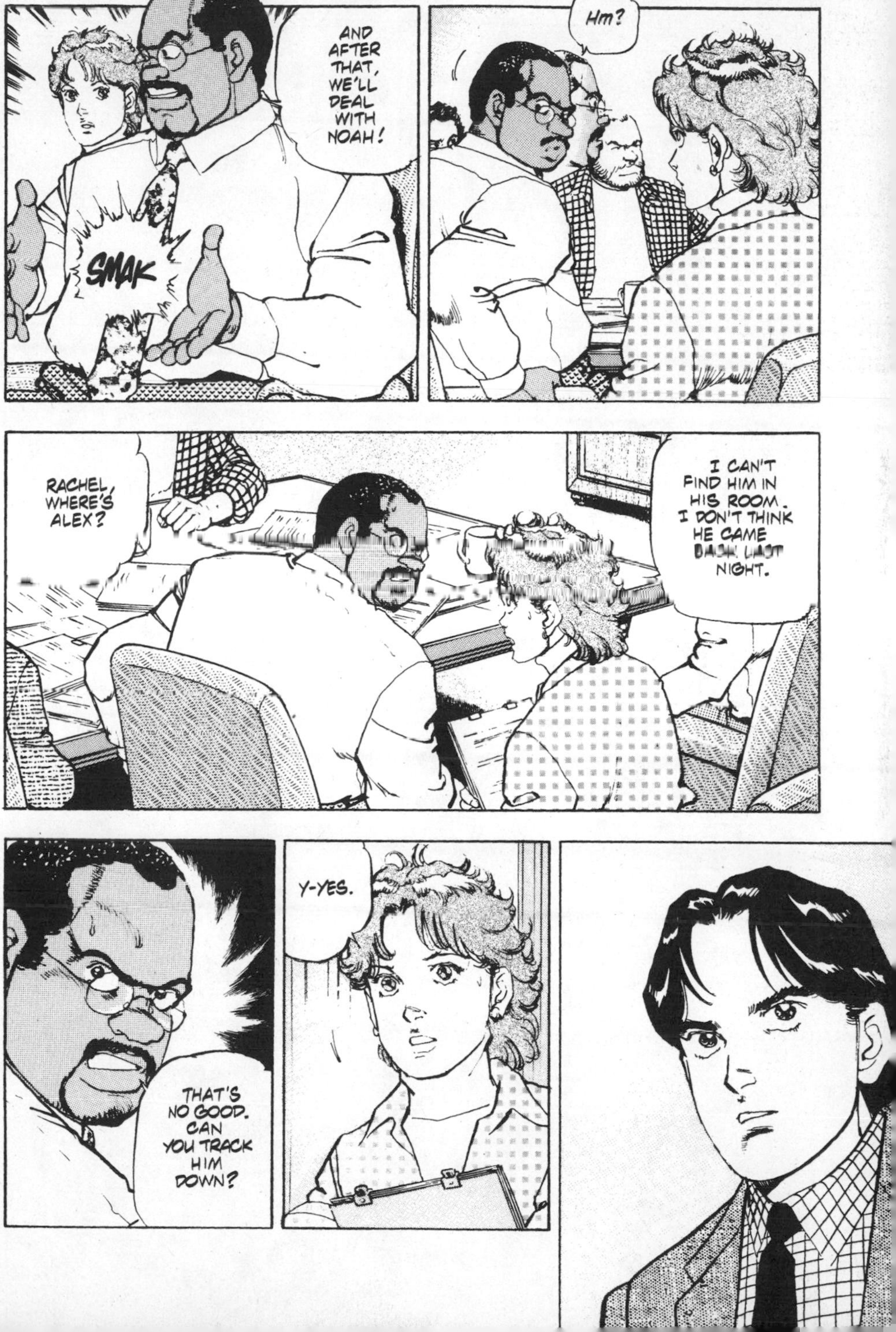
AND AFTER THAT, WE'LL DEAL WITH NOAH!
SMAK
Hm?
RACHEL, WHERE'S ALEX?
I CAN'T FIND HIM IN HIS ROOM. I DON'T THINK HE CAME BACK LAST NIGHT.
THAT'S NO GOOD. CAN YOU TRACK HIM DOWN?
Y-YES.

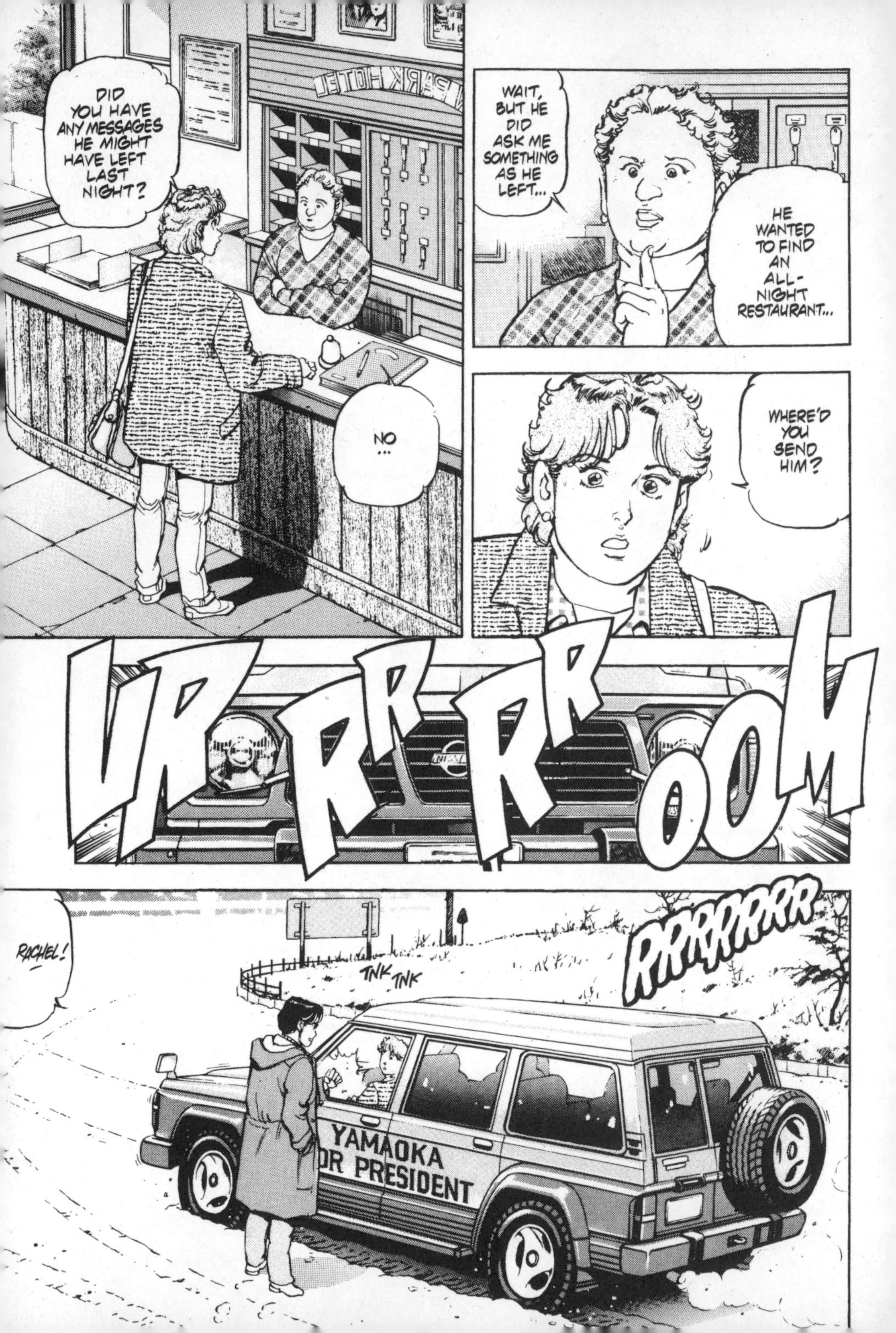

DID YOU HAVE ANY MESSAGES HE MIGHT HAVE LEFT LAST NIGHT?
NO ...
WAIT, BUT HE DID ASK ME SOMETHING AS HE LEFT...
HE WANTED TO FIND AN ALL-NIGHT RESTAURANT...
WHERE'D YOU SEND HIM?
VRRRROOM
RACHEL!
TNK TNK
RRRRRRRR
YAMAOKA FOR PRESIDENT

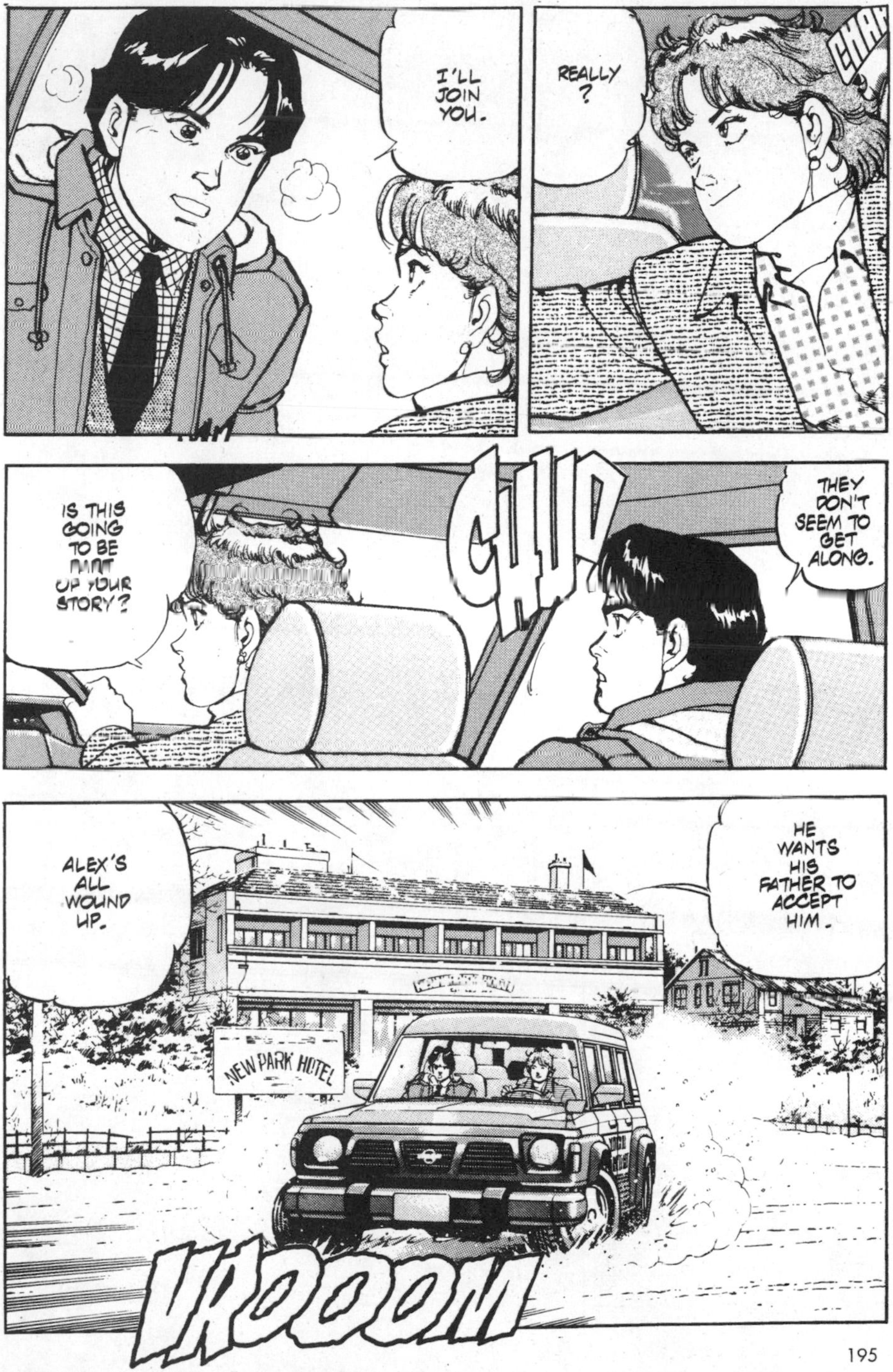

I'LL JOIN YOU.
REALLY?
IS THIS GOING TO BE PART OF YOUR STORY?
CHUD
THEY DON'T SEEM TO GET ALONG.
ALEX'S ALL WOUND UP.
HE WANTS HIS FATHER TO ACCEPT HIM.
NEW PARK HOTEL
VROOOM

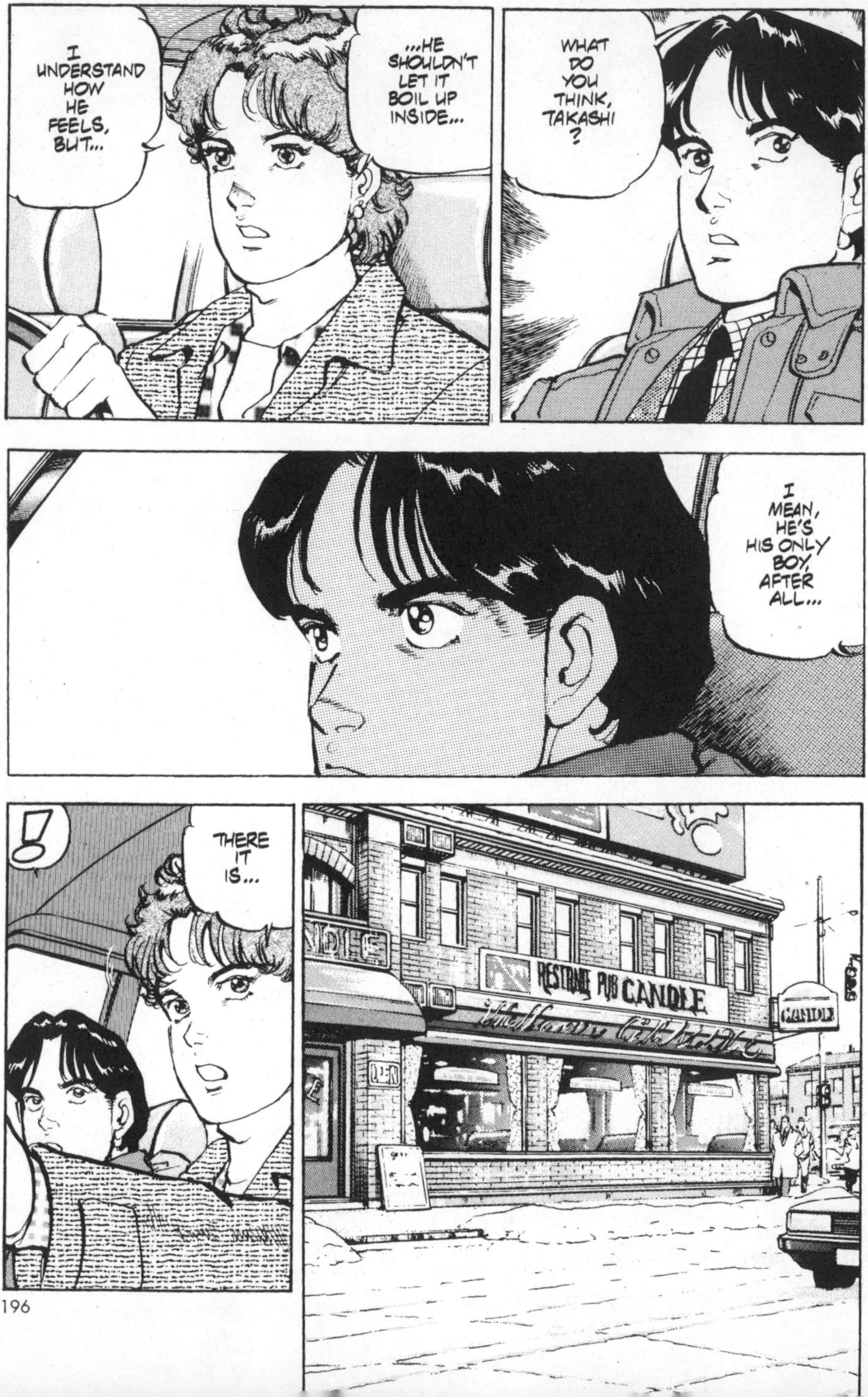
I UNDERSTAND HOW HE FEELS, BUT...
...HE SHOULDN'T LET IT BOIL UP INSIDE...
WHAT DO YOU THINK, TAKASHI?
I MEAN, HE'S HIS ONLY BOY, AFTER ALL...
!
THERE IT IS...
RESTRANT PUB CANDLE
CANDLE

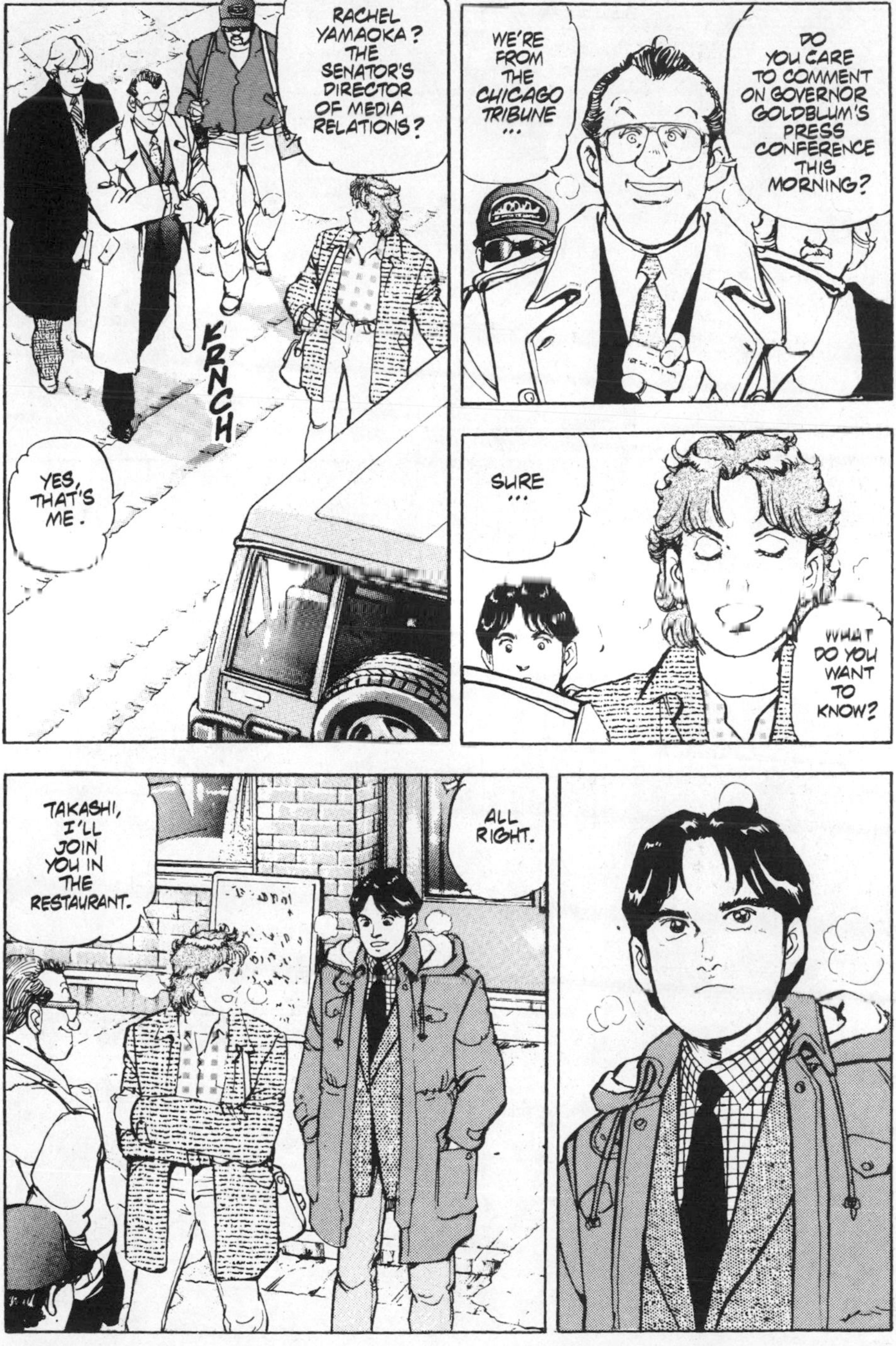

RACHEL YAMAOKA? THE SENATOR'S DIRECTOR OF MEDIA RELATIONS?
KRNCH
YES, THAT'S ME.
WE'RE FROM THE CHICAGO TRIBUNE ...
DO YOU CARE TO COMMENT ON GOVERNOR GOLDBLUM'S PRESS CONFERENCE THIS MORNING?
SURE ...
WHAT DO YOU WANT TO KNOW?
TAKASHI, I'LL JOIN YOU IN THE RESTAURANT.
ALL RIGHT.

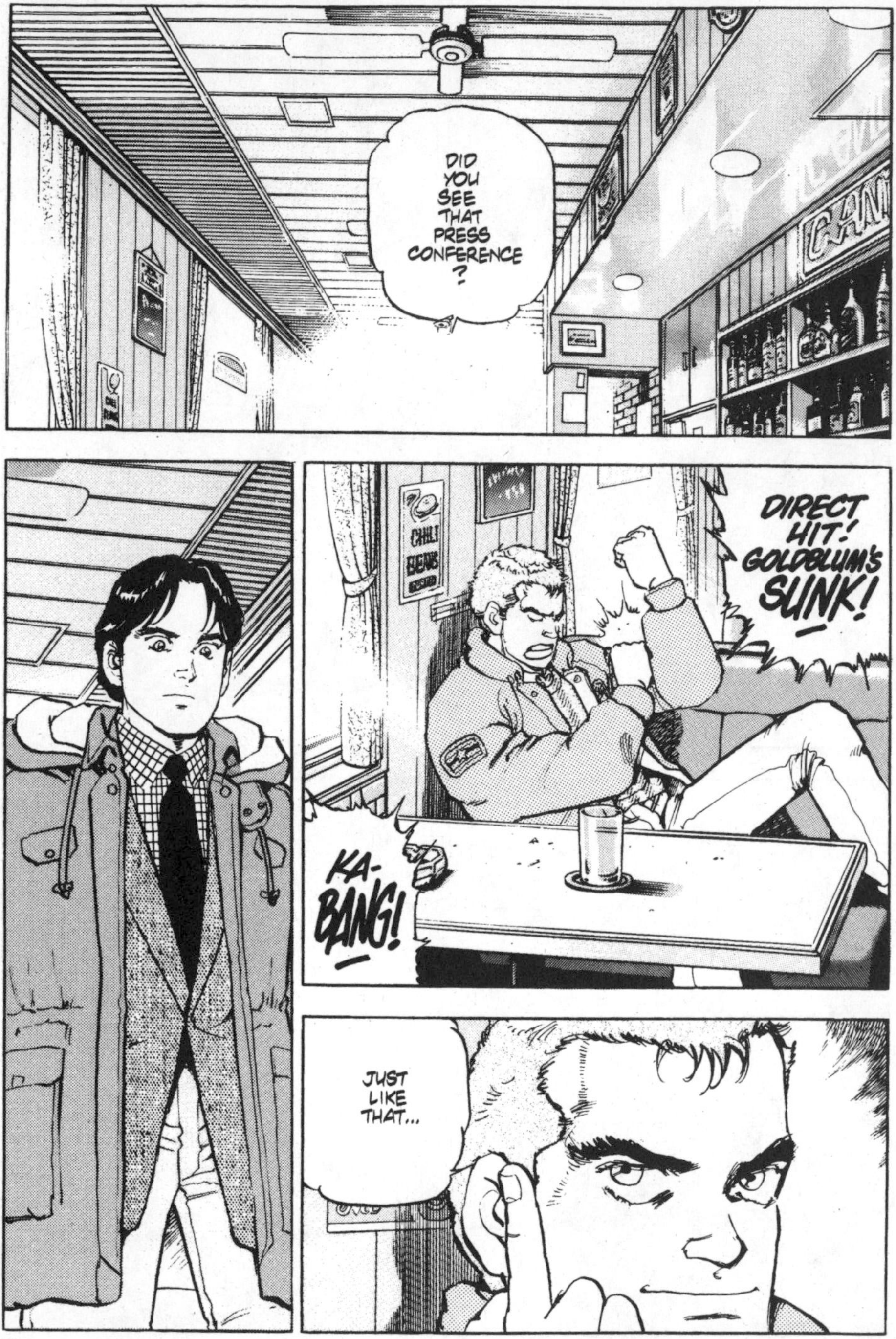
DID YOU SEE THAT PRESS CONFERENCE?
DIRECT HIT! GOLDBLUM'S SUNK!
KA-BANG!
JUST LIKE THAT...

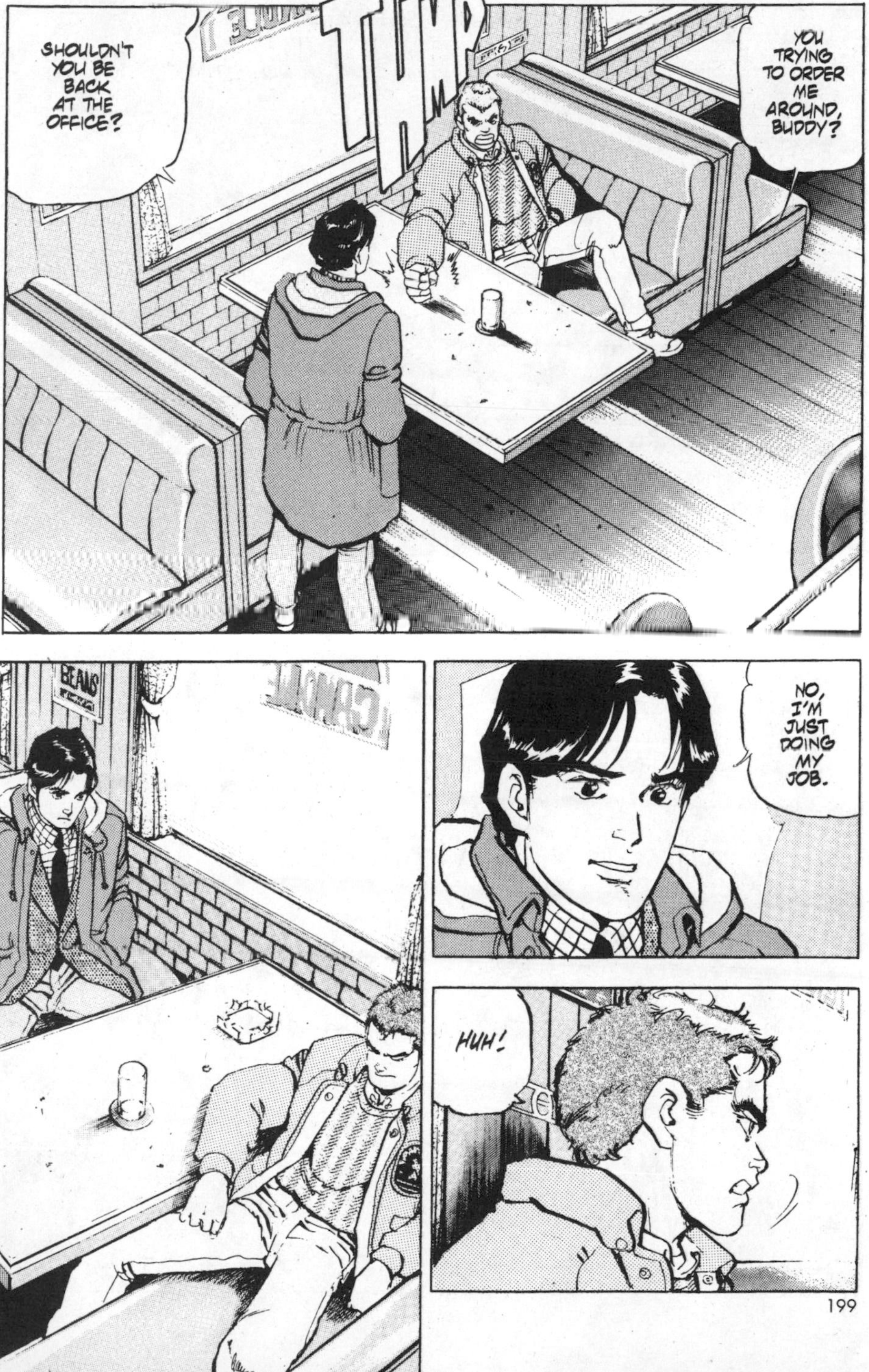
SHOULDN'T YOU BE BACK AT THE OFFICE?
THMP
YOU TRYING TO ORDER ME AROUND, BUDDY?
BEANS
NO, I'M JUST DOING MY JOB.
HUH!

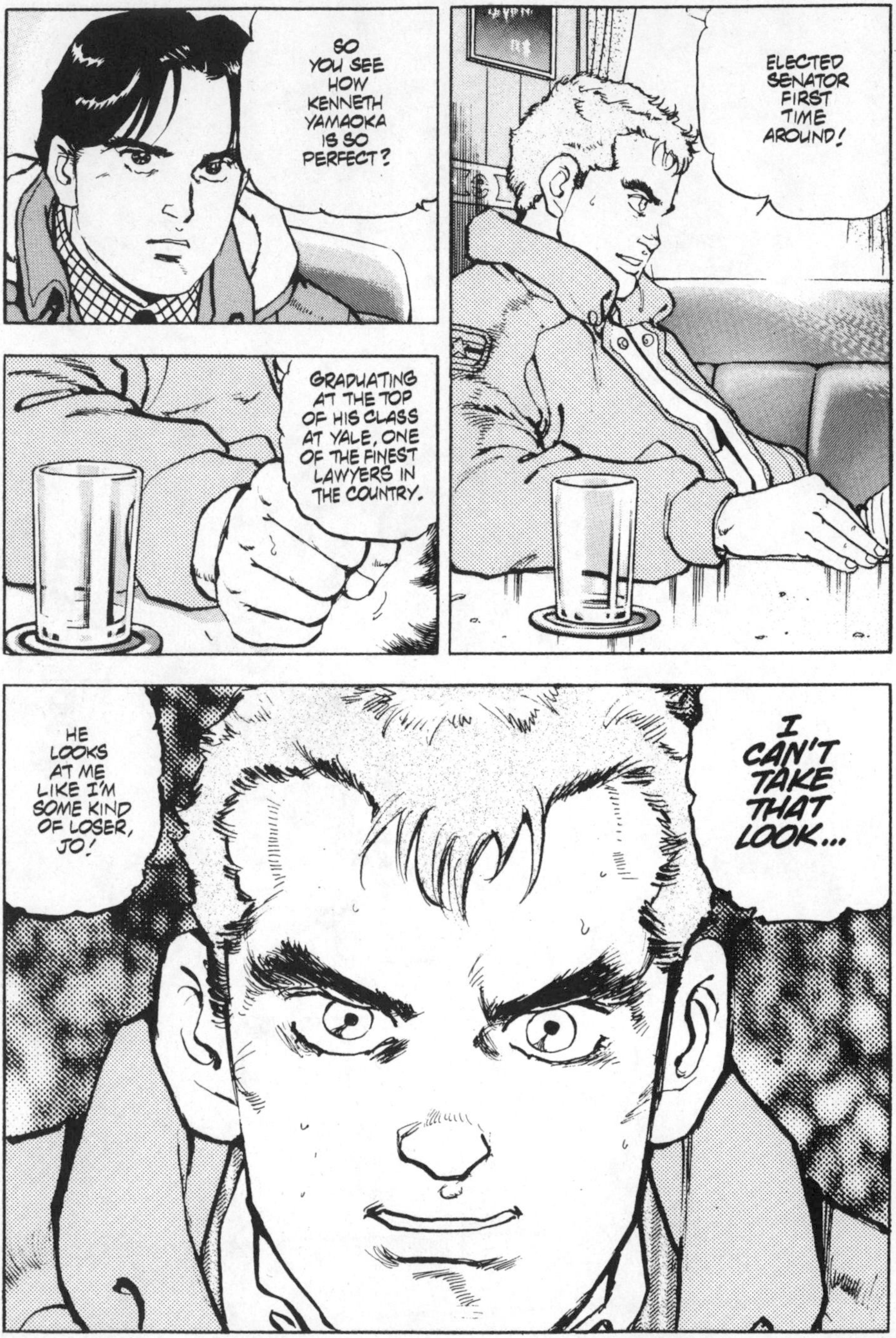
SO YOU SEE HOW KENNETH YAMAOKA IS SO PERFECT?
GRADUATING AT THE TOP OF HIS CLASS AT YALE, ONE OF THE FINEST LAWYERS IN THE COUNTRY.
ELECTED SENATOR FIRST TIME AROUND!
HE LOOKS AT ME LIKE I'M SOME KIND OF LOSER, JO!
I CAN'T TAKE THAT LOOK...

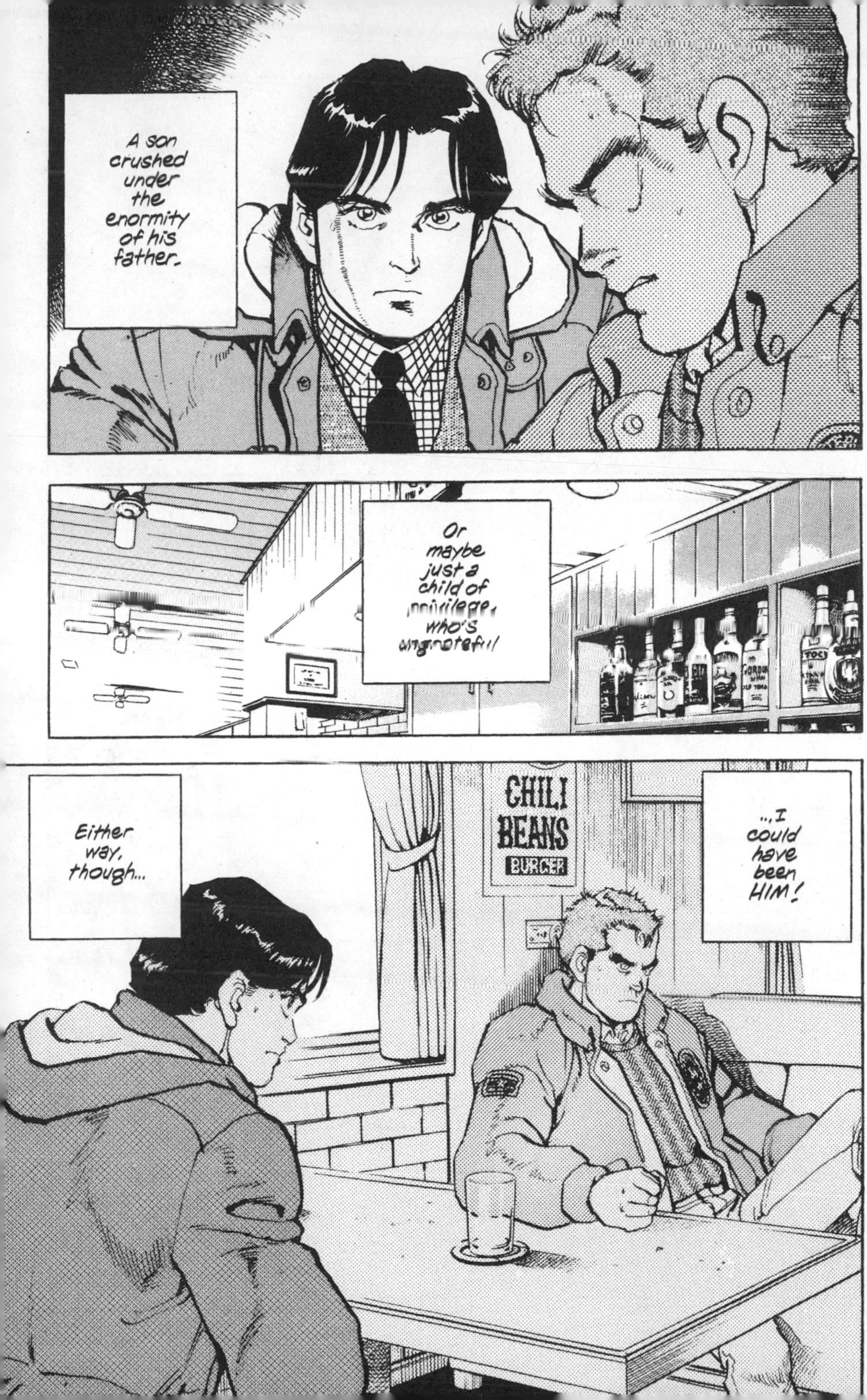
A son crushed under the enormity of his father.
Or maybe just a child of privilege, who's ungrateful
Either way, though...
CHILI BEANS
BURGER
...I could have been HIM!

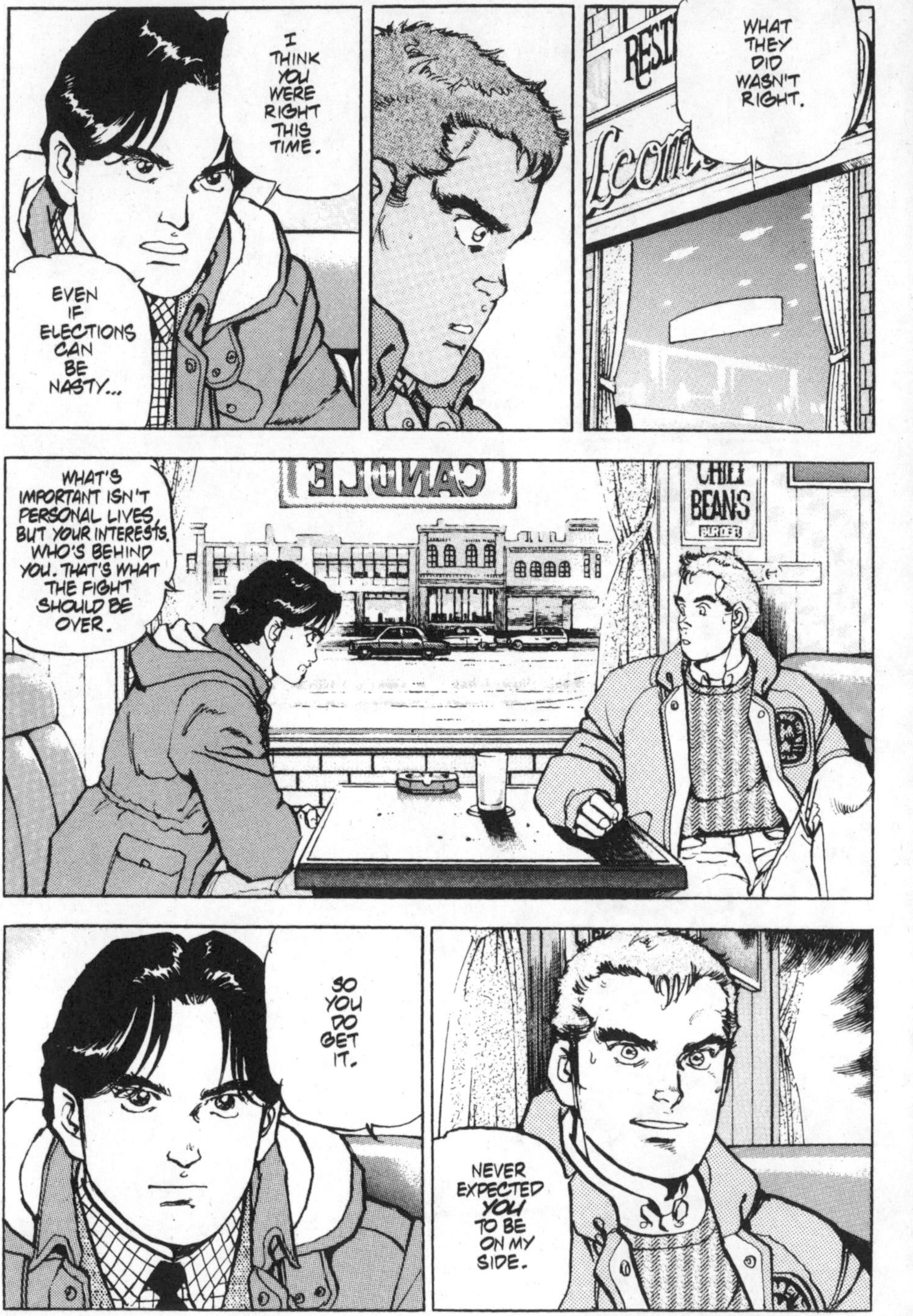
I THINK YOU WERE RIGHT THIS TIME.
EVEN IF ELECTIONS CAN BE NASTY...
WHAT THEY DID WASN'T RIGHT.
WHAT'S IMPORTANT ISN'T PERSONAL LIVES, BUT YOUR INTERESTS. WHO'S BEHIND YOU. THAT'S WHAT THE FIGHT SHOULD BE OVER.
CHILI BEANS
SO YOU DO GET IT.
NEVER EXPECTED YOU TO BE ON MY SIDE.

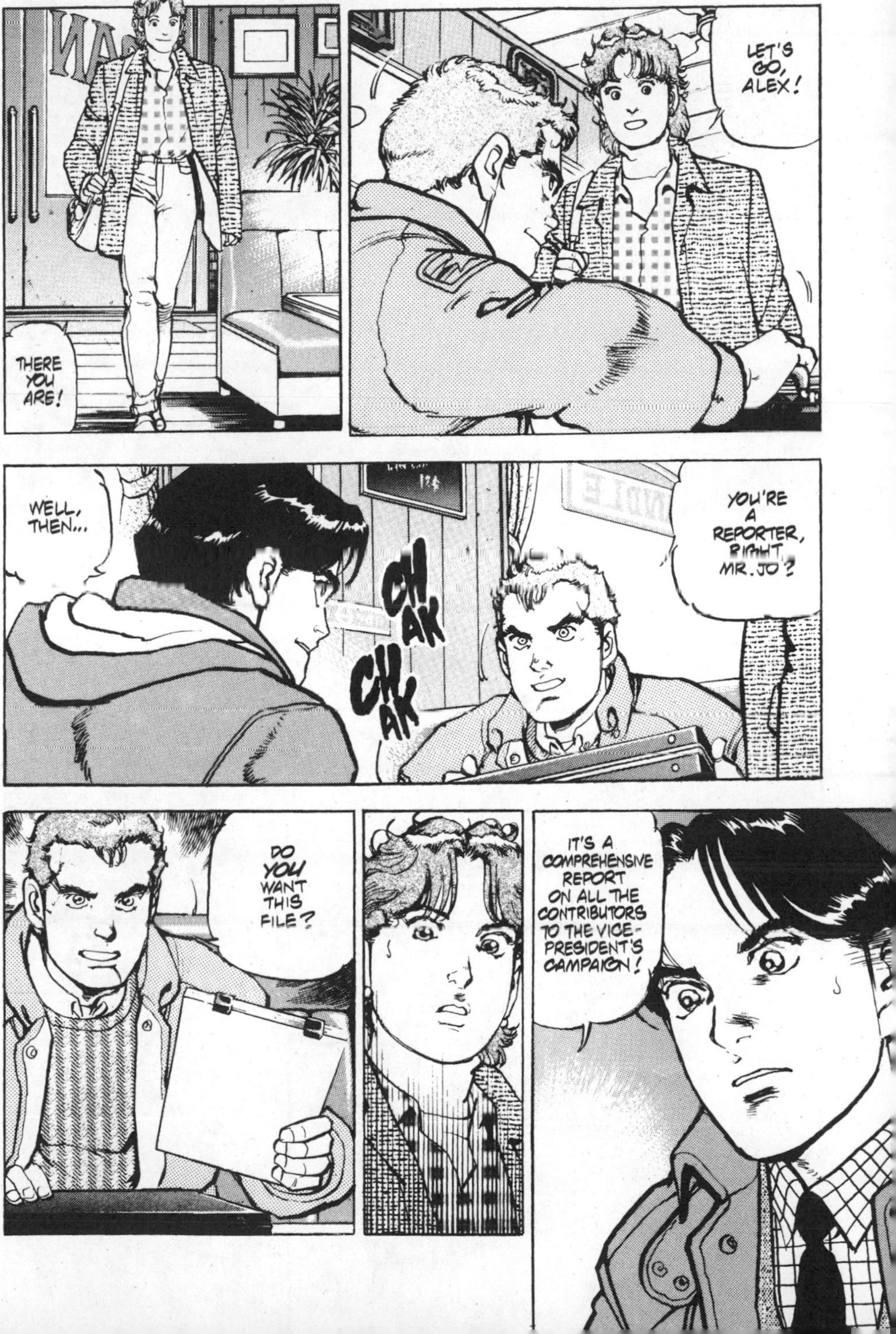
THERE YOU ARE!
LET'S GO, ALEX!
WELL, THEN...
CHAK CHAK
YOU'RE A REPORTER, RIGHT, MR. JO?
DO YOU WANT THIS FILE?
IT'S A COMPREHENSIVE REPORT ON ALL THE CONTRIBUTORS TO THE VICE-PRESIDENT'S CAMPAIGN!

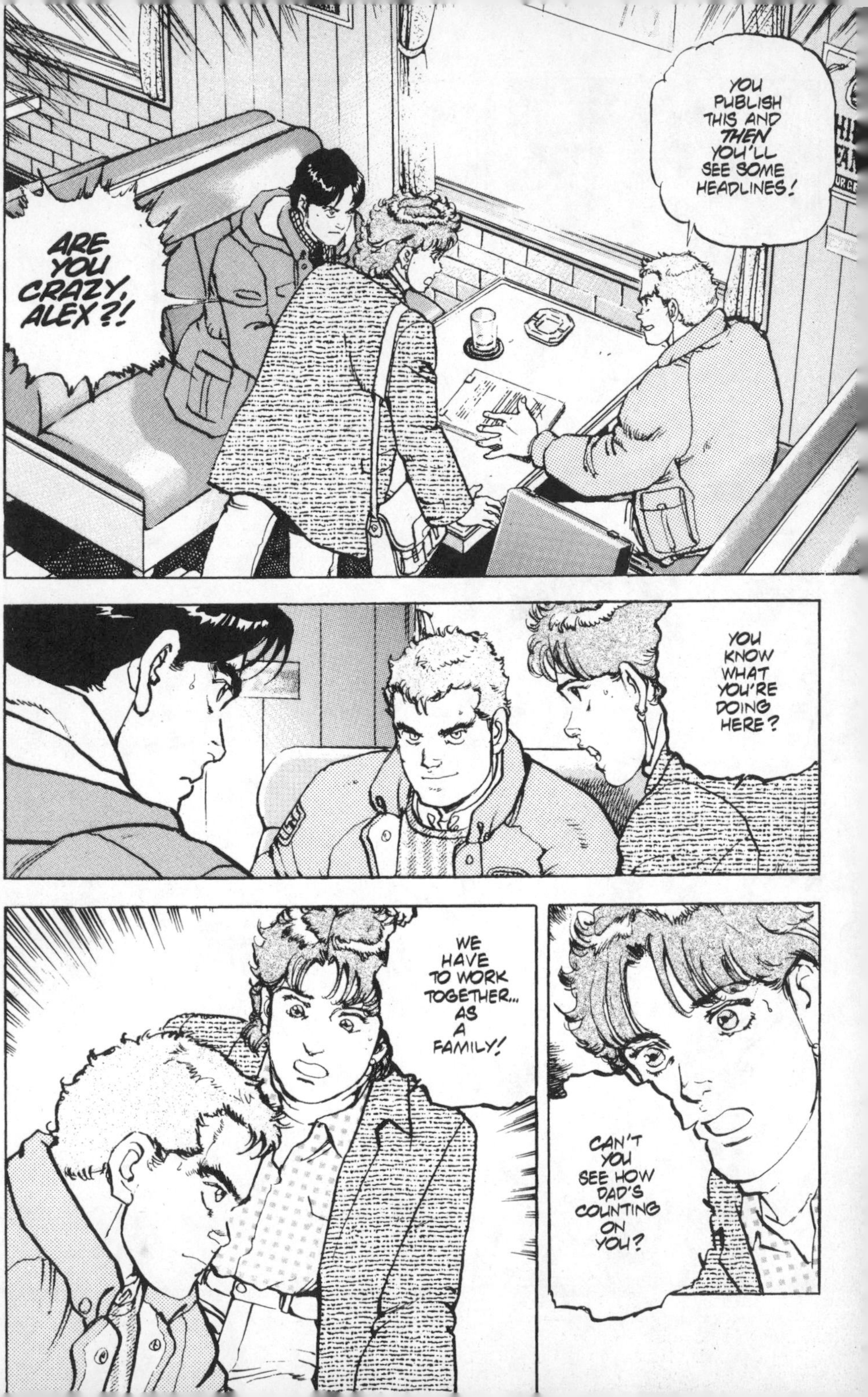
ARE YOU CRAZY, ALEX?!
YOU PUBLISH THIS AND THEN YOU'LL SEE SOME HEADLINES!
YOU KNOW WHAT YOU'RE DOING HERE?
WE HAVE TO WORK TOGETHER... AS A FAMILY!
CAN'T YOU SEE HOW DAD'S COUNTING ON YOU?

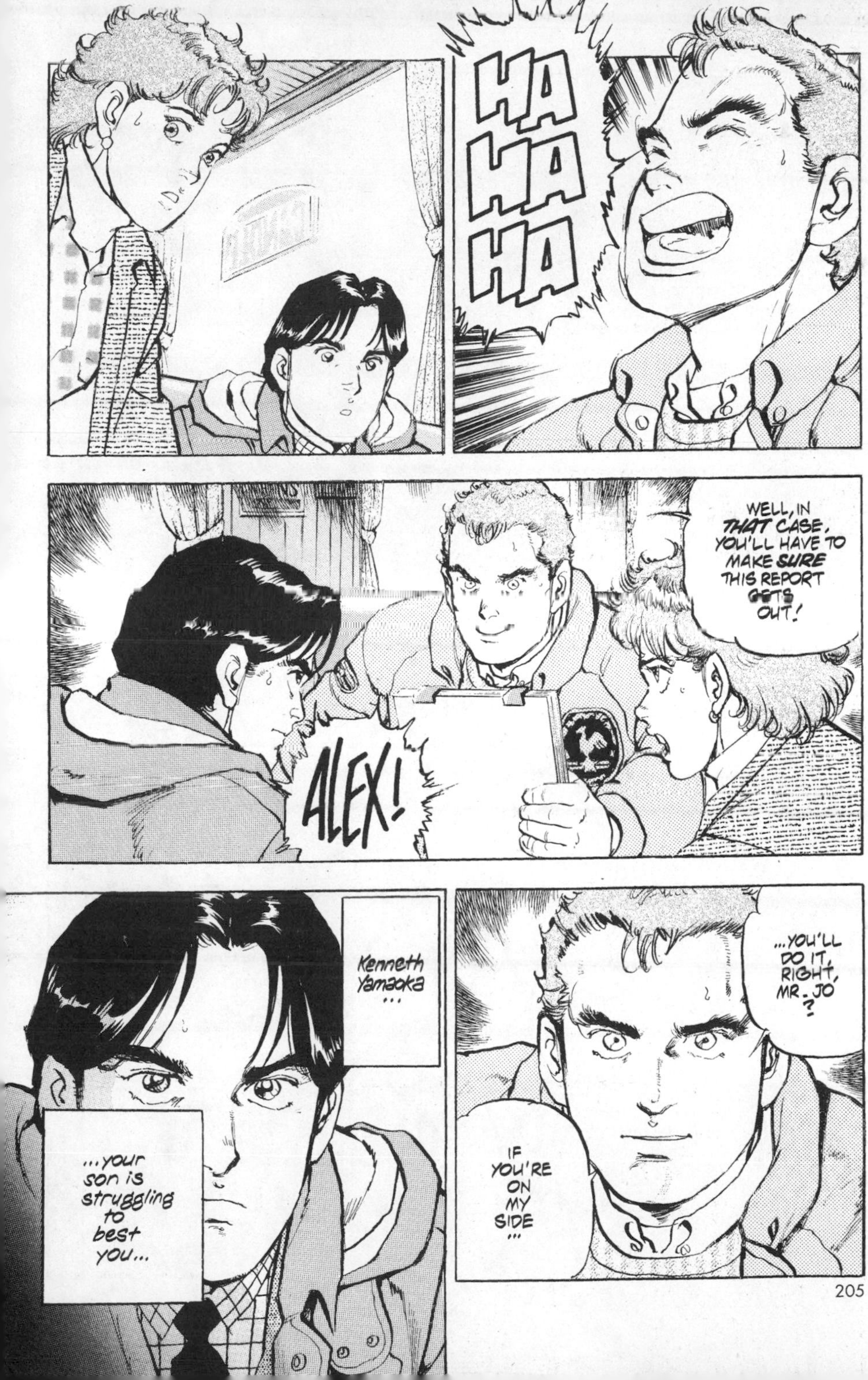

HA HA HA HA
WELL, IN THAT CASE, YOU'LL HAVE TO MAKE SURE THIS REPORT GETS OUT!
ALEX!
Kenneth Yamaoka...
...your son is struggling to best you...
...YOU'LL DO IT, RIGHT, MR. JO?
IF YOU'RE ON MY SIDE...

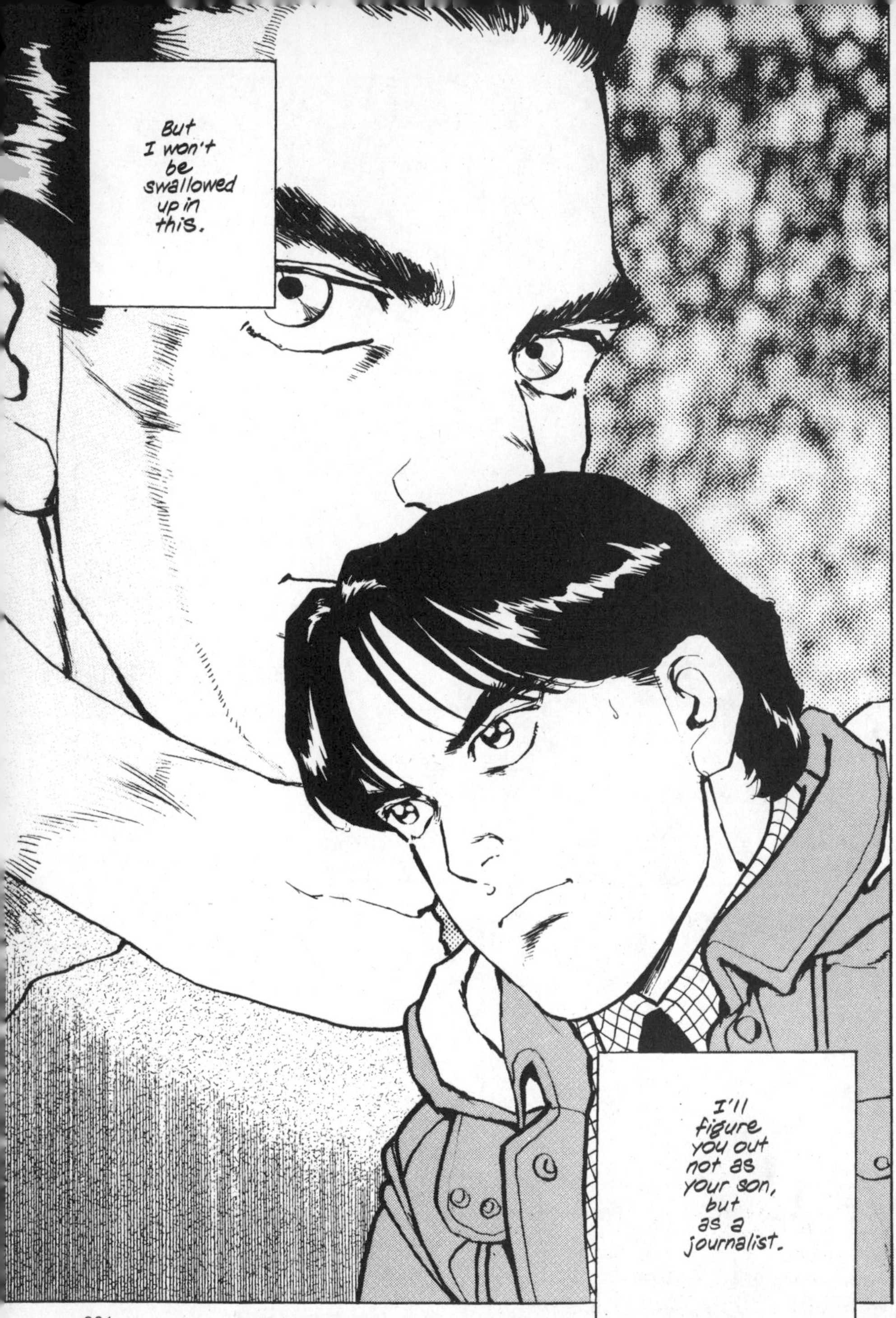
But I won't be swallowed up in this.
I'll figure you out not as your son, but as a journalist.

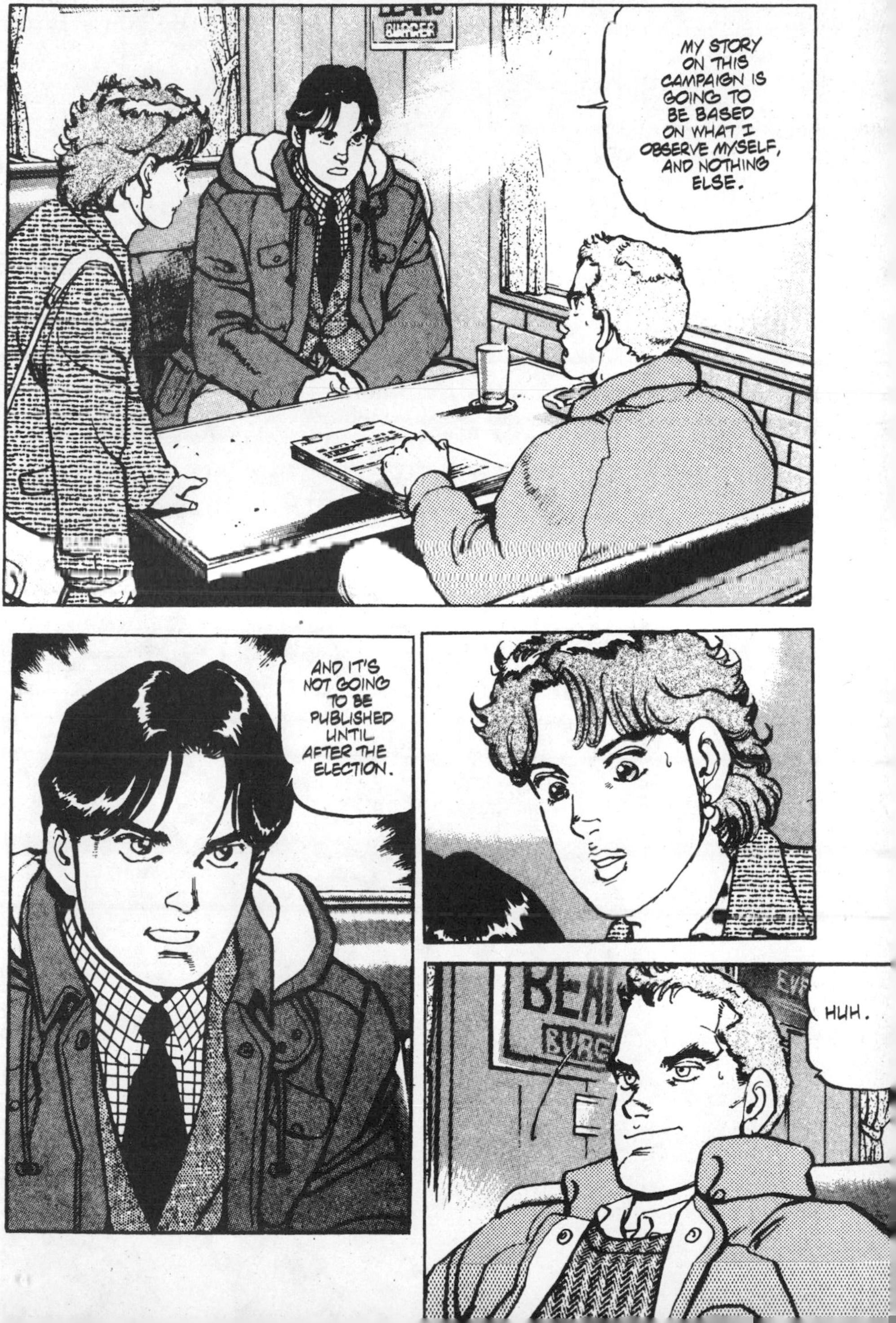
MY STORY ON THIS CAMPAIGN IS GOING TO BE BASED ON WHAT I OBSERVE MYSELF, AND NOTHING ELSE.
AND IT'S NOT GOING TO BE PUBLISHED UNTIL AFTER THE ELECTION.
HUH.

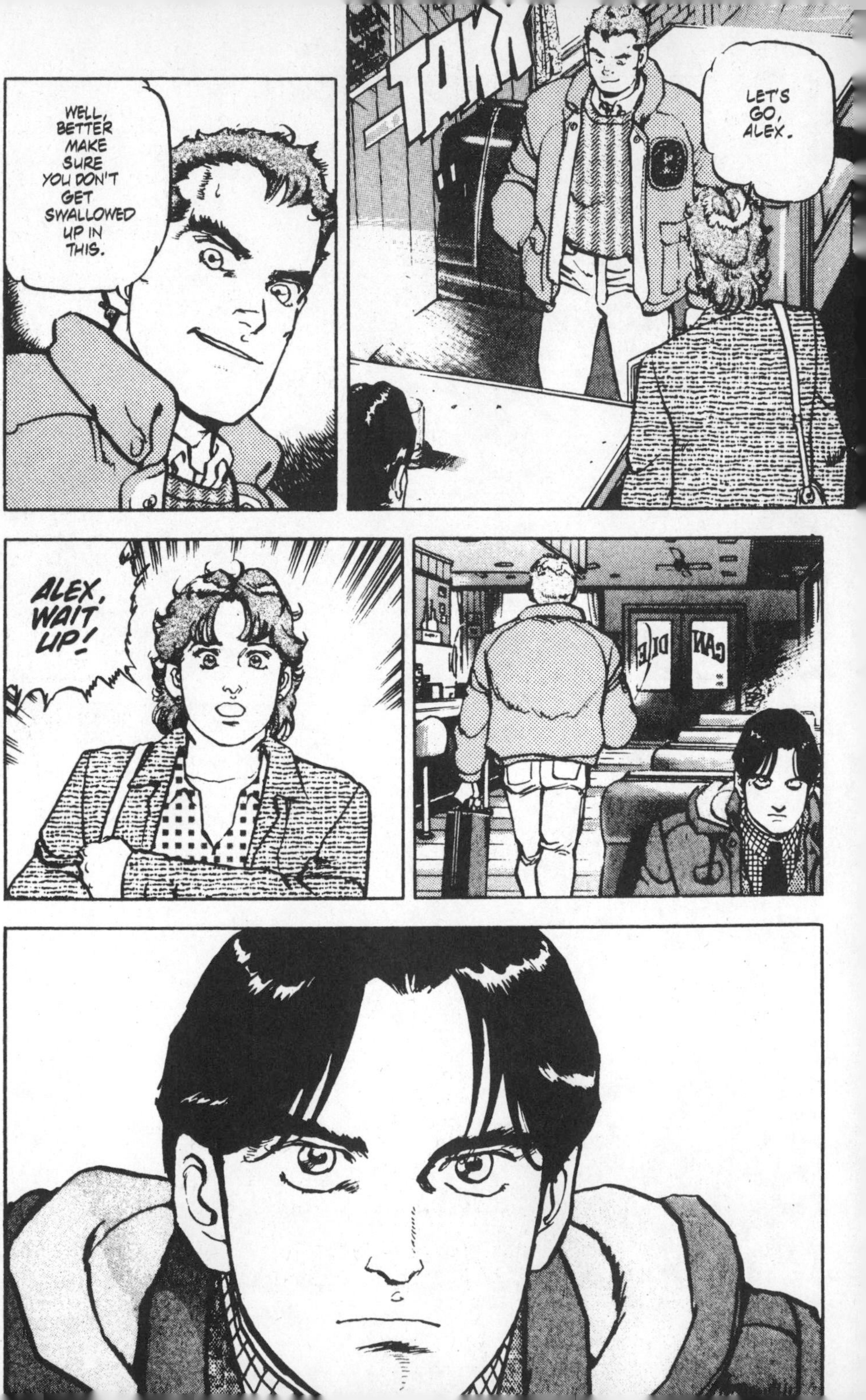
WELL, BETTER MAKE SURE YOU DON'T GET SWALLOWED UP IN THIS.
TOKK
LET'S GO, ALEX.
ALEX, WAIT UP!

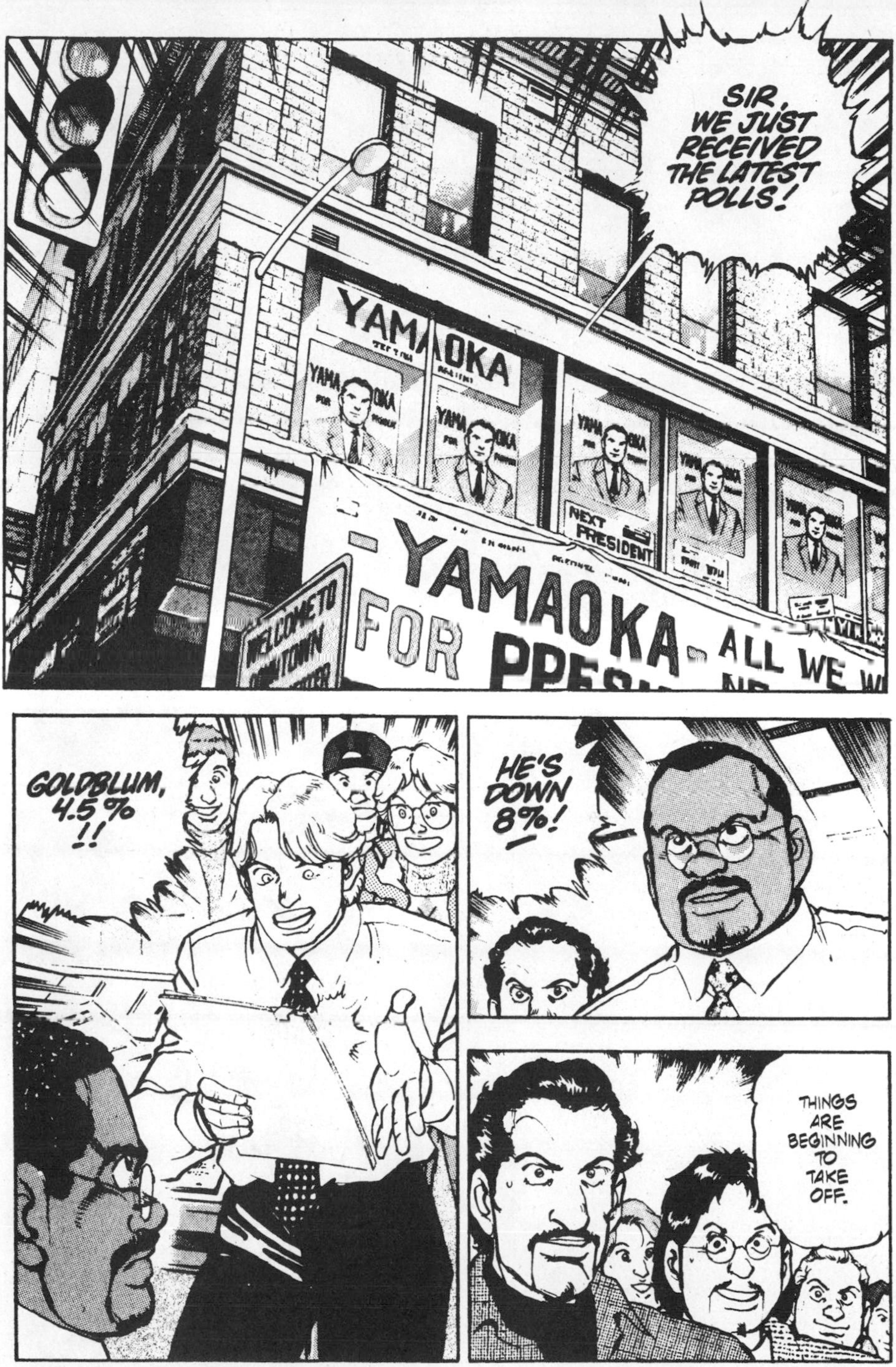
SIR, WE JUST RECEIVED THE LATEST POLLS!
YAMAOKA
NEXT PRESIDENT
-YAMAOKA-
FOR
ALL WE
GOLDBLUM, 4.5% !!
HE'S DOWN 8%!
THINGS ARE BEGINNING TO TAKE OFF.

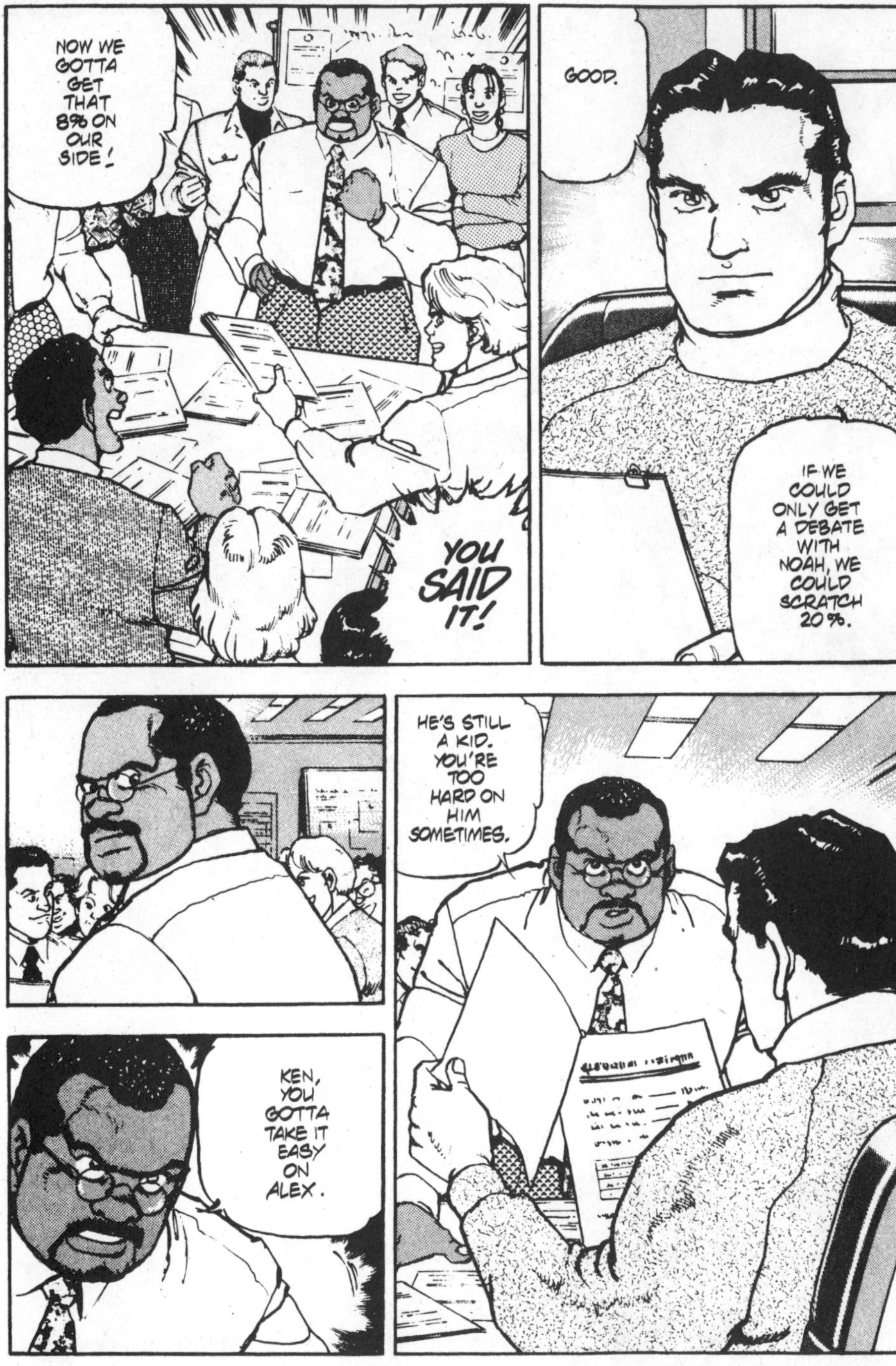
NOW WE GOTTA GET THAT 8% ON OUR SIDE!
YOU SAID IT!
GOOD.
IF WE COULD ONLY GET A DEBATE WITH NOAH, WE COULD SCRATCH 20%.
HE'S STILL A KID. YOU'RE TOO HARD ON HIM SOMETIMES.
KEN, YOU GOTTA TAKE IT EASY ON ALEX.

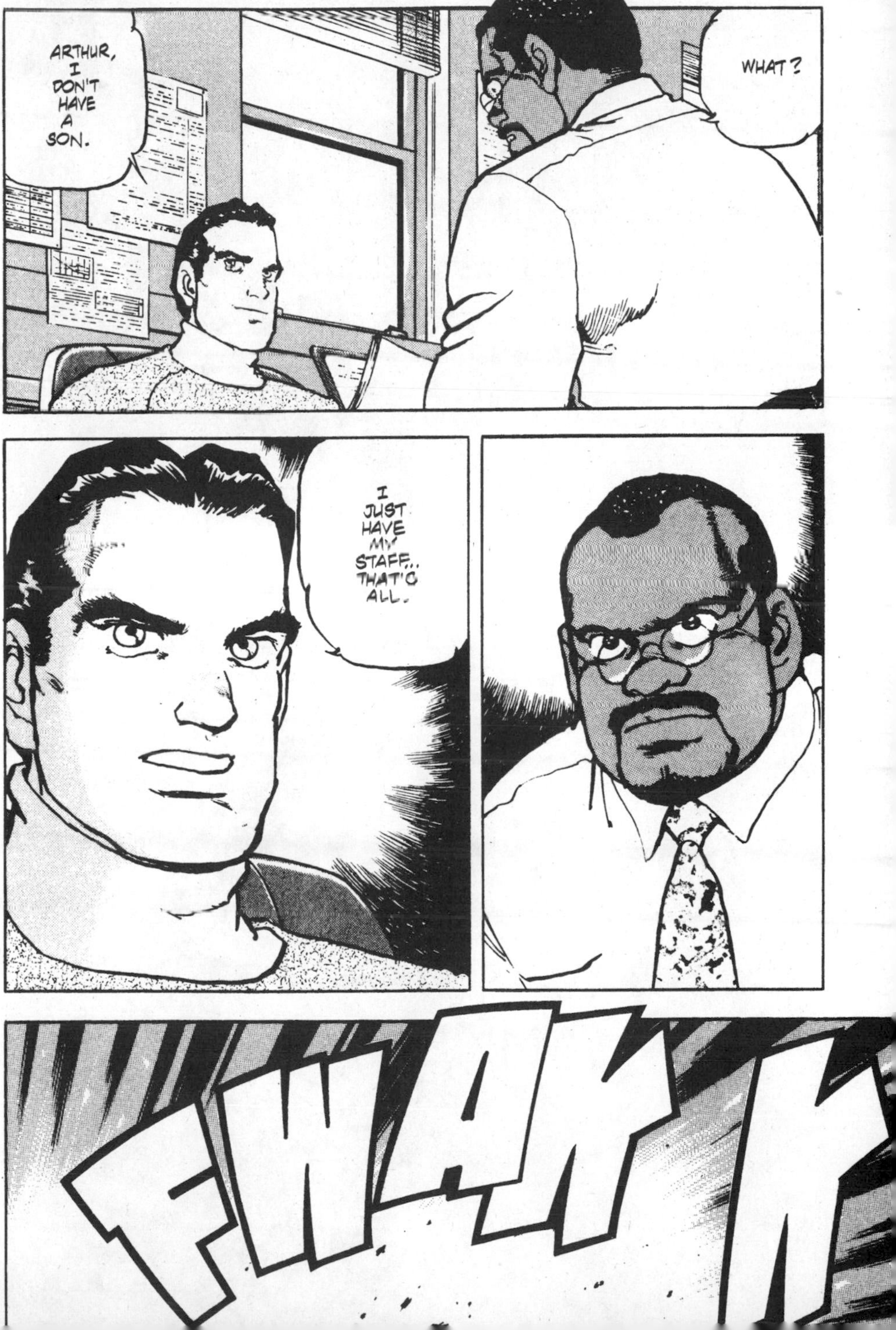
ARTHUR, I DON'T HAVE A SON.
WHAT?
I JUST HAVE MY STAFF... THAT'S ALL.
FWAKK

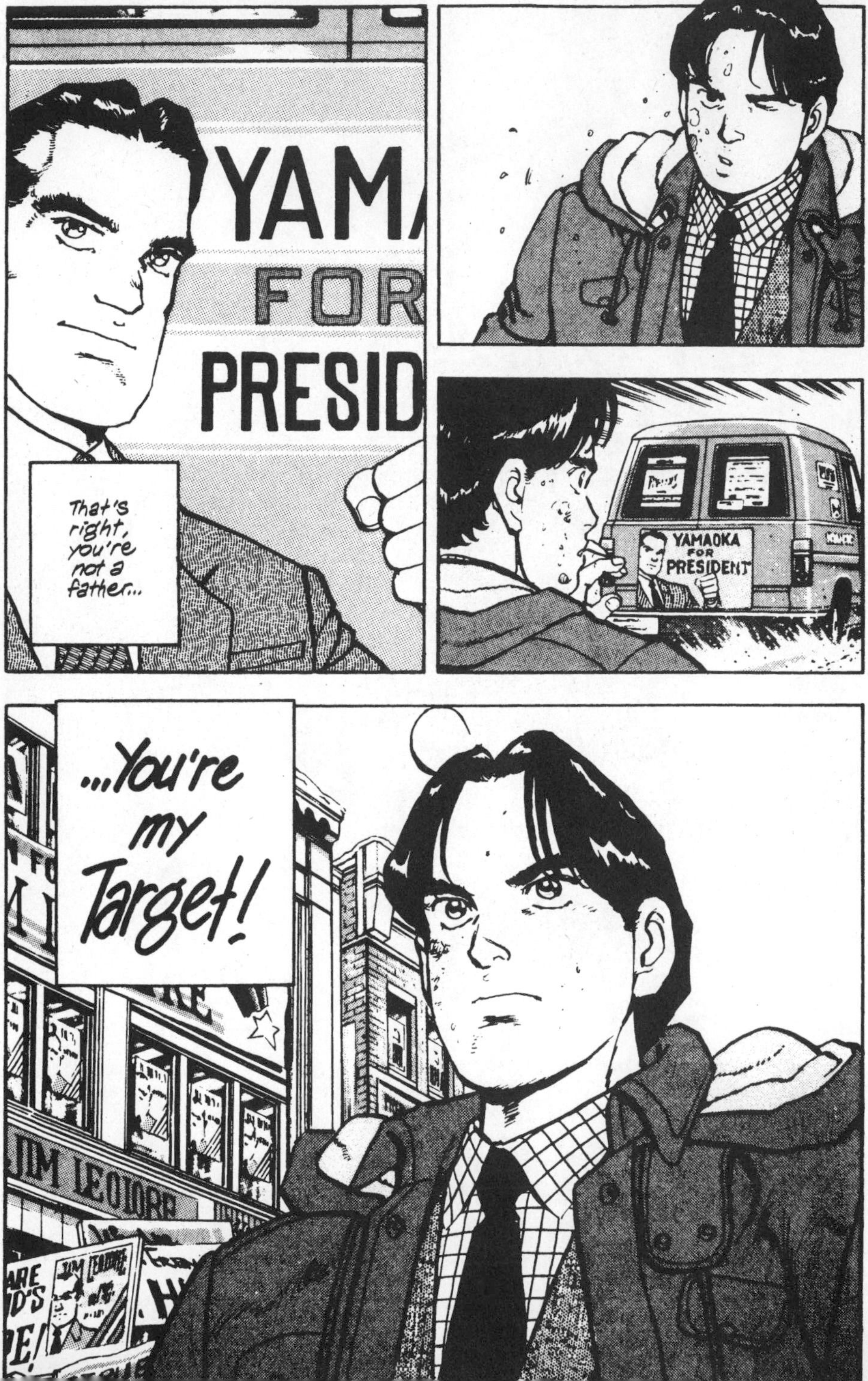
YAMA
FOR
PRESID
That's right, you're not a father...
YAMAOKA FOR PRESIDENT
...You're my Target!

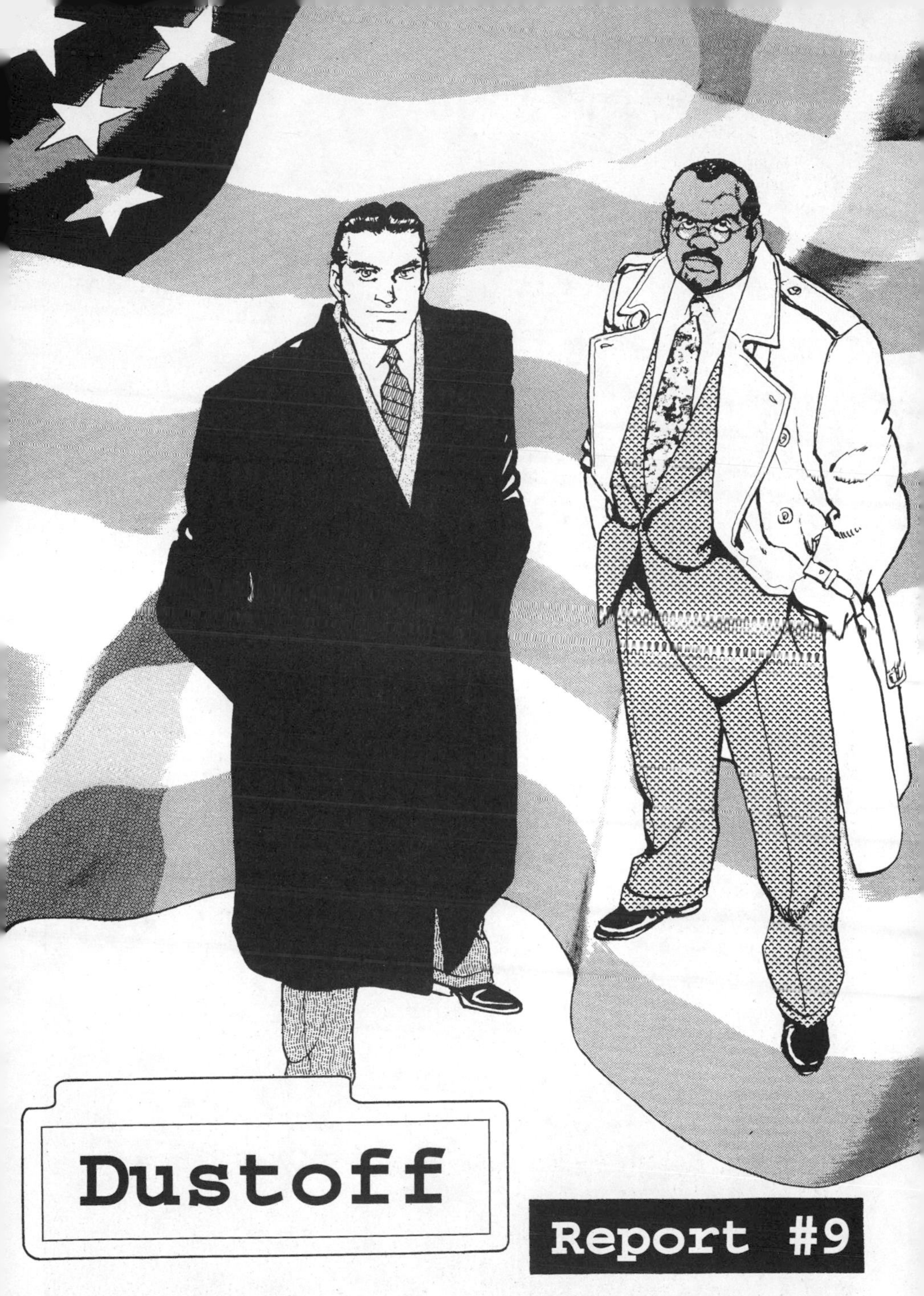
Dustoff
Report #9

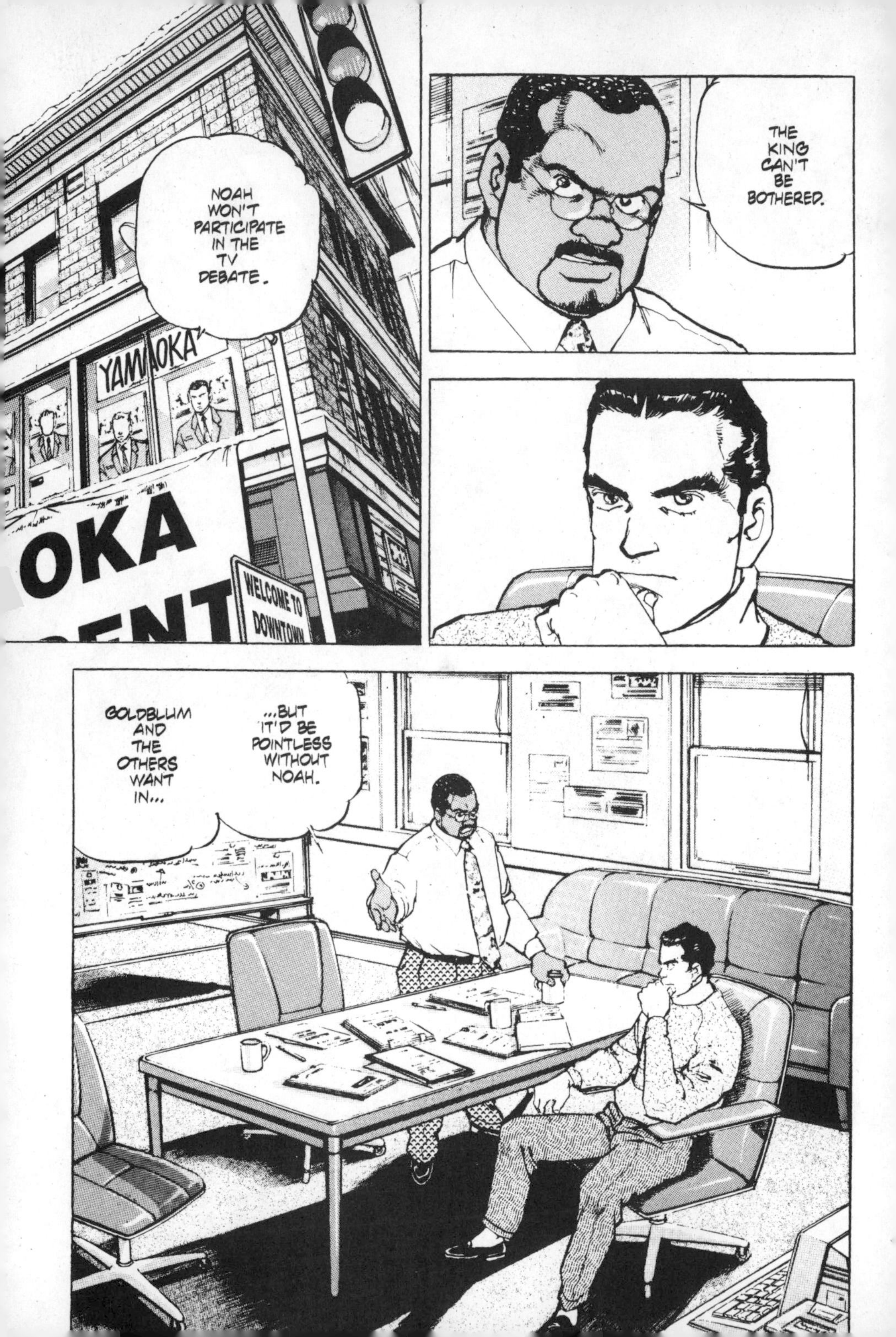

NOAH WON'T PARTICIPATE IN THE TV DEBATE.
YAMAOKA
OKA
WELCOME TO DOWNTOWN
THE KING CAN'T BE BOTHERED.
GOLDBLUM AND THE OTHERS WANT IN...
...BUT IT'D BE POINTLESS WITHOUT NOAH.

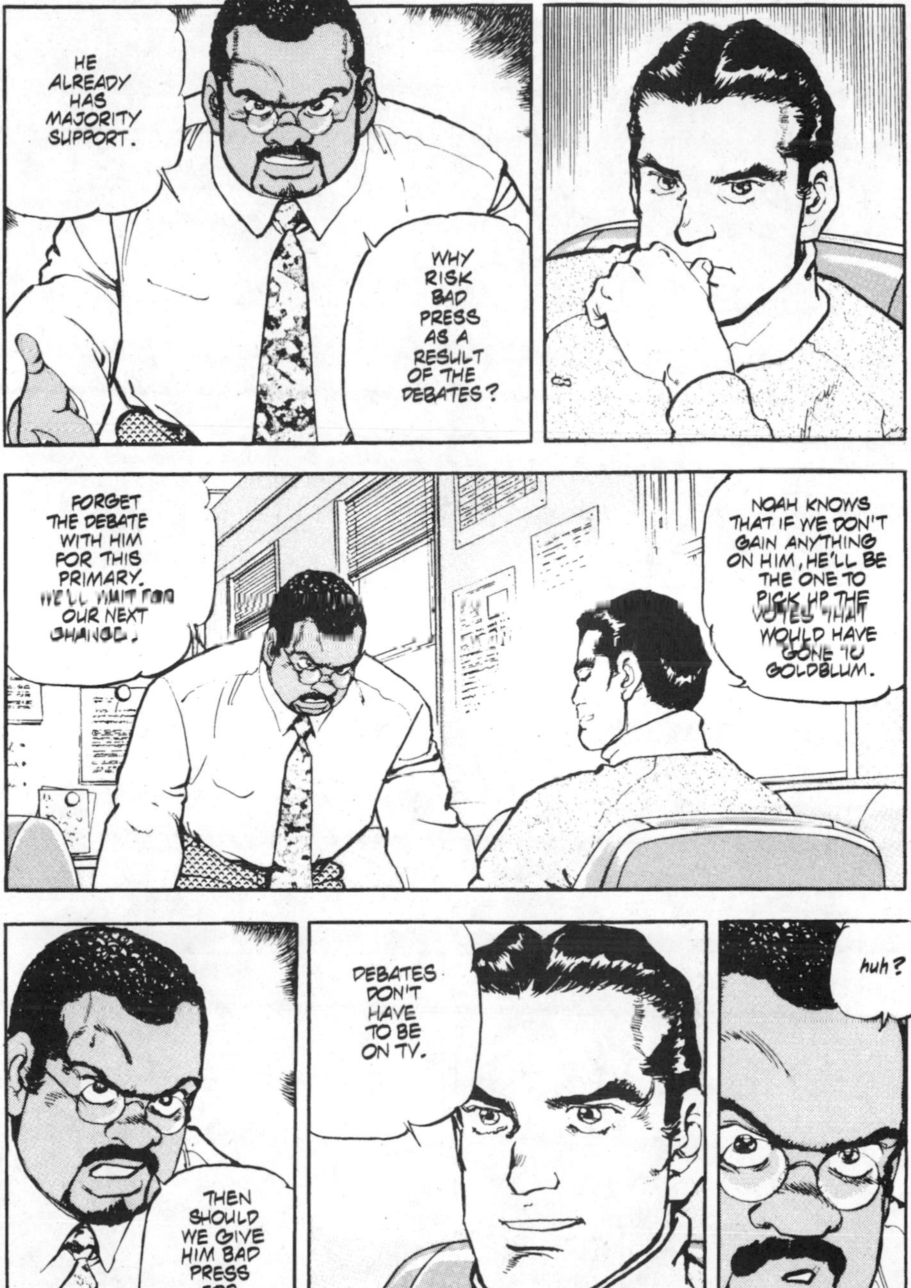
HE ALREADY HAS MAJORITY SUPPORT.
WHY RISK BAD PRESS AS A RESULT OF THE DEBATES?
FORGET THE DEBATE WITH HIM FOR THIS PRIMARY. WE'LL WAIT FOR OUR NEXT CHANCE.
NOAH KNOWS THAT IF WE DON'T GAIN ANYTHING ON HIM, HE'LL BE THE ONE TO PICK UP THE VOTES THAT WOULD HAVE GONE TO GOLDBLUM.
THEN SHOULD WE GIVE HIM BAD PRESS FOR BEING A COWARD?
DEBATES DON'T HAVE TO BE ON TV.
huh?

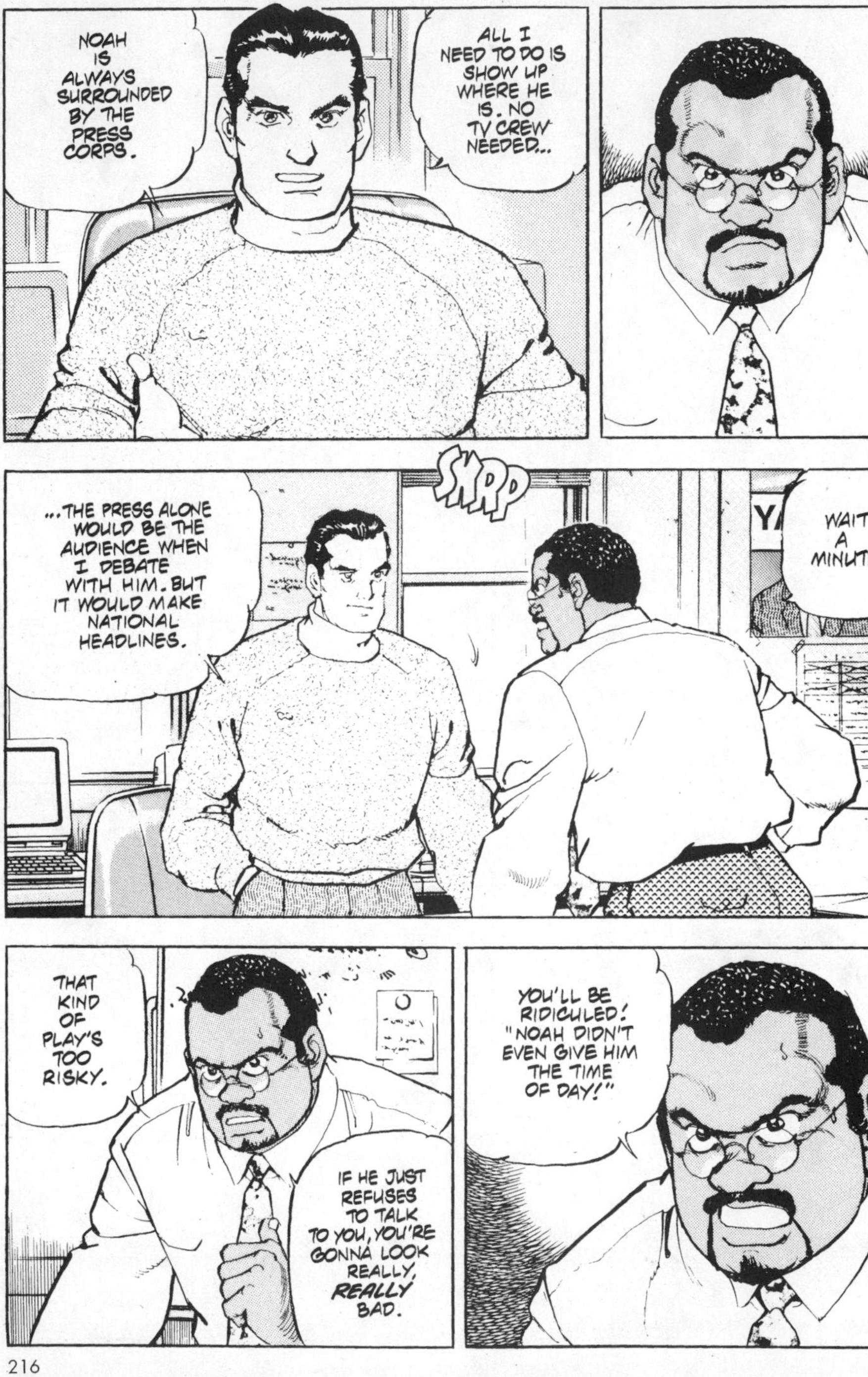
NOAH IS ALWAYS SURROUNDED BY THE PRESS CORPS.
ALL I NEED TO DO IS SHOW UP WHERE HE IS. NO TV CREW NEEDED...
SKRP
...THE PRESS ALONE WOULD BE THE AUDIENCE WHEN I DEBATE WITH HIM. BUT IT WOULD MAKE NATIONAL HEADLINES.
WAIT A MINUTE!
THAT KIND OF PLAY'S TOO RISKY.
IF HE JUST REFUSES TO TALK TO YOU, YOU'RE GONNA LOOK REALLY, REALLY BAD.
YOU'LL BE RIDICULED! "NOAH DIDN'T EVEN GIVE HIM THE TIME OF DAY!"

HE WON'T. HE CAN'T REFUSE ME.

YOU DON'T KNOW THAT FOR SURE! HE SAID NO TO THE TV DEBATE!

BUT IF HE REFUSES, HE'S NO LONGER THE KING.

I'M THE CHALLENGER. IF HE DOESN'T ADVANCE THEN I'LL HAVE TO MAKE THE FIRST MOVE.

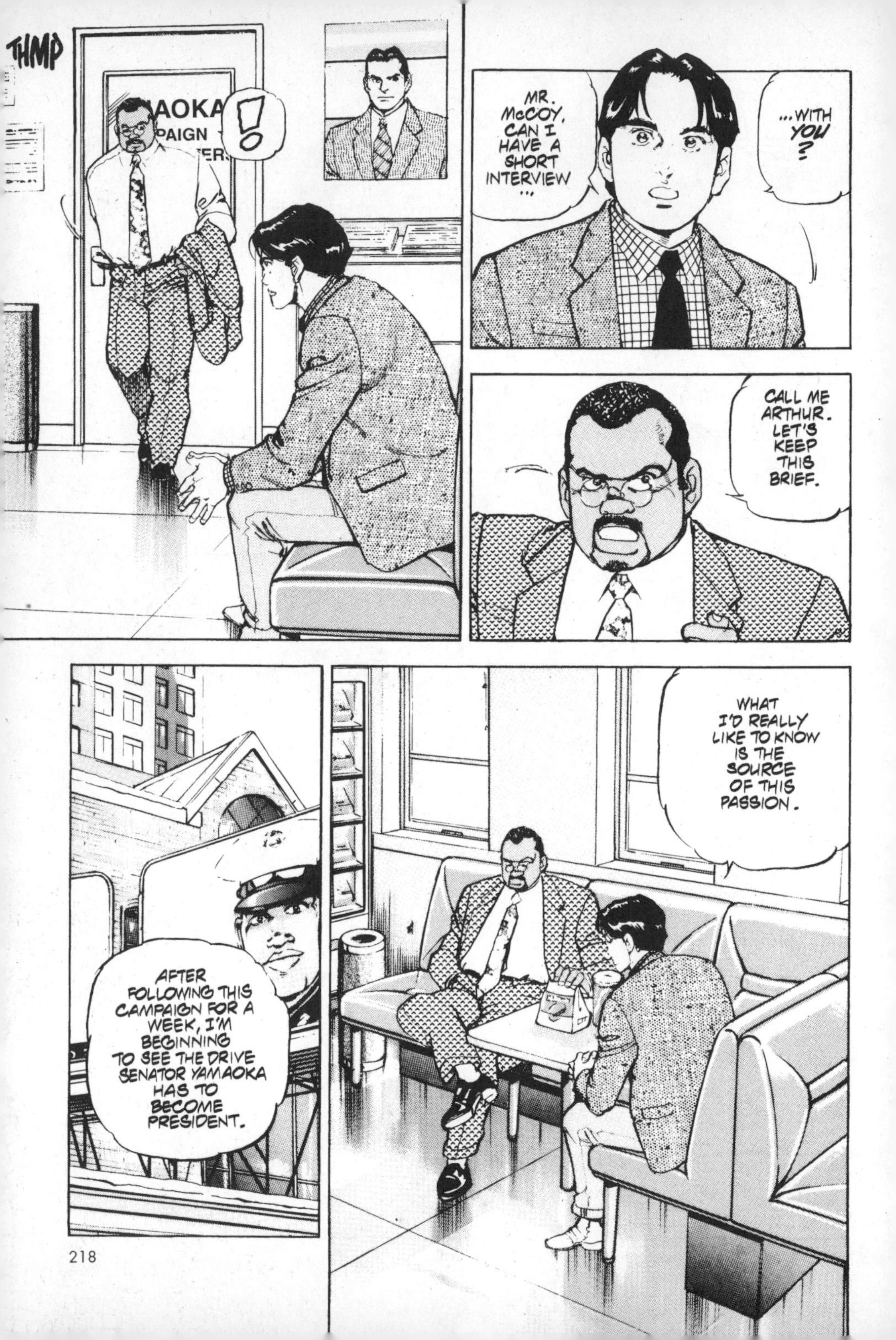
THMP
!
MR. McCOY, CAN I HAVE A SHORT INTERVIEW ...
...WITH YOU?
CALL ME ARTHUR. LET'S KEEP THIS BRIEF.
AFTER FOLLOWING THIS CAMPAIGN FOR A WEEK, I'M BEGINNING TO SEE THE DRIVE SENATOR YAMAOKA HAS TO BECOME PRESIDENT.
WHAT I'D REALLY LIKE TO KNOW IS THE SOURCE OF THIS PASSION.

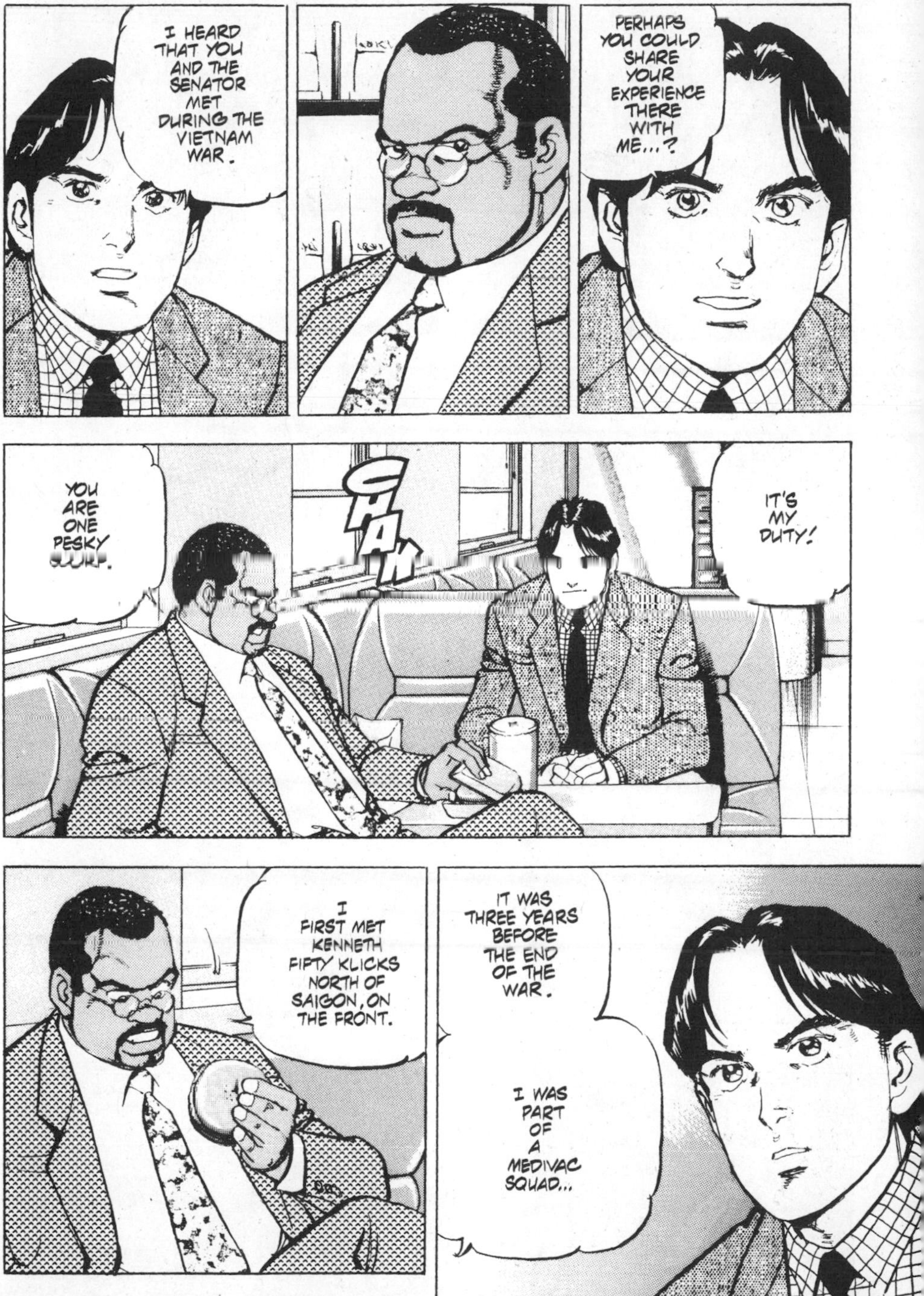
I HEARD THAT YOU AND THE SENATOR MET DURING THE VIETNAM WAR.
PERHAPS YOU COULD SHARE YOUR EXPERIENCE THERE WITH ME...?
YOU ARE ONE PESKY
CHAM
IT'S MY DUTY!
I FIRST MET KENNETH FIFTY KLICKS NORTH OF SAIGON, ON THE FRONT.
IT WAS THREE YEARS BEFORE THE END OF THE WAR.
I WAS PART OF A MEDIVAC SQUAD...

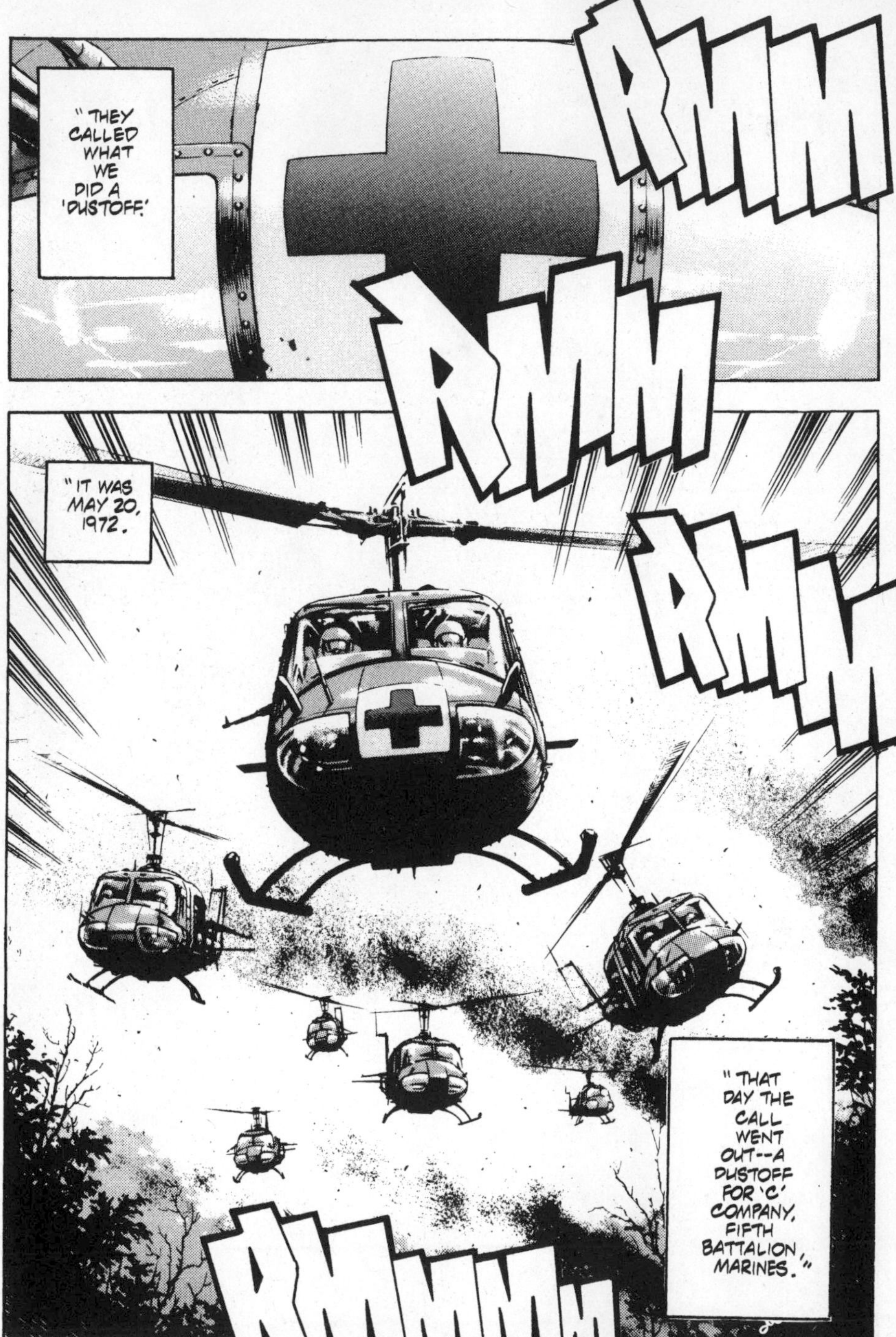

"THEY CALLED WHAT WE DID A 'DUSTOFF.'
RMMM
RMM
"IT WAS MAY 20, 1972.
RMMM
RMMMMMM
"THAT DAY THE CALL WENT OUT--A DUSTOFF FOR 'C' COMPANY, FIFTH BATTALION, MARINES."

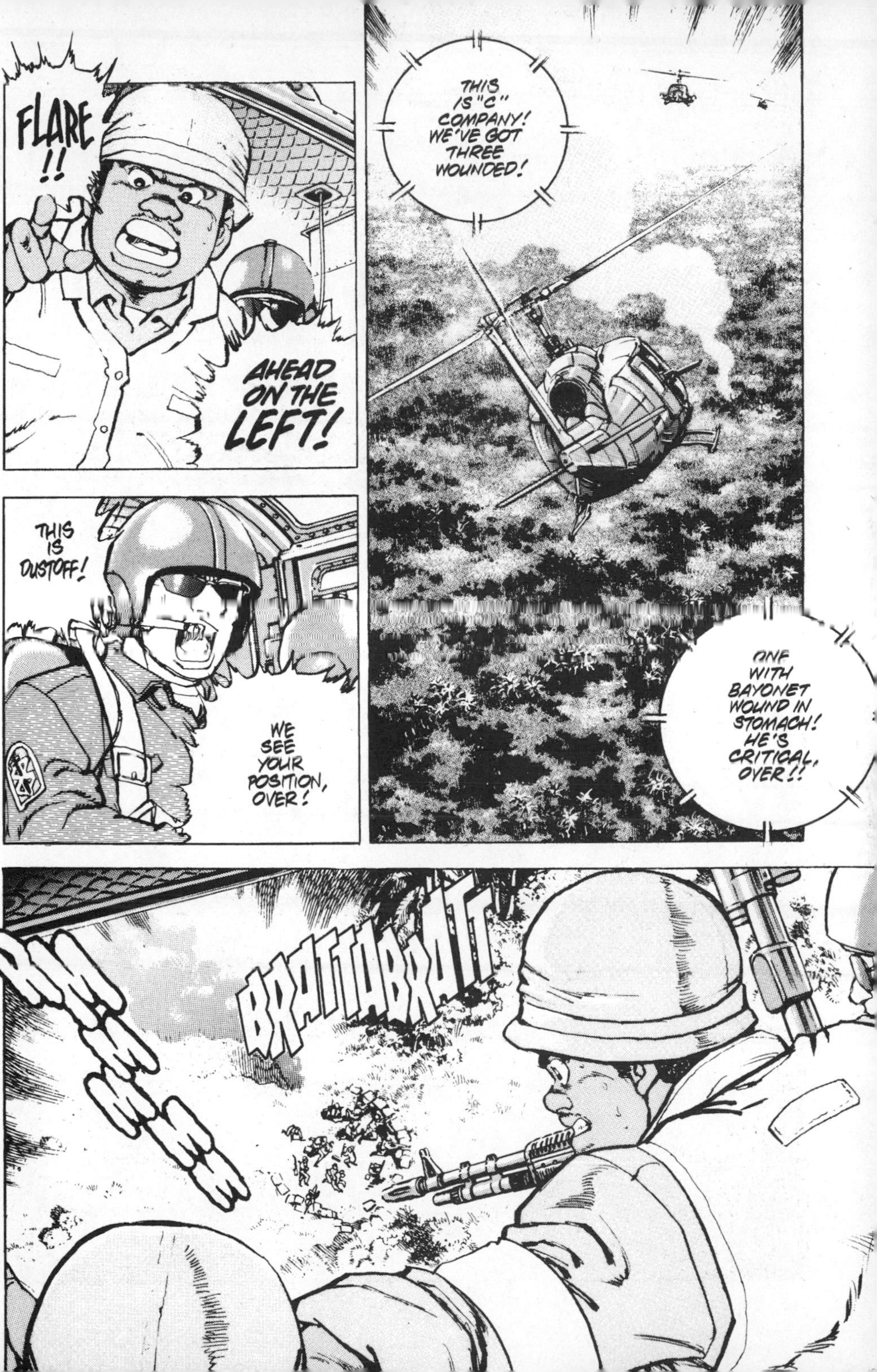
FLARE !!
AHEAD ON THE LEFT!
THIS IS DUSTOFF!
WE SEE YOUR POSITION, OVER!
THIS IS "C" COMPANY! WE'VE GOT THREE WOUNDED!
ONE WITH BAYONET WOUND IN STOMACH! HE'S CRITICAL, OVER!!
BRATTABRATT

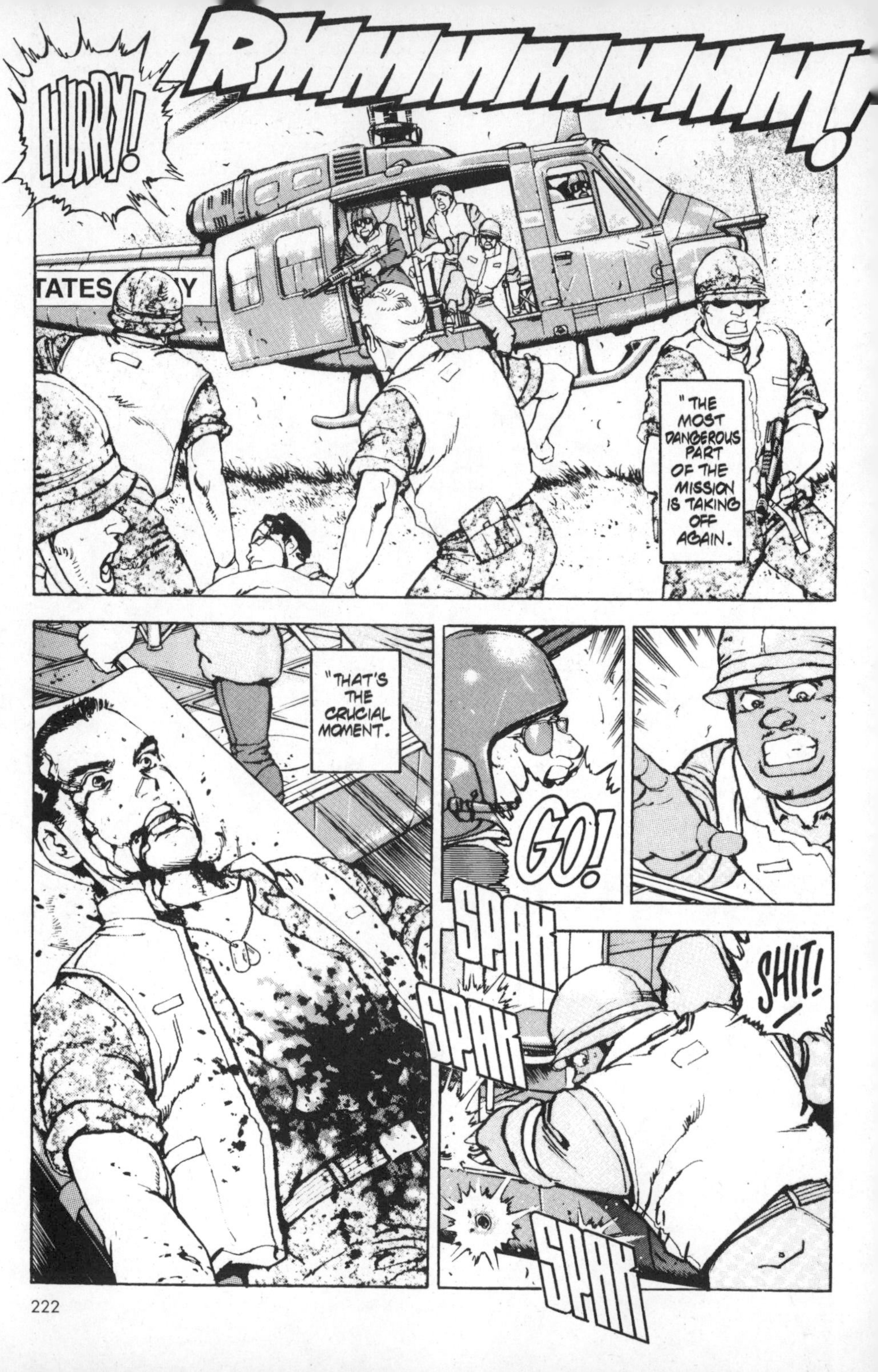
HURRY!
RHMMMMMMMM!
TATES Y
"THE MOST DANGEROUS PART OF THE MISSION IS TAKING OFF AGAIN.
"THAT'S THE CRUCIAL MOMENT.
GO!
SPAK
SPAK
SHIT!
SPAK

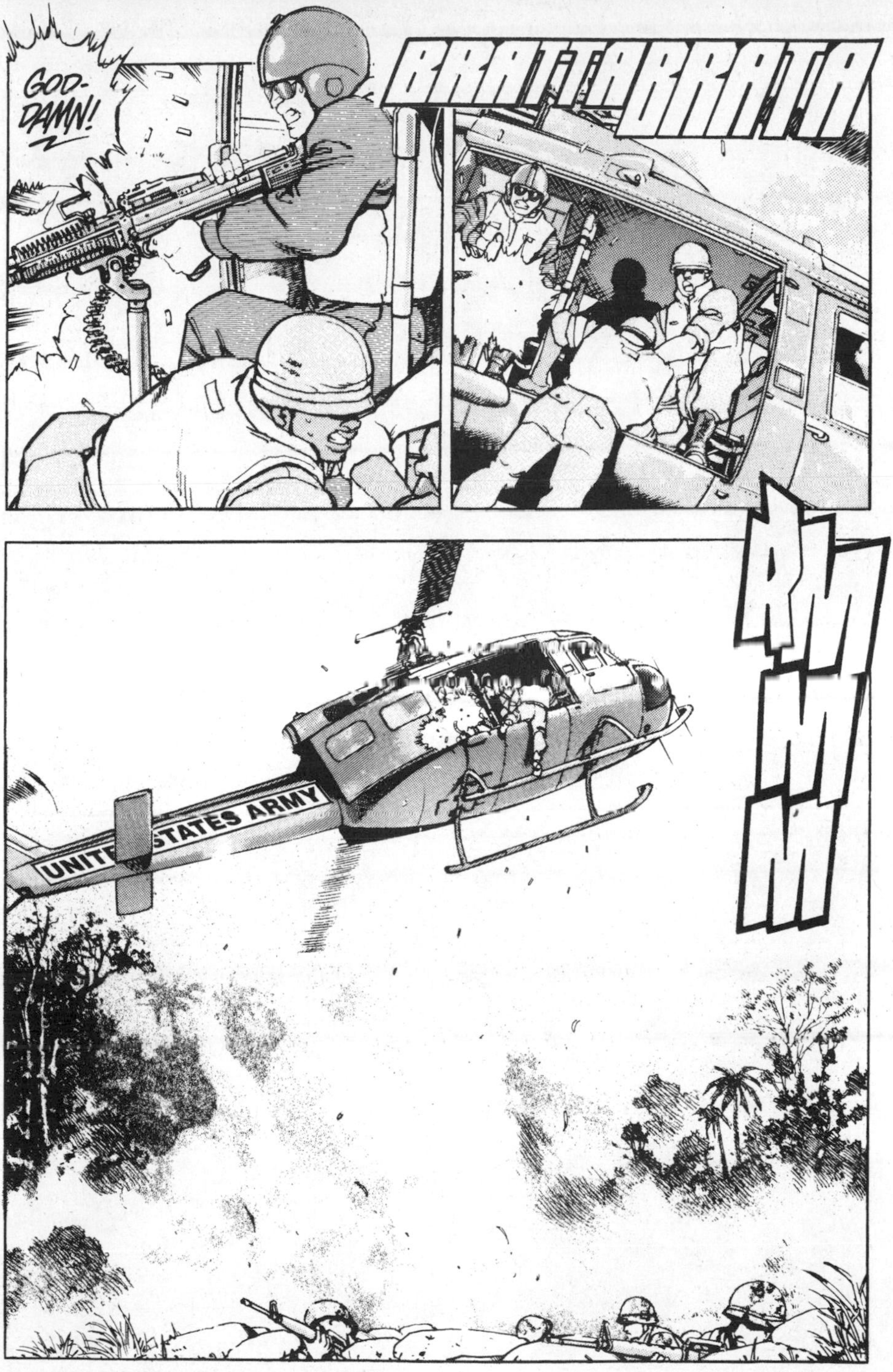
GOD-DAMN!
BRATATA BRATATA
UNITED STATES ARMY
RMMMMM

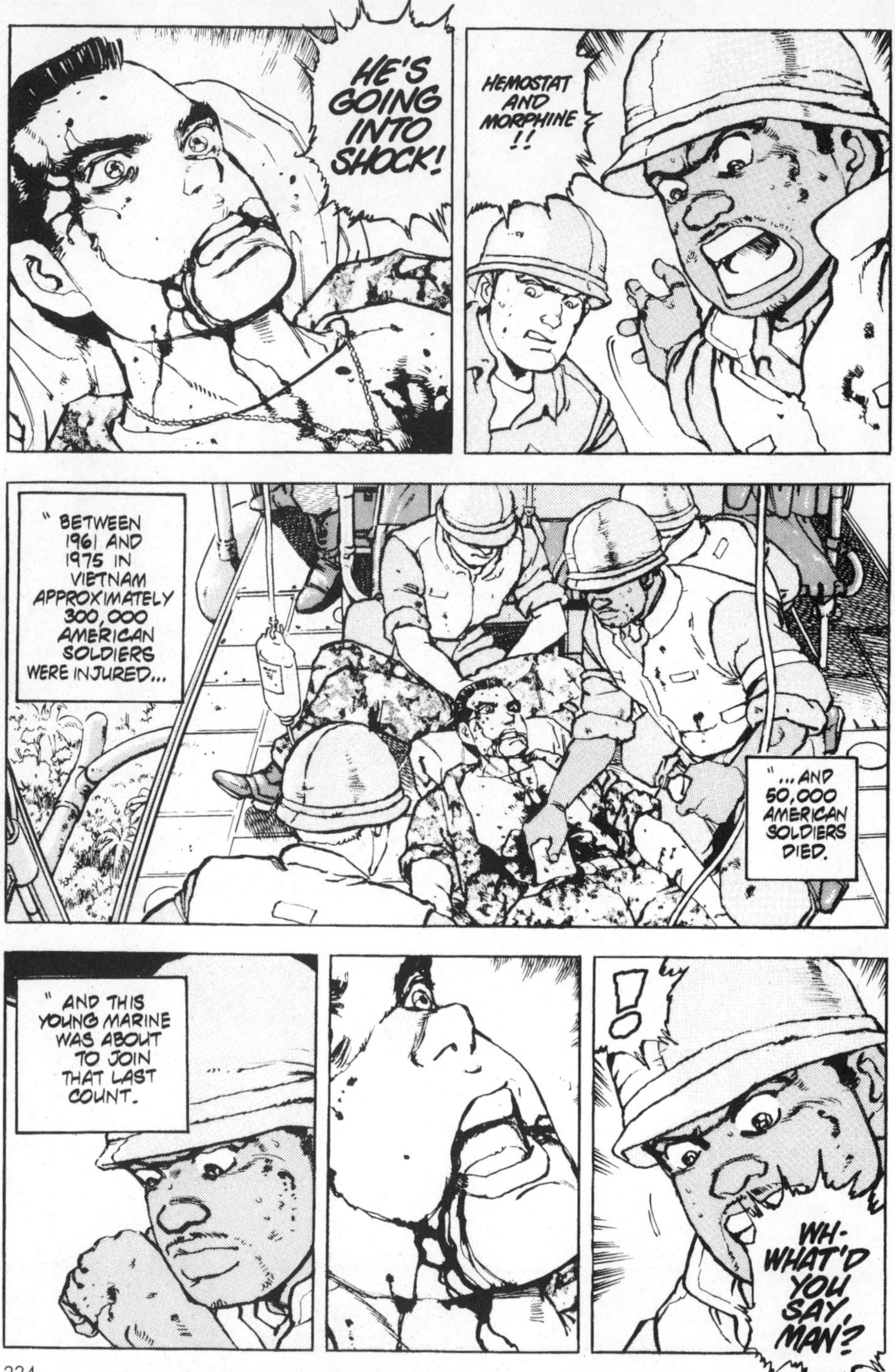
HE'S GOING INTO SHOCK!
HEMOSTAT AND MORPHINE !!
" BETWEEN 1961 AND 1975 IN VIETNAM APPROXIMATELY 300,000 AMERICAN SOLDIERS WERE INJURED...
"...AND 50,000 AMERICAN SOLDIERS DIED.
" AND THIS YOUNG MARINE WAS ABOUT TO JOIN THAT LAST COUNT.
!
WH-WHAT'D YOU SAY, MAN?

I-I'M SORRY... I CAN'T... COME BACK.

I'M G-GOING... TO BECOME PRESIDENT!

HEY, C'MON, HANG IN THERE!

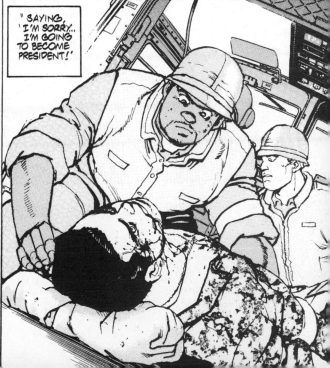

" SAYING, 'I'M SORRY... I'M GOING TO BECOME PRESIDENT!'

" IN HIS DELIRIUM, HE WAS CALLING OUT TO SOMEONE, DESPERATELY.

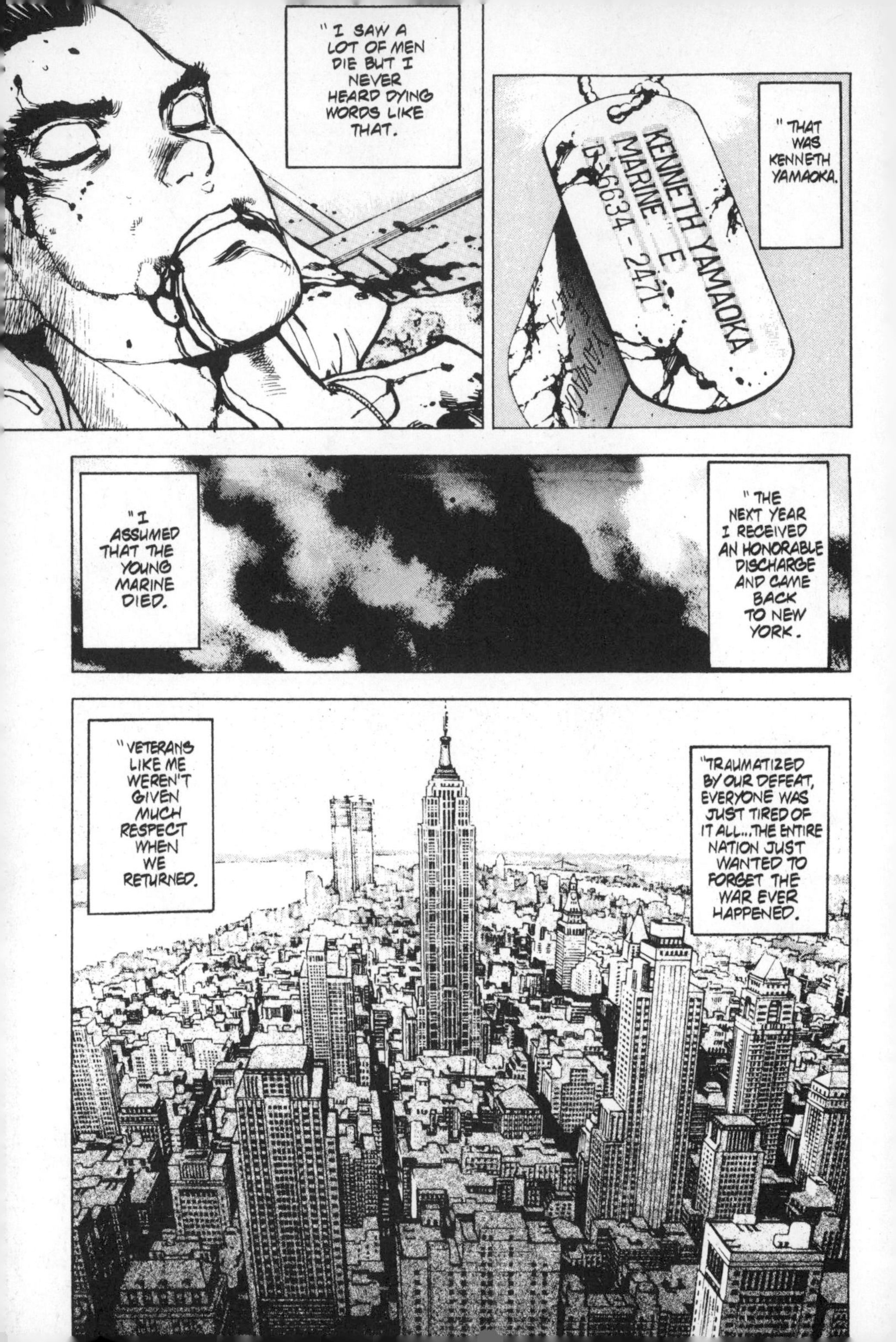
"I SAW A LOT OF MEN DIE BUT I NEVER HEARD DYING WORDS LIKE THAT.
KENNETH YAMAOKA
MARINE E
"THAT WAS KENNETH YAMAOKA.
"I ASSUMED THAT THE YOUNG MARINE DIED.
"THE NEXT YEAR I RECEIVED AN HONORABLE DISCHARGE AND CAME BACK TO NEW YORK.
"VETERANS LIKE ME WEREN'T GIVEN MUCH RESPECT WHEN WE RETURNED.
"TRAUMATIZED BY OUR DEFEAT, EVERYONE WAS JUST TIRED OF IT ALL...THE ENTIRE NATION JUST WANTED TO FORGET THE WAR EVER HAPPENED.

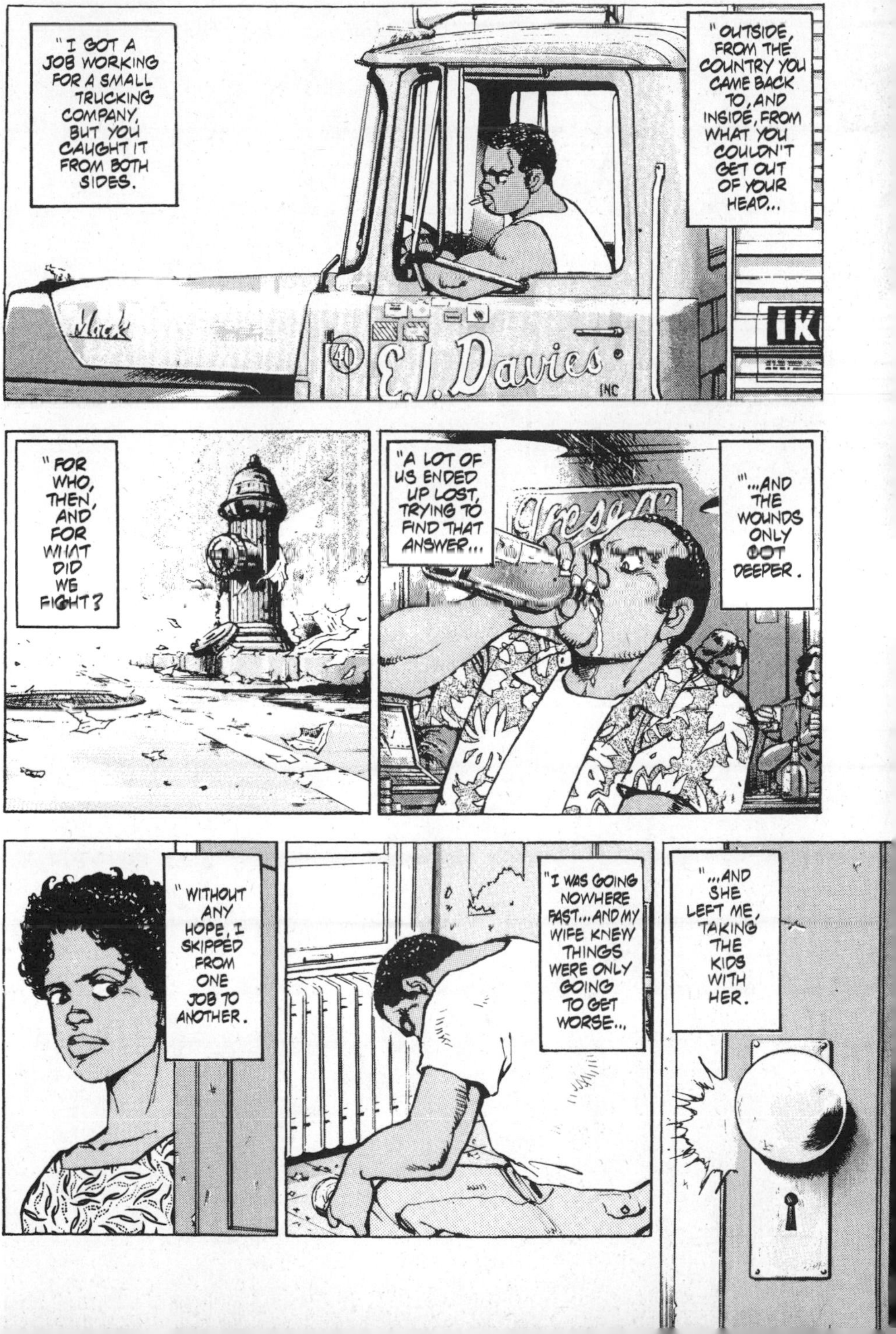
"I GOT A JOB WORKING FOR A SMALL TRUCKING COMPANY, BUT YOU CAUGHT IT FROM BOTH SIDES.
"OUTSIDE, FROM THE COUNTRY YOU CAME BACK TO, AND INSIDE, FROM WHAT YOU COULDN'T GET OUT OF YOUR HEAD...
Mack
E.J. Davies INC
"FOR WHO, THEN, AND FOR WHAT DID WE FIGHT?
"A LOT OF US ENDED UP LOST, TRYING TO FIND THAT ANSWER...
"...AND THE WOUNDS ONLY GOT DEEPER.
"WITHOUT ANY HOPE, I SKIPPED FROM ONE JOB TO ANOTHER.
"I WAS GOING NOWHERE FAST...AND MY WIFE KNEW THINGS WERE ONLY GOING TO GET WORSE...
"...AND SHE LEFT ME, TAKING THE KIDS WITH HER.

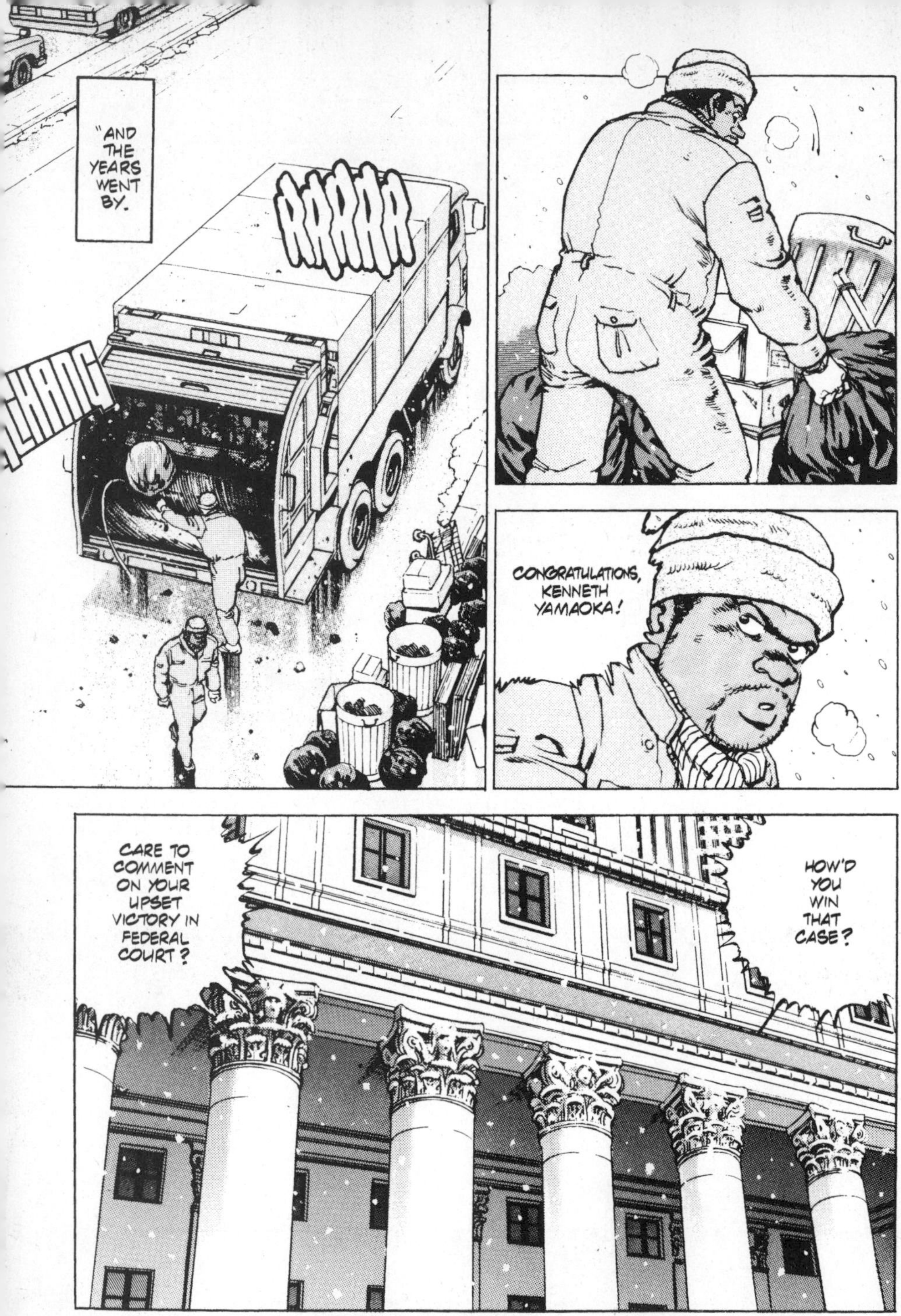
"AND THE YEARS WENT BY.
RRRRR
KLANG
CONGRATULATIONS, KENNETH YAMAOKA!
CARE TO COMMENT ON YOUR UPSET VICTORY IN FEDERAL COURT?
HOW'D YOU WIN THAT CASE?

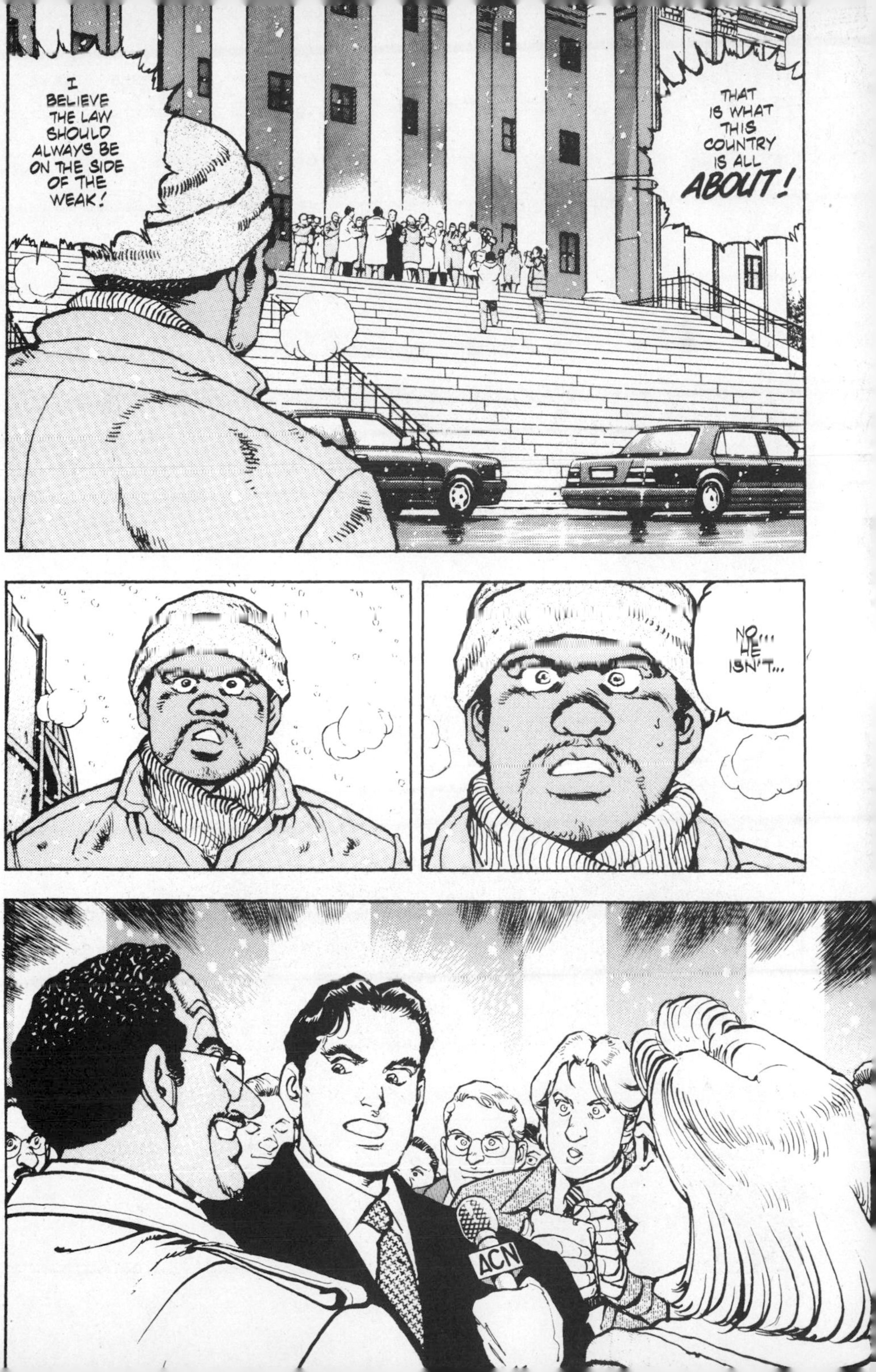
I BELIEVE THE LAW SHOULD ALWAYS BE ON THE SIDE OF THE WEAK!
THAT IS WHAT THIS COUNTRY IS ALL ABOUT!
NO... HE ISN'T...
ACN

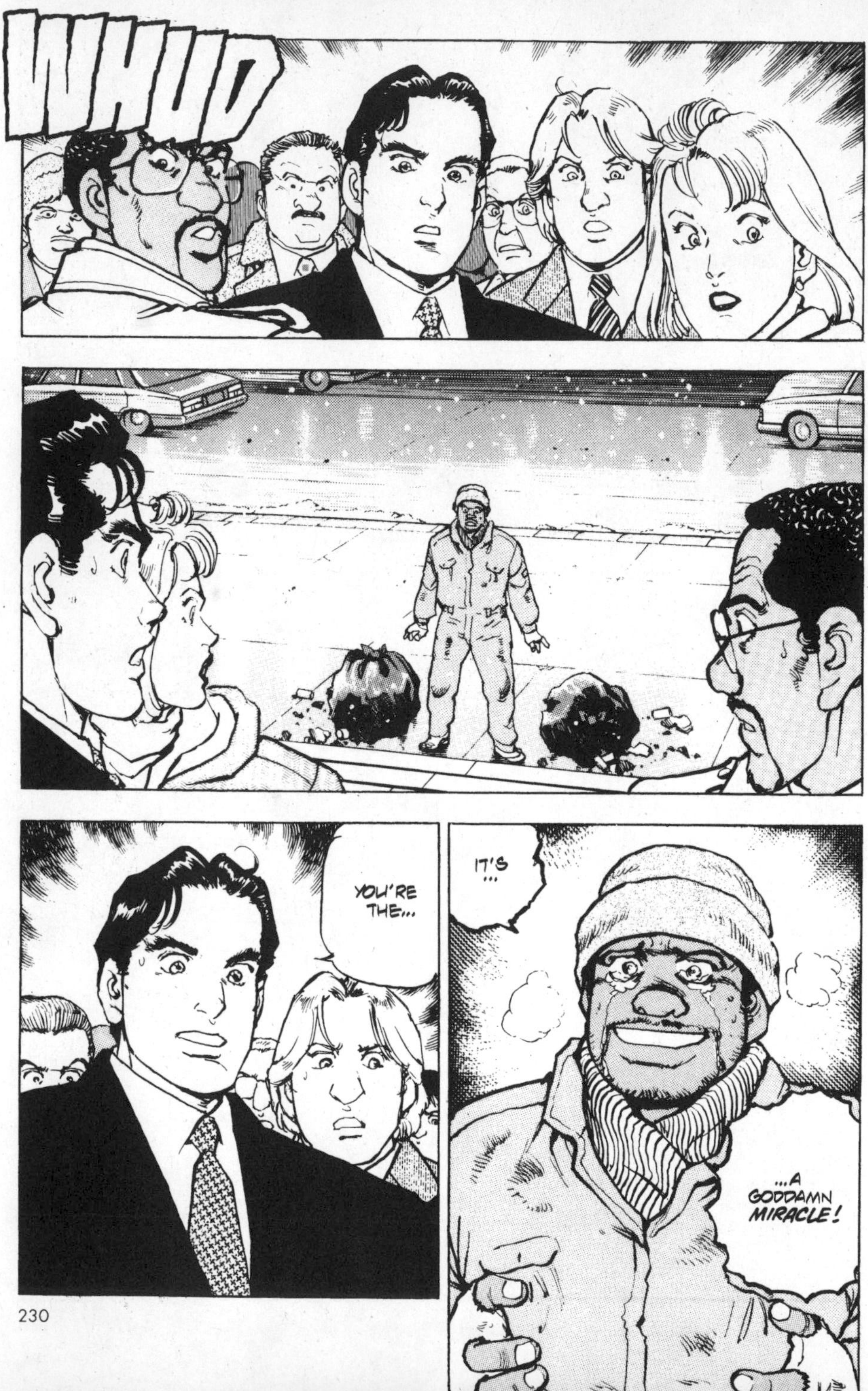
WHUD
YOU'RE THE...
IT'S ...
...A GODDAMN MIRACLE!

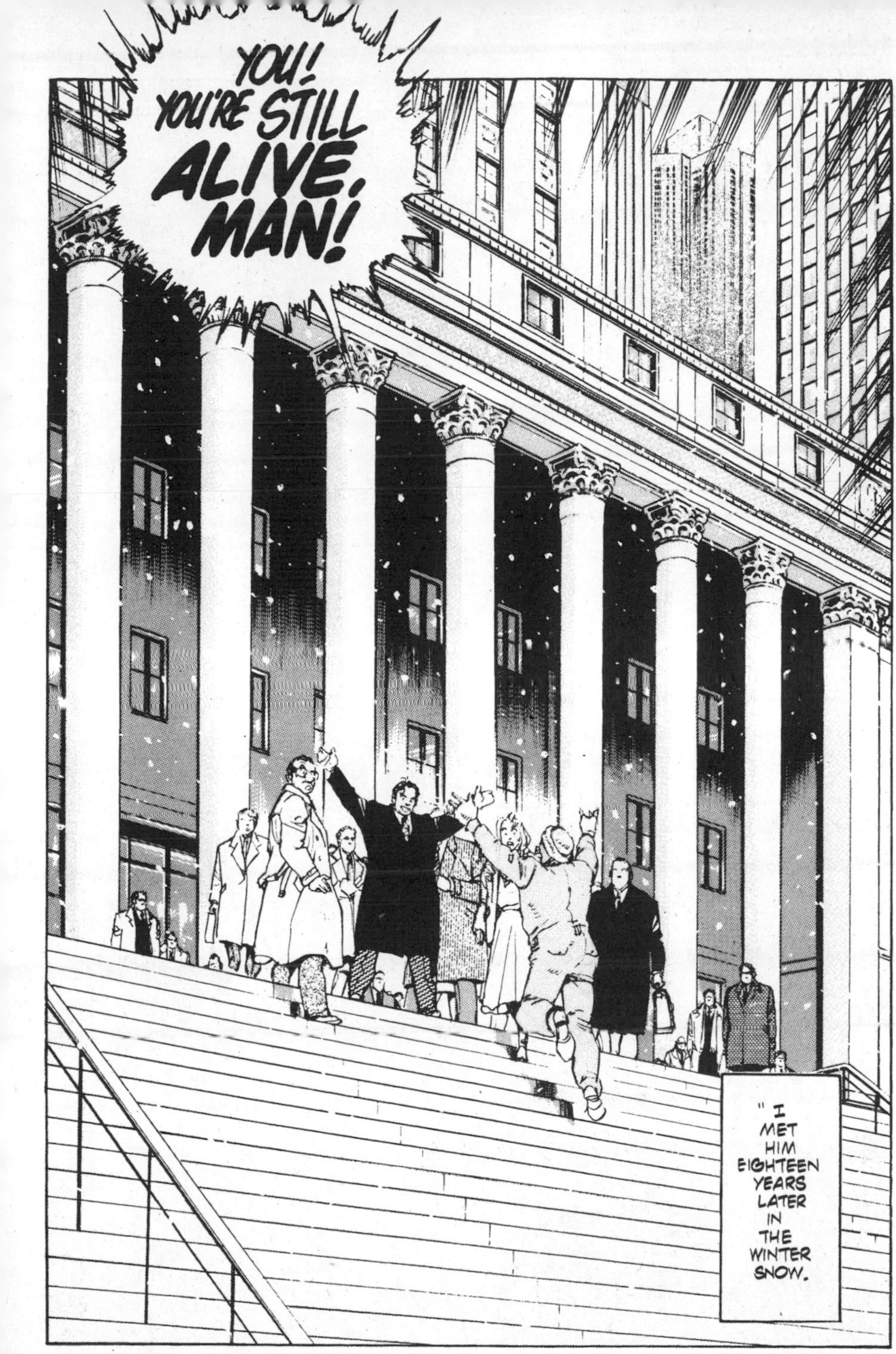
YOU! YOU'RE STILL ALIVE, MAN!
"I MET HIM EIGHTEEN YEARS LATER IN THE WINTER SNOW.

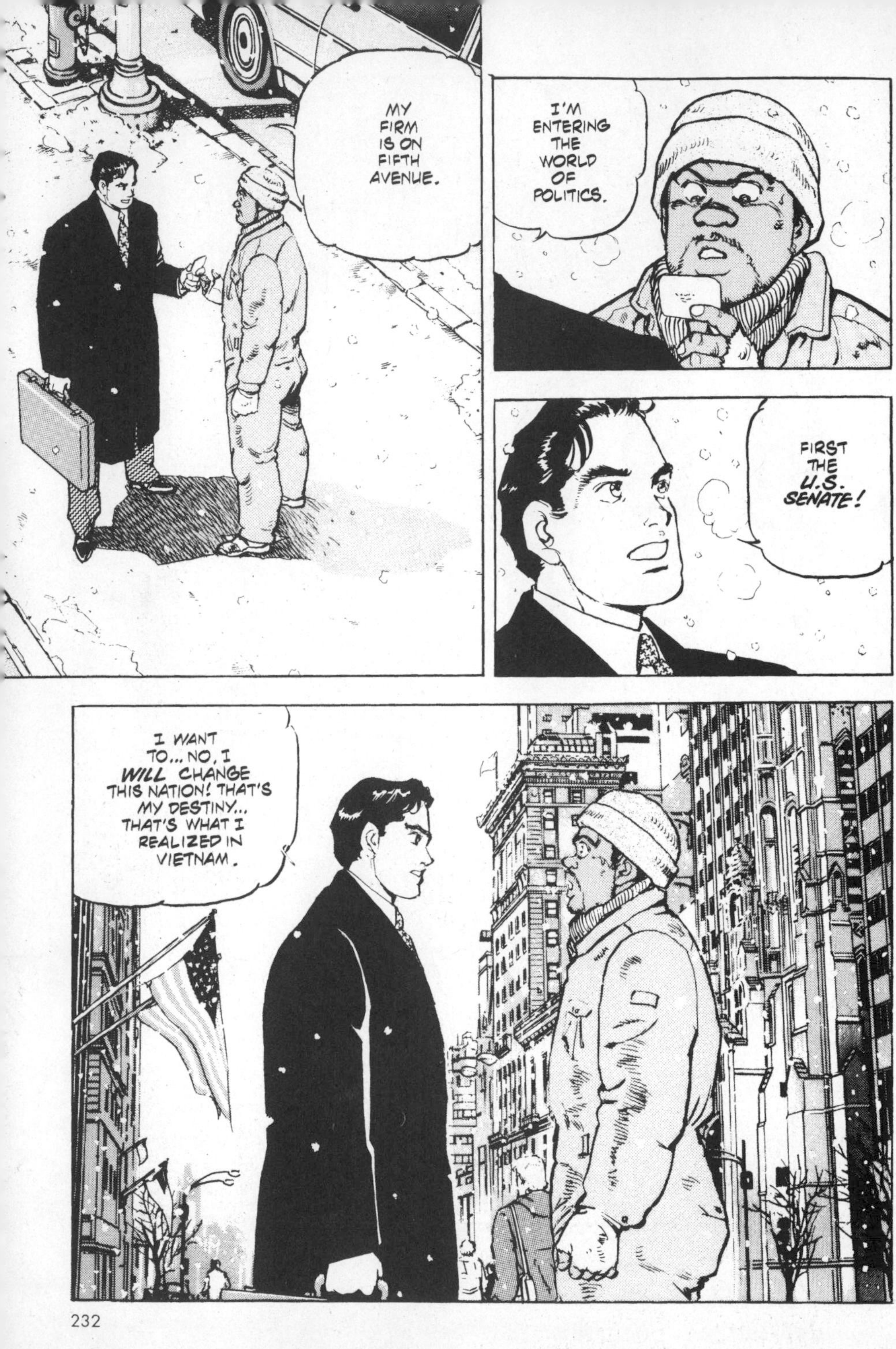
MY FIRM IS ON FIFTH AVENUE.
I'M ENTERING THE WORLD OF POLITICS.
FIRST THE U.S. SENATE!
I WANT TO... NO, I WILL CHANGE THIS NATION! THAT'S MY DESTINY... THAT'S WHAT I REALIZED IN VIETNAM.

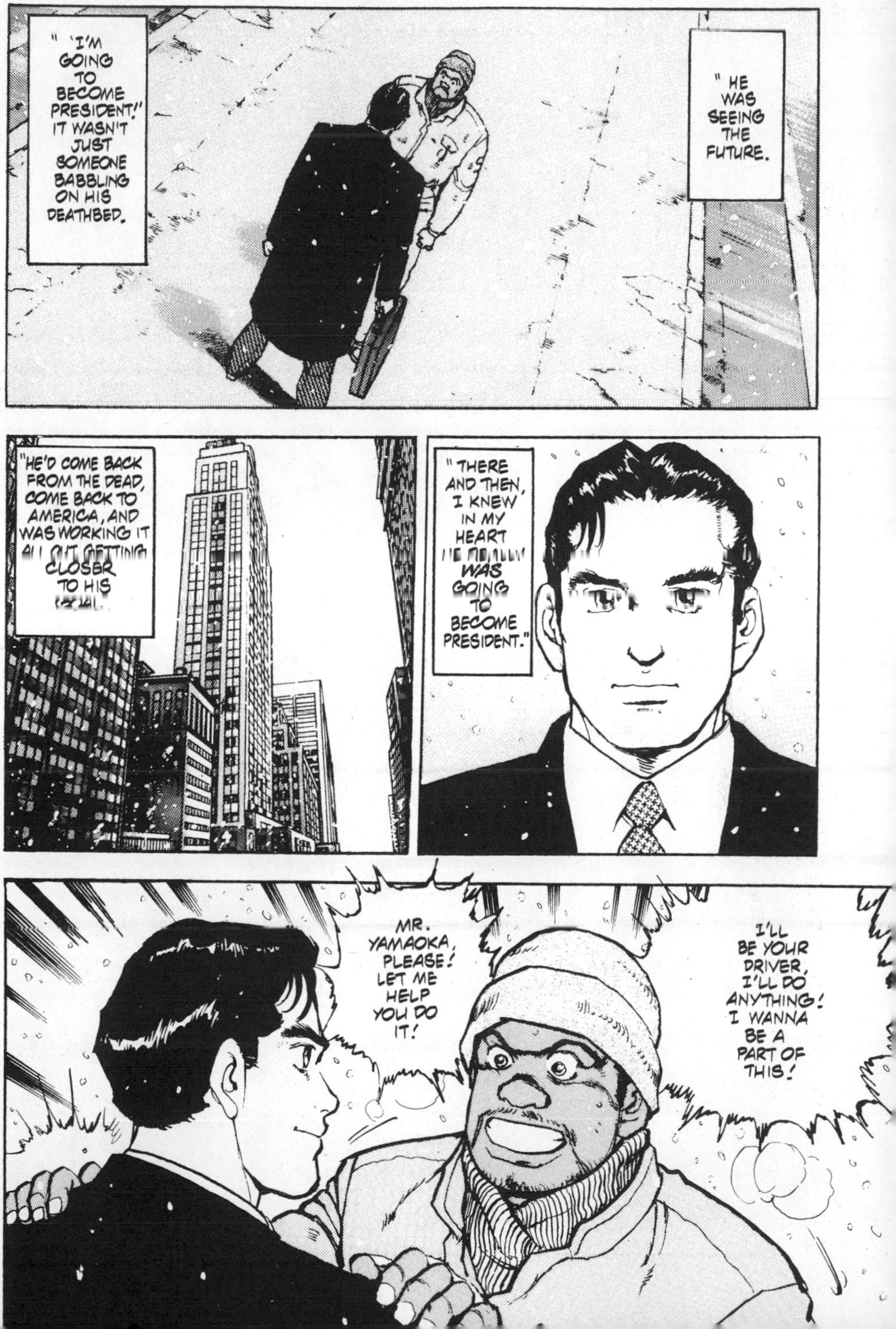
" 'I'M GOING TO BECOME PRESIDENT!' IT WASN'T JUST SOMEONE BABBLING ON HIS DEATHBED.
" HE WAS SEEING THE FUTURE.
"HE'D COME BACK FROM THE DEAD, COME BACK TO AMERICA, AND WAS WORKING IT ALL OUT GETTING CLOSER TO HIS
" THERE AND THEN, I KNEW IN MY HEART
WAS GOING TO BECOME PRESIDENT."
MR. YAMAOKA, PLEASE! LET ME HELP YOU DO IT!
I'LL BE YOUR DRIVER, I'LL DO ANYTHING! I WANNA BE A PART OF THIS!

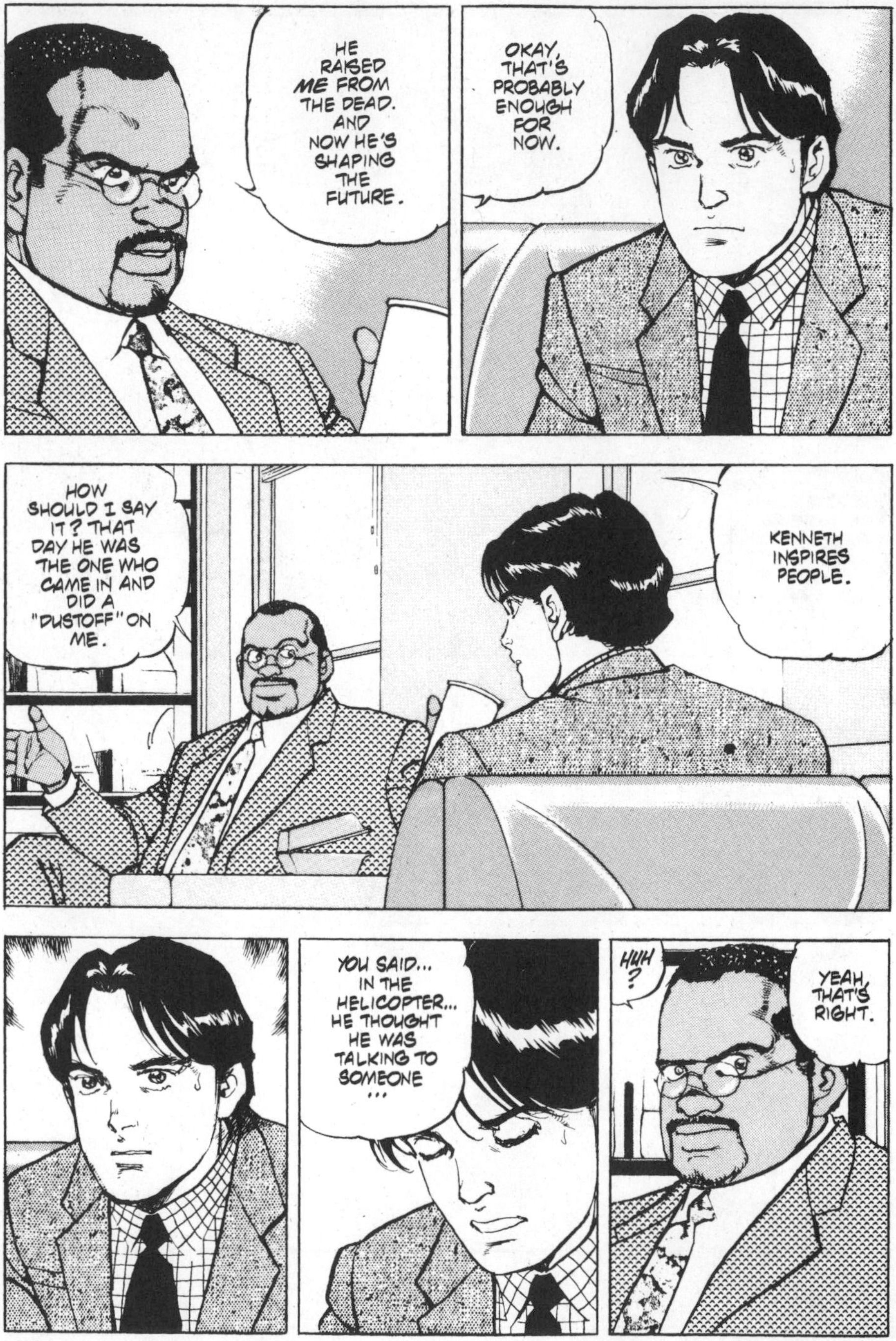
HE RAISED ME FROM THE DEAD. AND NOW HE'S SHAPING THE FUTURE.
OKAY, THAT'S PROBABLY ENOUGH FOR NOW.
HOW SHOULD I SAY IT? THAT DAY HE WAS THE ONE WHO CAME IN AND DID A "DUSTOFF" ON ME.
KENNETH INSPIRES PEOPLE.
YOU SAID... IN THE HELICOPTER... HE THOUGHT HE WAS TALKING TO SOMEONE ...
HUH?
YEAH, THAT'S RIGHT.

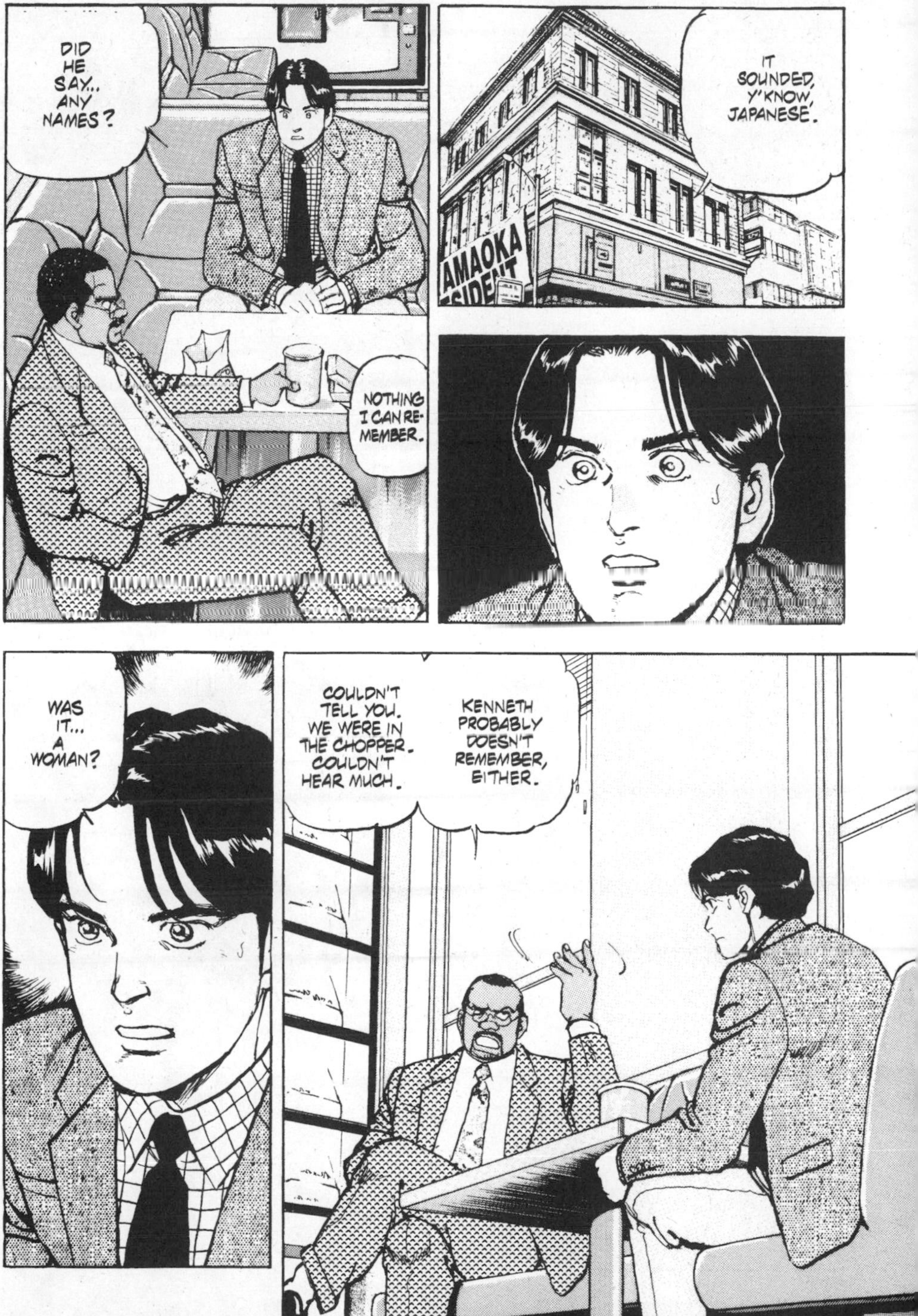
DID HE SAY... ANY NAMES?
NOTHING I CAN REMEMBER.
IT SOUNDED, Y'KNOW, JAPANESE.
AMAOKA
SIDENT
WAS IT... A WOMAN?
COULDN'T TELL YOU. WE WERE IN THE CHOPPER. COULDN'T HEAR MUCH.
KENNETH PROBABLY DOESN'T REMEMBER, EITHER.

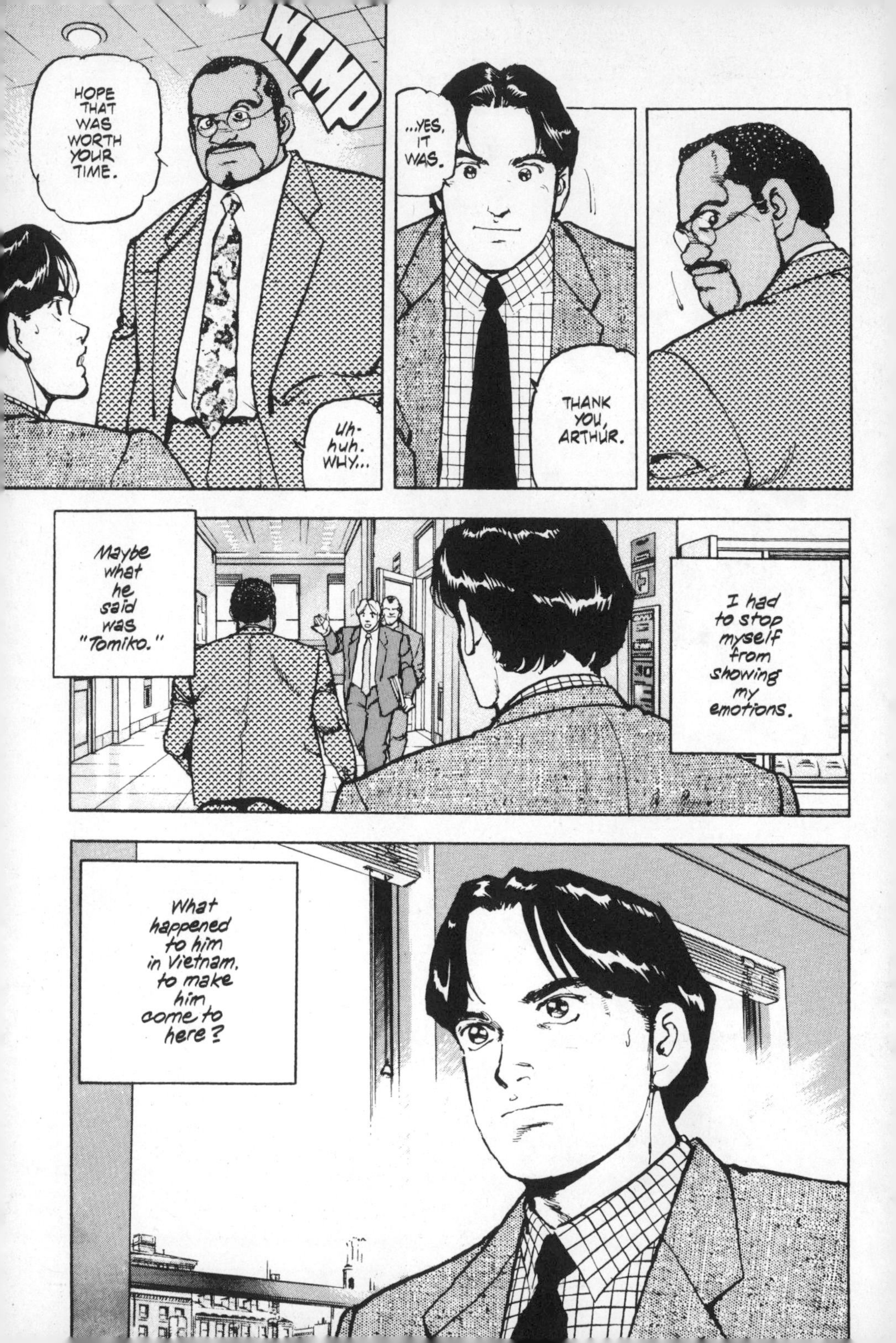
WTMP
HOPE THAT WAS WORTH YOUR TIME.
uh-huh. WHY...
...YES, IT WAS.
THANK YOU, ARTHUR.
Maybe what he said was "Tomiko."
I had to stop myself from showing my emotions.
What happened to him in Vietnam, to make him come to here?

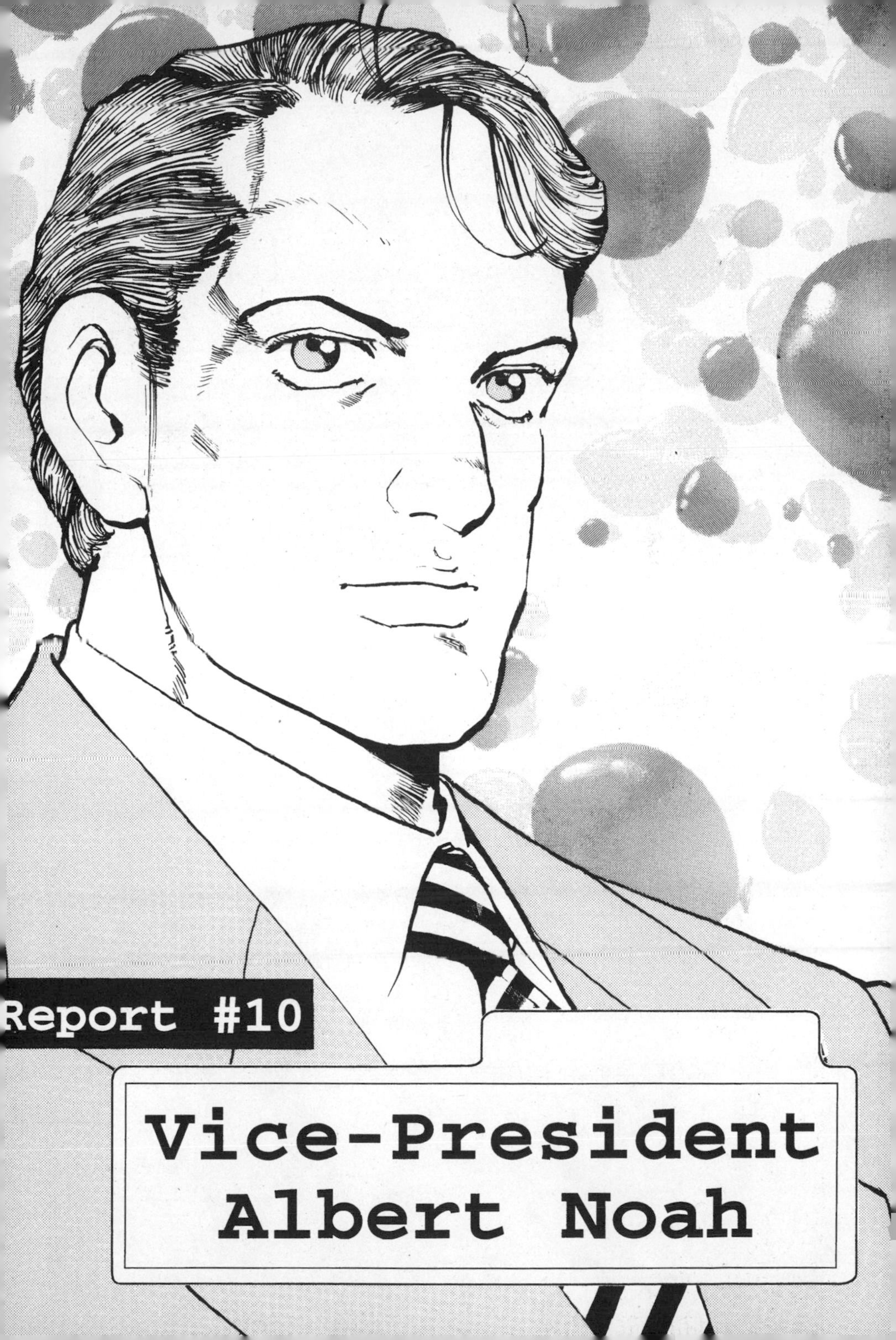
Report #10
Vice-President
Albert Noah

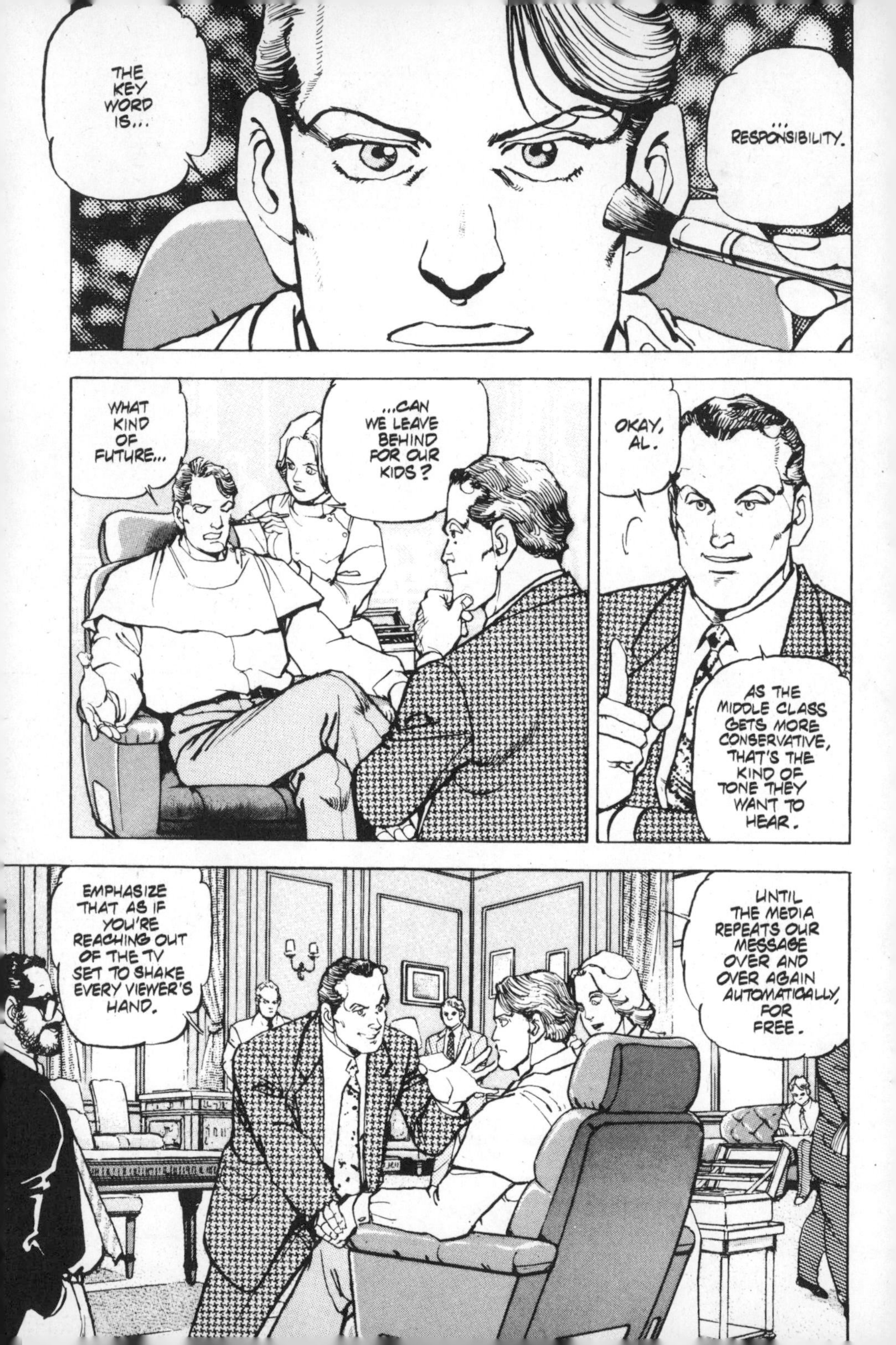
THE KEY WORD IS...
...RESPONSIBILITY.
WHAT KIND OF FUTURE...
...CAN WE LEAVE BEHIND FOR OUR KIDS?
OKAY, AL.
AS THE MIDDLE CLASS GETS MORE CONSERVATIVE, THAT'S THE KIND OF TONE THEY WANT TO HEAR.
EMPHASIZE THAT AS IF YOU'RE REACHING OUT OF THE TV SET TO SHAKE EVERY VIEWER'S HAND.
UNTIL THE MEDIA REPEATS OUR MESSAGE OVER AND OVER AGAIN AUTOMATICALLY, FOR FREE.

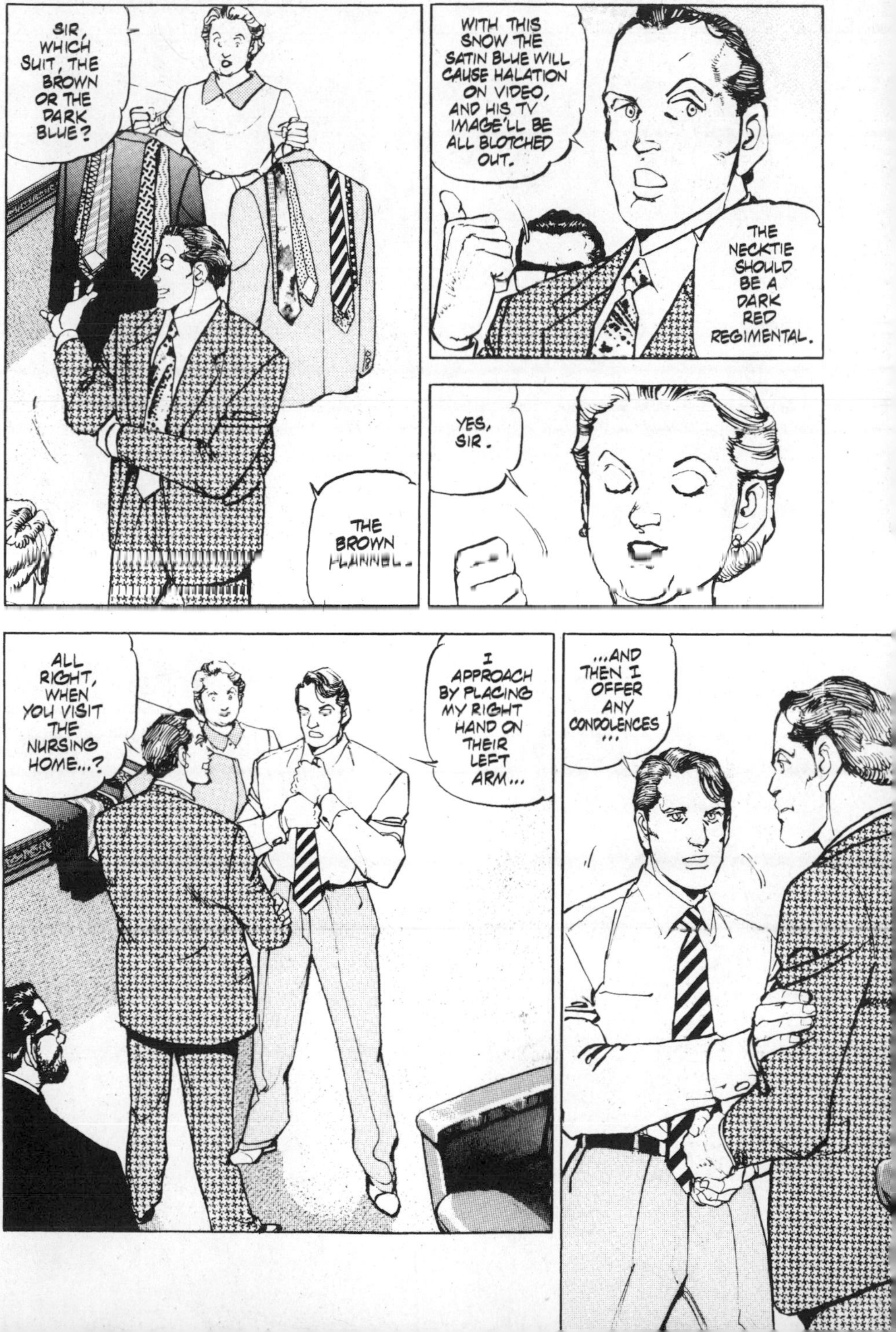
SIR, WHICH SUIT, THE BROWN OR THE DARK BLUE?
THE BROWN FLANNEL.
WITH THIS SNOW THE SATIN BLUE WILL CAUSE HALATION ON VIDEO, AND HIS TV IMAGE'LL BE ALL BLOTCHED OUT.
THE NECKTIE SHOULD BE A DARK RED REGIMENTAL.
YES, SIR.
ALL RIGHT, WHEN YOU VISIT THE NURSING HOME...?
I APPROACH BY PLACING MY RIGHT HAND ON THEIR LEFT ARM...
...AND THEN I OFFER ANY CONDOLENCES...

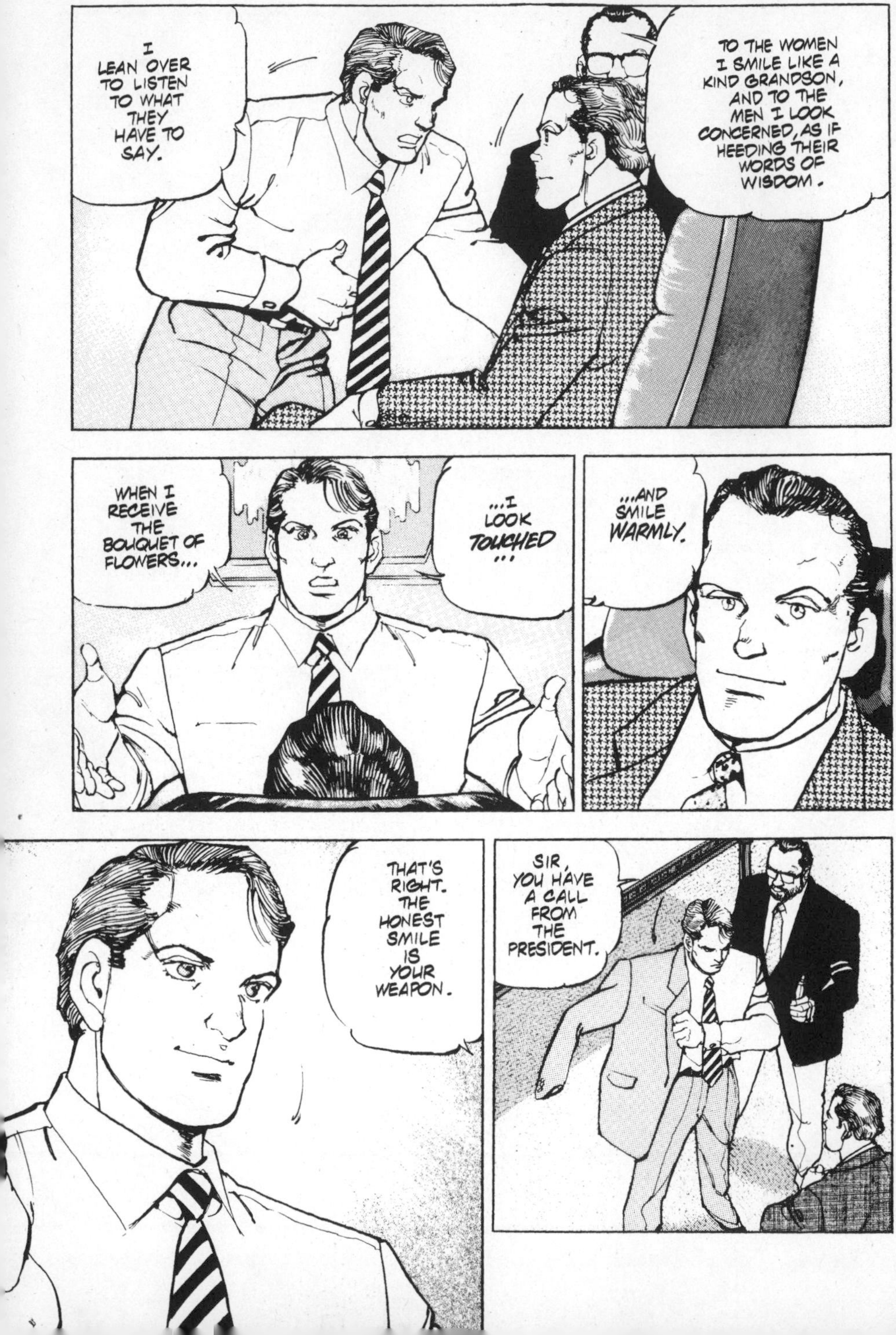
I LEAN OVER TO LISTEN TO WHAT THEY HAVE TO SAY.
TO THE WOMEN I SMILE LIKE A KIND GRANDSON, AND TO THE MEN I LOOK CONCERNED, AS IF HEEDING THEIR WORDS OF WISDOM.
WHEN I RECEIVE THE BOUQUET OF FLOWERS...
...I LOOK TOUCHED...
...AND SMILE WARMLY.
THAT'S RIGHT. THE HONEST SMILE IS YOUR WEAPON.
SIR, YOU HAVE A CALL FROM THE PRESIDENT.

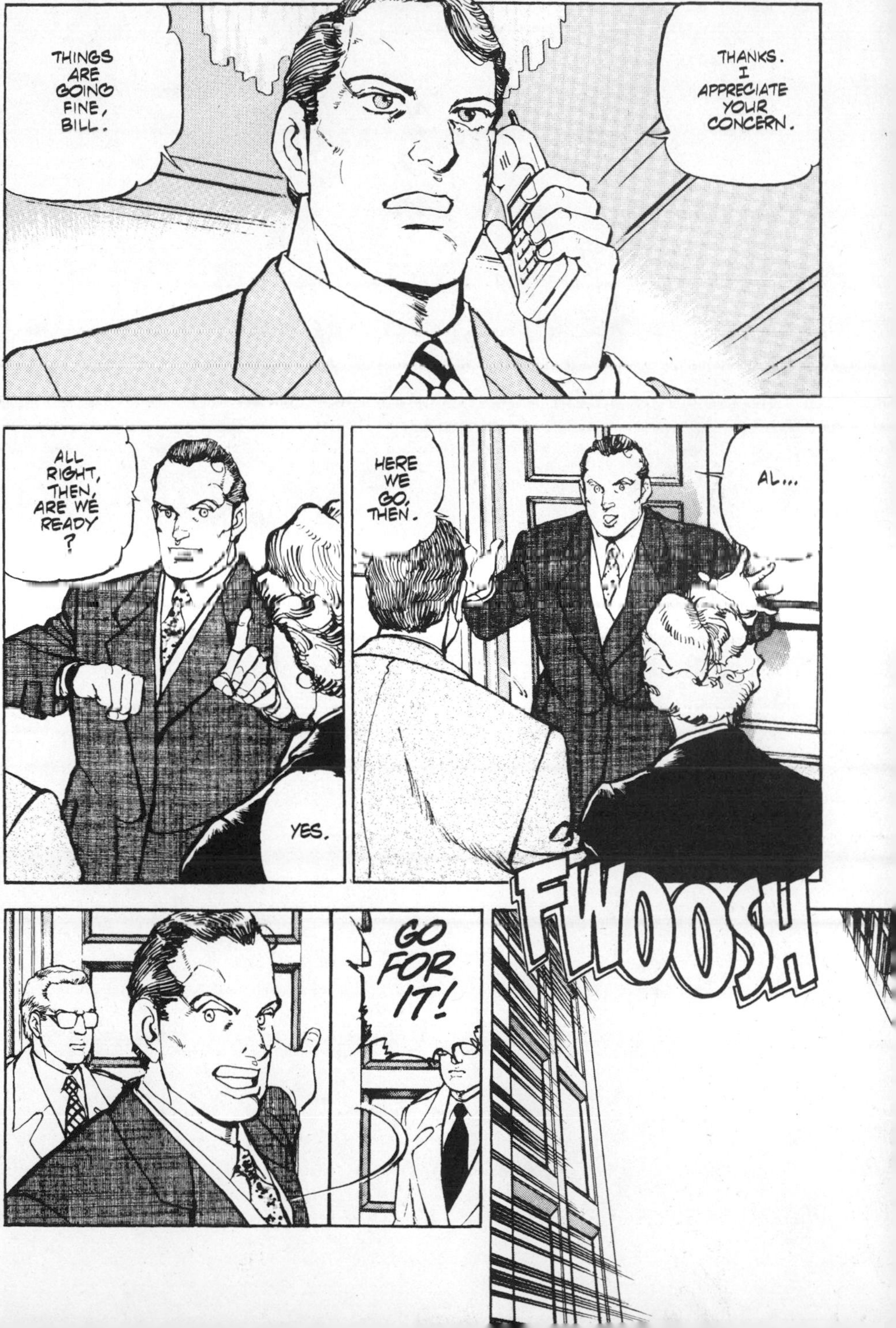
THINGS ARE GOING FINE, BILL.
THANKS. I APPRECIATE YOUR CONCERN.
ALL RIGHT, THEN, ARE WE READY?
YES.
HERE WE GO, THEN.
AL...
FWOOSH
GO FOR IT!

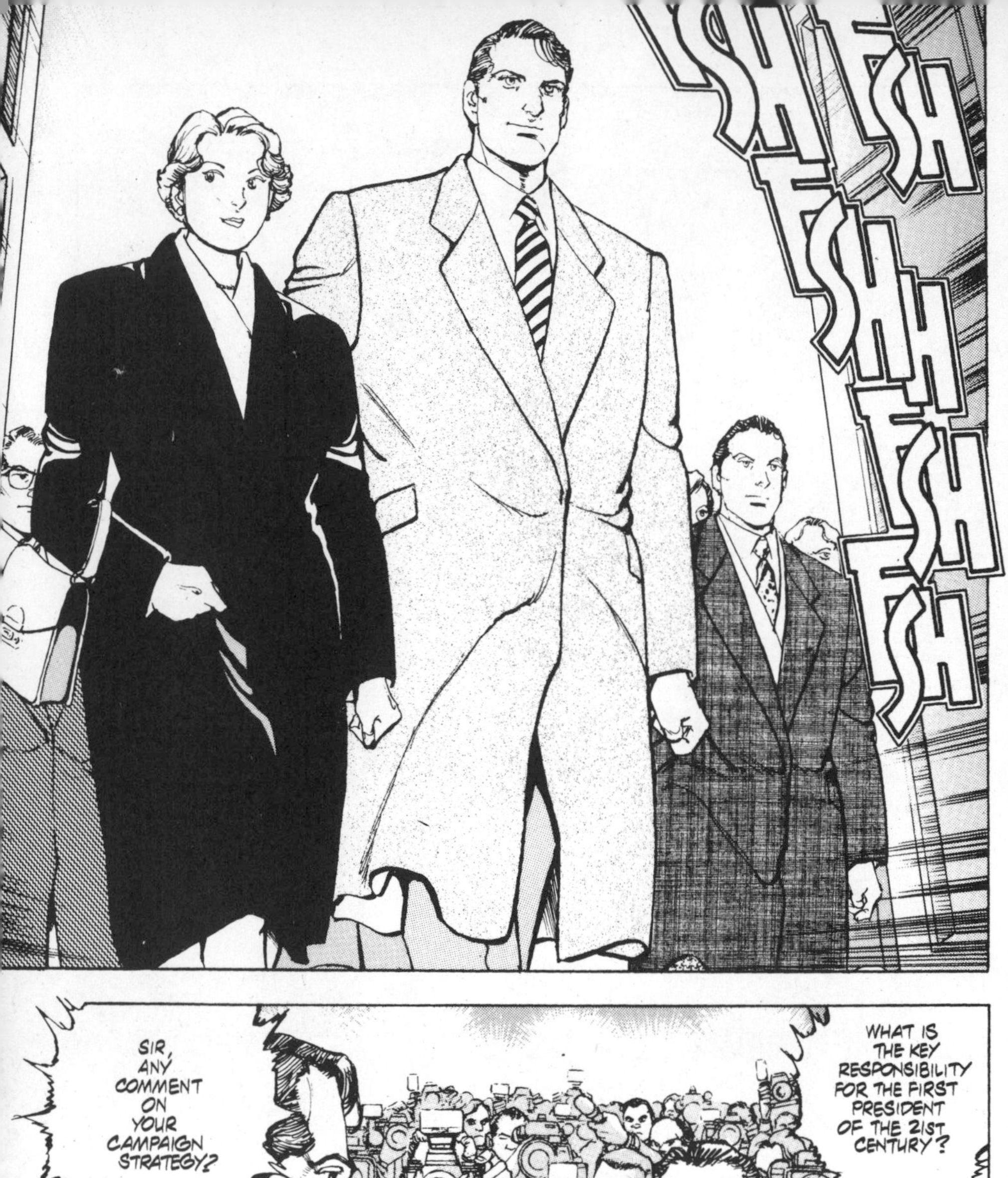
SH FSH FSH FSH FSH FSH

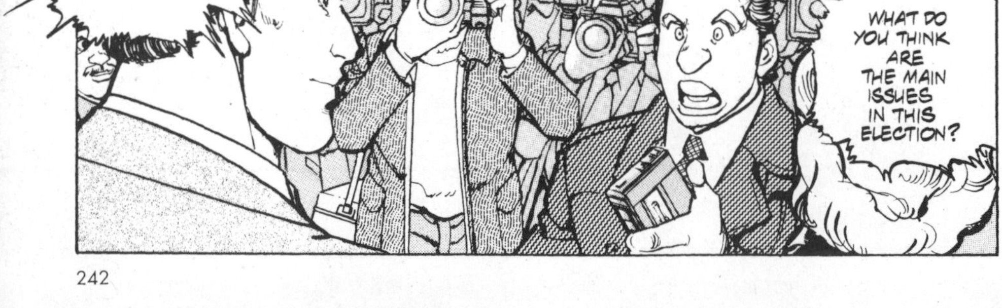
SIR, ANY COMMENT ON YOUR CAMPAIGN STRATEGY?
WHAT IS THE KEY RESPONSIBILITY FOR THE FIRST PRESIDENT OF THE 21ST CENTURY?
WHAT DO YOU THINK ARE THE MAIN ISSUES IN THIS ELECTION?

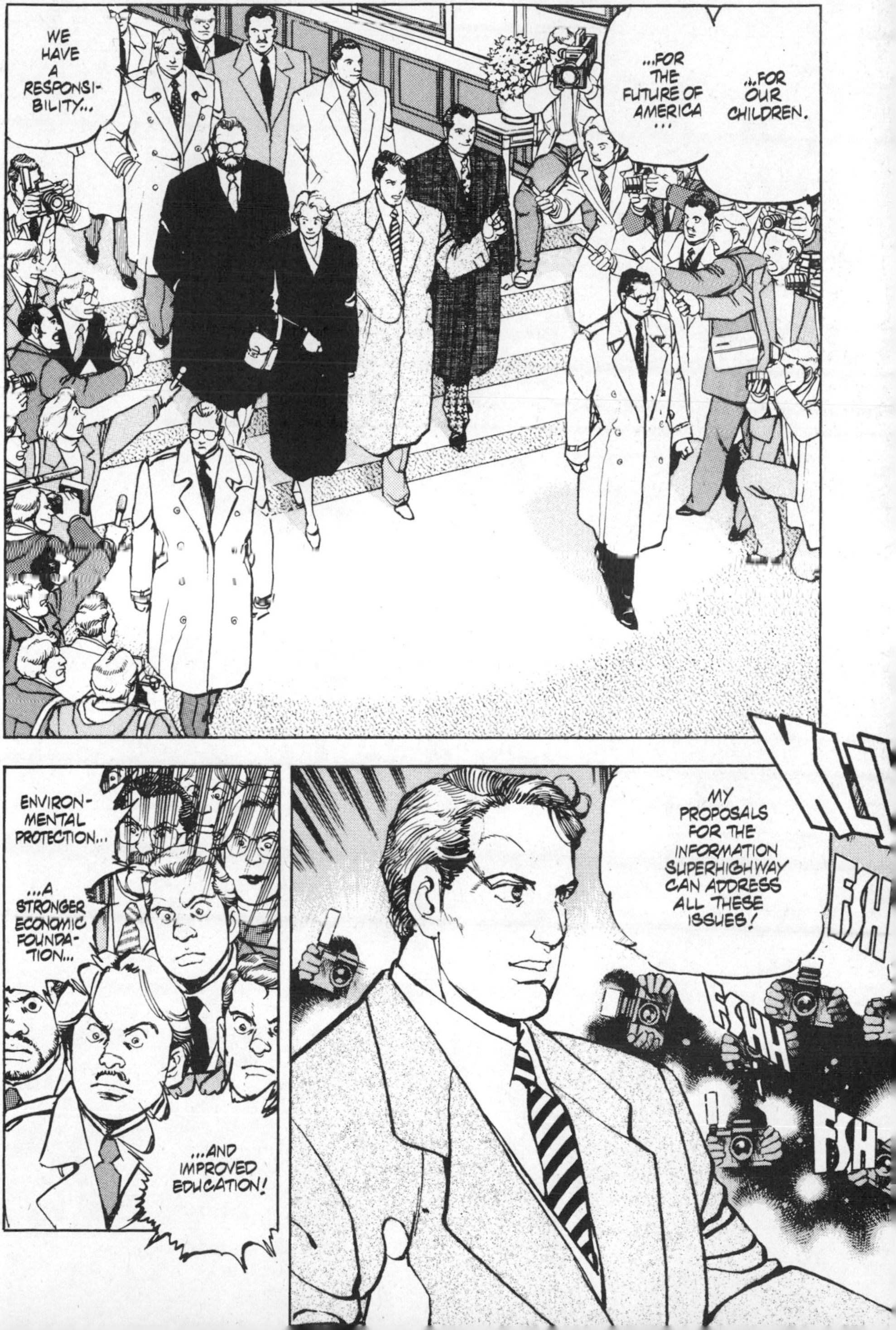
WE HAVE A RESPONSIBILITY...
...FOR THE FUTURE OF AMERICA...
...FOR OUR CHILDREN.
ENVIRONMENTAL PROTECTION...
...A STRONGER ECONOMIC FOUNDATION...
...AND IMPROVED EDUCATION!
MY PROPOSALS FOR THE INFORMATION SUPERHIGHWAY CAN ADDRESS ALL THESE ISSUES!
FSH
FSHH
FSH

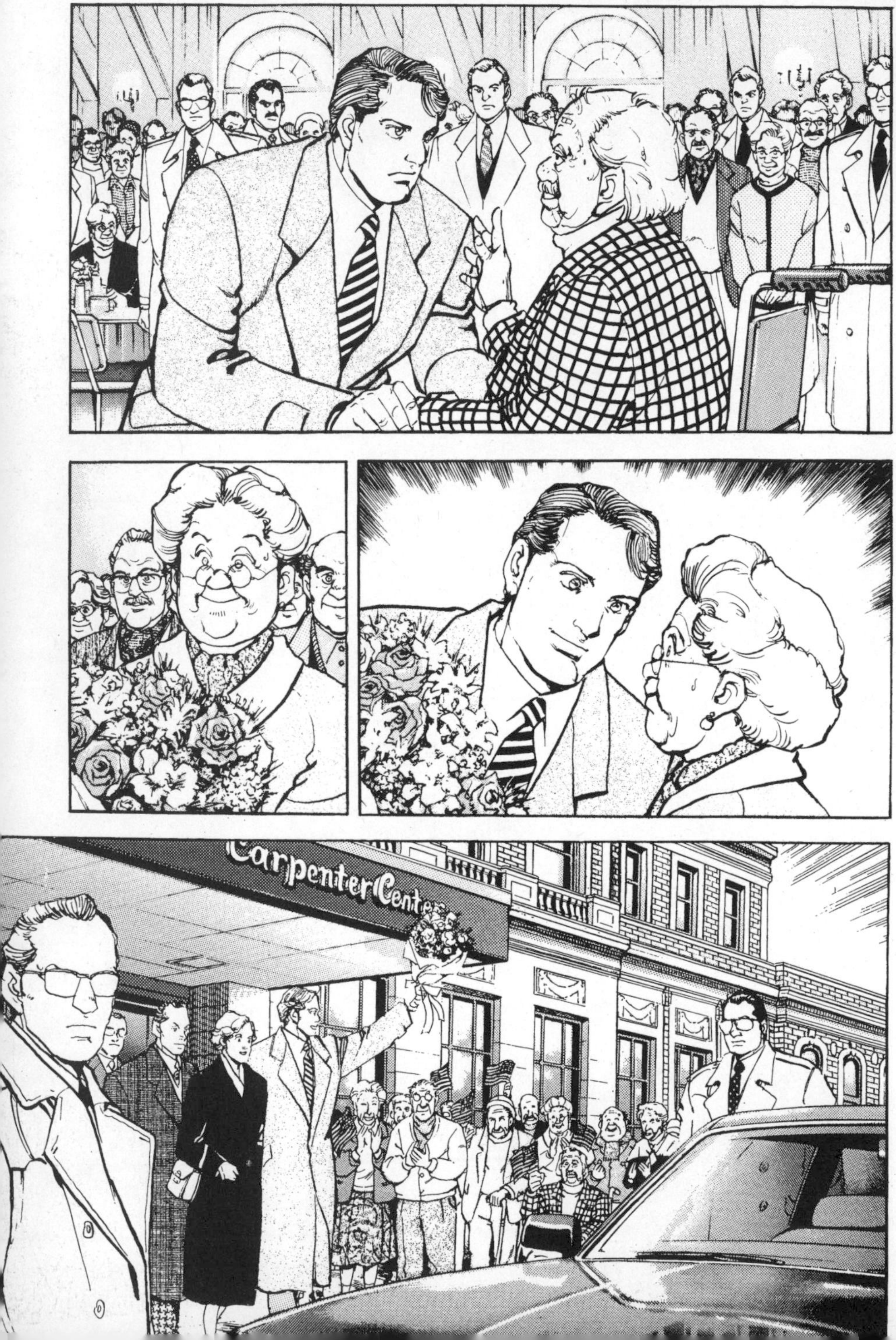
Carpenter Center

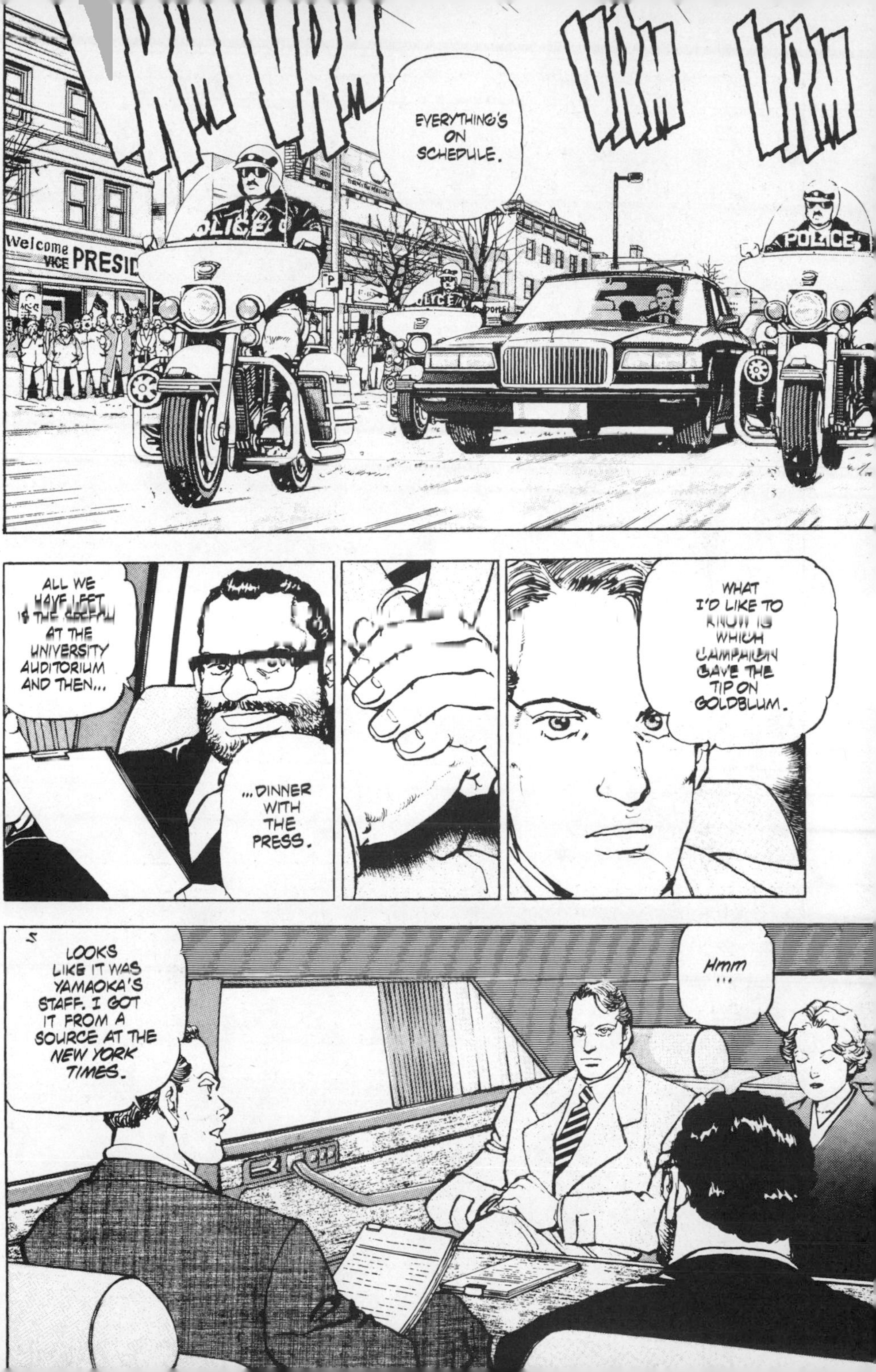
VRM VRM
EVERYTHING'S ON SCHEDULE.
VRM VRM
POLICE
Welcome VICE PRESID
POLICE
ALL WE HAVE LEFT IS THE SPEECH AT THE UNIVERSITY AUDITORIUM AND THEN...
...DINNER WITH THE PRESS.
WHAT I'D LIKE TO KNOW IS WHICH CAMPAIGN GAVE THE TIP ON GOLDBLUM.
LOOKS LIKE IT WAS YAMAOKA'S STAFF. I GOT IT FROM A SOURCE AT THE *NEW YORK TIMES*.
Hmm...

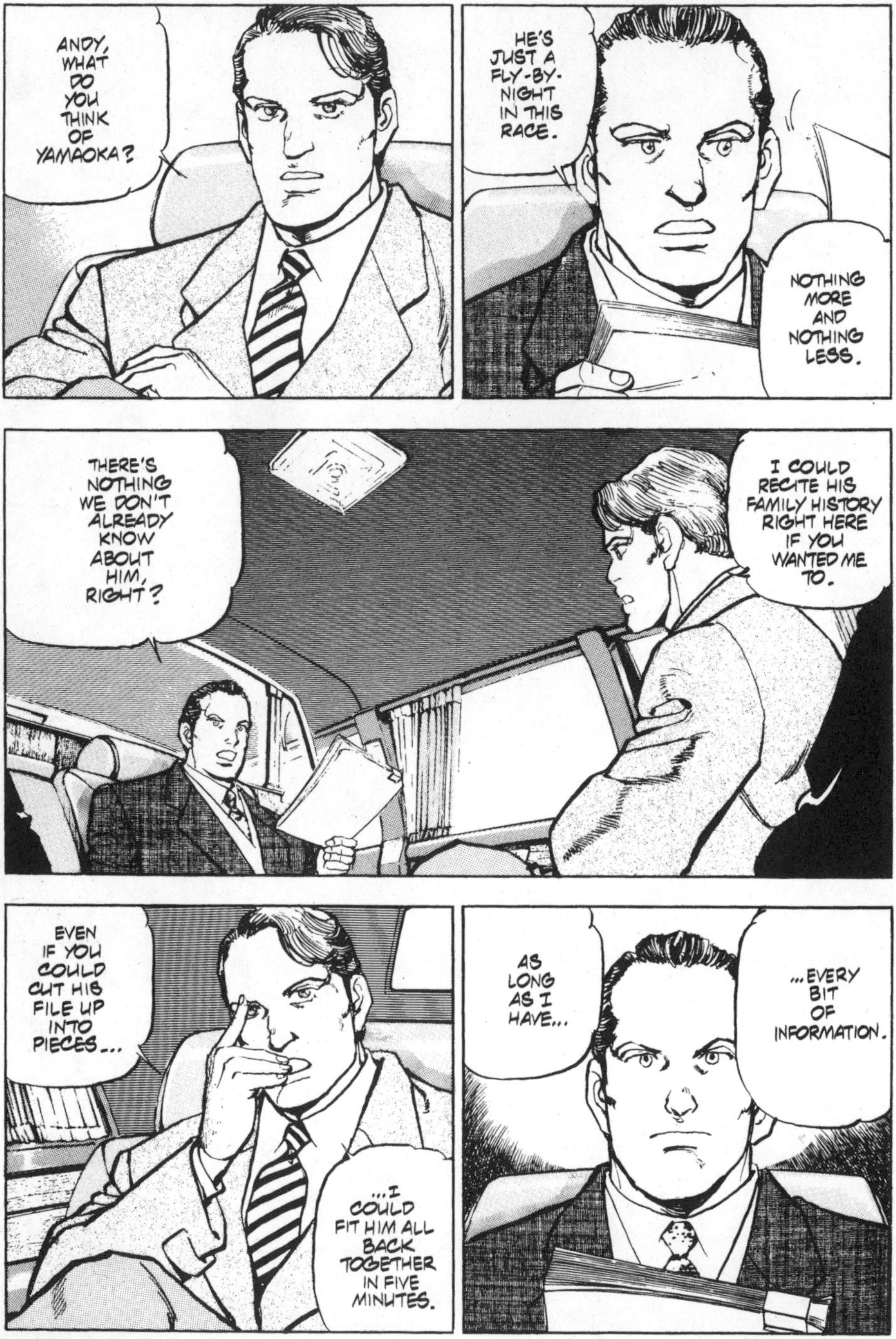
ANDY, WHAT DO YOU THINK OF YAMAOKA?
HE'S JUST A FLY-BY-NIGHT IN THIS RACE.
NOTHING MORE AND NOTHING LESS.
THERE'S NOTHING WE DON'T ALREADY KNOW ABOUT HIM, RIGHT?
I COULD RECITE HIS FAMILY HISTORY RIGHT HERE IF YOU WANTED ME TO.
EVEN IF YOU COULD CUT HIS FILE UP INTO PIECES...
...I COULD FIT HIM ALL BACK TOGETHER IN FIVE MINUTES.
AS LONG AS I HAVE...
...EVERY BIT OF INFORMATION.

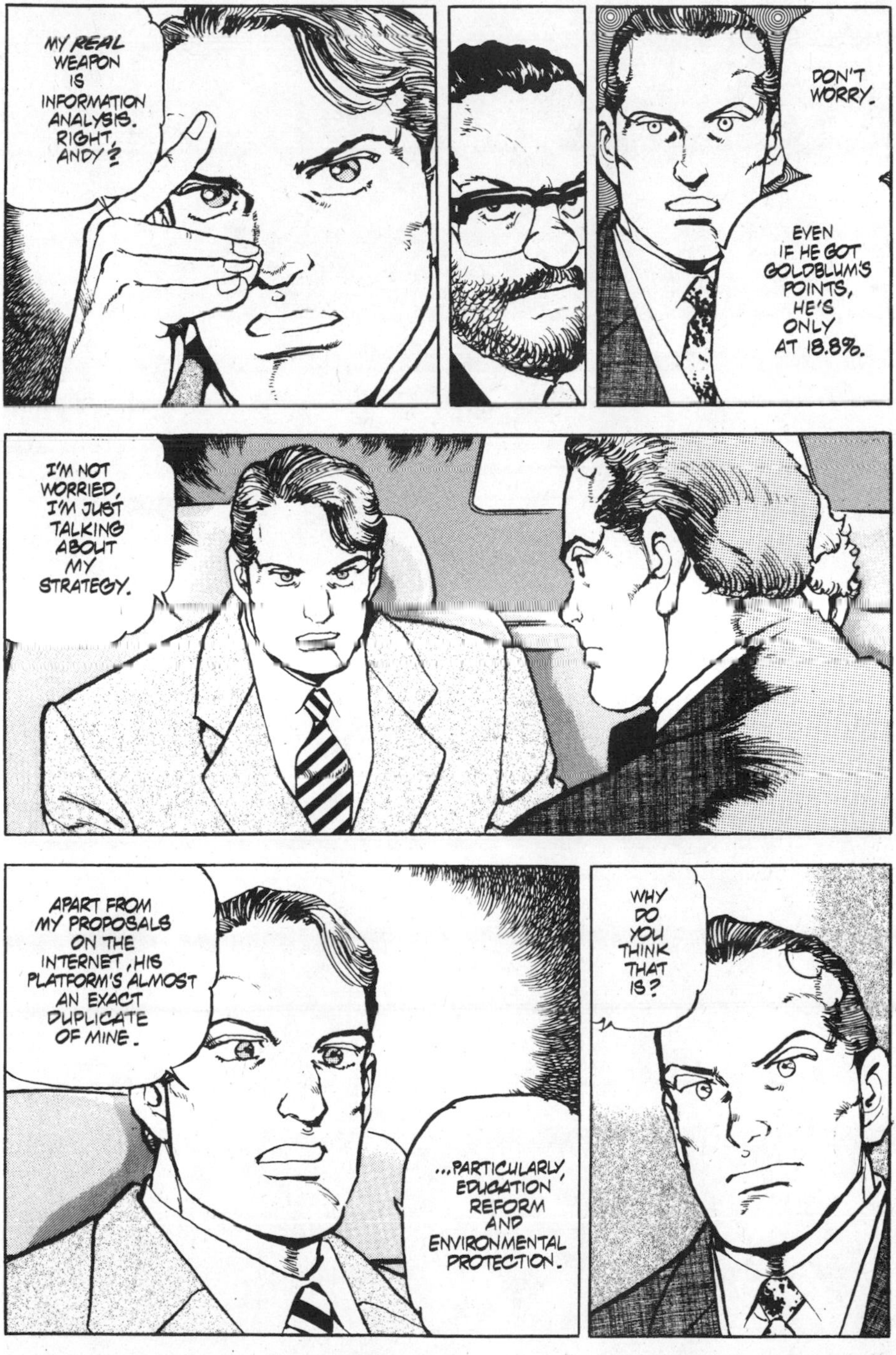
MY REAL WEAPON IS INFORMATION ANALYSIS. RIGHT, ANDY?
DON'T WORRY.
EVEN IF HE GOT GOLDBLUM'S POINTS, HE'S ONLY AT 18.8%.
I'M NOT WORRIED, I'M JUST TALKING ABOUT MY STRATEGY.
APART FROM MY PROPOSALS ON THE INTERNET, HIS PLATFORM'S ALMOST AN EXACT DUPLICATE OF MINE.
...PARTICULARLY, EDUCATION REFORM AND ENVIRONMENTAL PROTECTION.
WHY DO YOU THINK THAT IS?

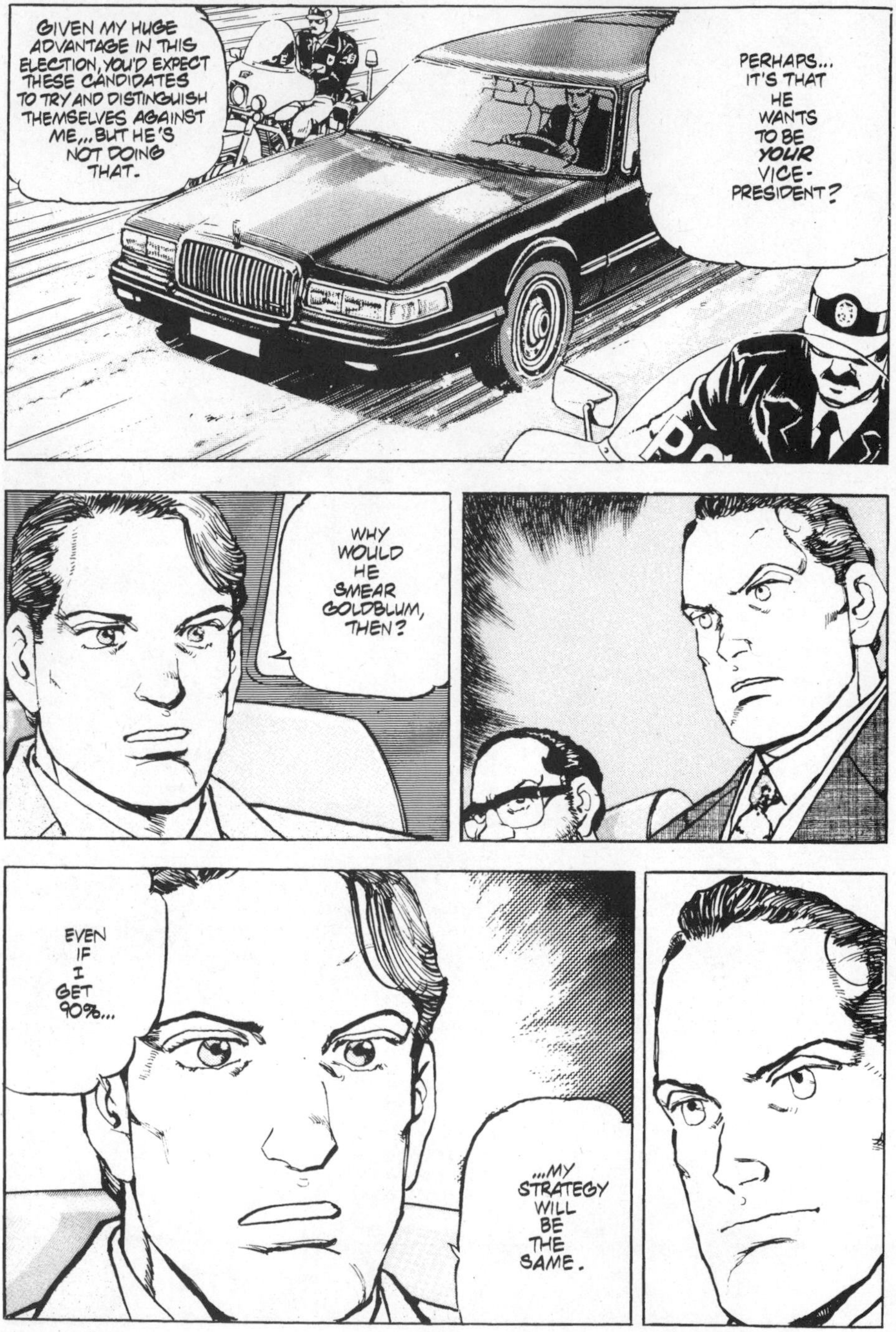
GIVEN MY HUGE ADVANTAGE IN THIS ELECTION, YOU'D EXPECT THESE CANDIDATES TO TRY AND DISTINGUISH THEMSELVES AGAINST ME... BUT HE'S NOT DOING THAT.
PERHAPS... IT'S THAT HE WANTS TO BE *YOUR* VICE-PRESIDENT?
WHY WOULD HE SMEAR GOLDBLUM, THEN?
EVEN IF I GET 90%...
...MY STRATEGY WILL BE THE SAME.

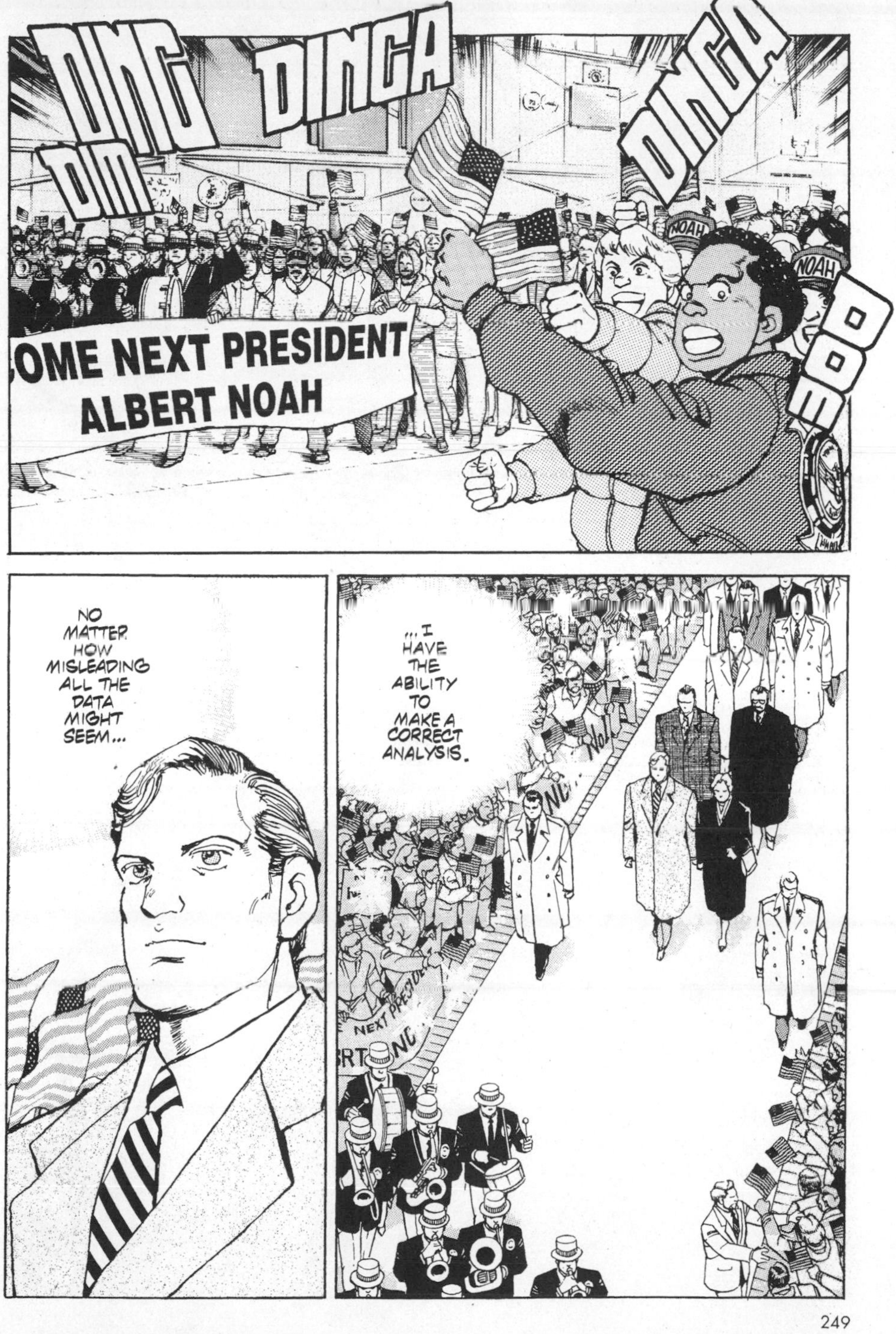
DINGA
DINGA
OME NEXT PRESIDENT
ALBERT NOAH
NOAH
NOAH
NO MATTER HOW MISLEADING ALL THE DATA MIGHT SEEM...
...I HAVE THE ABILITY TO MAKE A CORRECT ANALYSIS.

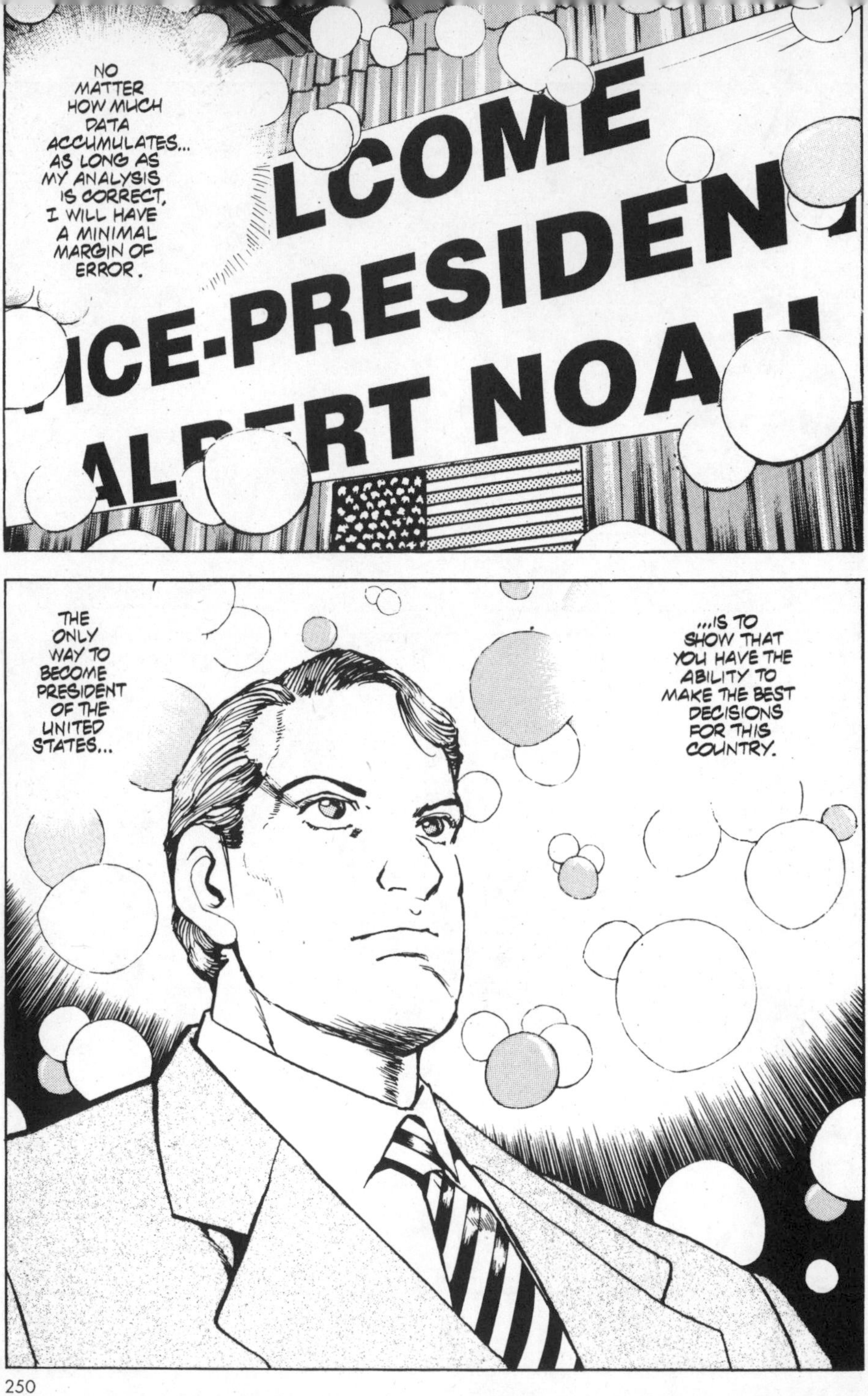
NO MATTER HOW MUCH DATA ACCUMULATES... AS LONG AS MY ANALYSIS IS CORRECT, I WILL HAVE A MINIMAL MARGIN OF ERROR.
LCOME
ICE-PRESIDEN
ALBERT NOA
THE ONLY WAY TO BECOME PRESIDENT OF THE UNITED STATES...
...IS TO SHOW THAT YOU HAVE THE ABILITY TO MAKE THE BEST DECISIONS FOR THIS COUNTRY.

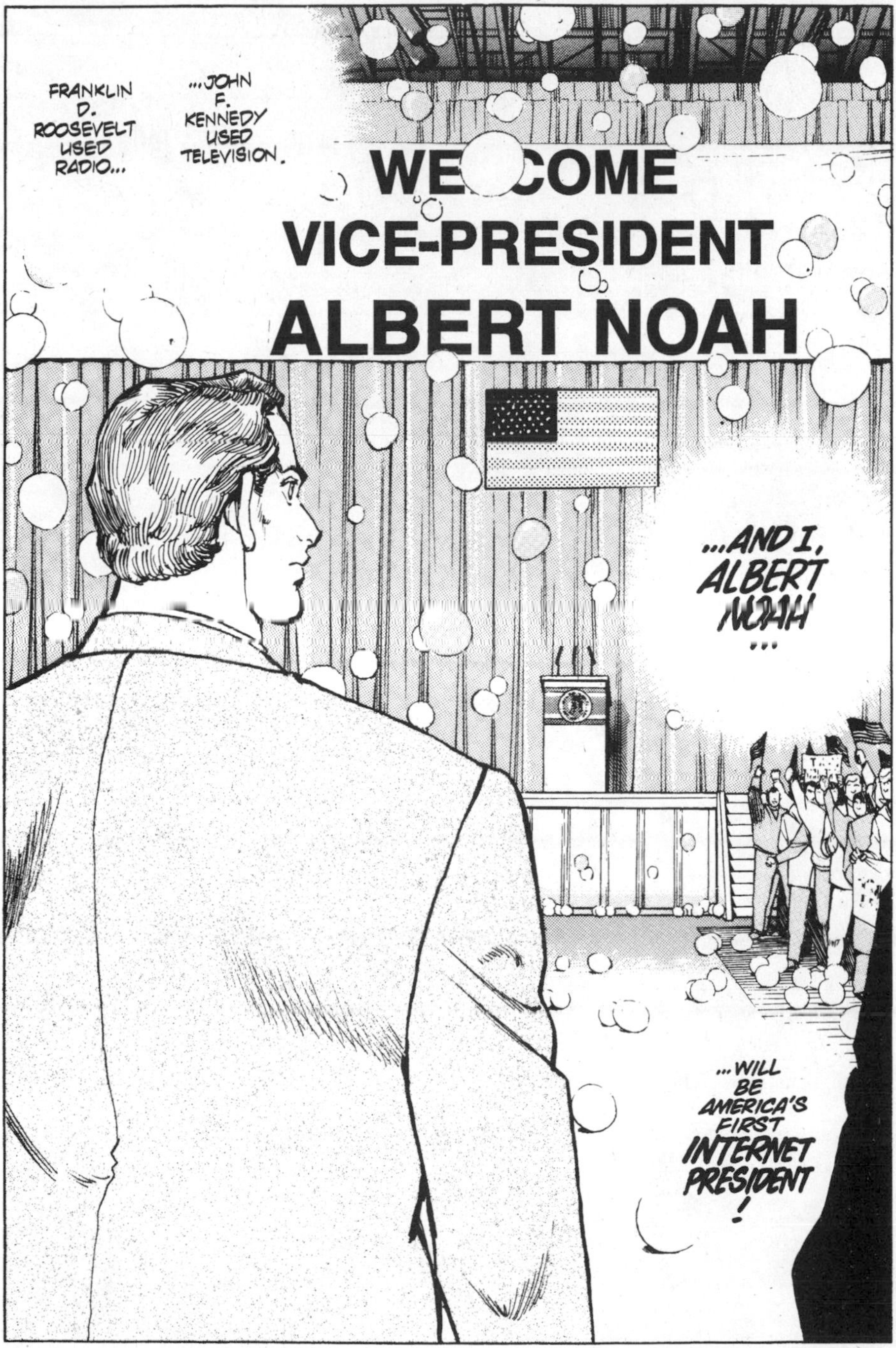
FRANKLIN D. ROOSEVELT USED RADIO...
...JOHN F. KENNEDY USED TELEVISION.
WELCOME VICE-PRESIDENT ALBERT NOAH
...AND I, ALBERT NOAH ...
...WILL BE AMERICA'S FIRST INTERNET PRESIDENT!

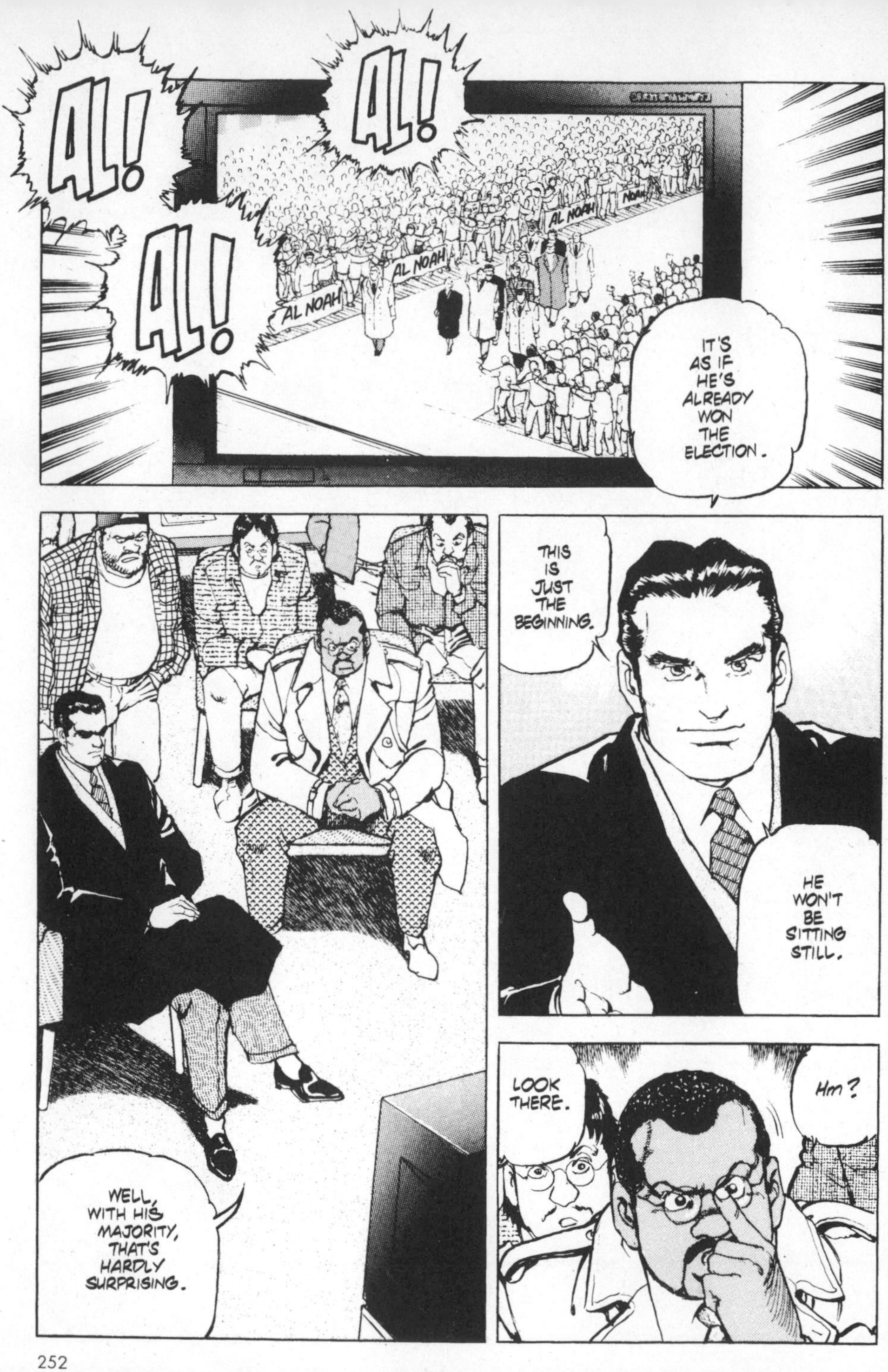
AL!
AL!
AL!
AL NOAH
AL NOAH
AL NOAH
NOAH
IT'S AS IF HE'S ALREADY WON THE ELECTION.
WELL, WITH HIS MAJORITY, THAT'S HARDLY SURPRISING.
THIS IS JUST THE BEGINNING.
HE WON'T BE SITTING STILL.
LOOK THERE.
Hm?

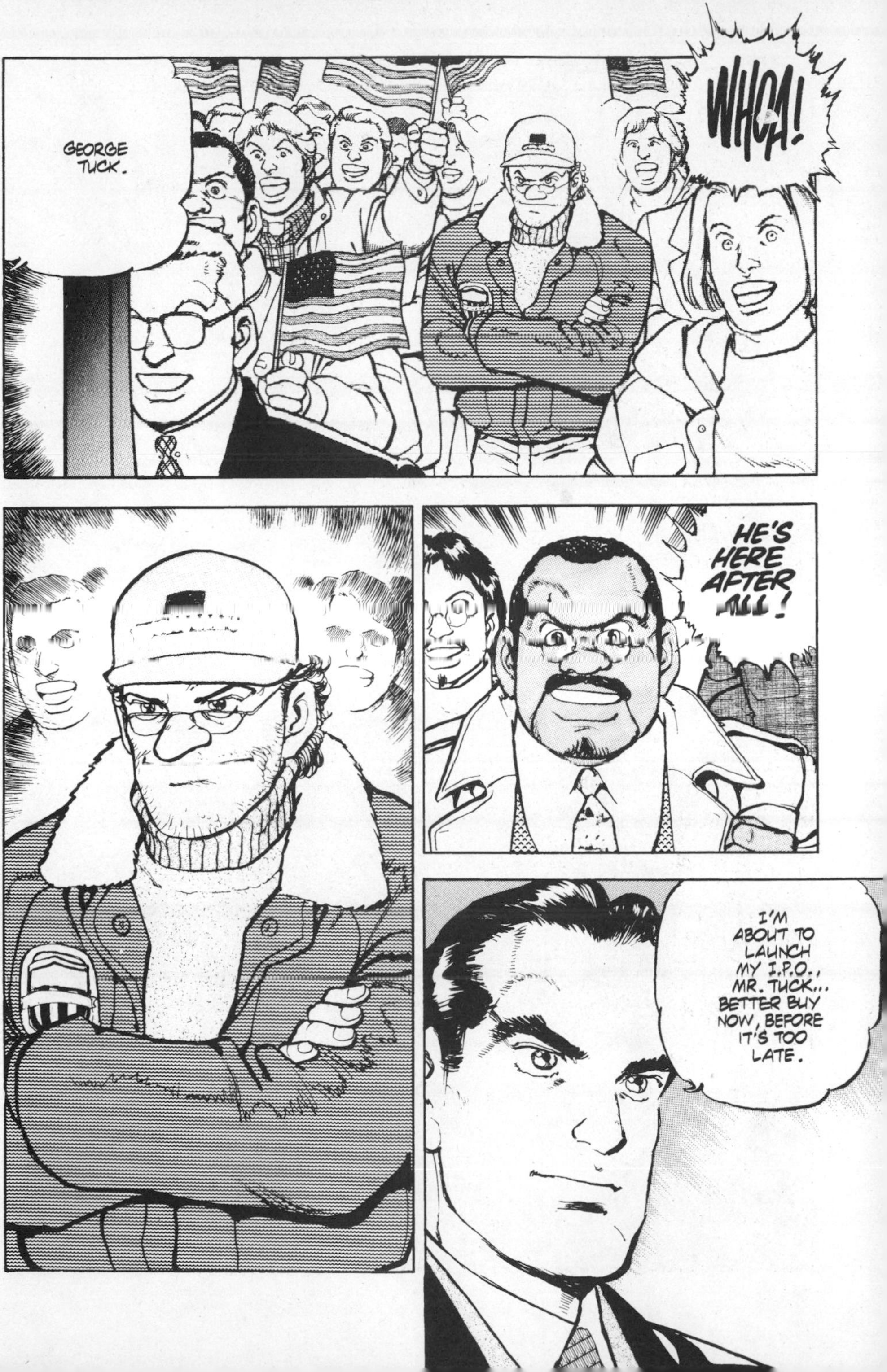
GEORGE TUCK.
WHOA!
HE'S HERE AFTER ALL!
I'M ABOUT TO LAUNCH MY I.P.O., MR. TUCK... BETTER BUY NOW, BEFORE IT'S TOO LATE.

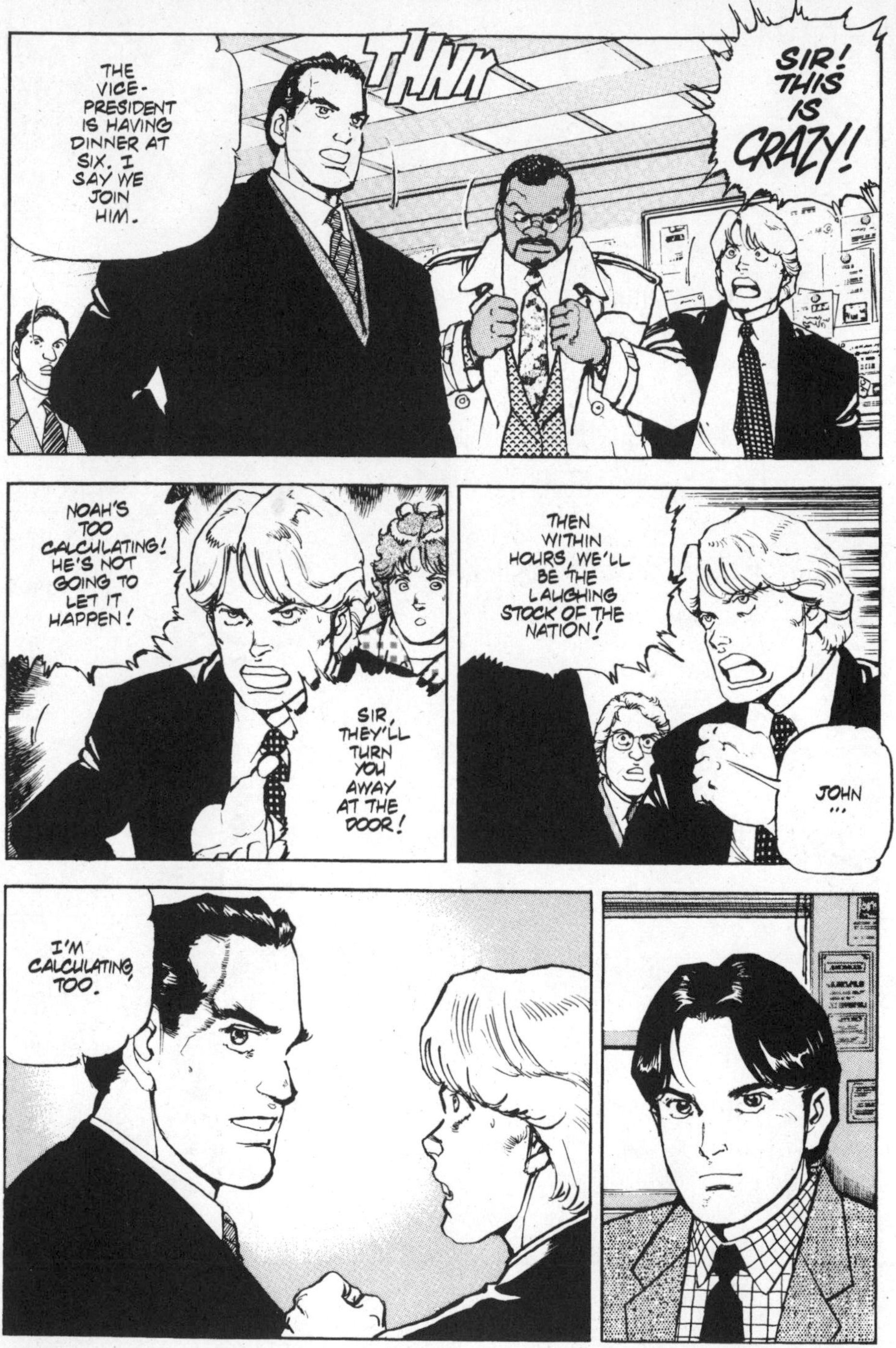
THE VICE-PRESIDENT IS HAVING DINNER AT SIX. I SAY WE JOIN HIM.
THNK
SIR! THIS IS CRAZY!
NOAH'S TOO CALCULATING! HE'S NOT GOING TO LET IT HAPPEN!
SIR, THEY'LL TURN YOU AWAY AT THE DOOR!
THEN WITHIN HOURS, WE'LL BE THE LAUGHING STOCK OF THE NATION!
JOHN ...
I'M CALCULATING, TOO.

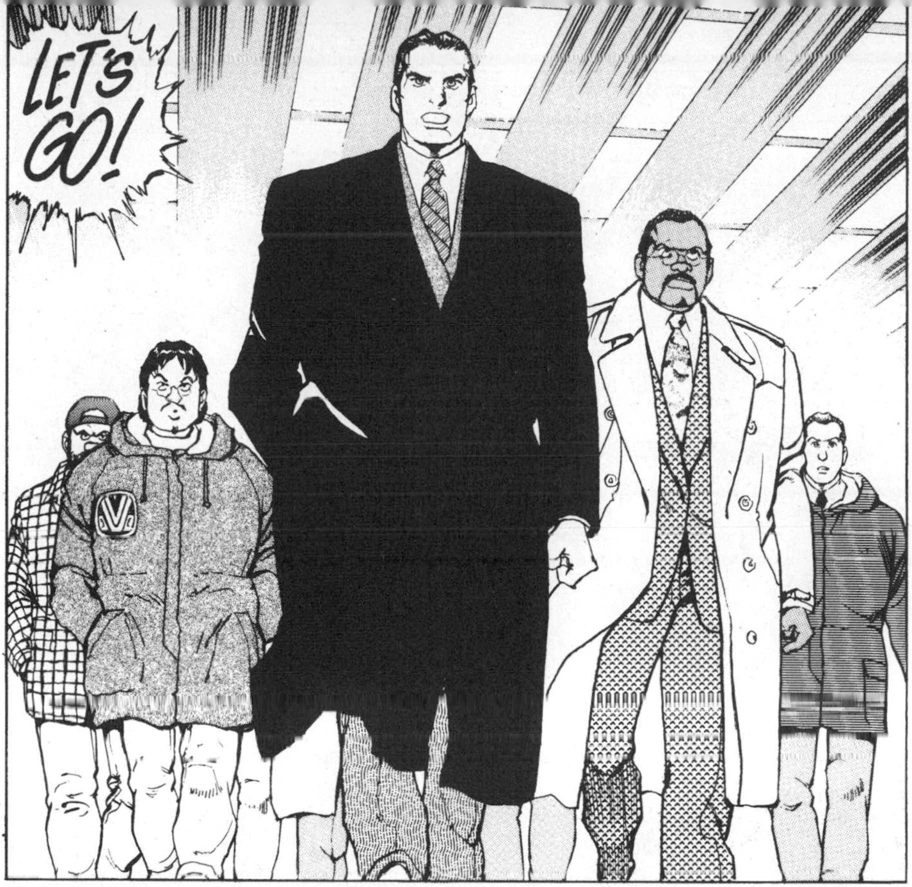
LET'S GO!
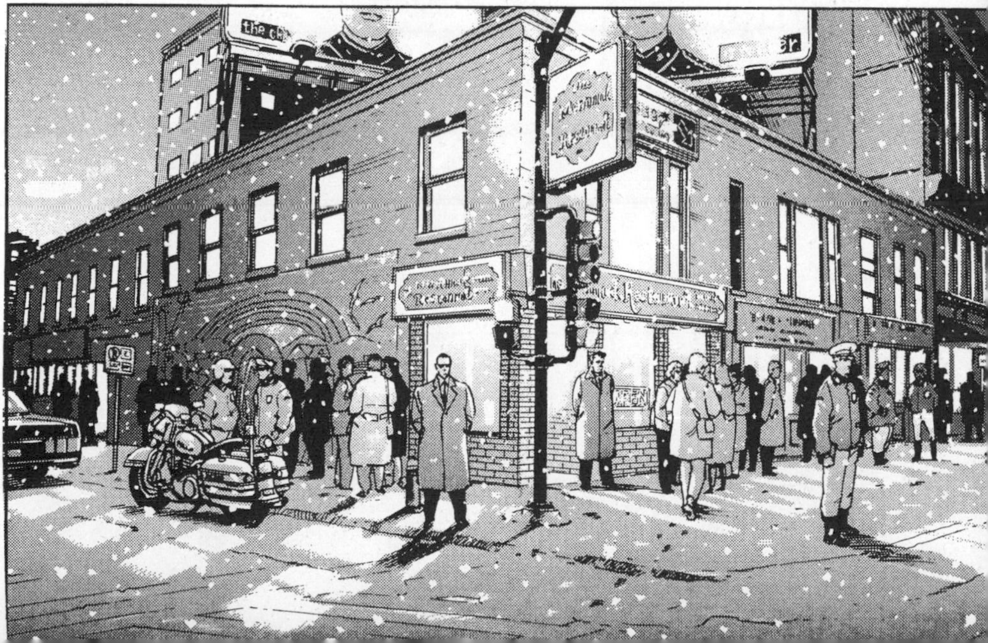

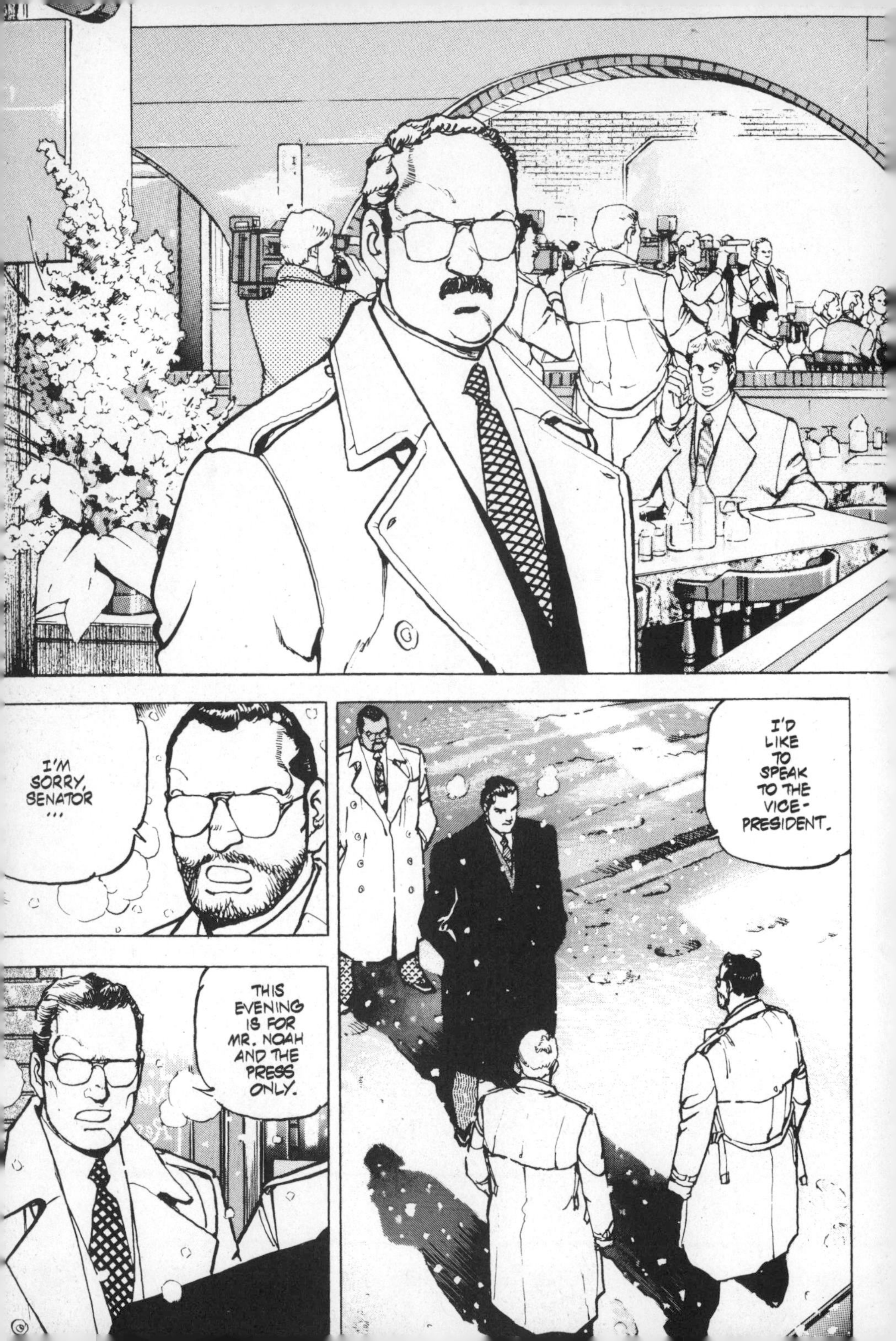
I'M SORRY, SENATOR ...
THIS EVENING IS FOR MR. NOAH AND THE PRESS ONLY.
I'D LIKE TO SPEAK TO THE VICE-PRESIDENT.

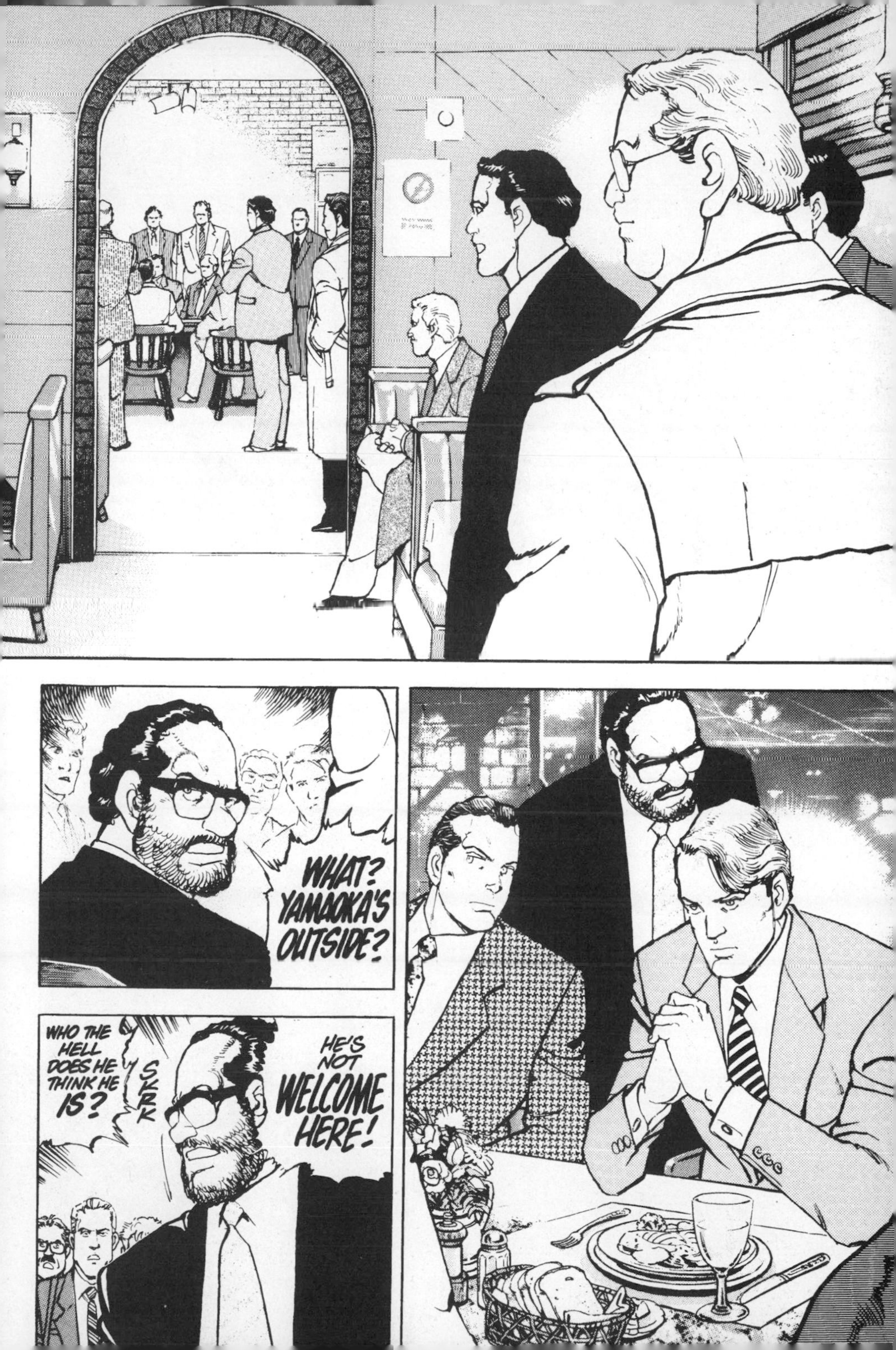
WHAT? YAMAOKA'S OUTSIDE?
WHO THE HELL DOES HE THINK HE IS?
SKRK
HE'S NOT WELCOME HERE!

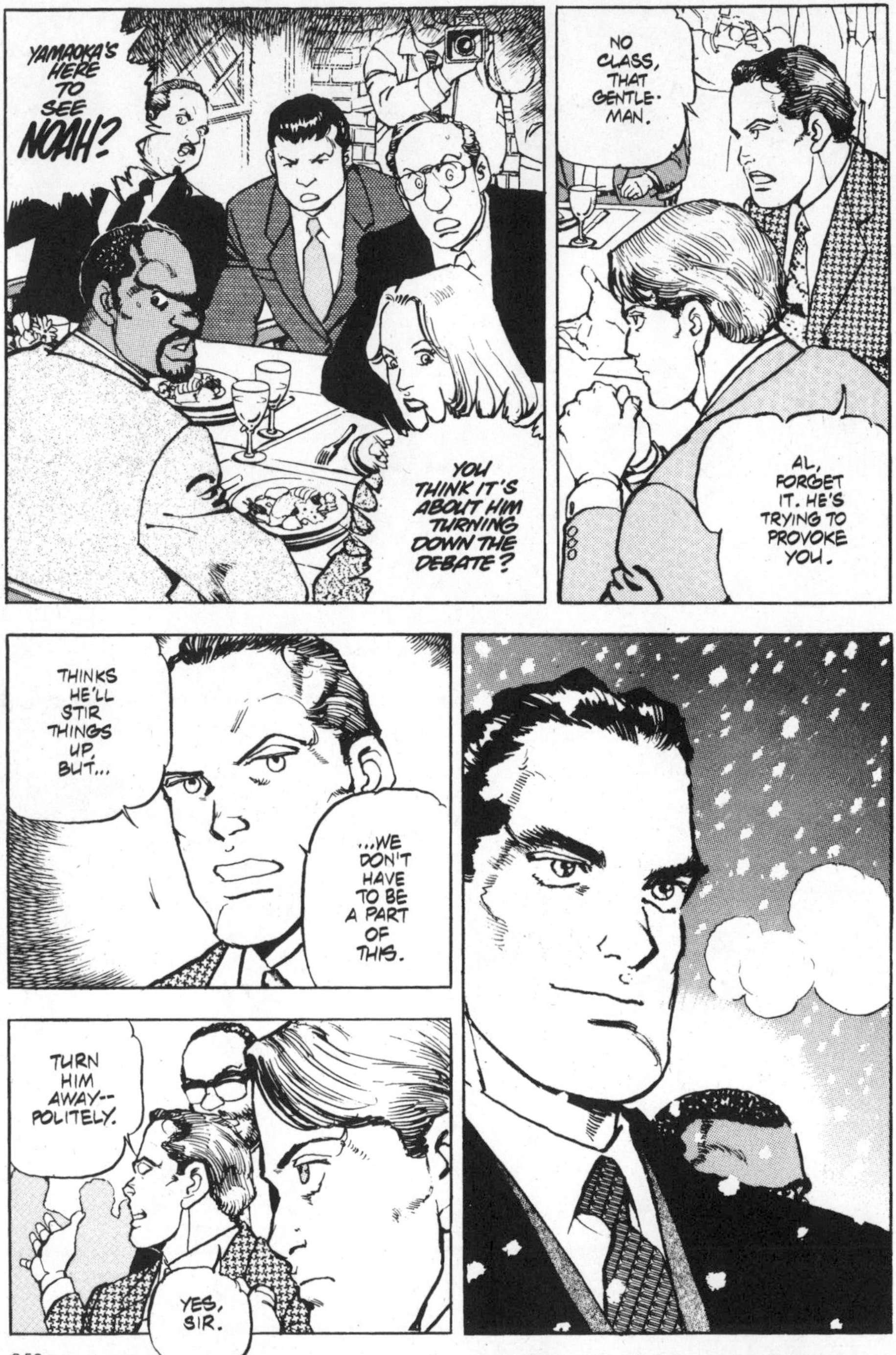
YAMAOKA'S HERE TO SEE NOAH?
YOU THINK IT'S ABOUT HIM TURNING DOWN THE DEBATE?
NO CLASS, THAT GENTLE-MAN.
AL, FORGET IT. HE'S TRYING TO PROVOKE YOU.
THINKS HE'LL STIR THINGS UP, BUT...
...WE DON'T HAVE TO BE A PART OF THIS.
TURN HIM AWAY--POLITELY.
YES, SIR.

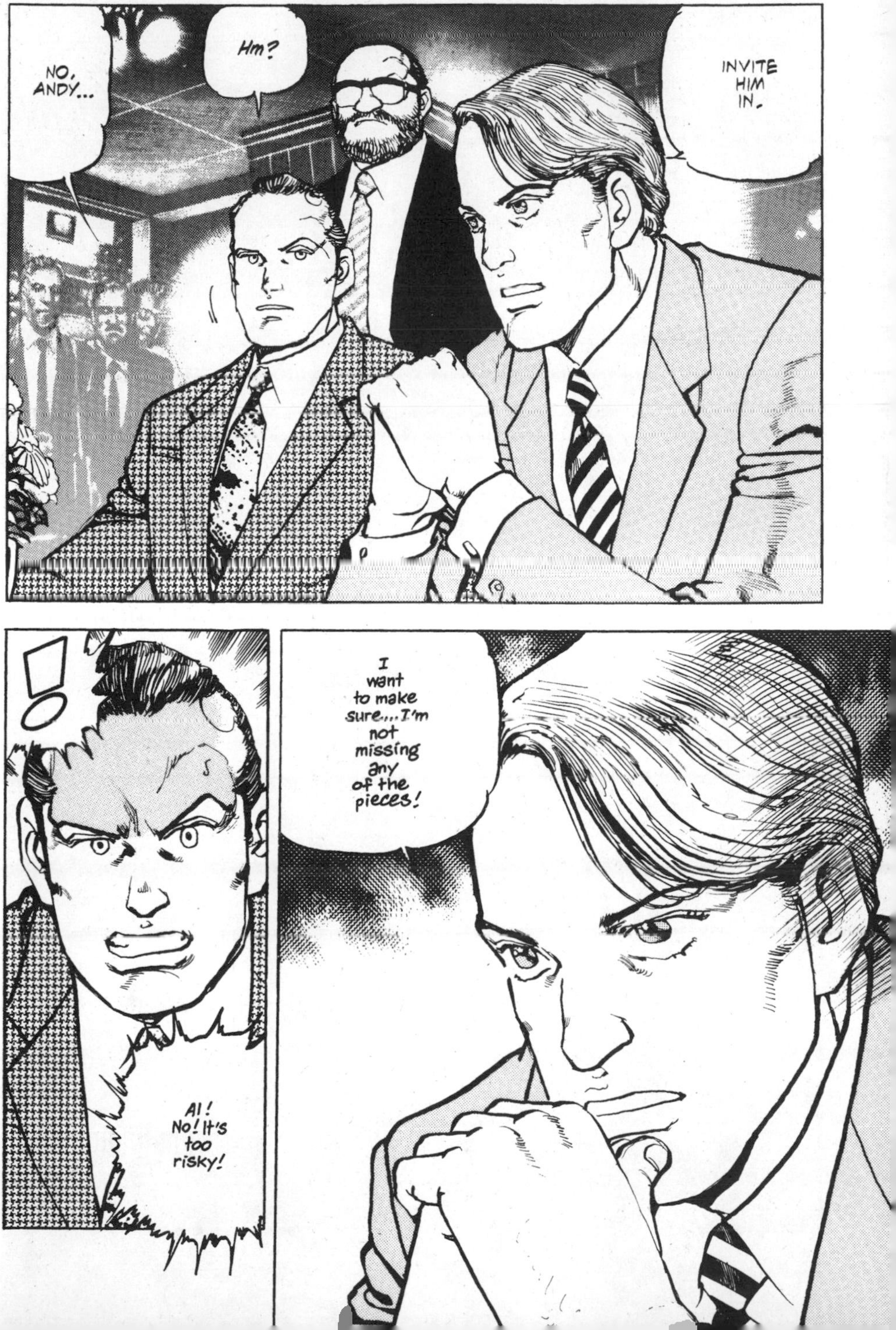
NO, ANDY...
Hm?
INVITE HIM IN.
!
Al! No! It's too risky!
I want to make sure... I'm not missing any of the pieces!

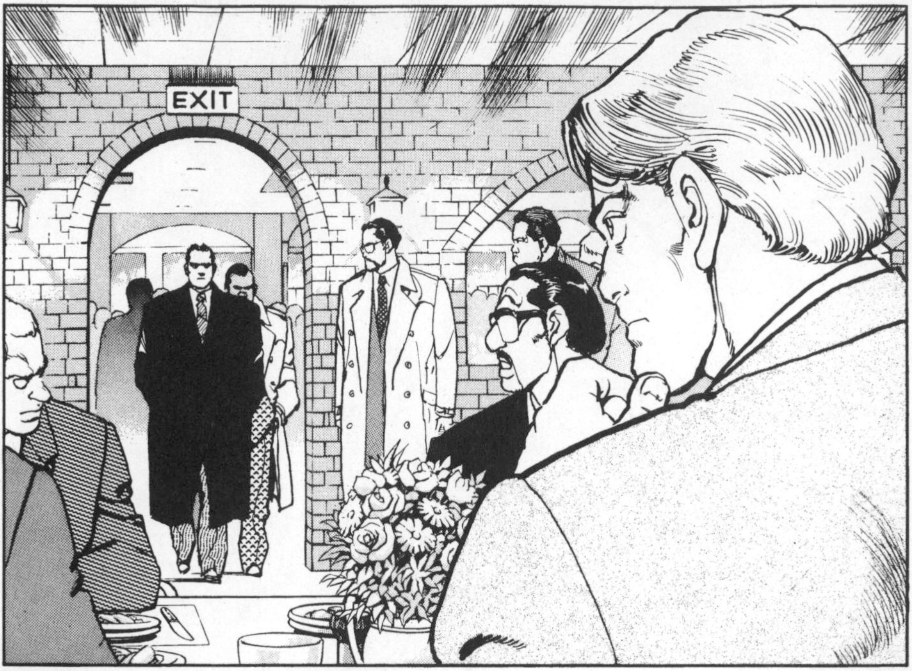
EXIT
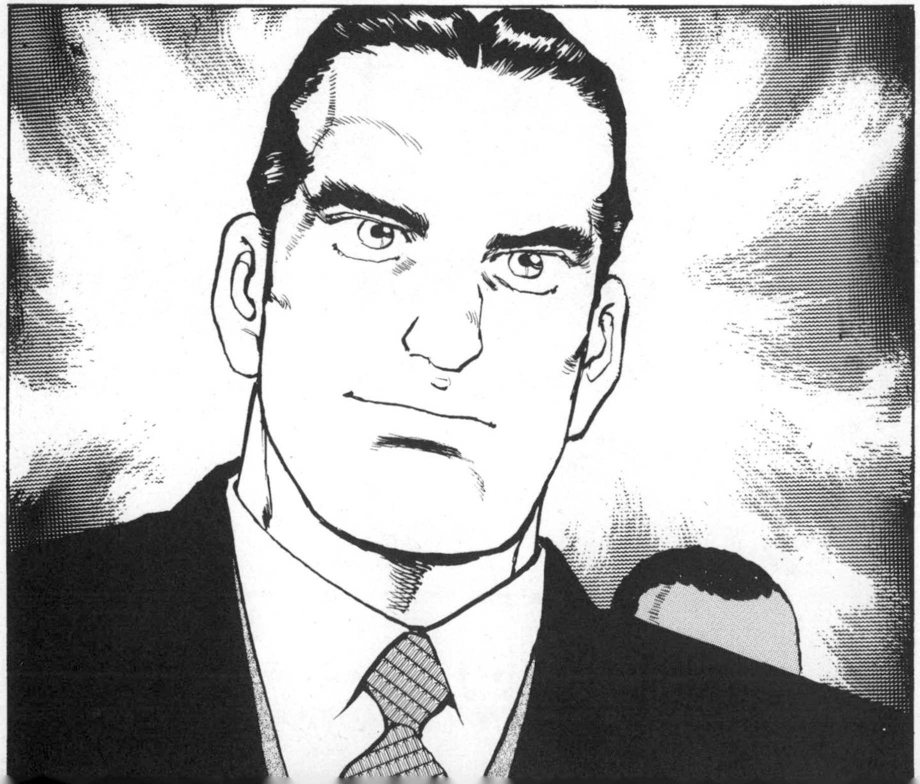

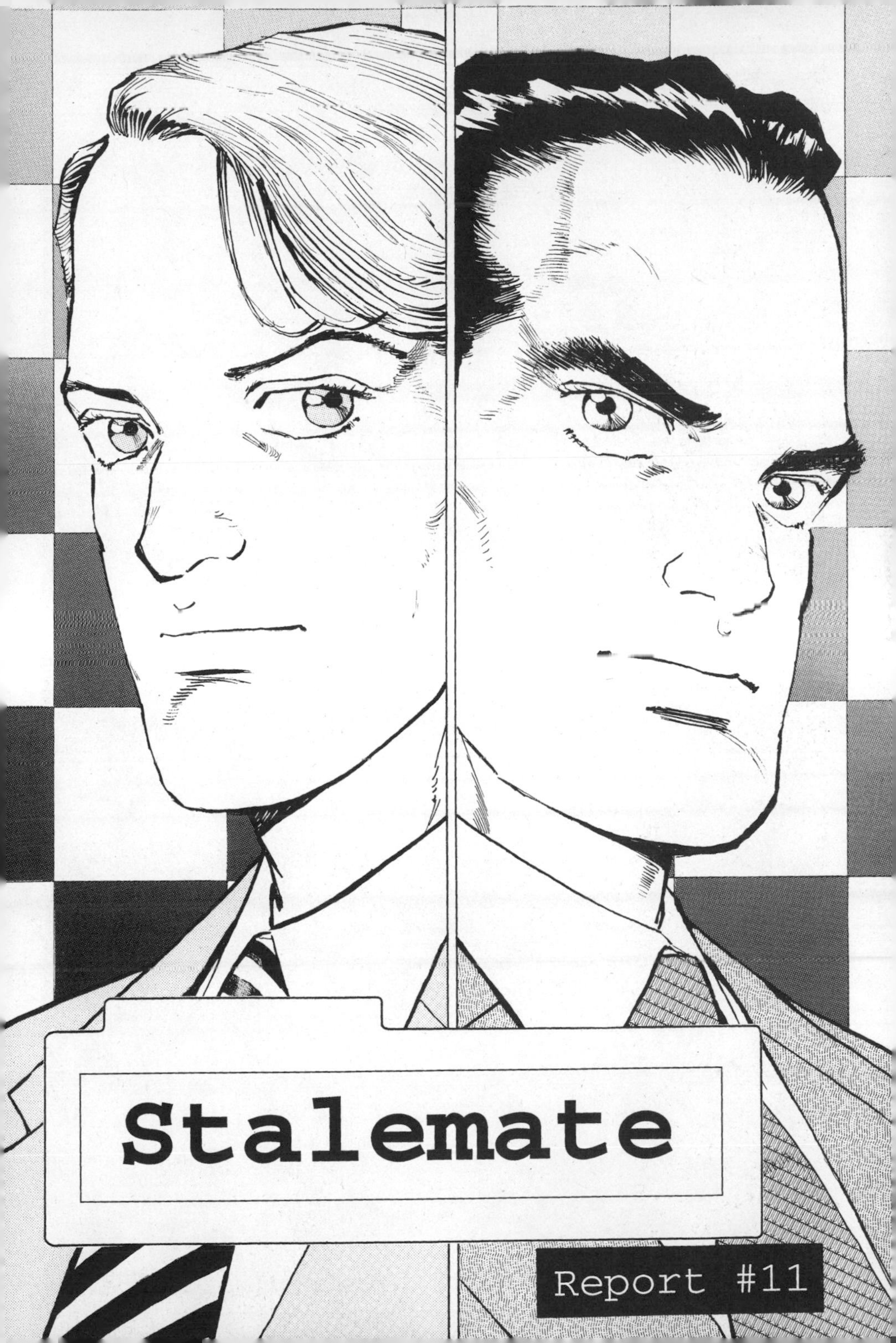
Stalemate
Report #11

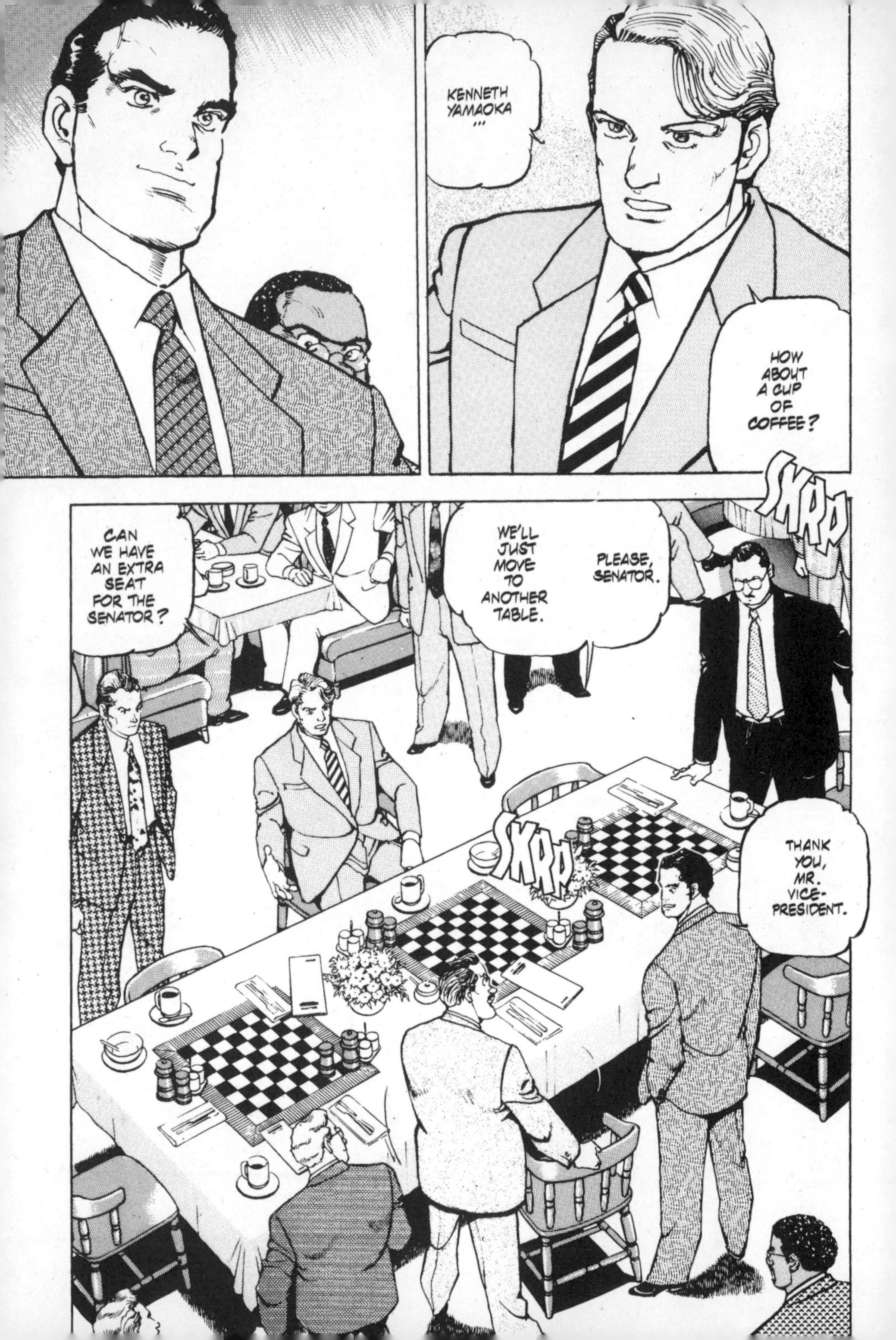
KENNETH YAMAOKA ...
HOW ABOUT A CUP OF COFFEE?
SKRP
CAN WE HAVE AN EXTRA SEAT FOR THE SENATOR?
WE'LL JUST MOVE TO ANOTHER TABLE.
PLEASE, SENATOR.
SKRP
THANK YOU, MR. VICE-PRESIDENT.

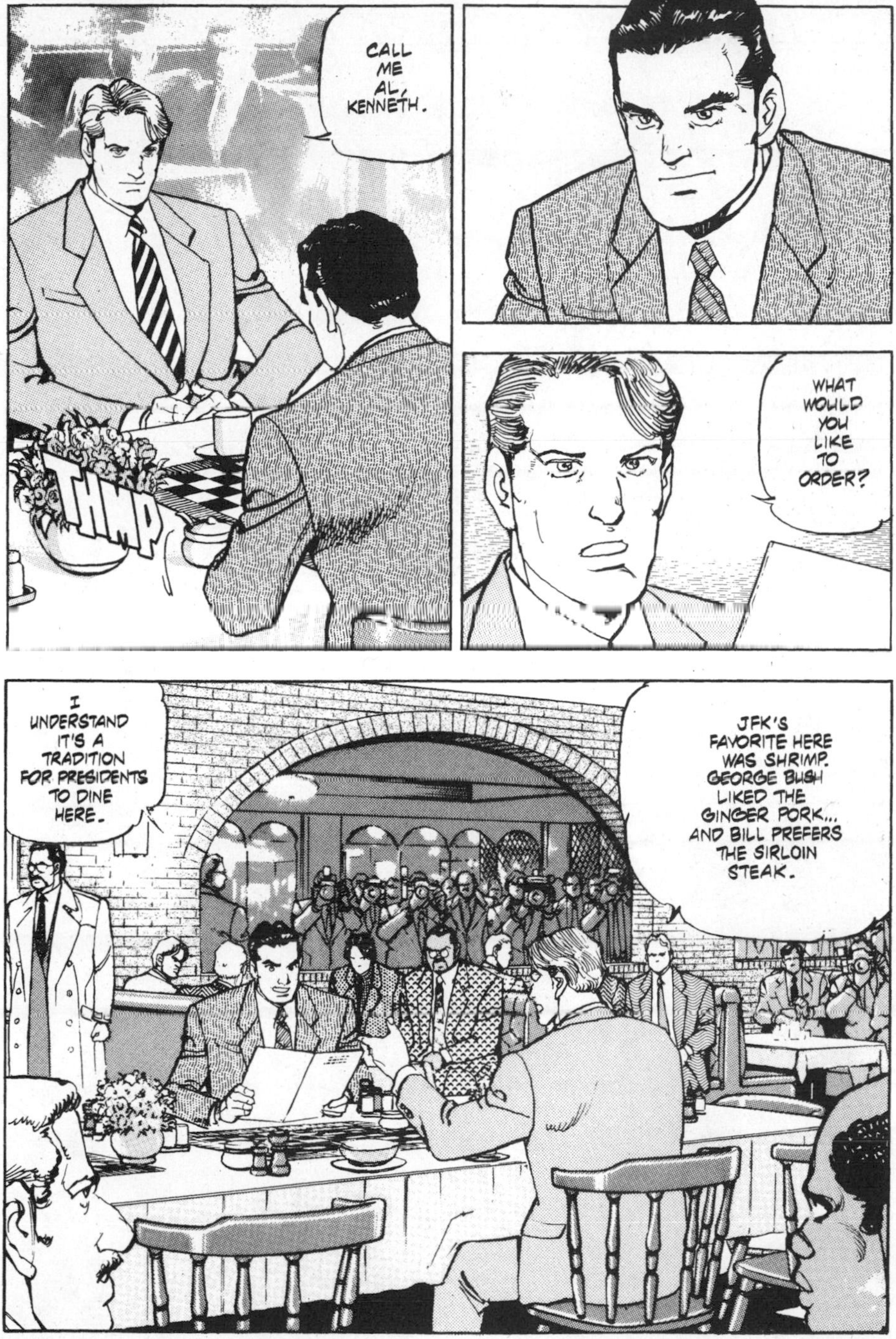
CALL ME AL, KENNETH.
THMP
WHAT WOULD YOU LIKE TO ORDER?
I UNDERSTAND IT'S A TRADITION FOR PRESIDENTS TO DINE HERE.
JFK'S FAVORITE HERE WAS SHRIMP. GEORGE BUSH LIKED THE GINGER PORK... AND BILL PREFERS THE SIRLOIN STEAK.

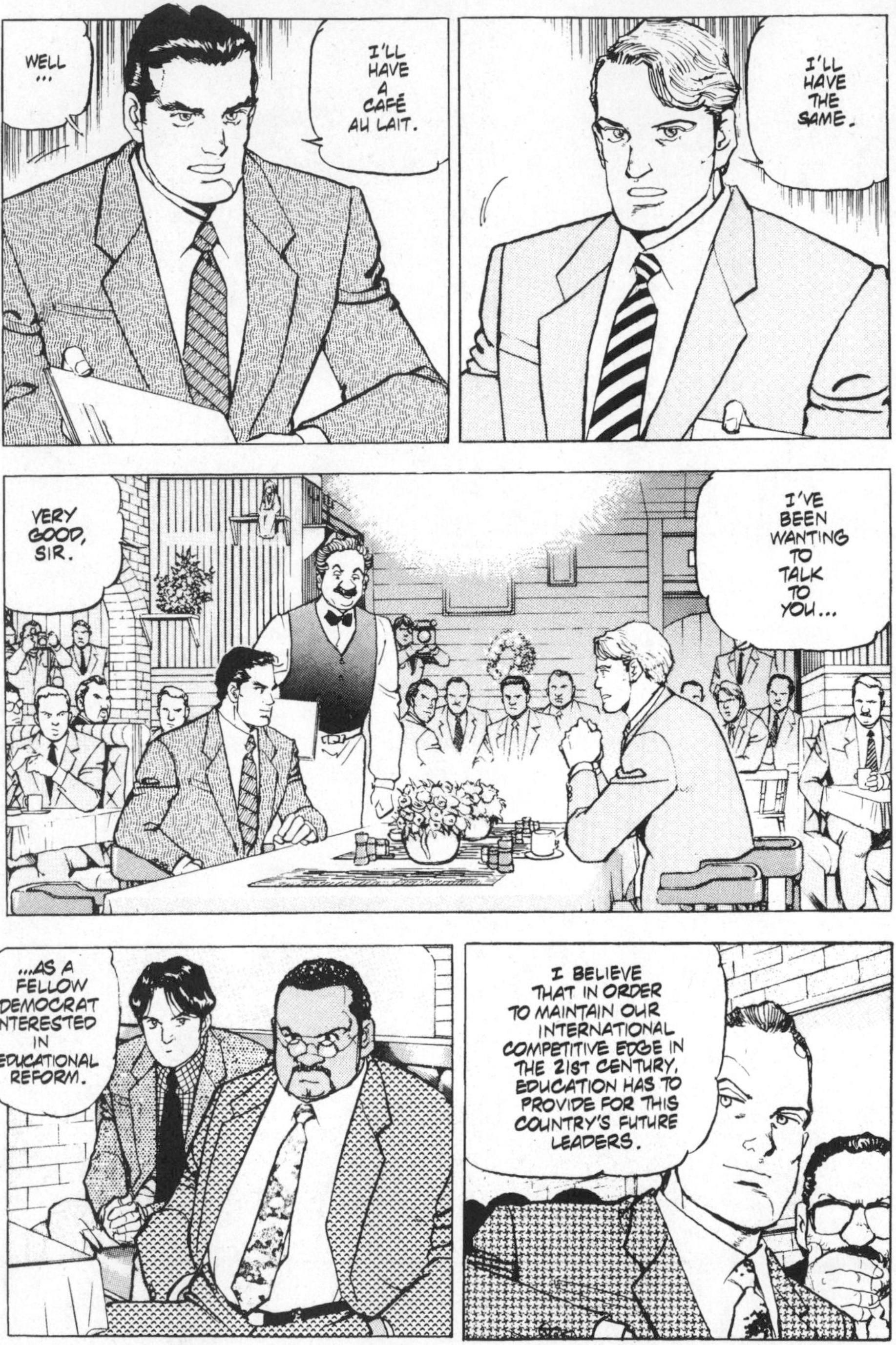
WELL ...
I'LL HAVE A CAFÉ AU LAIT.
I'LL HAVE THE SAME.
VERY GOOD, SIR.
I'VE BEEN WANTING TO TALK TO YOU...
...AS A FELLOW DEMOCRAT INTERESTED IN EDUCATIONAL REFORM.
I BELIEVE THAT IN ORDER TO MAINTAIN OUR INTERNATIONAL COMPETITIVE EDGE IN THE 21ST CENTURY, EDUCATION HAS TO PROVIDE FOR THIS COUNTRY'S FUTURE LEADERS.

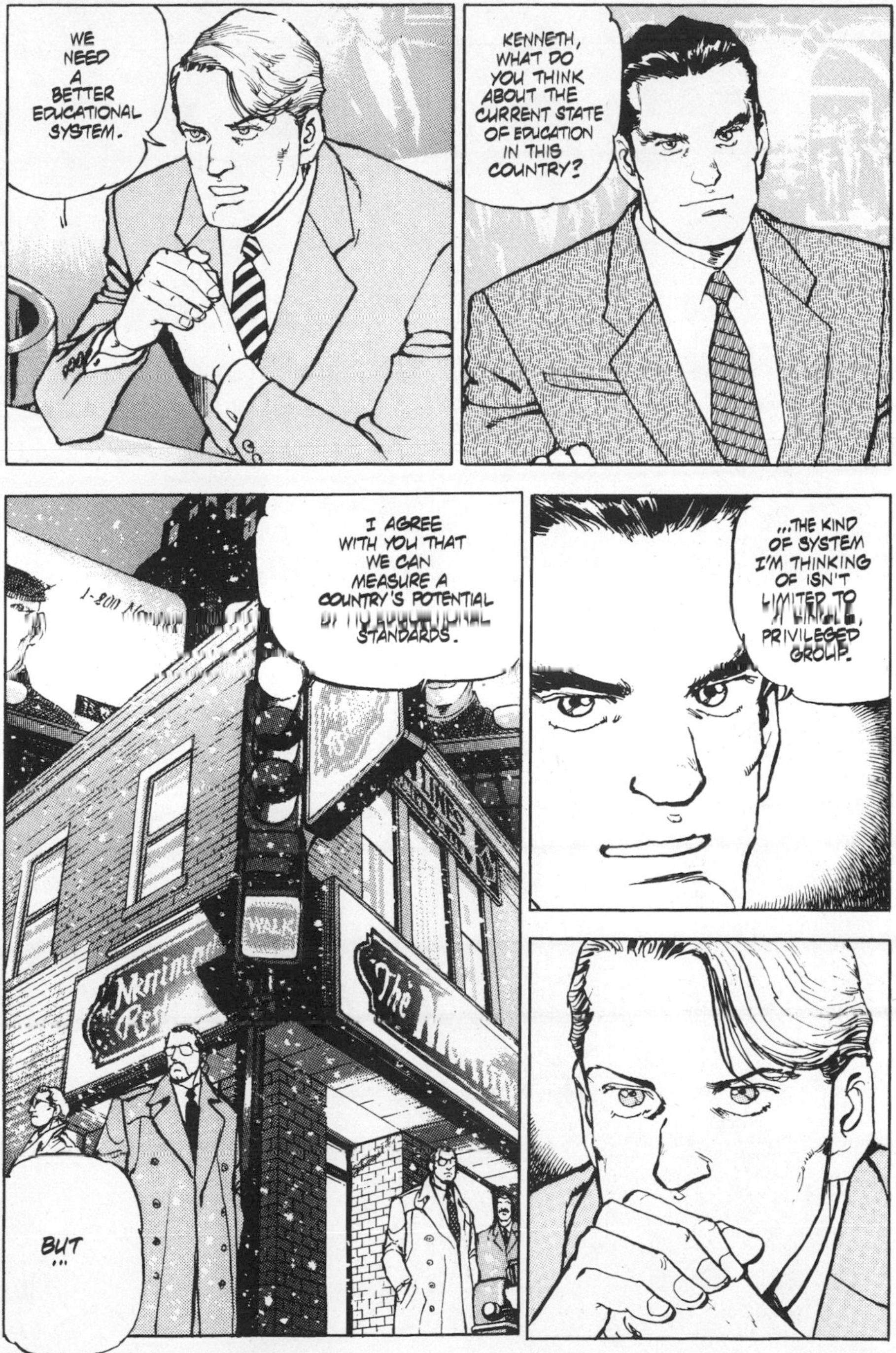
WE NEED A BETTER EDUCATIONAL SYSTEM.
KENNETH, WHAT DO YOU THINK ABOUT THE CURRENT STATE OF EDUCATION IN THIS COUNTRY?
I AGREE WITH YOU THAT WE CAN MEASURE A COUNTRY'S POTENTIAL
STANDARDS.
WALK
BUT...
...THE KIND OF SYSTEM I'M THINKING OF ISN'T LIMITED TO
PRIVILEGED GROUP.

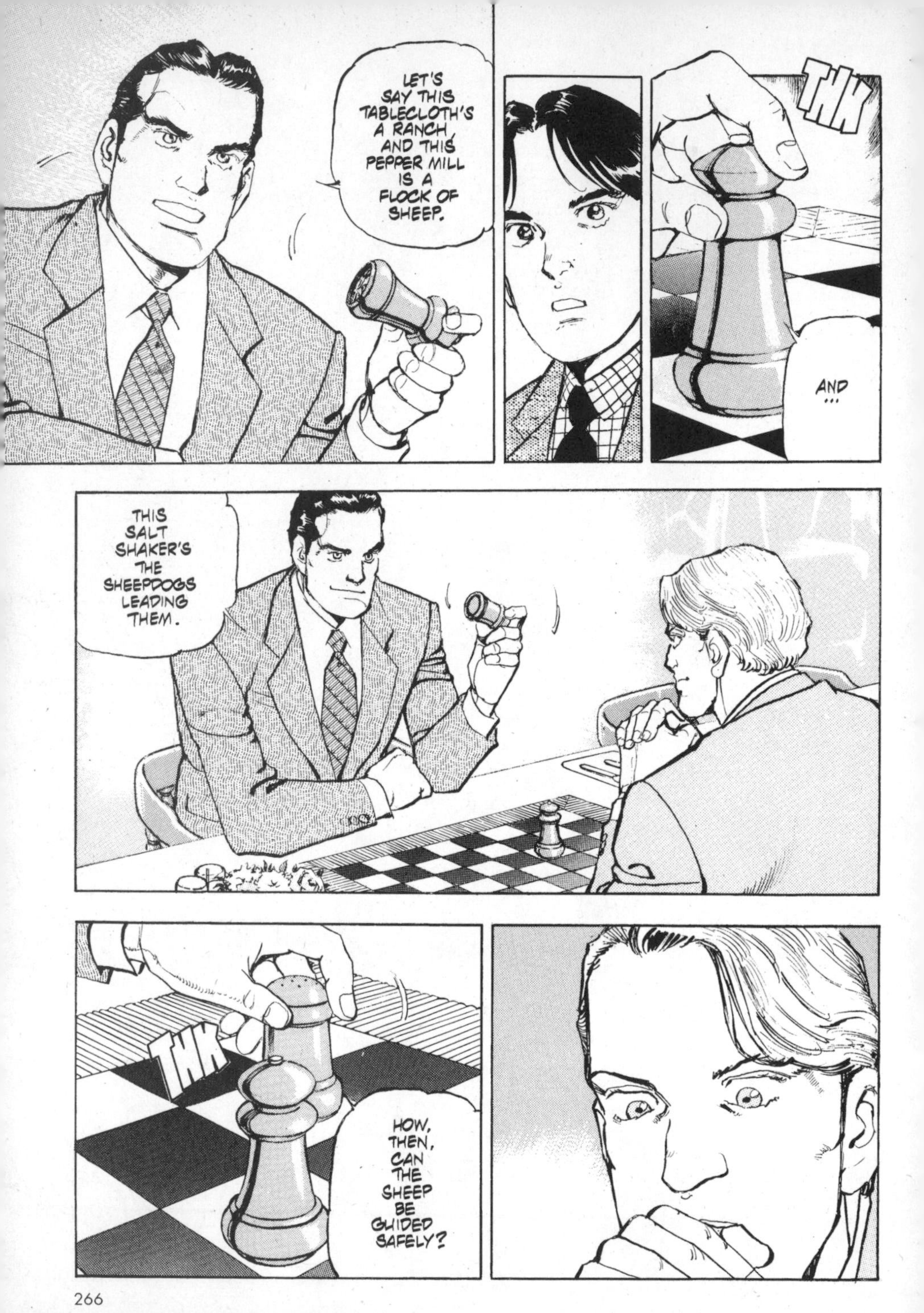
LET'S SAY THIS TABLECLOTH'S A RANCH, AND THIS PEPPER MILL IS A FLOCK OF SHEEP.
THK
AND ...
THIS SALT SHAKER'S THE SHEEPDOGS LEADING THEM.
THK
HOW, THEN, CAN THE SHEEP BE GUIDED SAFELY?

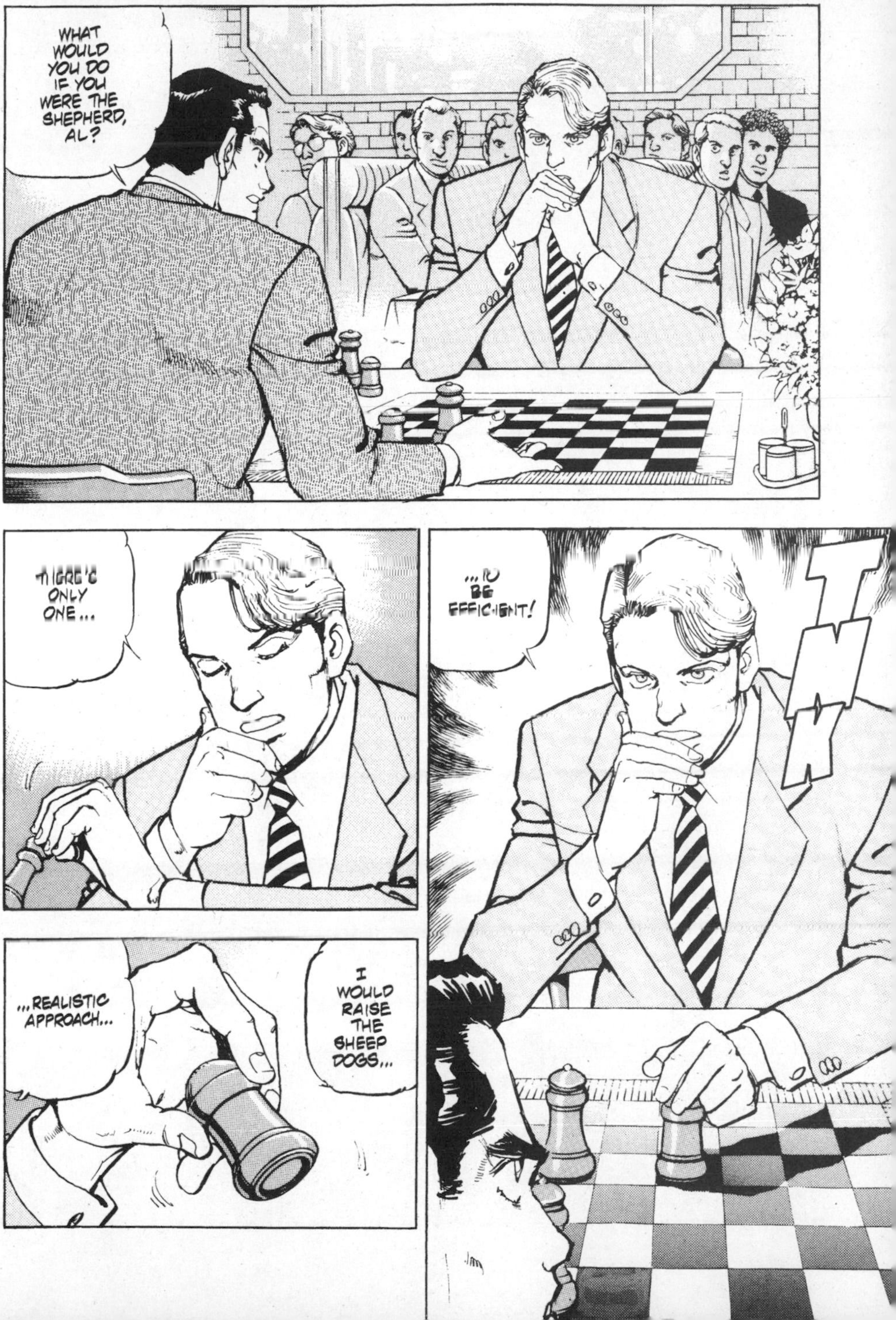
WHAT WOULD YOU DO IF YOU WERE THE SHEPHERD, AL?
THERE'S ONLY ONE...
...REALISTIC APPROACH...
I WOULD RAISE THE SHEEP DOGS...
...TO BE EFFICIENT!
TNK

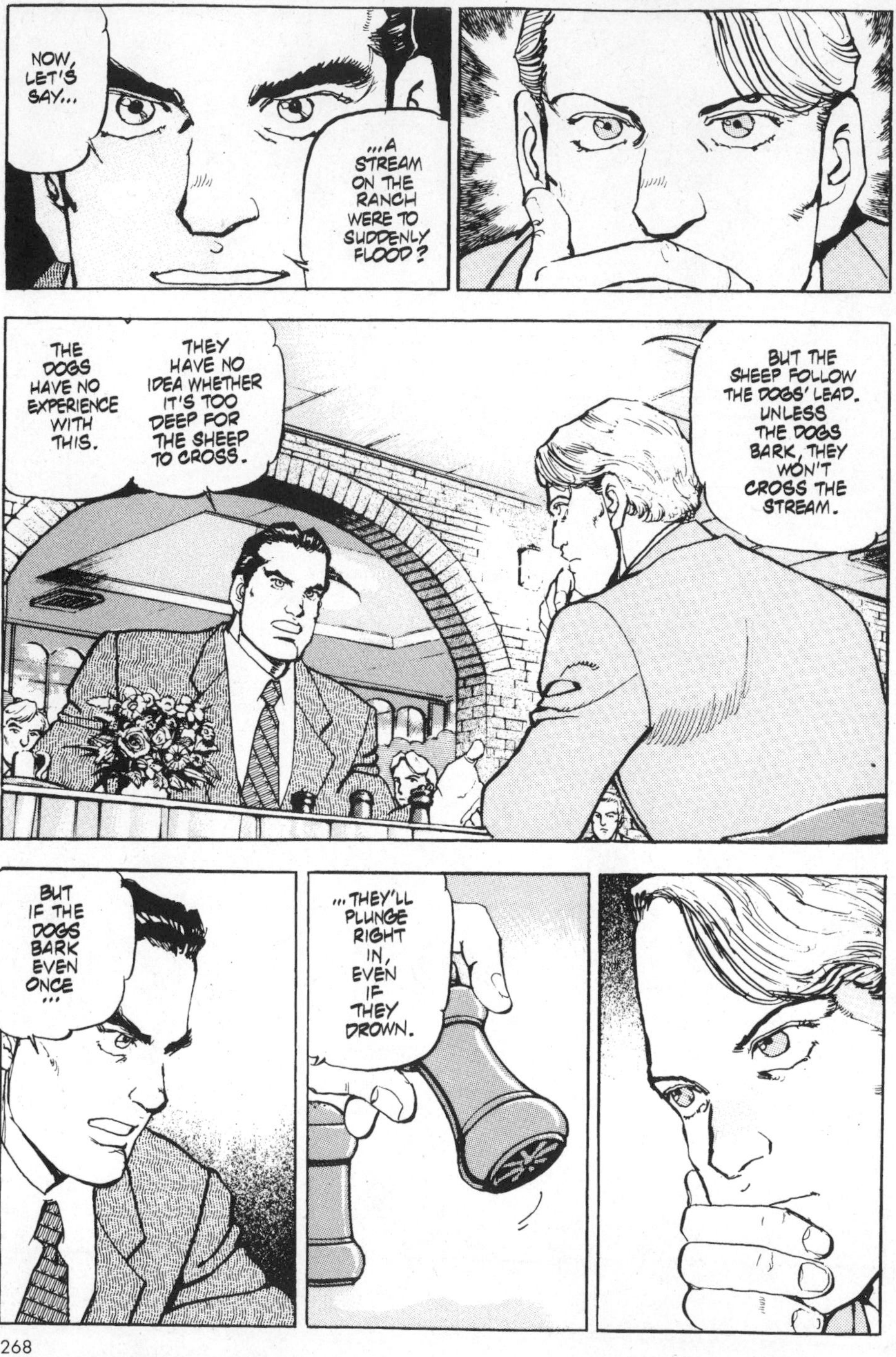
NOW, LET'S SAY...
...A STREAM ON THE RANCH WERE TO SUDDENLY FLOOD?
THE DOGS HAVE NO EXPERIENCE WITH THIS.
THEY HAVE NO IDEA WHETHER IT'S TOO DEEP FOR THE SHEEP TO CROSS.
BUT THE SHEEP FOLLOW THE DOGS' LEAD. UNLESS THE DOGS BARK, THEY WON'T CROSS THE STREAM.
BUT IF THE DOGS BARK EVEN ONCE...
...THEY'LL PLUNGE RIGHT IN, EVEN IF THEY DROWN.

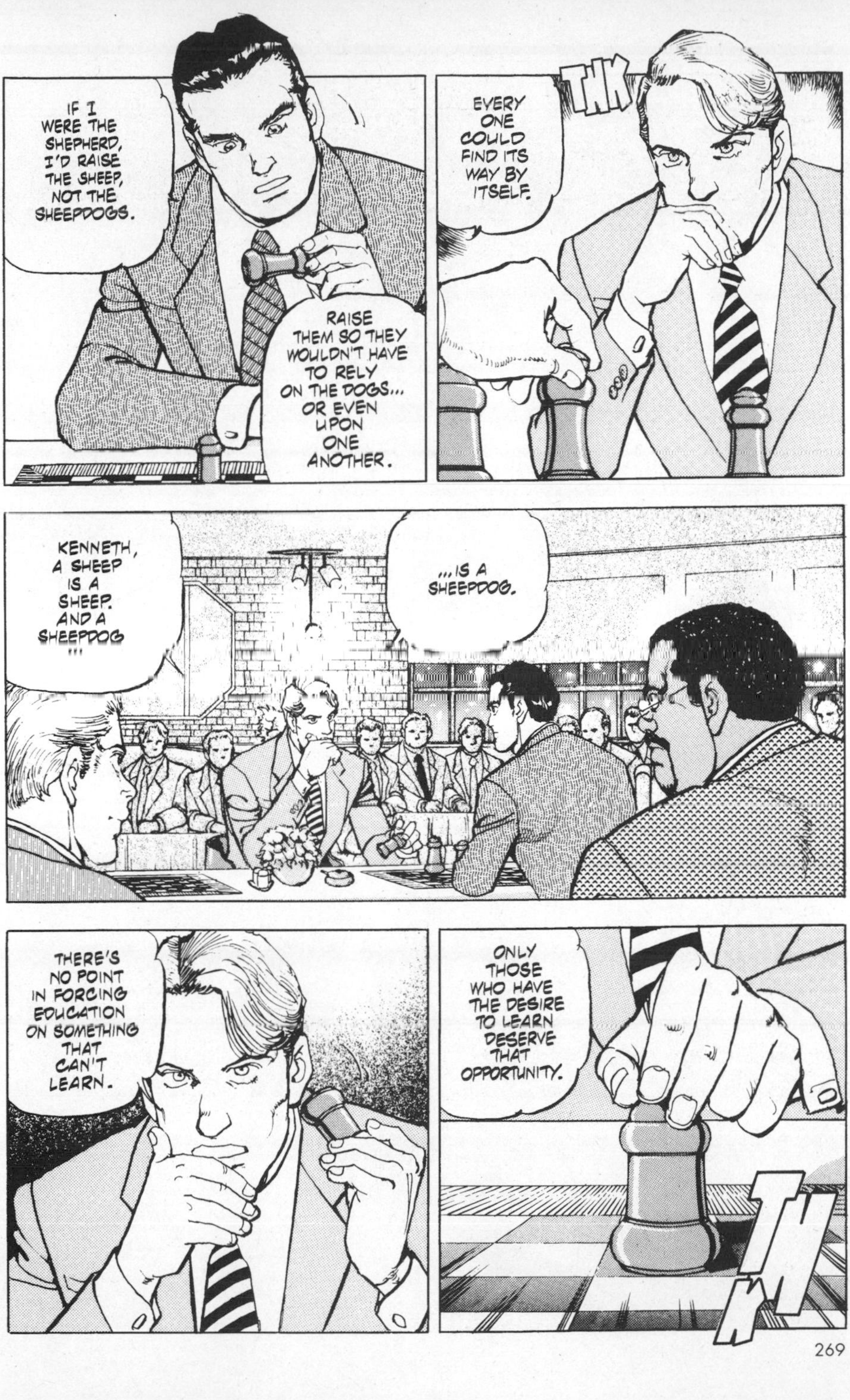
IF I WERE THE SHEPHERD, I'D RAISE THE SHEEP, NOT THE SHEEPDOGS.
RAISE THEM SO THEY WOULDN'T HAVE TO RELY ON THE DOGS... OR EVEN UPON ONE ANOTHER.
THK
EVERY ONE COULD FIND ITS WAY BY ITSELF.
KENNETH, A SHEEP IS A SHEEP. AND A SHEEPDOG ...
...IS A SHEEPDOG.
THERE'S NO POINT IN FORCING EDUCATION ON SOMETHING THAT CAN'T LEARN.
ONLY THOSE WHO HAVE THE DESIRE TO LEARN DESERVE THAT OPPORTUNITY.
THNK

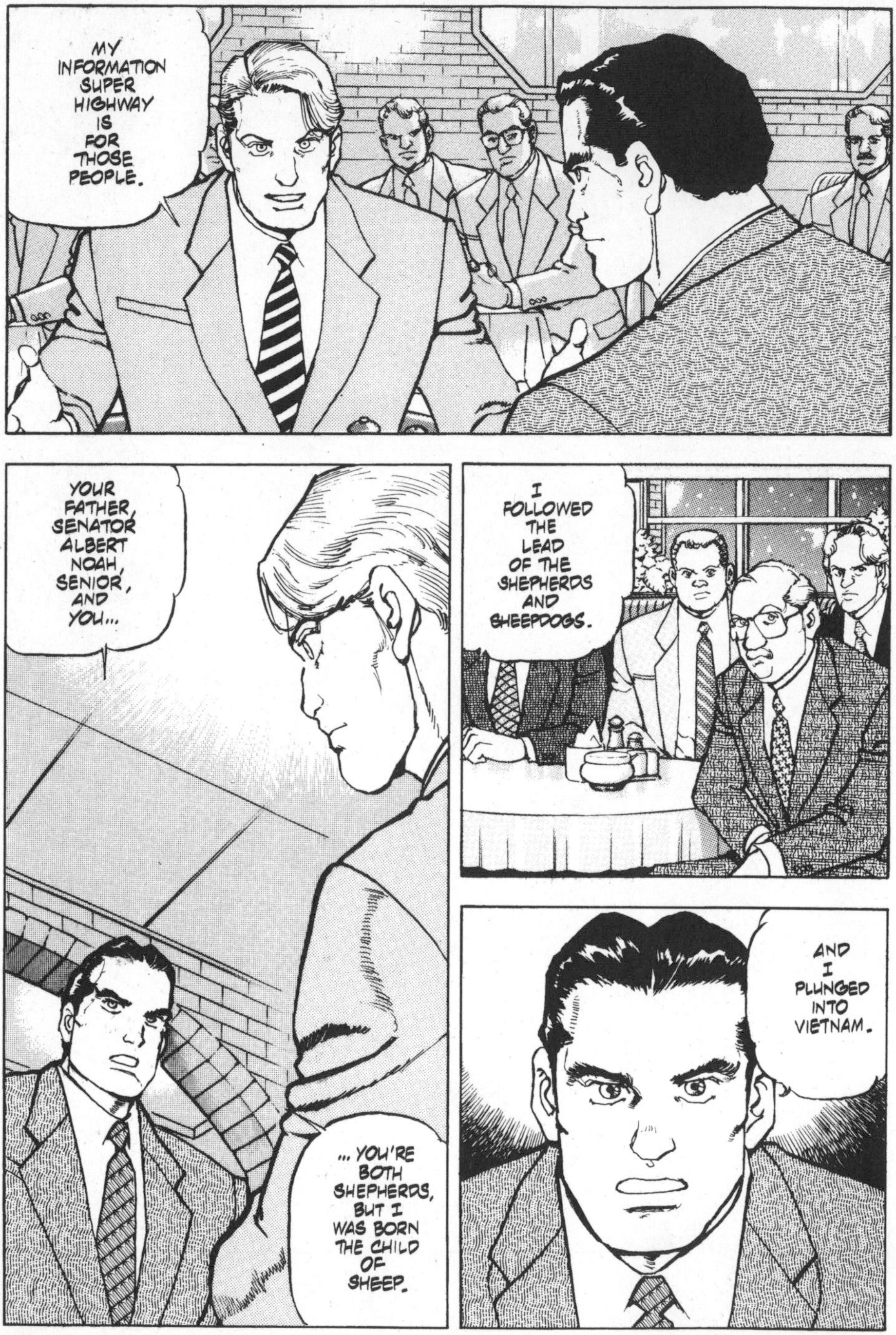
MY INFORMATION SUPER HIGHWAY IS FOR THOSE PEOPLE.
YOUR FATHER, SENATOR ALBERT NOAH, SENIOR, AND YOU...
...YOU'RE BOTH SHEPHERDS, BUT I WAS BORN THE CHILD OF SHEEP.
I FOLLOWED THE LEAD OF THE SHEPHERDS AND SHEEPDOGS.
AND I PLUNGED INTO VIETNAM.

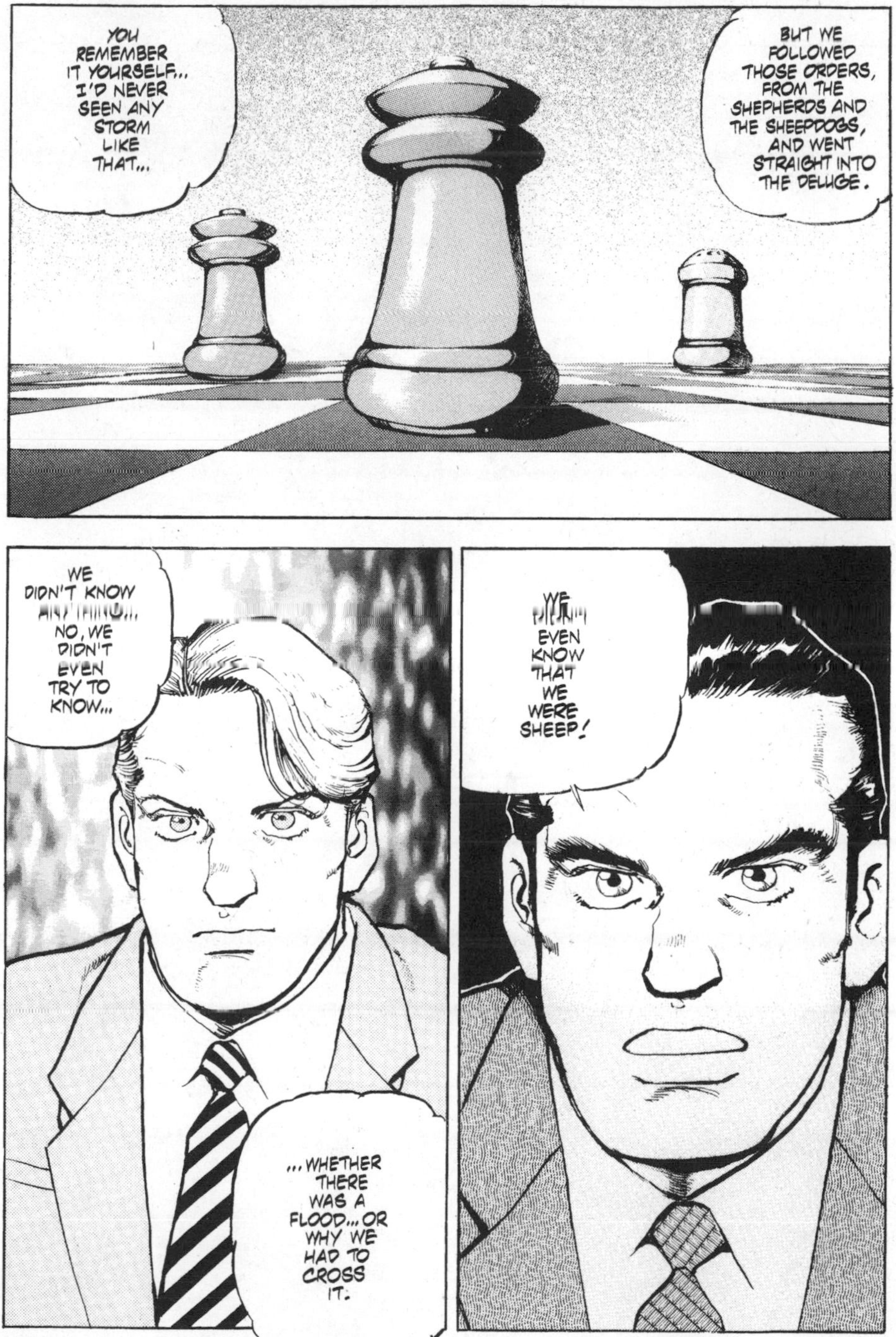
YOU REMEMBER IT YOURSELF... I'D NEVER SEEN ANY STORM LIKE THAT...
BUT WE FOLLOWED THOSE ORDERS, FROM THE SHEPHERDS AND THE SHEEPDOGS, AND WENT STRAIGHT INTO THE DELUGE.
WE DIDN'T KNOW
NO, WE DIDN'T EVEN TRY TO KNOW...
...WHETHER THERE WAS A FLOOD...OR WHY WE HAD TO CROSS IT.
WE
EVEN KNOW THAT WE WERE SHEEP!

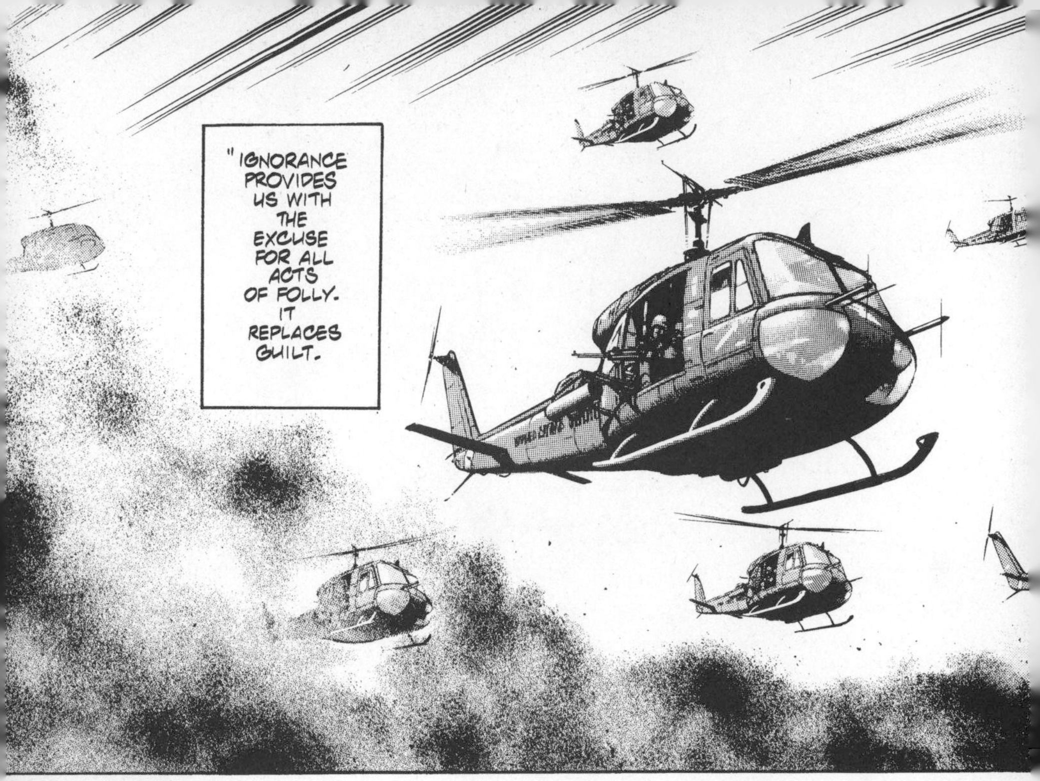
"IGNORANCE PROVIDES US WITH THE EXCUSE FOR ALL ACTS OF FOLLY. IT REPLACES GUILT.
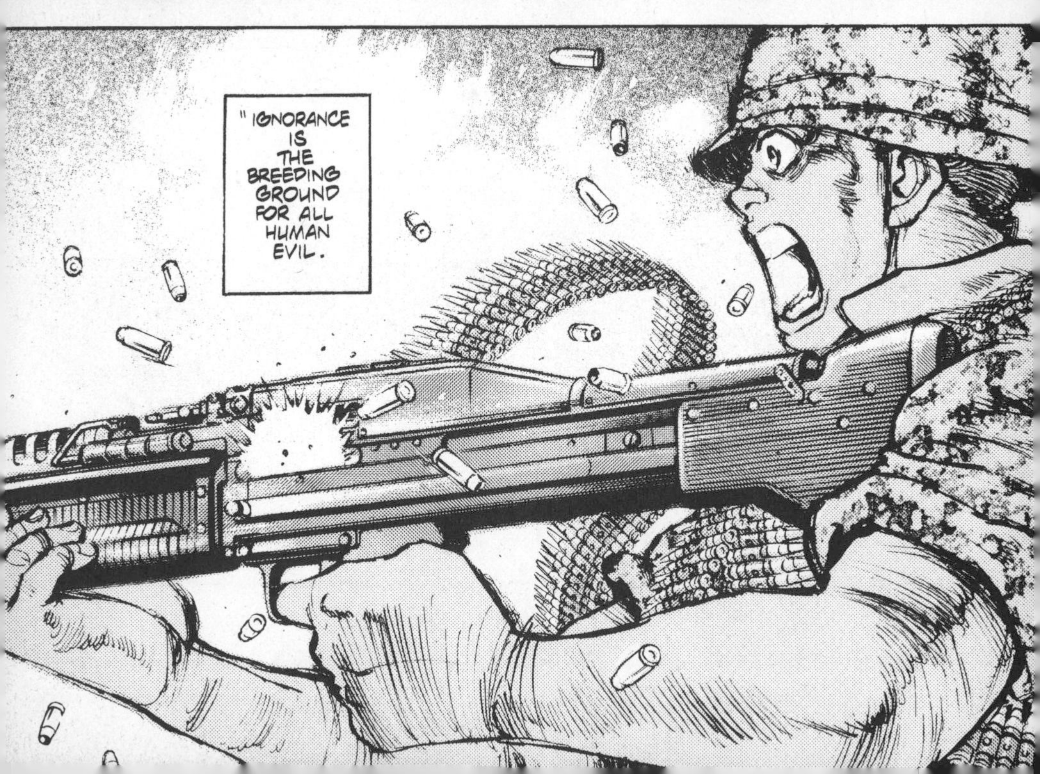
"IGNORANCE IS THE BREEDING GROUND FOR ALL HUMAN EVIL.

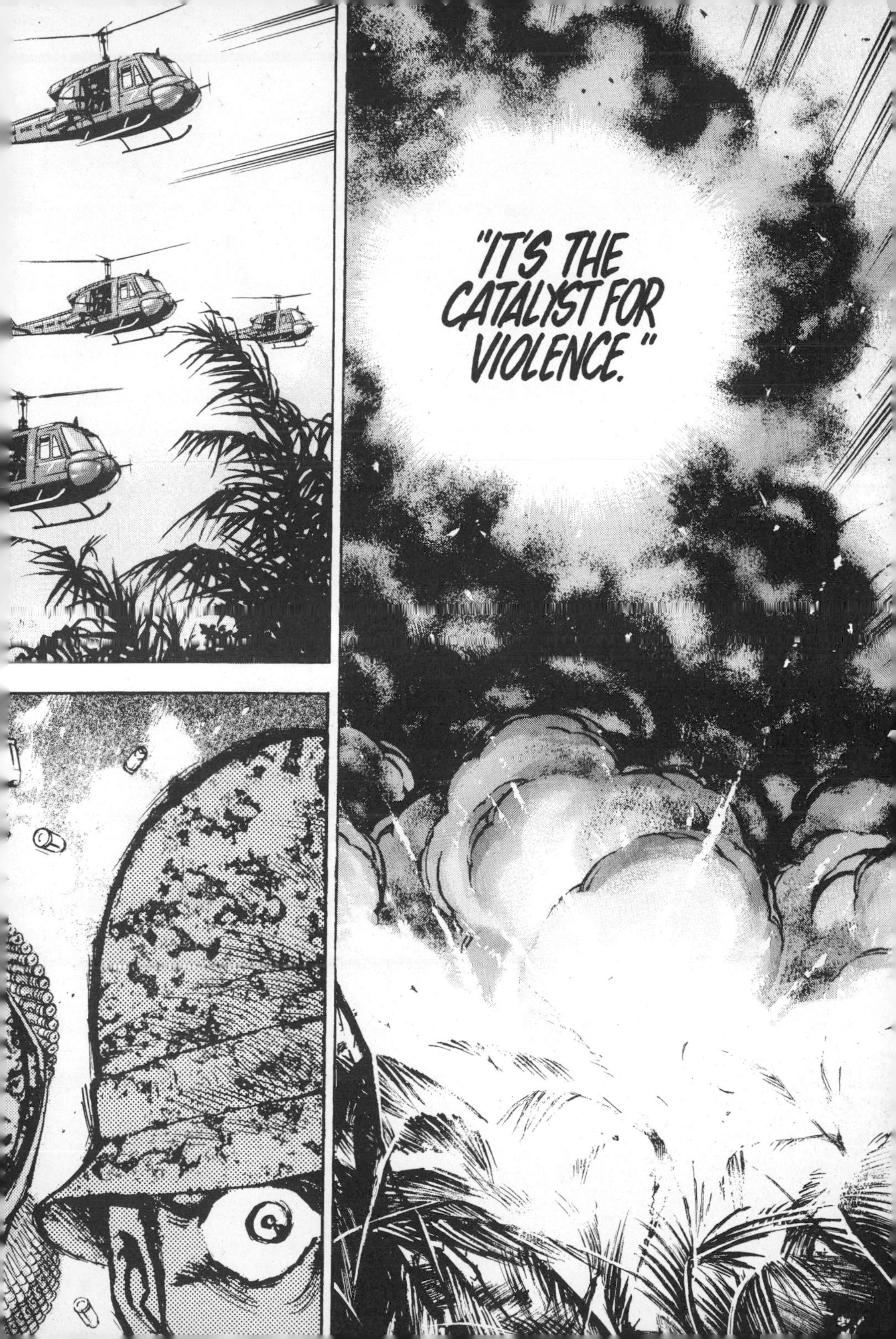
"IT'S THE CATALYST FOR VIOLENCE."

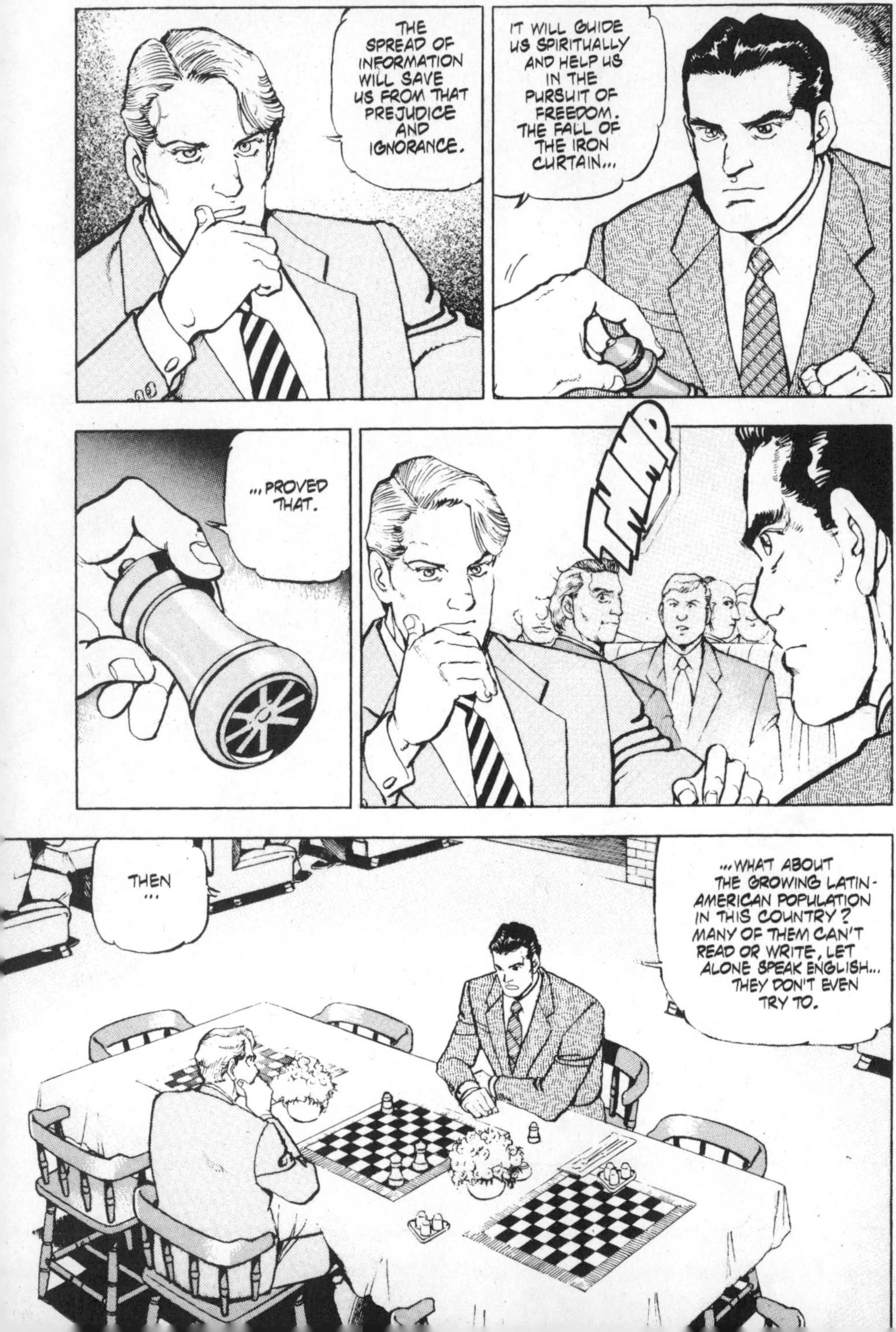
THE SPREAD OF INFORMATION WILL SAVE US FROM THAT PREJUDICE AND IGNORANCE.
IT WILL GUIDE US SPIRITUALLY AND HELP US IN THE PURSUIT OF FREEDOM. THE FALL OF THE IRON CURTAIN...
...PROVED THAT.
THEN ...
...WHAT ABOUT THE GROWING LATIN-AMERICAN POPULATION IN THIS COUNTRY? MANY OF THEM CAN'T READ OR WRITE, LET ALONE SPEAK ENGLISH... THEY DON'T EVEN TRY TO.

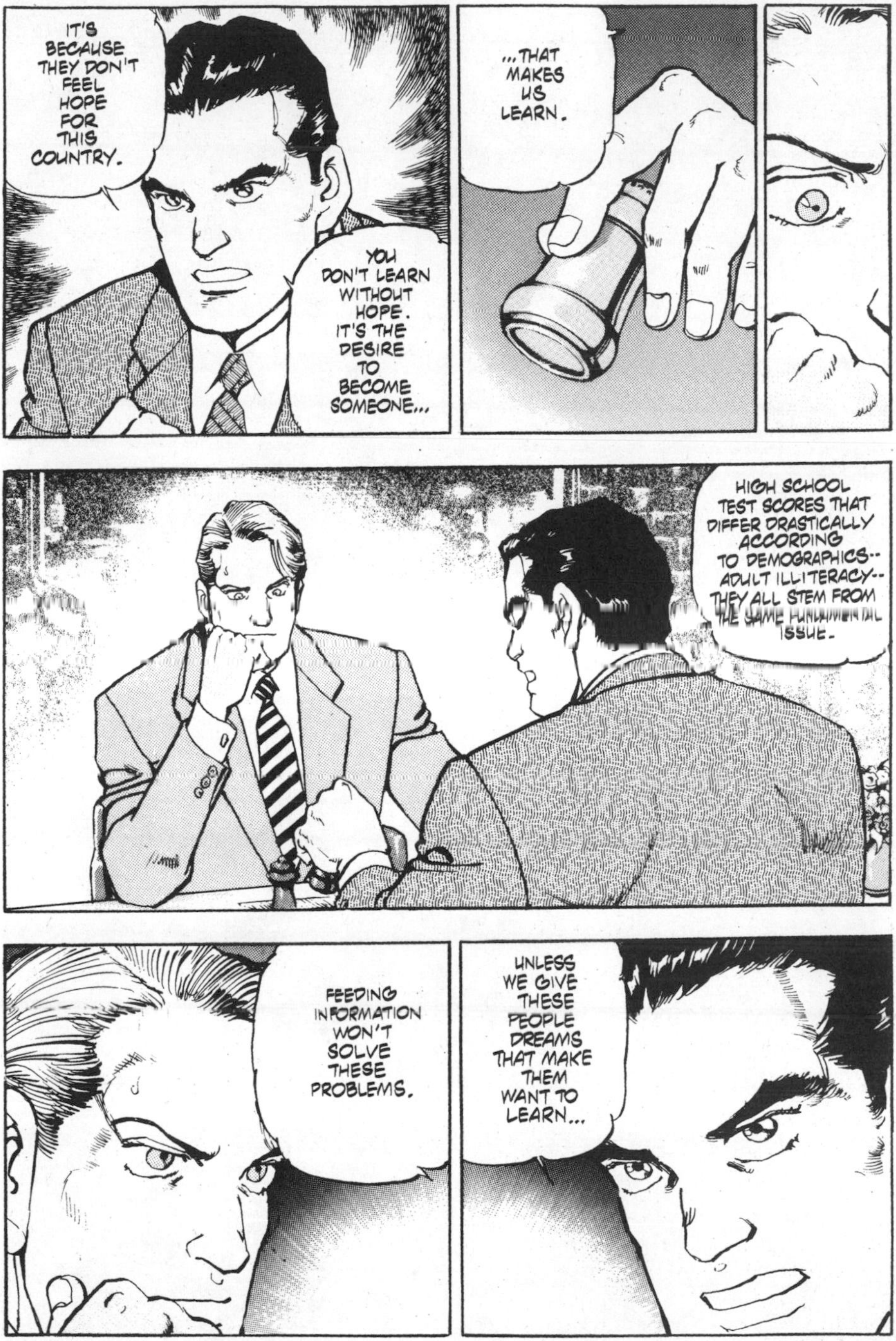
IT'S BECAUSE THEY DON'T FEEL HOPE FOR THIS COUNTRY.
YOU DON'T LEARN WITHOUT HOPE. IT'S THE DESIRE TO BECOME SOMEONE...
...THAT MAKES US LEARN.
HIGH SCHOOL TEST SCORES THAT DIFFER DRASTICALLY ACCORDING TO DEMOGRAPHICS-- ADULT ILLITERACY-- THEY ALL STEM FROM THE SAME FUNDAMENTAL ISSUE.
FEEDING INFORMATION WON'T SOLVE THESE PROBLEMS.
UNLESS WE GIVE THESE PEOPLE DREAMS THAT MAKE THEM WANT TO LEARN...

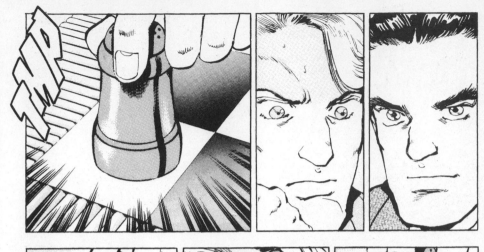

...THE SHEEP WILL NEVER CROSS THE STREAM ON THEIR OWN!

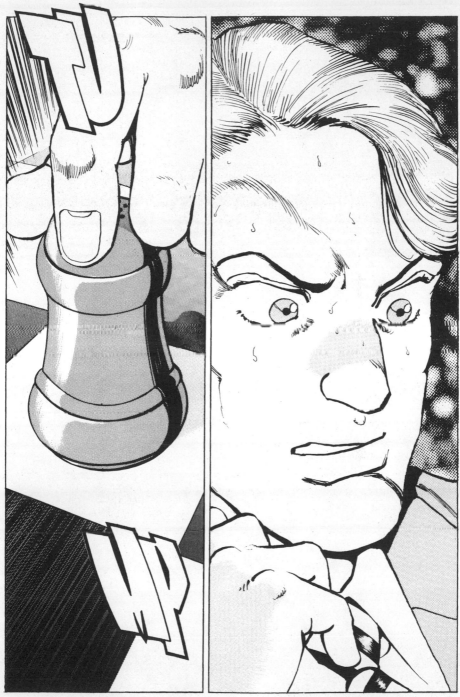

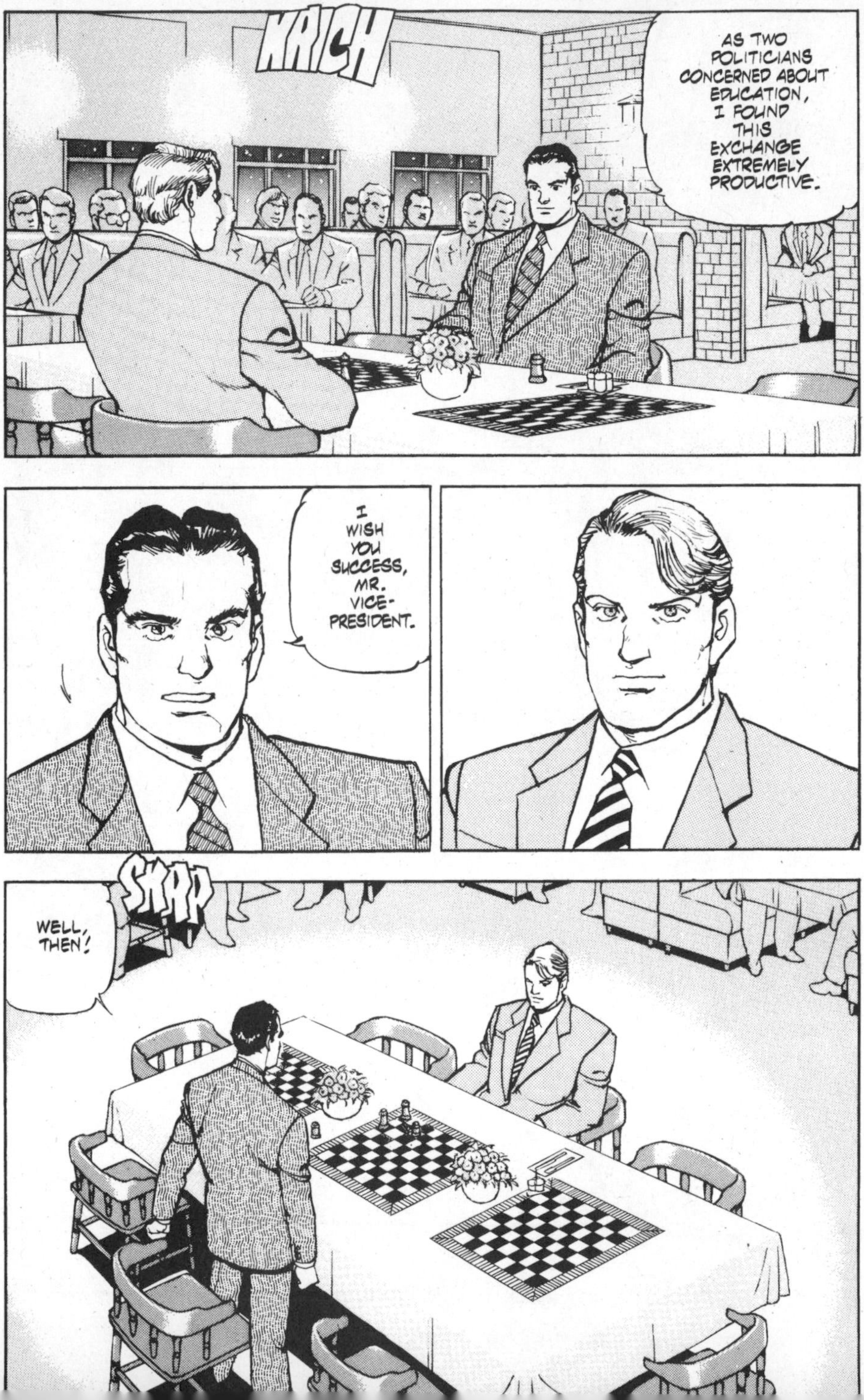
KRICH
AS TWO POLITICIANS CONCERNED ABOUT EDUCATION, I FOUND THIS EXCHANGE EXTREMELY PRODUCTIVE.
I WISH YOU SUCCESS, MR. VICE-PRESIDENT.
SKRP
WELL, THEN!

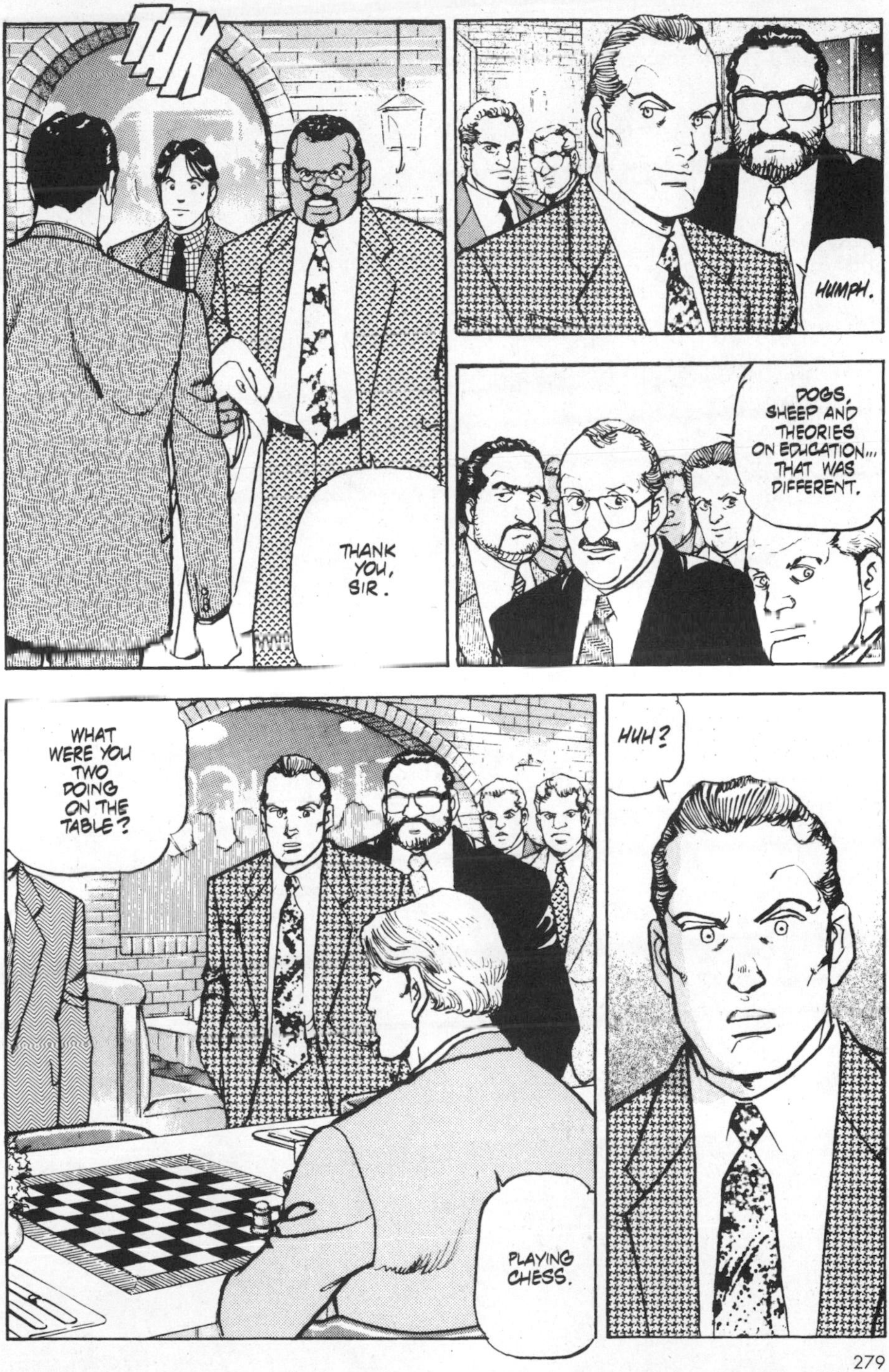
TAK
THANK YOU, SIR.
HUMPH.
DOGS, SHEEP AND THEORIES ON EDUCATION... THAT WAS DIFFERENT.
WHAT WERE YOU TWO DOING ON THE TABLE?
PLAYING CHESS.
HUH?

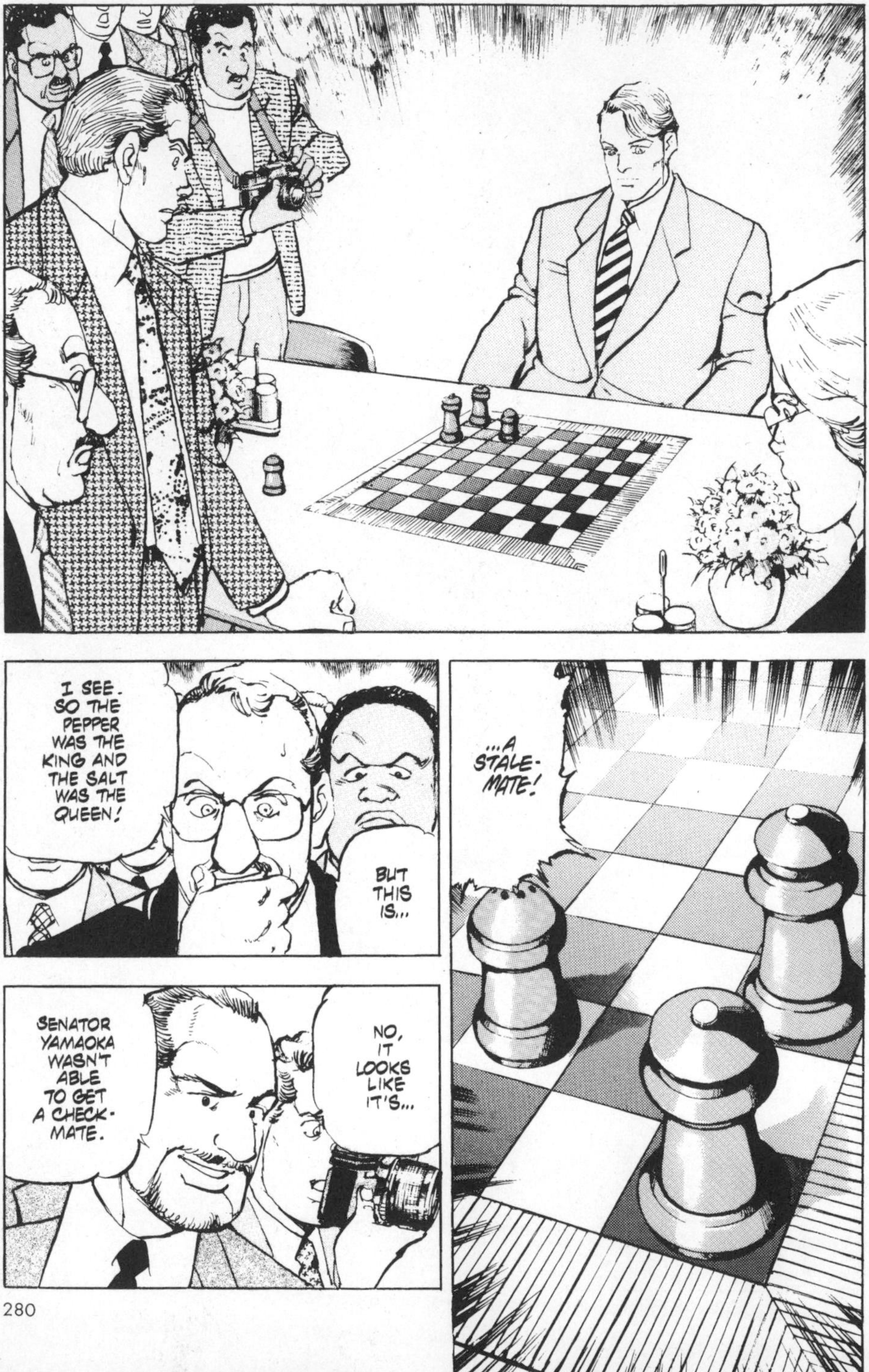
I SEE. SO THE PEPPER WAS THE KING AND THE SALT WAS THE QUEEN!
BUT THIS IS...
SENATOR YAMAOKA WASN'T ABLE TO GET A CHECKMATE.
NO, IT LOOKS LIKE IT'S...
...A STALEMATE!

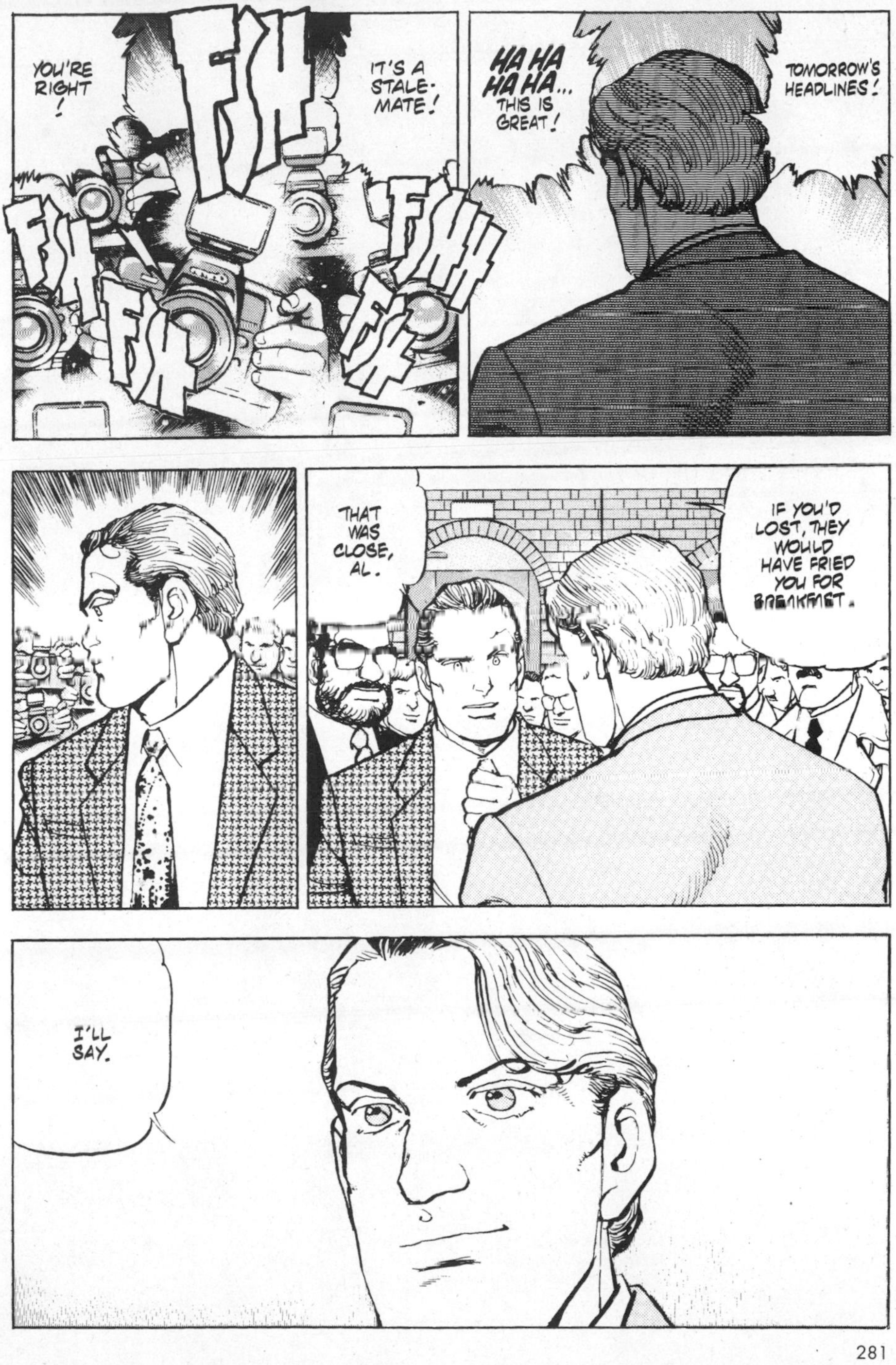
YOU'RE RIGHT!
IT'S A STALE-MATE!
HA HA HA HA... THIS IS GREAT!
TOMORROW'S HEADLINES!
THAT WAS CLOSE, AL.
IF YOU'D LOST, THEY WOULD HAVE FRIED YOU FOR BREAKFAST.
I'LL SAY.

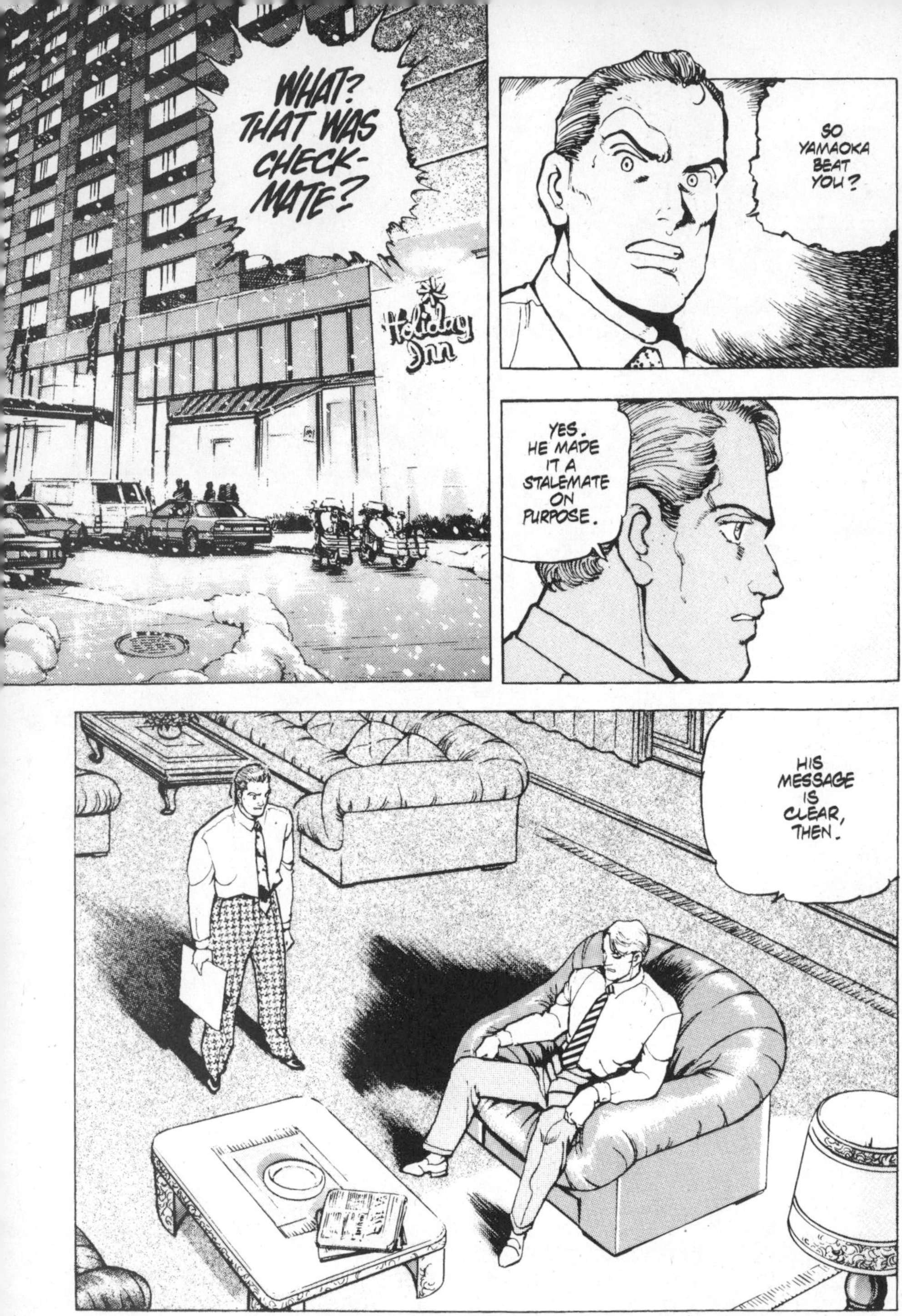
WHAT? THAT WAS CHECK-MATE?
Holiday Inn
SO YAMAOKA BEAT YOU?
YES. HE MADE IT A STALEMATE ON PURPOSE.
HIS MESSAGE IS CLEAR, THEN.

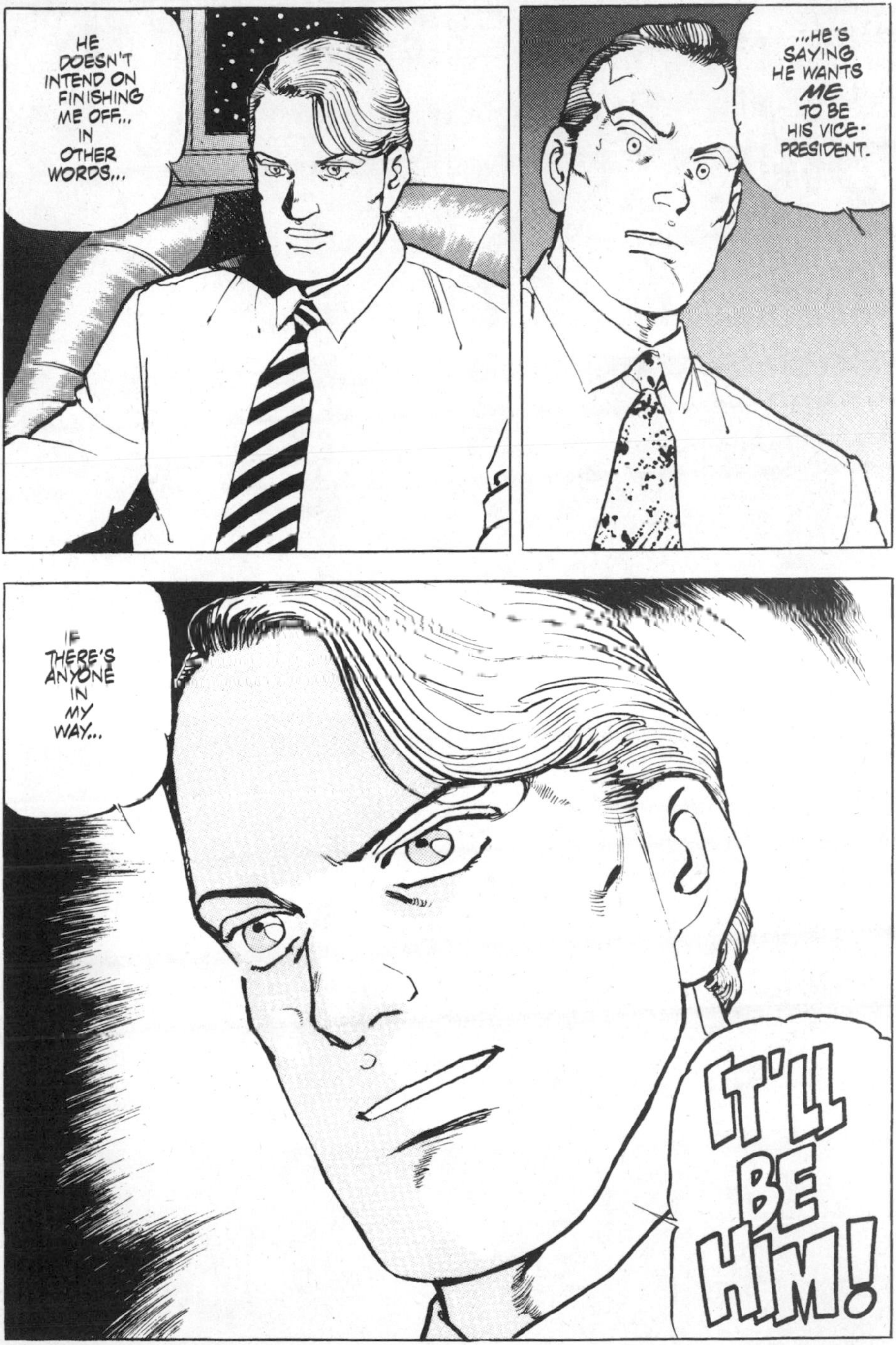
HE DOESN'T INTEND ON FINISHING ME OFF... IN OTHER WORDS...
...HE'S SAYING HE WANTS *ME* TO BE HIS VICE-PRESIDENT.
IF THERE'S ANYONE IN MY WAY...
IT'LL BE HIM!

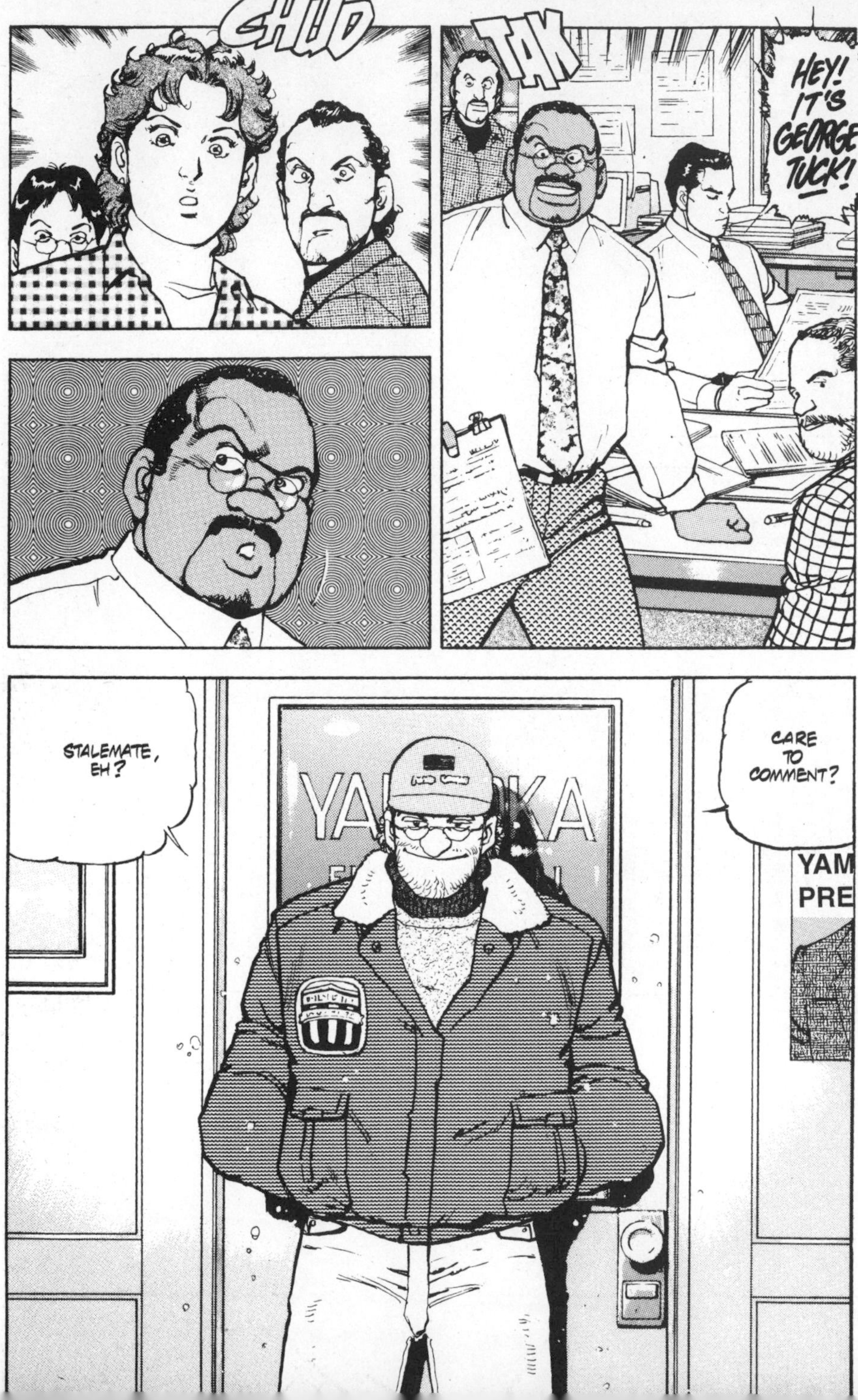
CHUD
TAK
HEY! IT'S GEORGE TUCK!
STALEMATE, EH?
CARE TO COMMENT?

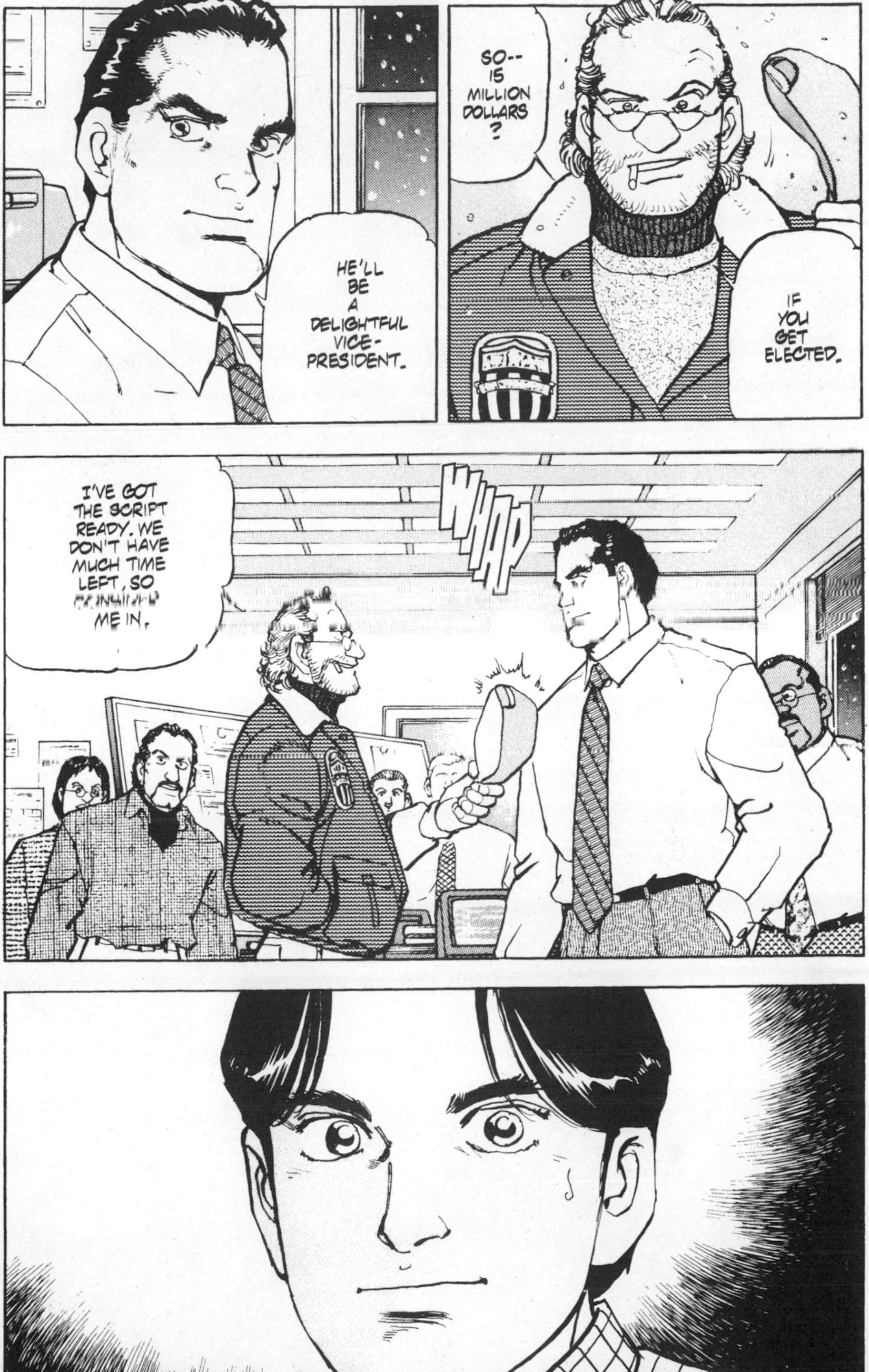
SO-- 15 MILLION DOLLARS?
HE'LL BE A DELIGHTFUL VICE-PRESIDENT.
IF YOU GET ELECTED.
I'VE GOT THE SCRIPT READY. WE DON'T HAVE MUCH TIME LEFT, SO ME IN.
WHAP

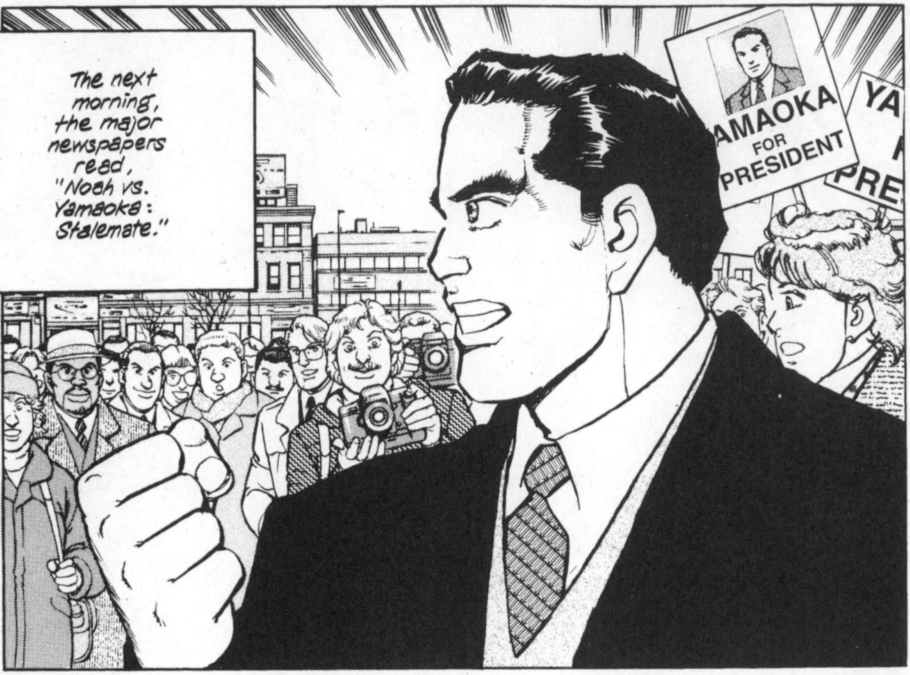
The next morning, the major newspapers read, "Noah vs. Yamaoka: Stalemate."
YAMAOKA FOR PRESIDENT
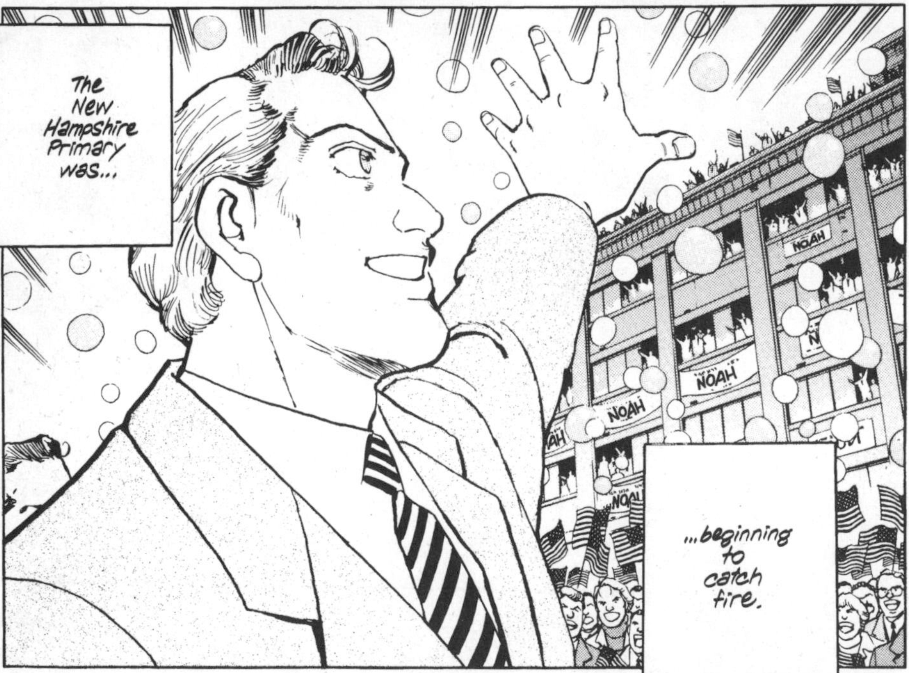
The New Hampshire Primary was...
NOAH
NOAH
NOAH
...beginning to catch fire.

The Spin

Report #12

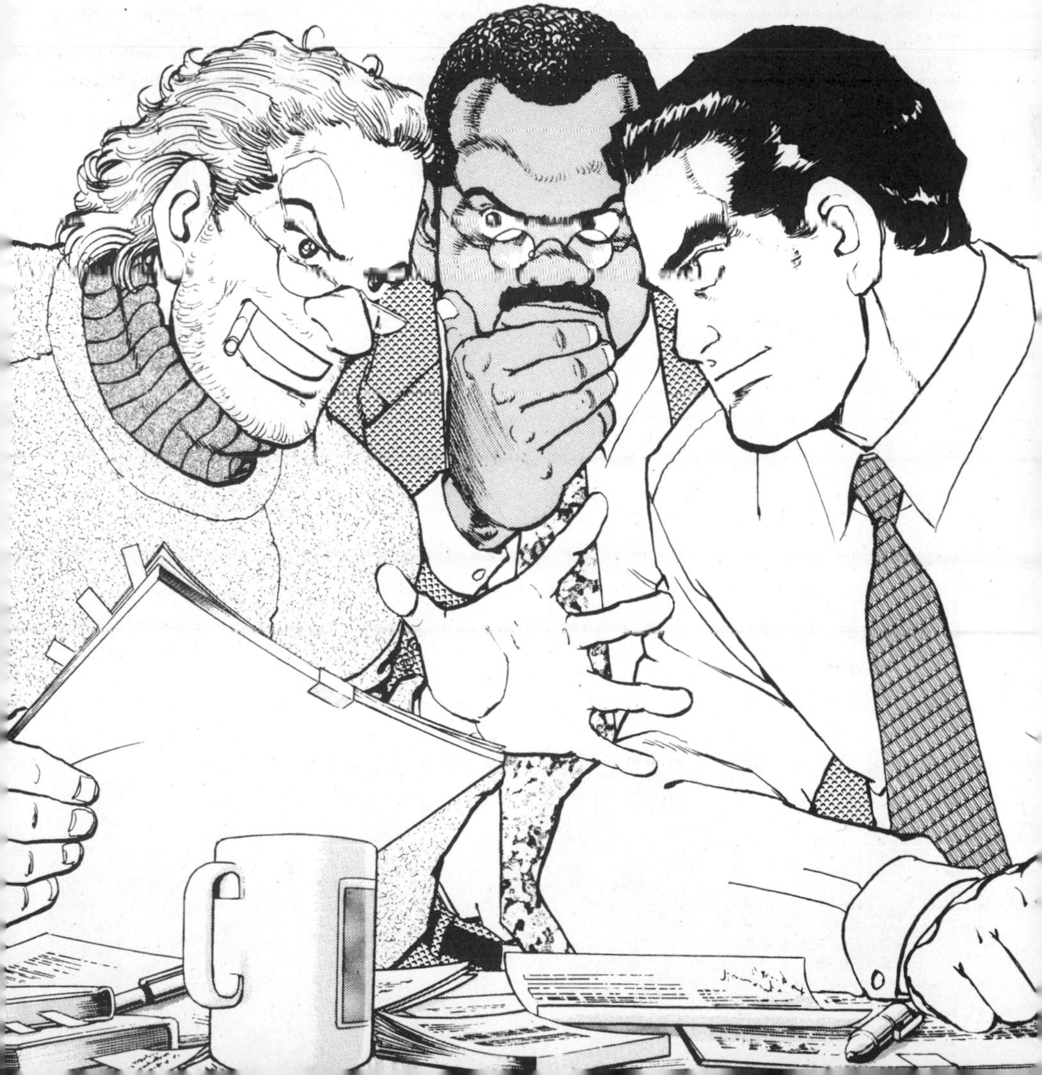

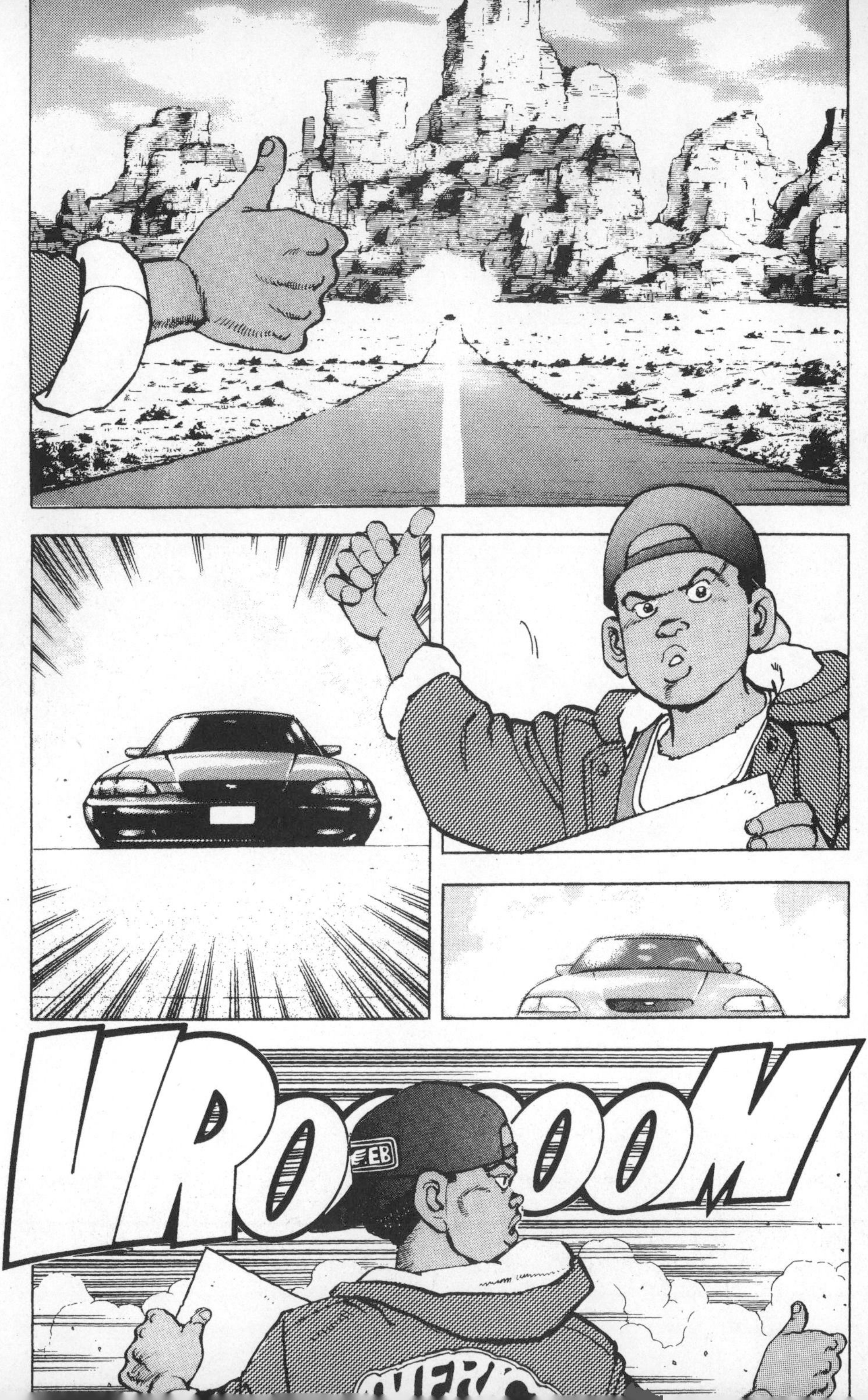
VRO
OOM

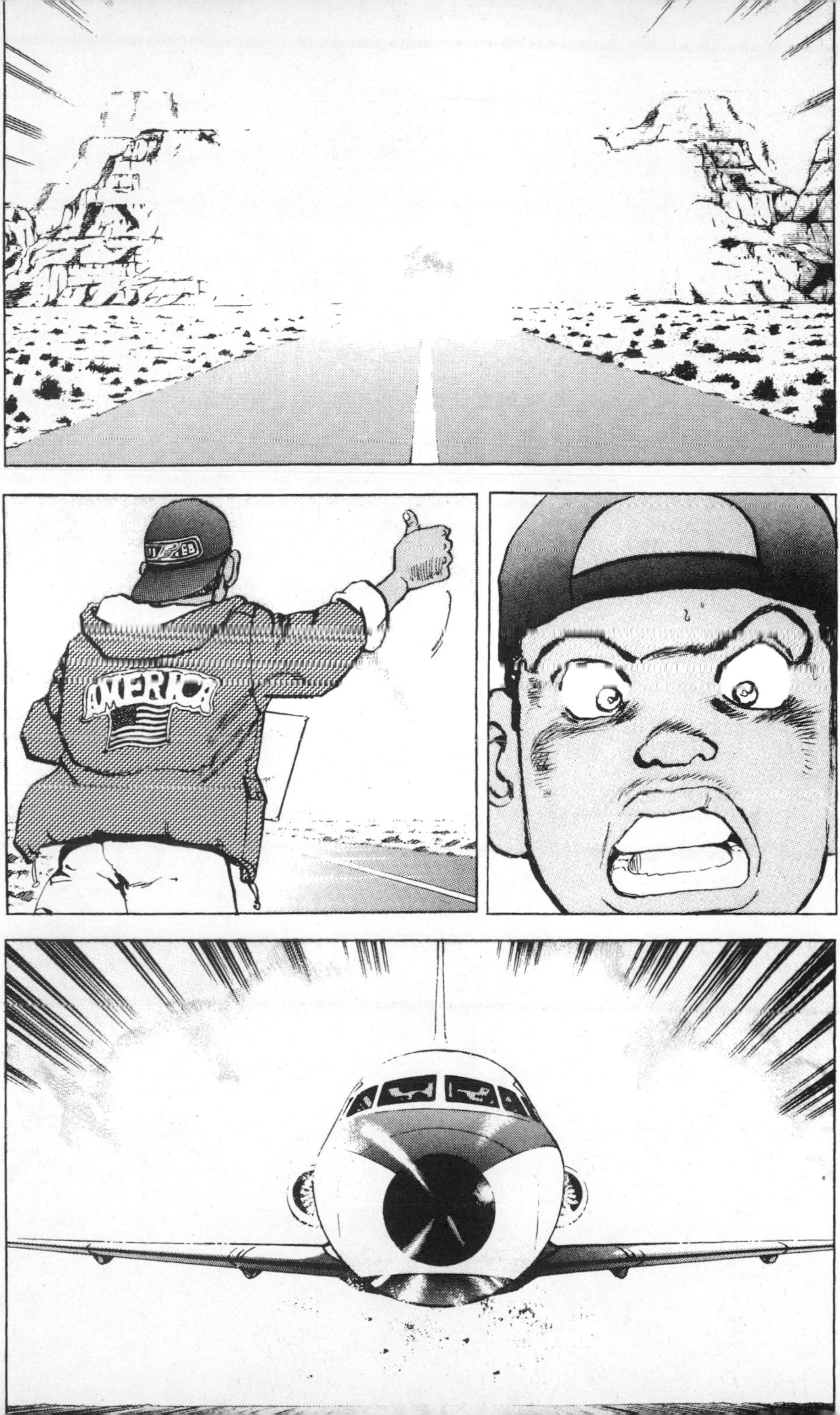
AMERICA

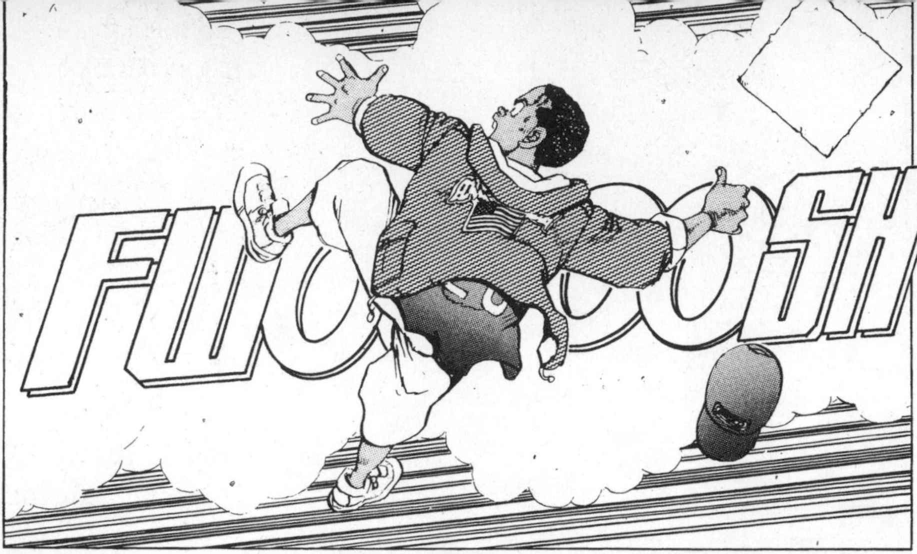
FUOOOOSH

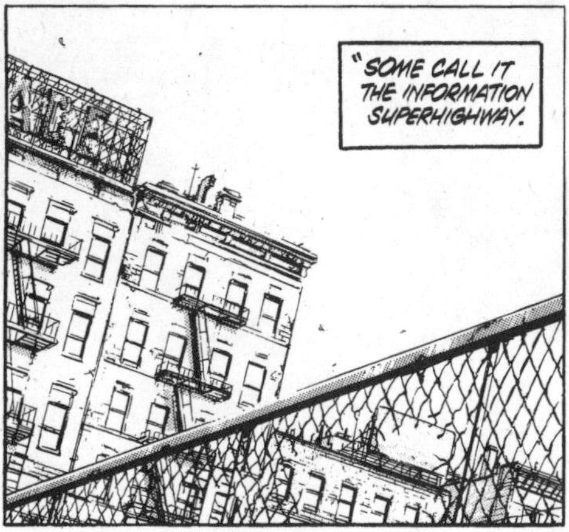
"SOME CALL IT THE INFORMATION SUPERHIGHWAY.

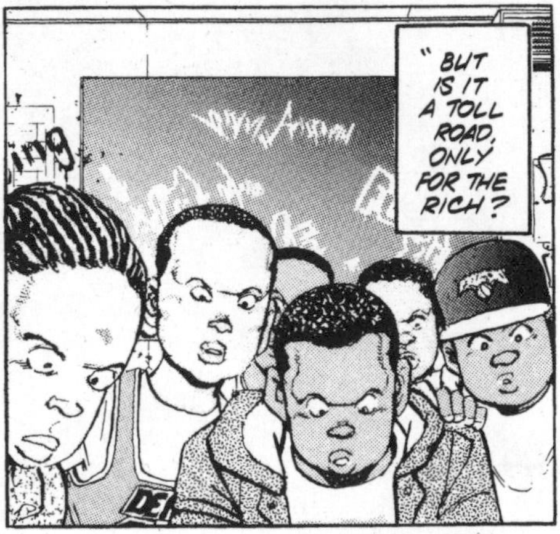
"BUT IS IT A TOLL ROAD, ONLY FOR THE RICH?

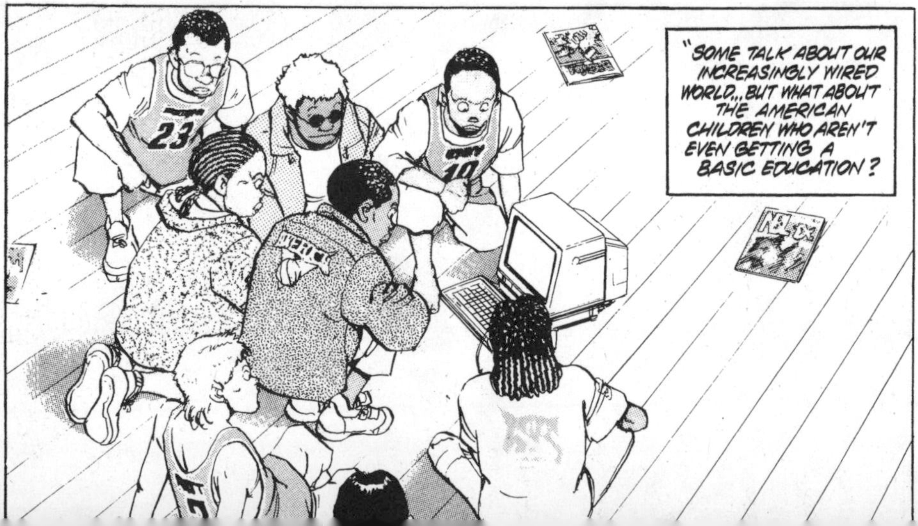
"SOME TALK ABOUT OUR INCREASINGLY WIRED WORLD... BUT WHAT ABOUT THE AMERICAN CHILDREN WHO AREN'T EVEN GETTING A BASIC EDUCATION?

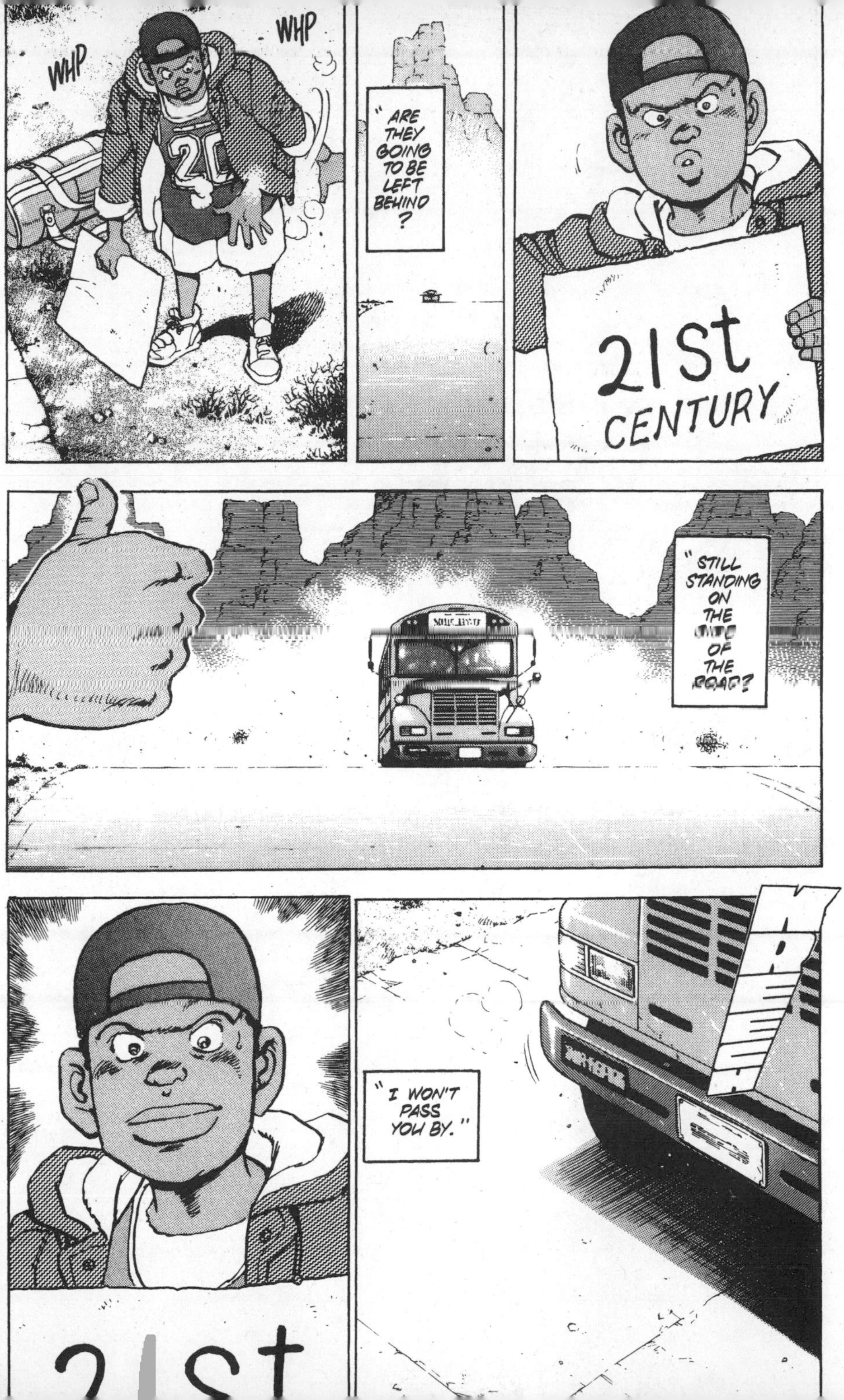
WHP
WHP
"ARE THEY GOING TO BE LEFT BEHIND?
21St CENTURY
"STILL STANDING ON THE OF THE ROAD?
"I WON'T PASS YOU BY."
21St

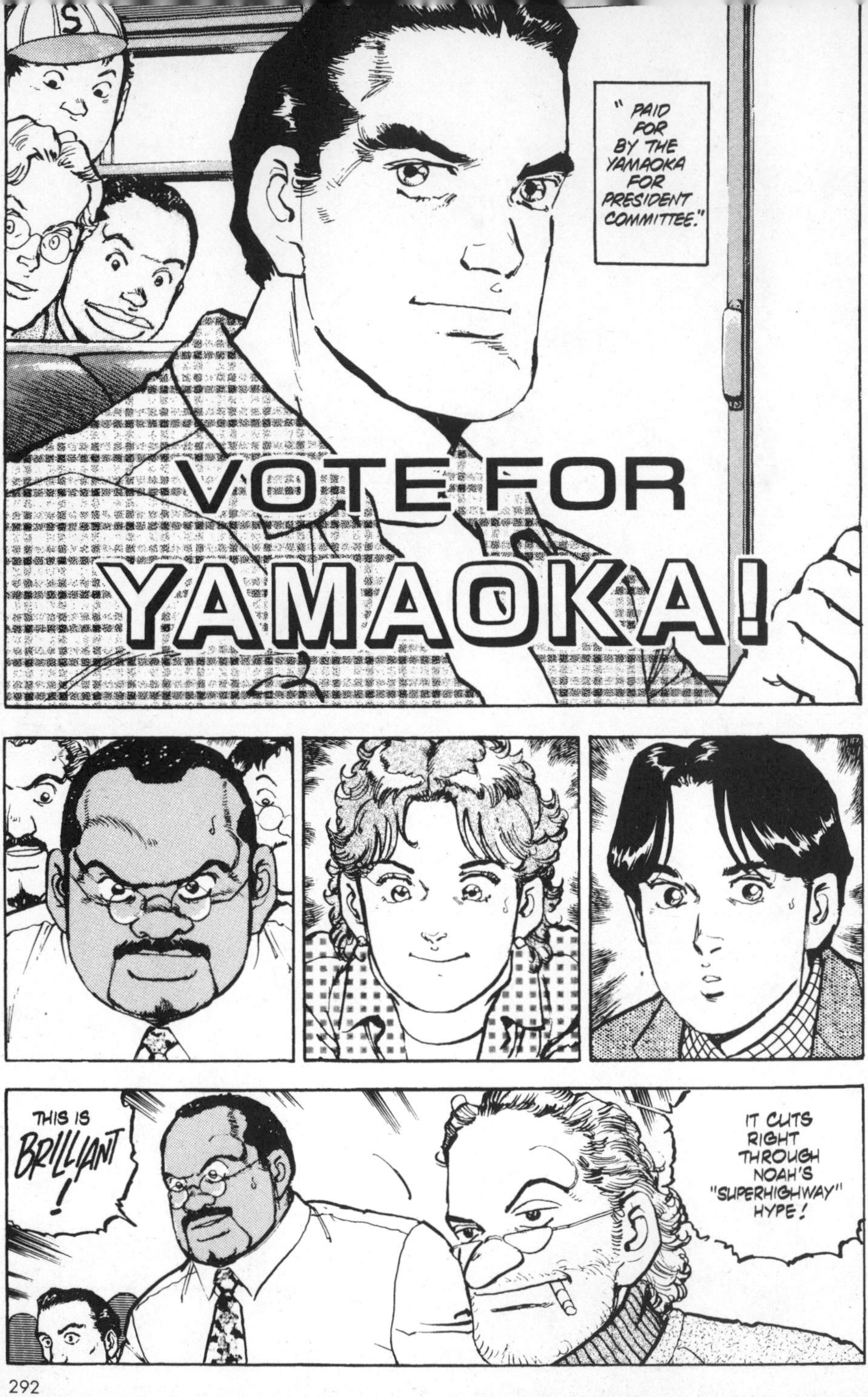
"PAID FOR BY THE YAMAOKA FOR PRESIDENT COMMITTEE."
VOTE FOR YAMAOKA!
THIS IS BRILLIANT!
IT CUTS RIGHT THROUGH NOAH'S "SUPERHIGHWAY" HYPE!

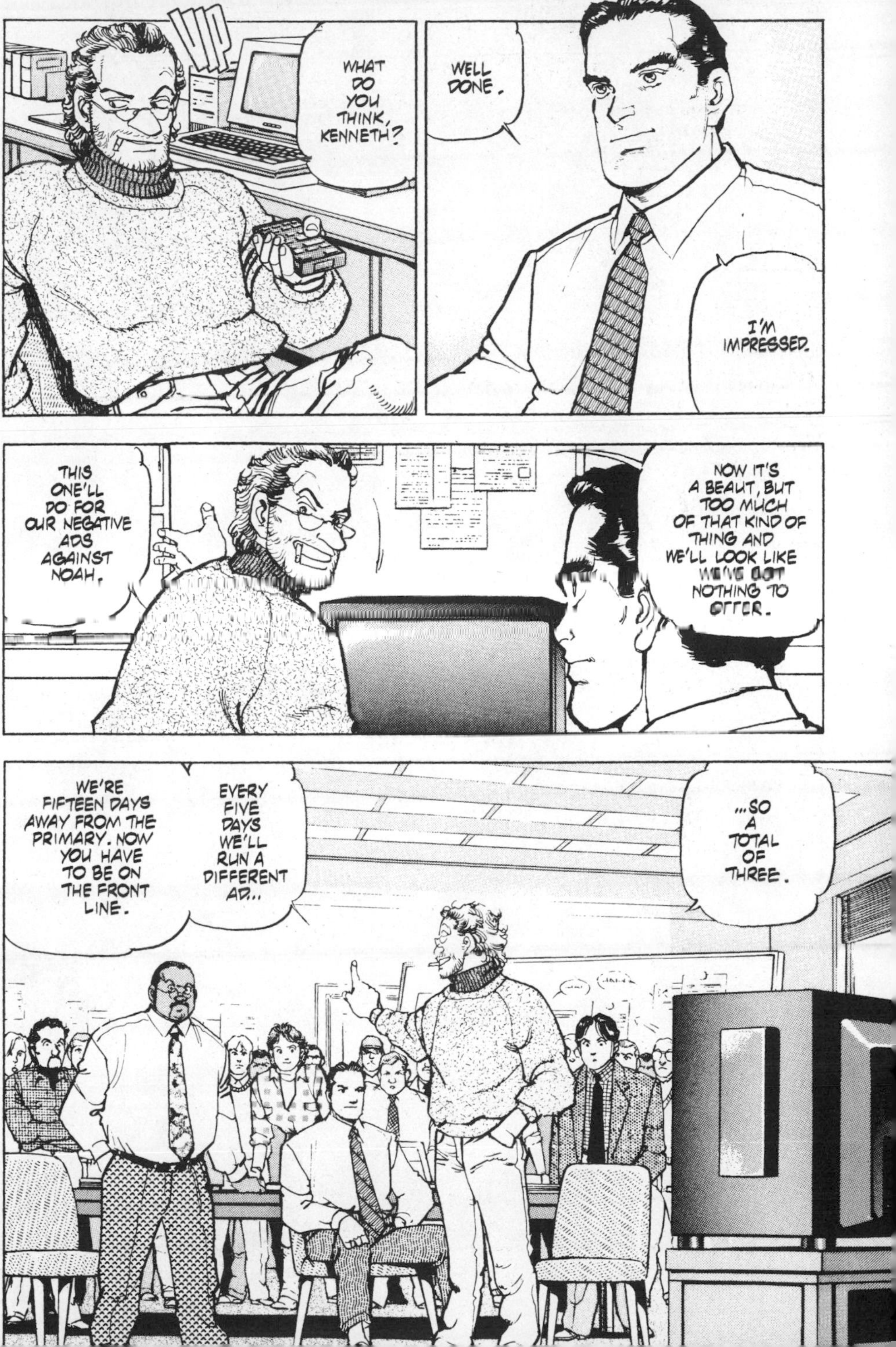
VIP
WHAT DO YOU THINK, KENNETH?
WELL DONE.
I'M IMPRESSED.
THIS ONE'LL DO FOR OUR NEGATIVE ADS AGAINST NOAH.
NOW IT'S A BEAUT, BUT TOO MUCH OF THAT KIND OF THING AND WE'LL LOOK LIKE WE'VE GOT NOTHING TO OFFER.
WE'RE FIFTEEN DAYS AWAY FROM THE PRIMARY. NOW YOU HAVE TO BE ON THE FRONT LINE.
EVERY FIVE DAYS WE'LL RUN A DIFFERENT AD...
...SO A TOTAL OF THREE.

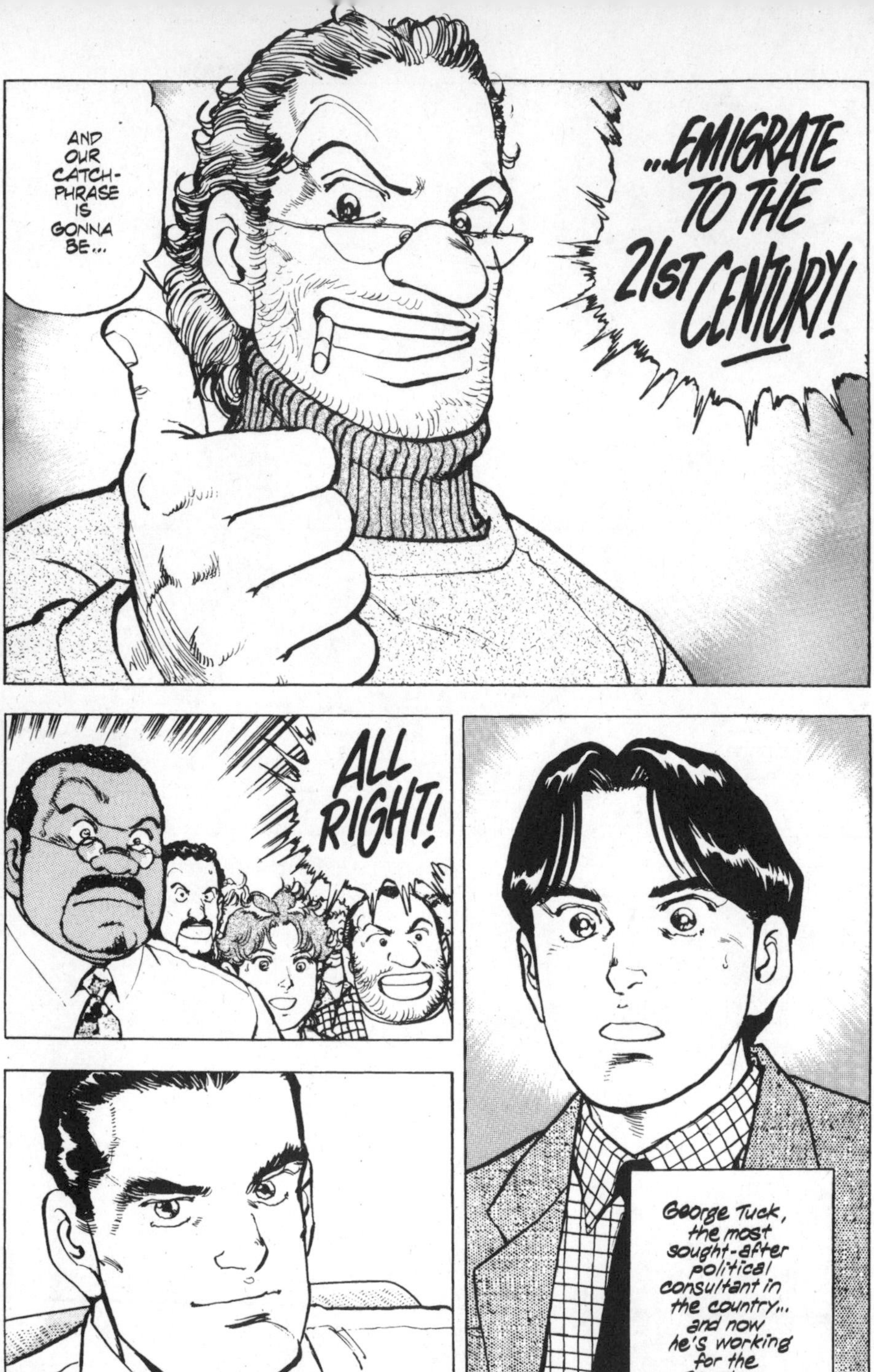

AND OUR CATCH-PHRASE IS GONNA BE...
...EMIGRATE TO THE 21ST CENTURY!
ALL RIGHT!
George Tuck, the most sought-after political consultant in the country... and now he's working for the Senator.

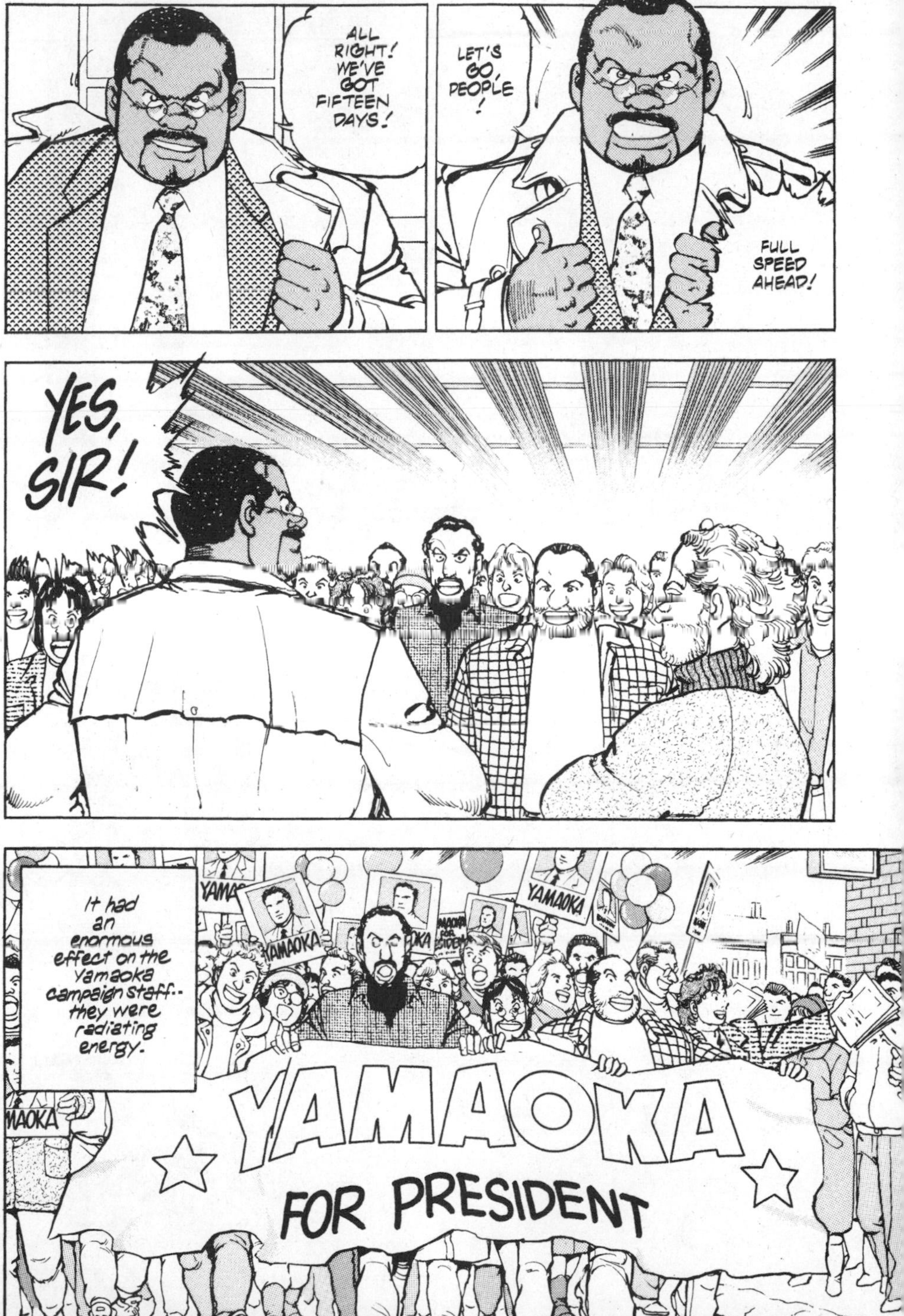
ALL RIGHT! WE'VE GOT FIFTEEN DAYS!
LET'S GO, PEOPLE!
FULL SPEED AHEAD!
YES, SIR!
It had an enormous effect on the Yamaoka campaign staff... they were radiating energy.
YAMAOKA
YAMAOKA
YAMAOKA
YAMAOKA FOR PRESIDENT

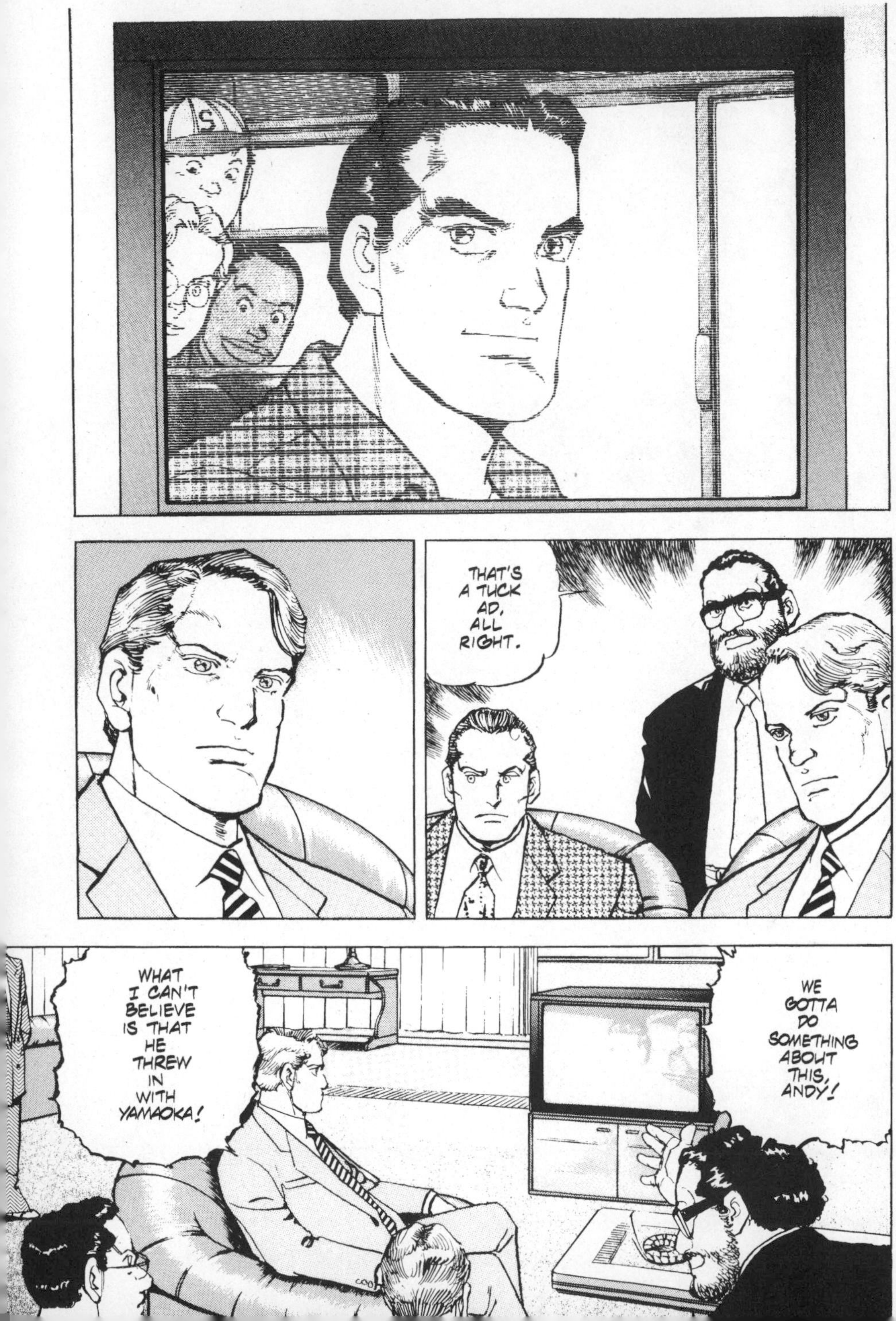
THAT'S A TUCK AD, ALL RIGHT.
WHAT I CAN'T BELIEVE IS THAT HE THREW IN WITH YAMAOKA!
WE GOTTA DO SOMETHING ABOUT THIS, ANDY!

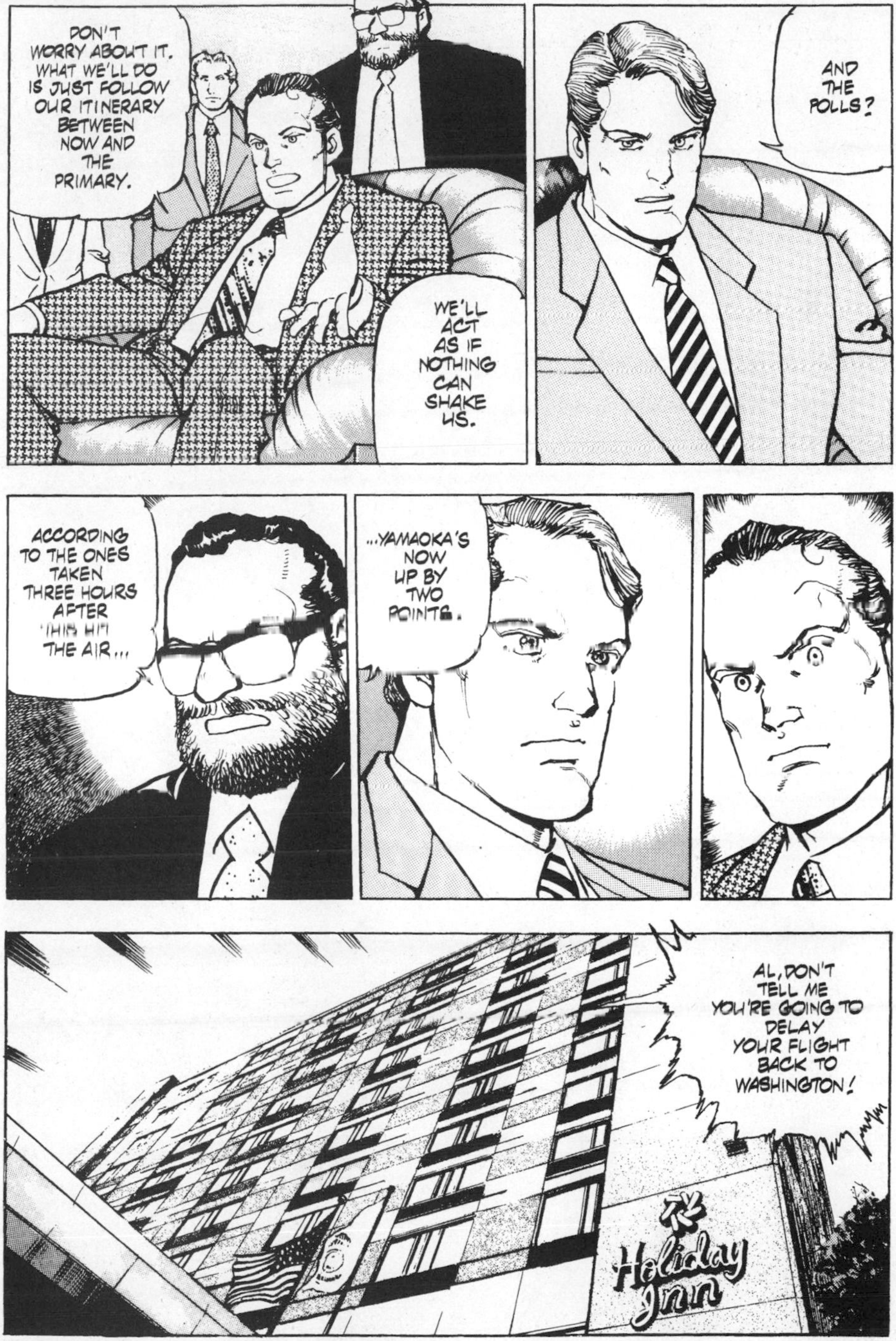
DON'T WORRY ABOUT IT. WHAT WE'LL DO IS JUST FOLLOW OUR ITINERARY BETWEEN NOW AND THE PRIMARY.
WE'LL ACT AS IF NOTHING CAN SHAKE US.
AND THE POLLS?
ACCORDING TO THE ONES TAKEN THREE HOURS AFTER THIS HIT THE AIR...
...YAMAOKA'S NOW UP BY TWO POINTS.
AL, DON'T TELL ME YOU'RE GOING TO DELAY YOUR FLIGHT BACK TO WASHINGTON!
Holiday Inn

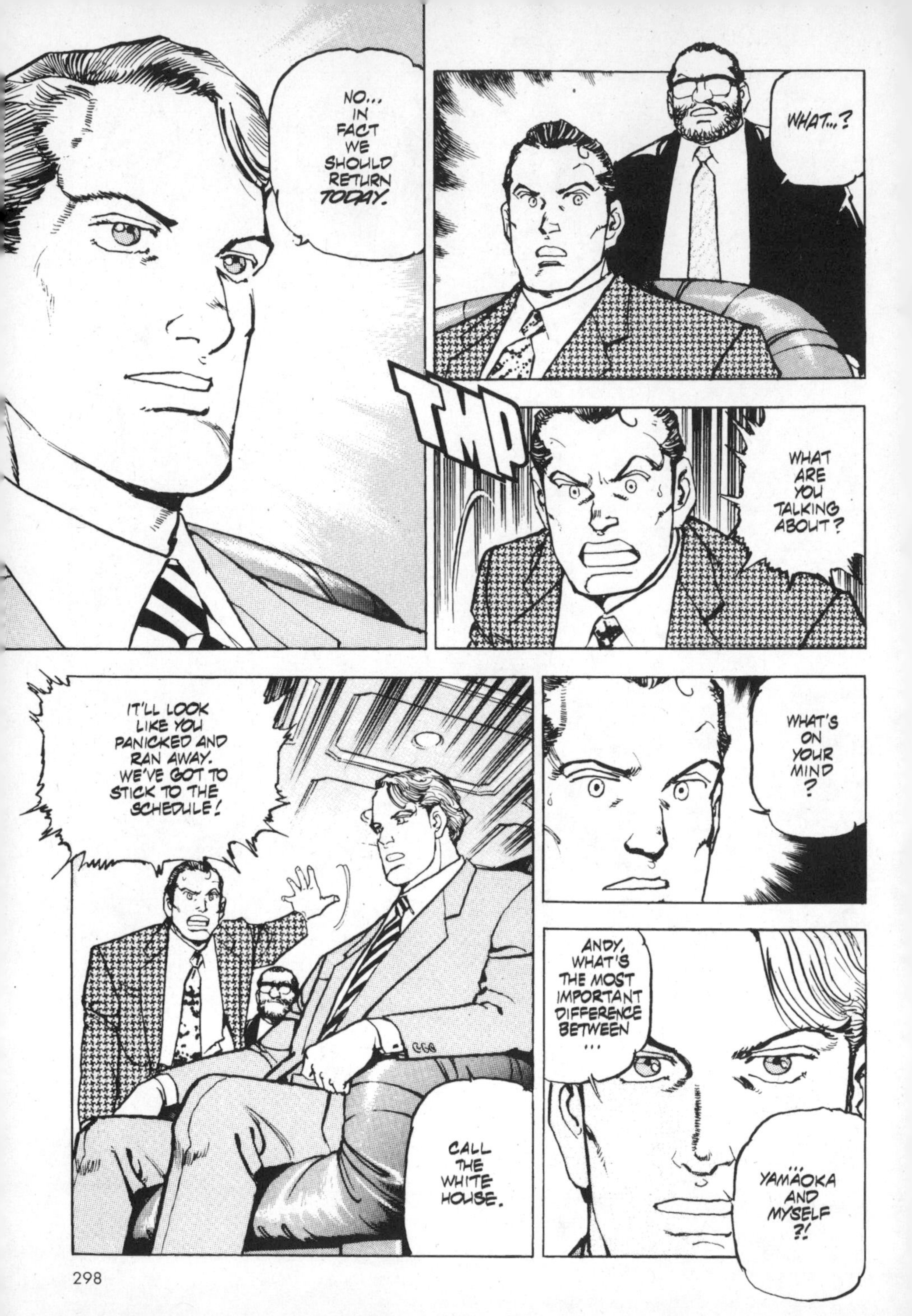
NO... IN FACT WE SHOULD RETURN TODAY.
WHAT...?
TMP
WHAT ARE YOU TALKING ABOUT?
IT'LL LOOK LIKE YOU PANICKED AND RAN AWAY. WE'VE GOT TO STICK TO THE SCHEDULE!
CALL THE WHITE HOUSE.
WHAT'S ON YOUR MIND?
ANDY, WHAT'S THE MOST IMPORTANT DIFFERENCE BETWEEN ...
...YAMAOKA AND MYSELF?!

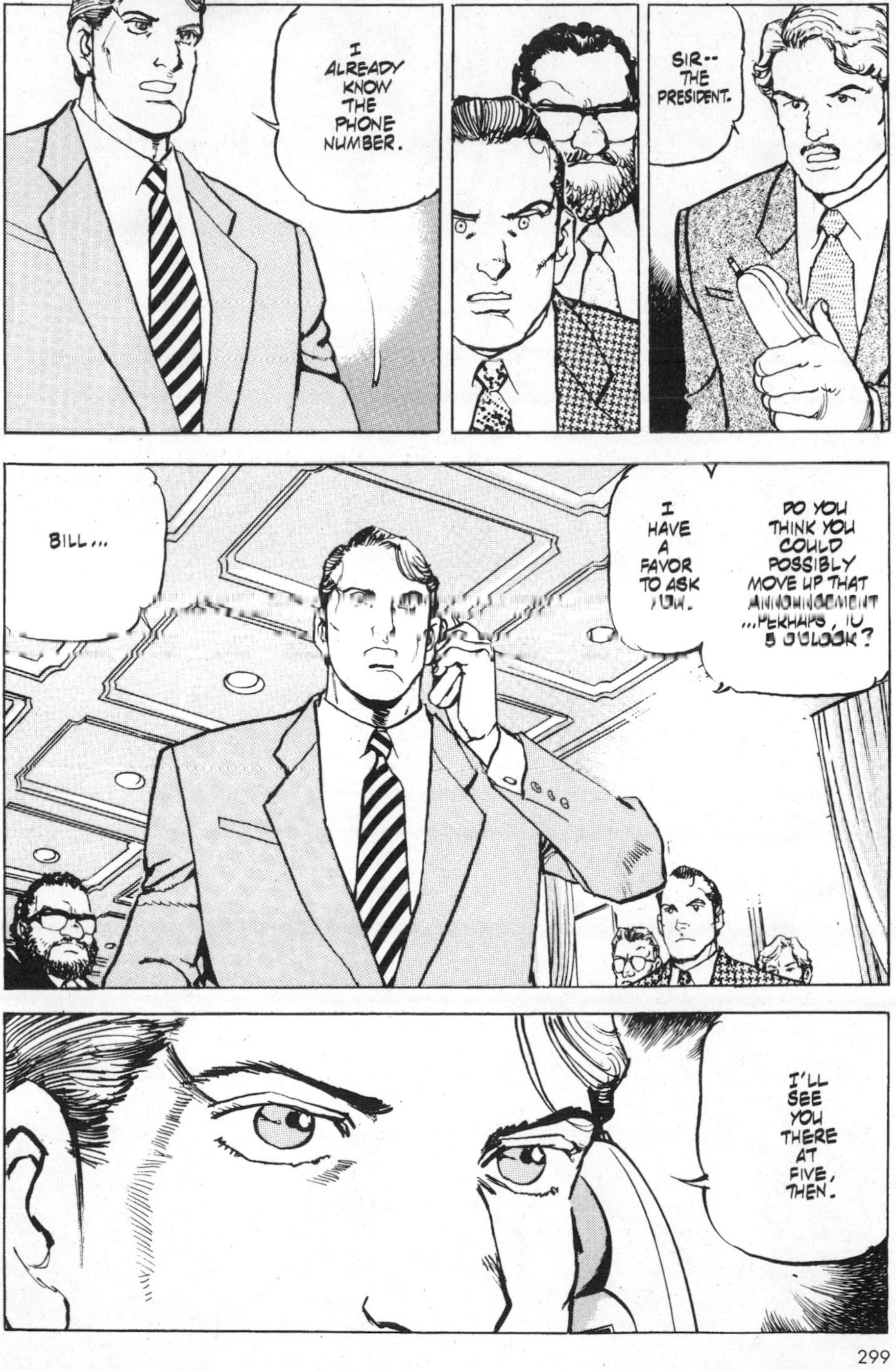
I ALREADY KNOW THE PHONE NUMBER.
SIR-- THE PRESIDENT.
BILL...
I HAVE A FAVOR TO ASK YOU.
DO YOU THINK YOU COULD POSSIBLY MOVE UP THAT ANNOUNCEMENT ...PERHAPS, TO 5 O'CLOCK?
I'LL SEE YOU THERE AT FIVE, THEN.

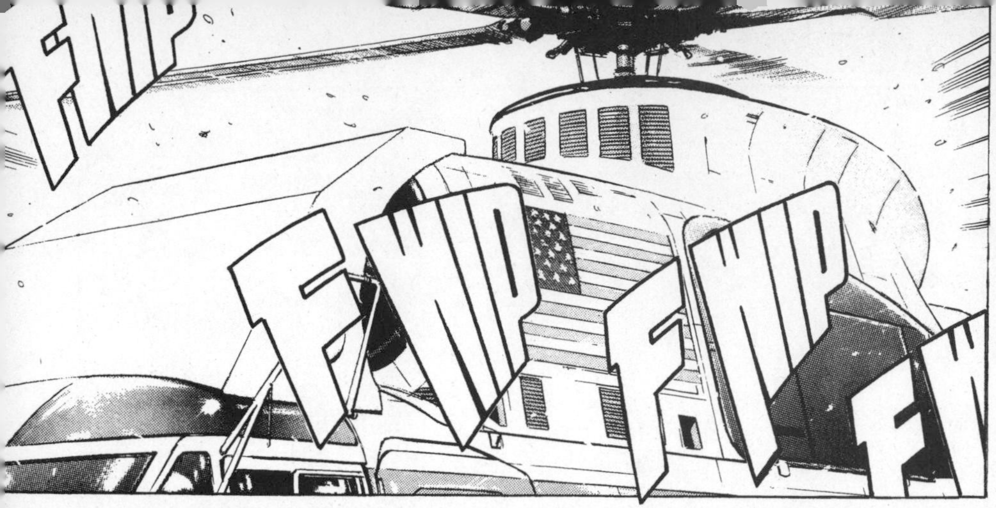
FWIP
FWIP FWIP
FW

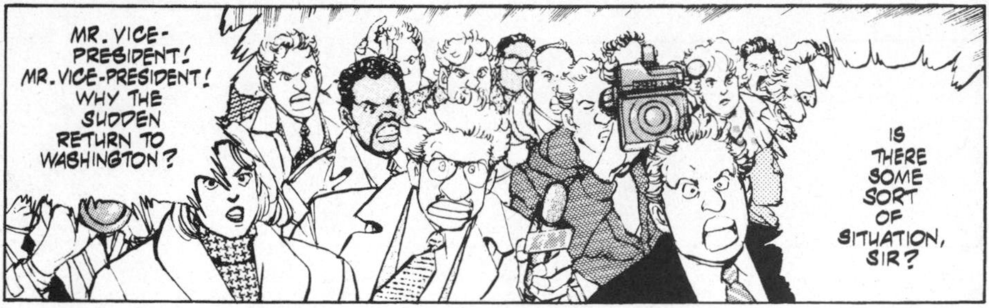
MR. VICE-PRESIDENT! MR. VICE-PRESIDENT! WHY THE SUDDEN RETURN TO WASHINGTON?
IS THERE SOME SORT OF SITUATION, SIR?

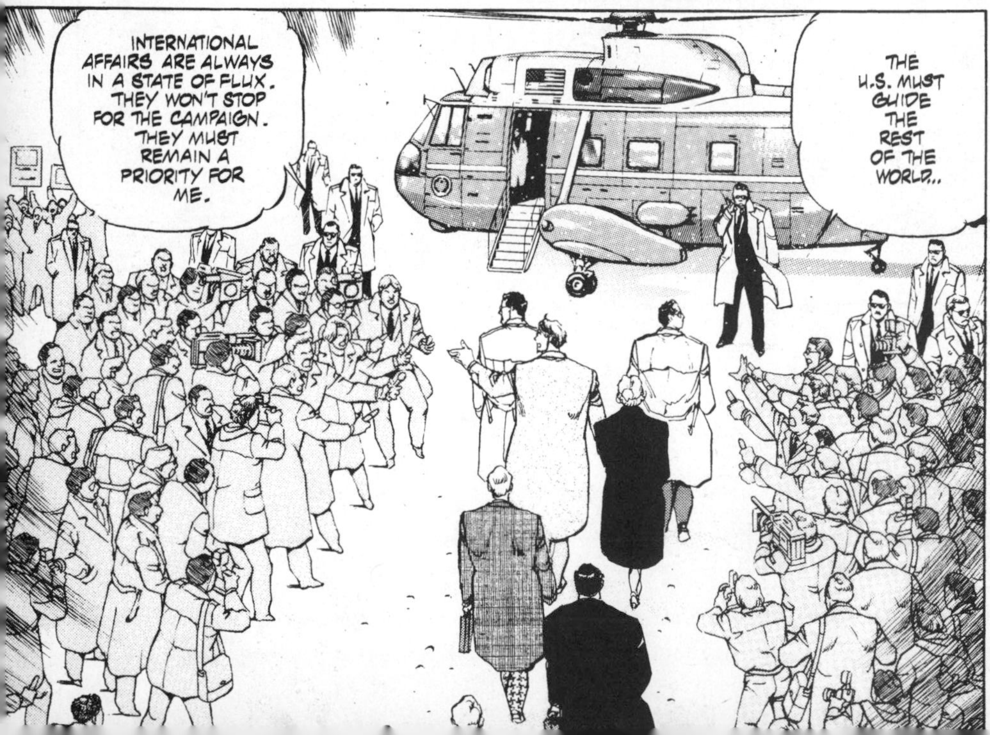
INTERNATIONAL AFFAIRS ARE ALWAYS IN A STATE OF FLUX. THEY WON'T STOP FOR THE CAMPAIGN. THEY MUST REMAIN A PRIORITY FOR ME.
THE U.S. MUST GUIDE THE REST OF THE WORLD...

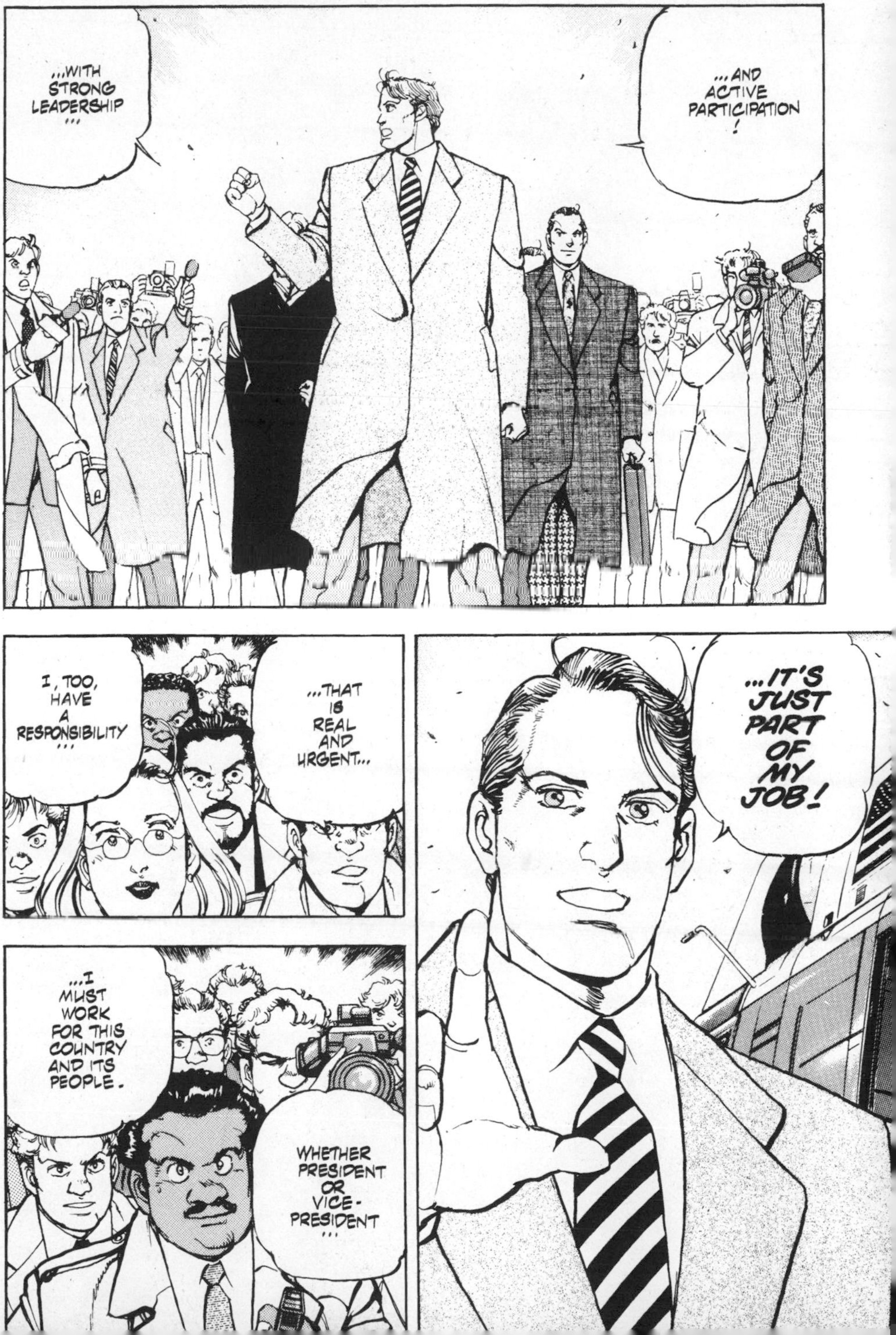
...WITH STRONG LEADERSHIP ...
...AND ACTIVE PARTICIPATION !
I, TOO, HAVE A RESPONSIBILITY ...
...THAT IS REAL AND URGENT...
...I MUST WORK FOR THIS COUNTRY AND ITS PEOPLE.
WHETHER PRESIDENT OR VICE-PRESIDENT ...
...IT'S JUST PART OF MY JOB!

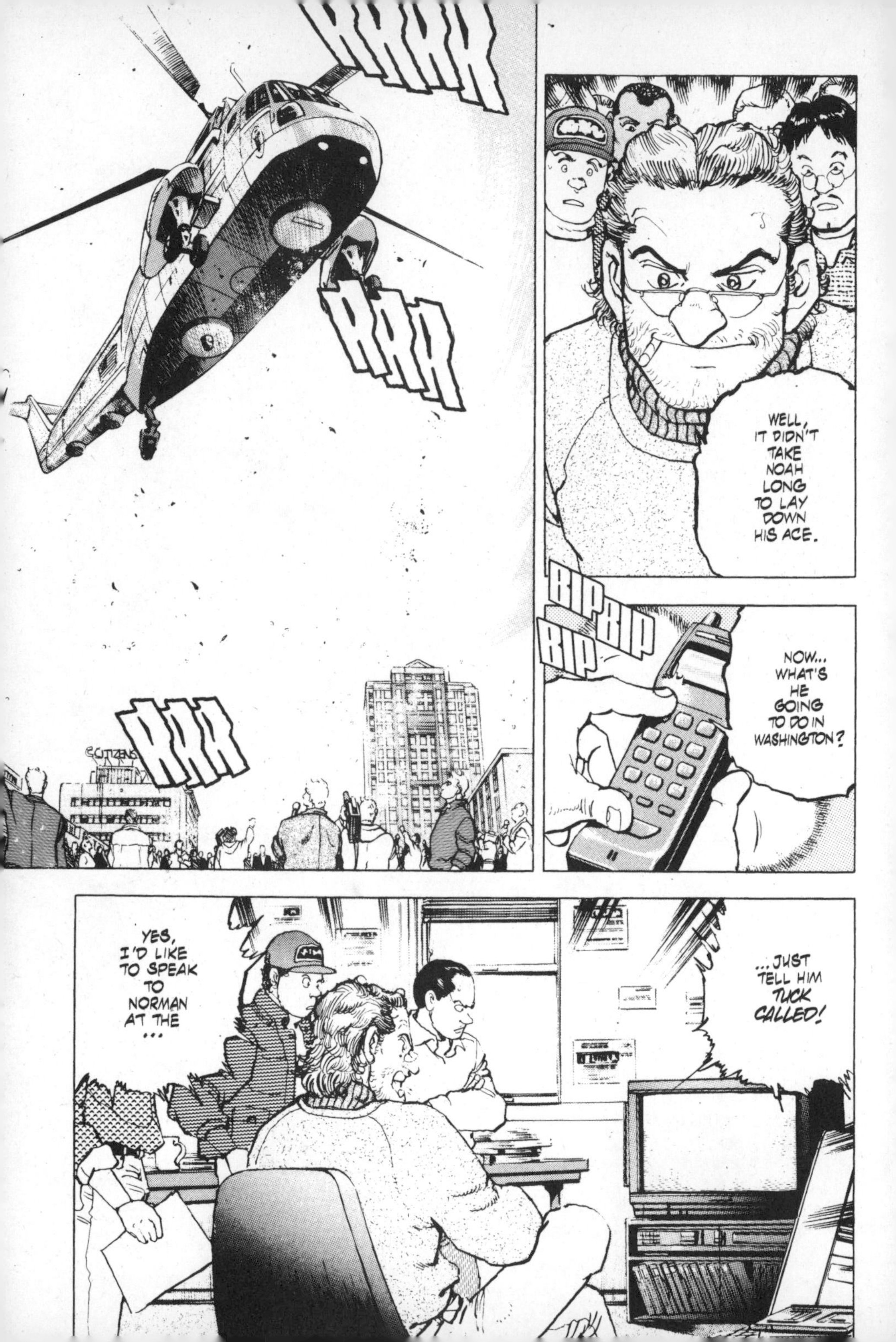
CITIZENS
WELL, IT DIDN'T TAKE NOAH LONG TO LAY DOWN HIS ACE.
BIP BIP BIP
NOW... WHAT'S HE GOING TO DO IN WASHINGTON?
YES, I'D LIKE TO SPEAK TO NORMAN AT THE ...
...JUST TELL HIM TUCK CALLED!

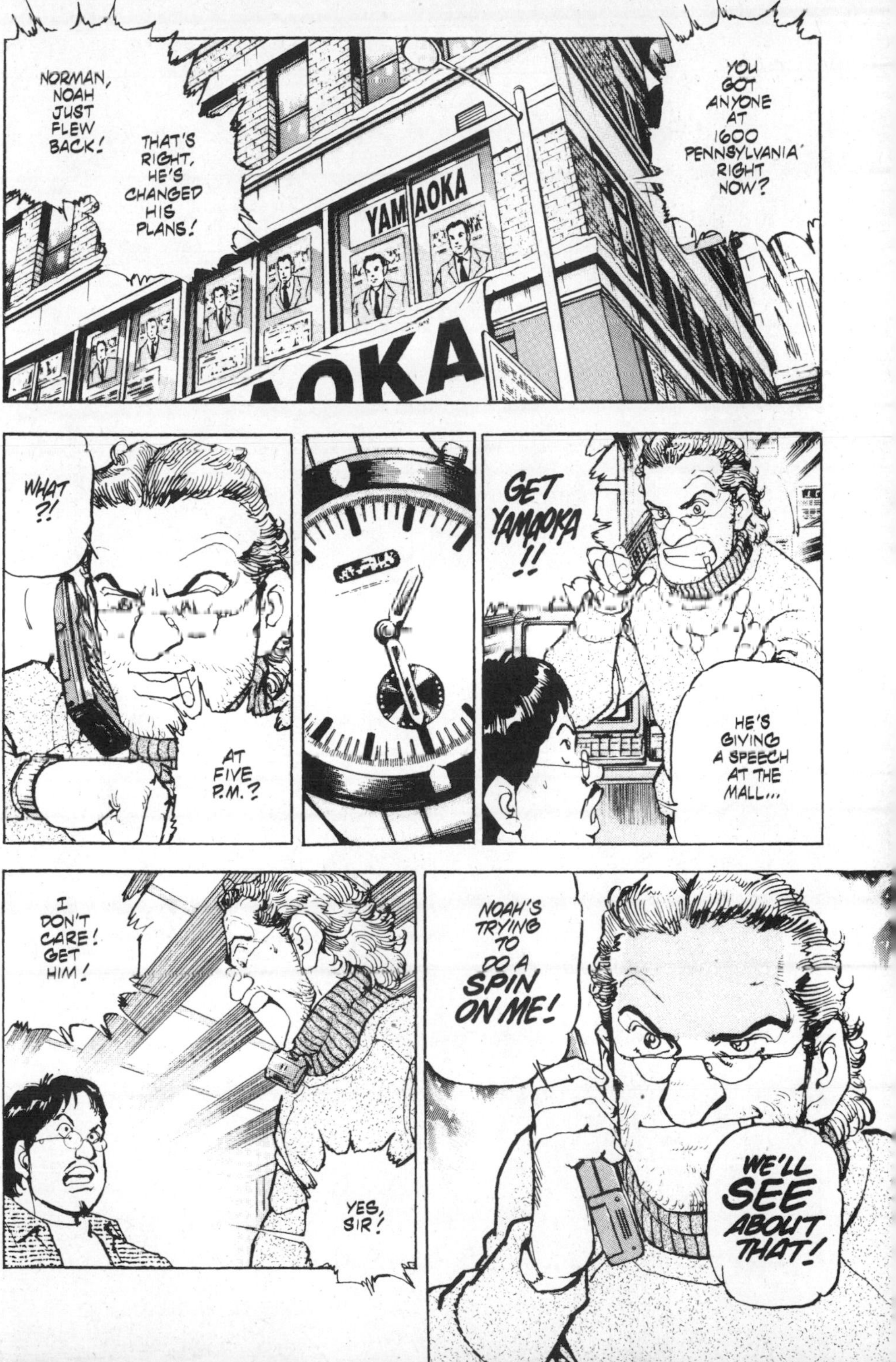
NORMAN, NOAH JUST FLEW BACK!
THAT'S RIGHT, HE'S CHANGED HIS PLANS!
YOU GOT ANYONE AT 1600 PENNSYLVANIA RIGHT NOW?
YAMAOKA
YAMAOKA
AOKA
WHAT?!
AT FIVE P.M.?
GET YAMAOKA!!
HE'S GIVING A SPEECH AT THE MALL...
I DON'T CARE! GET HIM!
YES, SIR!
NOAH'S TRYING TO DO A SPIN ON ME!
WE'LL SEE ABOUT THAT!

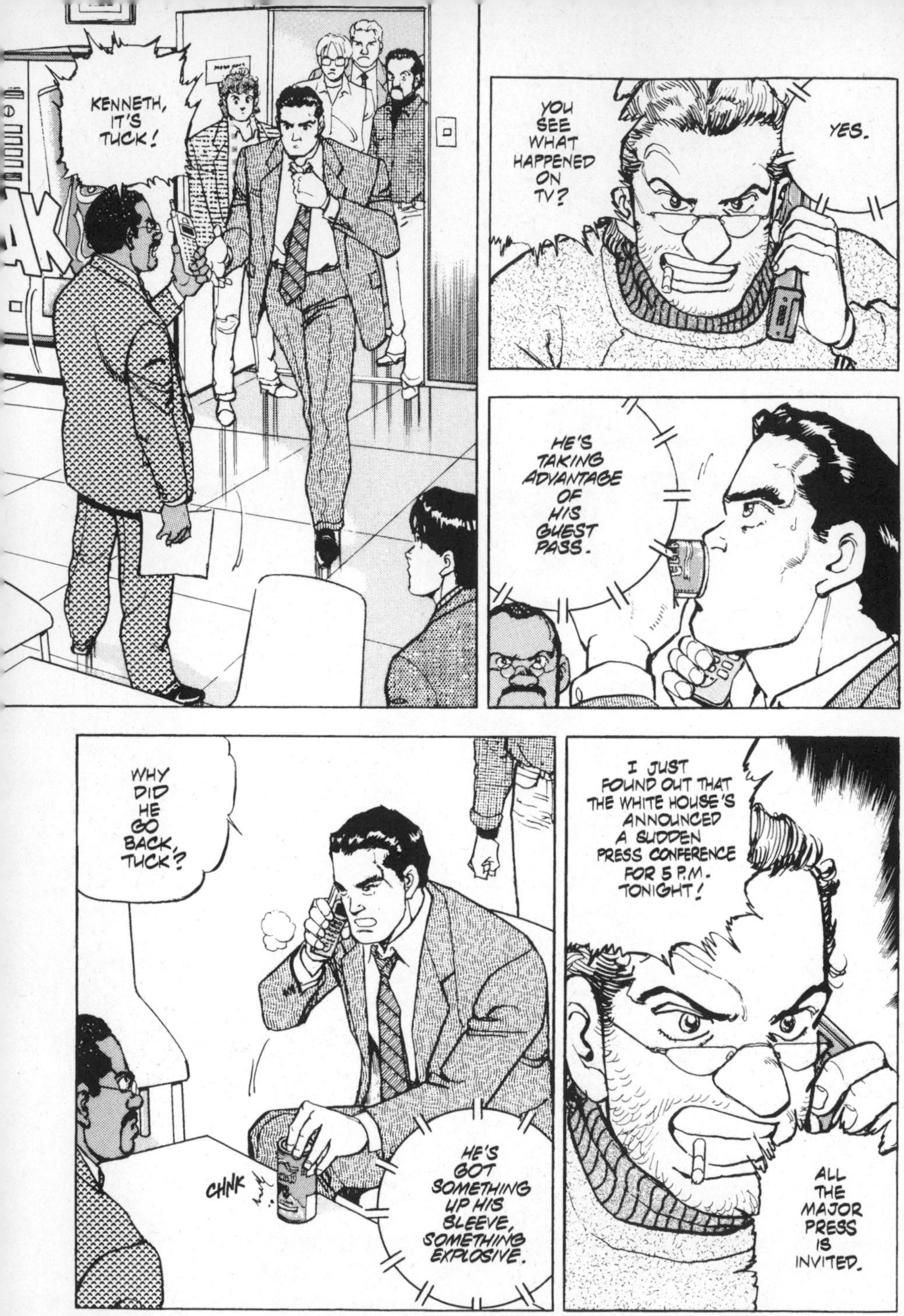
KENNETH, IT'S TUCK!
YOU SEE WHAT HAPPENED ON TV?
YES.
HE'S TAKING ADVANTAGE OF HIS GUEST PASS.
WHY DID HE GO BACK, TUCK?
CHNK
HE'S GOT SOMETHING UP HIS SLEEVE, SOMETHING EXPLOSIVE.
I JUST FOUND OUT THAT THE WHITE HOUSE'S ANNOUNCED A SUDDEN PRESS CONFERENCE FOR 5 P.M. TONIGHT!
ALL THE MAJOR PRESS IS INVITED.

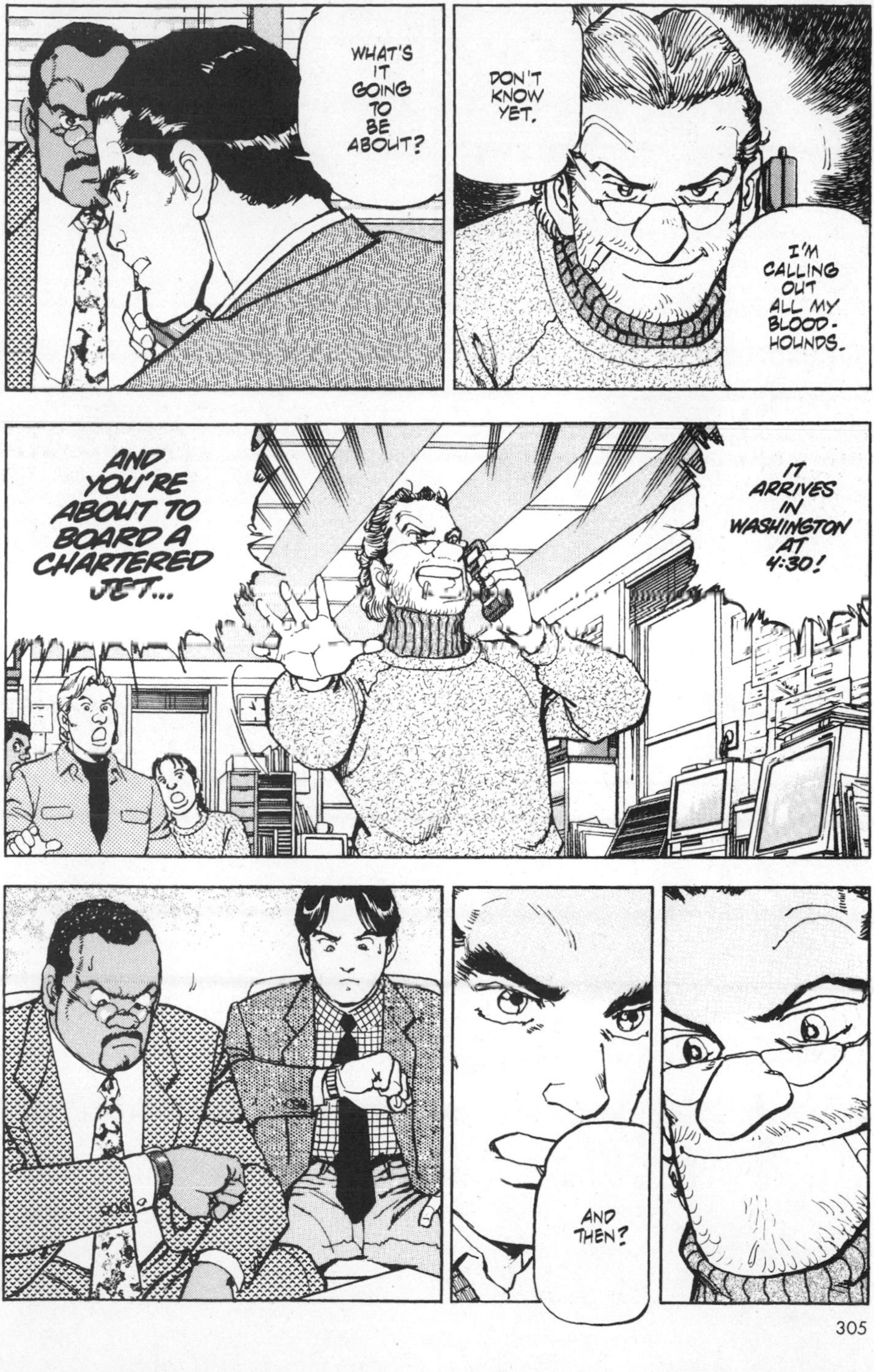
WHAT'S IT GOING TO BE ABOUT?
DON'T KNOW YET.
I'M CALLING OUT ALL MY BLOOD-HOUNDS.
AND YOU'RE ABOUT TO BOARD A CHARTERED JET...
IT ARRIVES IN WASHINGTON AT 4:30!
AND THEN?

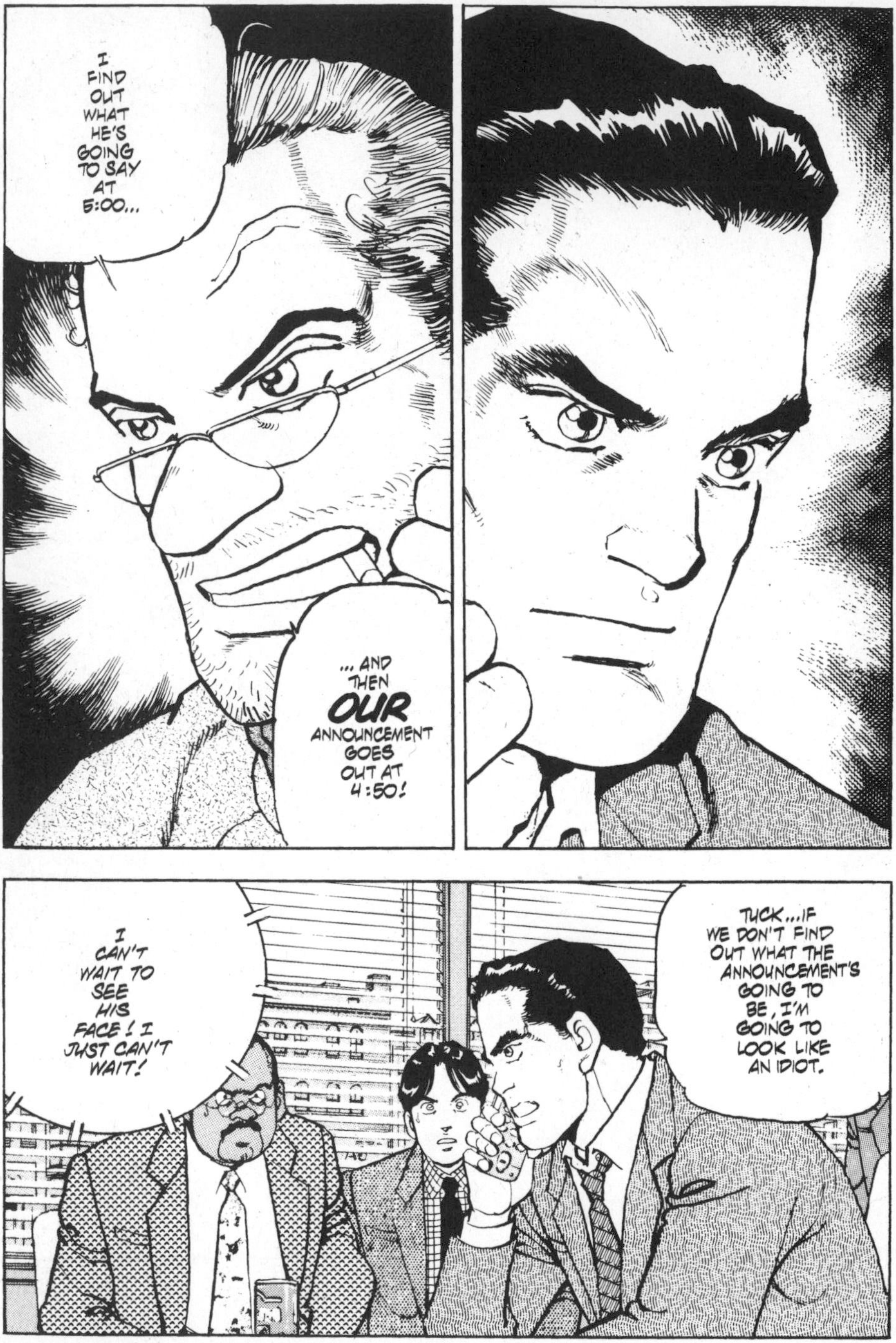
I FIND OUT WHAT HE'S GOING TO SAY AT 5:00...
...AND THEN OUR ANNOUNCEMENT GOES OUT AT 4:50!
I CAN'T WAIT TO SEE HIS FACE! I JUST CAN'T WAIT!
TUCK...IF WE DON'T FIND OUT WHAT THE ANNOUNCEMENT'S GOING TO BE, I'M GOING TO LOOK LIKE AN IDIOT.

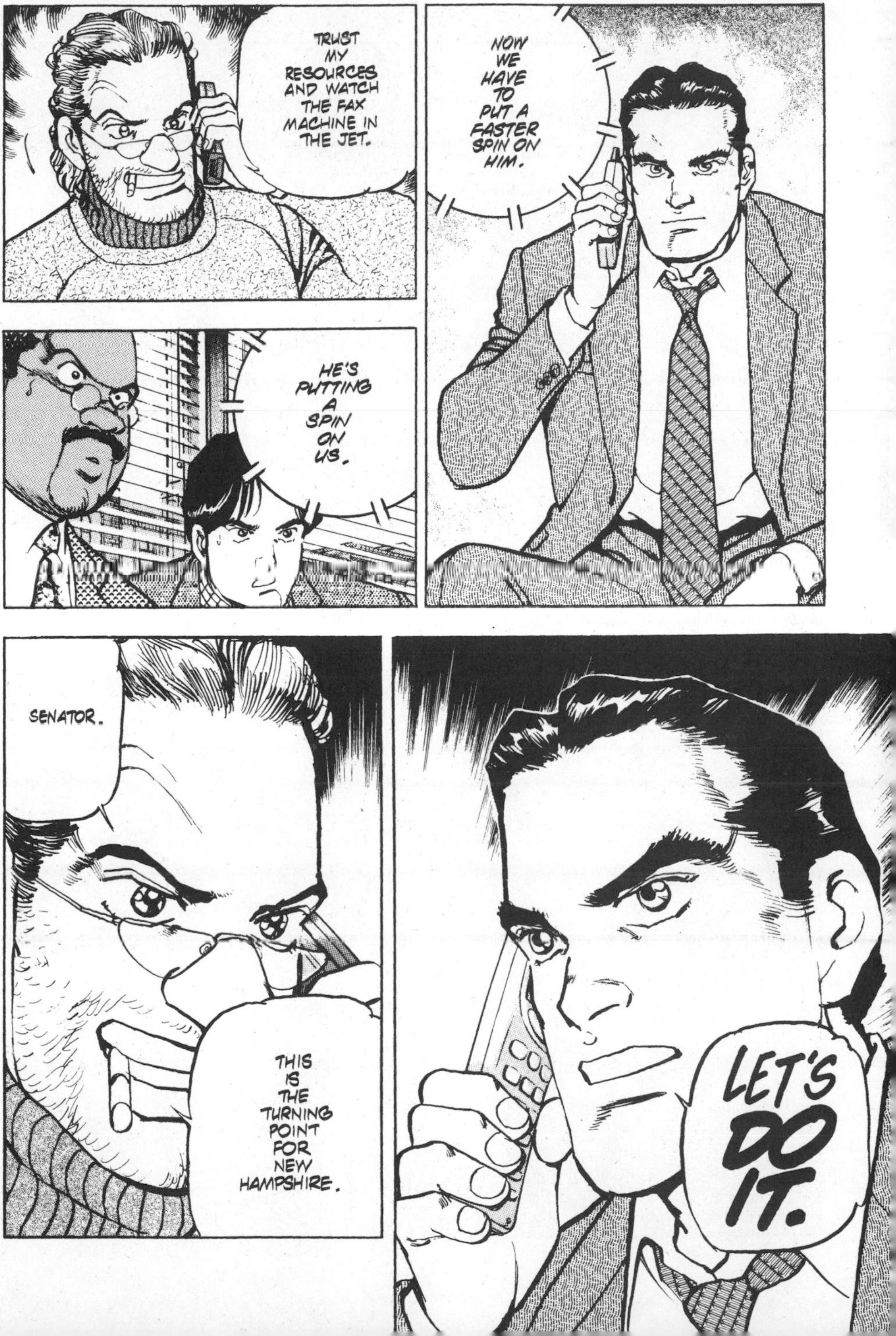
TRUST MY RESOURCES AND WATCH THE FAX MACHINE IN THE JET.
HE'S PUTTING A SPIN ON US.
NOW WE HAVE TO PUT A FASTER SPIN ON HIM.
SENATOR.
THIS IS THE TURNING POINT FOR NEW HAMPSHIRE.
LET'S DO IT.

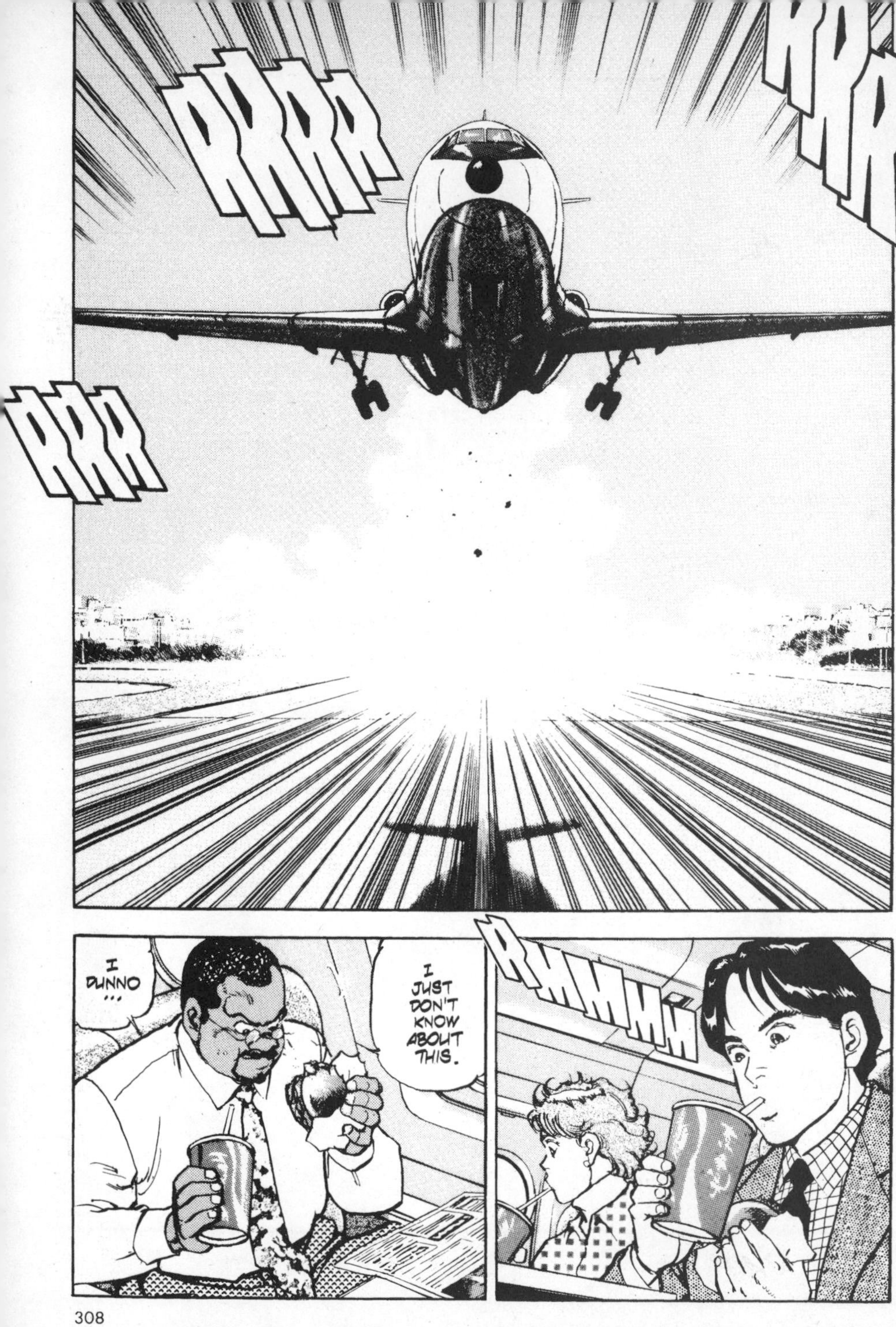
RRRR
RRR
RRR
I DUNNO...
I JUST DON'T KNOW ABOUT THIS.
RMMMM

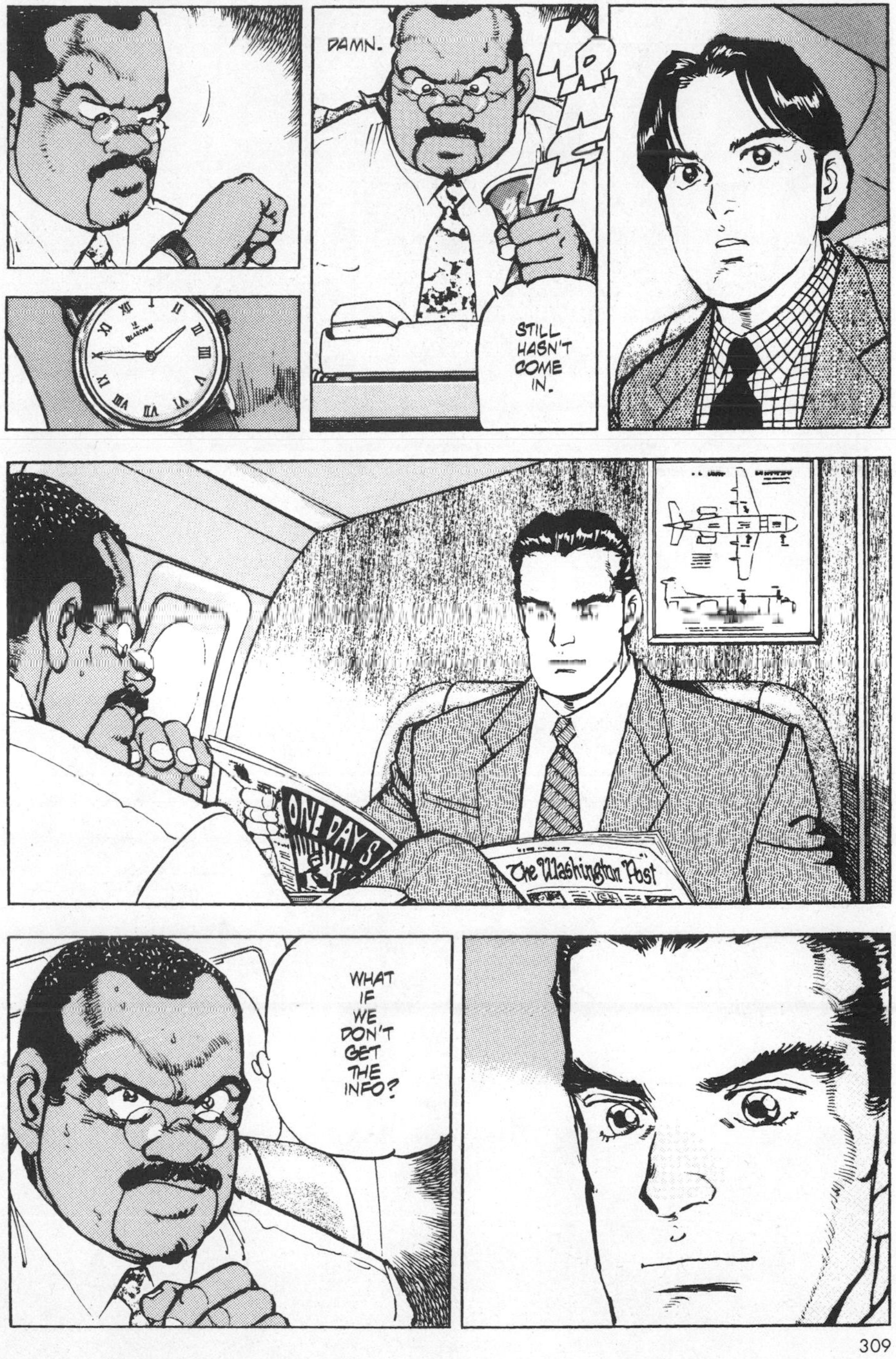
DAMN.
KRUNCH
STILL HASN'T COME IN.
ONE DAY S
The Washington Post
WHAT IF WE DON'T GET THE INFO?

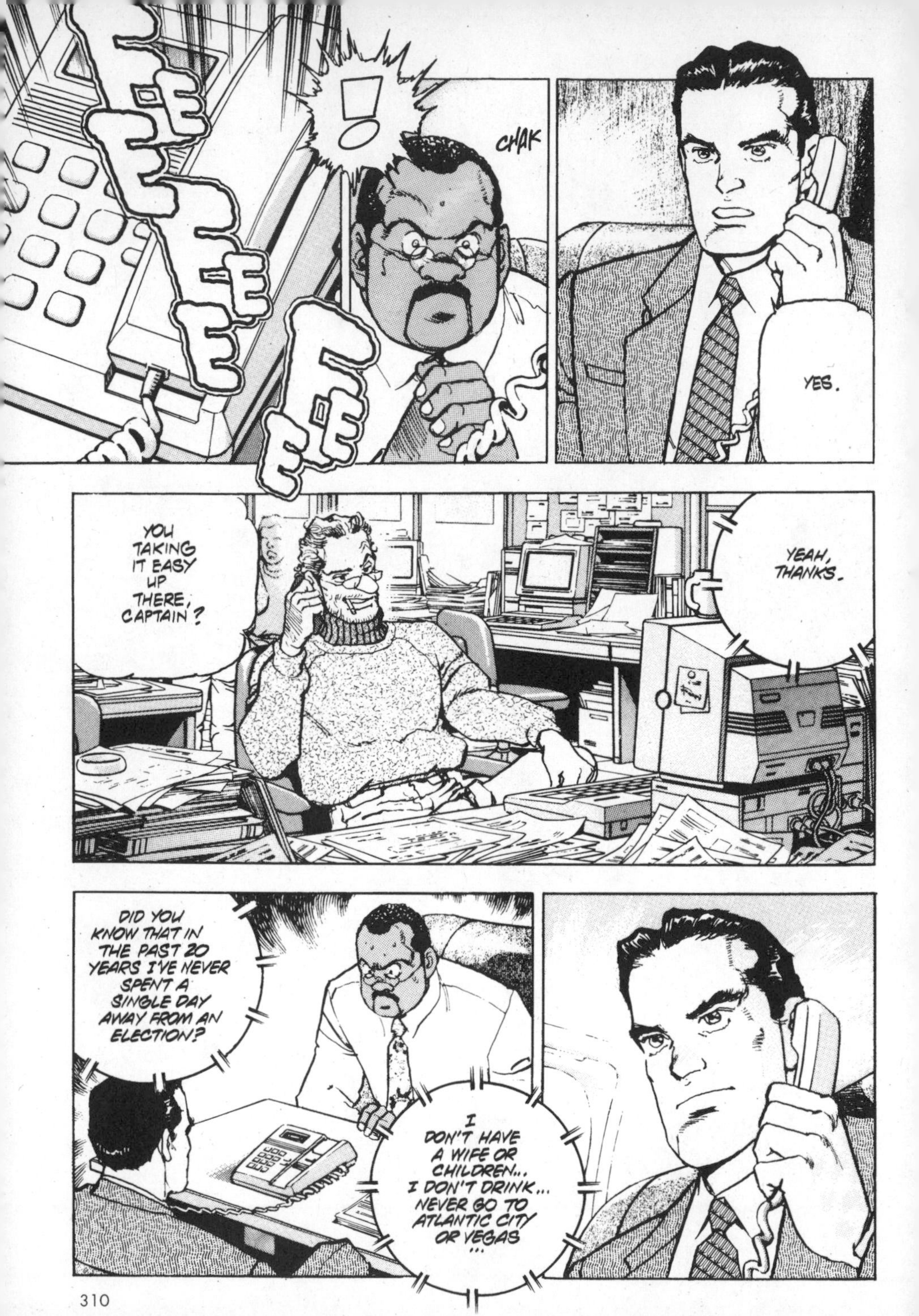
EEEEEEE
!
CHAK
YES.
YOU TAKING IT EASY UP THERE, CAPTAIN?
YEAH, THANKS.
DID YOU KNOW THAT IN THE PAST 20 YEARS I'VE NEVER SPENT A SINGLE DAY AWAY FROM AN ELECTION?
I DON'T HAVE A WIFE OR CHILDREN... I DON'T DRINK... NEVER GO TO ATLANTIC CITY OR VEGAS ...

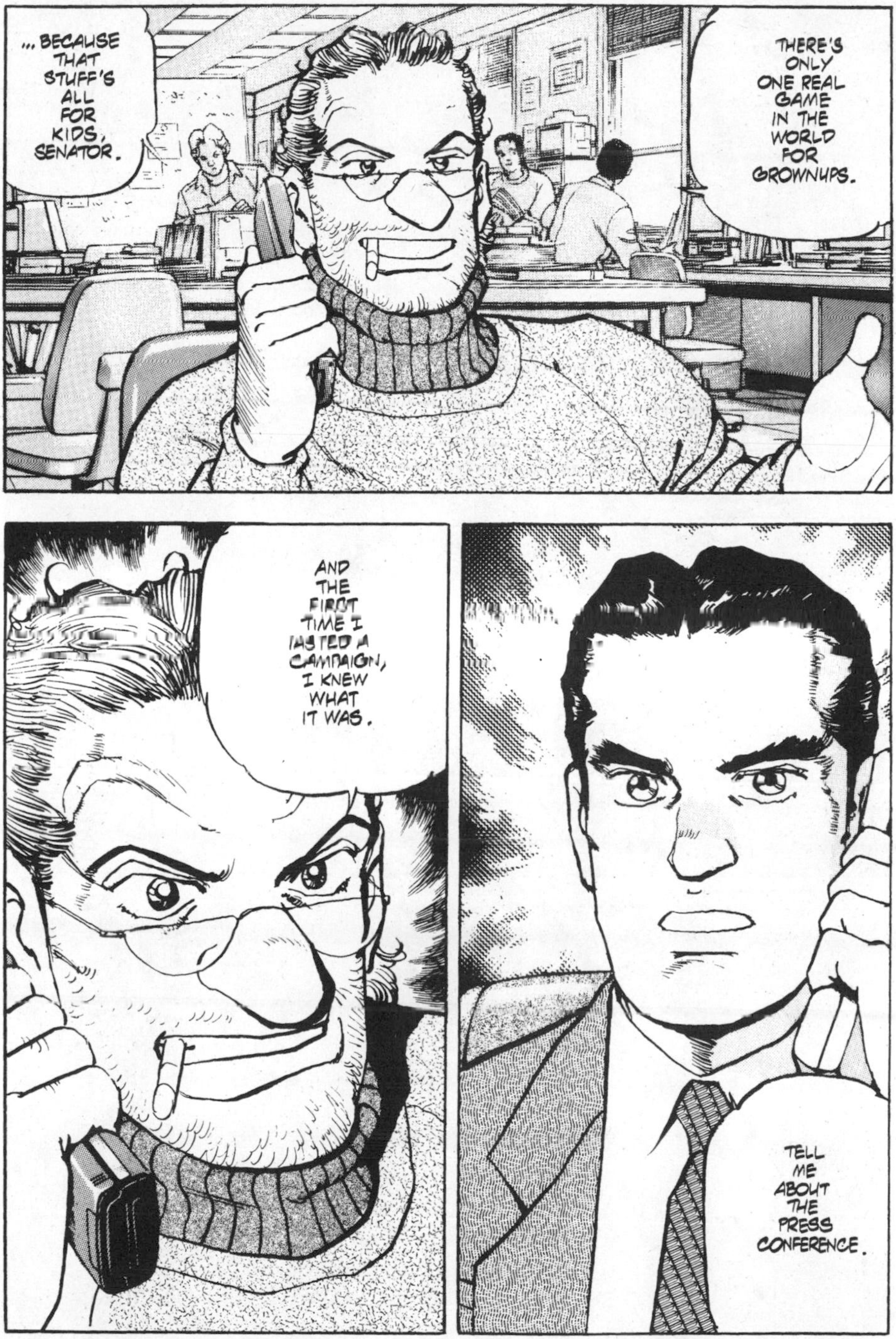
...BECAUSE THAT STUFF'S ALL FOR KIDS, SENATOR.
THERE'S ONLY ONE REAL GAME IN THE WORLD FOR GROWNUPS.
AND THE FIRST TIME I TASTED A CAMPAIGN, I KNEW WHAT IT WAS.
TELL ME ABOUT THE PRESS CONFERENCE.

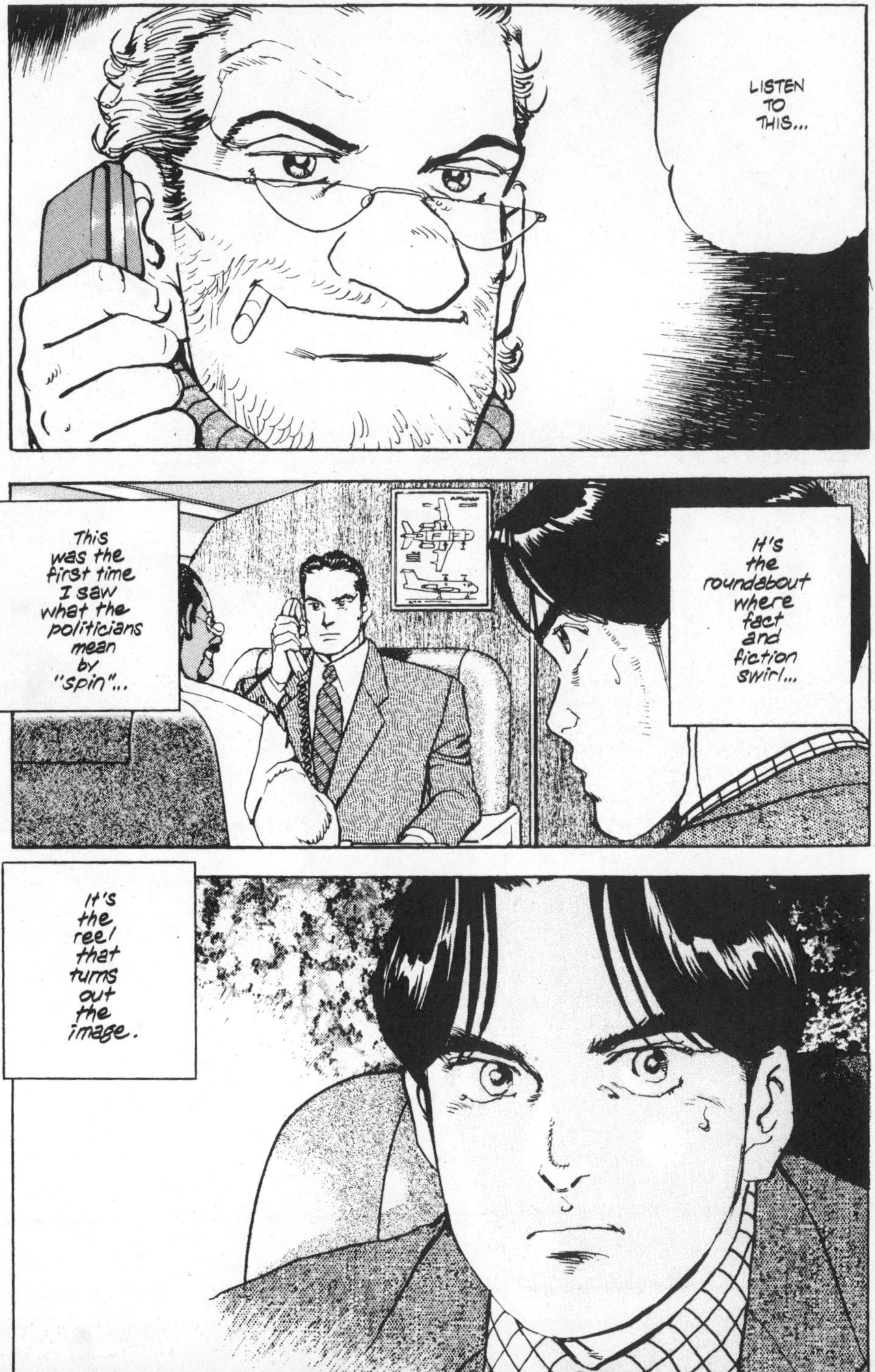
LISTEN TO THIS...
This was the first time I saw what the politicians mean by "spin"...
It's the roundabout where fact and fiction swirl...
It's the reel that turns out the image.

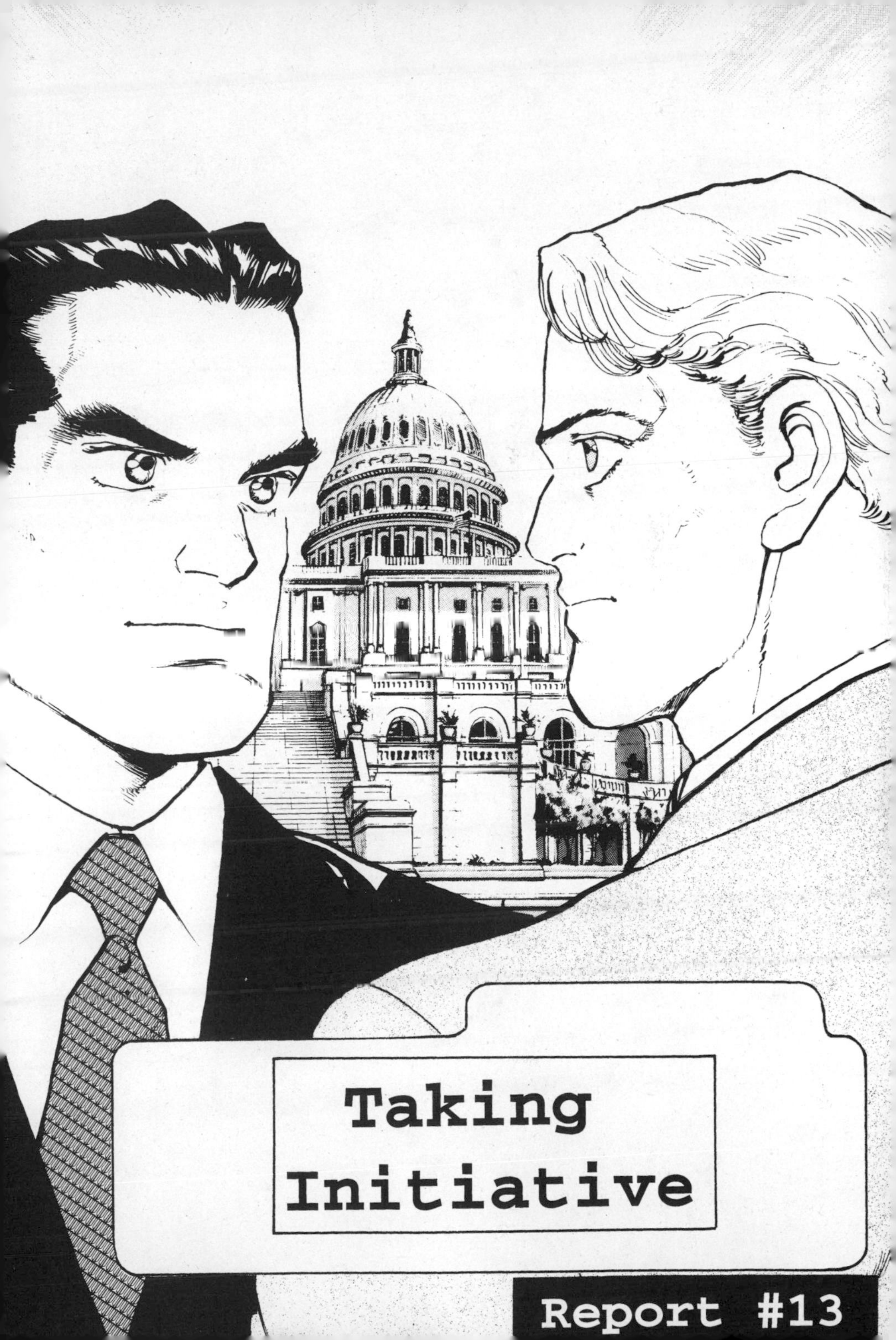
Taking Initiative
Report #13

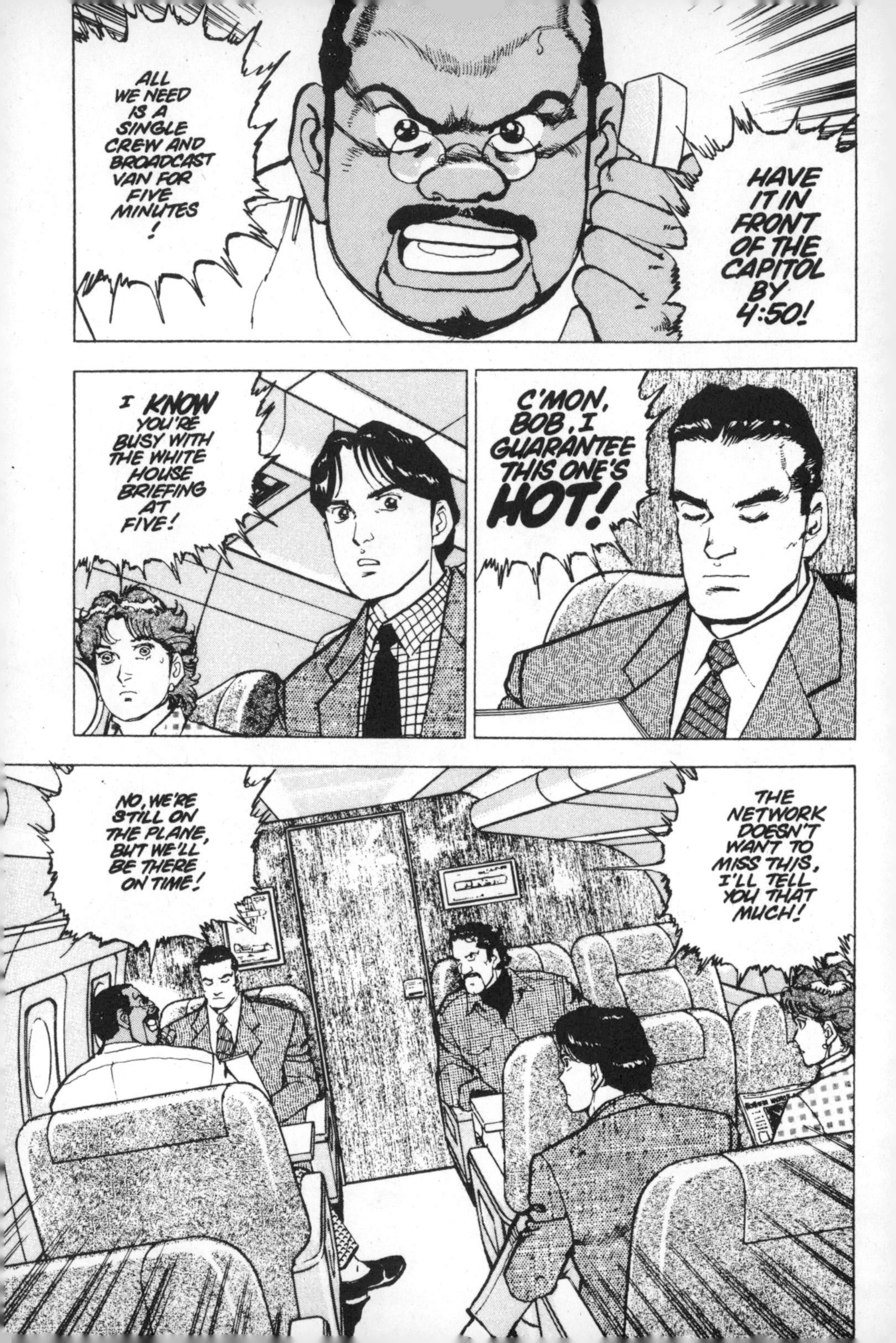
ALL WE NEED IS A SINGLE CREW AND BROADCAST VAN FOR FIVE MINUTES!
HAVE IT IN FRONT OF THE CAPITOL BY 4:50!
I KNOW YOU'RE BUSY WITH THE WHITE HOUSE BRIEFING AT FIVE!
C'MON, BOB. I GUARANTEE THIS ONE'S HOT!
NO, WE'RE STILL ON THE PLANE, BUT WE'LL BE THERE ON TIME!
THE NETWORK DOESN'T WANT TO MISS THIS, I'LL TELL YOU THAT MUCH!

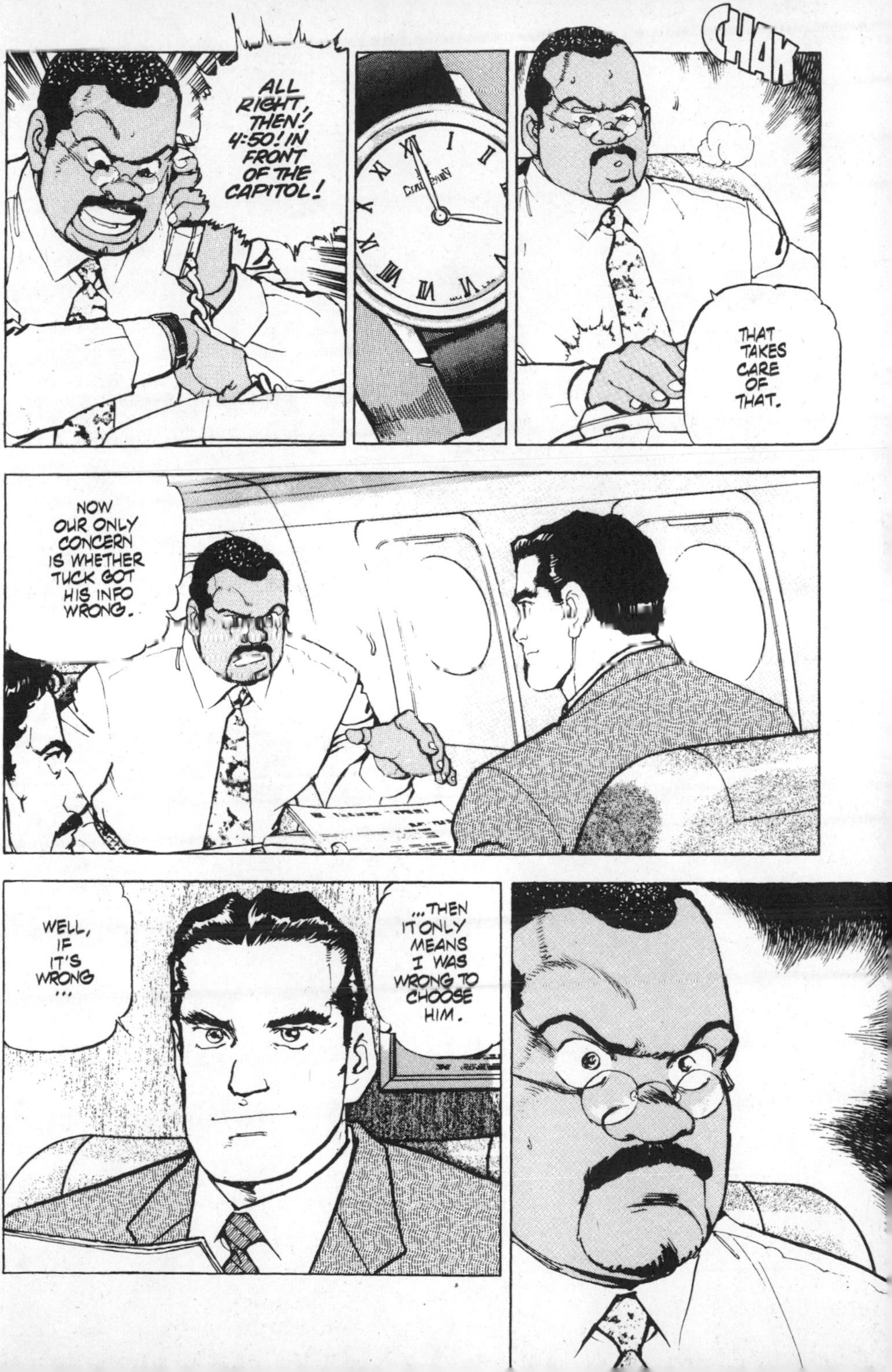
ALL RIGHT, THEN! 4:50! IN FRONT OF THE CAPITOL!
CHAK
THAT TAKES CARE OF THAT.
NOW OUR ONLY CONCERN IS WHETHER TUCK GOT HIS INFO WRONG.
WELL, IF IT'S WRONG...
...THEN IT ONLY MEANS I WAS WRONG TO CHOOSE HIM.

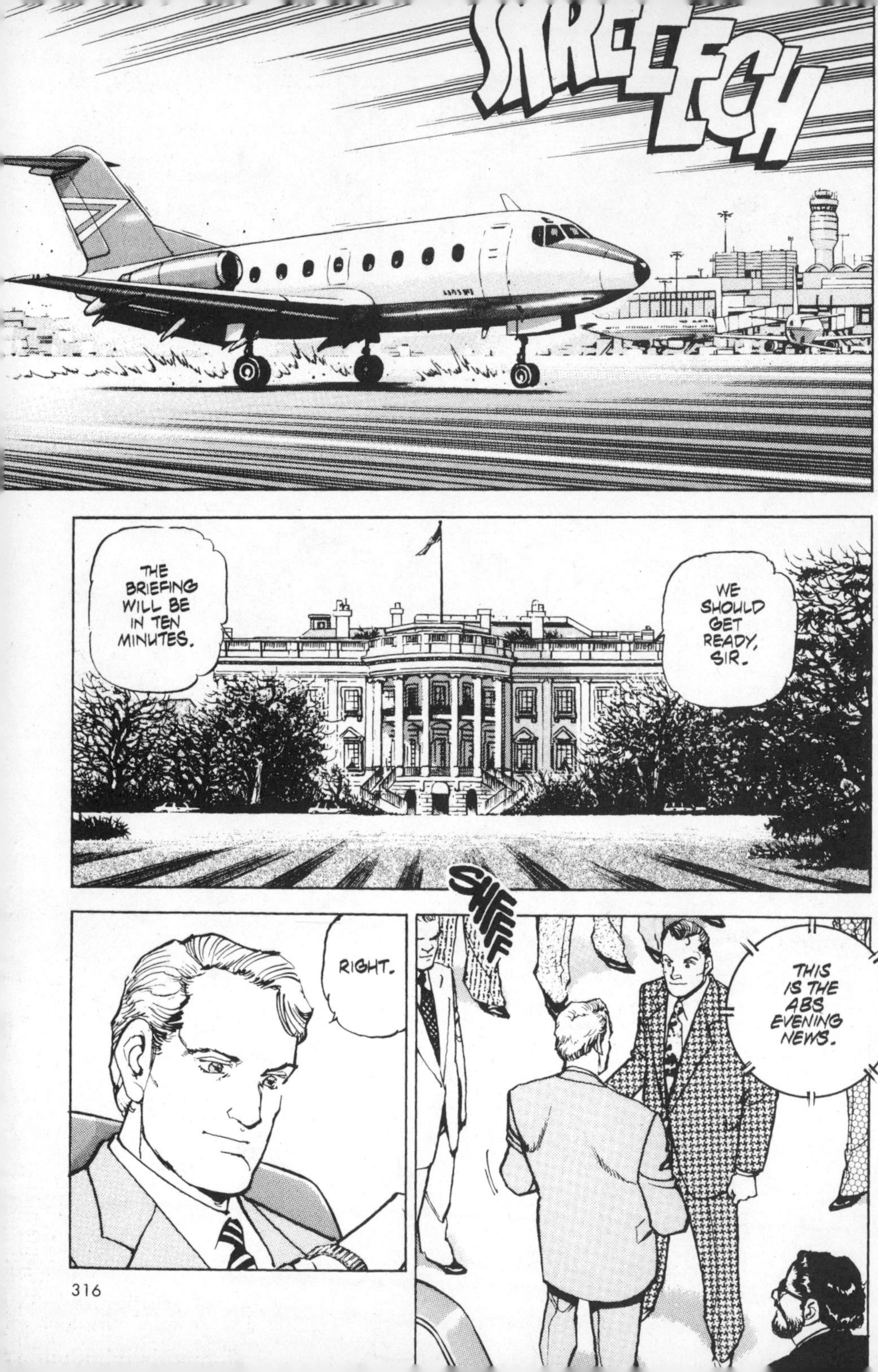
SKREEECH
THE BRIEFING WILL BE IN TEN MINUTES.
WE SHOULD GET READY, SIR.
RIGHT.
SHFF
THIS IS THE ABS EVENING NEWS.

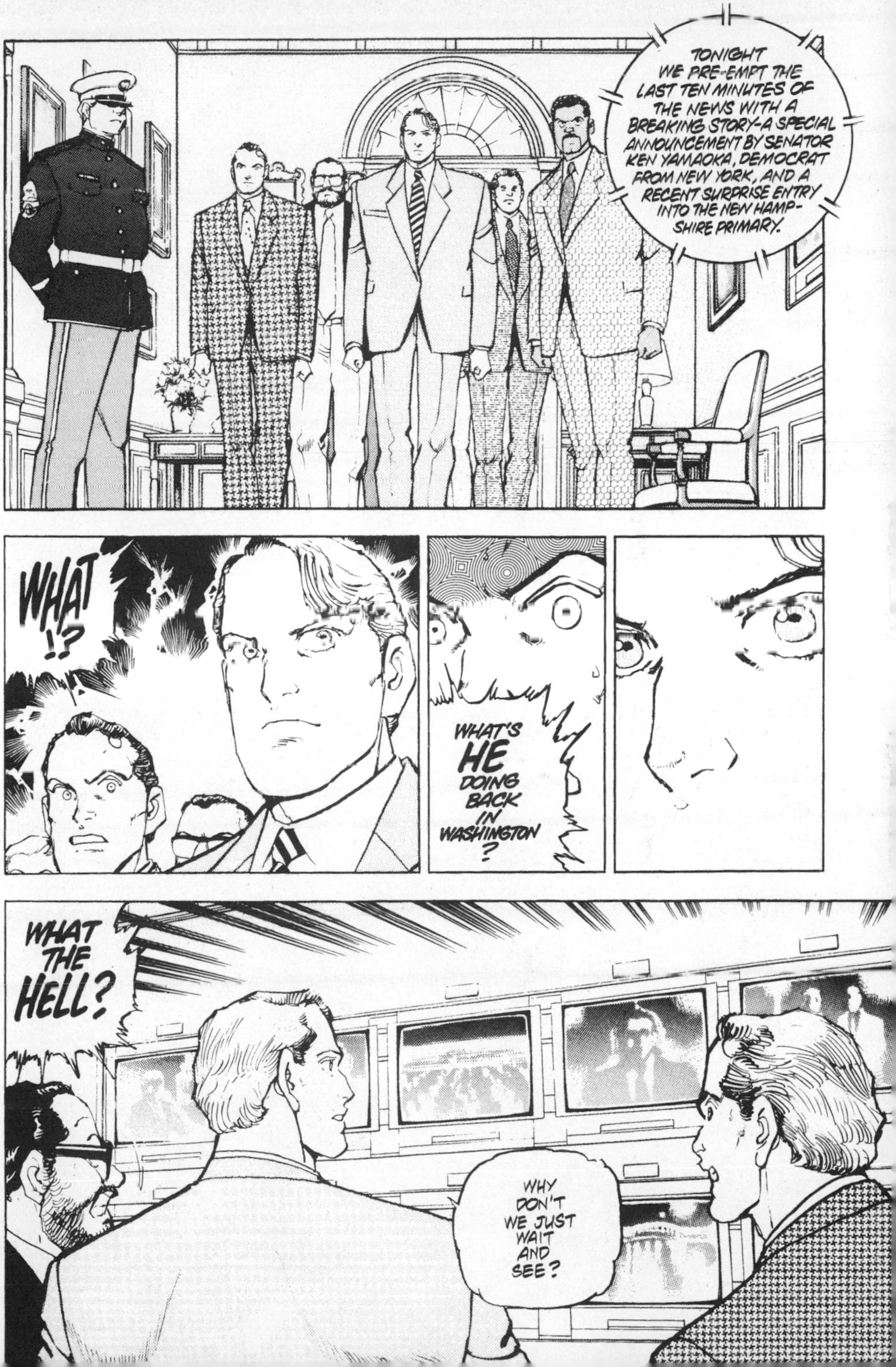
TONIGHT WE PRE-EMPT THE LAST TEN MINUTES OF THE NEWS WITH A BREAKING STORY–A SPECIAL ANNOUNCEMENT BY SENATOR KEN YAMAOKA, DEMOCRAT FROM NEW YORK, AND A RECENT SURPRISE ENTRY INTO THE NEW HAMPSHIRE PRIMARY.
WHAT !?
WHAT'S HE DOING BACK IN WASHINGTON ?
WHAT THE HELL?
WHY DON'T WE JUST WAIT AND SEE?

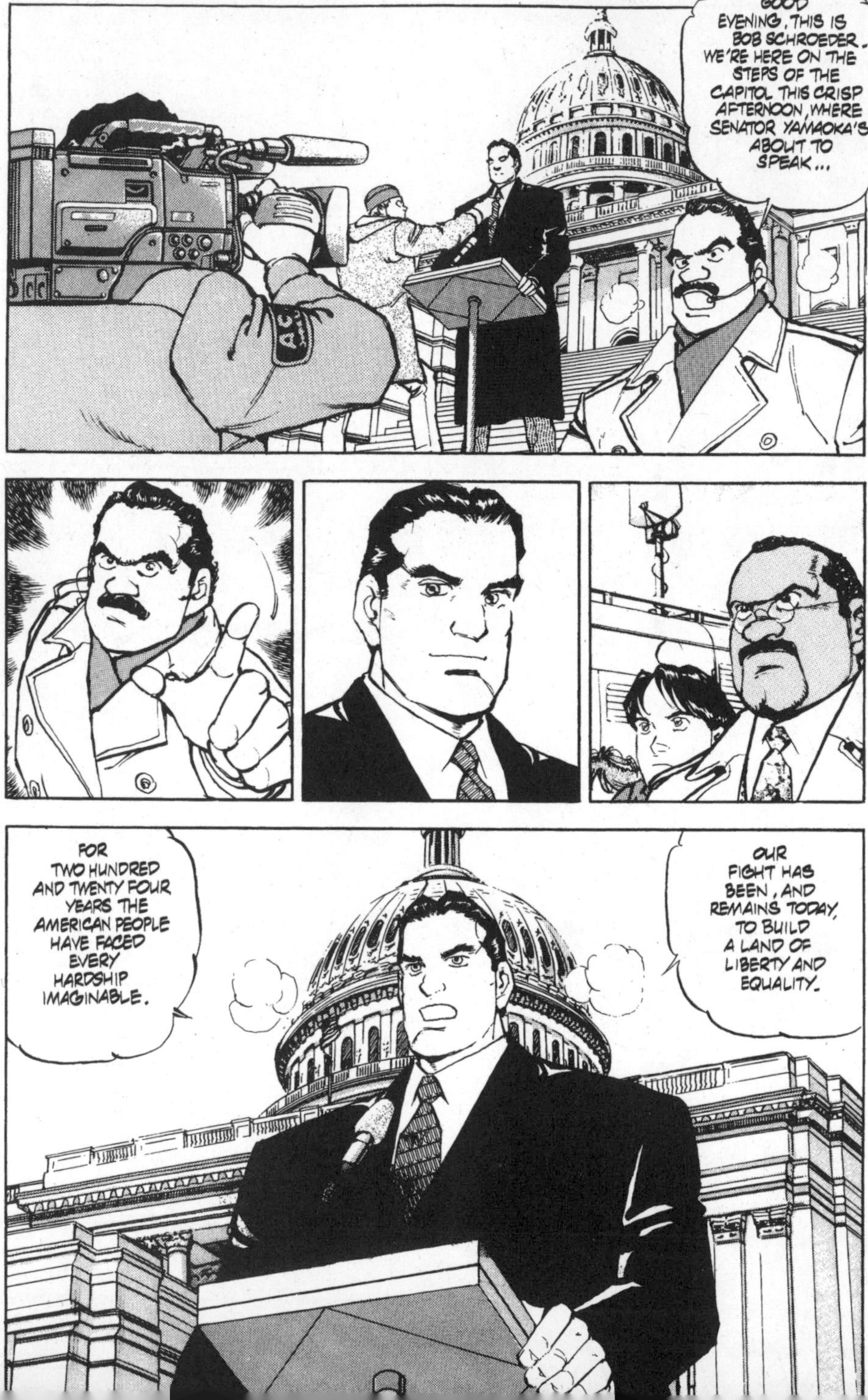
GOOD EVENING, THIS IS BOB SCHROEDER. WE'RE HERE ON THE STEPS OF THE CAPITOL THIS CRISP AFTERNOON, WHERE SENATOR YAMAOKA'S ABOUT TO SPEAK...
FOR TWO HUNDRED AND TWENTY FOUR YEARS THE AMERICAN PEOPLE HAVE FACED EVERY HARDSHIP IMAGINABLE.
OUR FIGHT HAS BEEN, AND REMAINS TODAY, TO BUILD A LAND OF LIBERTY AND EQUALITY.

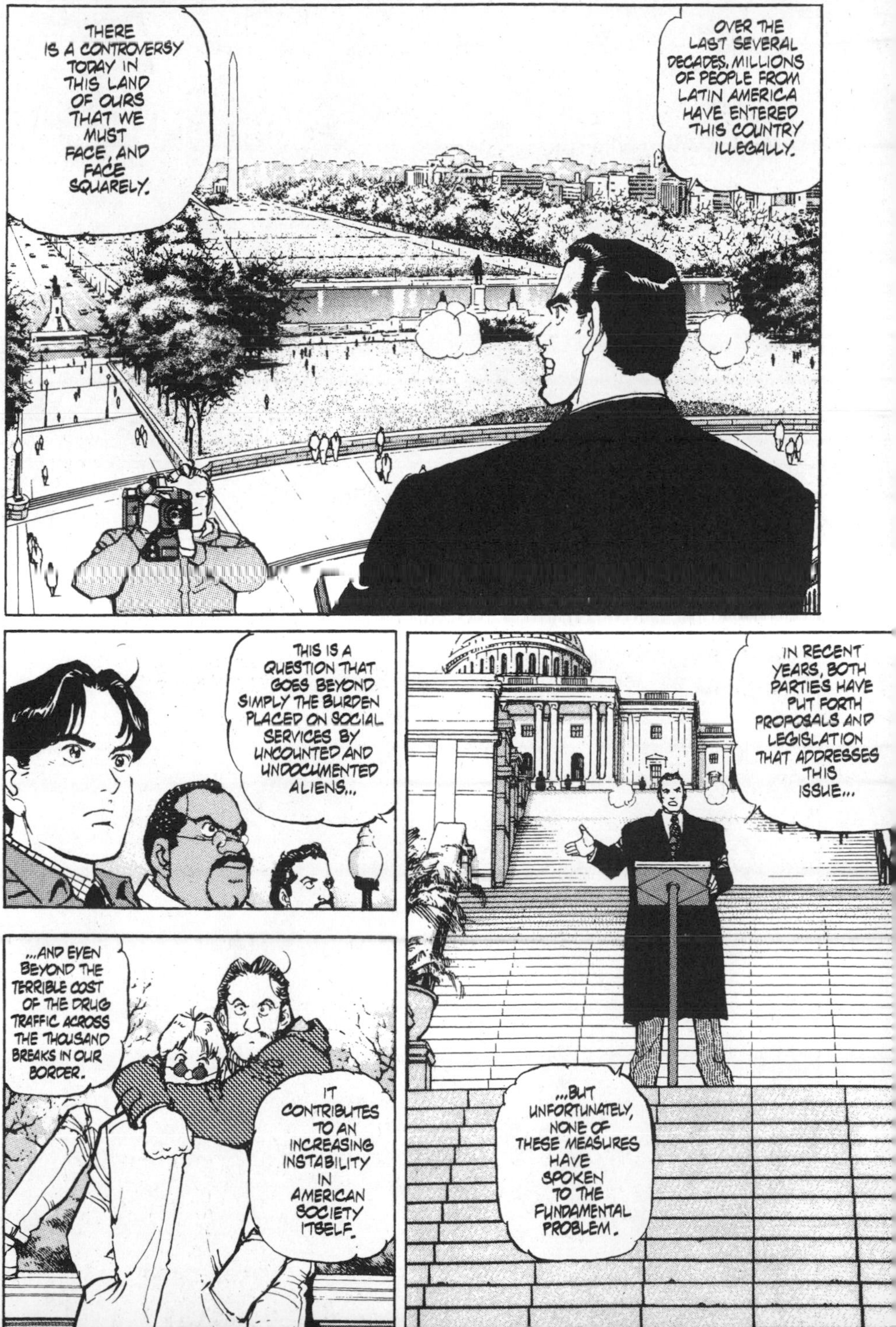
THERE IS A CONTROVERSY TODAY IN THIS LAND OF OURS THAT WE MUST FACE, AND FACE SQUARELY.
OVER THE LAST SEVERAL DECADES, MILLIONS OF PEOPLE FROM LATIN AMERICA HAVE ENTERED THIS COUNTRY ILLEGALLY.
THIS IS A QUESTION THAT GOES BEYOND SIMPLY THE BURDEN PLACED ON SOCIAL SERVICES BY UNCOUNTED AND UNDOCUMENTED ALIENS...
...AND EVEN BEYOND THE TERRIBLE COST OF THE DRUG TRAFFIC ACROSS THE THOUSAND BREAKS IN OUR BORDER.
IT CONTRIBUTES TO AN INCREASING INSTABILITY IN AMERICAN SOCIETY ITSELF.
IN RECENT YEARS, BOTH PARTIES HAVE PUT FORTH PROPOSALS AND LEGISLATION THAT ADDRESSES THIS ISSUE...
...BUT UNFORTUNATELY, NONE OF THESE MEASURES HAVE SPOKEN TO THE FUNDAMENTAL PROBLEM.

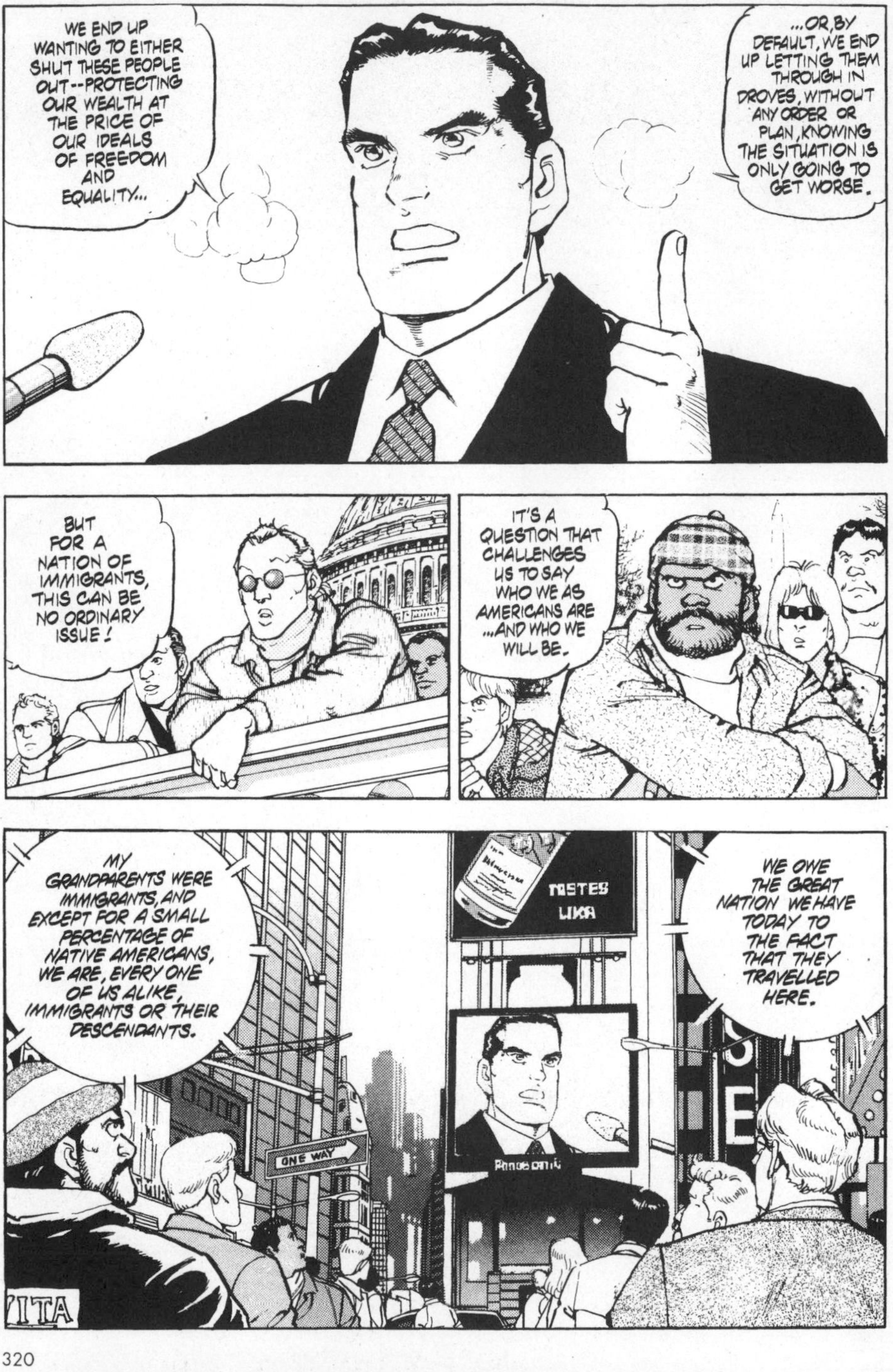
WE END UP WANTING TO EITHER SHUT THESE PEOPLE OUT--PROTECTING OUR WEALTH AT THE PRICE OF OUR IDEALS OF FREEDOM AND EQUALITY...
...OR, BY DEFAULT, WE END UP LETTING THEM THROUGH IN DROVES, WITHOUT ANY ORDER OR PLAN, KNOWING THE SITUATION IS ONLY GOING TO GET WORSE.
BUT FOR A NATION OF IMMIGRANTS, THIS CAN BE NO ORDINARY ISSUE!
IT'S A QUESTION THAT CHALLENGES US TO SAY WHO WE AS AMERICANS ARE ...AND WHO WE WILL BE.
MY GRANDPARENTS WERE IMMIGRANTS, AND EXCEPT FOR A SMALL PERCENTAGE OF NATIVE AMERICANS, WE ARE, EVERY ONE OF US ALIKE, IMMIGRANTS OR THEIR DESCENDANTS.
WE OWE THE GREAT NATION WE HAVE TODAY TO THE FACT THAT THEY TRAVELLED HERE.
ONE WAY
VITA

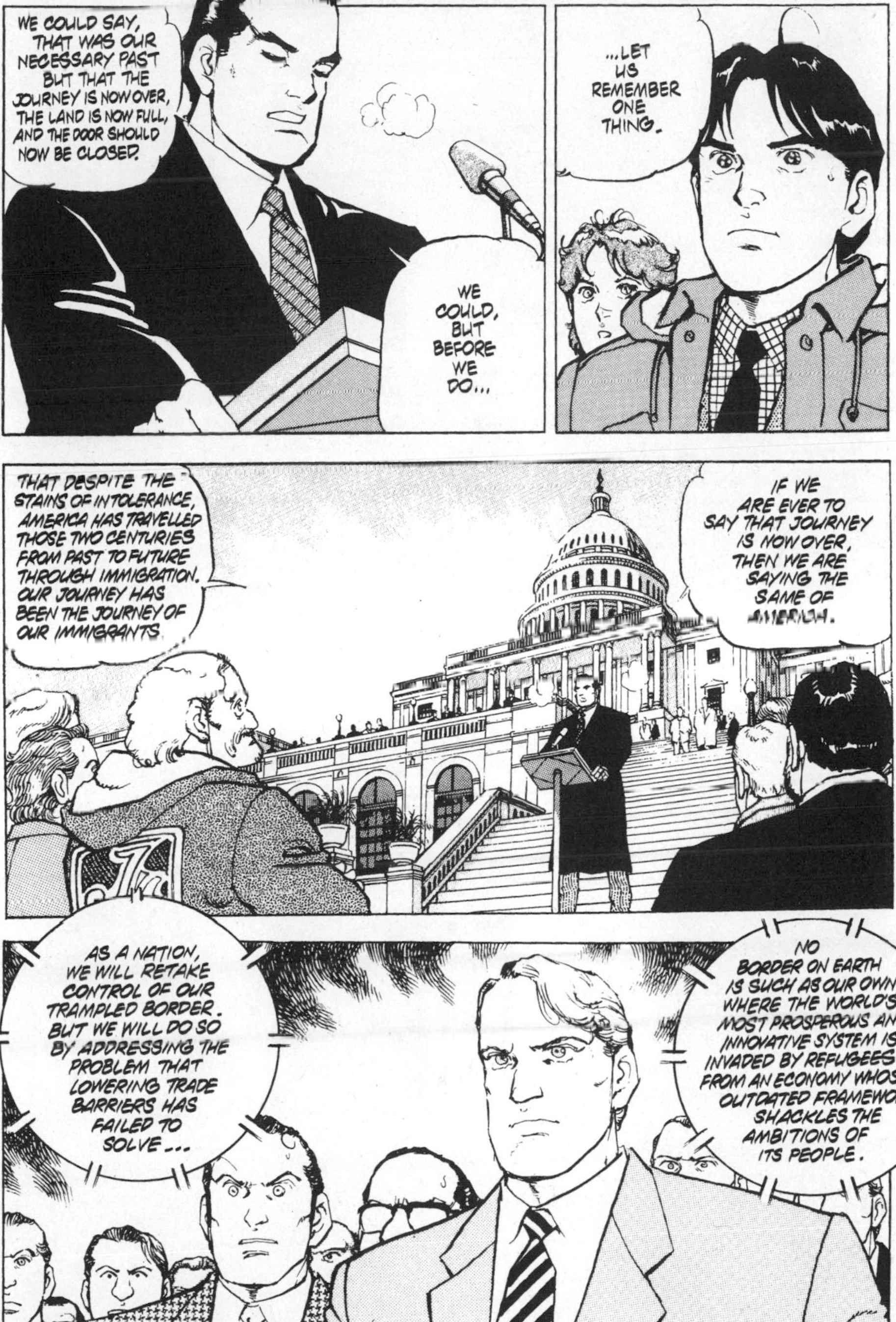
WE COULD SAY, THAT WAS OUR NECESSARY PAST BUT THAT THE JOURNEY IS NOW OVER, THE LAND IS NOW FULL, AND THE DOOR SHOULD NOW BE CLOSED.
WE COULD, BUT BEFORE WE DO...
...LET US REMEMBER ONE THING.
THAT DESPITE THE STAINS OF INTOLERANCE, AMERICA HAS TRAVELLED THOSE TWO CENTURIES FROM PAST TO FUTURE THROUGH IMMIGRATION. OUR JOURNEY HAS BEEN THE JOURNEY OF OUR IMMIGRANTS.
IF WE ARE EVER TO SAY THAT JOURNEY IS NOW OVER, THEN WE ARE SAYING THE SAME OF AMERICA.
AS A NATION, WE WILL RETAKE CONTROL OF OUR TRAMPLED BORDER. BUT WE WILL DO SO BY ADDRESSING THE PROBLEM THAT LOWERING TRADE BARRIERS HAS FAILED TO SOLVE...
NO BORDER ON EARTH IS SUCH AS OUR OWN, WHERE THE WORLD'S MOST PROSPEROUS AND INNOVATIVE SYSTEM IS INVADED BY REFUGEES FROM AN ECONOMY WHOSE OUTDATED FRAMEWORK SHACKLES THE AMBITIONS OF ITS PEOPLE.

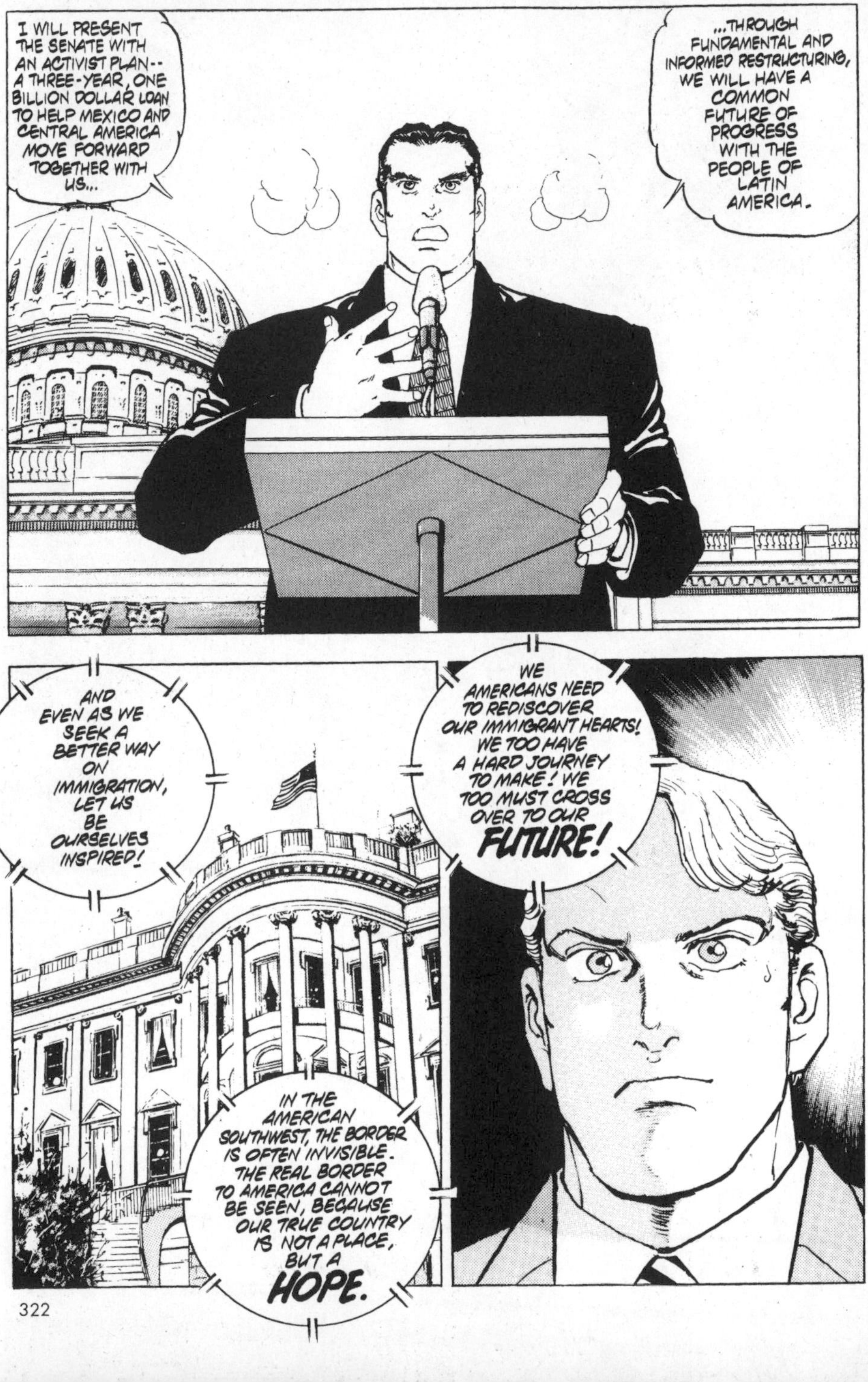
I WILL PRESENT THE SENATE WITH AN ACTIVIST PLAN-- A THREE-YEAR, ONE BILLION DOLLAR LOAN TO HELP MEXICO AND CENTRAL AMERICA MOVE FORWARD TOGETHER WITH US...
...THROUGH FUNDAMENTAL AND INFORMED RESTRUCTURING, WE WILL HAVE A COMMON FUTURE OF PROGRESS WITH THE PEOPLE OF LATIN AMERICA.
AND EVEN AS WE SEEK A BETTER WAY ON IMMIGRATION, LET US BE OURSELVES INSPIRED!
IN THE AMERICAN SOUTHWEST, THE BORDER IS OFTEN INVISIBLE. THE REAL BORDER TO AMERICA CANNOT BE SEEN, BECAUSE OUR TRUE COUNTRY IS NOT A PLACE, BUT A HOPE.
WE AMERICANS NEED TO REDISCOVER OUR IMMIGRANT HEARTS! WE TOO HAVE A HARD JOURNEY TO MAKE! WE TOO MUST CROSS OVER TO OUR FUTURE!

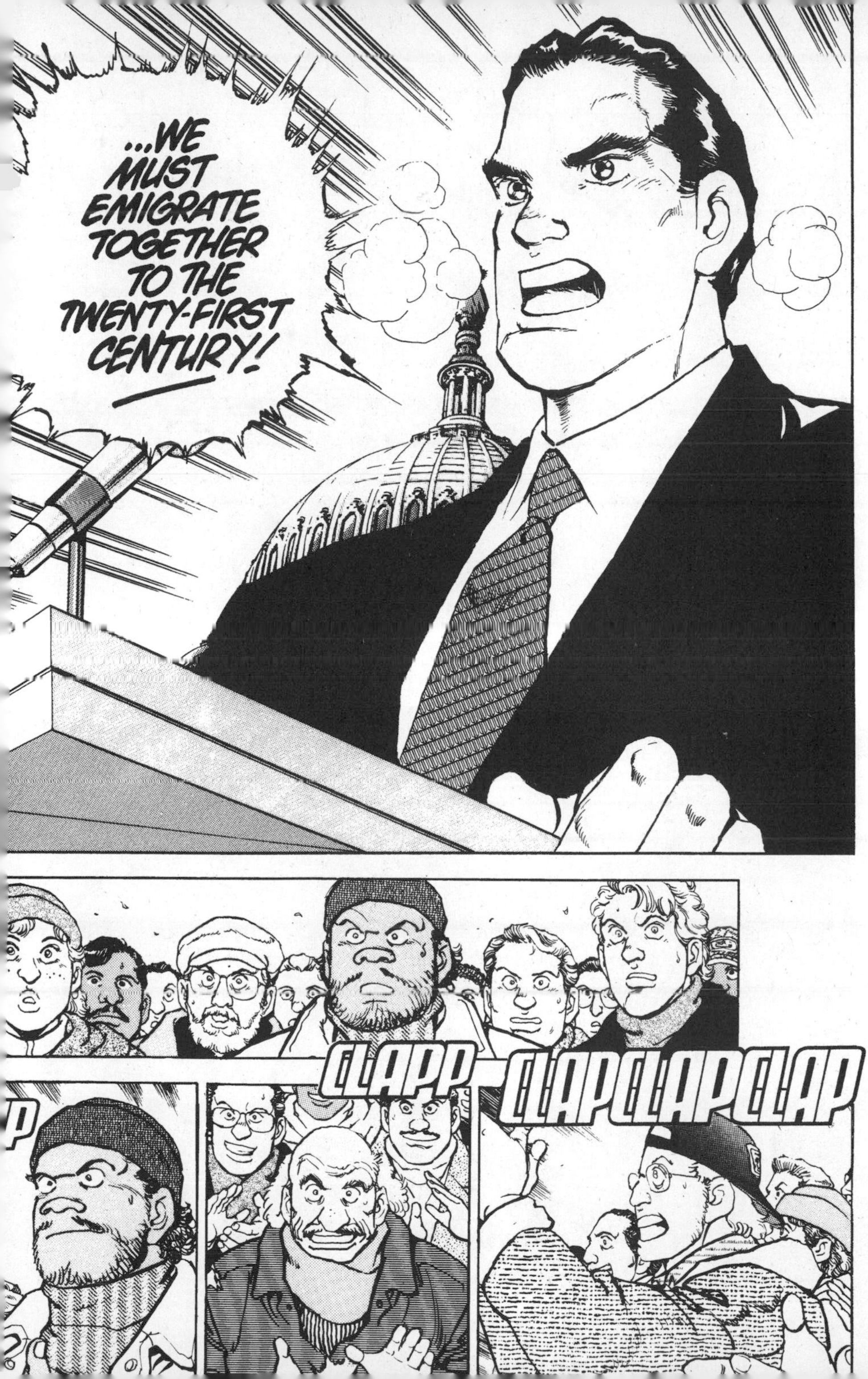
...WE MUST EMIGRATE TOGETHER TO THE TWENTY-FIRST CENTURY!
CLAPP
CLAPCLAPCLAP

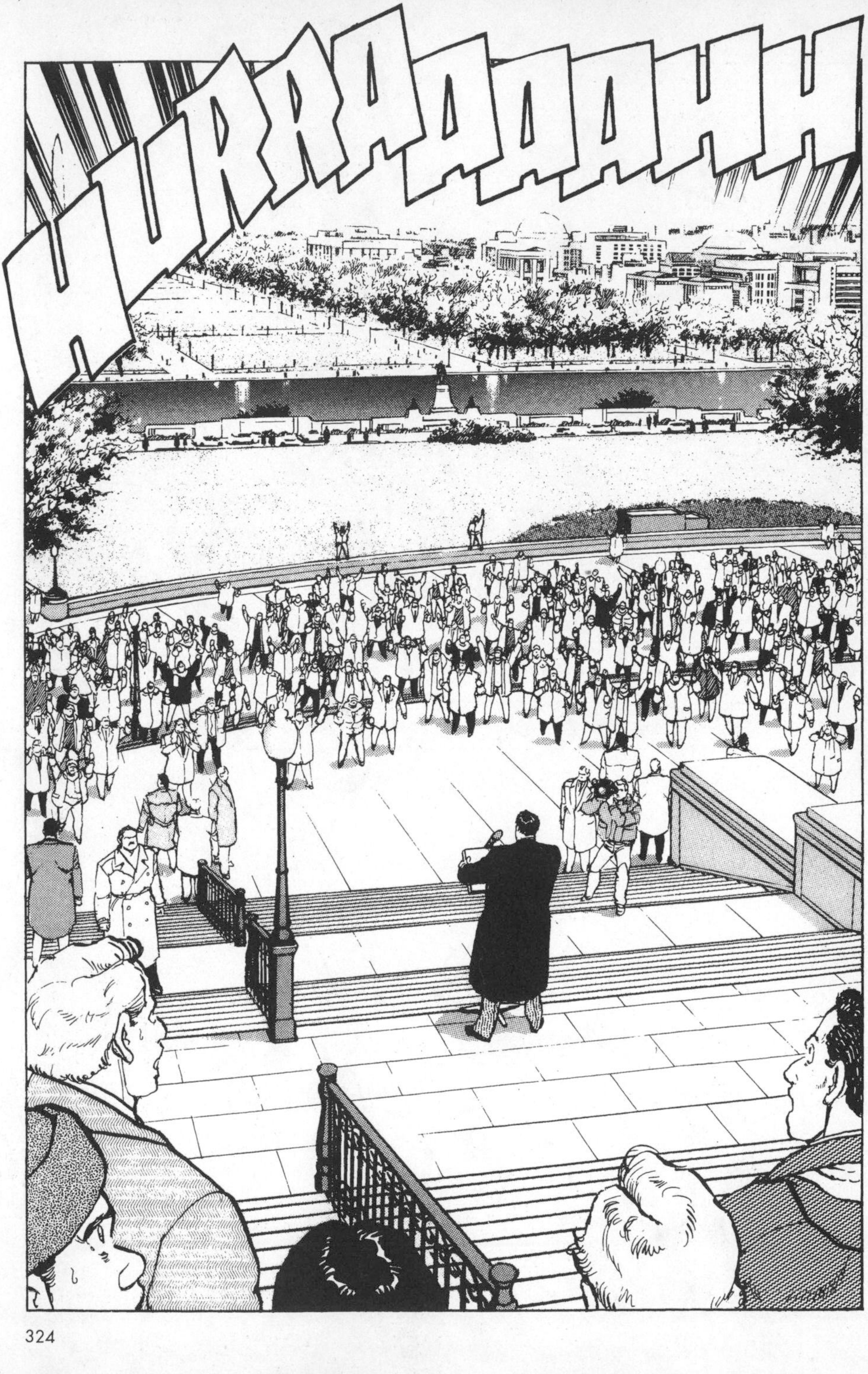
HURRAAAAHH

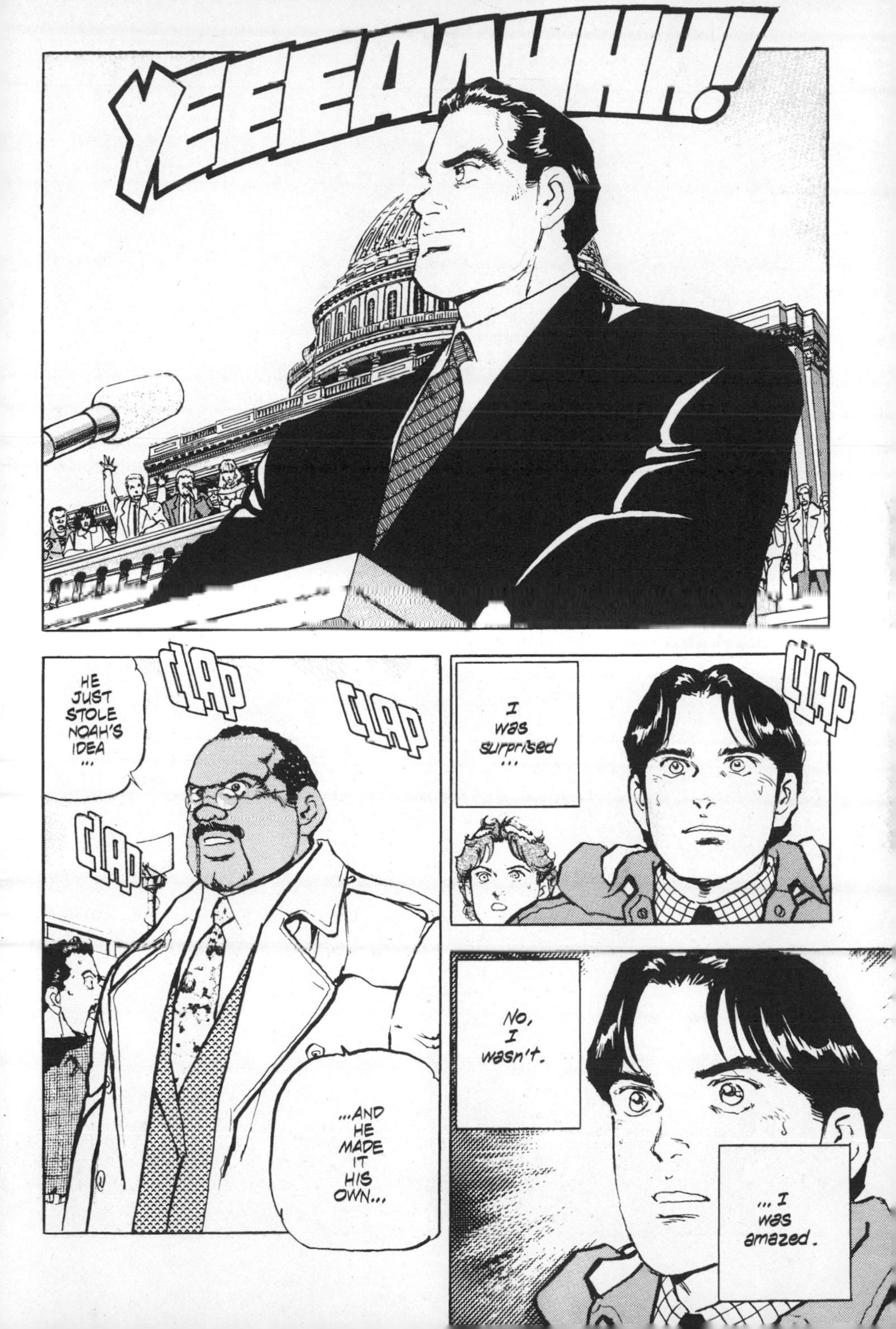
YEEEAHHH!
HE JUST STOLE NOAH'S IDEA ...
CLAP
CLAP
CLAP
...AND HE MADE IT HIS OWN...
I was surprised ...
CLAP
No, I wasn't.
... I was amazed.

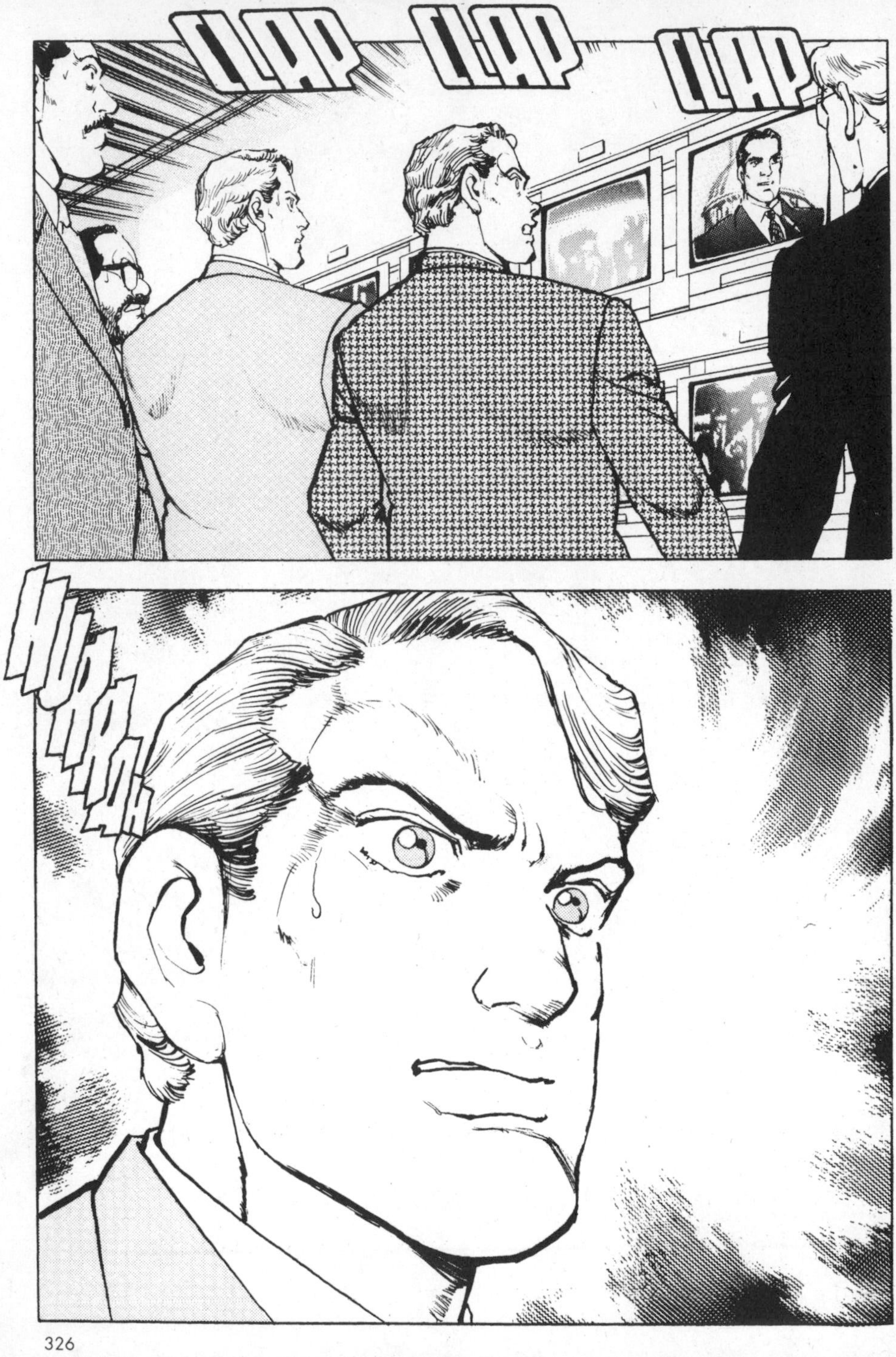
CLAP CLAP CLAP
HURRAH

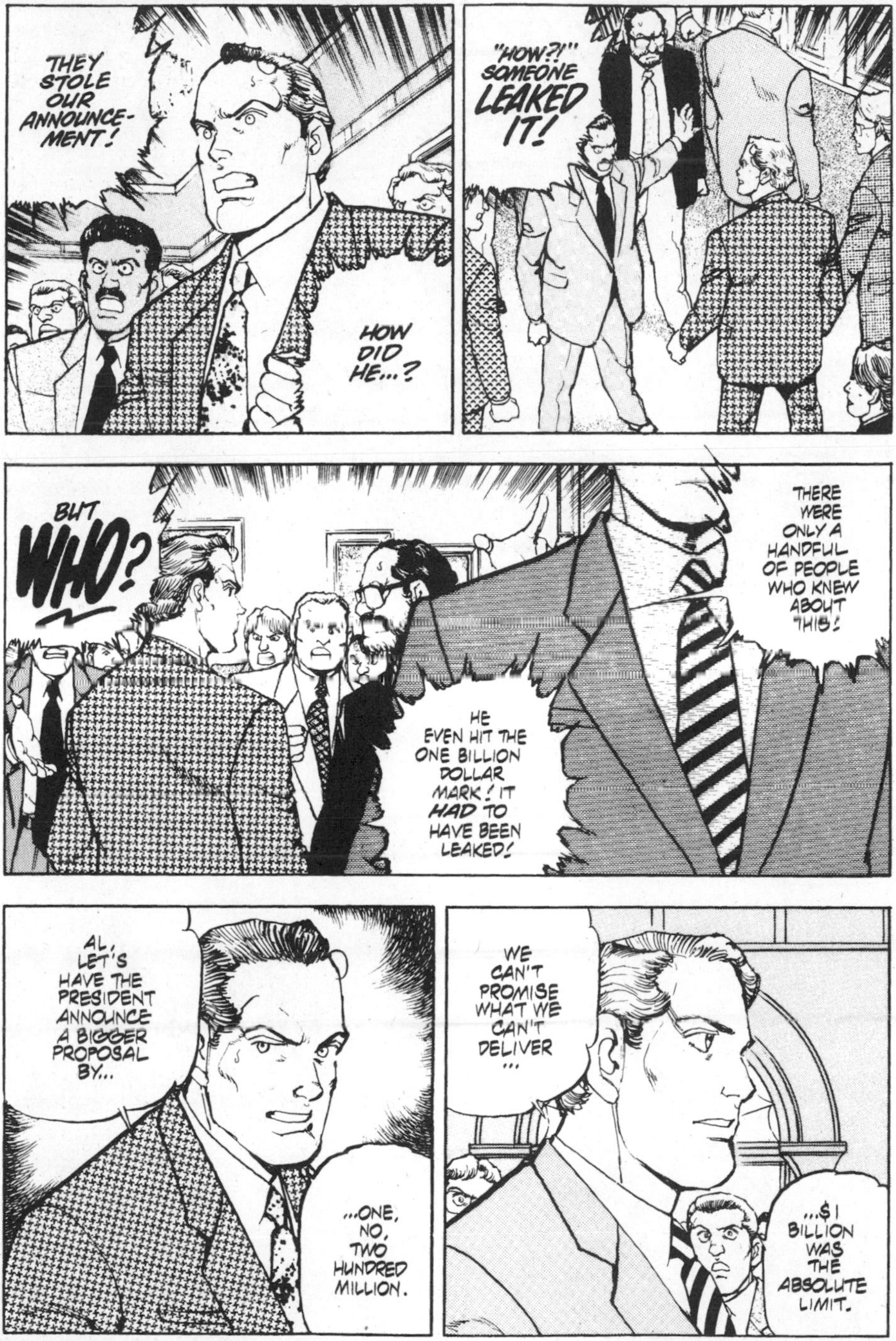
THEY STOLE OUR ANNOUNCE-MENT!
HOW DID HE...?
"HOW?!" SOMEONE LEAKED IT!
BUT WHO?
THERE WERE ONLY A HANDFUL OF PEOPLE WHO KNEW ABOUT THIS!
HE EVEN HIT THE ONE BILLION DOLLAR MARK! IT HAD TO HAVE BEEN LEAKED!
AL, LET'S HAVE THE PRESIDENT ANNOUNCE A BIGGER PROPOSAL BY...
...ONE, NO, TWO HUNDRED MILLION.
WE CAN'T PROMISE WHAT WE CAN'T DELIVER ...
...$1 BILLION WAS THE ABSOLUTE LIMIT.

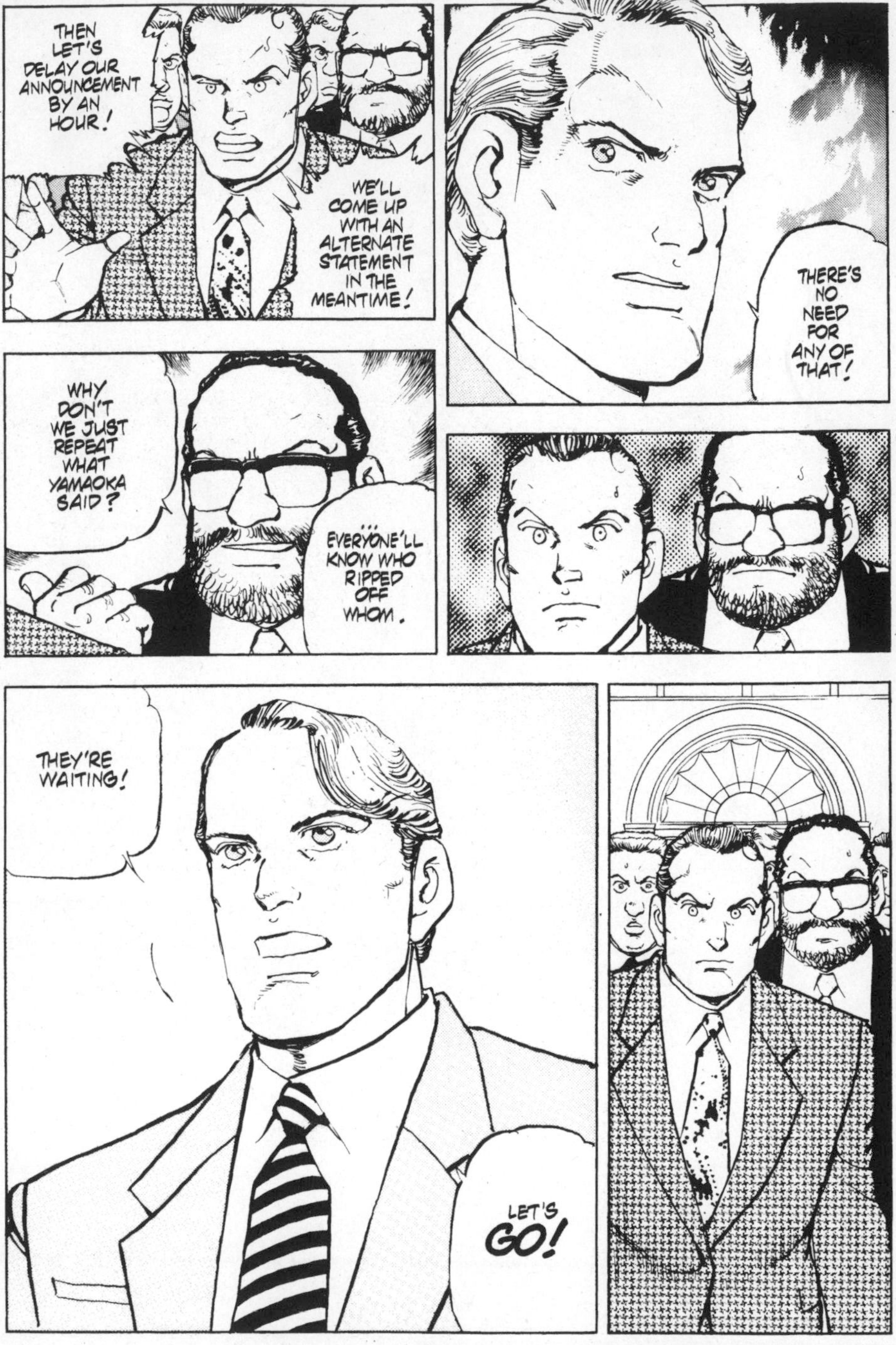
THEN LET'S DELAY OUR ANNOUNCEMENT BY AN HOUR!
WE'LL COME UP WITH AN ALTERNATE STATEMENT IN THE MEANTIME!
THERE'S NO NEED FOR ANY OF THAT!
WHY DON'T WE JUST REPEAT WHAT YAMAOKA SAID?
...EVERYONE'LL KNOW WHO RIPPED OFF WHOM.
THEY'RE WAITING!
LET'S GO!

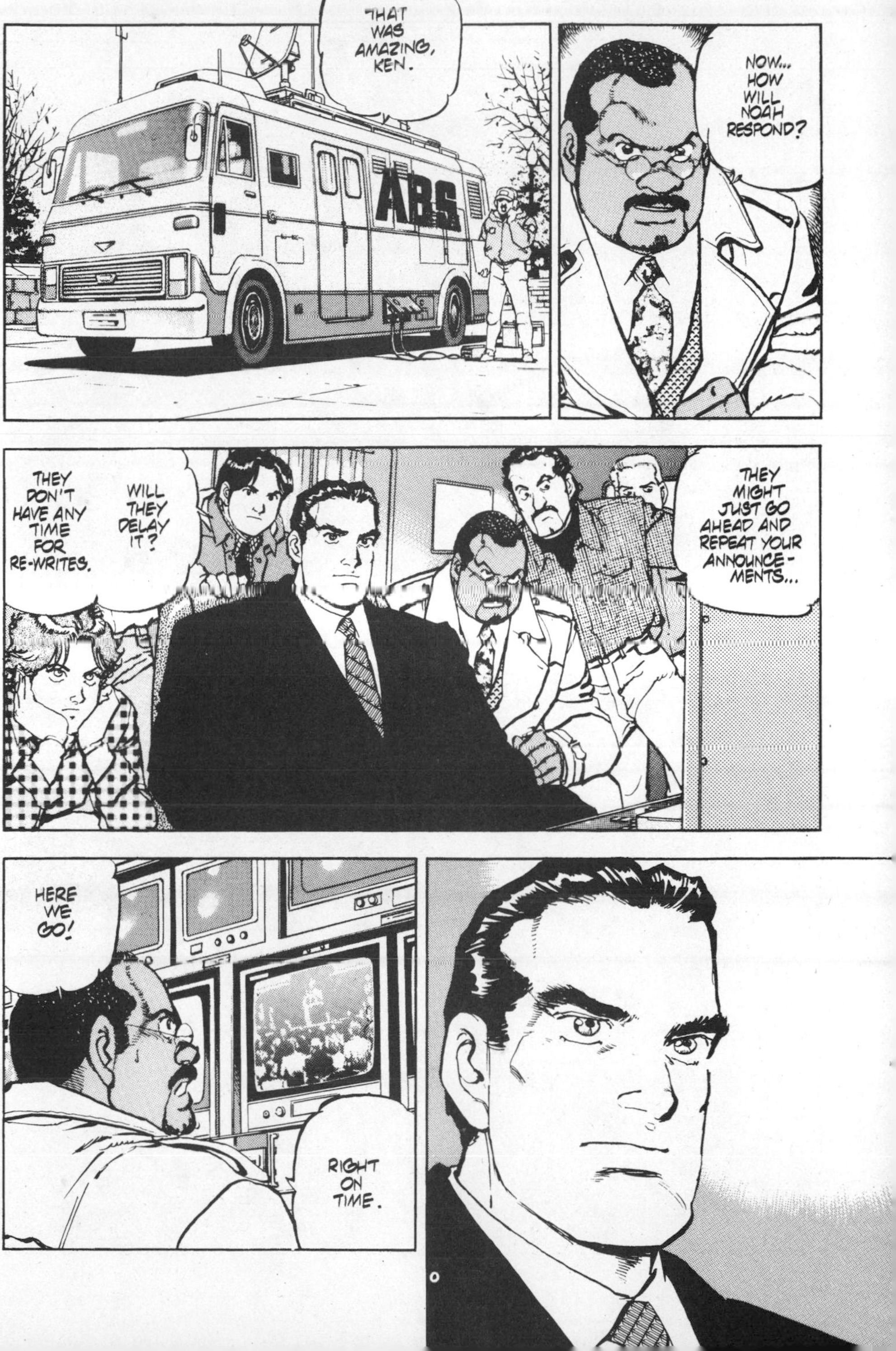
THAT WAS AMAZING, KEN.
NOW... HOW WILL NOAH RESPOND?
THEY DON'T HAVE ANY TIME FOR RE-WRITES.
WILL THEY DELAY IT?
THEY MIGHT JUST GO AHEAD AND REPEAT YOUR ANNOUNCE-MENTS...
HERE WE GO!
RIGHT ON TIME.

WHITE HOU
LOOK AT THAT GRIN!

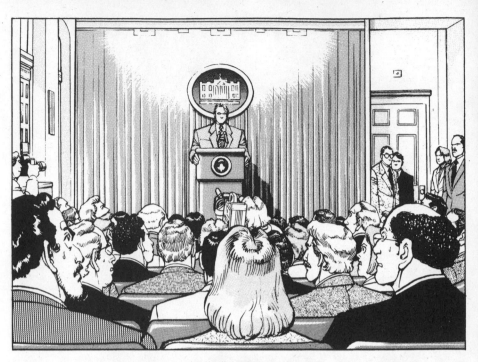

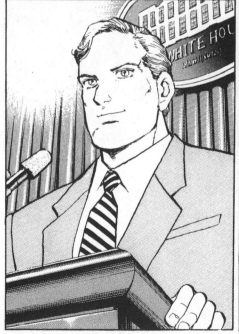

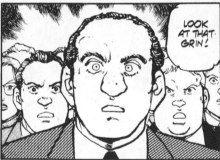

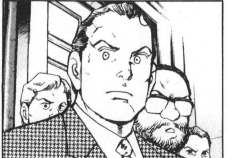

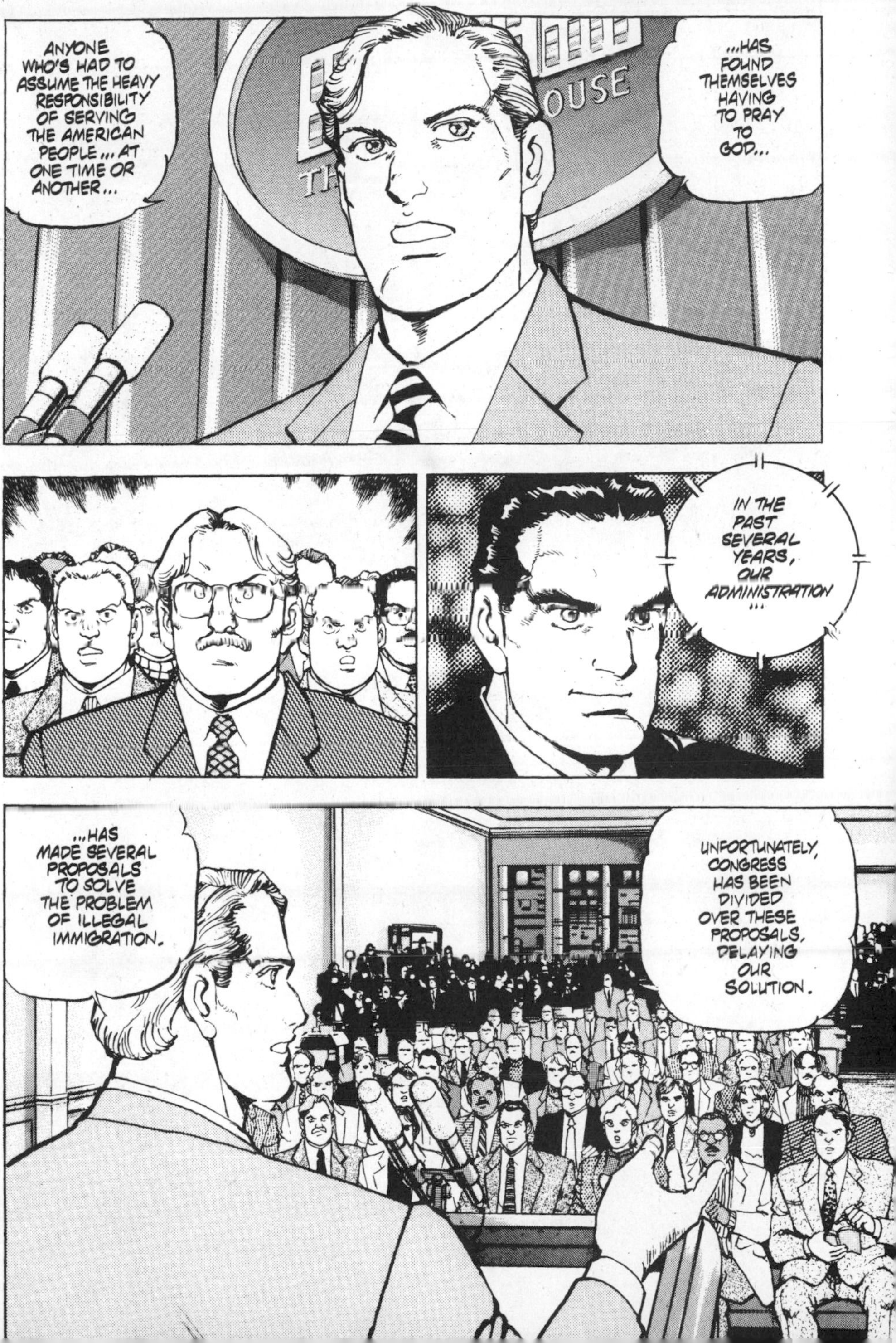
ANYONE WHO'S HAD TO ASSUME THE HEAVY RESPONSIBILITY OF SERVING THE AMERICAN PEOPLE ... AT ONE TIME OR ANOTHER ...
...HAS FOUND THEMSELVES HAVING TO PRAY TO GOD...
IN THE PAST SEVERAL YEARS, OUR ADMINISTRATION ...
...HAS MADE SEVERAL PROPOSALS TO SOLVE THE PROBLEM OF ILLEGAL IMMIGRATION.
UNFORTUNATELY, CONGRESS HAS BEEN DIVIDED OVER THESE PROPOSALS, DELAYING OUR SOLUTION.

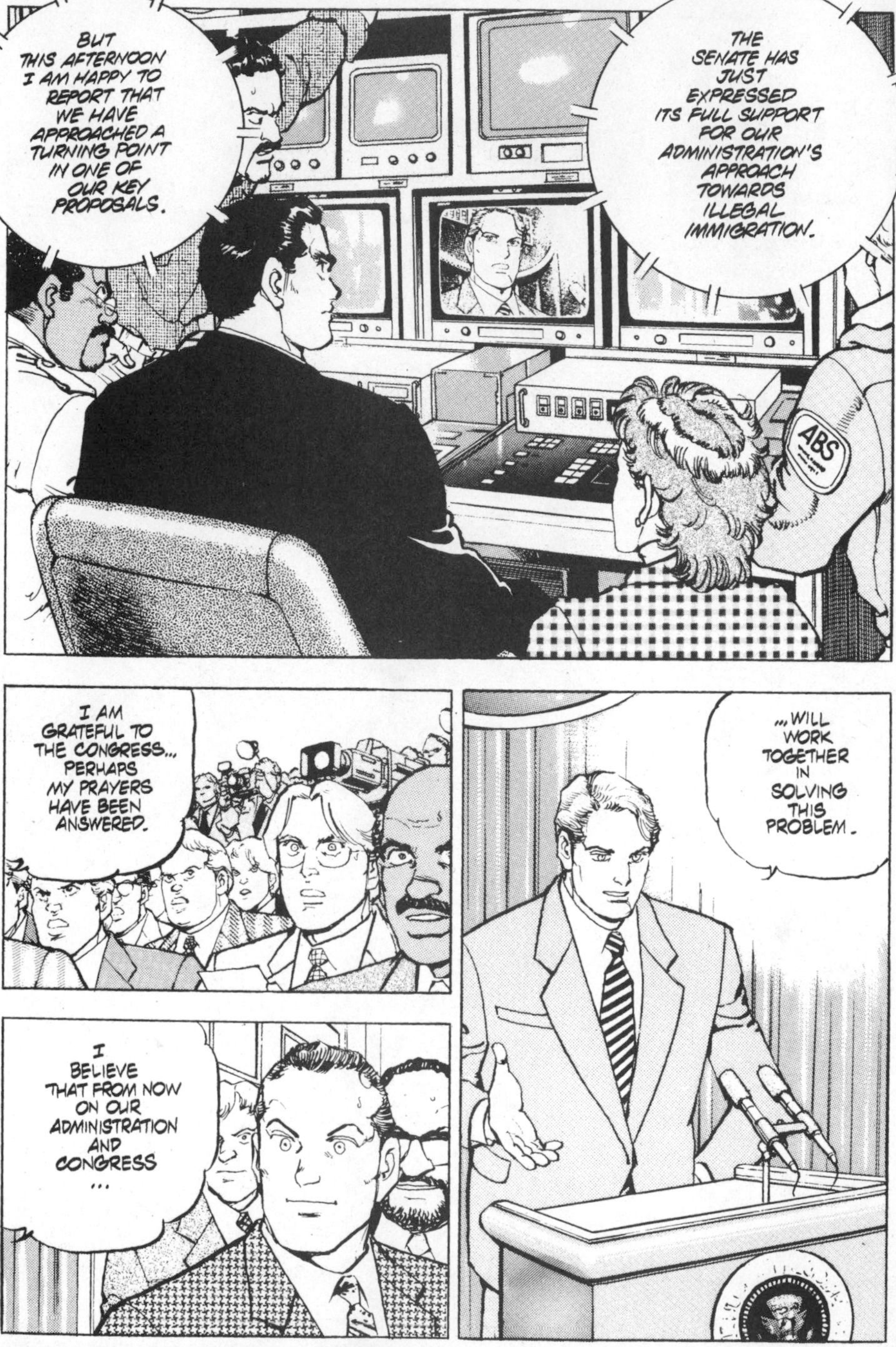
BUT THIS AFTERNOON I AM HAPPY TO REPORT THAT WE HAVE APPROACHED A TURNING POINT IN ONE OF OUR KEY PROPOSALS.
THE SENATE HAS JUST EXPRESSED ITS FULL SUPPORT FOR OUR ADMINISTRATION'S APPROACH TOWARDS ILLEGAL IMMIGRATION.
I AM GRATEFUL TO THE CONGRESS... PERHAPS MY PRAYERS HAVE BEEN ANSWERED.
I BELIEVE THAT FROM NOW ON OUR ADMINISTRATION AND CONGRESS ...
...WILL WORK TOGETHER IN SOLVING THIS PROBLEM.
ABS

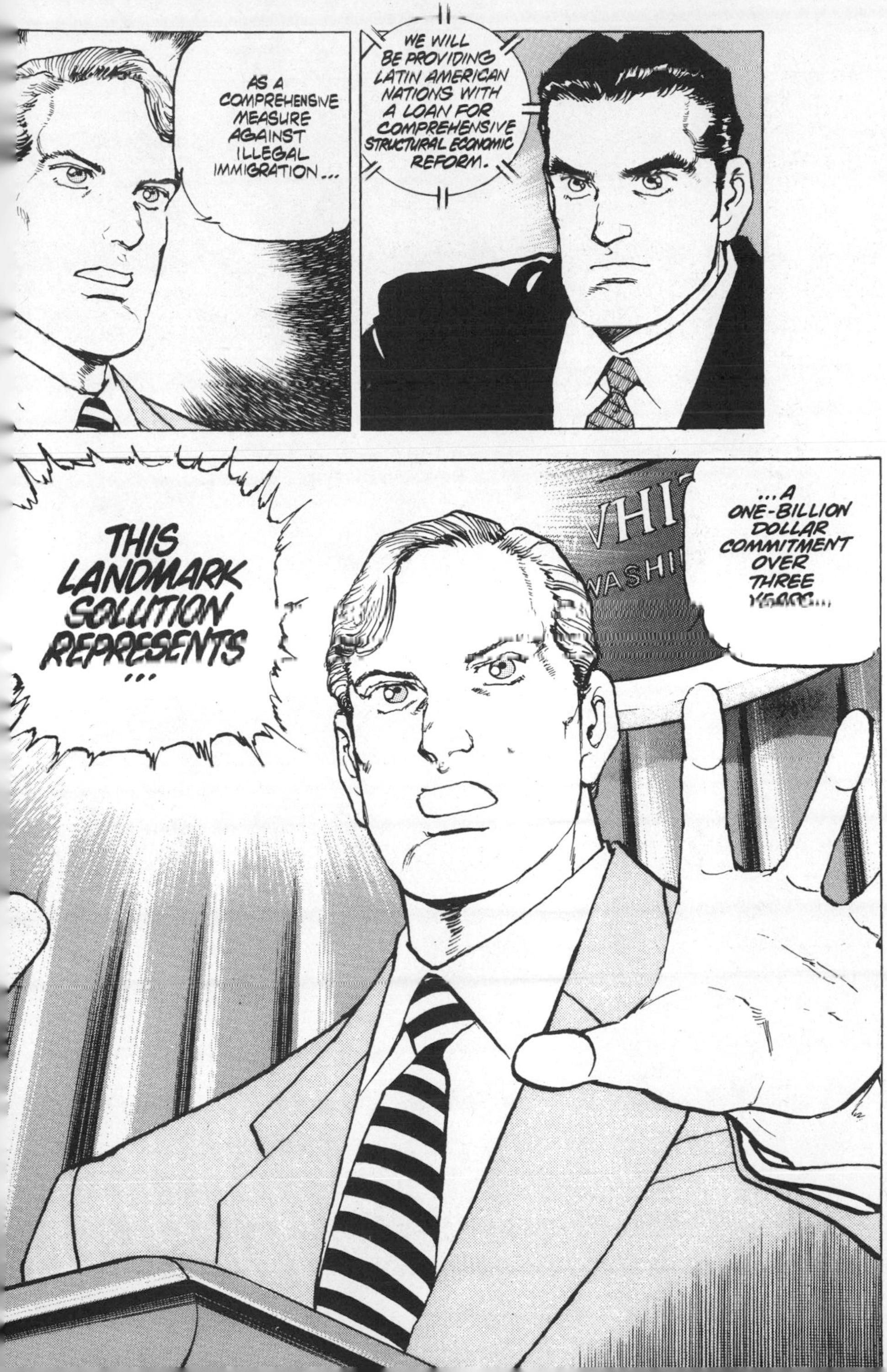
AS A COMPREHENSIVE MEASURE AGAINST ILLEGAL IMMIGRATION...
WE WILL BE PROVIDING LATIN AMERICAN NATIONS WITH A LOAN FOR COMPREHENSIVE STRUCTURAL ECONOMIC REFORM.
THIS LANDMARK SOLUTION REPRESENTS...
...A ONE-BILLION DOLLAR COMMITMENT OVER THREE YEARS...

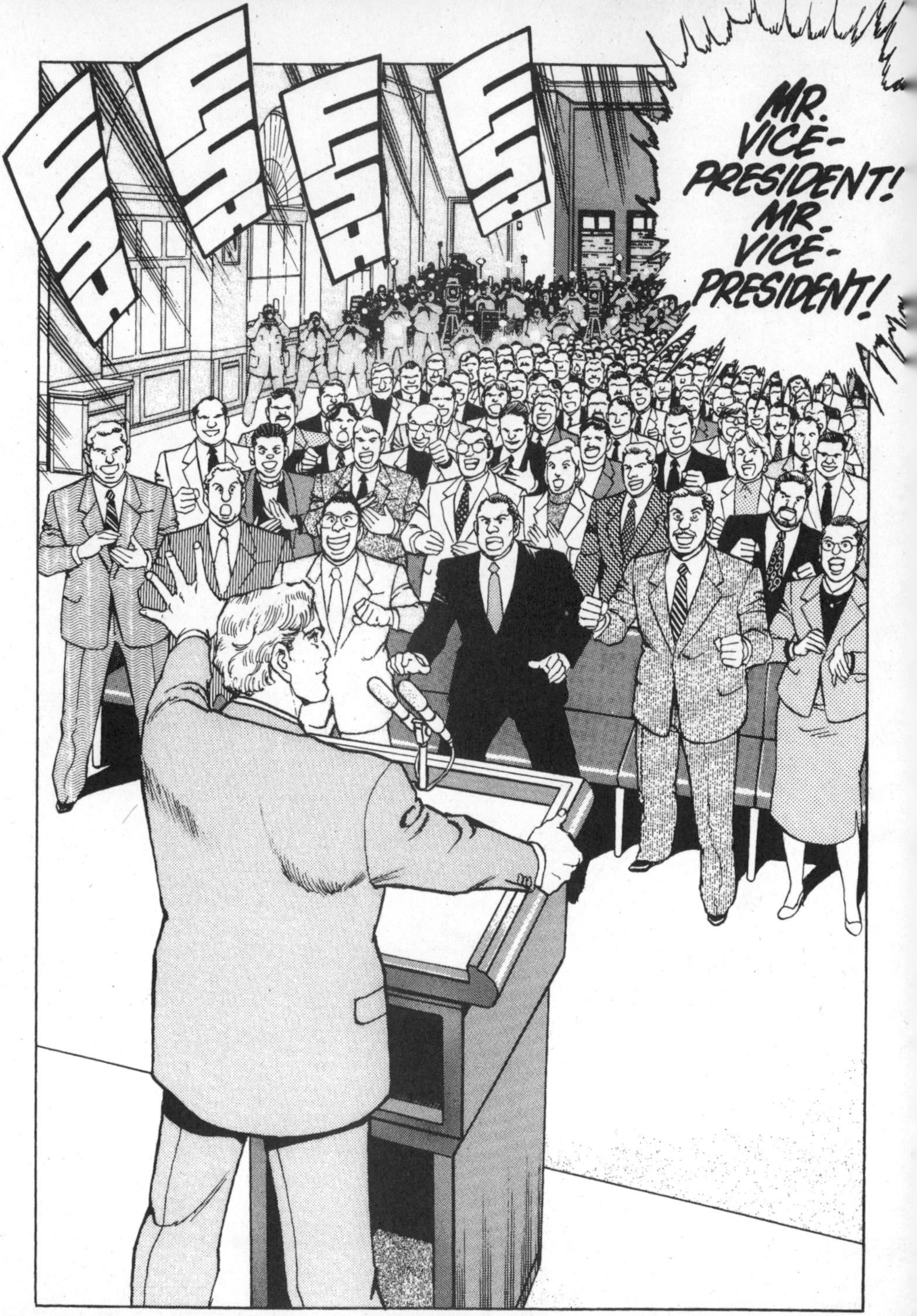
MR. VICE-PRESIDENT! MR. VICE-PRESIDENT!

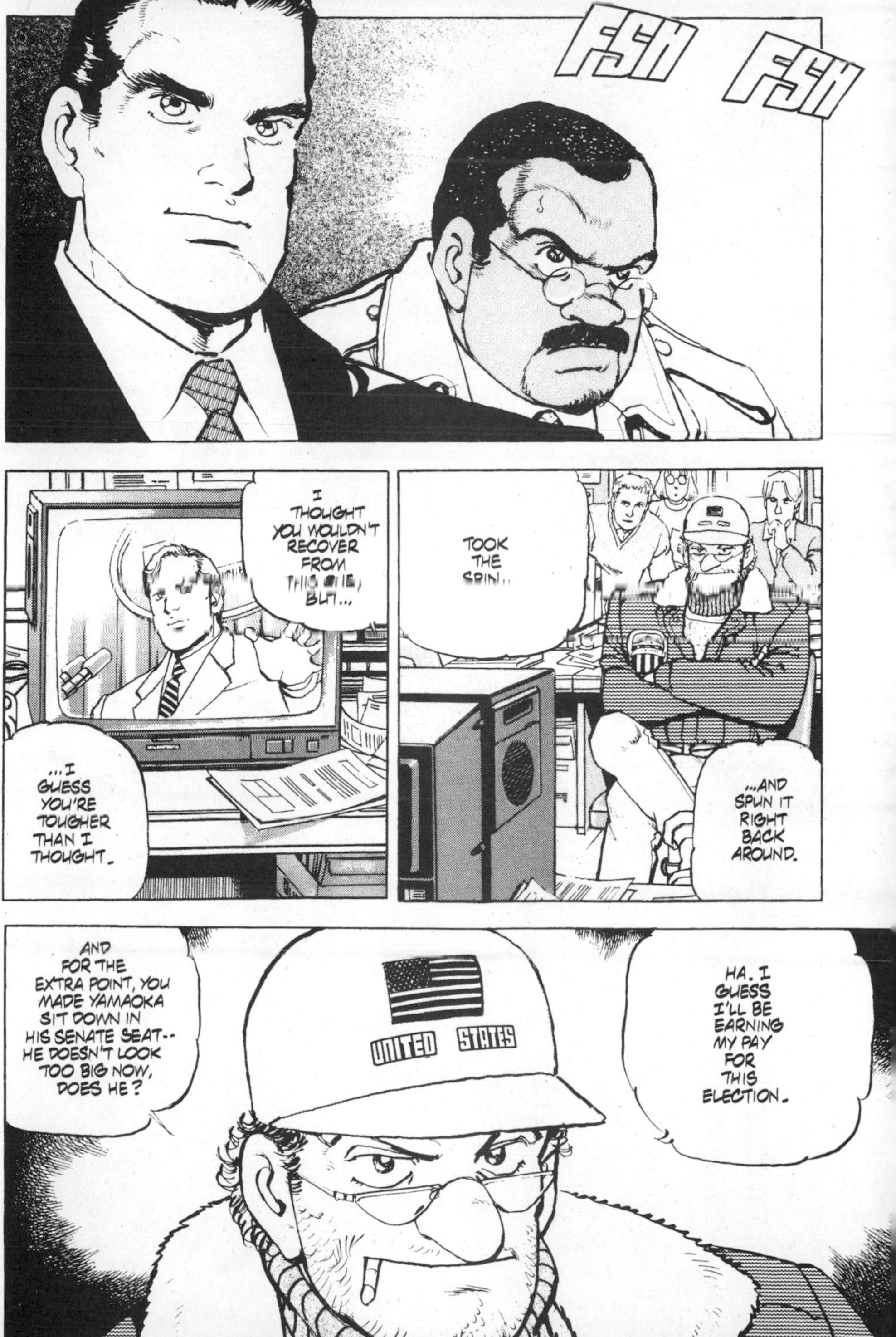
FSH FSH
I THOUGHT YOU WOULDN'T RECOVER FROM BUT...
...I GUESS YOU'RE TOUGHER THAN I THOUGHT.
TOOK THE SPIN...
...AND SPUN IT RIGHT BACK AROUND.
AND FOR THE EXTRA POINT, YOU MADE YAMAOKA SIT DOWN IN HIS SENATE SEAT-- HE DOESN'T LOOK TOO BIG NOW, DOES HE?
UNITED STATES
HA. I GUESS I'LL BE EARNING MY PAY FOR THIS ELECTION.

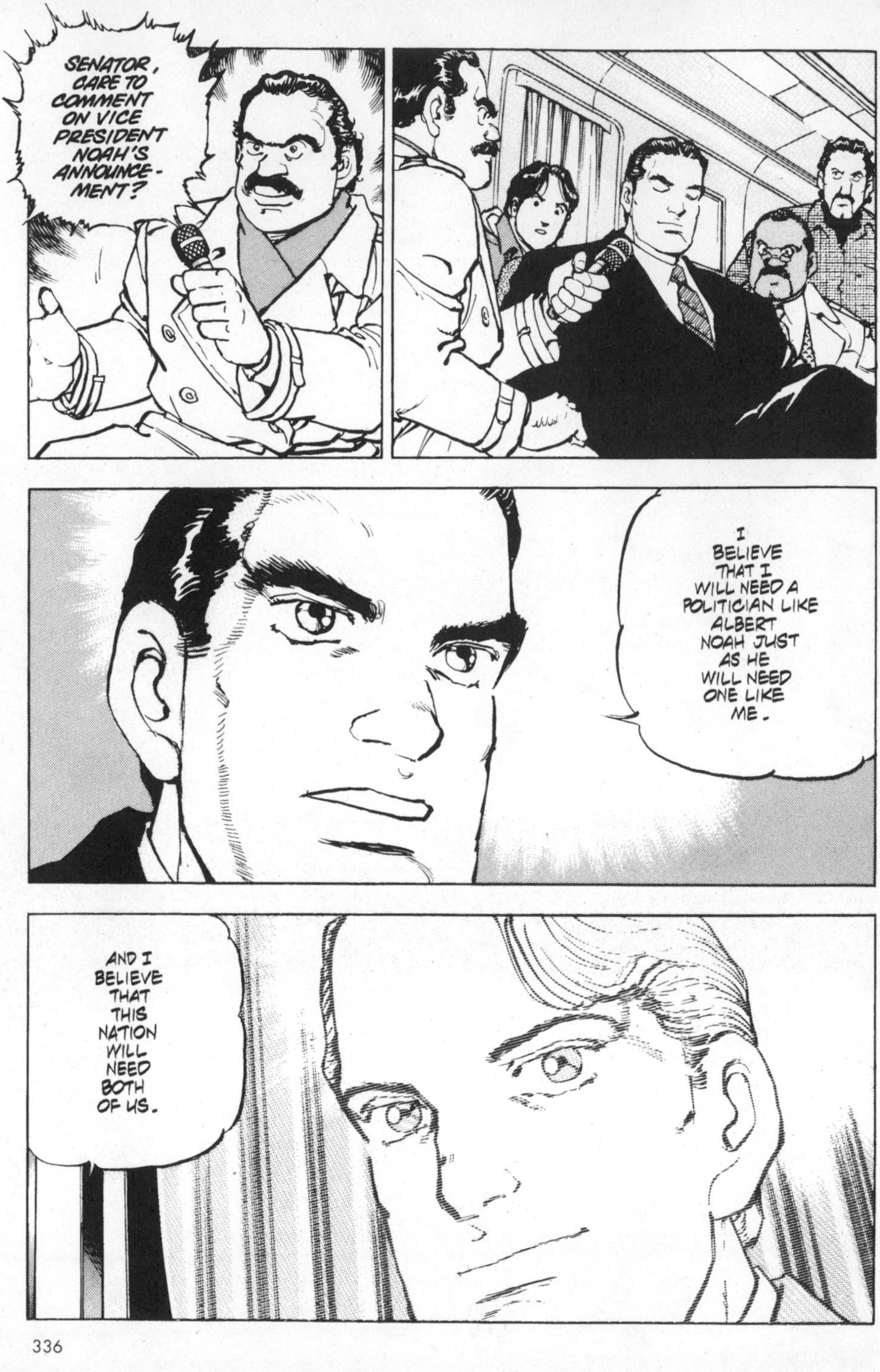
SENATOR, CARE TO COMMENT ON VICE PRESIDENT NOAH'S ANNOUNCEMENT?
I BELIEVE THAT I WILL NEED A POLITICIAN LIKE ALBERT NOAH JUST AS HE WILL NEED ONE LIKE ME.
AND I BELIEVE THAT THIS NATION WILL NEED BOTH OF US.

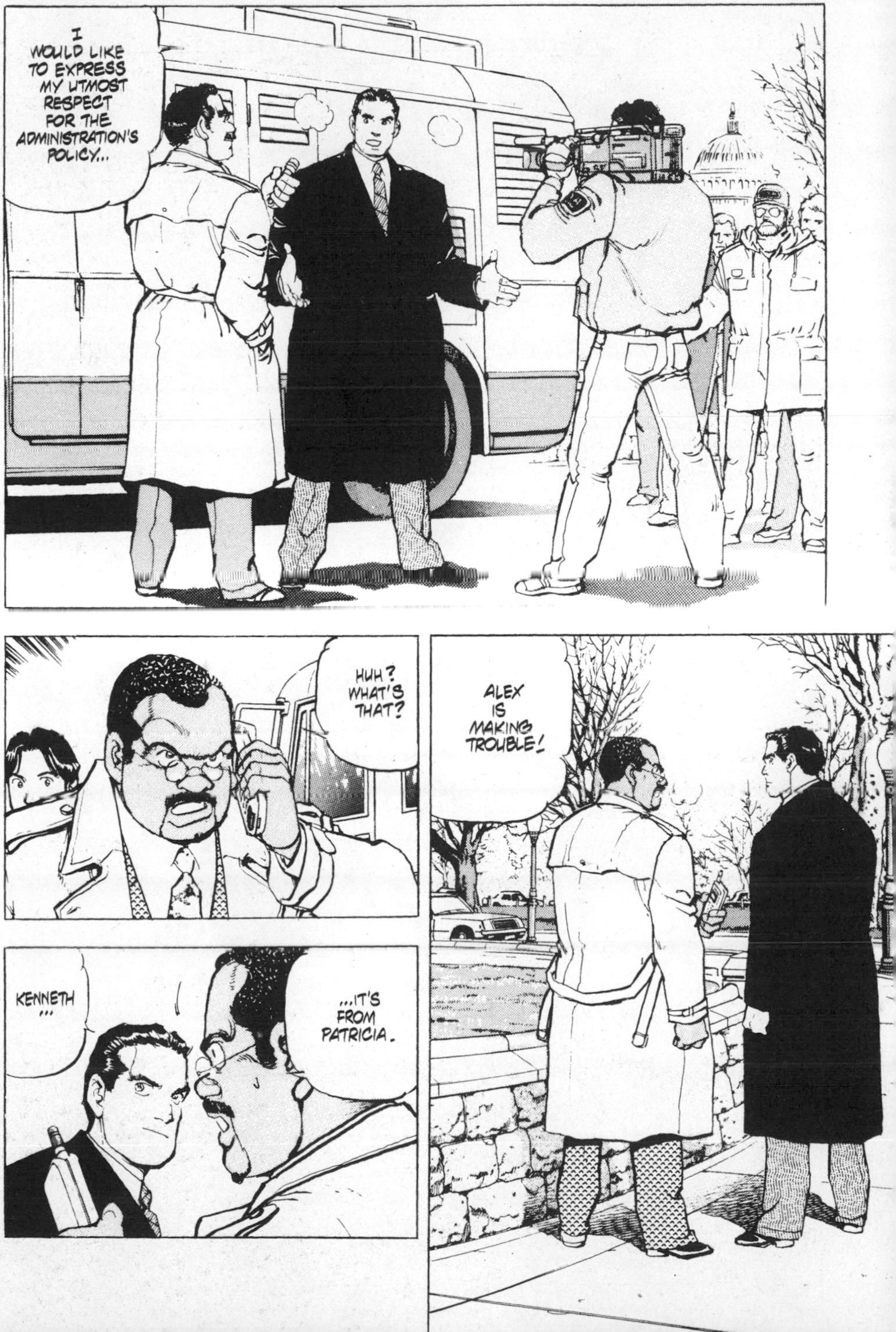
I WOULD LIKE TO EXPRESS MY UTMOST RESPECT FOR THE ADMINISTRATION'S POLICY...
HUH? WHAT'S THAT?
KENNETH ...
...IT'S FROM PATRICIA.
ALEX IS MAKING TROUBLE!

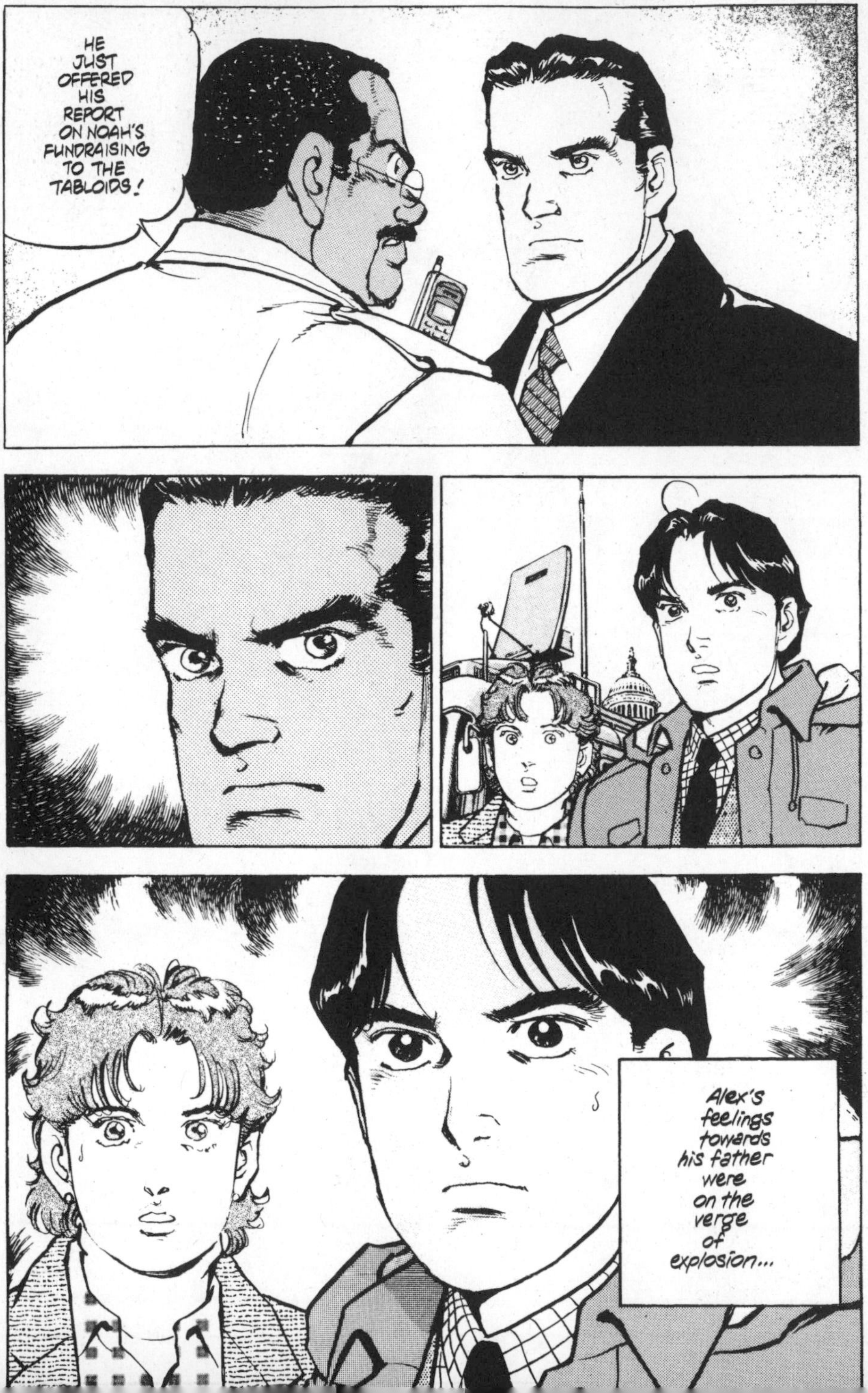
HE JUST OFFERED HIS REPORT ON NOAH'S FUNDRAISING TO THE TABLOIDS!
Alex's feelings towards his father were on the verge of explosion...

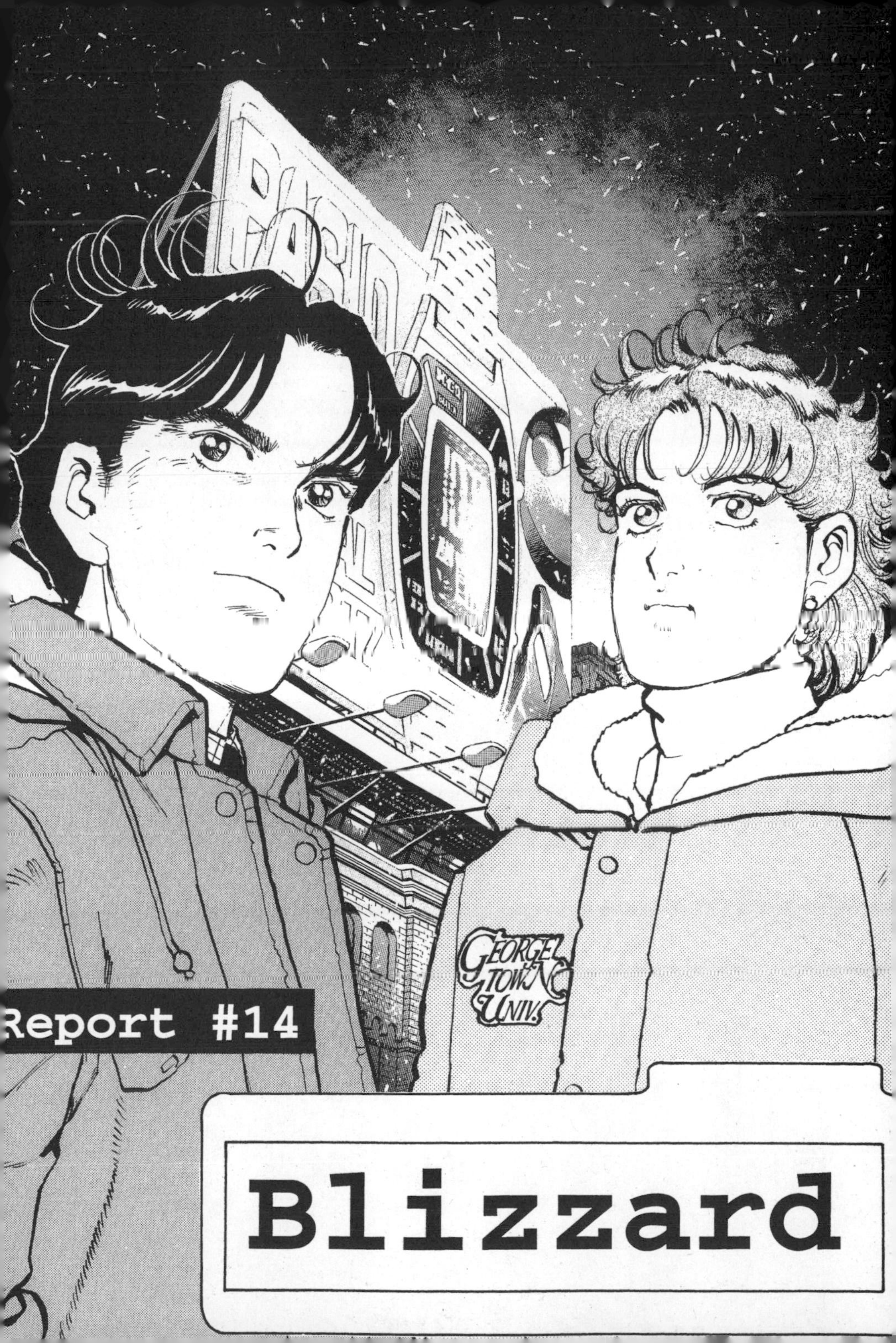
GEORGETOWN UNIV.
Report #14
Blizzard

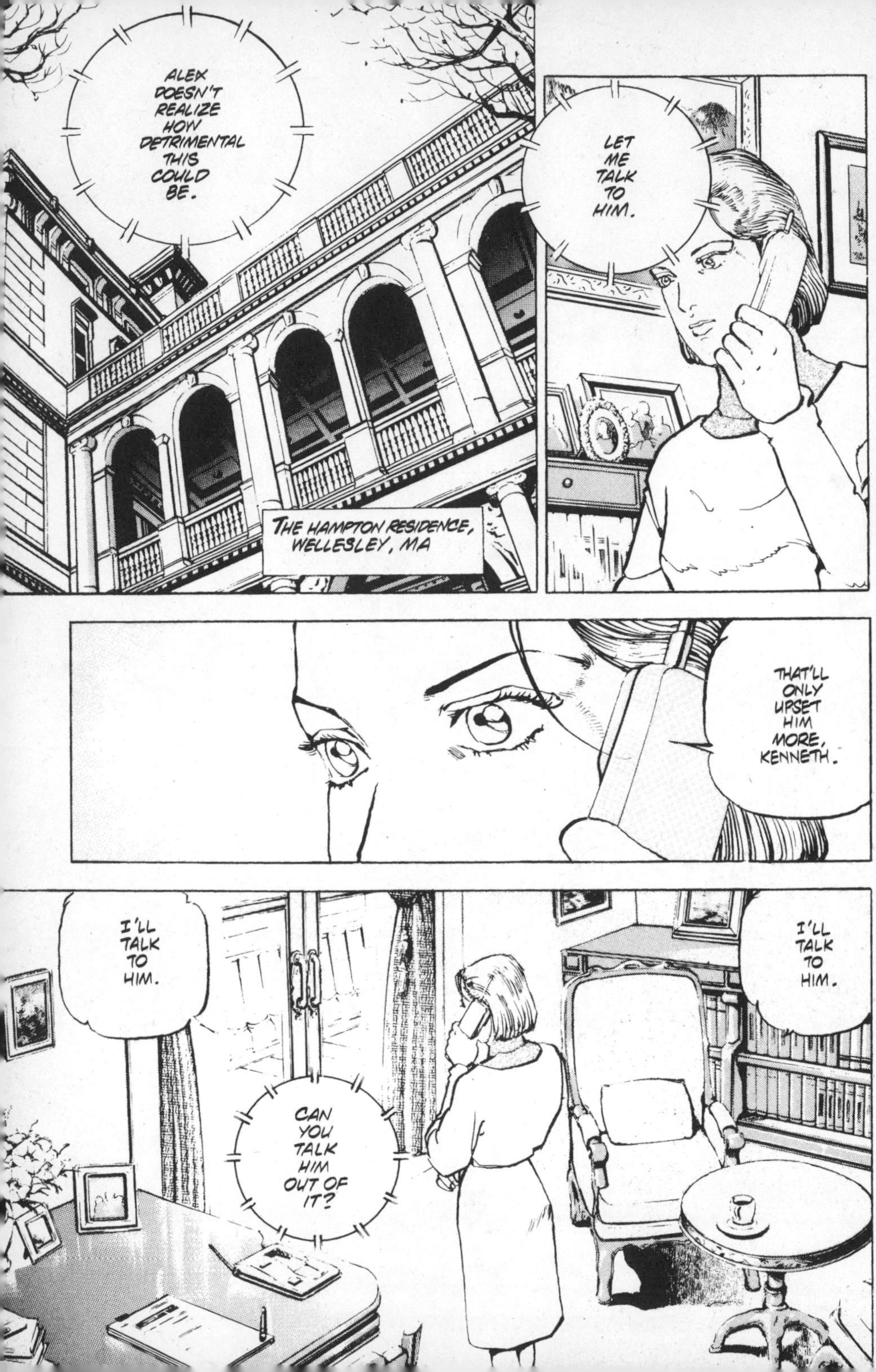
ALEX DOESN'T REALIZE HOW DETRIMENTAL THIS COULD BE.
THE HAMPTON RESIDENCE, WELLESLEY, MA
LET ME TALK TO HIM.
THAT'LL ONLY UPSET HIM MORE, KENNETH.
I'LL TALK TO HIM.
CAN YOU TALK HIM OUT OF IT?
I'LL TALK TO HIM.

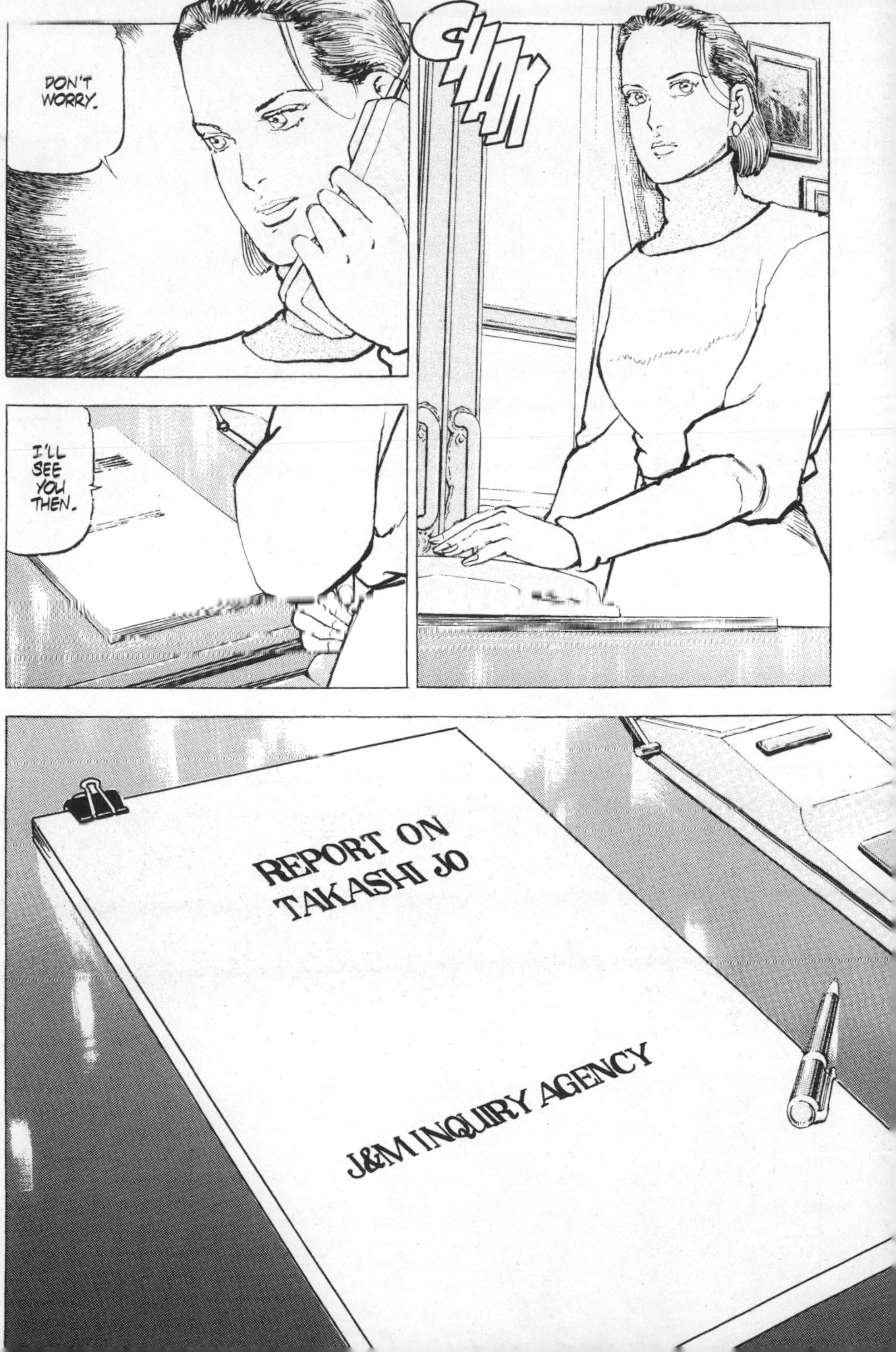
DON'T WORRY.
CHAN
I'LL SEE YOU THEN.
REPORT ON TAKASHI JO
J&M INQUIRY AGENCY

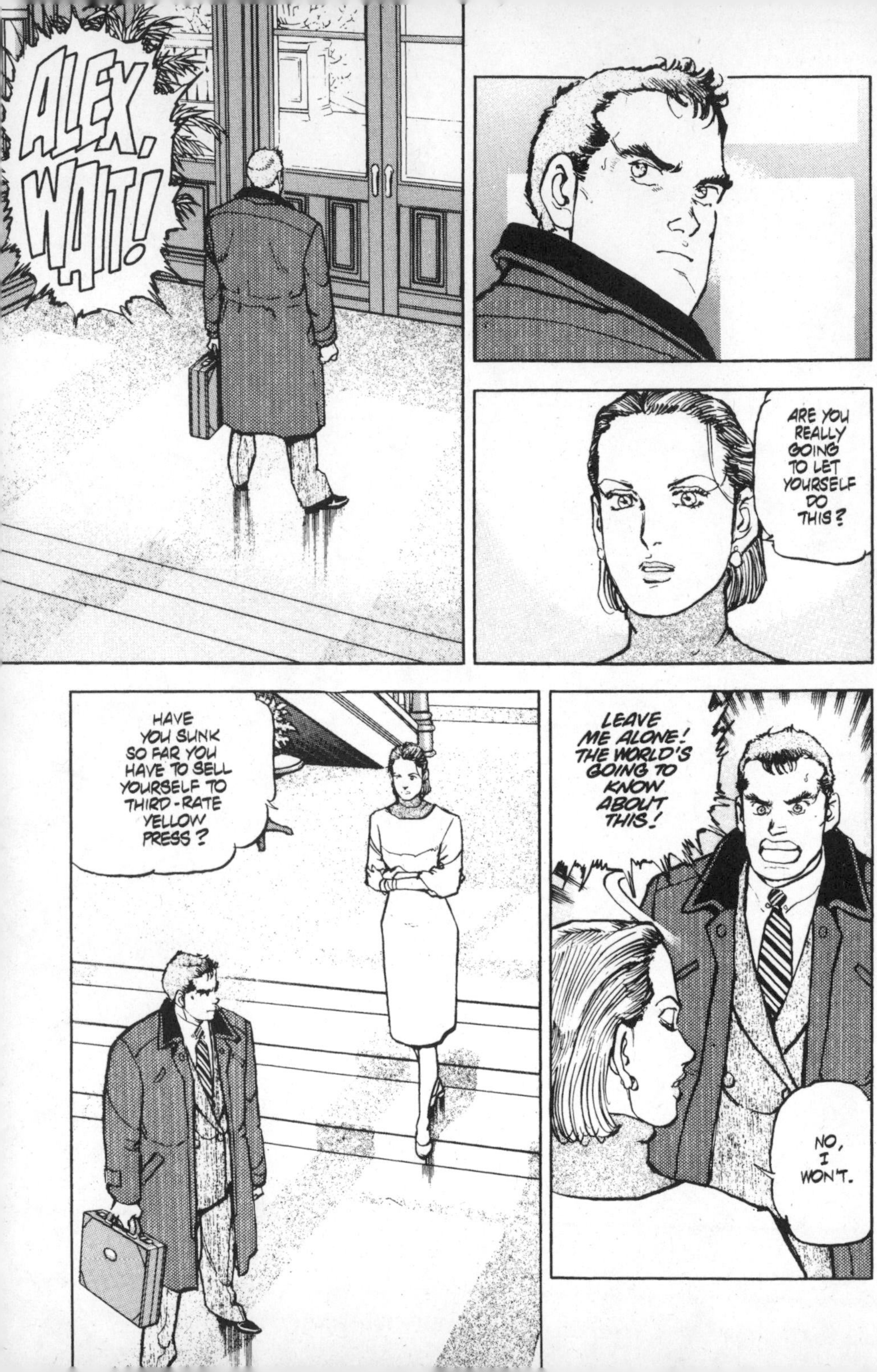
ALEX, WAIT!
ARE YOU REALLY GOING TO LET YOURSELF DO THIS?
HAVE YOU SUNK SO FAR YOU HAVE TO SELL YOURSELF TO THIRD-RATE YELLOW PRESS?
LEAVE ME ALONE! THE WORLD'S GOING TO KNOW ABOUT THIS!
NO, I WON'T.

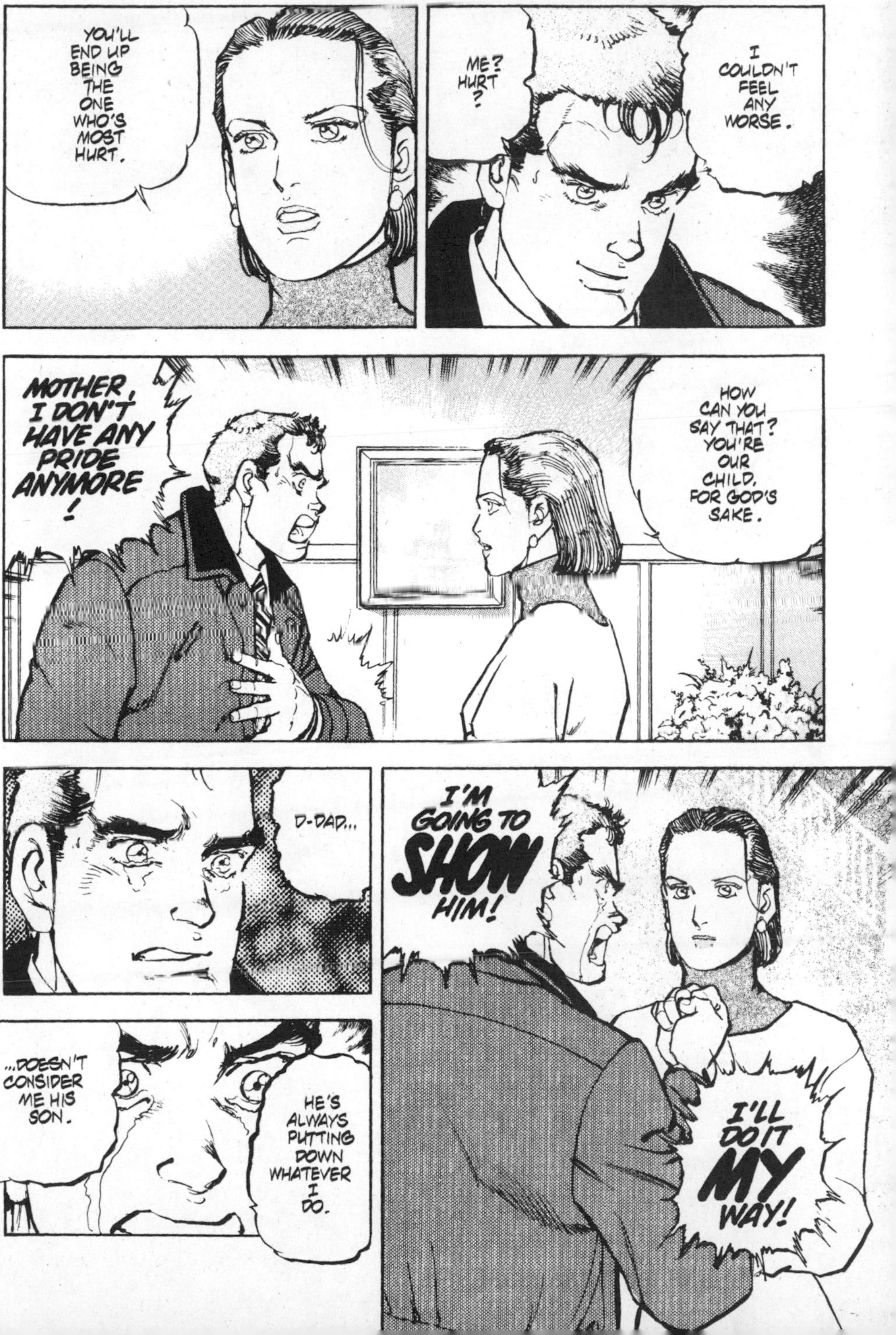
YOU'LL END UP BEING THE ONE WHO'S MOST HURT.
ME? HURT?
I COULDN'T FEEL ANY WORSE.
MOTHER, I DON'T HAVE ANY PRIDE ANYMORE!
HOW CAN YOU SAY THAT? YOU'RE OUR CHILD, FOR GOD'S SAKE.
D-DAD...
...DOESN'T CONSIDER ME HIS SON.
HE'S ALWAYS PUTTING DOWN WHATEVER I DO.
I'M GOING TO SHOW HIM!
I'LL DO IT MY WAY!

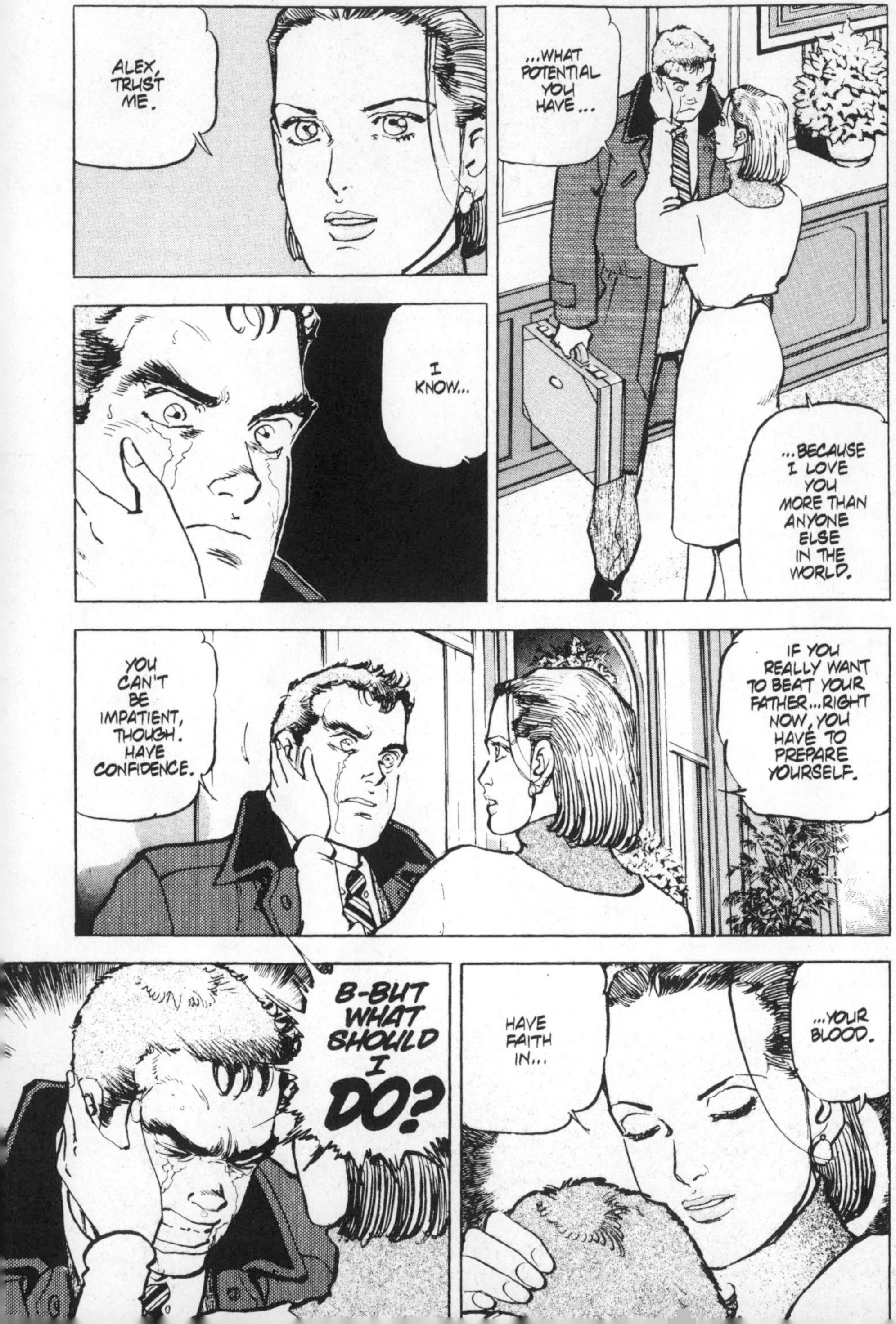

ALEX, TRUST ME.
...WHAT POTENTIAL YOU HAVE...
I KNOW...
...BECAUSE I LOVE YOU MORE THAN ANYONE ELSE IN THE WORLD.
YOU CAN'T BE IMPATIENT, THOUGH. HAVE CONFIDENCE.
IF YOU REALLY WANT TO BEAT YOUR FATHER...RIGHT NOW, YOU HAVE TO PREPARE YOURSELF.
B-BUT WHAT SHOULD I DO?
HAVE FAITH IN...
...YOUR BLOOD.

YOU'RE NOT ONLY THE SON OF KENNETH YAMAOKA. YOU'RE A CHILD OF *MY* FAMILY. YOU'RE A HAMPTON!

YOU'RE...

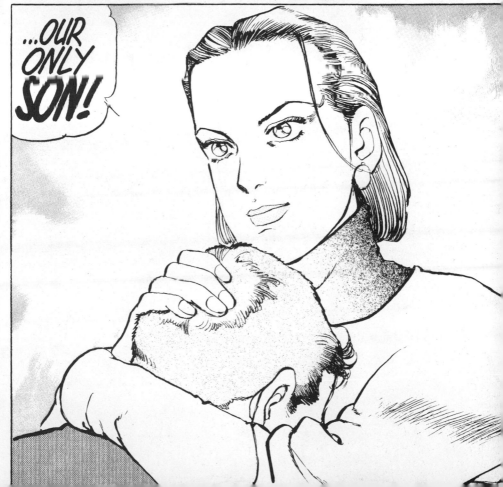

...OUR ONLY SON!

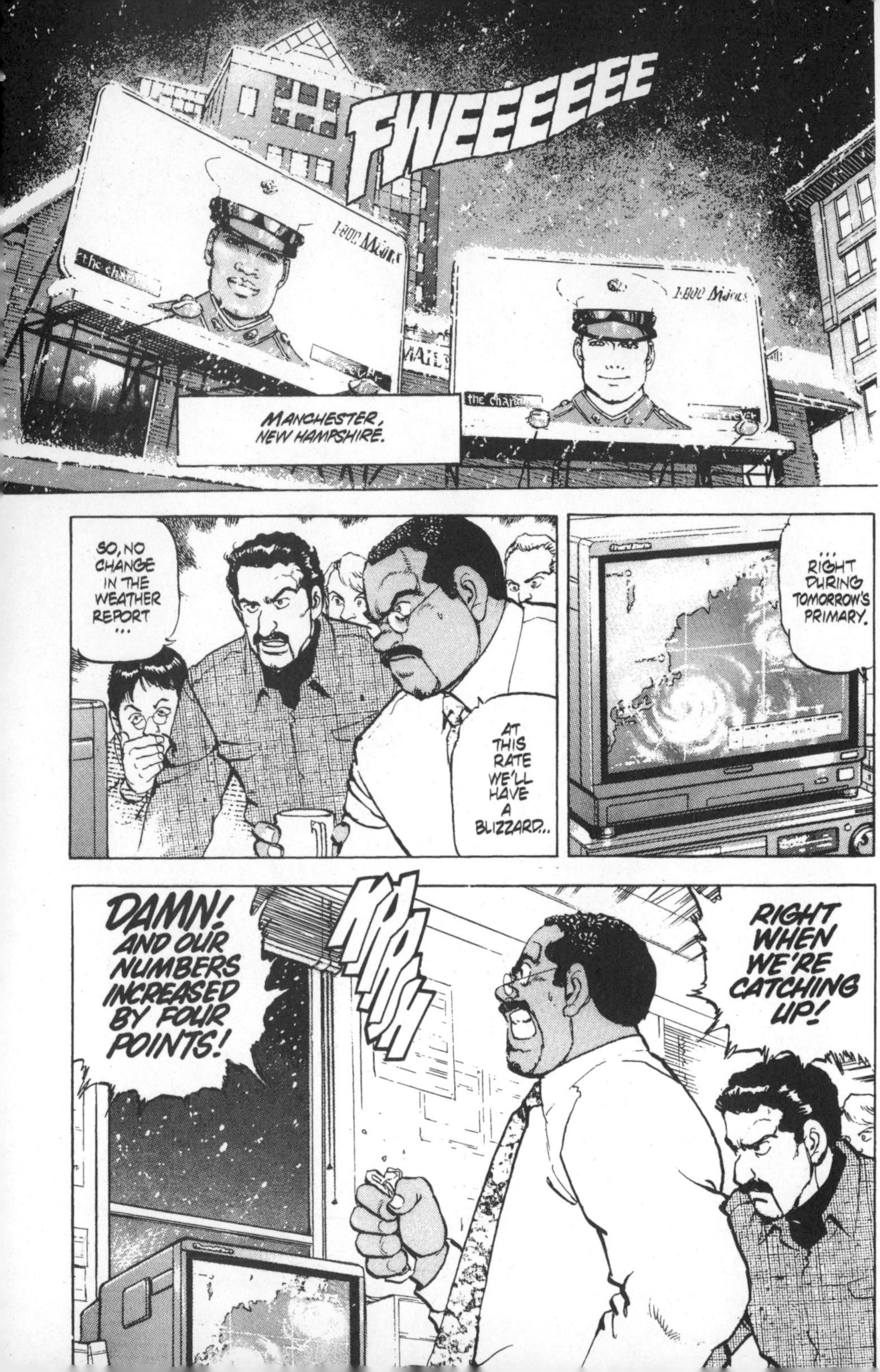
FWEEEEEE
MANCHESTER, NEW HAMPSHIRE.
SO, NO CHANGE IN THE WEATHER REPORT ...
AT THIS RATE WE'LL HAVE A BLIZZARD...
...RIGHT DURING TOMORROW'S PRIMARY.
DAMN! AND OUR NUMBERS INCREASED BY FOUR POINTS!
KRASH
RIGHT WHEN WE'RE CATCHING UP!

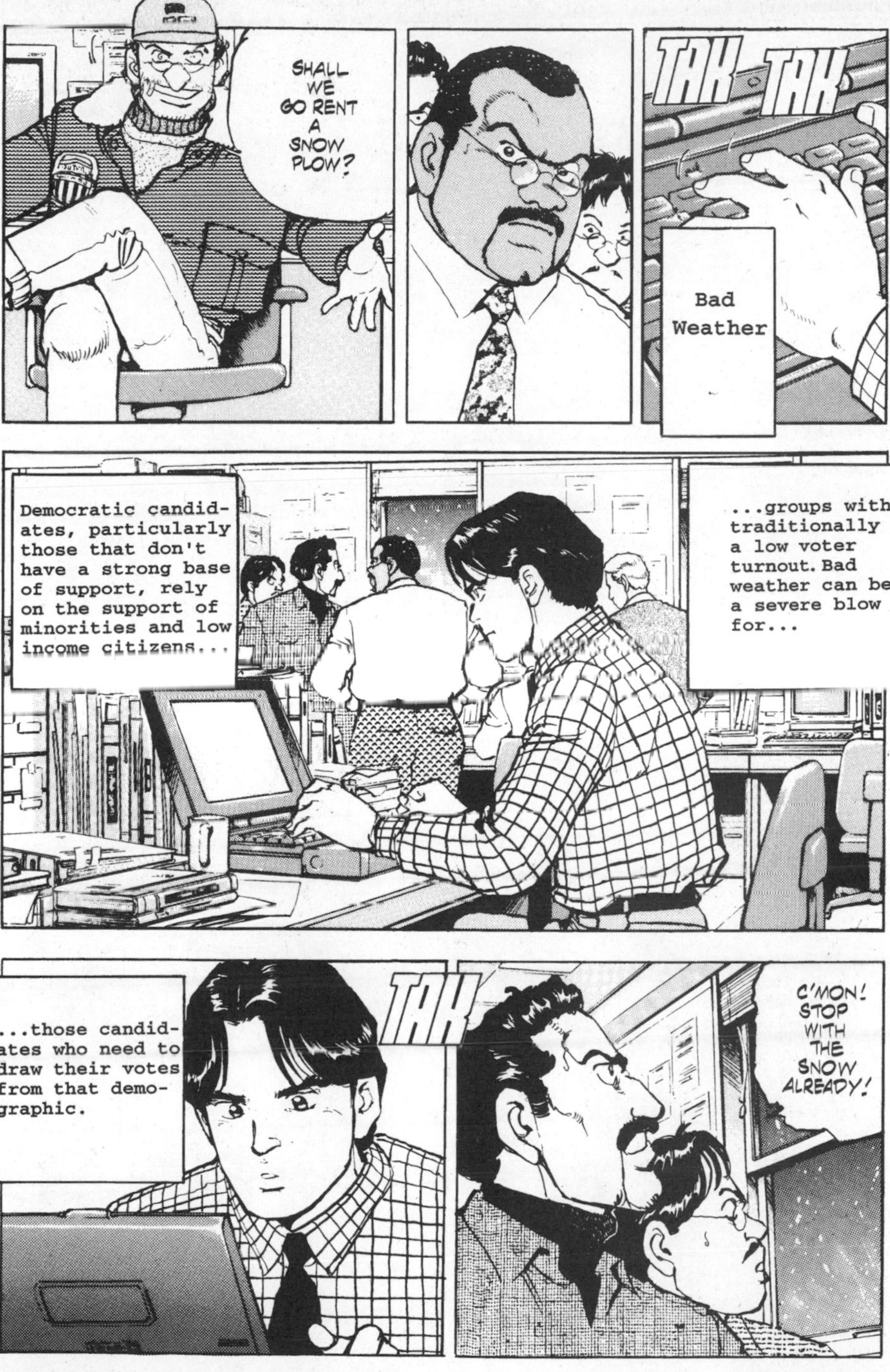
SHALL WE GO RENT A SNOW PLOW?
TAK TAK
Bad Weather
Democratic candidates, particularly those that don't have a strong base of support, rely on the support of minorities and low income citizens...
...groups with traditionally a low voter turnout. Bad weather can be a severe blow for...
...those candidates who need to draw their votes from that demographic.
TAK
C'MON! STOP WITH THE SNOW ALREADY!

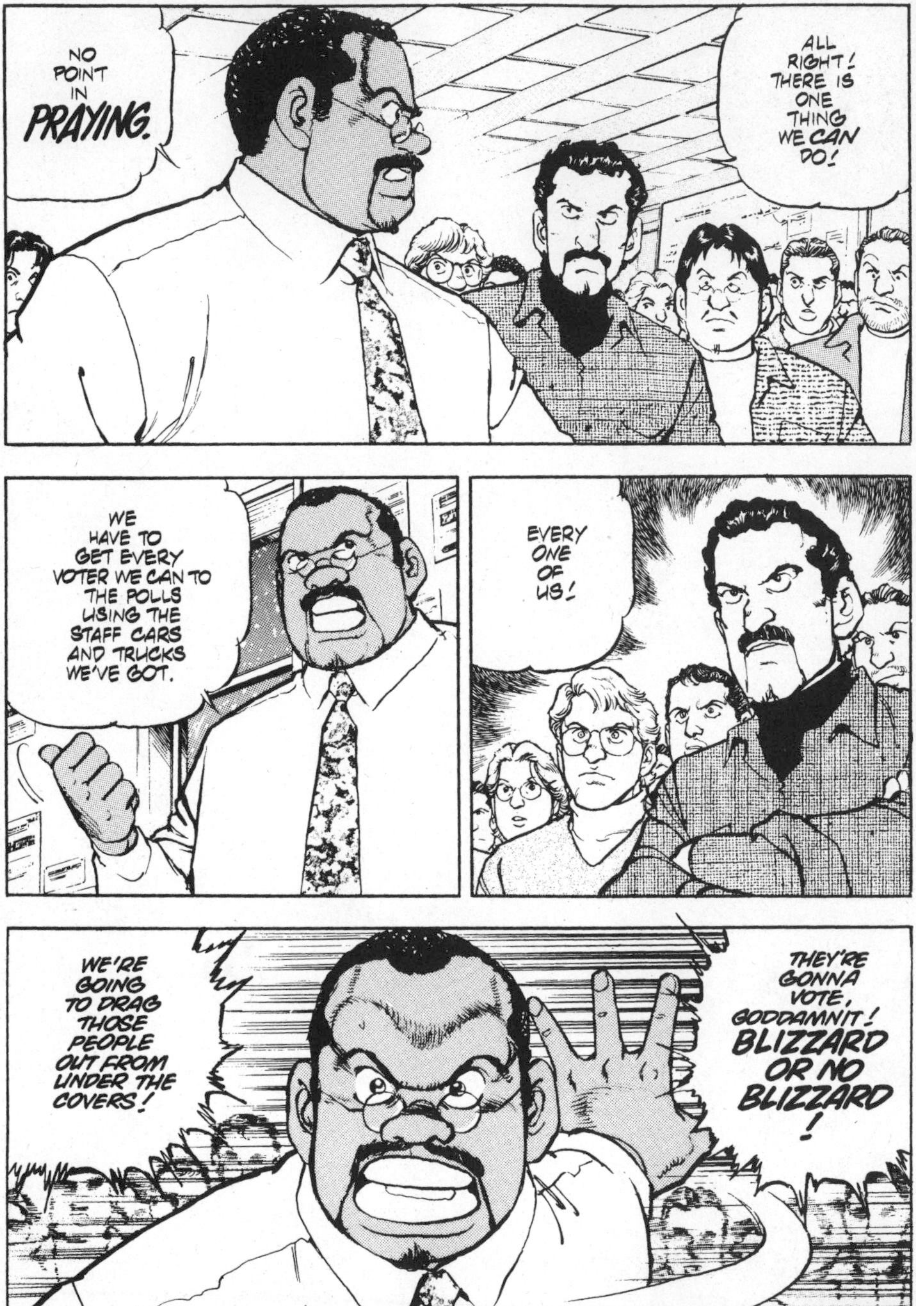
NO POINT IN PRAYING.
ALL RIGHT! THERE IS ONE THING WE CAN DO!
WE HAVE TO GET EVERY VOTER WE CAN TO THE POLLS USING THE STAFF CARS AND TRUCKS WE'VE GOT.
EVERY ONE OF US!
WE'RE GOING TO DRAG THOSE PEOPLE OUT FROM UNDER THE COVERS!
THEY'RE GONNA VOTE, GODDAMNIT! BLIZZARD OR NO BLIZZARD!

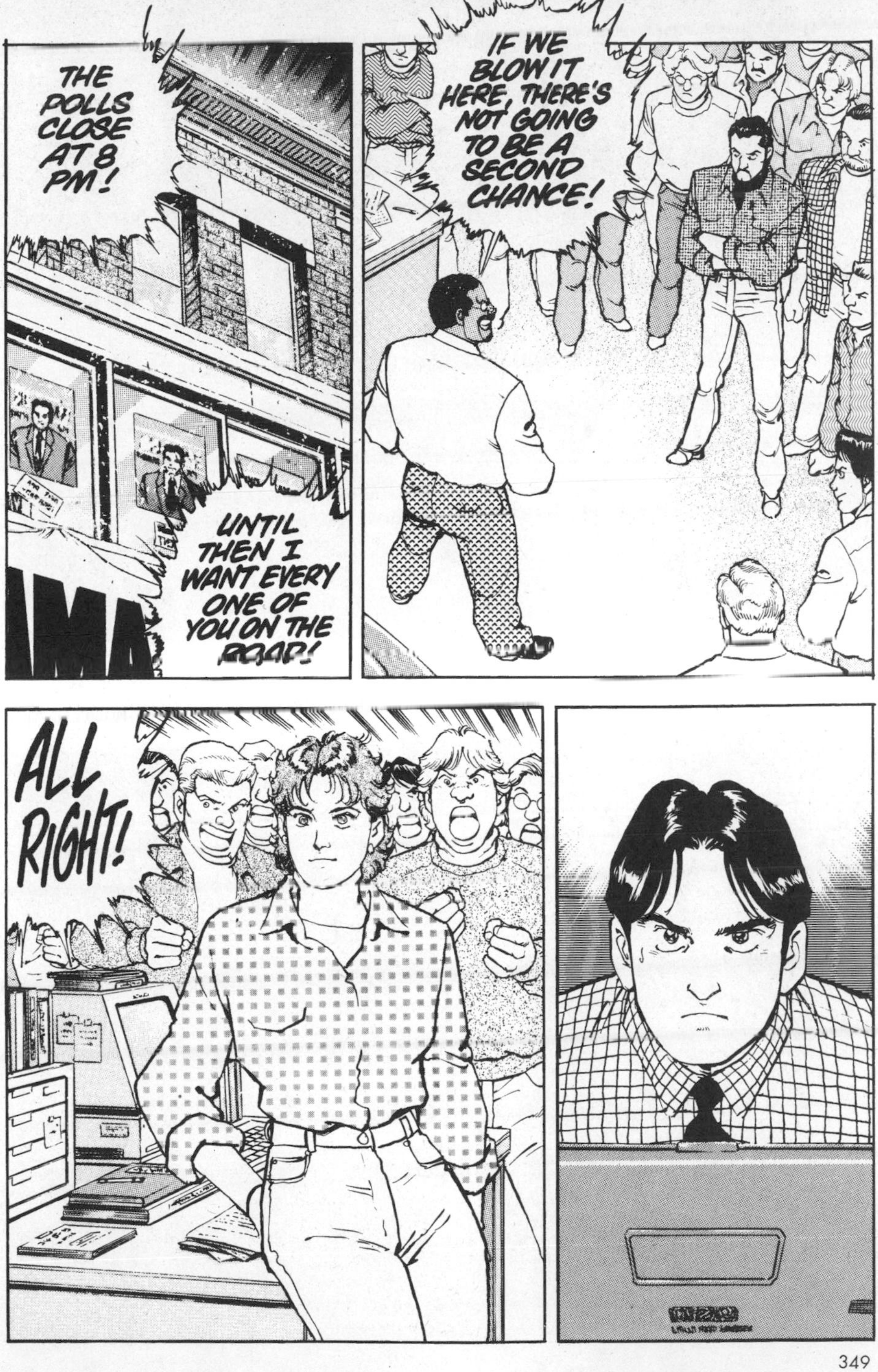
THE POLLS CLOSE AT 8 PM!
UNTIL THEN I WANT EVERY ONE OF YOU ON THE ROAD!
IF WE BLOW IT HERE, THERE'S NOT GOING TO BE A SECOND CHANCE!
ALL RIGHT!

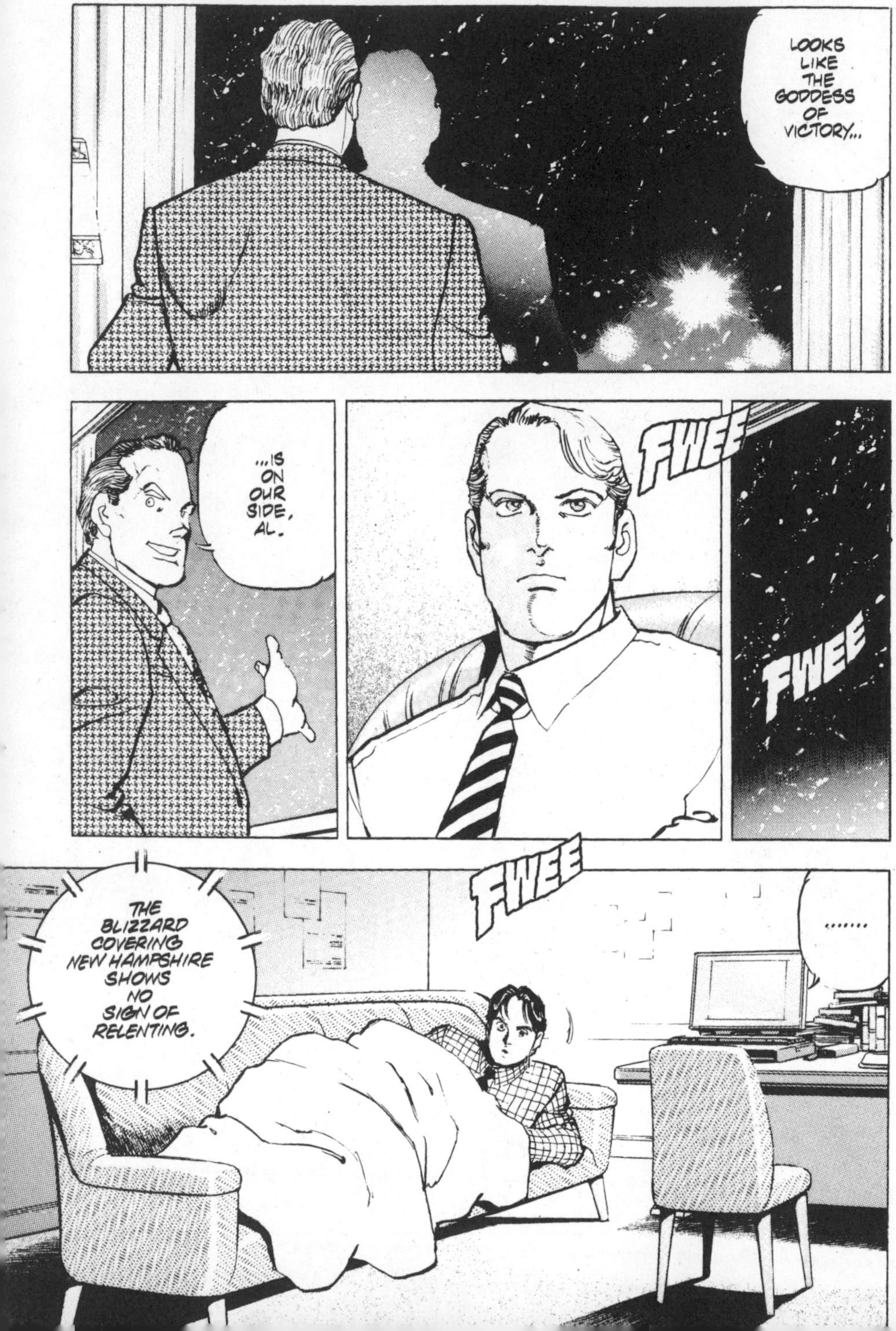
LOOKS LIKE THE GODDESS OF VICTORY...
...IS ON OUR SIDE, AL.
FWEE
FWEE
FWEE
THE BLIZZARD COVERING NEW HAMPSHIRE SHOWS NO SIGN OF RELENTING.
....

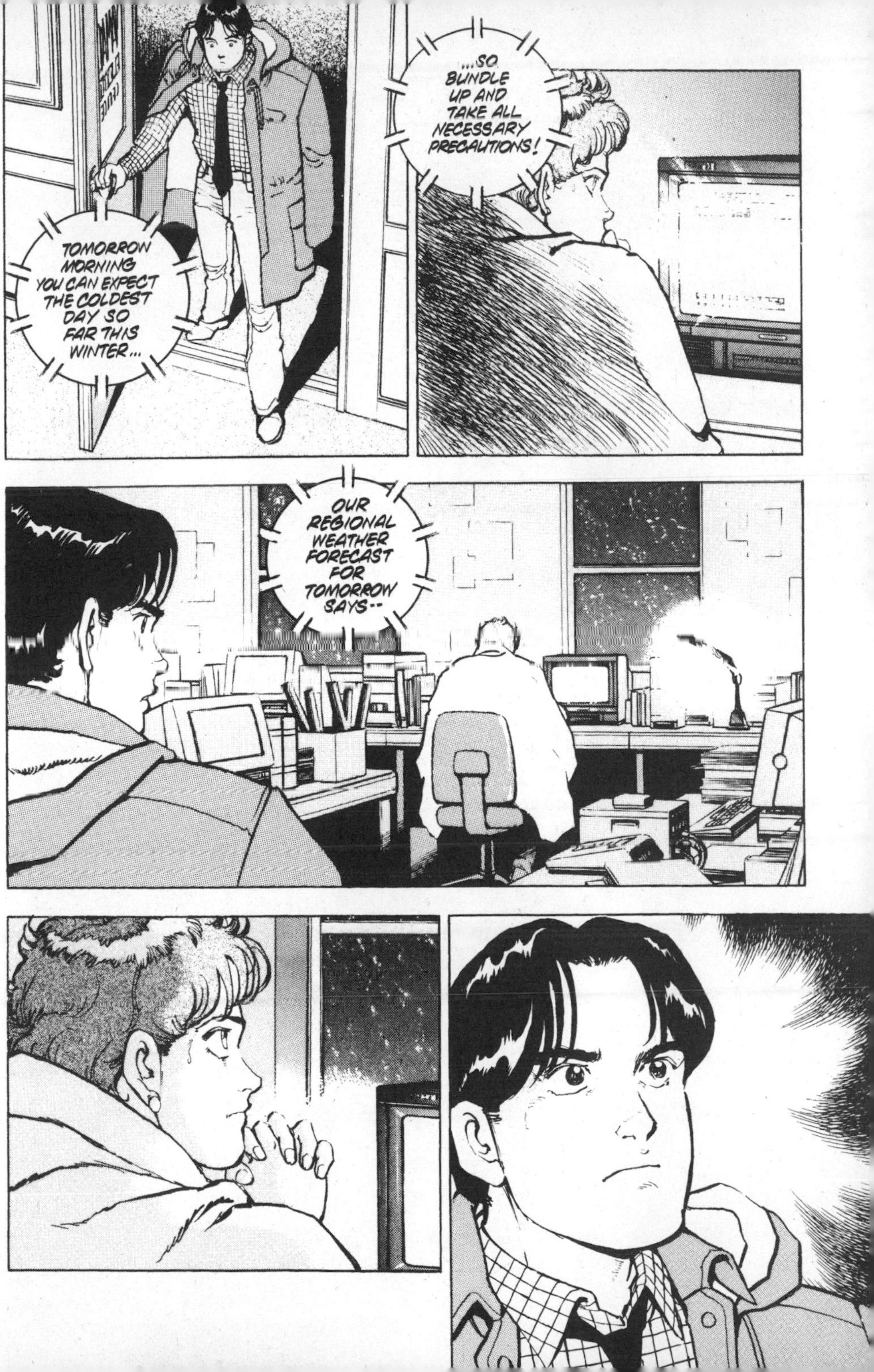
TOMORROW MORNING YOU CAN EXPECT THE COLDEST DAY SO FAR THIS WINTER...
...SO BUNDLE UP AND TAKE ALL NECESSARY PRECAUTIONS!
OUR REGIONAL WEATHER FORECAST FOR TOMORROW SAYS--

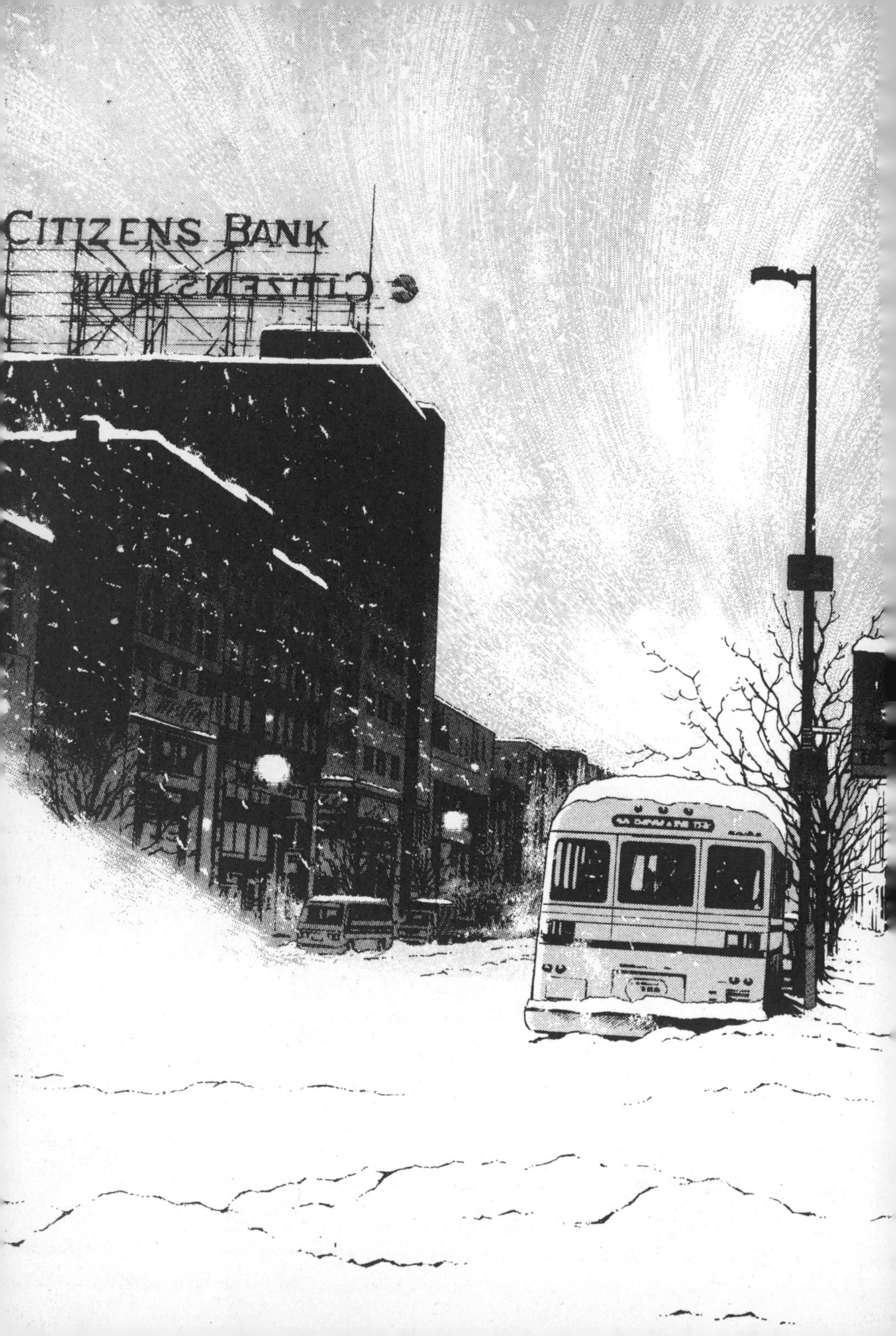
CITIZENS BANK

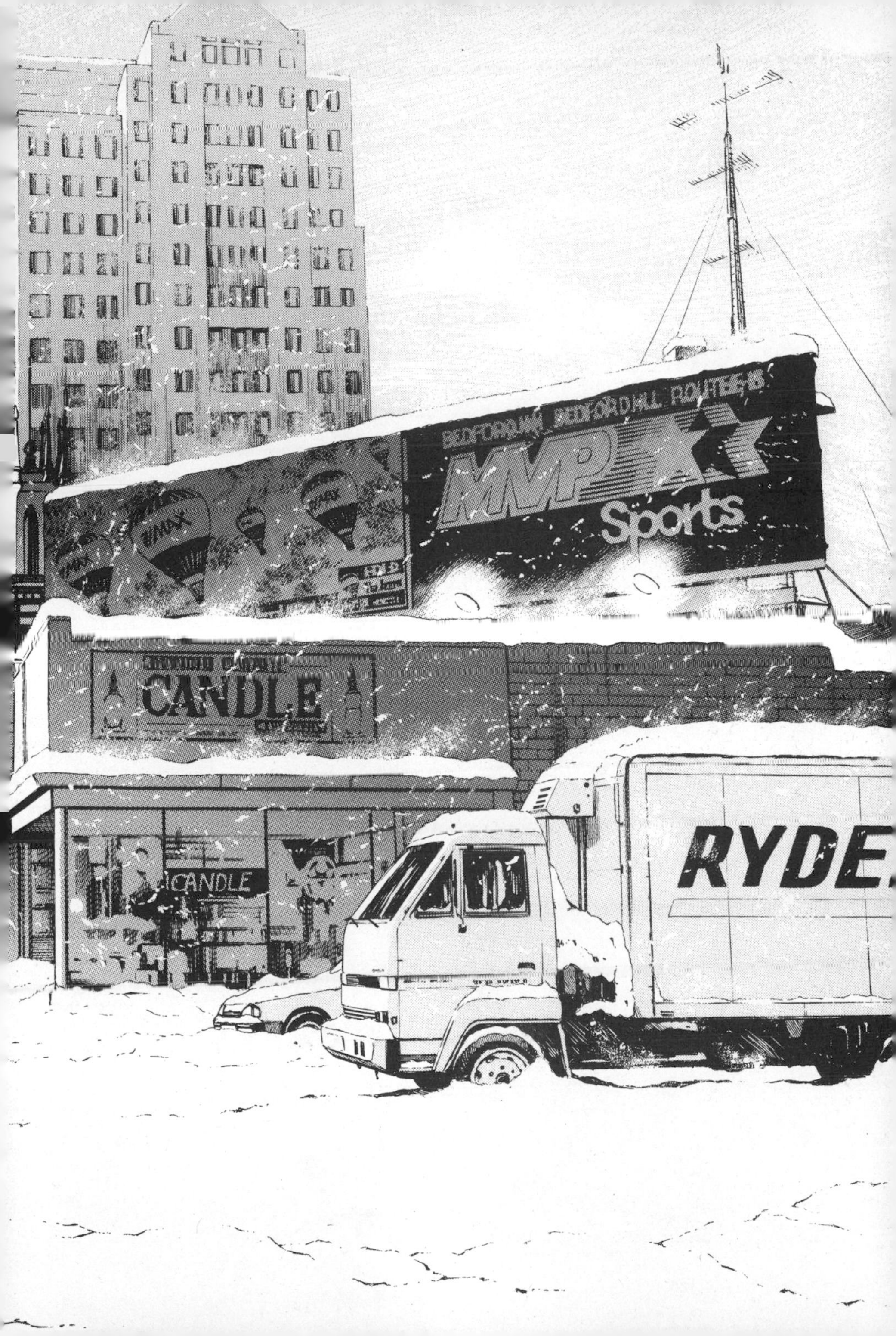
Sports
CANDLE
CANDLE
RYDE

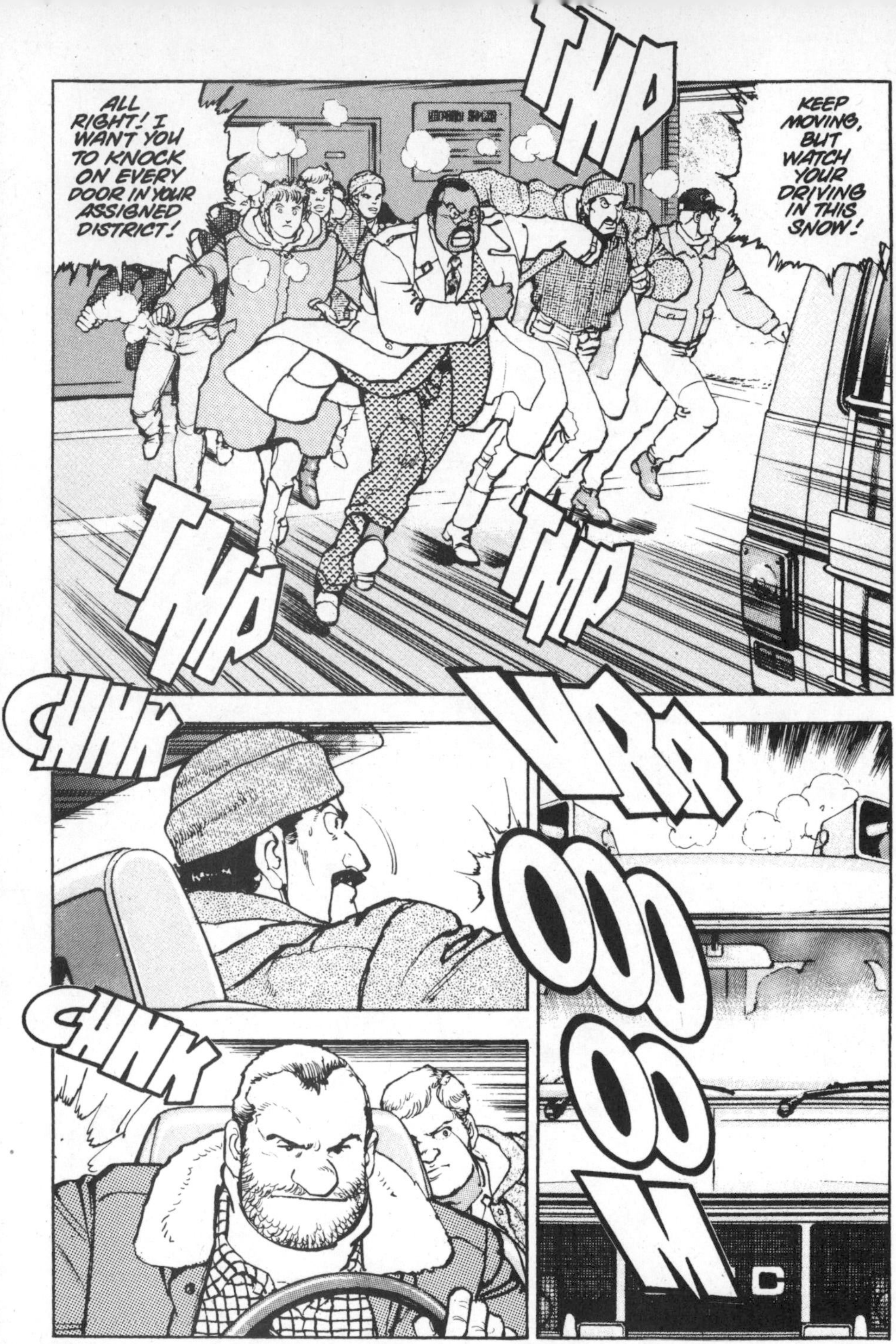
THMP
ALL RIGHT! I WANT YOU TO KNOCK ON EVERY DOOR IN YOUR ASSIGNED DISTRICT!
KEEP MOVING, BUT WATCH YOUR DRIVING IN THIS SNOW!
THMP
THMP
CHNK
VRR
OOOOOM
CHNK

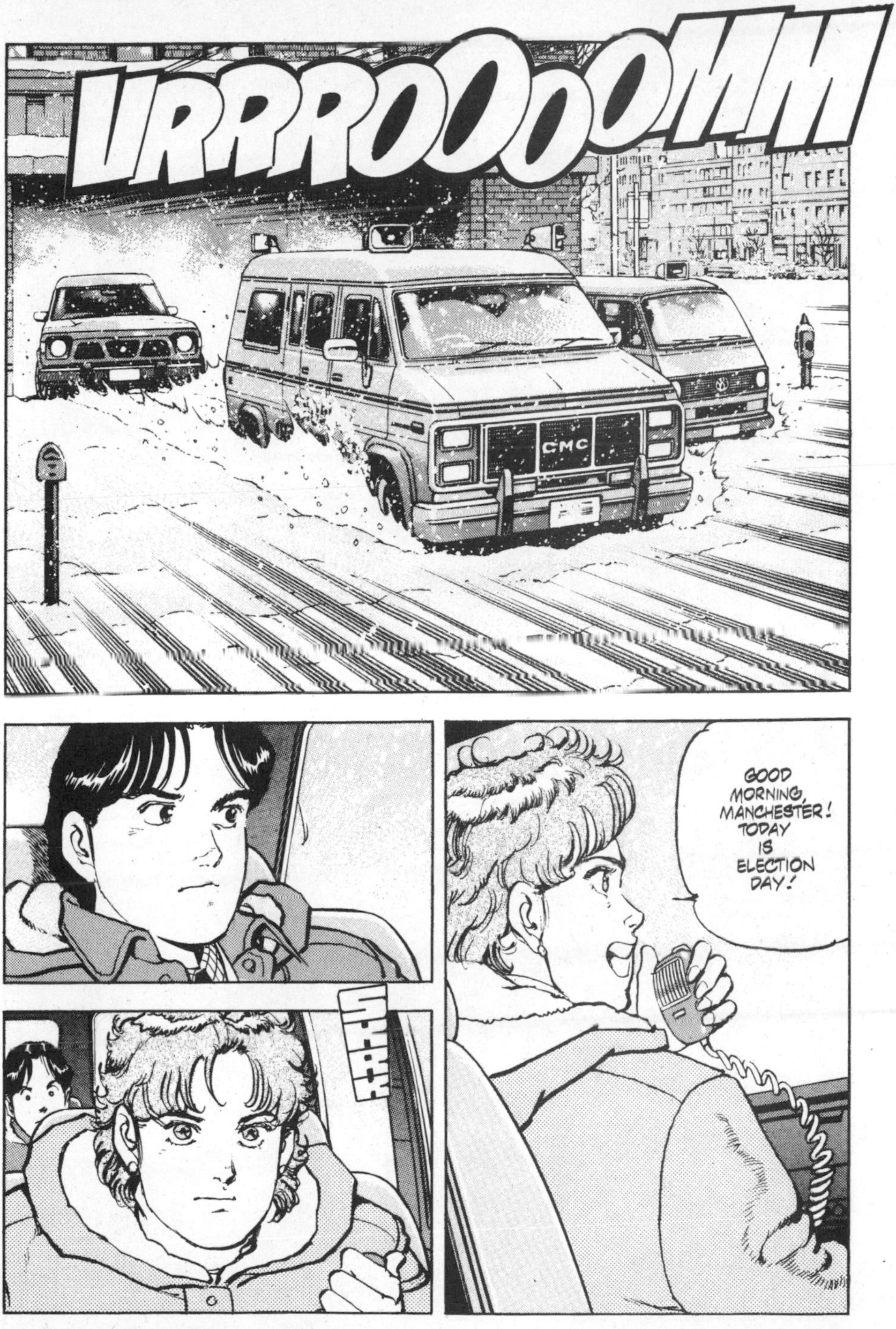
URRROOOOOMM
GMC
GOOD MORNING, MANCHESTER! TODAY IS ELECTION DAY!
SKKK

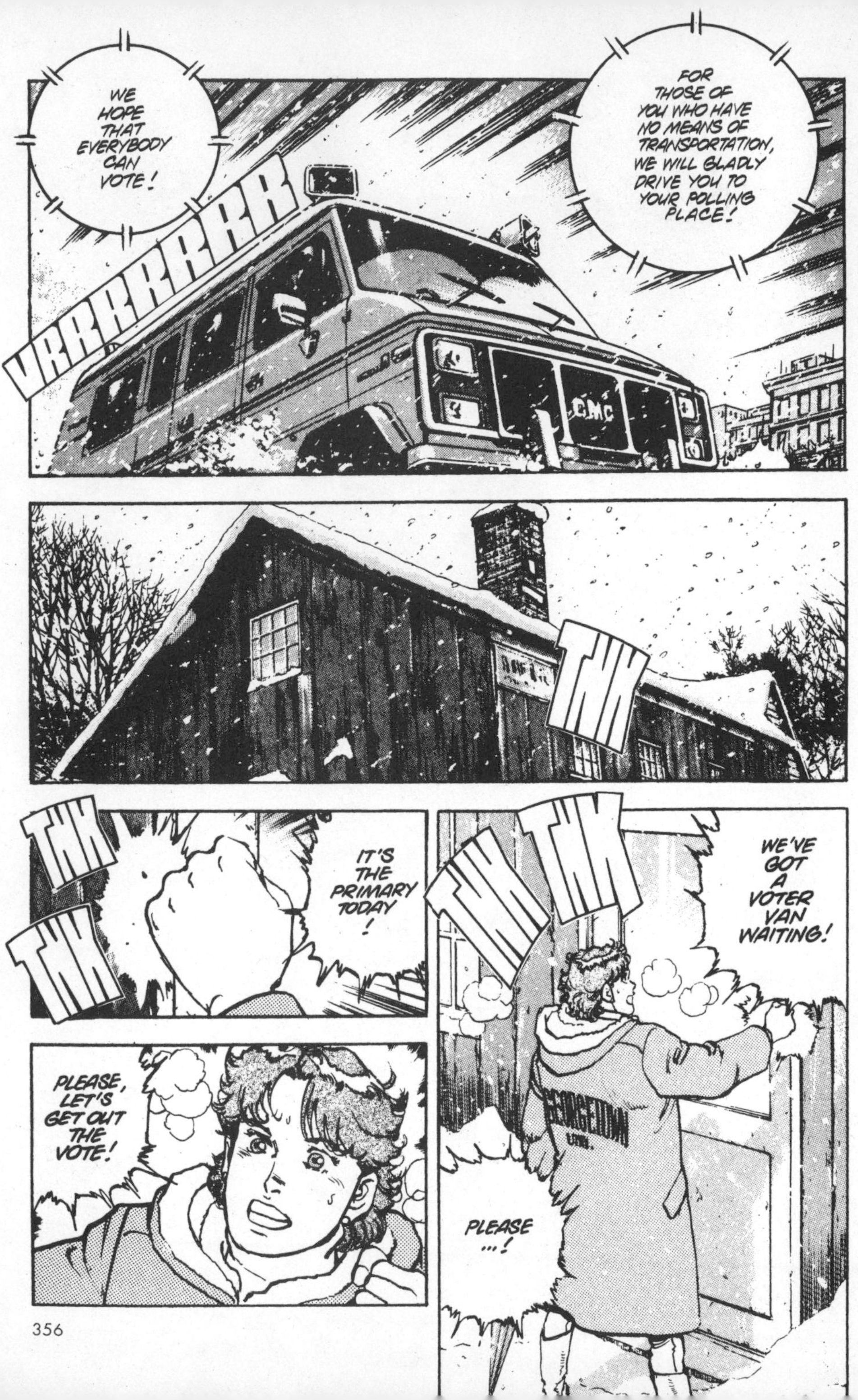
WE HOPE THAT EVERYBODY CAN VOTE!
VRRRRRRR
FOR THOSE OF YOU WHO HAVE NO MEANS OF TRANSPORTATION, WE WILL GLADLY DRIVE YOU TO YOUR POLLING PLACE!
THK
THK
THK
IT'S THE PRIMARY TODAY!
PLEASE, LET'S GET OUT THE VOTE!
THK
THK
WE'VE GOT A VOTER VAN WAITING!
PLEASE ...!

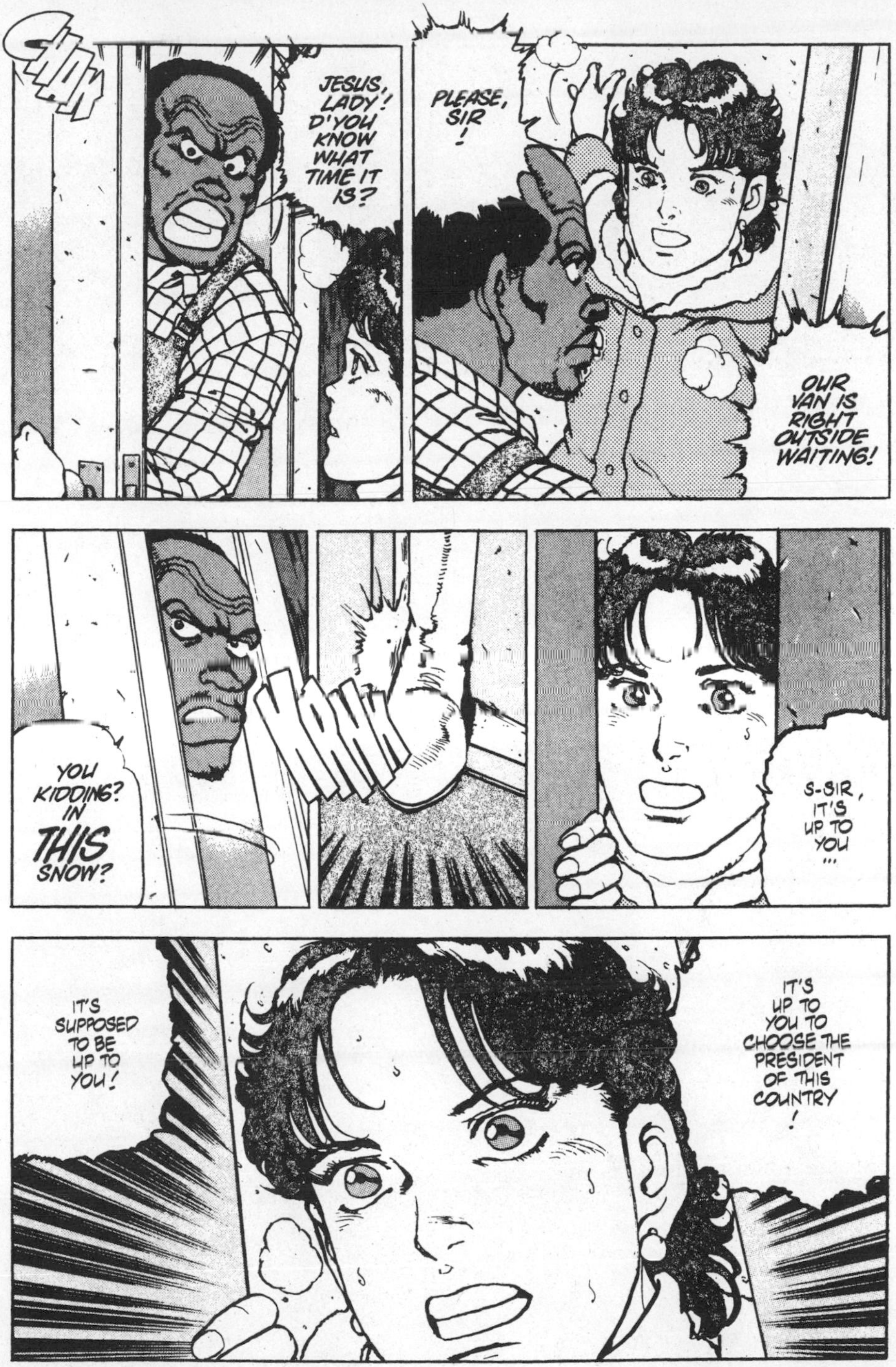
CHAK
JESUS, LADY! D'YOU KNOW WHAT TIME IT IS?
PLEASE, SIR!
OUR VAN IS RIGHT OUTSIDE WAITING!
YOU KIDDING? IN THIS SNOW?
S-SIR, IT'S UP TO YOU...
IT'S SUPPOSED TO BE UP TO YOU!
IT'S UP TO YOU TO CHOOSE THE PRESIDENT OF THIS COUNTRY!

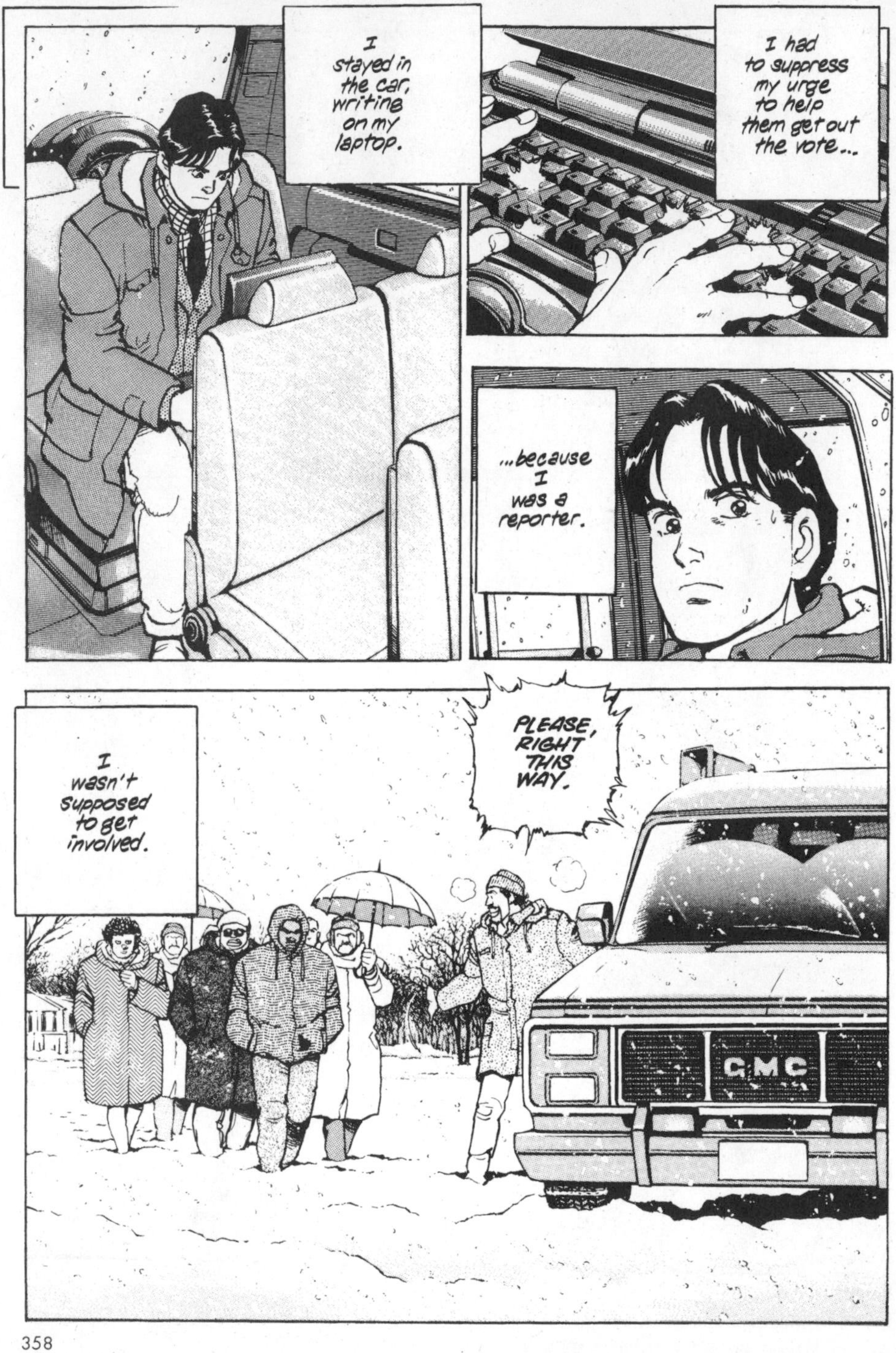
I stayed in the car, writing on my laptop.
I had to suppress my urge to help them get out the vote...
...because I was a reporter.
I wasn't supposed to get involved.
PLEASE, RIGHT THIS WAY.
GMC

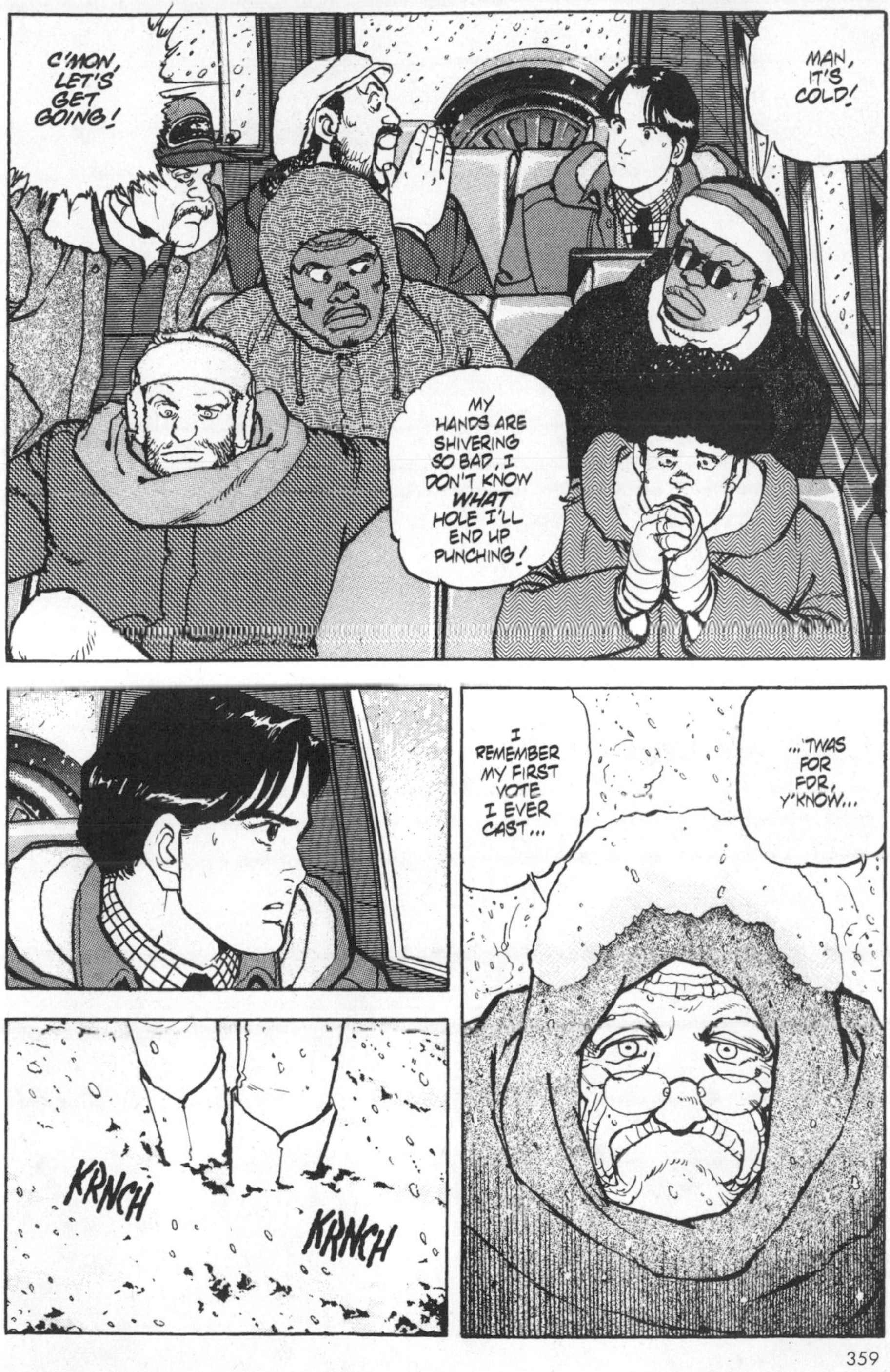
C'MON, LET'S GET GOING!
MAN, IT'S COLD!
MY HANDS ARE SHIVERING SO BAD, I DON'T KNOW WHAT HOLE I'LL END UP PUNCHING!
KRNCH
KRNCH
I REMEMBER MY FIRST VOTE I EVER CAST...
...'TWAS FOR FOR, Y'KNOW...

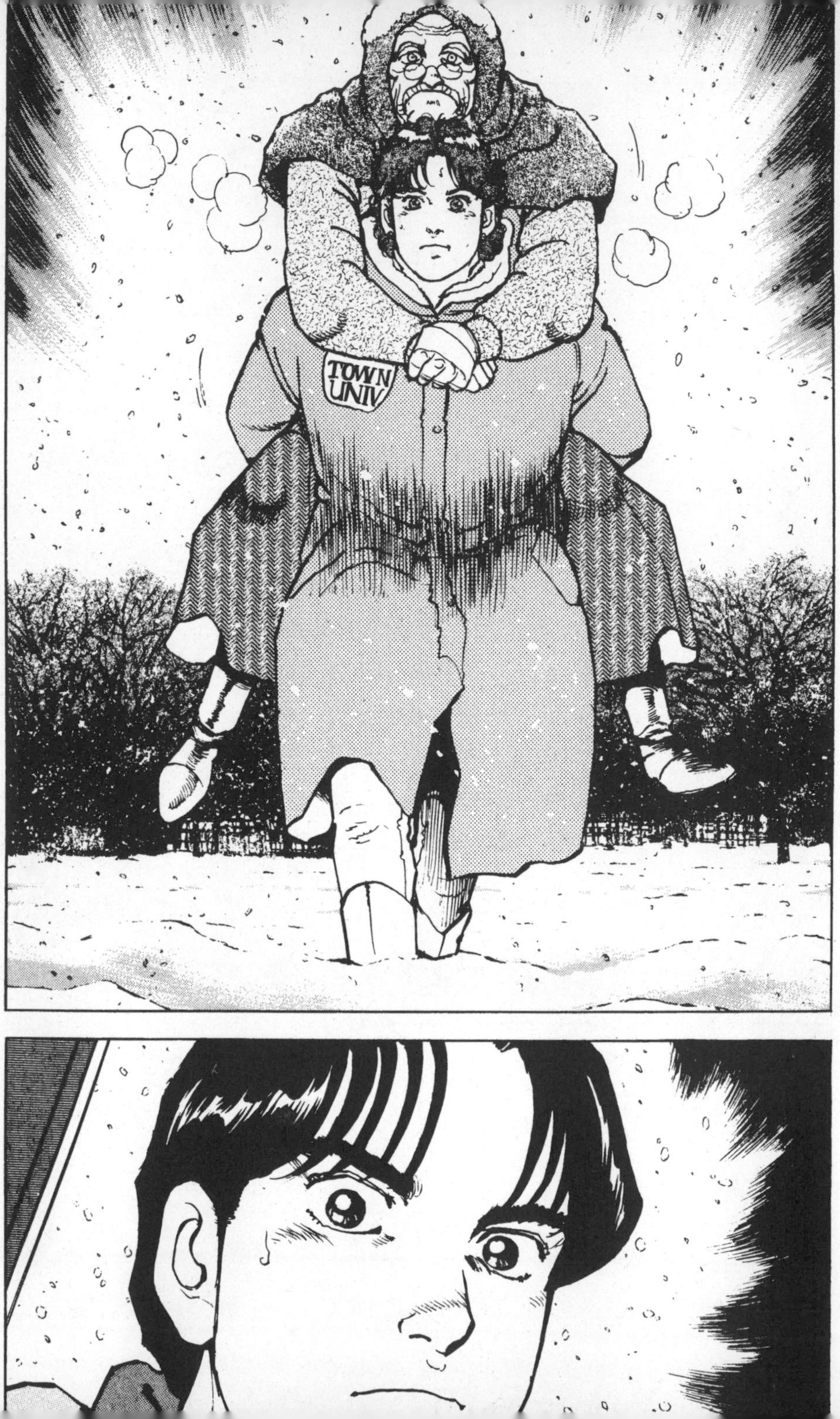
TOWN UNIV

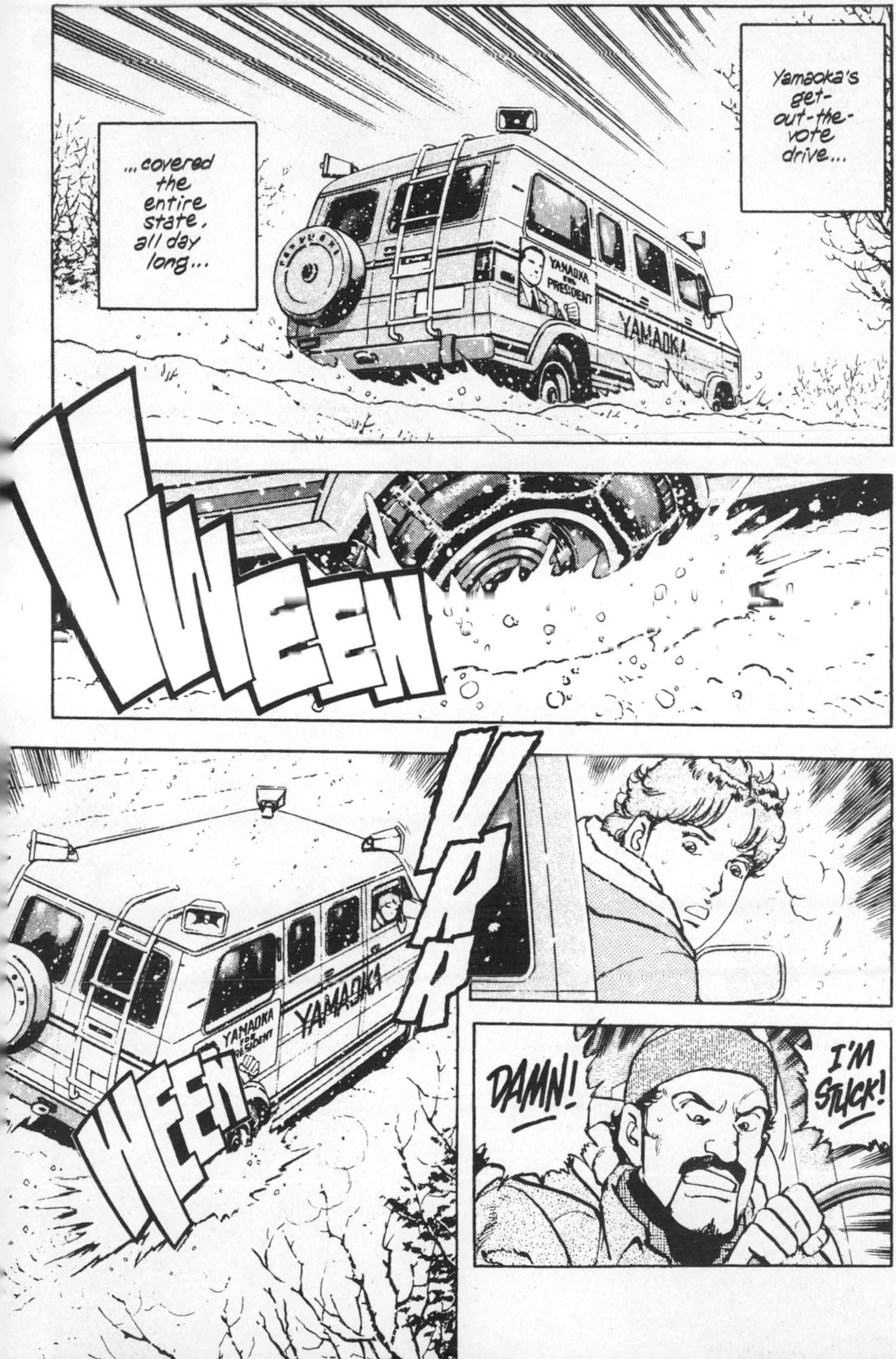
Yamaoka's get-out-the-vote drive...
...covered the entire state, all day long...
YAMAOKA FOR PRESIDENT
YAMAOKA
VVWEEN
YAMAOKA FOR PRESIDENT
YAMAOKA
WEEN
VRR
DAMN!
I'M STUCK!

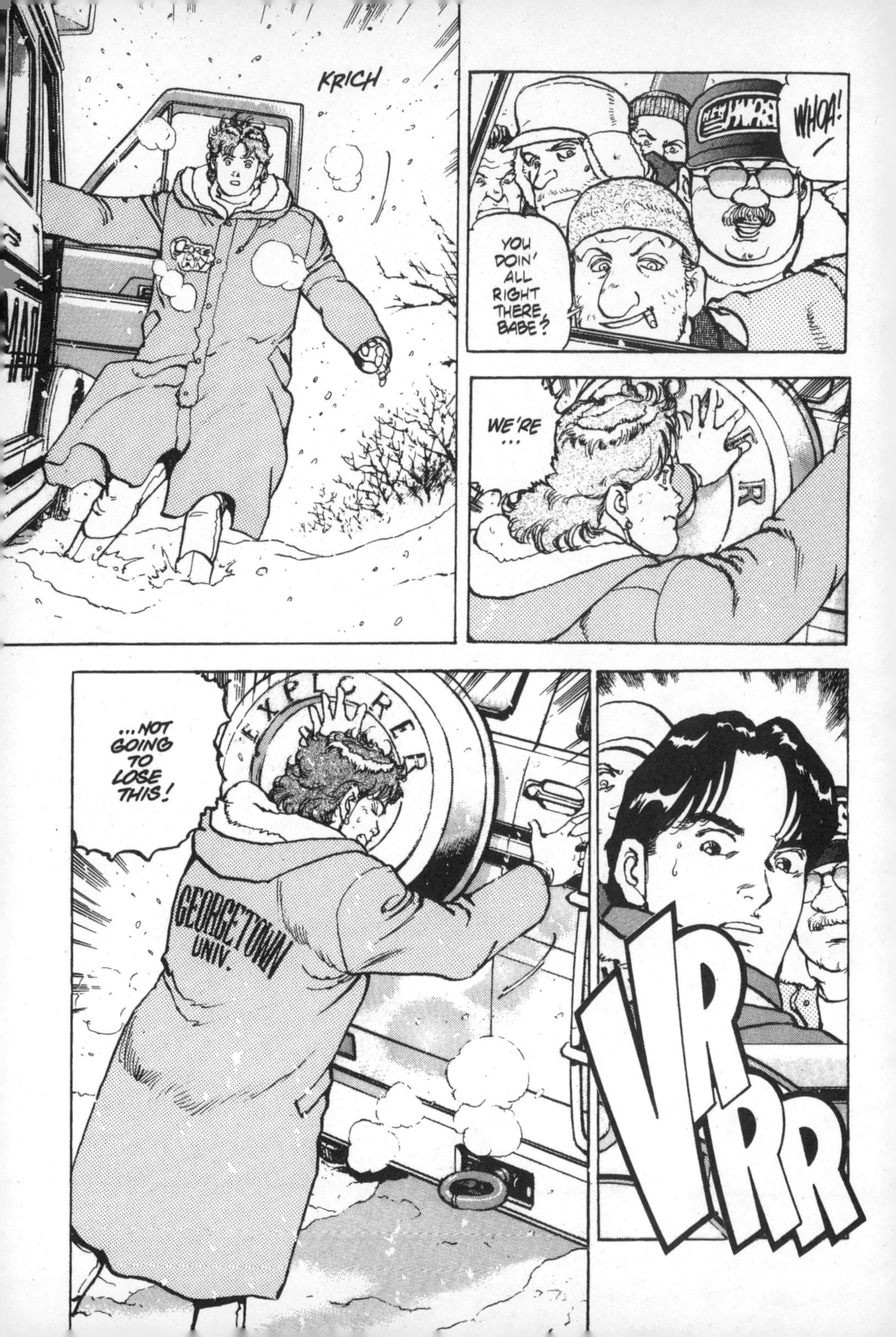
KRICH
WHOA!
YOU DOIN' ALL RIGHT THERE BABE?
WE'RE ...
...NOT GOING TO LOSE THIS!
GEORGETOWN UNIV.
VRRRR

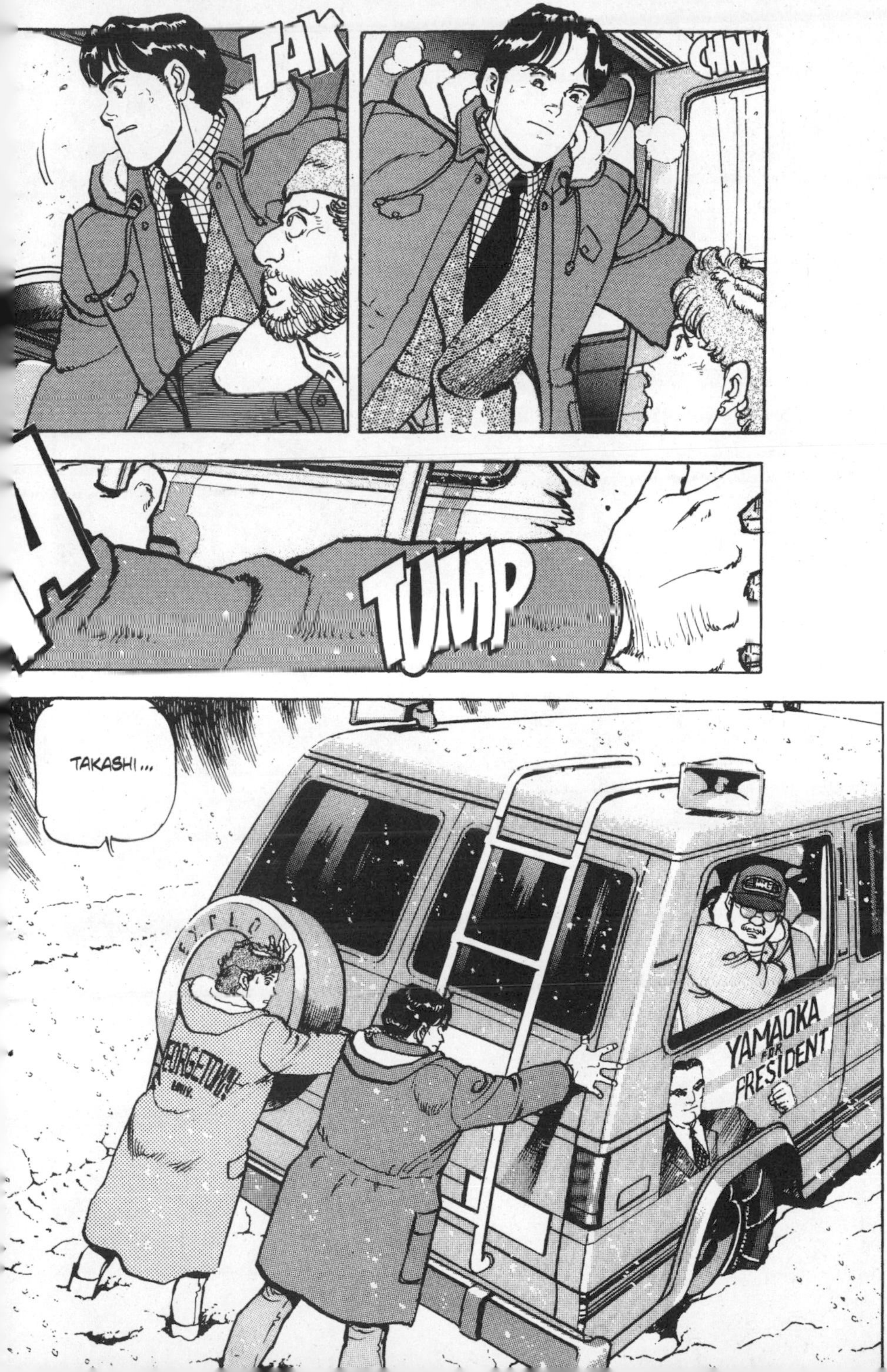

TAK
CHNK
TUMP
TAKASHI...
GEORGETOWN
YAMAOKA FOR PRESIDENT

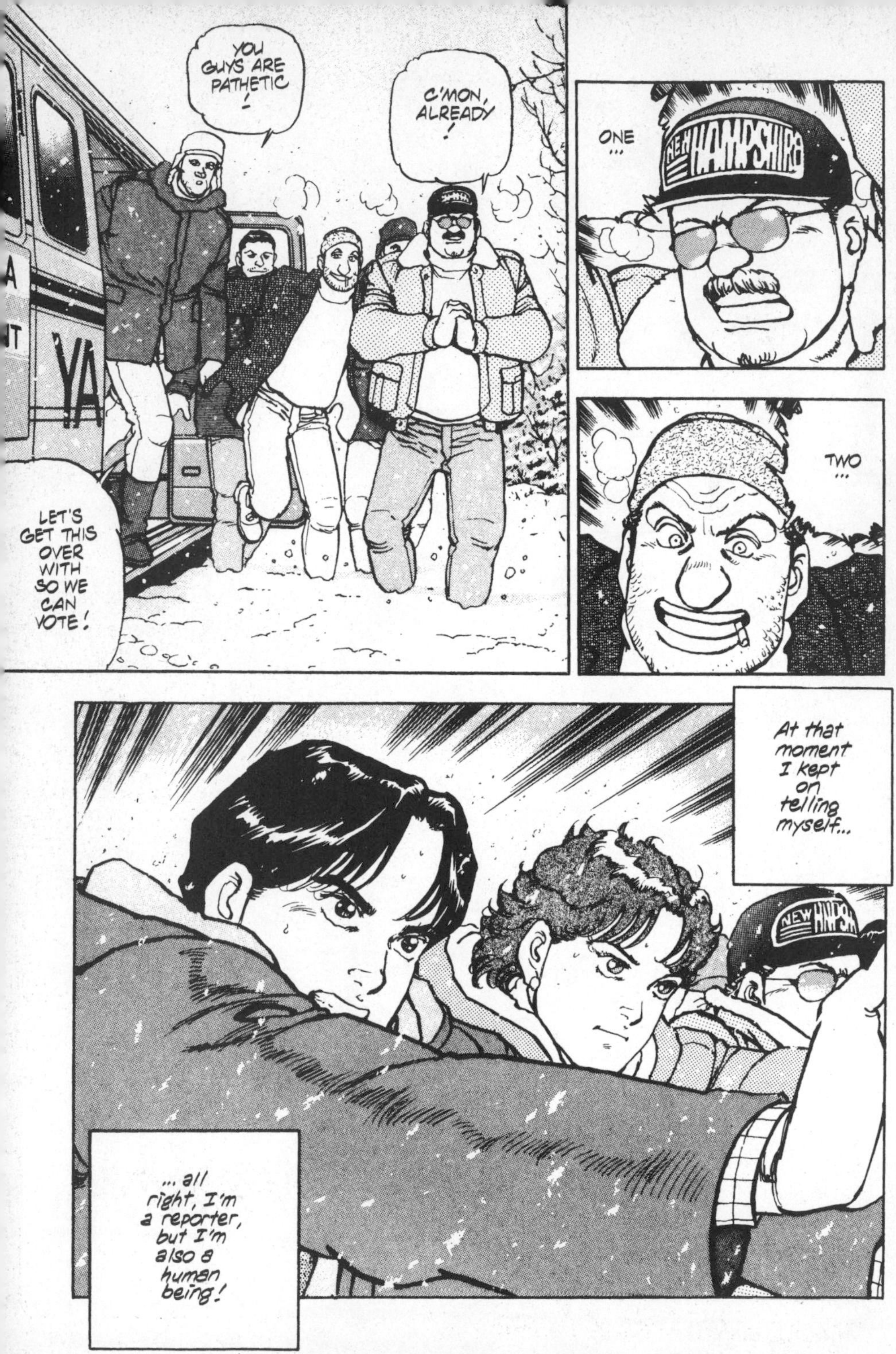
YOU GUYS ARE PATHETIC!
C'MON, ALREADY!
LET'S GET THIS OVER WITH SO WE CAN VOTE!
ONE ...
NEW HAMPSHIRE
TWO ...
At that moment I kept on telling myself...
NEW HAMPSH
... all right, I'm a reporter, but I'm also a human being!

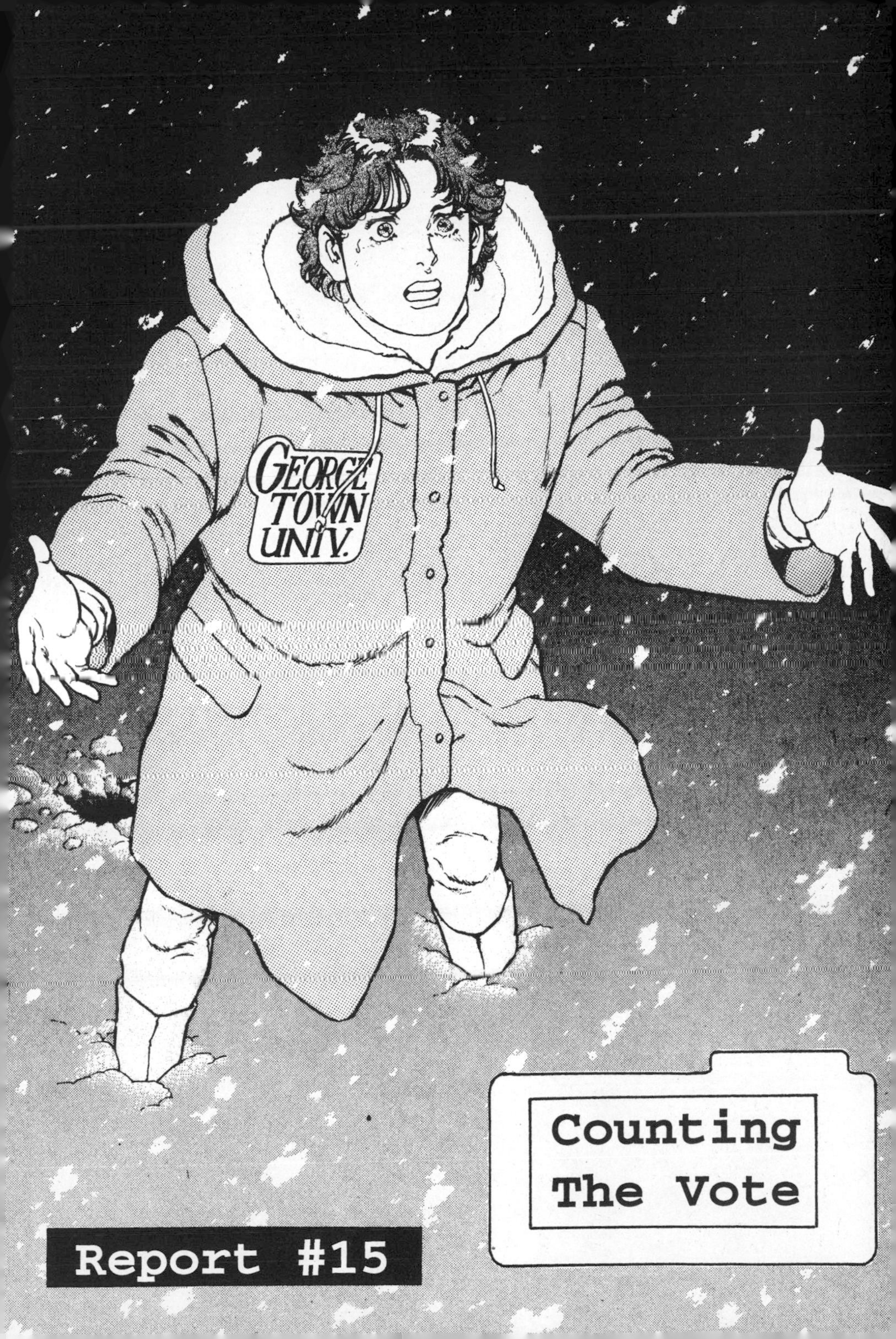
GEORGE TOWN UNIV.
Counting The Vote
Report #15

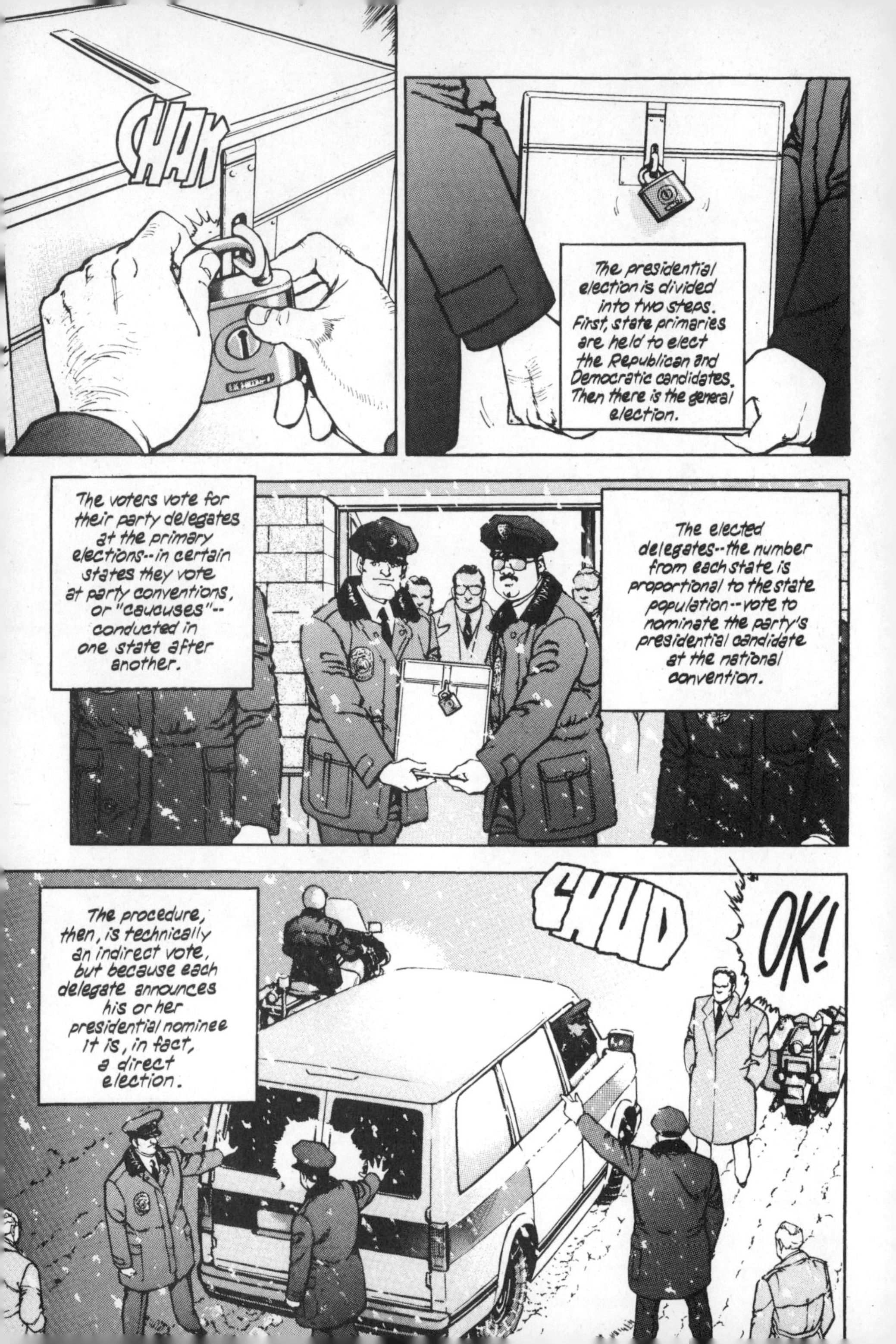
CHAK
The presidential election is divided into two steps. First, state primaries are held to elect the Republican and Democratic candidates. Then there is the general election.
The voters vote for their party delegates at the primary elections--in certain states they vote at party conventions, or "caucuses"--conducted in one state after another.
The elected delegates--the number from each state is proportional to the state population--vote to nominate the party's presidential candidate at the national convention.
The procedure, then, is technically an indirect vote, but because each delegate announces his or her presidential nominee it is, in fact, a direct election.
CHUD
OK!

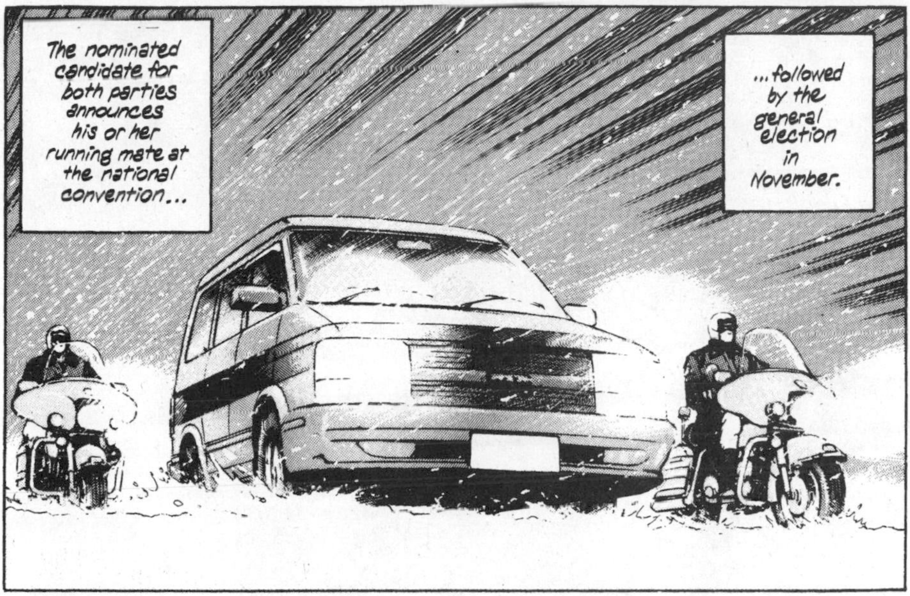
The nominated candidate for both parties announces his or her running mate at the national convention...
...followed by the general election in November.

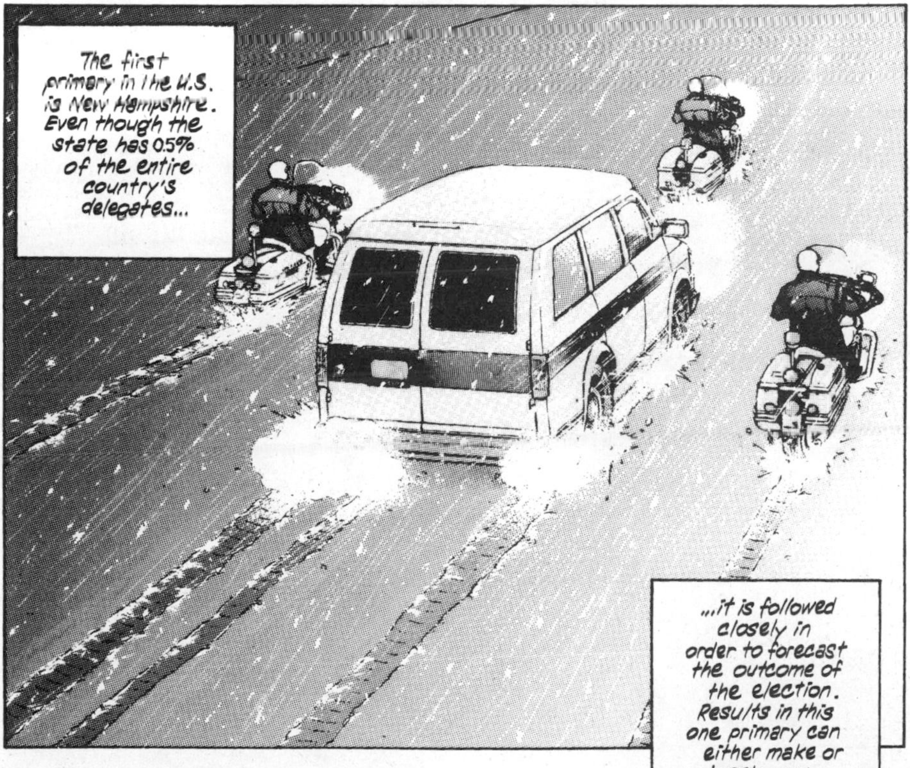
The first primary in the U.S. is New Hampshire. Even though the state has 0.5% of the entire country's delegates...
...it is followed closely in order to forecast the outcome of the election. Results in this one primary can either make or break you.

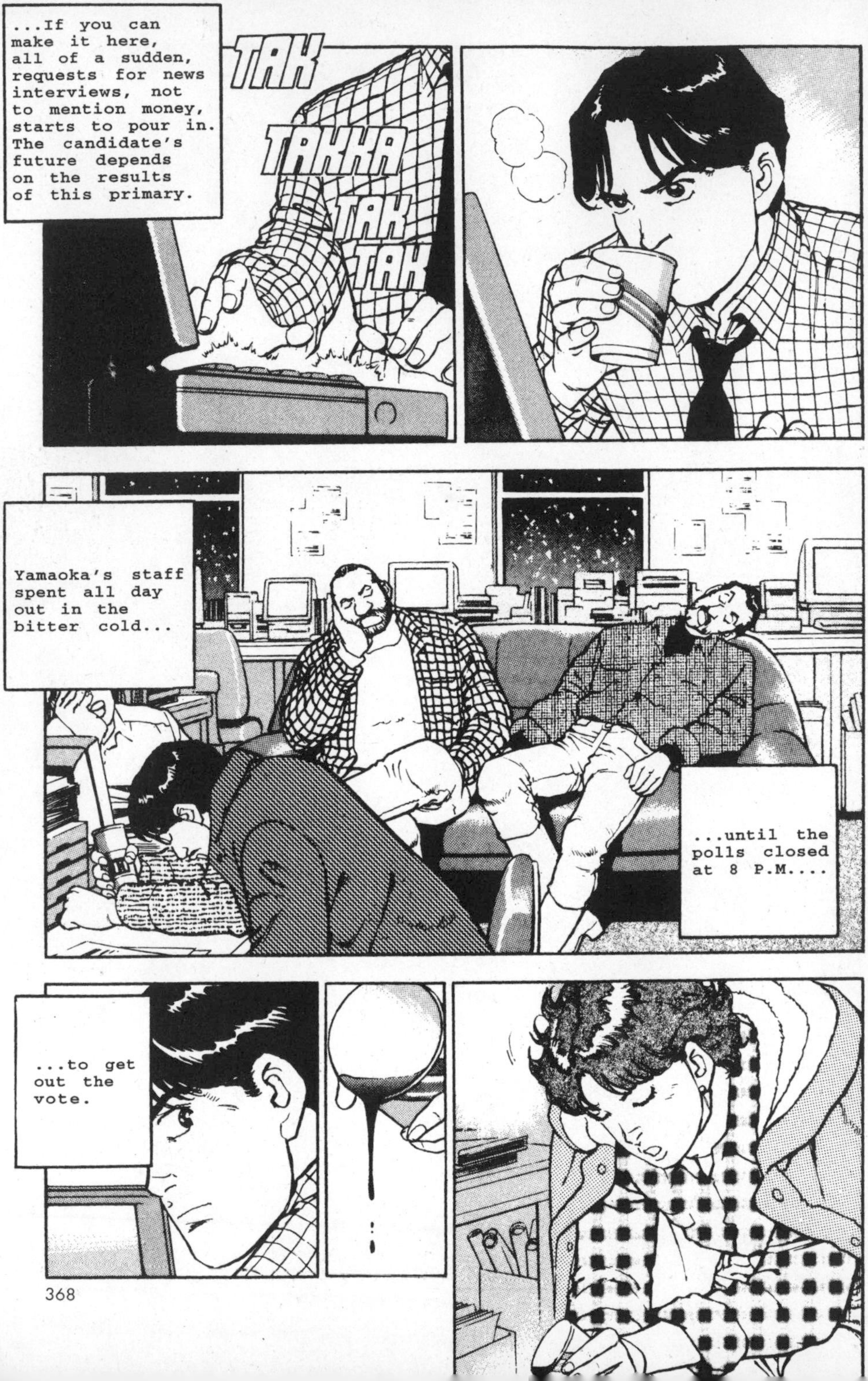
...If you can make it here, all of a sudden, requests for news interviews, not to mention money, starts to pour in. The candidate's future depends on the results of this primary.
TAK
TAKKA
TAK
TAK
Yamaoka's staff spent all day out in the bitter cold...
...until the polls closed at 8 P.M....
...to get out the vote.

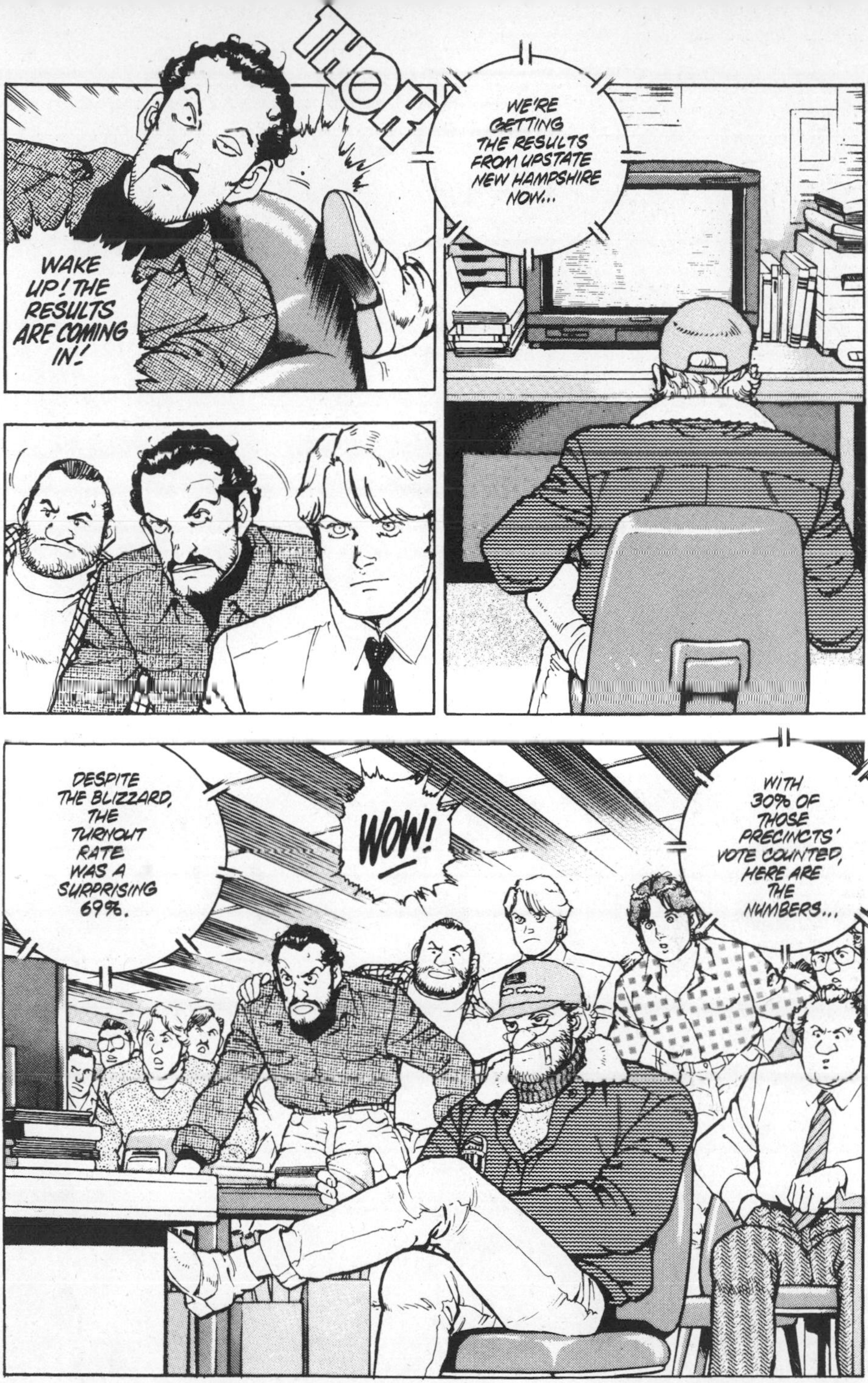
THOK
WAKE UP! THE RESULTS ARE COMING IN!
WE'RE GETTING THE RESULTS FROM UPSTATE NEW HAMPSHIRE NOW...
DESPITE THE BLIZZARD, THE TURNOUT RATE WAS A SURPRISING 69%.
WOW!
WITH 30% OF THOSE PRECINCTS' VOTE COUNTED, HERE ARE THE NUMBERS...

ABS NEWS

NOAH TAKES A COMMANDING LEAD AT 55.5%. WOODSMAN IS SECOND AT 16.9%.

YAMAOKA IS THIRD AT 14.5%. GOLDBLUM, UNTIL A FEW WEEKS AGO FAVORED AT NUMBER TWO IN THE POLLS, SEEMS TO SHOW THE EFFECTS OF RECENT SCANDAL, TRAILING AT FOURTH WITH 9.3%.

DUE TO THE BLIZZARD, THE BALLOT-COUNT FROM SOUTHERN NEW HAMPSHIRE HAS BEEN DELAYED.

...WE'RE NOW STARTING TO GET RESULTS IN FROM THE SOUTHERN PRECINCTS. NOAH AGAIN HAS TAKEN THE LEAD. YAMAOKA IS ON THE RISE, HOWEVER, MAKING A CHALLENGE FOR SECOND...

NOAH	53.8%
WOODSMAN	17.4%
YAMAOKA	16.2%
GOLDBLUM	8.6%

81% OF THE VOTES ARE IN.

NOAH	**51.7%**
YAMAOKA	**19.6%**
WOODSMAN	**19.4%**
GOLDBLUM	**6.8%**

YES! WE TOUCHED SECOND!

C'MON... C'MON...

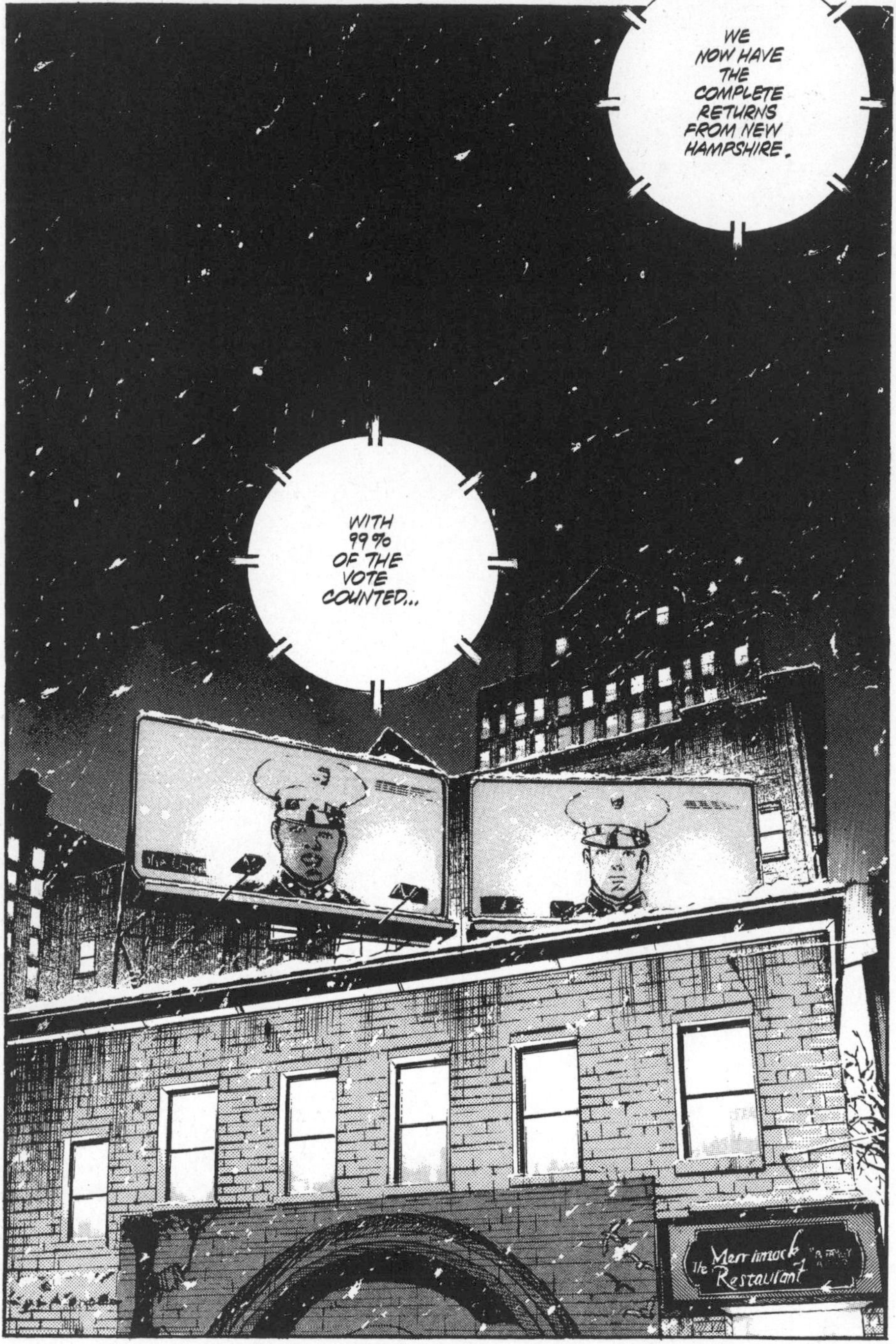
WE NOW HAVE THE COMPLETE RETURNS FROM NEW HAMPSHIRE.
WITH 99% OF THE VOTE COUNTED...
The Merrimack Restaurant

NOAH	48.6%
YAMAOKA	26.8%
WOODSMAN	17.2%
GOLDBLUM	5.2%

YES!

WE BROKE NOAH'S MAJORITY!

WE MADE IT! UP TO NUMBER TWO, AND A QUARTER OF THE VOTE!

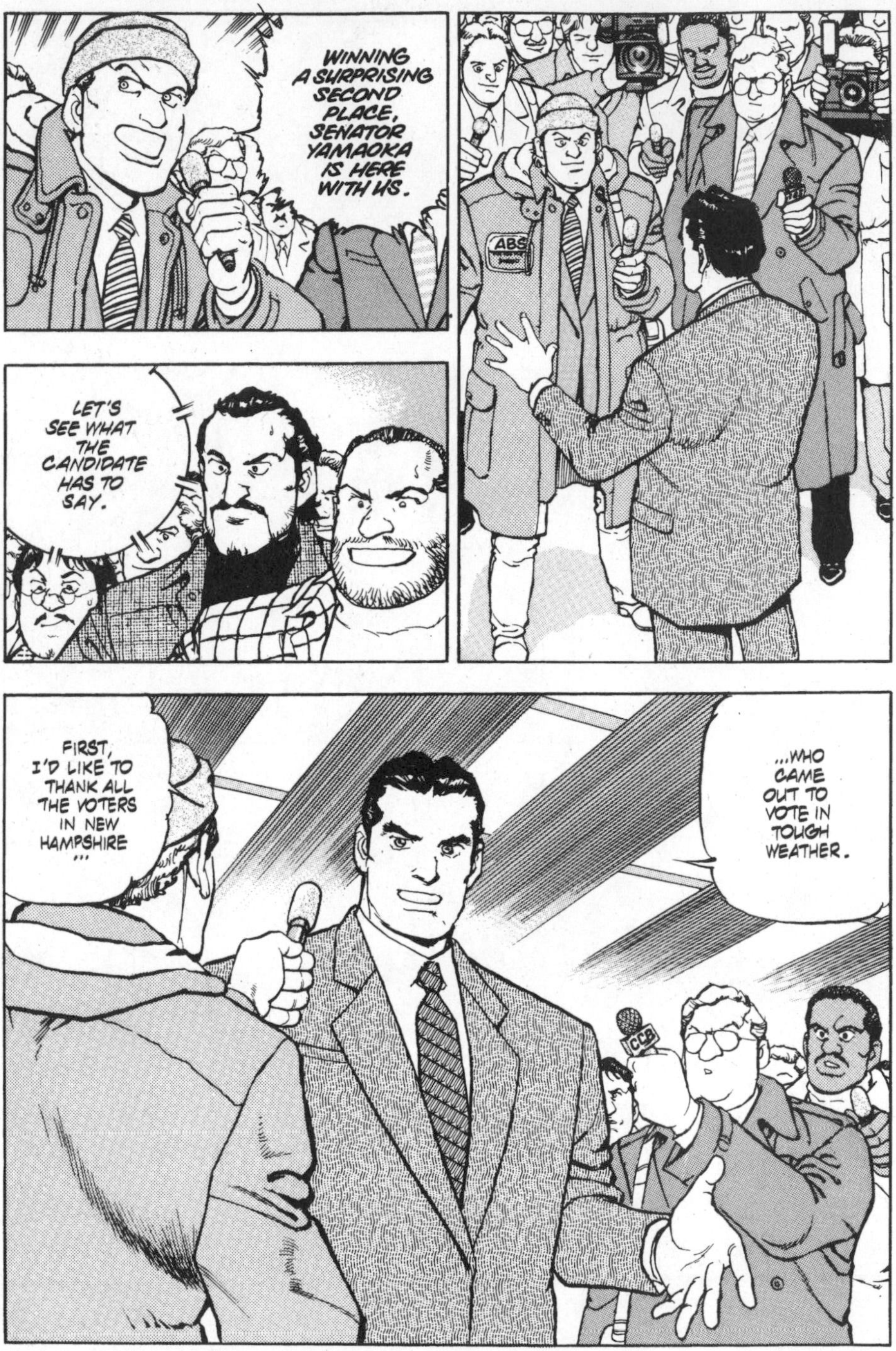
WINNING A SURPRISING SECOND PLACE, SENATOR YAMAOKA IS HERE WITH US.
LET'S SEE WHAT THE CANDIDATE HAS TO SAY.
ABS
FIRST, I'D LIKE TO THANK ALL THE VOTERS IN NEW HAMPSHIRE ...
...WHO CAME OUT TO VOTE IN TOUGH WEATHER.
CCB

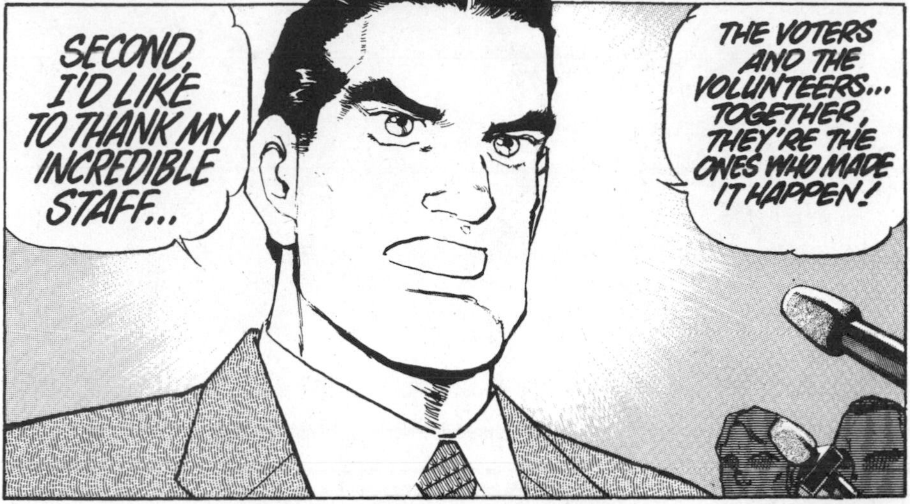
SECOND, I'D LIKE TO THANK MY INCREDIBLE STAFF...
THE VOTERS AND THE VOLUNTEERS... TOGETHER, THEY'RE THE ONES WHO MADE IT HAPPEN!

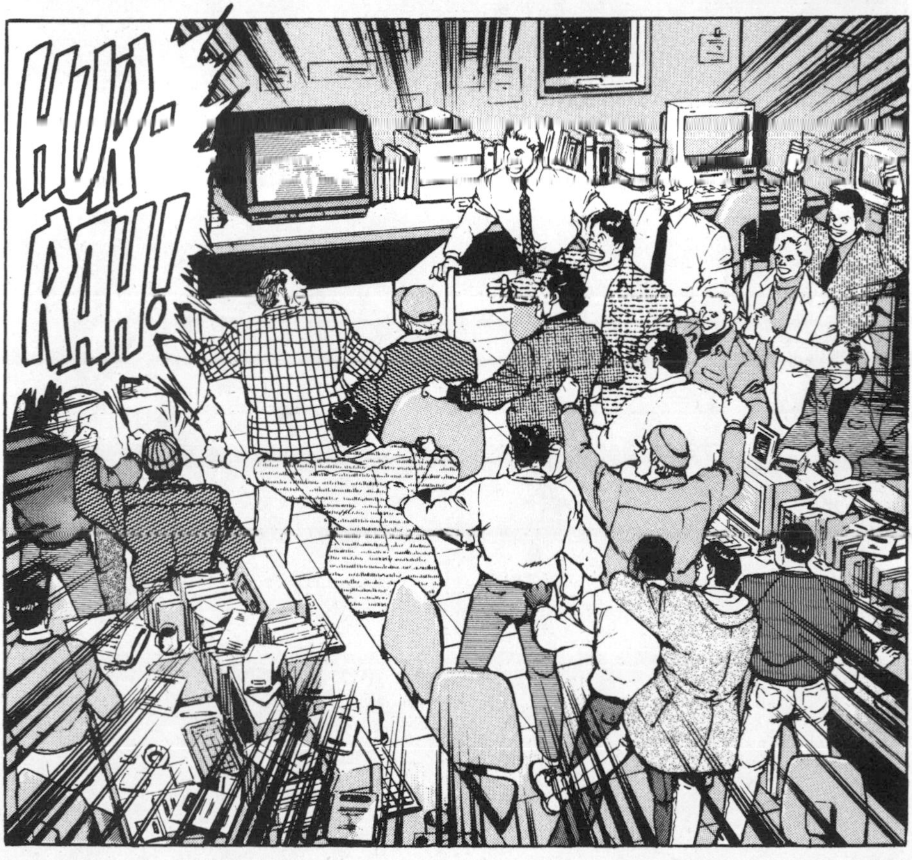
HUR-RAH!

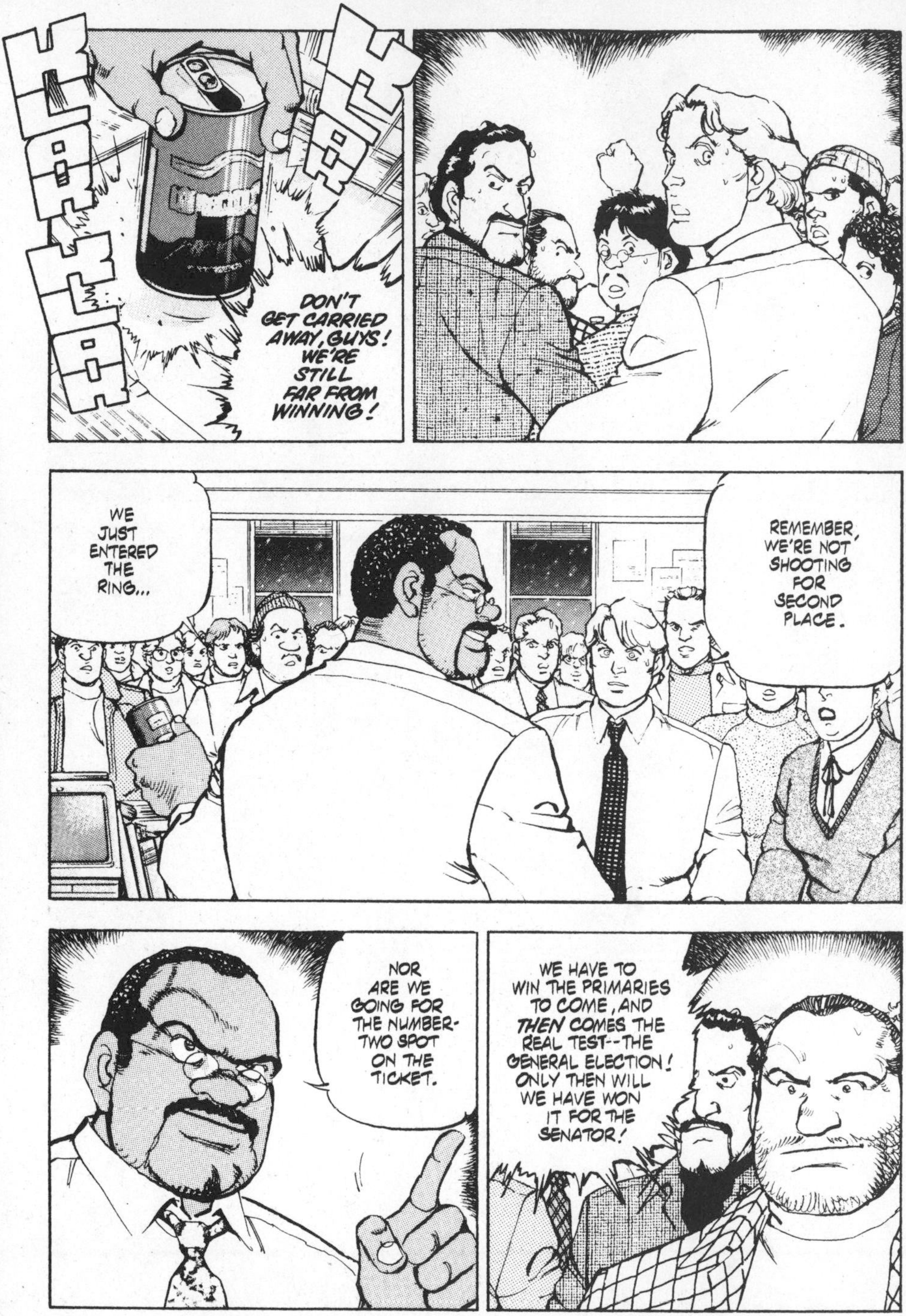

KLAK KLAK
KLAK
DON'T GET CARRIED AWAY, GUYS! WE'RE STILL FAR FROM WINNING!
WE JUST ENTERED THE RING...
REMEMBER, WE'RE NOT SHOOTING FOR SECOND PLACE.
NOR ARE WE GOING FOR THE NUMBER-TWO SPOT ON THE TICKET.
WE HAVE TO WIN THE PRIMARIES TO COME, AND *THEN* COMES THE REAL TEST--THE GENERAL ELECTION! ONLY THEN WILL WE HAVE WON IT FOR THE SENATOR!

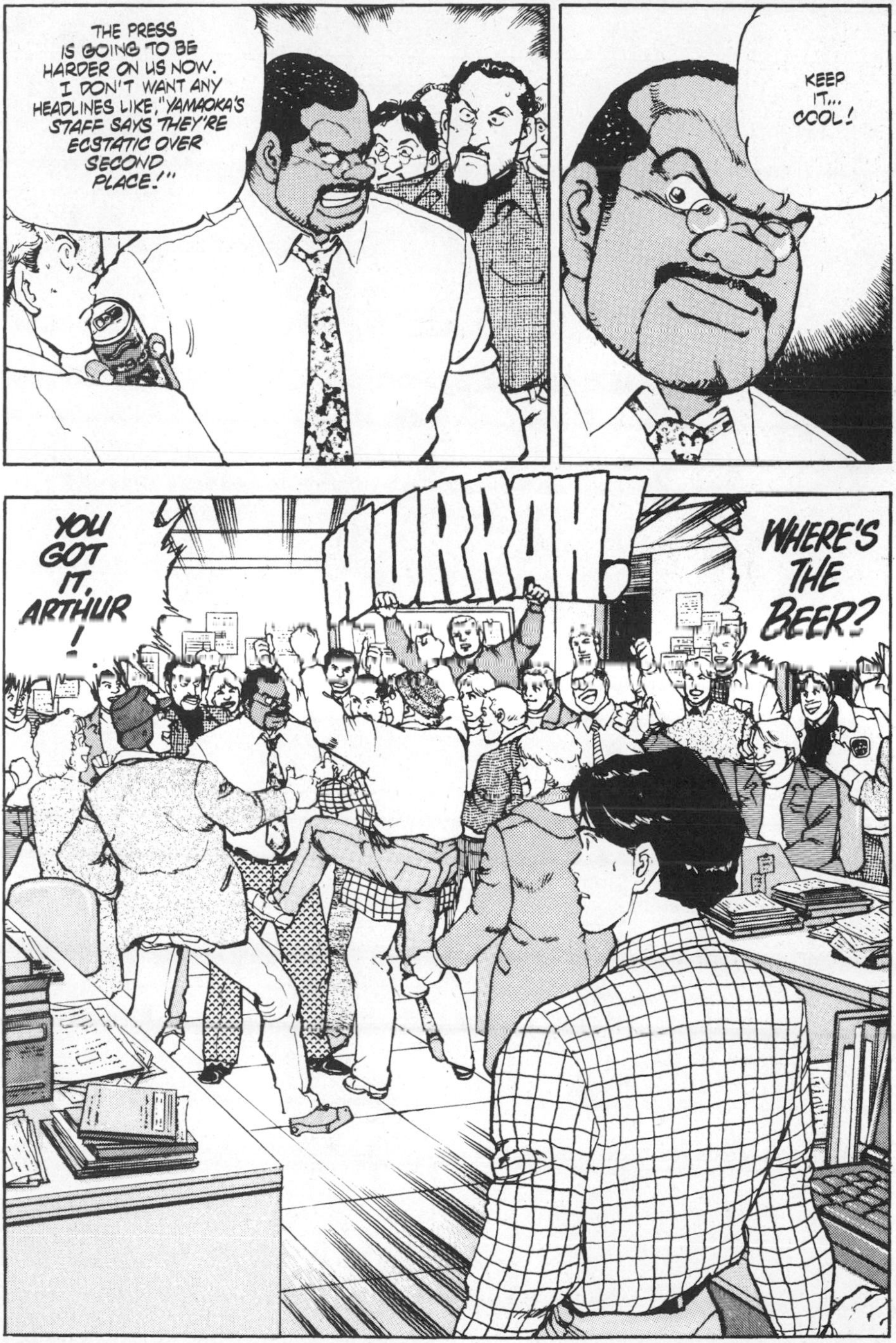
THE PRESS IS GOING TO BE HARDER ON US NOW. I DON'T WANT ANY HEADLINES LIKE, "YAMAOKA'S STAFF SAYS THEY'RE ECSTATIC OVER SECOND PLACE!"
KEEP IT... COOL!
YOU GOT IT, ARTHUR!
HURRAH!
WHERE'S THE BEER?

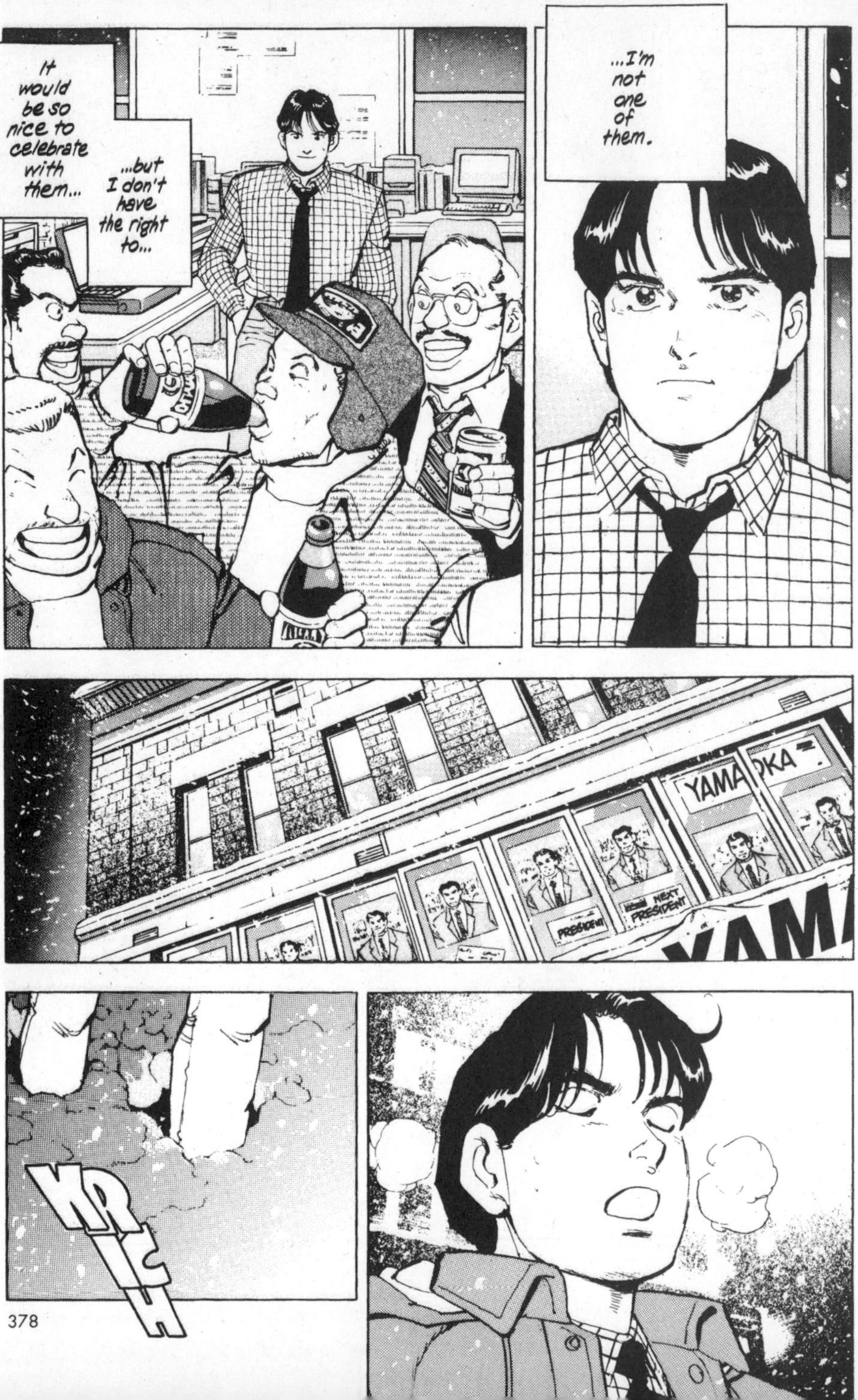
It would be so nice to celebrate with them...
...but I don't have the right to...
...I'm not one of them.
YAMAOKA
PRESIDENT
NEXT PRESIDENT
YAMA

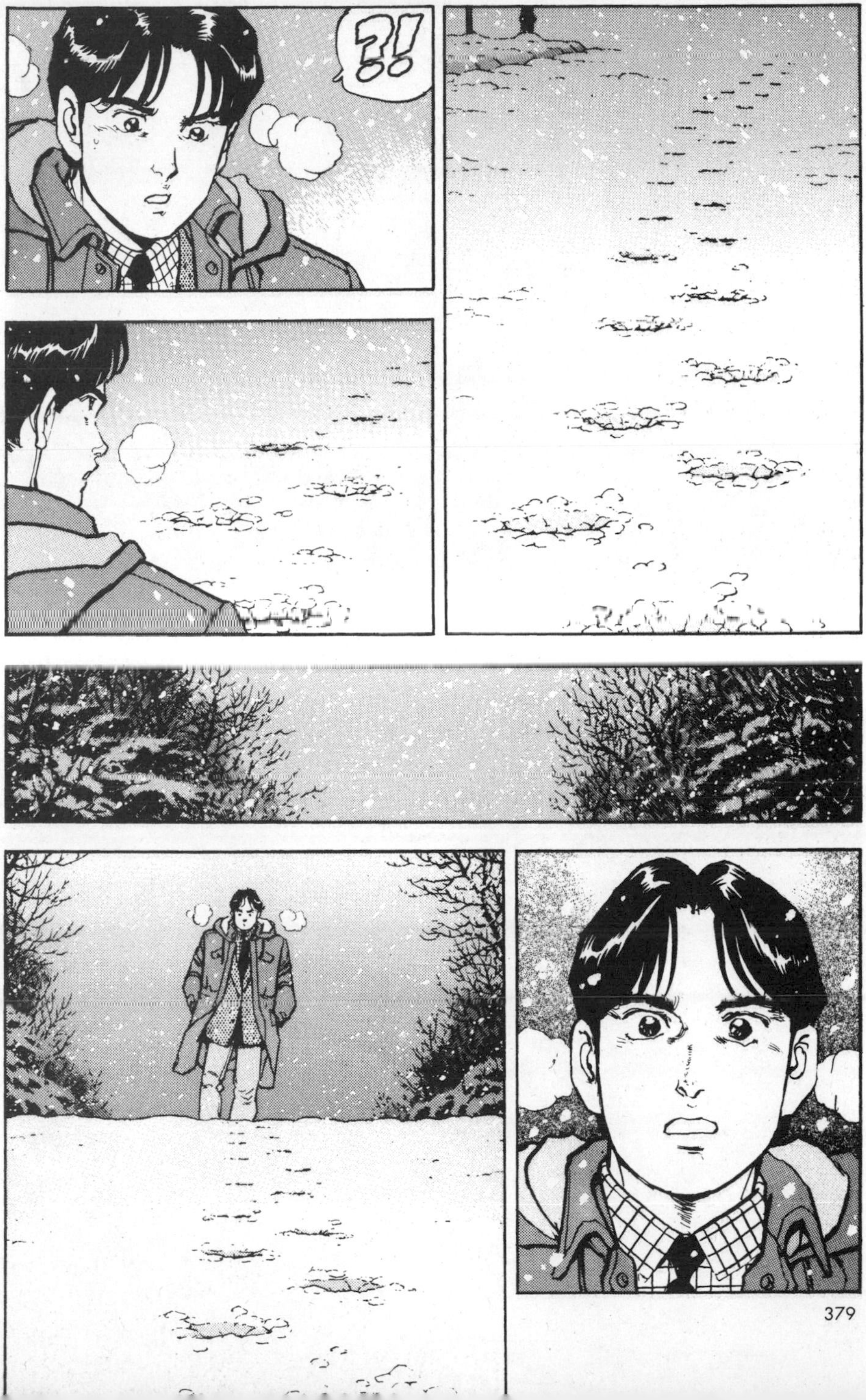
?!

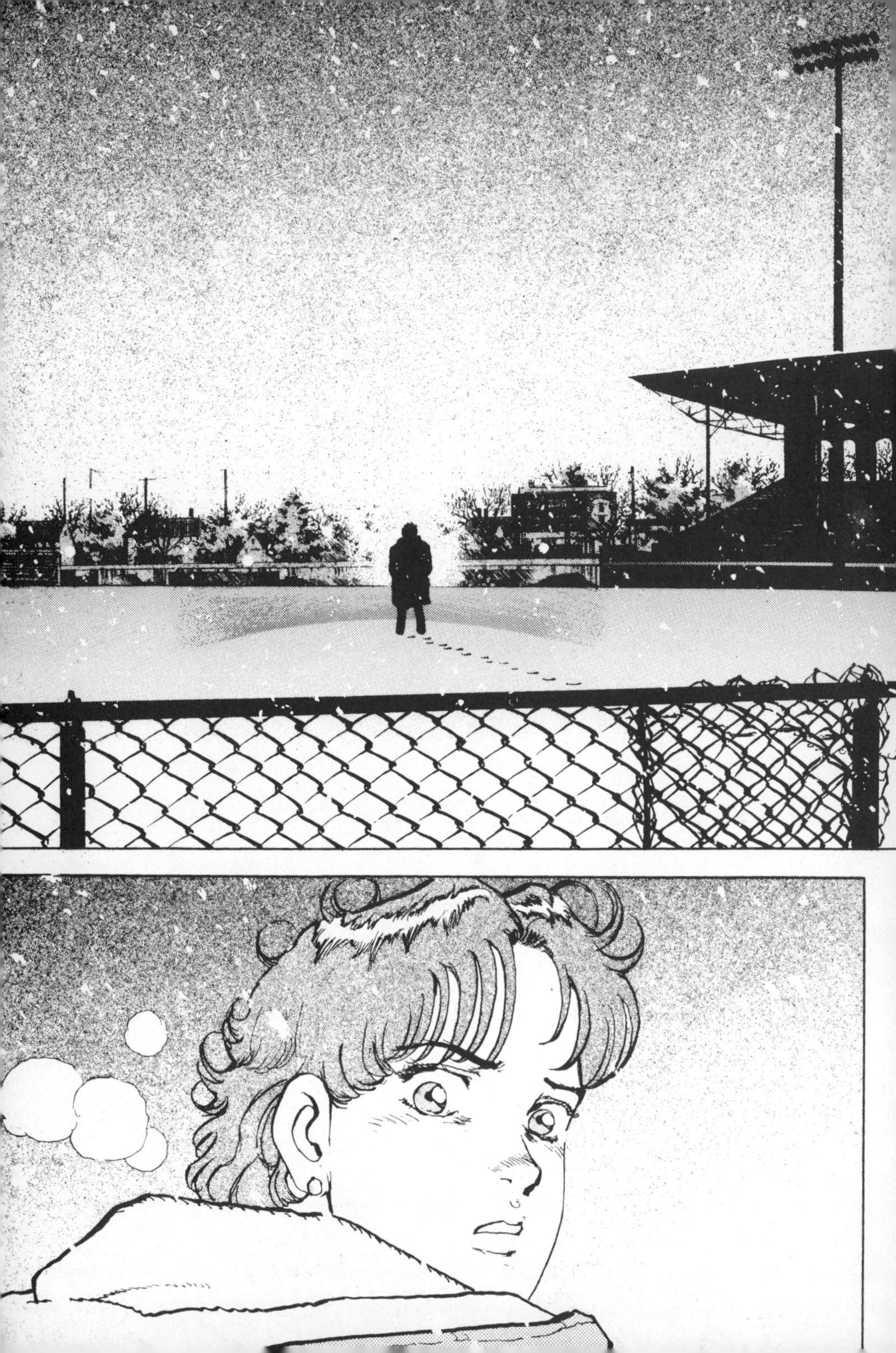

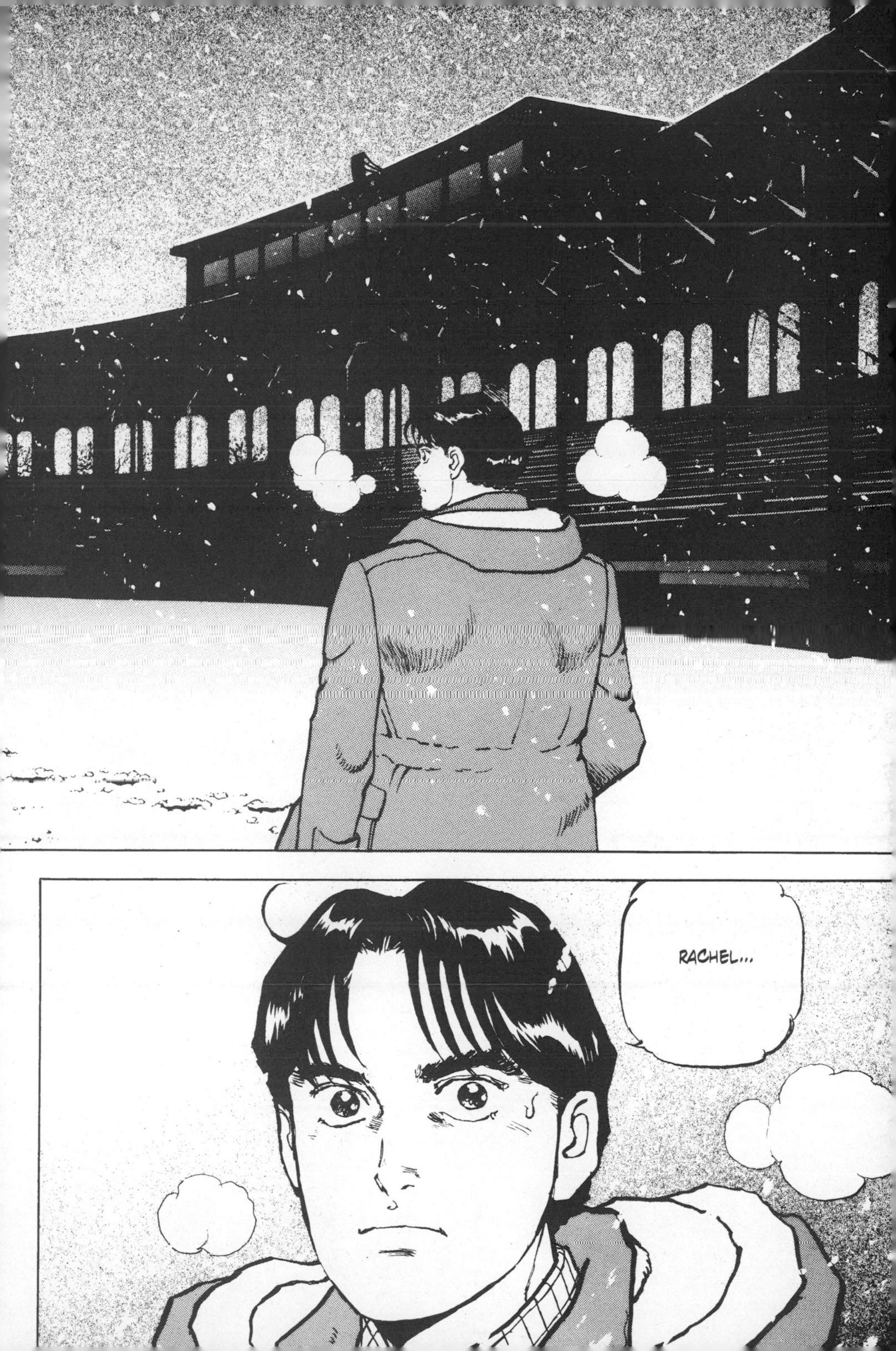
RACHEL...

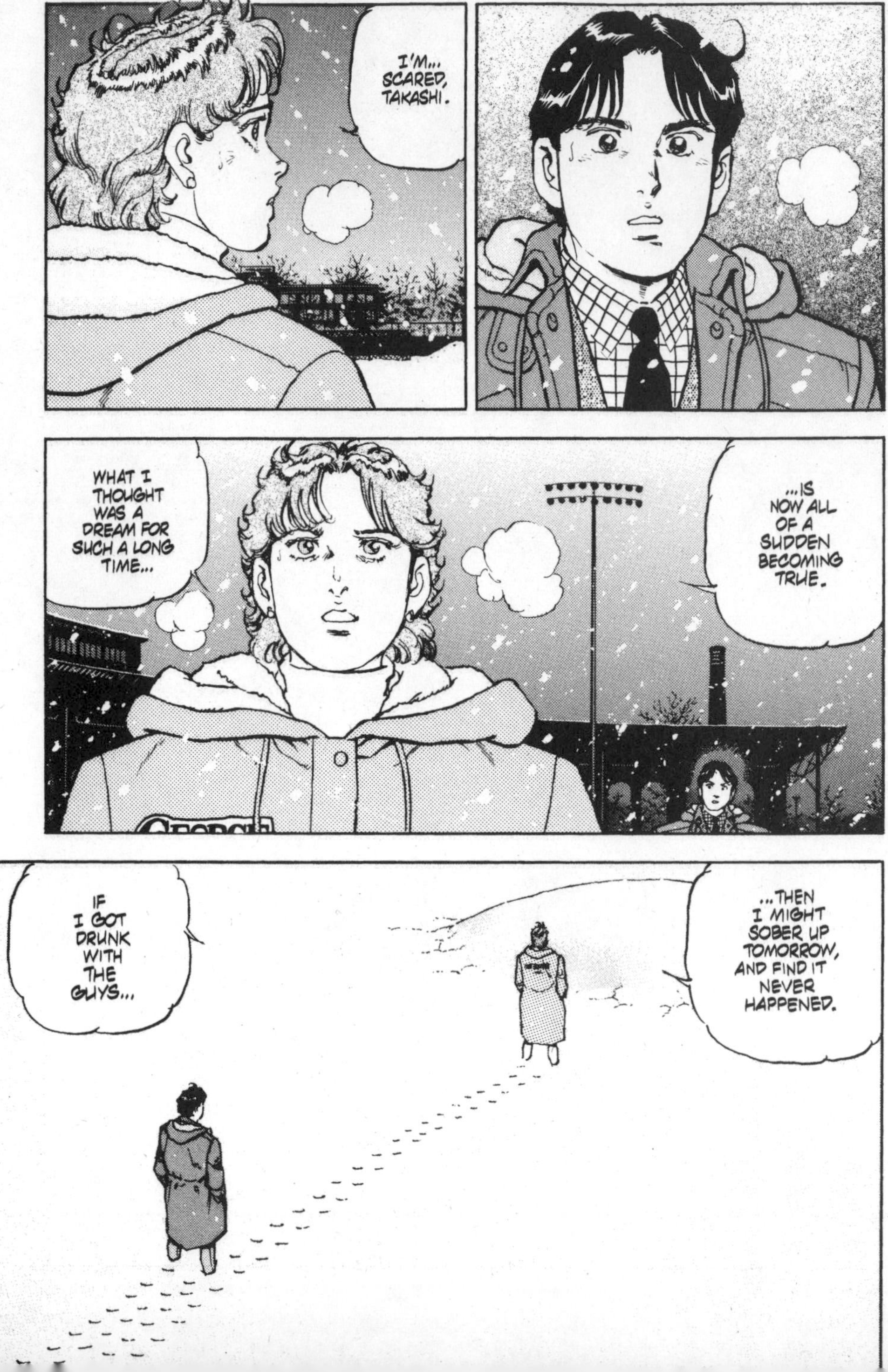
I'M... SCARED, TAKASHI.
WHAT I THOUGHT WAS A DREAM FOR SUCH A LONG TIME...
...IS NOW ALL OF A SUDDEN BECOMING TRUE.
IF I GOT DRUNK WITH THE GUYS...
...THEN I MIGHT SOBER UP TOMORROW, AND FIND IT NEVER HAPPENED.

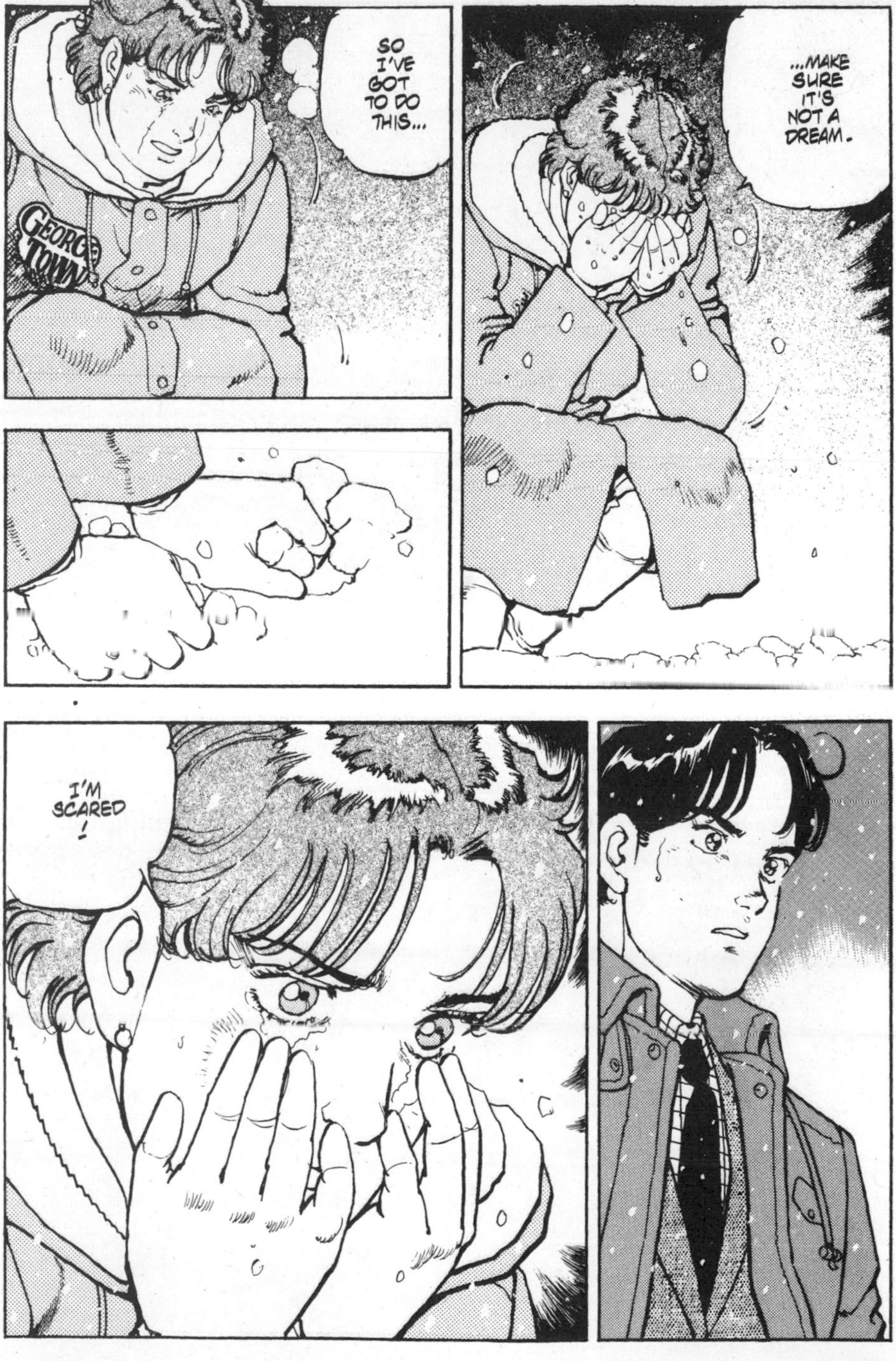
SO I'VE GOT TO DO THIS...
GEORGETOWN
...MAKE SURE IT'S NOT A DREAM.
I'M SCARED!

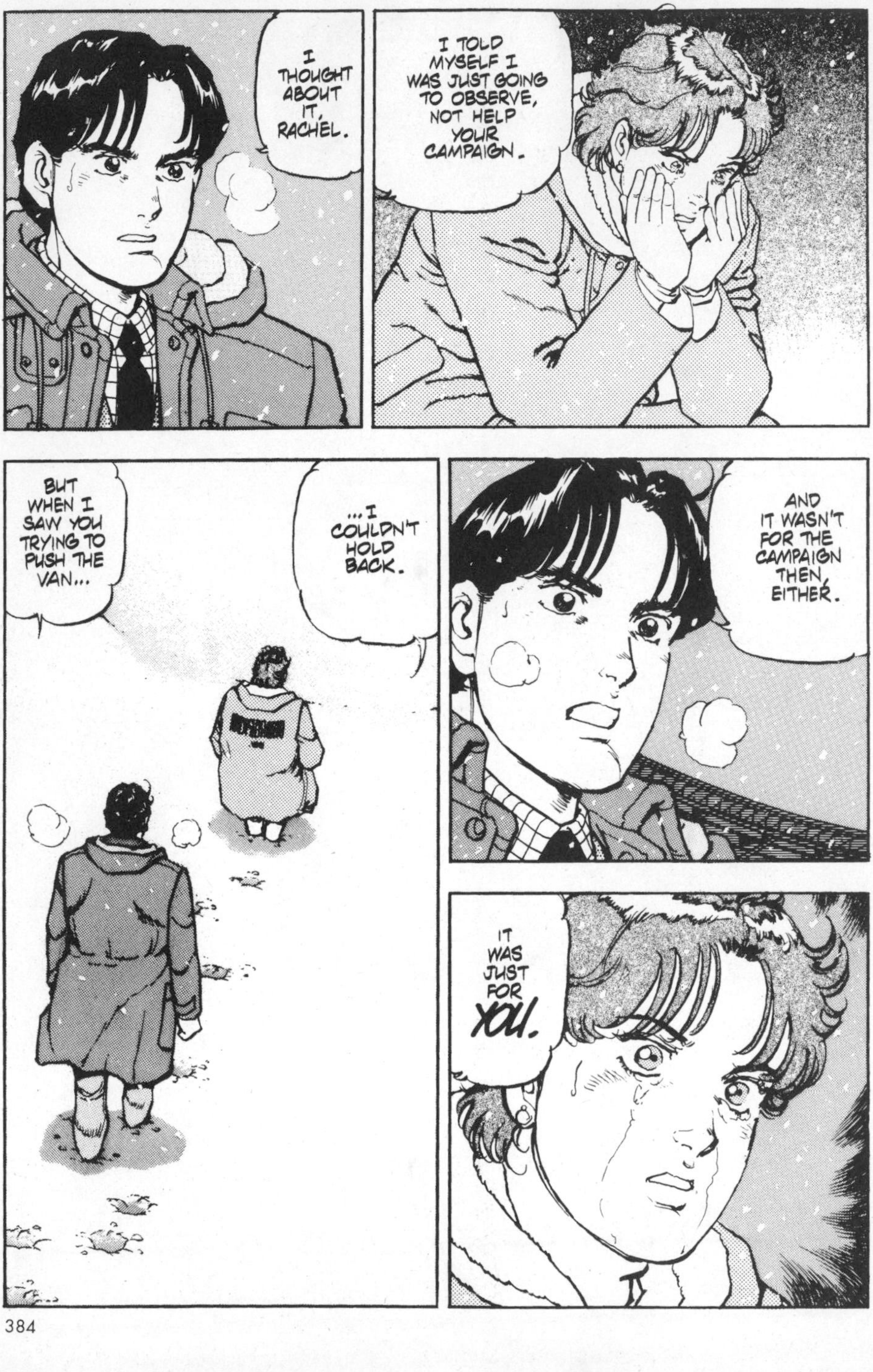
I THOUGHT ABOUT IT, RACHEL.
I TOLD MYSELF I WAS JUST GOING TO OBSERVE, NOT HELP YOUR CAMPAIGN.
BUT WHEN I SAW YOU TRYING TO PUSH THE VAN...
...I COULDN'T HOLD BACK.
AND IT WASN'T FOR THE CAMPAIGN THEN, EITHER.
IT WAS JUST FOR YOU.

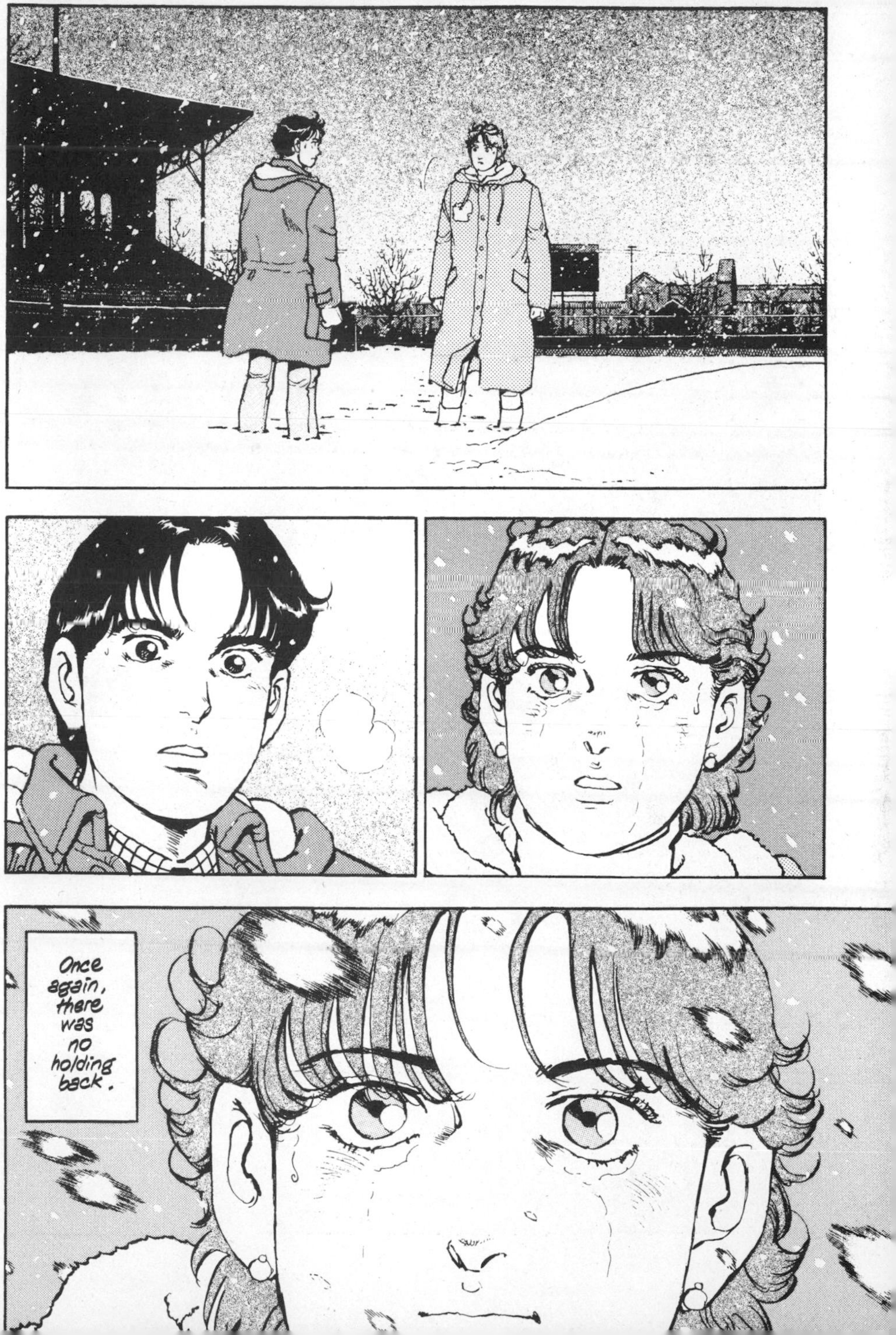
Once again, there was no holding back.

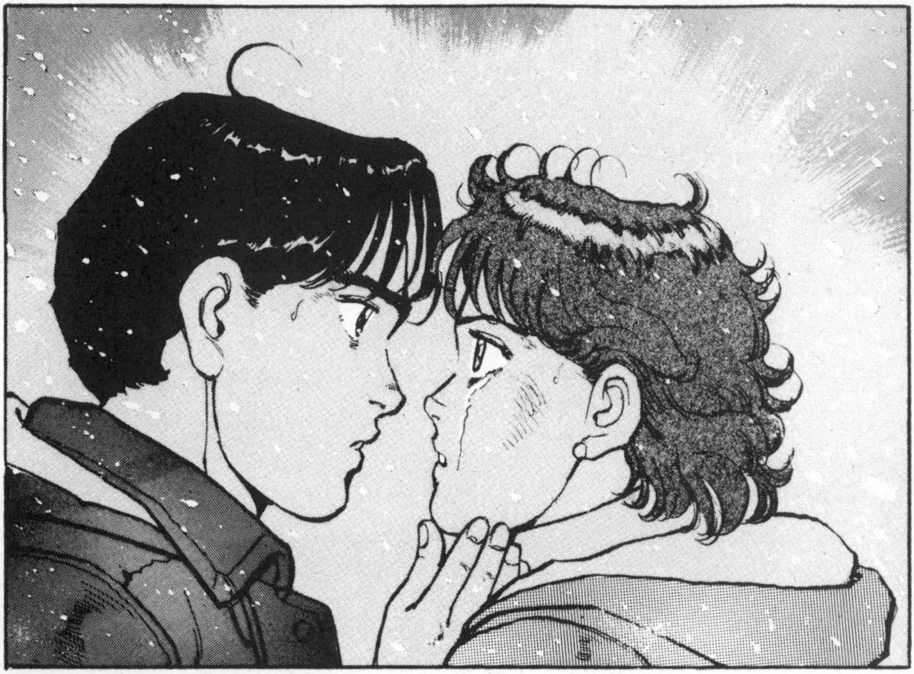

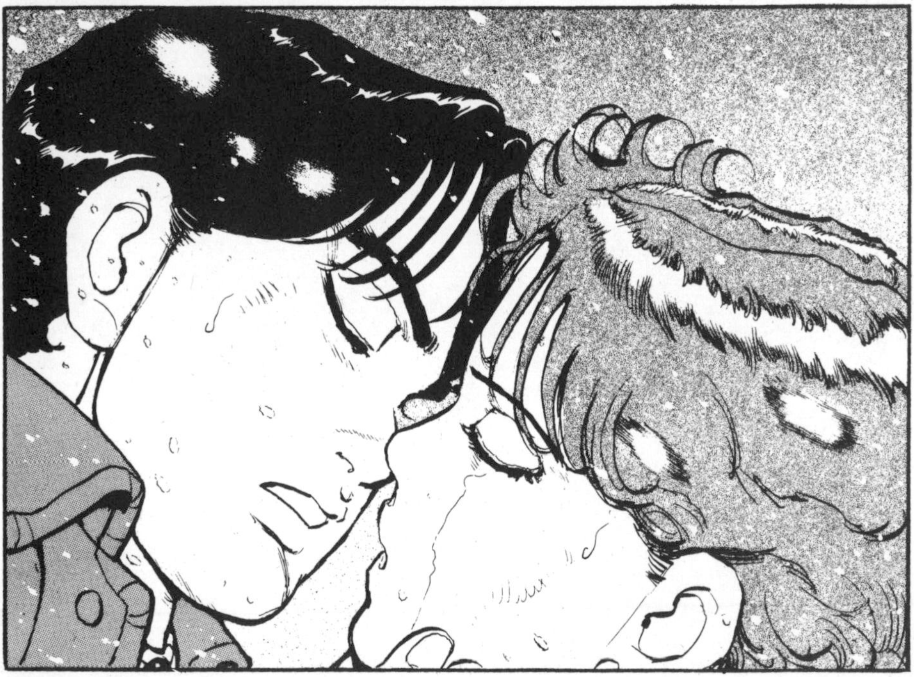

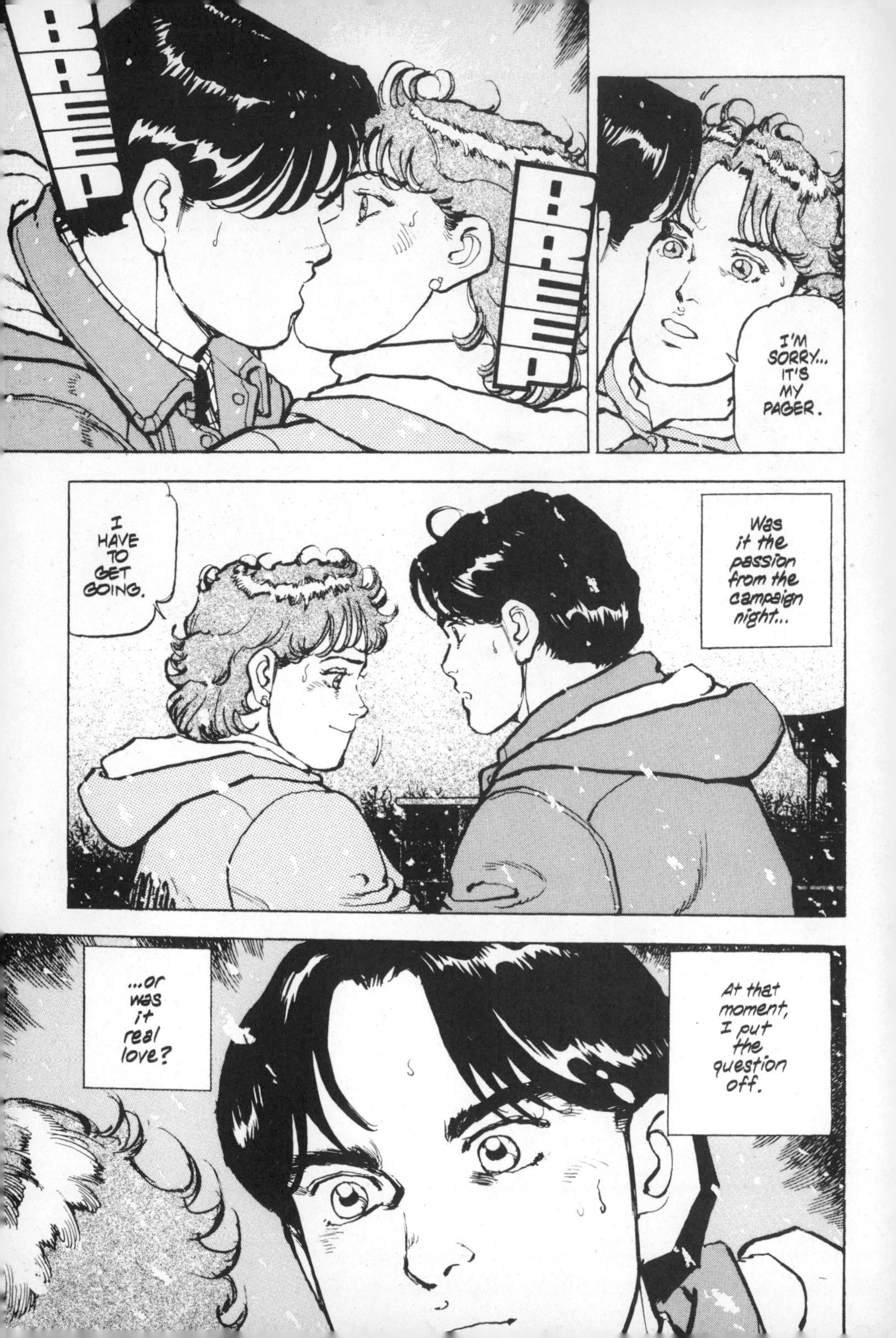
BREEP
BREEP
I'M SORRY... IT'S MY PAGER.
I HAVE TO GET GOING.
Was it the passion from the campaign night...
...or was it real love?
At that moment, I put the question off.

Offense/ Defense

Report #16

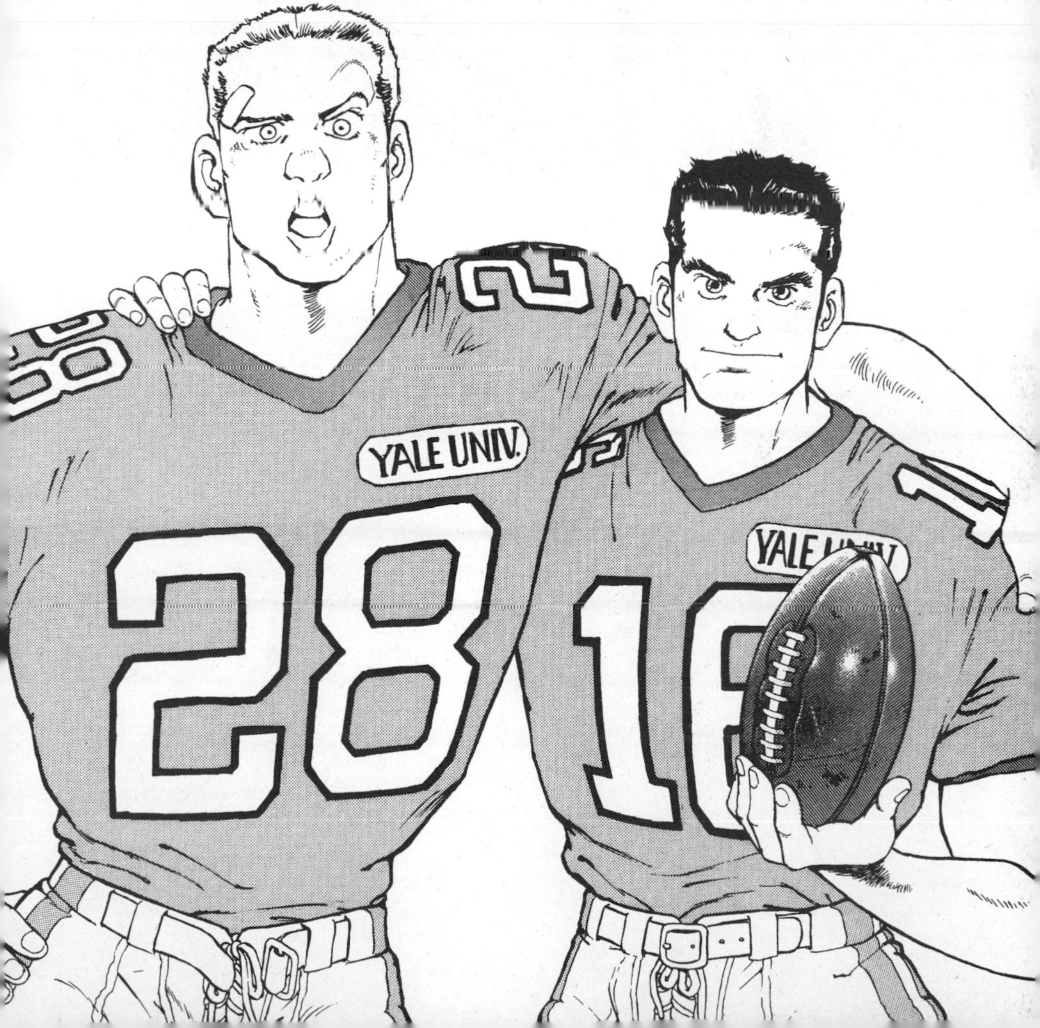
YALE UNIV.
28

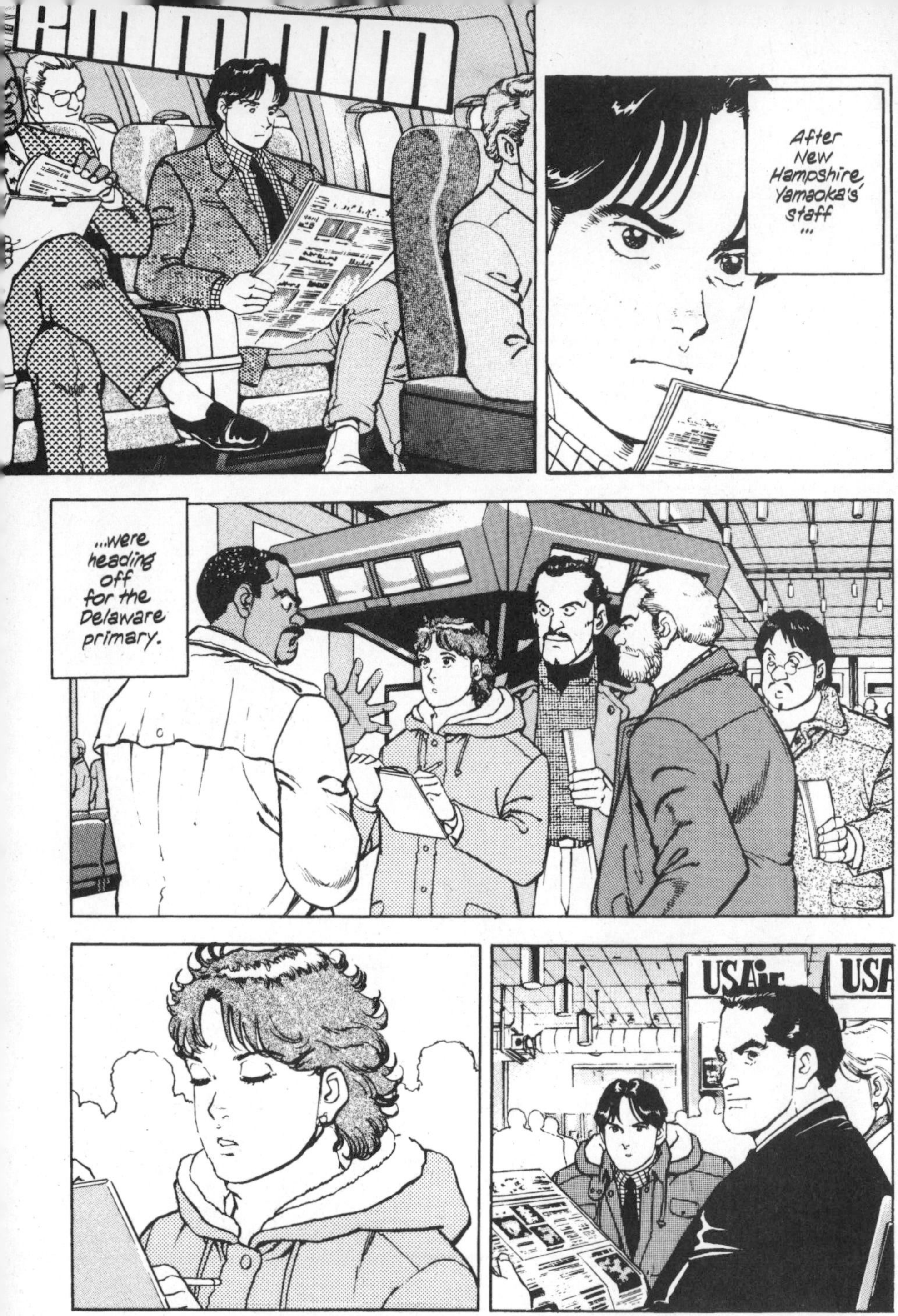
After New Hampshire, Yamaoka's staff ...
...were heading off for the Delaware primary.
USAir

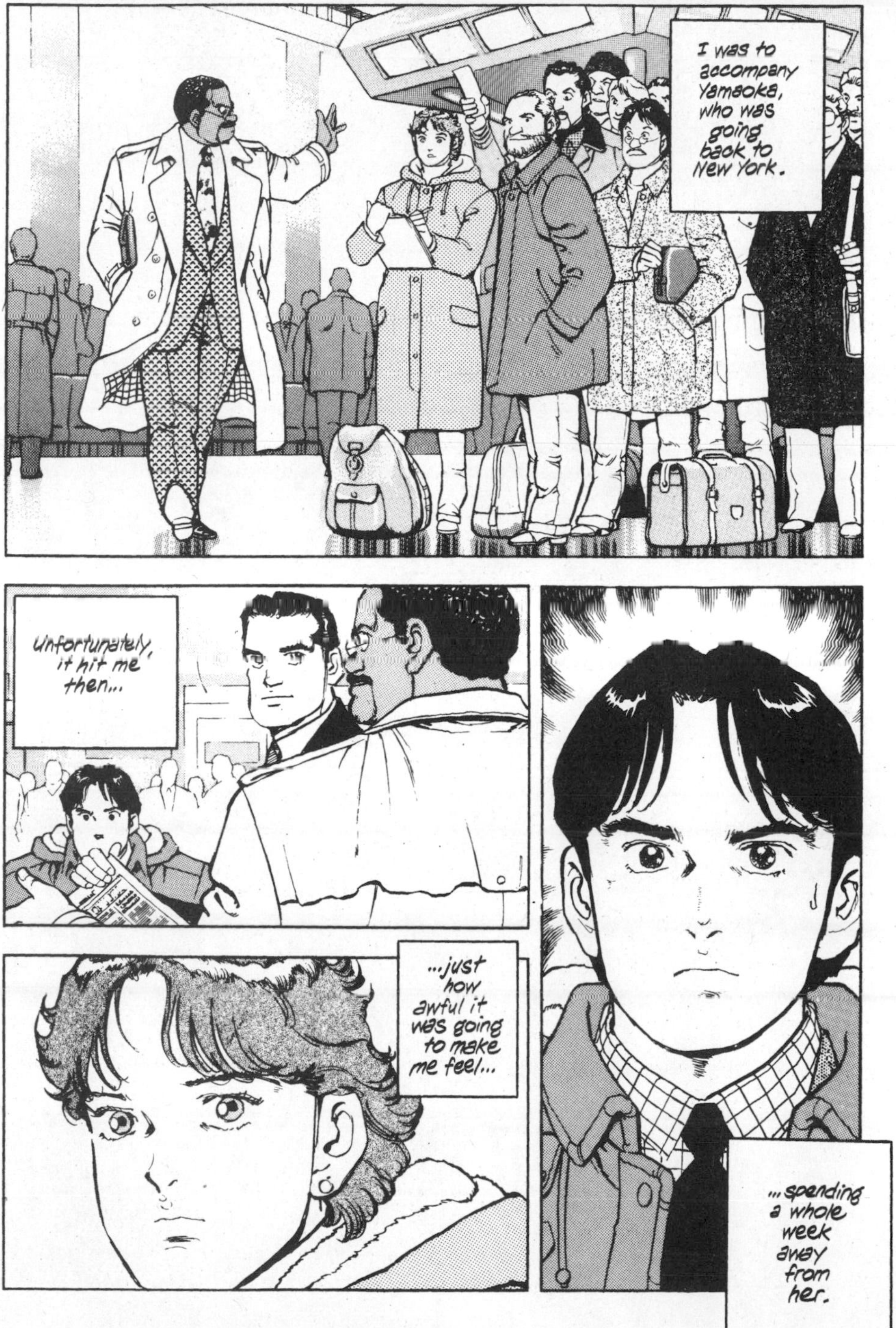
I was to accompany Yamaoka, who was going back to New York.
Unfortunately, it hit me then...
...just how awful it was going to make me feel...
...spending a whole week away from her.

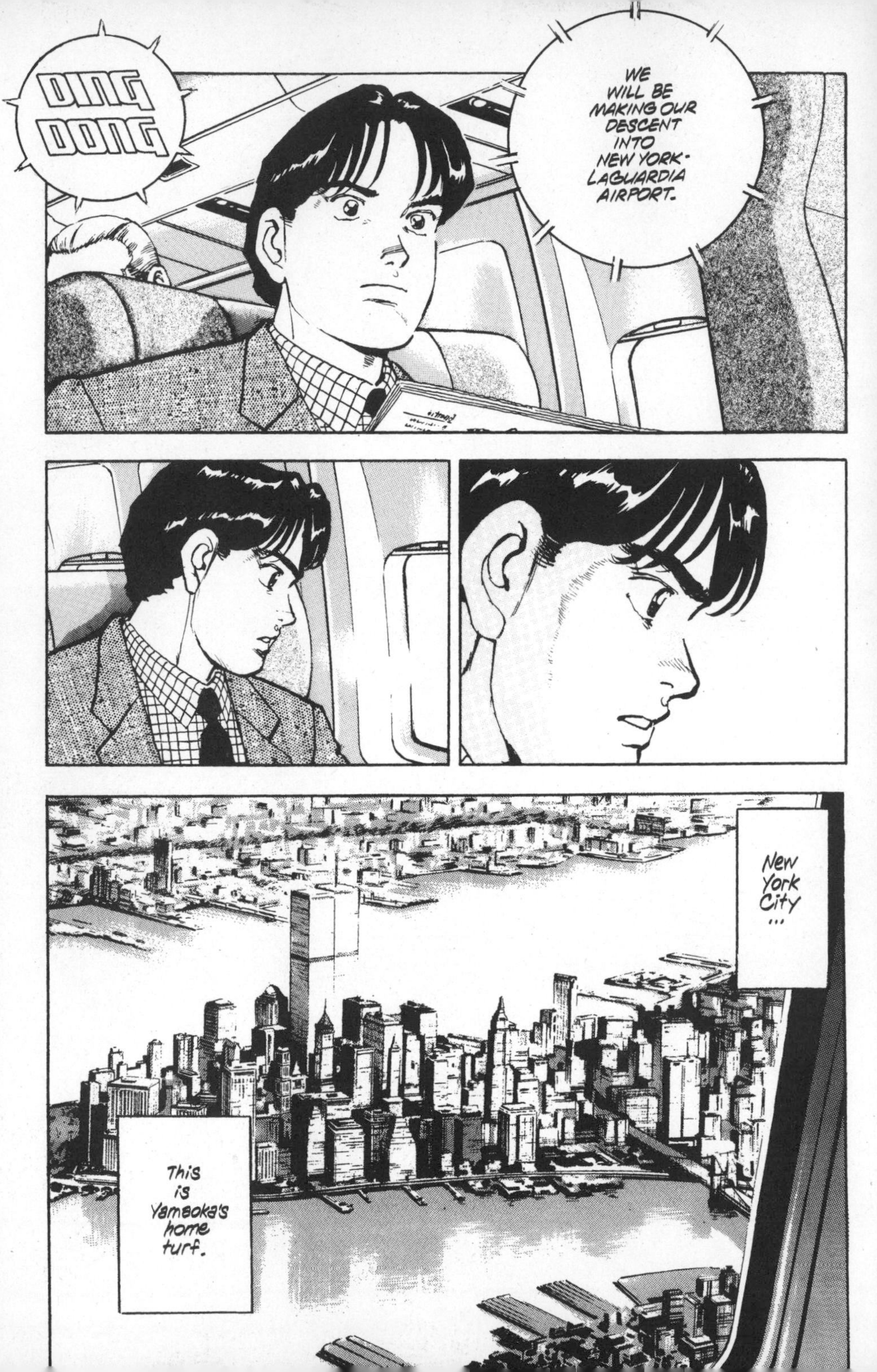
DING DONG
WE WILL BE MAKING OUR DESCENT INTO NEW YORK-LAGUARDIA AIRPORT.
New York City ...
This is Yamaoka's home turf.

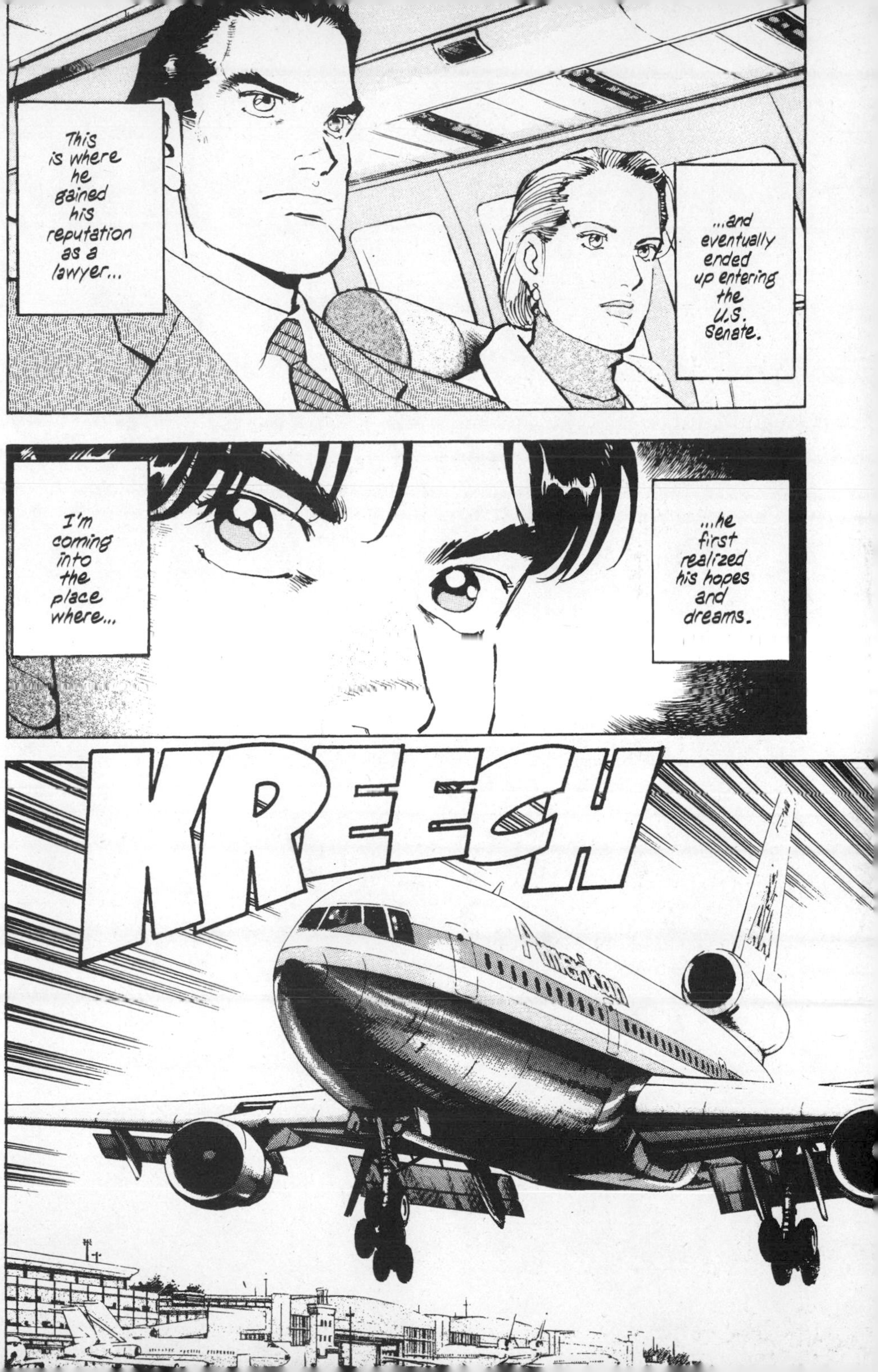
This is where he gained his reputation as a lawyer...
...and eventually ended up entering the U.S. Senate.
I'm coming into the place where...
...he first realized his hopes and dreams.
KREECH

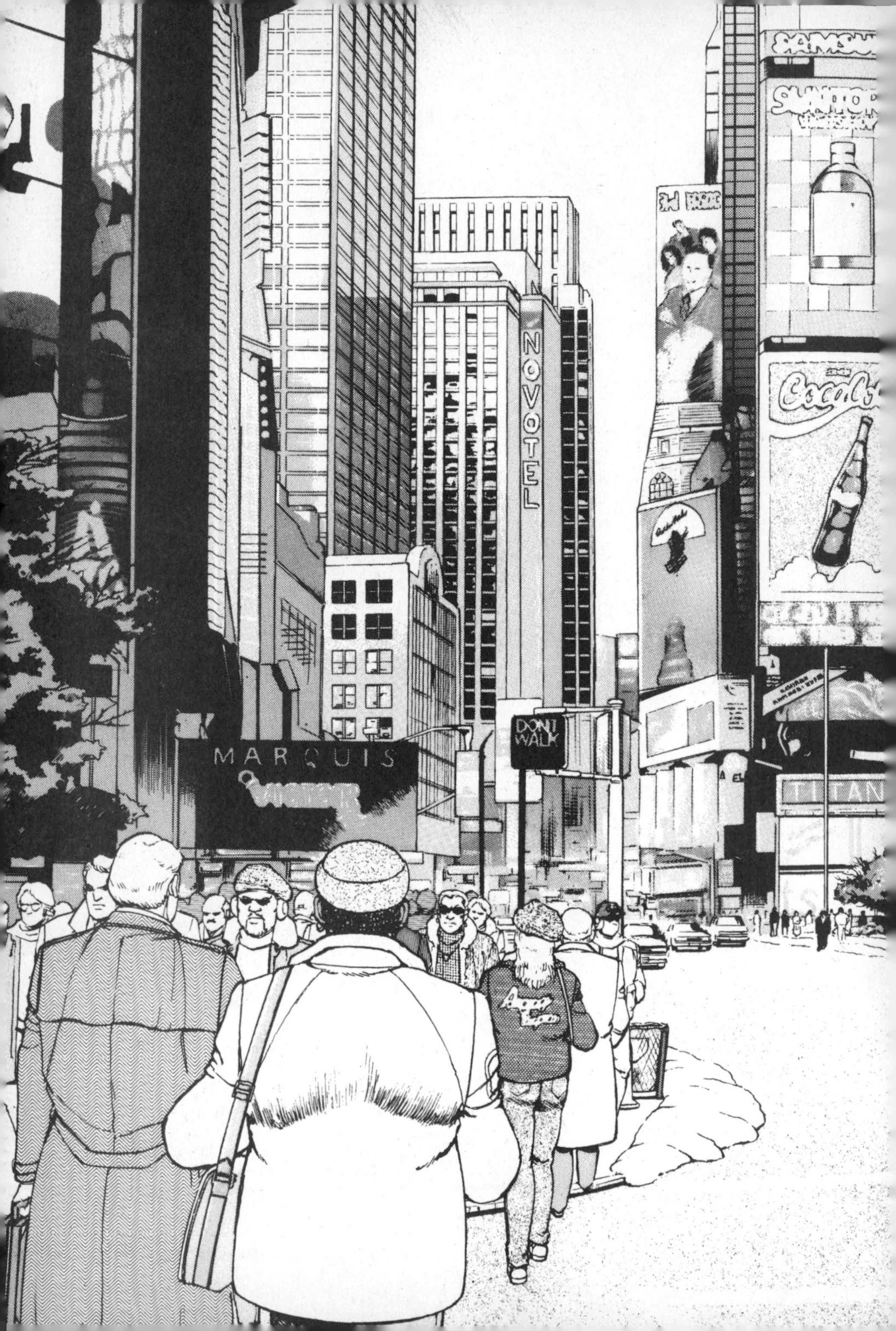
NOVOTEL
MARQUIS
DON'T WALK

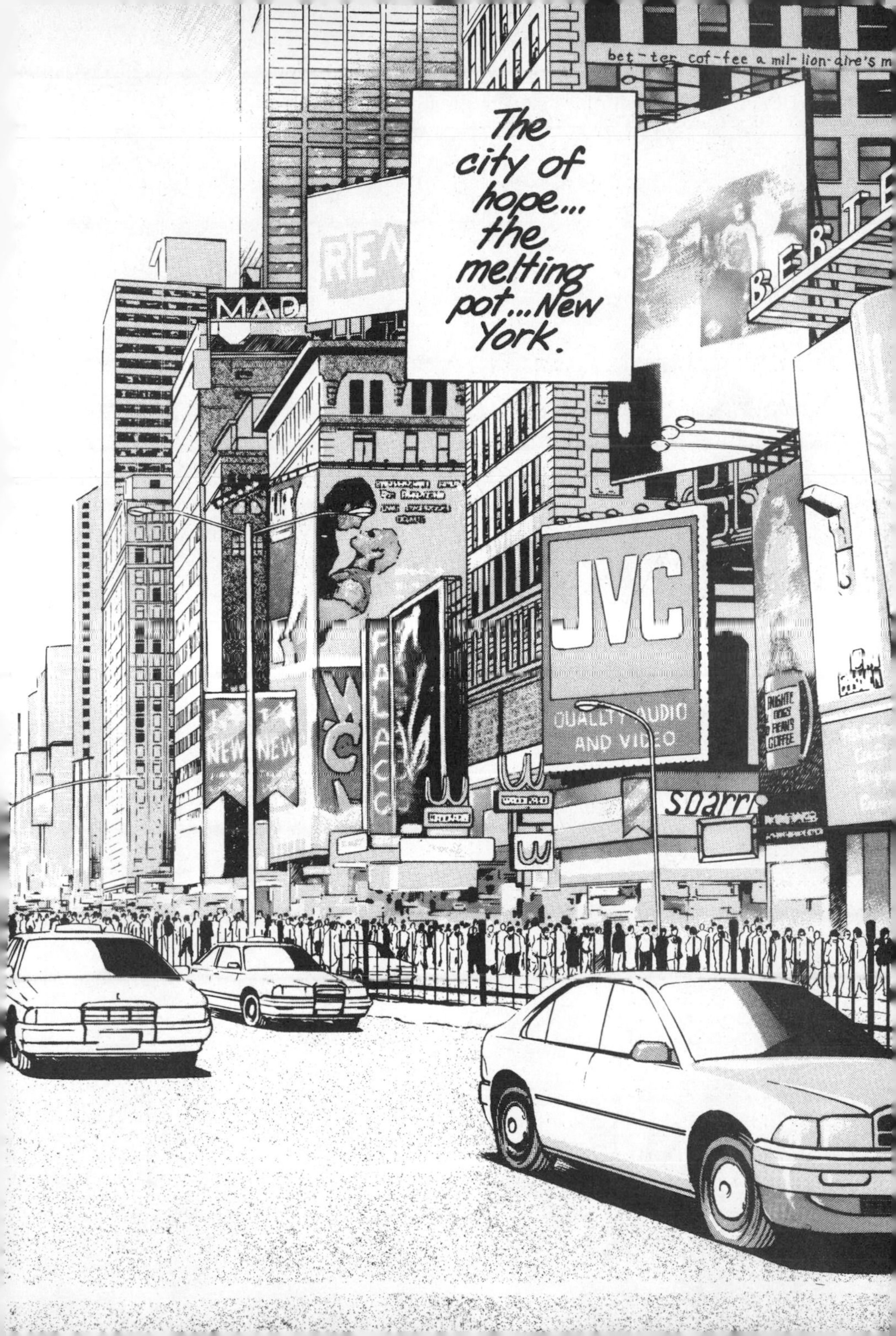
bet-ter cof-fee a mil-lion-aire's m
The city of hope... the melting pot... New York.
MAD
JVC
QUALITY AUDIO AND VIDEO
NEW NEW

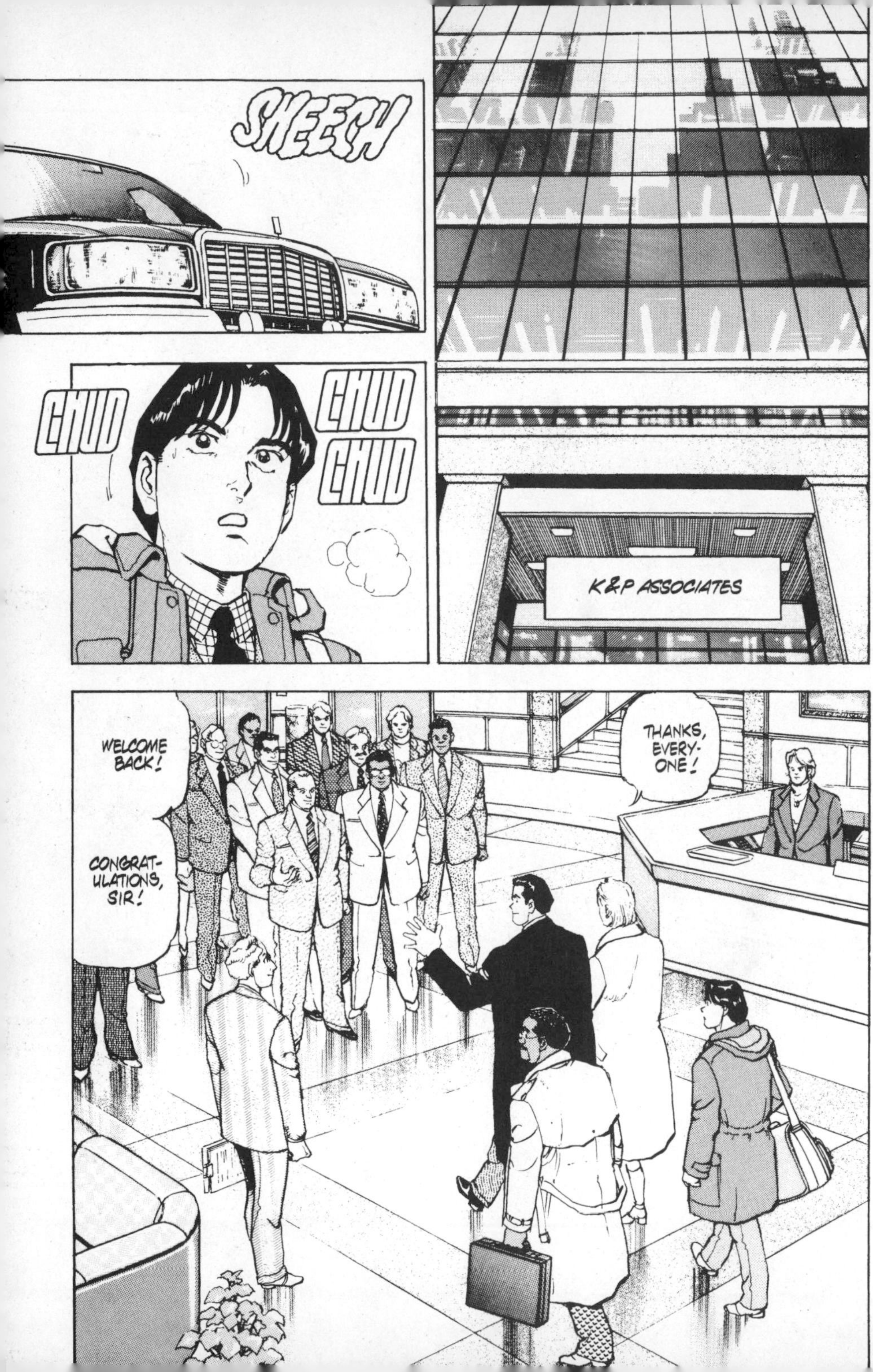
SHEECH
CHUD
CHUD CHUD
K&P ASSOCIATES
WELCOME BACK!
CONGRAT-ULATIONS, SIR!
THANKS, EVERY-ONE!

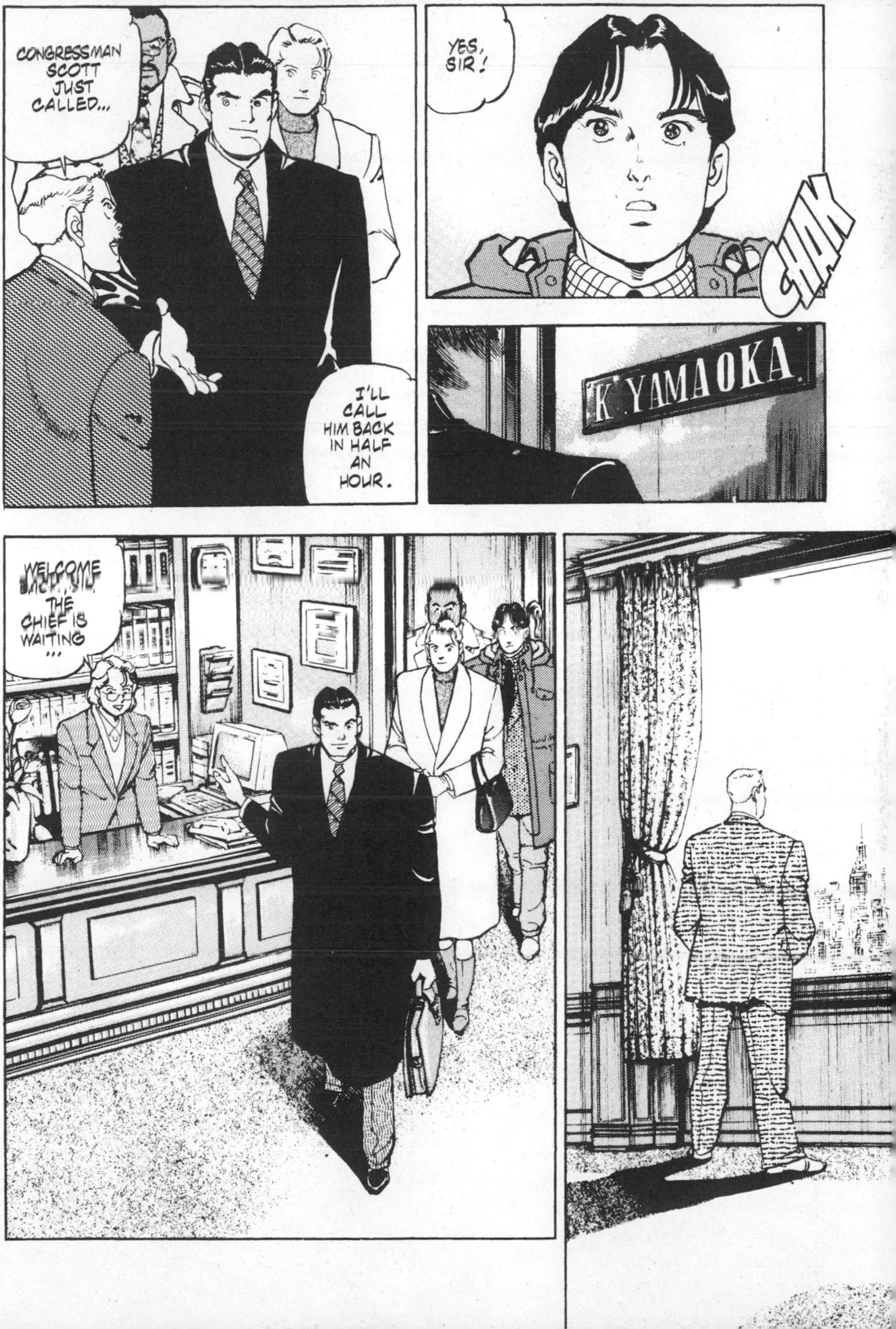
CONGRESSMAN SCOTT JUST CALLED...
I'LL CALL HIM BACK IN HALF AN HOUR.
YES, SIR!
CHAK
K. YAMAOKA
WELCOME BACK, SIR. THE CHIEF IS WAITING...

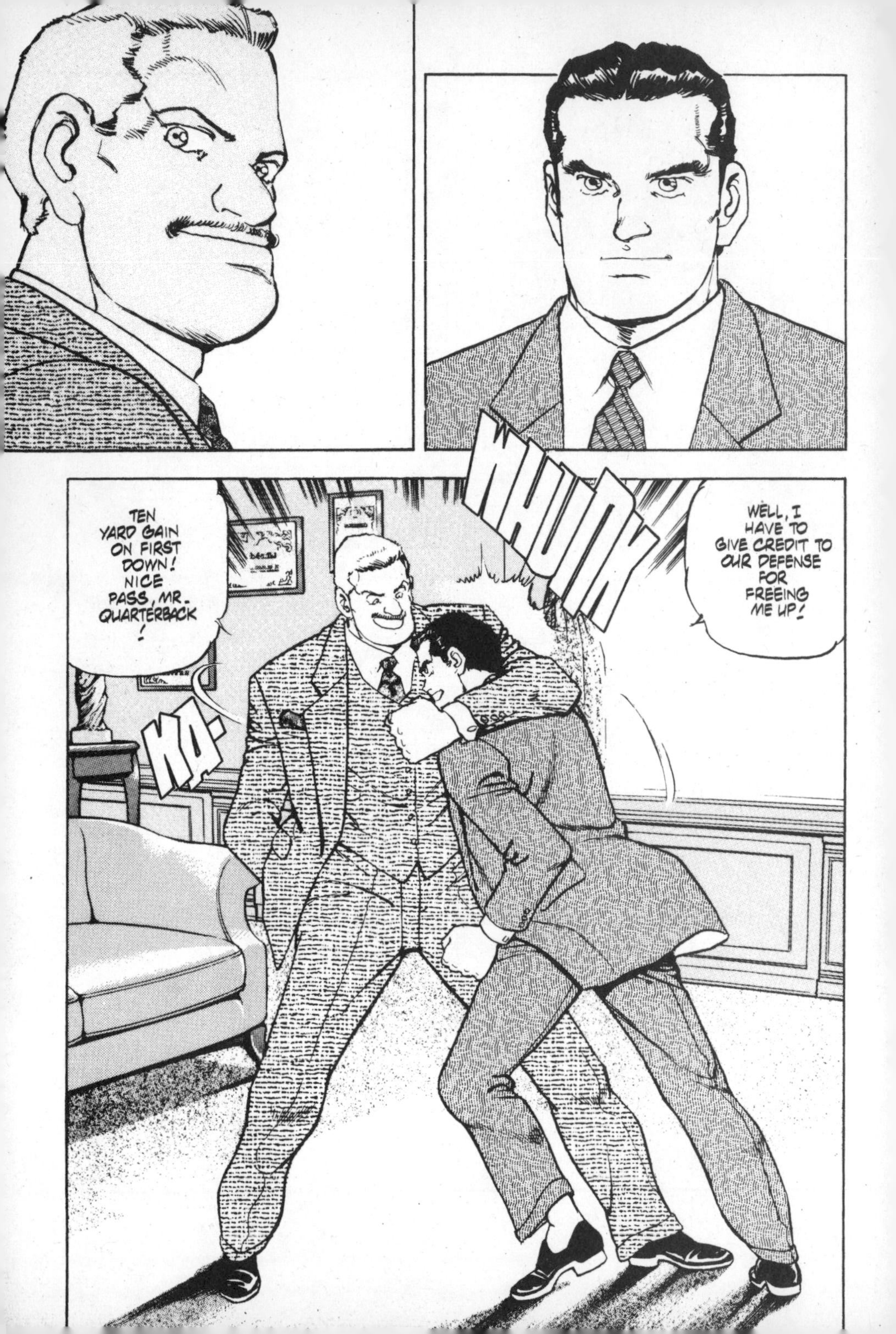
WHUMP
TEN YARD GAIN ON FIRST DOWN! NICE PASS, MR. QUARTERBACK!
WELL, I HAVE TO GIVE CREDIT TO OUR DEFENSE FOR FREEING ME UP!
KA-

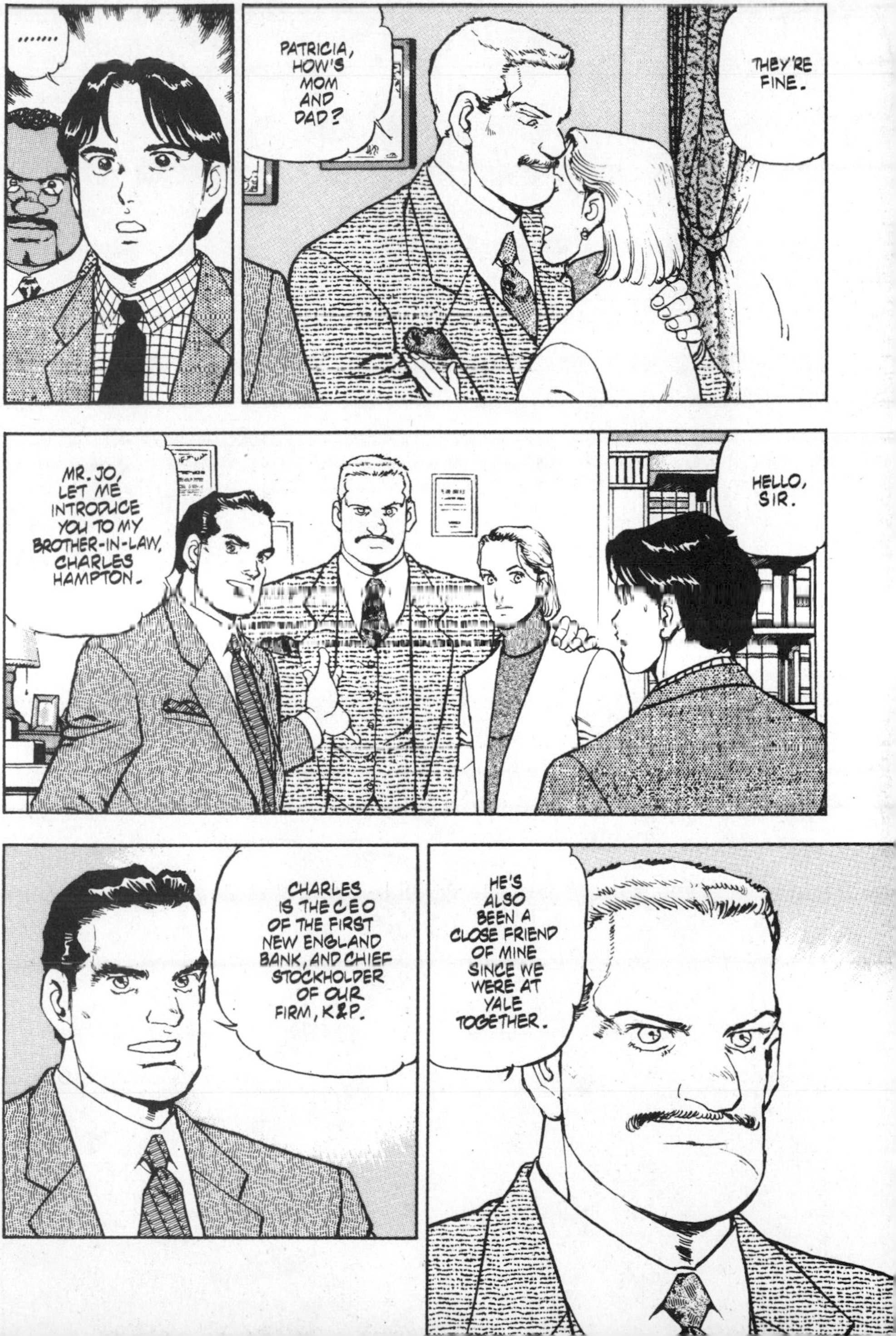
....
PATRICIA, HOW'S MOM AND DAD?
THEY'RE FINE.
MR. JO, LET ME INTRODUCE YOU TO MY BROTHER-IN-LAW, CHARLES HAMPTON.
HELLO, SIR.
CHARLES IS THE CEO OF THE FIRST NEW ENGLAND BANK, AND CHIEF STOCKHOLDER OF OUR FIRM, K&P.
HE'S ALSO BEEN A CLOSE FRIEND OF MINE SINCE WE WERE AT YALE TOGETHER.

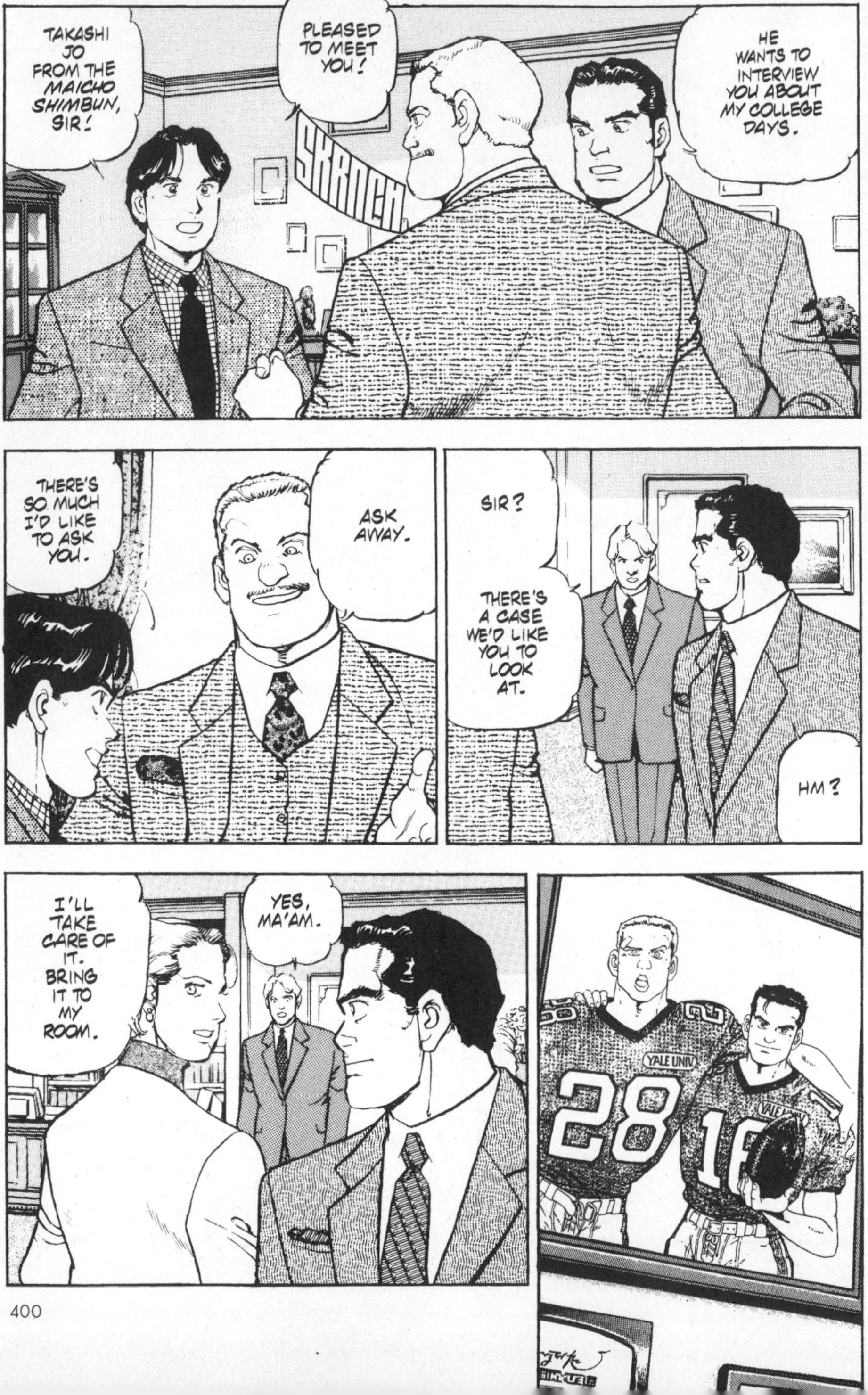
TAKASHI JO FROM THE *MAICHO SHIMBUN*, SIR!
PLEASED TO MEET YOU!
SKRNCH
HE WANTS TO INTERVIEW YOU ABOUT MY COLLEGE DAYS.
THERE'S SO MUCH I'D LIKE TO ASK YOU.
ASK AWAY.
SIR?
THERE'S A CASE WE'D LIKE YOU TO LOOK AT.
HM?
I'LL TAKE CARE OF IT. BRING IT TO MY ROOM.
YES, MA'AM.
YALE UNIV
28

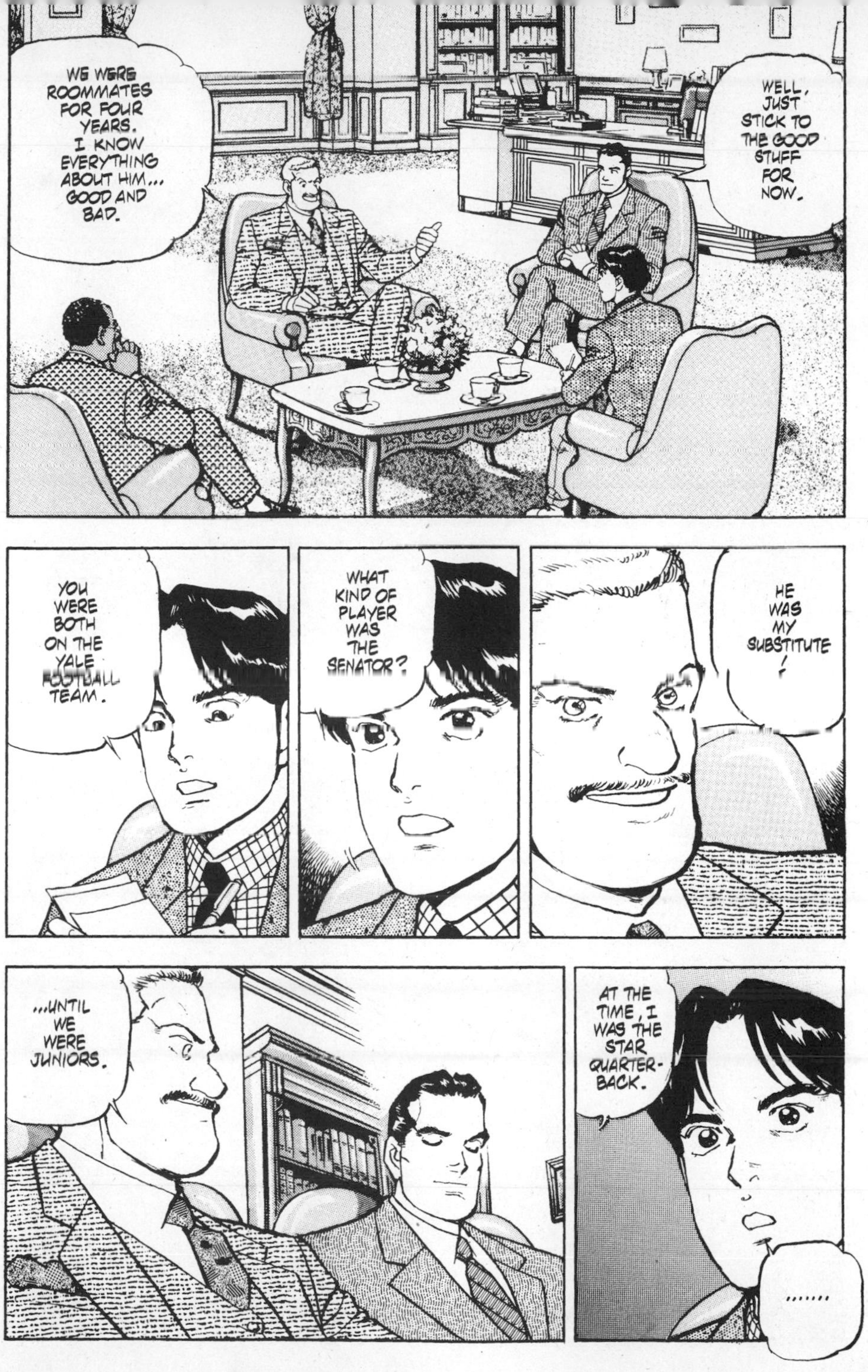
WE WERE ROOMMATES FOR FOUR YEARS. I KNOW EVERYTHING ABOUT HIM... GOOD AND BAD.
WELL, JUST STICK TO THE GOOD STUFF FOR NOW.
YOU WERE BOTH ON THE YALE FOOTBALL TEAM.
WHAT KIND OF PLAYER WAS THE SENATOR?
HE WAS MY SUBSTITUTE!
...UNTIL WE WERE JUNIORS.
AT THE TIME, I WAS THE STAR QUARTER-BACK.
....

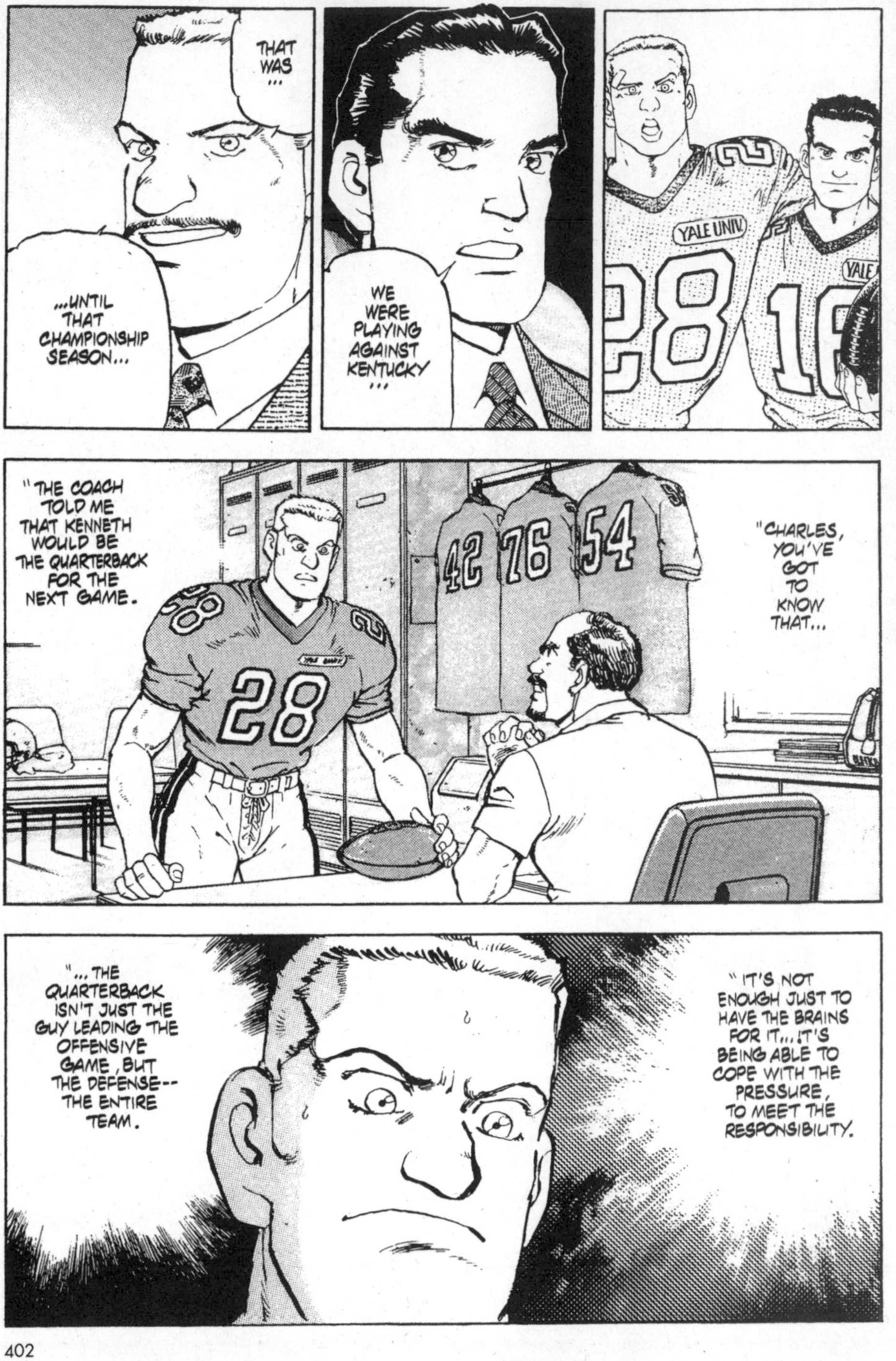
THAT WAS ...
...UNTIL THAT CHAMPIONSHIP SEASON...
WE WERE PLAYING AGAINST KENTUCKY ...
YALE UNIV.
28
YALE
16
"THE COACH TOLD ME THAT KENNETH WOULD BE THE QUARTERBACK FOR THE NEXT GAME.
42
76
54
"CHARLES, YOU'VE GOT TO KNOW THAT...
28
"... THE QUARTERBACK ISN'T JUST THE GUY LEADING THE OFFENSIVE GAME, BUT THE DEFENSE-- THE ENTIRE TEAM.
"IT'S NOT ENOUGH JUST TO HAVE THE BRAINS FOR IT... IT'S BEING ABLE TO COPE WITH THE PRESSURE, TO MEET THE RESPONSIBILITY.

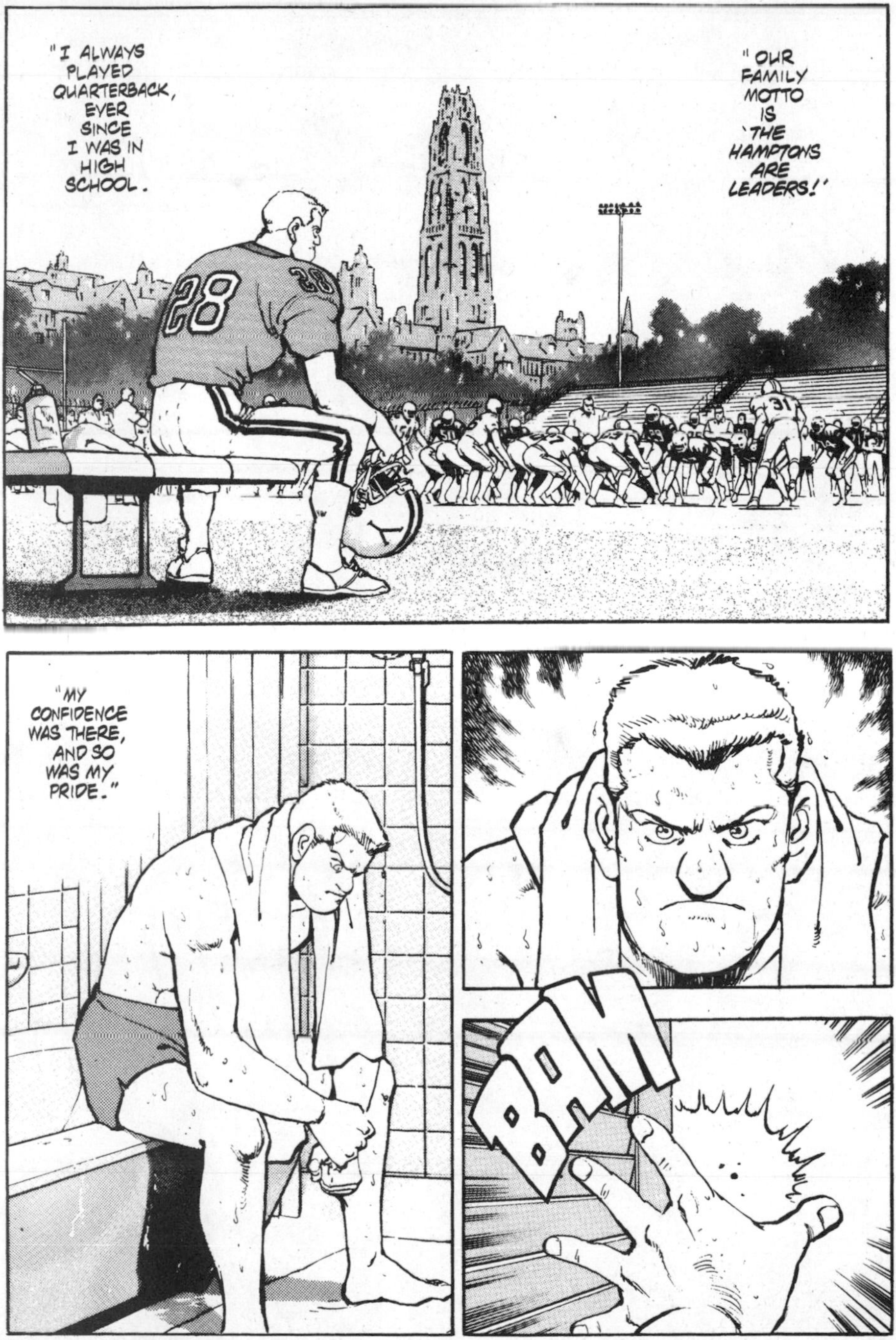
"I ALWAYS PLAYED QUARTERBACK, EVER SINCE I WAS IN HIGH SCHOOL.
"OUR FAMILY MOTTO IS `THE HAMPTONS ARE LEADERS!'
"MY CONFIDENCE WAS THERE, AND SO WAS MY PRIDE."
BAM

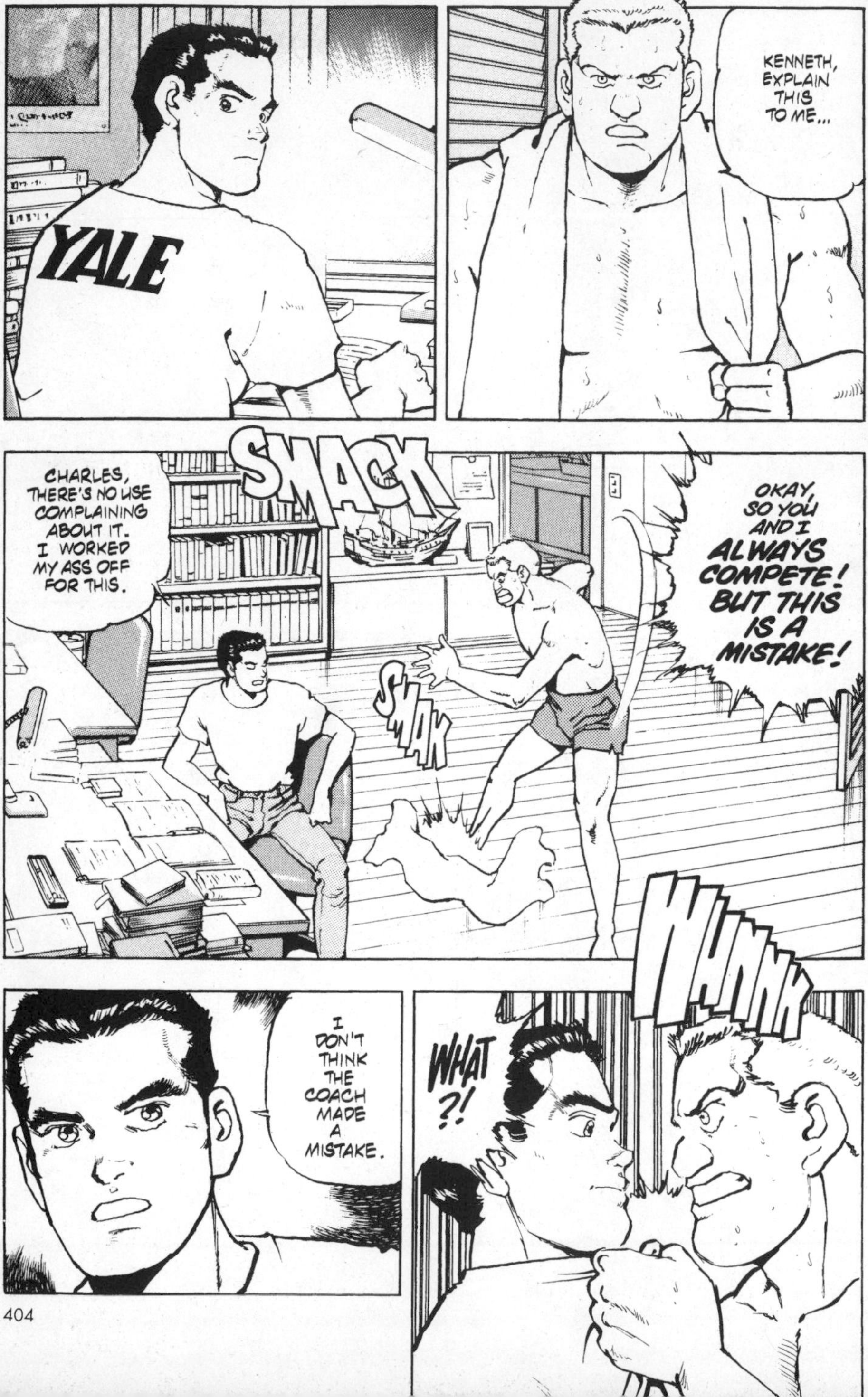
YALE
KENNETH, EXPLAIN THIS TO ME...
SMACK
CHARLES, THERE'S NO USE COMPLAINING ABOUT IT. I WORKED MY ASS OFF FOR THIS.
SMAK
OKAY, SO YOU AND I ALWAYS COMPETE! BUT THIS IS A MISTAKE!
I DON'T THINK THE COACH MADE A MISTAKE.
WHAT ?!
WHUNNK

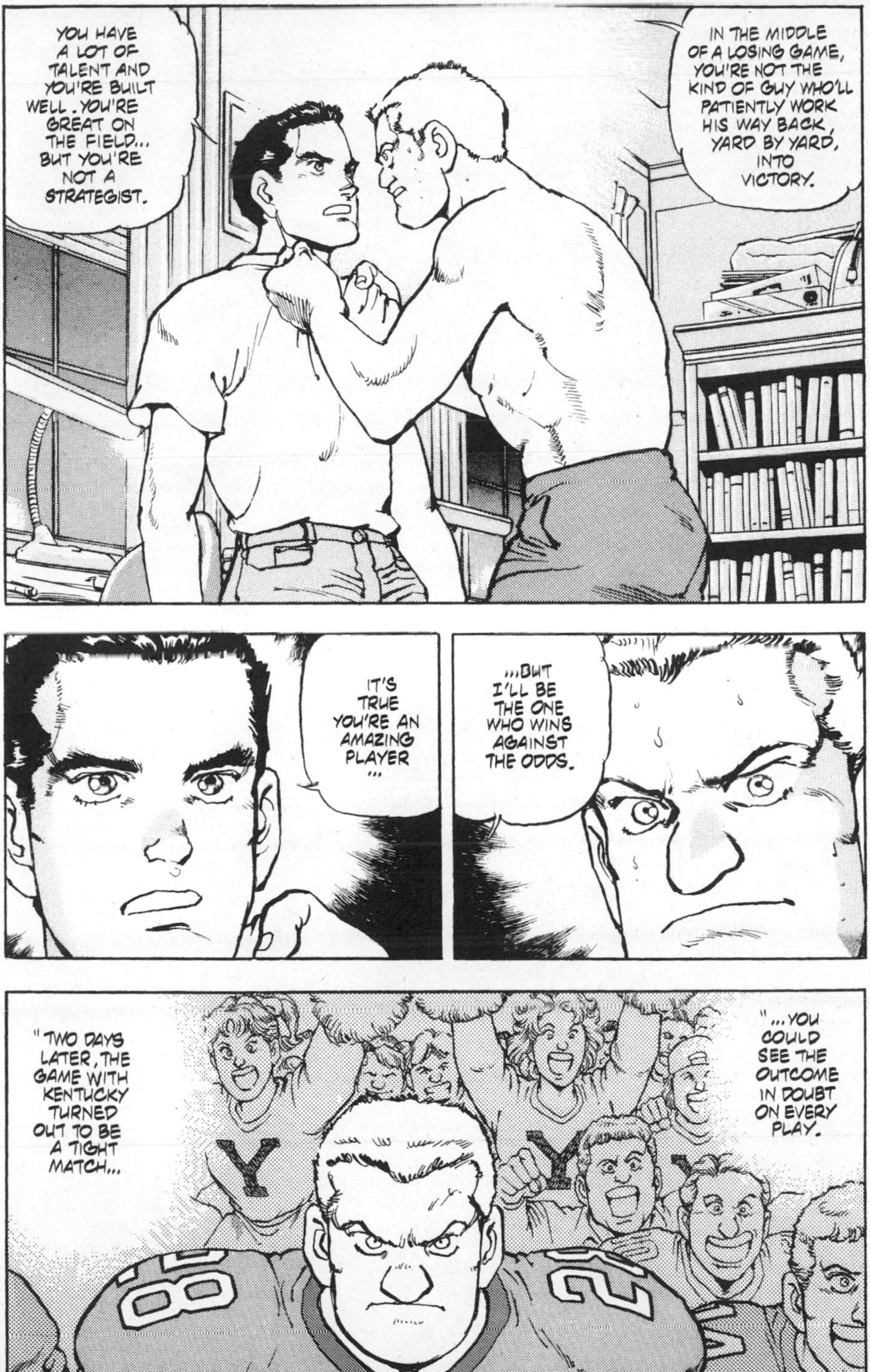
YOU HAVE A LOT OF TALENT AND YOU'RE BUILT WELL. YOU'RE GREAT ON THE FIELD... BUT YOU'RE NOT A STRATEGIST.
IN THE MIDDLE OF A LOSING GAME, YOU'RE NOT THE KIND OF GUY WHO'LL PATIENTLY WORK HIS WAY BACK, YARD BY YARD, INTO VICTORY.
IT'S TRUE YOU'RE AN AMAZING PLAYER ...
...BUT I'LL BE THE ONE WHO WINS AGAINST THE ODDS.
"TWO DAYS LATER, THE GAME WITH KENTUCKY TURNED OUT TO BE A TIGHT MATCH...
"...YOU COULD SEE THE OUTCOME IN DOUBT ON EVERY PLAY.

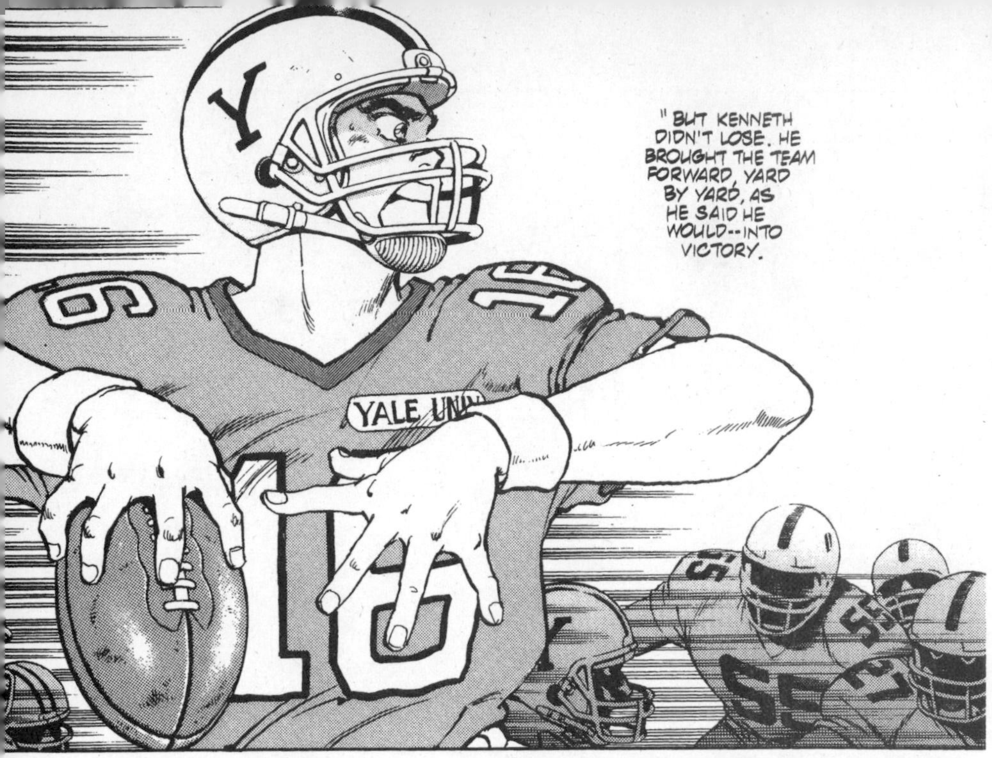
"BUT KENNETH DIDN'T LOSE. HE BROUGHT THE TEAM FORWARD, YARD BY YARD, AS HE SAID HE WOULD--INTO VICTORY.

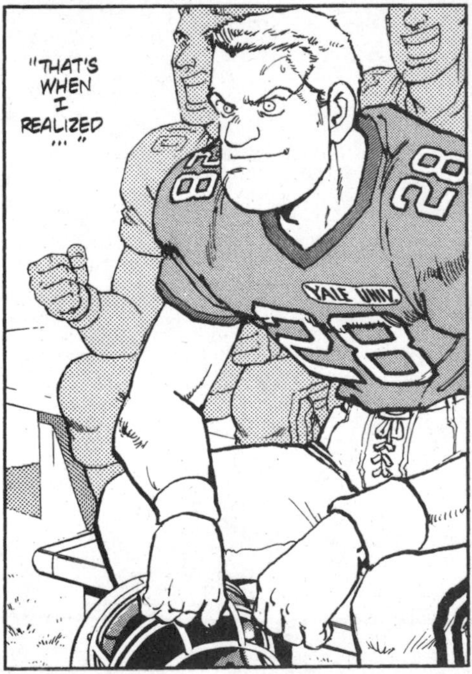
"THAT'S WHEN I REALIZED ..."

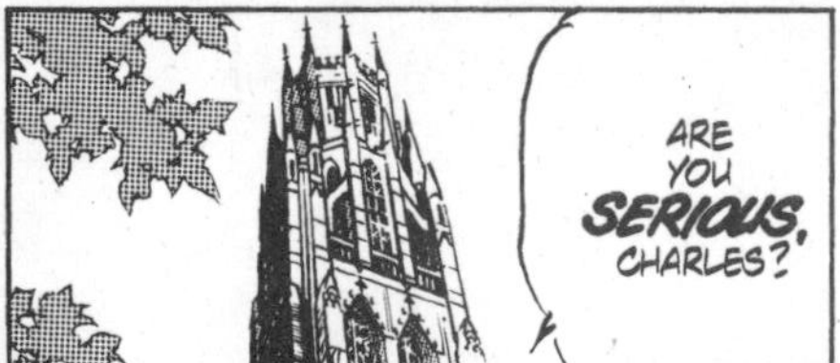
ARE YOU **SERIOUS**, CHARLES?

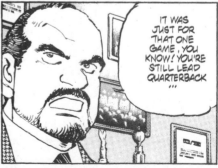

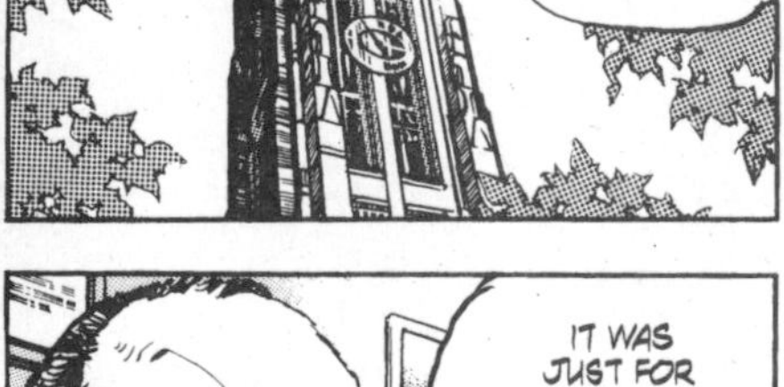
IT WAS JUST FOR THAT ONE GAME, YOU KNOW! YOU'RE STILL LEAD QUARTERBACK ...

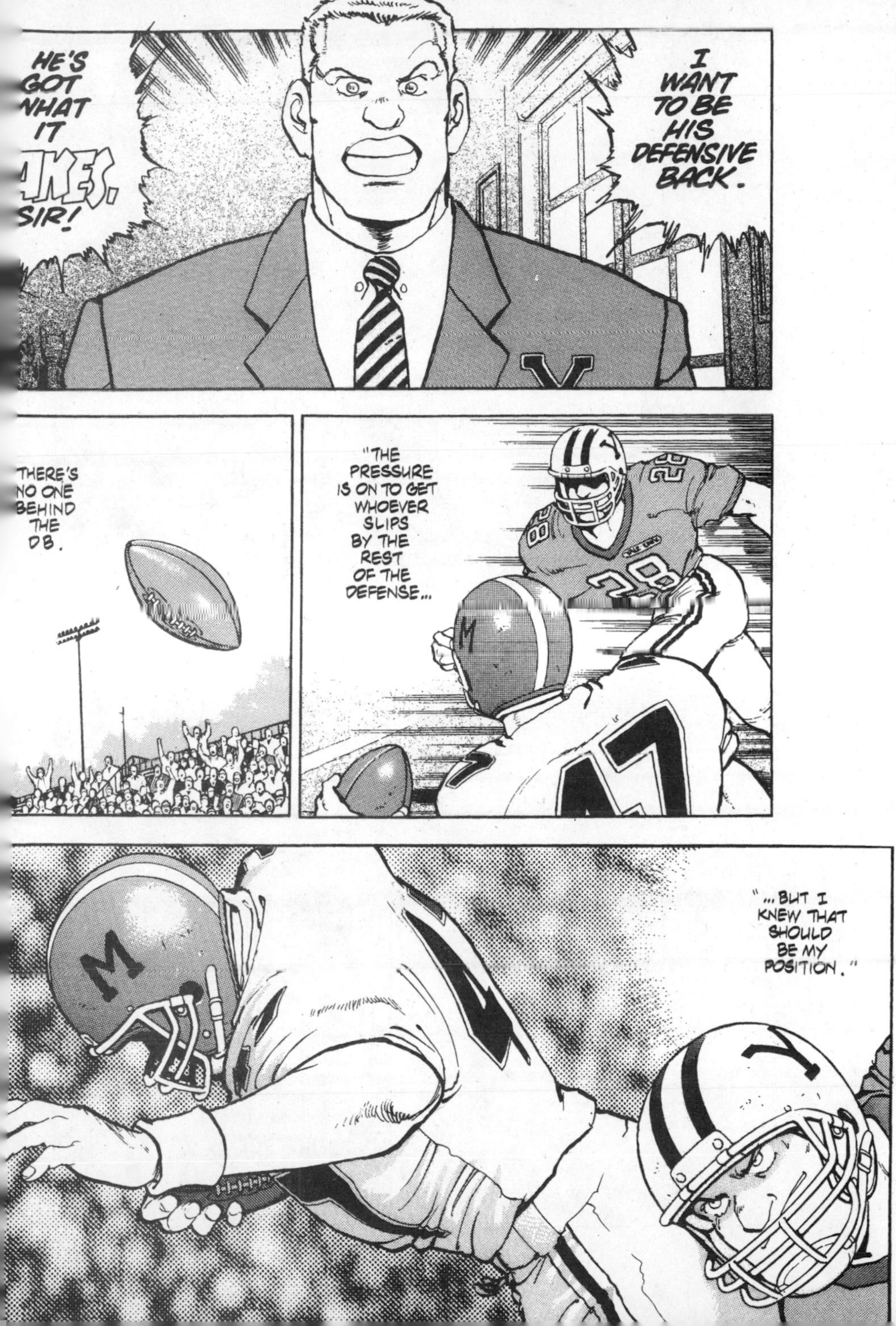
HE'S GOT WHAT IT TAKES, SIR!
I WANT TO BE HIS DEFENSIVE BACK.
THERE'S NO ONE BEHIND THE DB.
"THE PRESSURE IS ON TO GET WHOEVER SLIPS BY THE REST OF THE DEFENSE...
"...BUT I KNEW THAT SHOULD BE MY POSITION."

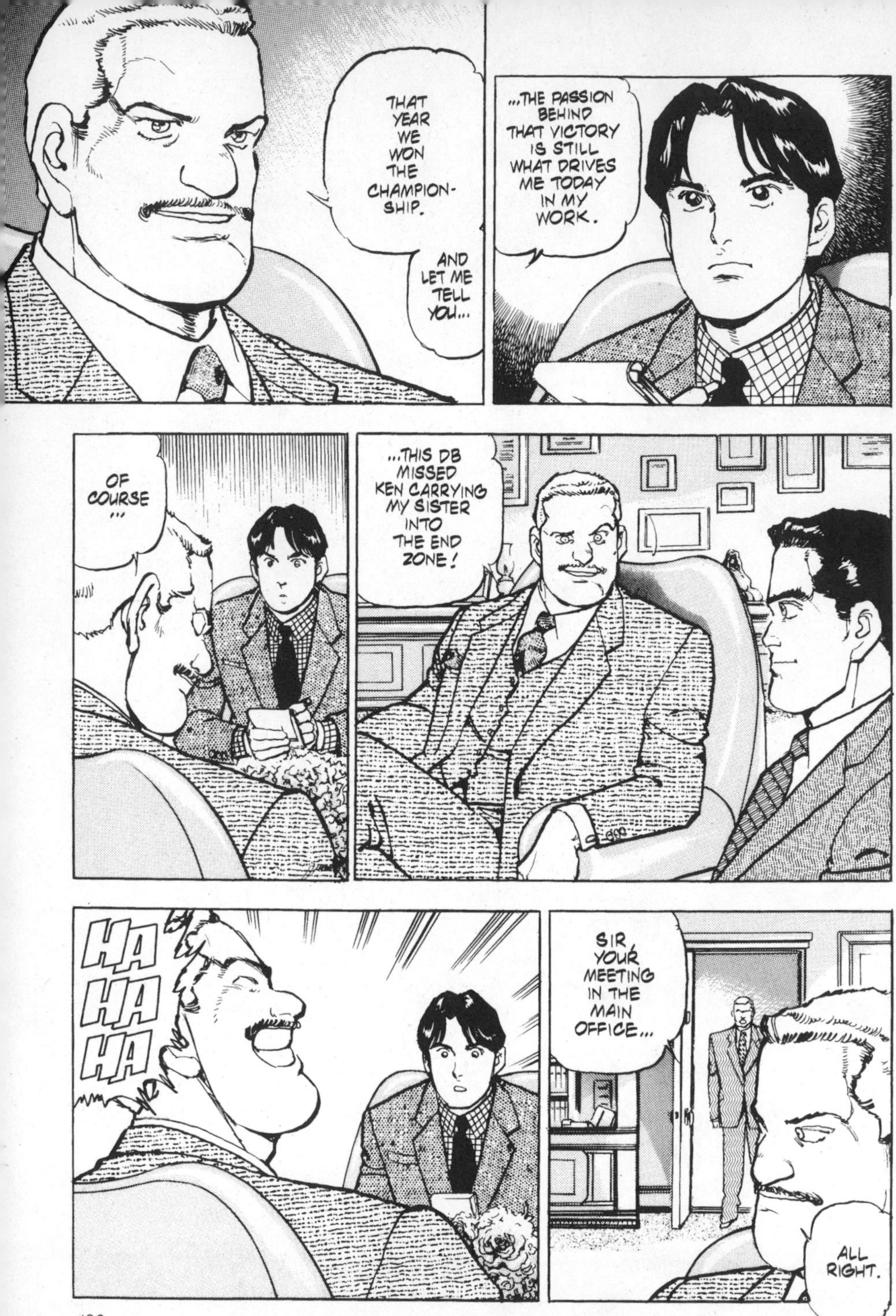
THAT YEAR WE WON THE CHAMPION-SHIP.
AND LET ME TELL YOU...
...THE PASSION BEHIND THAT VICTORY IS STILL WHAT DRIVES ME TODAY IN MY WORK.
OF COURSE ...
...THIS DB MISSED KEN CARRYING MY SISTER INTO THE END ZONE!
HA HA HA
SIR YOUR MEETING IN THE MAIN OFFICE...
ALL RIGHT.

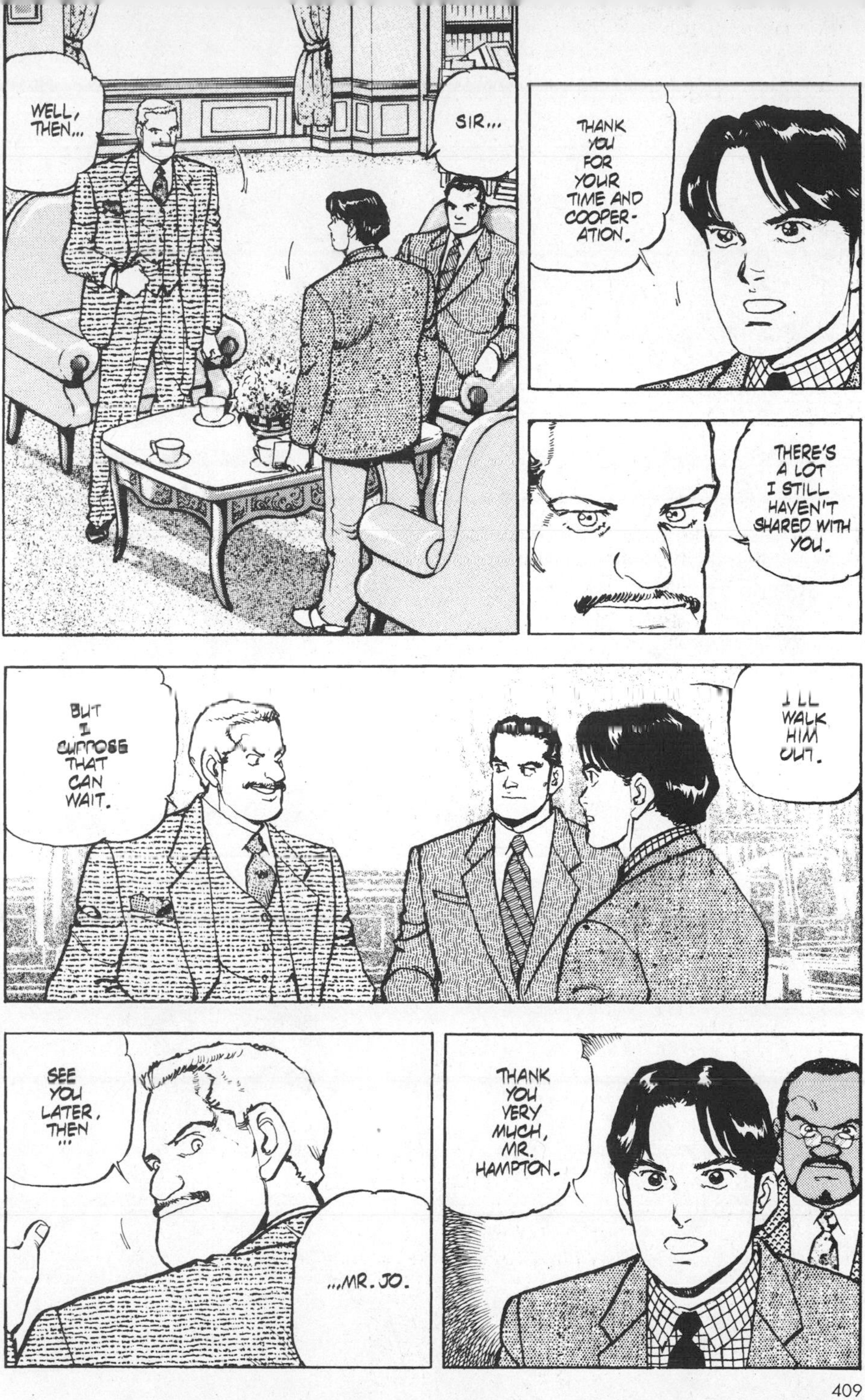
WELL, THEN...
SIR...
THANK YOU FOR YOUR TIME AND COOPERATION.
THERE'S A LOT I STILL HAVEN'T SHARED WITH YOU.
BUT I SUPPOSE THAT CAN WAIT.
I'LL WALK HIM OUT.
SEE YOU LATER, THEN ...
...MR. JO.
THANK YOU VERY MUCH, MR. HAMPTON.

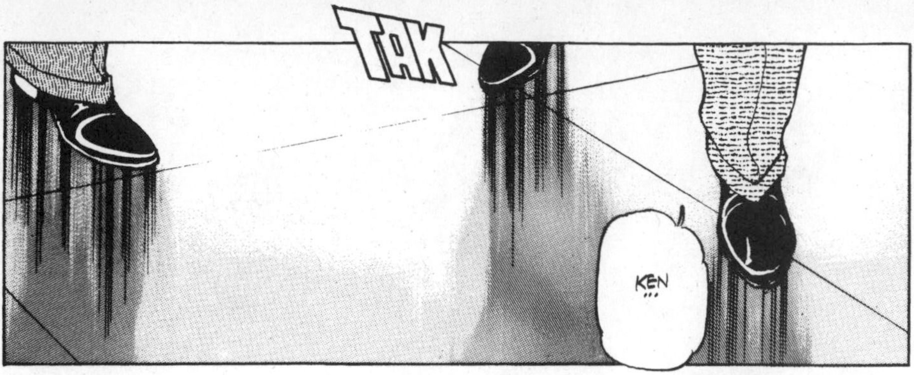
TAK
KEN ...

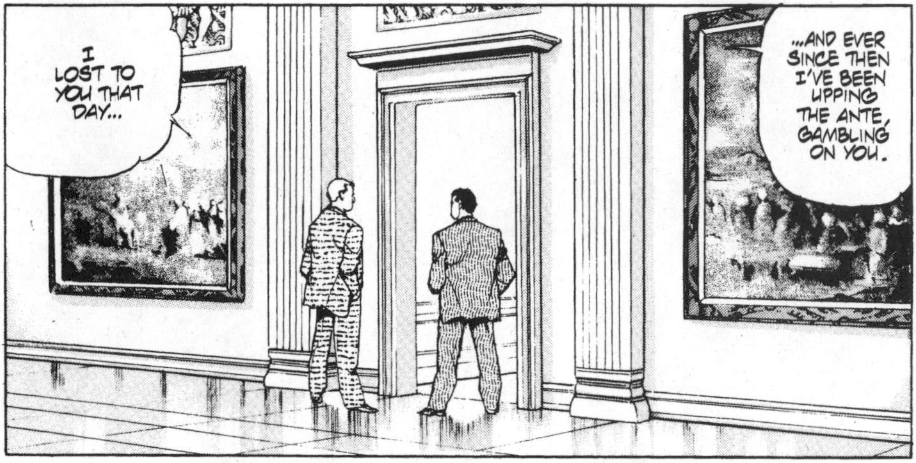
I LOST TO YOU THAT DAY...
...AND EVER SINCE THEN I'VE BEEN UPPING THE ANTE, GAMBLING ON YOU.

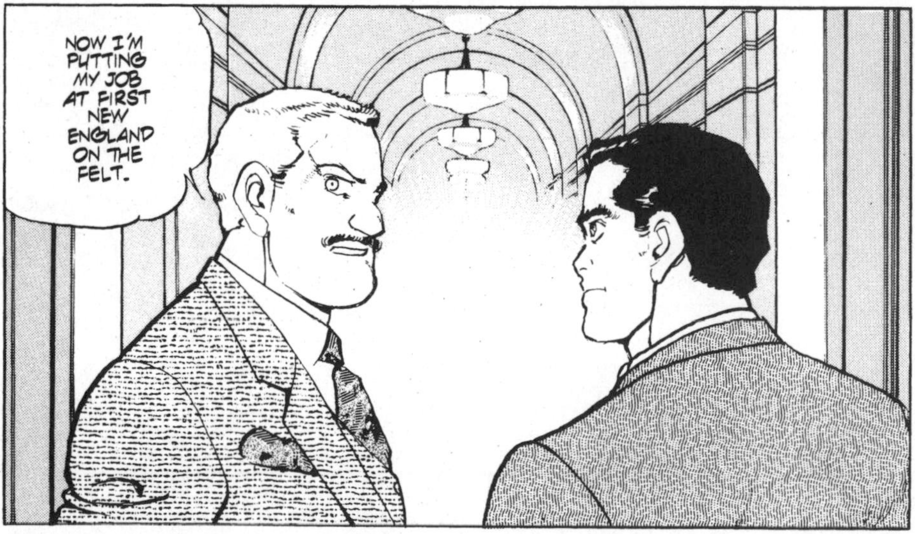
NOW I'M PUTTING MY JOB AT FIRST NEW ENGLAND ON THE FELT.

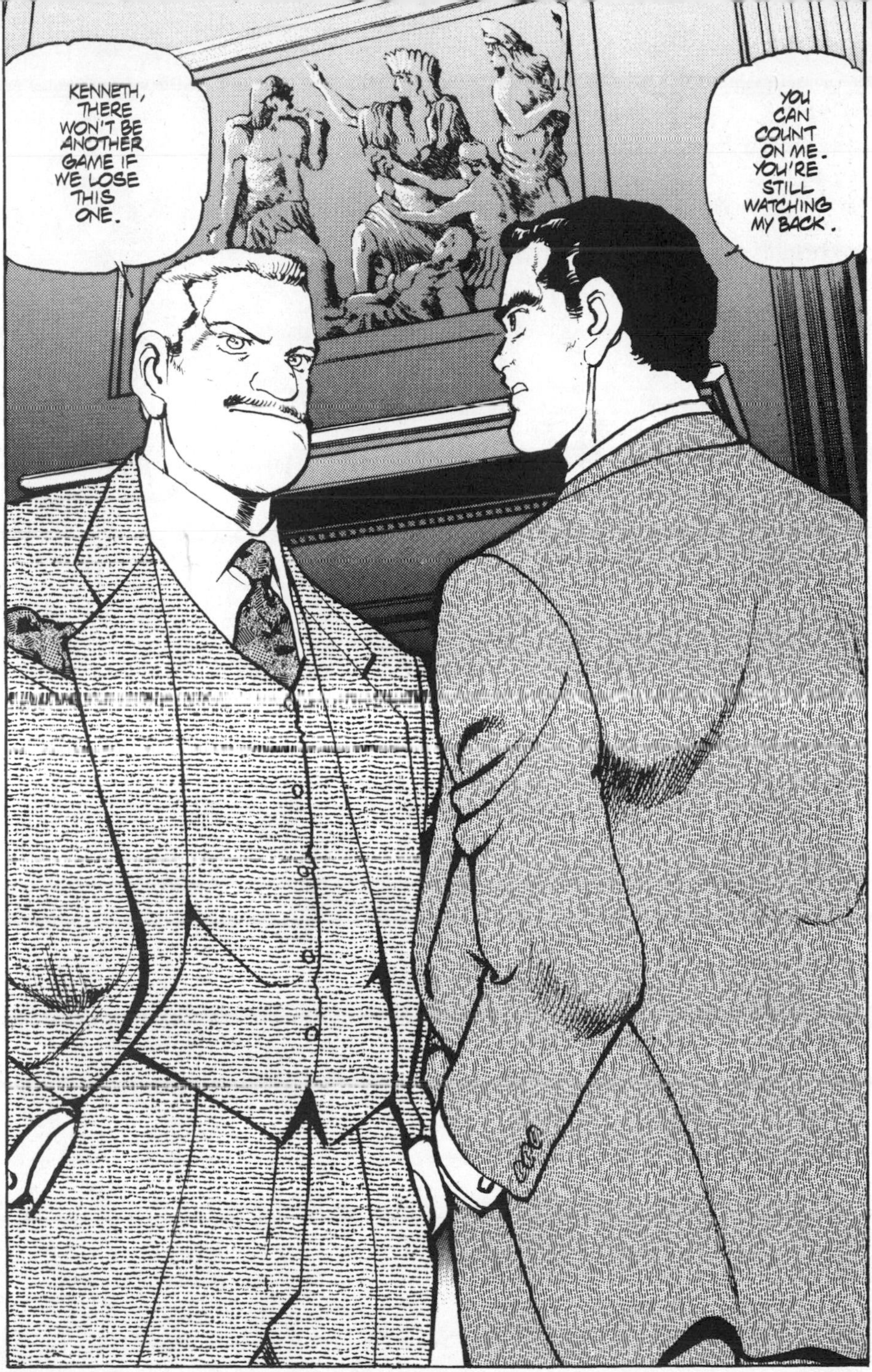
KENNETH, THERE WON'T BE ANOTHER GAME IF WE LOSE THIS ONE.
YOU CAN COUNT ON ME. YOU'RE STILL WATCHING MY BACK.

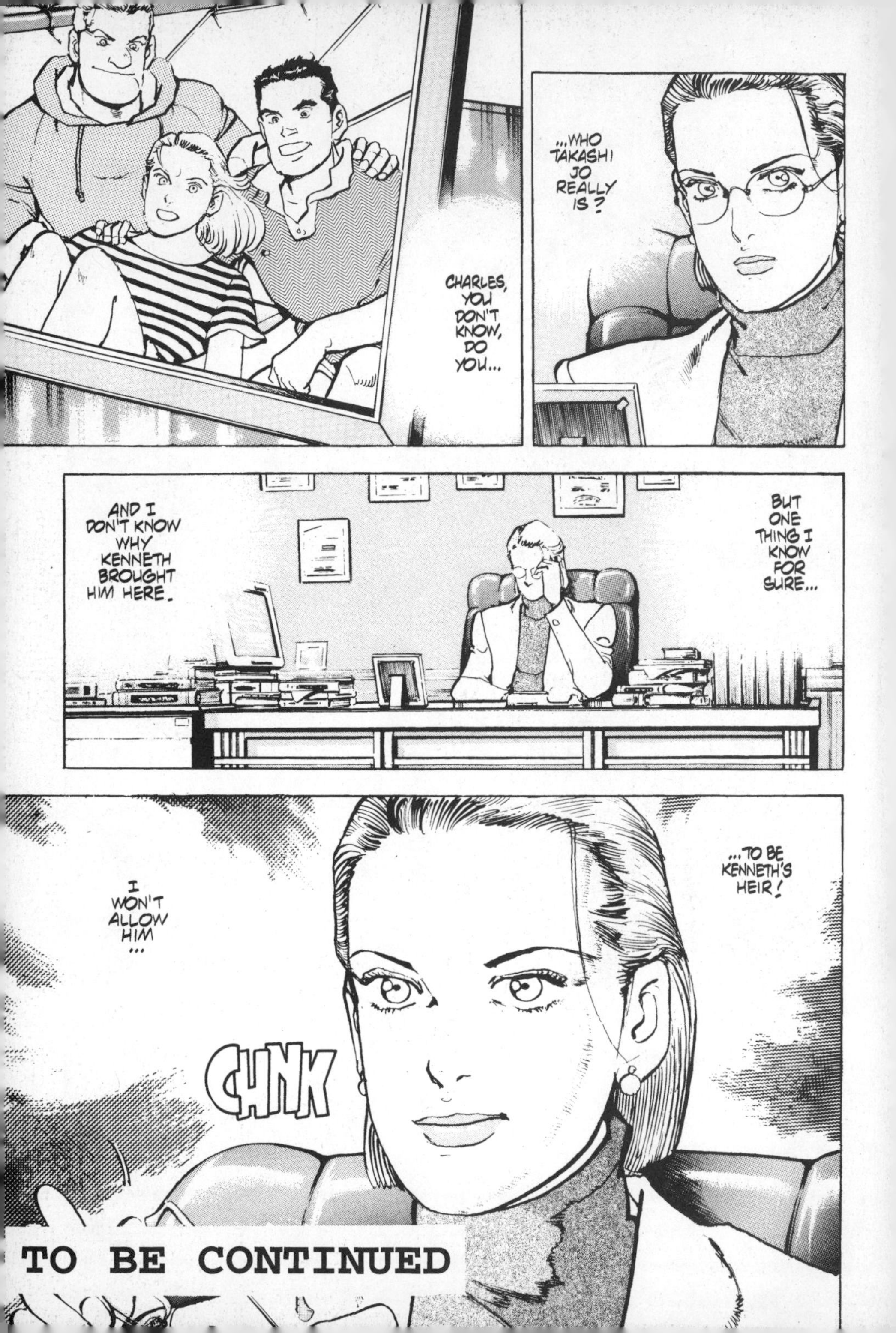
CHARLES, YOU DON'T KNOW, DO YOU...
...WHO TAKASHI JO REALLY IS?
AND I DON'T KNOW WHY KENNETH BROUGHT HIM HERE.
BUT ONE THING I KNOW FOR SURE...
I WON'T ALLOW HIM ...
...TO BE KENNETH'S HEIR!
CHNK
TO BE CONTINUED

HARD-HITTING POLITICS!

YAMAOKA FOR PRESIDENT

EAGLE

THE MAKING OF AN ASIAN-AMERICAN PRESIDENT

VOL.5: ON THE BATTLEFIELD

STORY AND ART BY KAIJI KAWAGUCHI

EAGLE: THE MAKING OF AN ASIAN-AMERICAN PRESIDENT

The monthly manga series by Kaiji Kawaguchi
The story of Kenneth Yamaoka: United States senator, Vietnam vet, and the first Japanese-American contender for the presidency.

100+ PAGES AN ISSUE!

VIZ COMICS™

Viz Comics
P.O. Box 77010
San Francisco, CA 94107
Phone: (800) 394-3042
Fax: (415) 348-8936
www.viz.com
www.j-pop.com
www.pulp-mag.com

Postscript

To the reader: Two congratulations!

First of all, congratulations on discovering in **Eagle** the world of *manga* (mawn-gah). At the risk of sounding like Dr. Evil about all this if you're already in the know, let me explain. Manga is what Japan did with comic books. Manga are comic books as mass media, comic books that compete with top-rated TV shows for the eyes of a hundred million people, comic books with full market saturation from grade schoolers to readers in their 50s. The original Japanese version of **Eagle** is serialized there in an all-comics magazine, appropriately called **Big Comic**, that reaches hundreds of thousands of readers every two weeks. And the highest-circulation manga magazines come out weekly and sell in the *millions*. Every once in a while, the American mainstream media will rediscover comic books in this country—sometimes with a patronizing note that "comics just aren't for kids anymore." In Japan, this need never occur; comics *are* the mainstream media. In America, comics-based movies and TV shows are a novelty; in Japan it is debated whether they have *too much* influence over movies, television, and even books. In Japan, comics draw talent and revenue away from those fields; people like Michael Crichton, Steven Spielberg and Steven Bochco might very well have ended up in the manga business.

If it seems I'm stressing the business rather than the creative side to you, it's because when it comes to comic books, America has no shortage of creative talent doing stories of all kinds for all ages. If you take the time to investigate online, or are lucky enough to have a first-class comics store in your neighborhood with helpful staff, you'll find works by Will Eisner and Daniel Clowes and Chris Ware and Warren Ellis, just to name a very few, and you'll find out what I mean. But notice those caveats. In Japan, comic books are something that come to *you*, wherever *you* are—on every streetcorner newsstand, on every train platform; they're even sold out of vending machines. What makes manga what it is, (for better and, as with any mass media, also for worse) is its business model. It's a very successful one that takes comic books that—were they in the American market—could, regardless of their quality or entertainment value, only hope to reach a few thousand readers, and sells them to millions.

Second congratulations: on discovering *this* manga, Kaiji Kawaguchi's **Eagle**. Over the past ten years, Mr. Kawaguchi has built a reputation as a solid storyteller with concepts that get a whole nation talking. He first did it in 1989 with **The Silent Service**, an epic that took the "rogue nuclear submarine" premise and used it to propose one path the world could take in the post-Cold War era. Kawaguchi's provocative tone was presented in such a matter-of-fact manner that **Silent Service** became a bestseller discussed on the floor of the Japanese Diet and covered by the **Los Angeles Times**. Now Kawaguchi, fascinated by the process in which Americans choose a leader who in turn shapes the whole world, uses the same methods to bring you **Eagle**. I read England's **The Economist** to get a valuable outsider's perspective on what's going on in my own country. Japan, perhaps our other most important ally across the ocean, has a perspective for us to consider as well.

In the real America, in the real Campaign 2000, the question of who would be the major-party candidates was settled within seven weeks of the New Hampshire Primary. In **Eagle** the debate is still open, the questions are still being asked. Its main character remains a mystery—Yamaoka's supreme arrogance and scheming approach goes with his ability to convey a sense of genuine idealism in public, and with his private assertion to the Vice-President that what Americans really need is not a man to lead them, but to be able to lead themselves. Lest anyone think the manga world is pointing fingers abroad, Sho Fumimura and Ryoichi Ikegami's *Sanctuary*, also available from Viz, portrayed a contemporary Japan whose political corruption and apathy is even worse.

Perhaps because it was about their own country, the creators of *Sanctuary* spoke more bluntly about the common problem we share with the Japanese as citizens of democracies—one politician actually shouts at the crowd that this election is supposed to be *their* fight, not just a fight between two candidates. It wasn't too long ago that many people here wished for the success of Bill Bradley or John McCain, and wondered if they might actually beat the front-runners...as if it were all some sort of spectator sport. We speak of candidates who were "unable to get their message out"—but isn't that backwards? Isn't it upon *us* to examine *them*? We may look at ten different models of DVD player before making a decision to buy, but we seem to vote only for the best-known candidate—despite the fact that it's not our DVD player that will write laws for us or might even send us off to war.

Especially in the age of the Web, which gives a more level ground to candidates, there is no excuse. You may in fact sincerely support the platforms of George Bush, Jr. or Al Gore, Jr. But before this Election Day, go to the sites of the Green, Reform, and Libertarian parties, and at least examine what they have to say. You are often told that to vote for a third-party candidate has no more practical effect than to split the affiliations associated with one major party, and give victory to the other. This not only makes the patronizing assumption that the American people could have no valid interests outside the Democratic and Republican platforms, it becomes a self-fulfilling prophecy against change.

Yes, it is unlikely for a third party to win the 2000 election. But just as election strategists think longer-term, and are even now looking down the road to 2004 or 2008, so should you, the citizen. If you find that a third party is closer to your own beliefs, you will not only *not* be wasting your vote to support them in 2000—you will also be doing exactly the right thing to see that they have a greater chance in the next election. Under U.S. law, if a third party gets as little as 5% of the popular vote, it qualifies for Federal matching funds. The major parties this year have announced that they will only admit to their Presidential debates those parties polling 15% or more—suggesting, among other things, that they are at least a little afraid of them. As well they should be, for as little as eight years ago, a third party got 19% of the vote. One last set of figures. In 1854 a new, third party was founded, in a time of national deadlock. As you might expect, they promptly lost when the next Presidential election came, in 1856. But in 1860, their candidate managed to scramble to 39%, and won. He was named Abraham Lincoln.

Carl Gustav Horn
Editor